KT-437-022

"So you agree that there is no debt between us? No lingering sense of injury?"

"I wouldna go that far," Jamie replied, very dry indeed. "Ye've got three fingers left. But there's nay debt, no. Not between us."

The man was sharp; he caught the faint emphasis on "us."

"Whatever disagreements you may have with my brother do not concern me," Pardloe said. "So long as they don't interfere with the business I am about to lay before you."

Jamie wondered just what John Grey had told his brother concerning the disagreements between them—but if it wasn't Pardloe's concern, it wasn't his either.

"Speak, then," he said, and felt a sudden knotting in his belly. They were the same words he'd said to John Grey, which had unleashed that final disastrous conversation. He had a strong foreboding that this wasn't going to end well, either.

By Diana Gabaldon

Outlander novels

Outlander
Dragonfly in Amber
Voyager
Drums of Autumn
The Fiery Cross
A Breath of Snow and Ashes
An Echo in the Bone
The Exile (graphic novel)
A Trail of Fire (collected novellas)

Lord John novels

Lord John and the Hellfire Club (novella)
Lord John and the Private Matter
Lord John and the Succubus (novella)
Lord John and the Brotherhood of the Blade
Lord John and the Haunted Soldier (novella)
Custom of the Army (novella)
Lord John and the Hand of Devils (collected novellas)
Plague of Zombies (novella)
The Scottish Prisoner

Diana Gabaldon is the *New York Times* bestselling author of the wildly popular Outlander novels and one work of non-fiction, as well as the bestselling series featuring Lord John Grey, an important character from the original series. She lives with her family and a lot of other assorted wildlife in Scottsdale, Arizona. Visit her website at www.dianagabaldon.com

DIANA GABALDON

The Scottish Prisoner

A Novel

An Orion paperback

First published in Great Britain in 2011
by Orion
This paperback edition published in 2012
by Orion Books
an imprint of The Orion Publishing Group Ltd,
Orion House, 5 Upper St Martin's Lane,
London WC2H 9EA

An Hachette UK company

1 3 5 7 9 10 8 6 4 2

Copyright © Diana Gabaldon 2011

The moral right of Diana Gabaldon to be identified as the author of this work has been asserted in accordance with the Copyright, Designs and Patents Act 1988.

All rights reserved. No part of this publication may be reproduced, stored in a retrieval system, or transmitted, in any form or by any means, electronic, mechanical, photocopying, recording or otherwise, without the prior permission of the copyright owner.

MORAY COUNCIL
LIBRARIES &
INFO.SERVICES

20 34 85 07

Askews & Holts

F

All the characters in this book are fictitious, and any resemblance to actual persons, living or dead, is purely coincidental.

A CIP catalogue record for this book is available from the British Library.

ISBN 978-1-4091-3519-7

Book design by Virginia Norey

Printed and bound in Great Britain by
CPI Group (UK) Ltd, Croydon, CR0 4YY

The Orion Publishing Group's policy is to use papers that are natural, renewable and recyclable products and made from wood grown in sustainable forests. The logging and manufacturing processes are expected to conform to the environmental regulations of the country of origin.

www.orionbooks.co.uk

To those selfless champions of a beautiful and beloved language who have so kindly helped me with Gaelic translations through the years:

Iain MacKinnon Taylor (and members of his family)
(Gaelic/*Gàidhlig*): *Voyager, Drums of Autumn,*
The Fiery Cross, and *A Breath of Snow and Ashes*

Catherine MacGregor and Catherine-Ann MacPhee
(Gaelic/*Gàidhlig*): *An Echo in the Bone,*
The Exile, and *The Scottish Prisoner*

Kevin Dooley (Irish/*Gaeilge*): *The Scottish Prisoner*

Moran Taing!

Contents

Acknowledgments *xiii*
Preface *xvii*
Prologue *xix*

SECTION I: *The Fate of Fuses*
1. April Fool *3*
2. Erse *10*
3. An Irishman, a Gentleman *23*
4. Not Good *39*
5. Why Am Not I at Peace? *50*
6. Summoning *74*

SECTION II: *Force Majeure*
7. When a Man Is Tired of London, He Is Tired of Life *81*
8. Debts of Honor *89*
9. Eros Rising *104*
10. Punch and Judy *123*
11. Vulgar Curiosity *141*
12. The Belly of a Flea *148*

13. By Darkness Met *163*
14. Fridstool *171*

SECTION III: *Beast in View*
15. The Return of Tobias Quinn *191*
16. Tower House *205*
17. Castle Athlone *217*
18. Fireside Tales *224*
19. Quagmire *234*
20. Stalking Horse *261*
21. A Poultice for Bruising *269*
22. Glastuig *281*
23. Plan B *290*
24. Clishmaclaver *297*
25. Escape from Athlone *306*
26. Opium Dreams *329*
27. Loyalty and Duty *335*
28. Amplexus *345*

SECTION IV: *A Tithe to Hell*
29. The Wild Hunt *365*
30. Particular Friends *375*
31. Betrayal *384*
32. Duello *393*
33. *Billets-Doux* *406*
34. All Heads Turn as the Hunt Goes By *416*
35. Justice *421*
36. *Teind* *439*
37. Sole Witness *443*

SECTION V: *Succession*
38. Redux *451*
39. The Fog Comes Down *464*
40. Gambit *478*
41. A Moonlicht Flicht *482*
42. Point of Departure *494*
43. Succession *498*

Author's Notes *509*

Acknowledgments

To Jennifer Hershey and Bill Massey, my editors, who have so gracefully and skillfully handled the business of editing a book simultaneously from two different countries, companies, and points of view . . .

To the delightful copy editor Kathy Lord, who knows how many esses there are in "nonplussed," and who repeatedly saves my bacon by knowing how old everybody is and how far it is from Point A to Point B, geography and chronology not being my strong points at all, at all . . .

Jessica Waters, editorial assistant, adept at juggling several huge wads of manuscript, requests for interviews, and miscellaneous snippets of this and that simultaneously . . .

Virginia Norey (aka "the Book Goddess"), who designed the elegant volume you hold . . .

Vincent La Scala, Maggie Hart, and the many, many hardworking and endlessly tolerant people in the production department at Random House . . .

Catherine-Ann MacPhee, that glowing daughter of Barra, actress, TV presenter, traditional singer, teacher, and recording artist—whose wonderful Gaelic recordings can be found at www.Greentrax.com—and who provided the marvelously nuanced translations of Scottish Gaelic for this book . . .

Kevin Dooley, fluent speaker of Irish, musician, storyteller, and author (see www.kevindooleyauthor.blogspot.com), for his lovely and thoughtful translations of the Irish Gaelic. Any loss of *fadas* (the little accent marks scattered over written Irish like ground black pepper) is the fault either of me or the unavoidable friction involved in typesetting, and we apologize if we inadvertently lost any, either way . . .

Catherine MacGregor (aka "Amazingly Perceptive and Generous Reader"), both for assistance in procuring and recording the Gaelic translations, helpful commentary on the manuscript, and for Eye-ball-Numbing Nitpickery . . .

Barbara Schnell and Sarah Meral, for the German bits . . .

Laura Bailey, for helpful information on gaiters and other items of eighteenth-century costume . . .

Allene Edwards, for Advanced Typo-spotting and Nitpickery . . .

Claudia Howard, Recorded Books producer, for her open-mindedness and courtesy while going about the tricky business of getting the audiobook of *The Scottish Prisoner* on sale simultaneously with the print version . . .

Malcolm Edwards and Orion Publishing, for their faith in and stout support of this book . . .

My husband, Doug Watkins, for helpful information on horses, mules, harness, and small boys . . .

Karen Henry, Czarina of Traffic and Aedile Curule of the Diana Gabaldon folder (in the Compuserve Books and Writers Forum), without whom I would have a lot more distraction and fewer words on paper, both for herding the bumblebees and for her detailed and helpful manuscript comments . . .

Susan Butler, for invaluable logistical assistance, household and dog management, and encyclopedic knowledge on how to ship things most expeditiously from Point A to Point B . . .

Jeremy Tolbert, Nikki Rowe, Michelle Moore, Loretta McKibben, and Janice Millford, for Web-based constructions and management . . . I can't clone myself, but they're the next best thing . . .

Lara, Suellen, Jari Backman, Wayne Sowry, and the dozens of other lovely people who've given me useful details and suggestions, or have remembered things for me that I had forgotten, but needed . . .

Vicki Pack and The Society for the Appreciation of the English Awesomesauce (Lord John's fan club), for moral support and a great T-shirt . . .

Elenna Loughlin, for the lovely author photo (taken in the eighteenth-century walled garden at Culloden House, near Inverness) . . .

Judy Lowstuter, Judie Rousselle, and the Ladies of Lallybroch, for the bench in the eighteenth-century walled garden at Culloden House, kindly dedicated to me and my books . . .

Allan Scott-Douglas, Ewen Dougan, and Louise Lewis for various Scots idioms, and for the correct spelling of "tattie" . . .

Betsy ("Betty") Mitchell, Bedelia, Eldon Garlock, Karen Henry ("Keren-happuch"), and Guero the mule (aka "Whitey")—for the use of their names, though I hasten to add that with the exception of Guero, none of the above has anything in common with the characters bearing those names . . .

Homer and JJ, for observations on dachshund puppies . . .

and

Danny Baror and Russell Galen—better agents, no one's ever had.

Preface

Chronology of the Novels: When to Read What?

The Lord John novellas and novels* are sequential, but are built to stand alone; you don't need to read them in order.

In terms of their relationship to the larger Outlander novels: These books are part of the overall series, but are focused for the most part on those times in Lord John's life

*There are also a couple of short stories—and will eventually be more—dealing with minor events, minor characters, and/or lacunae in the main books. These are presently published in various anthologies, but will eventually be collected in book form.

"A Leaf on the Wind of All Hallows" appears in the anthology *Songs of Love and Death* (edited by George R.R. Martin and Gardner Dozois). This is a short story set in WWII that tells the story of what *really* happened to Roger MacKenzie's parents, Jerry and Dolly.

"The Space Between" is a novella that will appear in an anthology titled *The Mad Scientist's Guide to World Domination* (edited by John Joseph Adams), which will likely appear sometime in 2012. This story is set mostly in Paris and involves Joan McKimmie (Marsali's younger sister), Michael Murray (Young Ian's older brother), the Comte St. Germain (no, of course he's not dead, don't be silly), and Mother Hildegarde.

when he's not "onstage" in the main novels. This particular book focuses also on a part of Jamie Fraser's life not covered in the main novels.

All of the Lord John novels take place between 1756 and 1766—this one is set in 1760—and in terms of the overall Outlander novels/timeline, they thus occur more or less in the middle of *Voyager.* So you can read any of them, in any order, once you've read *Voyager,* without getting lost.

Prologue

If you deal in death routinely, there are two paths. Either it becomes routine, in which case ye risk killing for nothing and thus lose your soul—for if the lives ye take are worth nothing, neither is yours.

Or you become that much more aware of the value of a life and that much more reluctant to take one without the direst necessity. That way you risk losing your own life—there are the quick and there are the dead, and I do not mean what St. Paul meant about that—but not your soul.

Soldiers manage by dividing themselves. They're one man in the killing, another at home, and the man that dandles his bairn on his knee has nothing to do wi' the man who crushed his enemy's throat with his boot. So he tells himself, sometimes successfully.

But it marks you, killing. No matter why it's done.

It's a brand upon your heart, and while it may heal, the mark canna be removed, save by a blade. All ye can hope for is a cleaner scar.

SECTION I

The Fate of Fuses

1

April Fool

Helwater, the Lake District
April 1, 1760

IT WAS SO COLD OUT, HE THOUGHT HIS COCK MIGHT BREAK off in his hand—if he could find it. The thought passed through his sleep-mazed mind like one of the small, icy drafts that darted through the loft, making him open his eyes.

He could find it now; had waked with his fist wrapped round it and desire shuddering and twitching over his skin like a cloud of midges. The dream was wrapped just as tightly round his mind, but he knew it would fray in seconds, shredded by the snores and farts of the other grooms. He needed her, needed to spill himself with the feel of her touch still on him.

Hanks stirred in his sleep, chuckled loudly, said something incoherent, and fell back into the void, murmuring, "Bugger, bugger, bugger . . ."

Jamie said something similar under his breath in the Gaelic and flung back his blanket. Damn the cold.

He made his way down the ladder into the half-warm, horse-smelling fug of the barn, nearly falling in his haste, ignoring a splinter in his bare foot. He hesitated in the dark, still urgent. The horses wouldn't care, but if they noticed him, they'd make enough noise, perhaps, to wake the others.

Wind struck the barn and went booming round the roof. A strong chilly draft with a scent of snow stirred the somnolence, and two or three of the horses shifted, grunting and whickering. Overhead, a murmured "'ugger" drifted down, accompanied by the sound of someone turning over and pulling the blanket up round his ears, defying reality.

Claire was still with him, vivid in his mind, solid in his hands. He could imagine that he smelled her hair in the scent of fresh hay. The memory of her mouth, those sharp white teeth . . . He rubbed his nipple, hard and itching beneath his shirt, and swallowed.

His eyes were long accustomed to the dark; he found the vacant loose box at the end of the row and leaned against its boards, cock already in his fist, body and mind yearning for his lost wife.

He'd have made it last if he could, but he was fearful lest the dream go altogether, and he surged into the memory, groaning. His knees gave way in the aftermath and he slid slowly down the boards of the box into the loose piled hay, shirt rucked round his thighs and his heart pounding like a kettledrum.

Lord, that she might be safe was his last conscious thought. *She and the child.*

HE PLUNGED at once into a sleep so deep and luxurious that when a hand shook him by the shoulder, he didn't spring to his feet but merely stirred sluggishly, momentarily befuddled by the prickle of hay on his bare legs. His instincts came back to life in sudden alarm and he flung himself over, getting his feet under him in the same motion that put his back against the wall of the loose box.

There was a gasp from the small form in the shadows before him, and he classified it as feminine just in time to restrain himself from reflexive violence.

"Who's that?" he demanded. He spoke low, his voice hoarse with sleep, and the form swayed back a little farther, exhibiting dubiousness.

He was in no mood for foolishness and shot out a hand, grabbing her by the arm. She squealed like a pig and he let go as though she were red-hot, cursing himself mentally as he heard the startled grunts and rustlings of his fellow grooms overhead.

"What the devil's that?" Crusoe demanded, in a voice like a clogged pipe. Jamie heard him clear his throat and spit thickly into his half-filled pot, then bellow down the ladder, "Who's there?"

The shadowy form was making wild motions, beseeching him to be silent. The horses were half awake, snorting with mild confusion but not panicked; they were used to Crusoe shouting in the night. He did it whenever he had the money to buy drink, waking from nightmares in a cold sweat, shrieking at his demons.

Jamie rubbed a hand over his face, trying to think. If Crusoe and Hanks didn't already know he was gone, they'd notice in the next few seconds.

"Rats in the feed," he shouted up. "I killed one." It was a feeble story; there were always rats in the feed, and no one would have stirred a finger to investigate their noises in the dead of night, let alone hunt them in the dark.

Hanks made a sound of disgust, rustling his bedclothes. "The Scotchman's buggering the horses again," he said conversationally to Crusoe, though clearly speaking loud enough to be heard below. "Ought to speak to his lordship about it."

Crusoe grunted angrily. "Well, whatever the fuck you're doin', MacKenzie, be quiet about it!" he shouted, and flung himself over on his pallet in a flurry of bother.

Jamie's heart was pounding again, with annoyed agitation. He reached for the young woman—no auld crone squealed like that—but slowly this time, and she made no demur when he took her by the arm. He led her down the stone-flagged aisle between the stalls and outside, shoving the sliding door to behind them with a rumble.

It was cold enough out to make him gasp, an icy wind flattening his shirt to his body and stealing his breath. The moon was obscured by racing cloud, but enough glow came from the sky for him to make out the identity of his intruder.

"What the *devil* d'ye want?" he snapped. "And how did ye ken where I was?" It had dawned on him that she hadn't just stumbled over him in the hay, for why would a lady's maid be poking about the stables at night? She'd come looking for him.

Betty lifted her chin.

"There's a man what wants to talk to you. He sent me to say. And I saw you come down from the loft."

That last sentence floated in the air between them, charged like a Leyden jar. Touch it, and there'd be a spark that would stand his hair on end. Christ. Did she have any notion what it *was* he'd been doing?

He caught the hint of a smirk on her face before a cloud shadow obscured it, and his ears went suddenly hot with rising blood.

"What man?" he said. "Where?"

"An Irishman," she said. "But a gentleman. He says to tell you the green branch will flower. And to meet him on the fells, where the old shepherd's hut is."

The shock of it nearly made him forget the cold, though the

wind was ripping through the linen of his shirt and he was shivering so hard that he found it hard to speak without his voice shaking. And *that* wouldn't do.

"I've nothing to do wi' any Irishmen," he snapped. "And if he comes back, ye may tell him so." He put a hand on the door, turning to go in. "I'm going to my bed. Good night to ye."

A light hand ran down his back and stopped just above his buttocks. He could feel the hair there bristle like a badger's, and not from the cold.

"Your bed'll be cold as death by now." She'd stepped close; he could feel the slight warmth of her body behind him, the heat of her breath through his shirt. And she still had her hand on him. Lower now. "Mine's a good deal warmer."

Holy Lord. Arse clenched, he moved deliberately away from her and pushed the door open.

"Good night," he said, without turning round, and stepped into the rustling, inquisitive dark of the stable. He saw her for an instant as he turned to shut the door, caught in the flickering moonlight, her eyes narrowed like an angry cat's.

HE MADE NO EFFORT to be quiet, climbing the ladder back to the loft. Hanks and Crusoe were pointedly silent, though he thought neither one was asleep. God knew what they'd say about tonight's incident, but he wasn't disposed to be worrit over that pair. He'd enough else to think on.

Betty, for one. For if anyone on Helwater estate knew his great secret, it was she. Betty had been Geneva Dunsany's lady's maid before becoming maid to her sister after Geneva's death. How much of a confidante had she been, though?

He could still feel the pressure of her hand on his backside and squirmed his arse irritably into his pallet, the straw under his blanket poking him. Damn the woman. She'd given him an eye when he'd first come to Helwater from Ardsmuir prison three years before, a paroled Jacobite traitor, but a lady's maid had little to do with a groom, and it was easy enough not to see her long-eyed glances when she came to tell him that Lady Geneva wanted her horse. Not so easy to avoid Lady Geneva.

He grimaced in the dark at thought of Geneva. He wasn't feeling charitable at the moment but crossed himself nonetheless and said a brief prayer for the repose of her soul, as he did whenever she came into his mind. He owed her that much, poor lass, no matter what she'd done to him.

But why the devil was Betty playing the loon now? Geneva had been dead more than two years, and Betty herself had come back to Helwater soon after her mistress's death in childbirth. She'd not spoken a word to him in the last six months; why go to the risk of coming to the stable at night—and, come to that, what had the silly wee bitch intended? Climbing the creaking ladder and sliding into his bed unannounced, with Hanks and Crusoe curled under their blankets six feet away, their great ears flapping? Sneaking him into the servants' attic?

She couldn't have meant to wait below for him; she hadn't known he'd come down. For that matter . . . she said she'd seen him descend the ladder, but she hadn't come to him then. Why not?

The logical answer presented itself, with a small jolt to the pit of his stomach. She hadn't been looking for him at all.

He sat bolt upright before the train of his thought had entirely finished, his body grasping the point at once. She'd come to meet someone else, and that meeting had been interrupted by his own inopportune appearance.

An intruder couldn't have hidden in an occupied stall or anywhere else . . . save the vacant loose box near the door.

And that's why she woke me, he thought, hands clenching on the blanket. *She had to draw me away, so the fellow could get out. Christ, he was in there with me!* His skin prickled with mingled embarrassment and fury. The notion that . . . could it be possible . . . surely he would have sensed someone . . . ?

But he wouldn't. He'd been so desperate to find solitude in which to reach Claire for that one necessary moment that he wouldn't have noticed a bear lurking in the shadows, provided it hadn't tried to interrupt him.

One of the cocks in the hen coop crowed, two more on its heels. A sleepy "Oh, fuuuck" came from a nearby pallet. A loud rustle of someone sitting up, and the hawking and snorting started. Hanks smoked heavily—when he could afford it—and took a good quarter hour to start breathing in the morning.

Jamie breathed deep himself, thinking. Then flung back his blanket and rose to meet what was likely to be an interesting day.

2

Erse

London
Argus House, residence of Harold,
Duke of Pardloe

LORD JOHN GREY EYED THE RIBBON-TIED PACKET ON HIS KNEE as though it were a bomb. In fact, it couldn't have been more explosive had it been filled with black powder and equipped with a fuse.

His attitude as he handed it to his brother must have reflected this knowledge, for Hal fixed him with a gimlet eye and raised one brow. He said nothing, though, flicking loose both ribbon and wrapping with an impatient gesture and bending his head at once over the thick sheaf of densely written sheets that emerged.

Grey couldn't stand to watch him read through Charles Carruthers's postmortem denunciation, recalling each damning page as Hal read it. He stood up and went to the window of the library that looked out into the back garden of Argus House, ignoring the swish of turning pages and the occasional blasphemous mutterings behind him.

Hal's three boys were playing a game of tigers and hunters,

leaping out at one another from behind the shrubbery with shrill roars, followed by shrieks of delight and yells of "Bang! Take that, you striped son of a bitch!"

The nurse seated on the edge of the fish pool, keeping a tight grip on baby Dottie's gown, looked up at this but merely rolled her eyes with a martyred expression. *Flesh and blood has its limits,* her expression said clearly, and she resumed paddling a hand in the water, luring one of the big goldfish close so that Dottie could drop bits of bread to it.

John longed to be down there with them. It was a rare day for early April, and he felt the pulse of it in his blood, urging him to be outside, running barefoot through young grass. *Running naked down into the water . . .* The sun was high, flooding warm through the glass of the French windows, and he closed his eyes and turned his face up to it.

Siverly. The name floated in the darkness behind his eyes, pasted across the blank face of an imagined cartoon major, drawn in uniform, an outsize sword brandished in his hand and bags of money stuffed into the back of his breeches, obscene bulges under the skirt of his coat. One or two had fallen to the ground, bursting open so that you could see the contents—coin in one, the other filled with what looked like poppets, small wooden doll-like things. Each one with a tiny knife through its heart.

Hal swore in German behind him. He must have reached the part about the rifles; German oaths were reserved for the most stringent occasions, French being used for minor things like a burnt dinner, and Latin for formal insults committed to paper. Minnie wouldn't let either Hal or John swear in English in the house, not wanting the boys to acquire low habits. John could have told her it was too late for such caution but didn't.

He turned round to see Hal on his feet, pale with rage, a sheet of paper crumpled in one hand.

"How dare he? How *dare* he?"

A small knot he hadn't known was there dissolved under John's ribs. His brother had built his own regiment, the 46th, out of his own blood and bones; no one was less likely to overlook or condone military malfeasance. Still, Hal's response reassured him.

"You believe Carruthers, then?"

Hal glared at him.

"Don't you? You knew the man."

He *had* known Charles Carruthers—in more than one sense.

"Yes, I believed him when he told me about Siverly in Canada, and *that*"—he nodded at the papers, thrown in a sprawl across Hal's desk—"is even more convincing. You'd think he'd been a lawyer."

He could still see Carruthers's face, pale in the dimness of his attic room in the little garrison town of Gareon, drawn with ill health but set with grim determination to live long enough to see justice done. Charlie hadn't lived that long, but long enough to write down every detail of the case against Major Gerald Siverly and to entrust it to Grey.

He was the fuse that would detonate this particular bomb. And he was all too familiar with what happened to fuses, once lit.

"WHAT IS THIS?" Hal was frowning at one of the papers. Grey put down the book in his hand and came to look. The paper was in Carruthers's handwriting, as painstakingly executed as the rest; Carruthers had known he was setting down evidence for a court-martial and had done his best to make it legible.

It *was* legible—insofar as Grey could make out the various letters that composed the words. But the words themselves looked like nothing he had ever seen before.

Éistigí, Fir na dtrí náisiún.
Éistigí, le glór na hadhairc ag caoineadh san goath.
Ag teácht as an oiche.

Tá sí ag teacht.
Tá an Banrion ag teacht.
Sé na deonaigh, le gruaig agus súil in bhfiainne,
Ag leanúint lucht mhóir an Bhanríon.

It looked like the sheerest gibberish. At the same time, there was something . . . civilized—was that the word?—in its appearance. The words bore all manner of strange accents and looked like no language with which Grey was familiar, and yet the text was punctuated in what seemed a logical fashion. It was laid out upon the page in the style of verse, with evident stanzas and what certainly looked like a repeated refrain—perhaps it was the text of a song?

"Have you ever seen anything like that before?" he asked Hal. His brother shook his head, still frowning.

"No. It looks vaguely as though someone had made an effort to transliterate Greek, using the Roman alphabet—but the words certainly aren't Greek."

"Nor Hebrew," Grey said, peering at the first line. "Russian, perhaps? Turkish?"

"Perhaps," Hal said dubiously. "But why, for God's sake?"

Grey ran through in his mind what he knew of Carruthers's career but turned up no particular connections with exotic languages. Neither had Charlie ever struck him as being remarkably well educated; he was always getting into a muddle over his bills when Grey first knew him, through simple inability to add, and his French was fluent but uncouth.

"Everything else in the packet pertains to Siverly and his misdeeds. So logically this must, too."

"Was Carruthers particularly logical?" Hal eyed the stack of papers. "He's legible, I'll give him that. You knew him a great deal better than I, though—what d'you think?"

Grey thought a lot of things, most of which he didn't intend to speak out loud. He had known Charlie Carruthers fairly well—in the Biblical sense, among others—though for only a short time and that time, more than ten years ago. Their meeting in Canada the year before had been brief—but Charlie had known Grey very well, too. He'd known who to trust with his inflammatory legacy.

"Not particularly logical, no," he answered slowly. "Rather determined, though. Once he'd made up his mind to something, he'd see it through."

And he nearly had. In spite of a failing heart, Carruthers had clung to life stubbornly, compiling this damning mass of testimony, determined to bring Major Gerald Siverly to justice.

"Blessed are those who hunger and thirst for justice," he had whispered in John's ear, during their last meeting. Grey picked up the little stack of papers and shuffled them neatly into order, smelling in memory the scent of that attic room in Gareon, near Quebec. Pine boards, hot with a stifling turpentine perfume. Soured milk and the moldy sweetness of mouse droppings. The scent of Charlie's skin, sweating with heat and with illness. The touch of his deformed hand on Grey's face, a light touch but strong with the force of memory.

"I hunger, John," he'd said, his breath heavy with approaching death. "And you thirst. You won't fail me."

Grey didn't intend to. With slow deliberation, he tapped the papers on the table, squaring them, and set them neatly down.

"Is there enough here, do you think?" he asked his brother. Enough to cause a general court-martial to be called, he meant—enough to convict Siverly of corruption, of abuse of his office. Of misconduct amounting to the murder of his own men. Siverly did not belong to Hal's regiment, but he did belong to the army to which Hal—and Grey himself, come to that—had given most of their lives.

"More than enough," Hal said, rubbing a hand over his chin. It was late in the day; the bristles of his beard made a tiny rasping sound. "If the witnesses can be found. If they'll speak." He spoke abstractedly, though, still puzzling over the mysterious sheet.

> *Do chuir siad na Róisíní Bhán ar an bealach go bua.*
> *Agus iad toilteannach agus buail le híobáirt an teannta ifrinn.*
> *Iad ag leanúint le bealach glór an Bhanríon.*

"Do choo-ir see-ad na Royseenee . . ." he read aloud, slowly. "Is it a cipher, do you suppose? Or a code?"

"Is there a difference?"

"Yes, there is," Hal said absently. He held it up to the light from the window, presumably to see if anything showed through, then bent and held it over the fire.

Grey stopped his involuntary move to snatch the paper; there were ways of doing secret writing, and most of those showed up with heat. Though why one would add an overtly mysterious code to a paper with hidden writing, thus drawing attention to it . . .

The paper was beginning to scorch and curl at the edges, but nothing was showing up save the original words, cryptic as ever. Hal pulled it back and dropped it smoking on the desk, shaking his fingers.

"For what the observation is worth," Grey said, gingerly picking up the hot sheet, "I don't see why Carruthers would trouble himself with encoding this particular document. Given the rest of it, I mean."

Hal compressed his lips but nodded. "The rest of it" included specific denunciations of a number of men—some of them powerful—who had been involved in Siverly's defalcations. If Carruthers trusted Grey to handle such incendiary stuff, what might he have balked at?

"Besides, Charlie knew he was dying," Grey said more quietly. He laid the sheet on top of the others and again began to tidy them into a square. "He left this packet addressed to me. He expected me to use it. Why would he have tried to conceal some part of the information from me?"

Hal shrugged, acknowledging the argument.

"Then why is it here? Included by mistake?" Even as he suggested this, he was shaking his head. The packet itself had been meticulously assembled, with documents in chronological order. Some of the papers were Carruthers's own testimony; some were statements signed by other witnesses; some were original army documents—or perhaps copies made by a clerk. It was impossible to tell, unless the original had borne a stamp. The whole bundle spoke of care, precision—and the passion that had driven Carruthers past his own weakness in order to accomplish Siverly's destruction.

"It is Carruthers's hand?" Unable to let a puzzle alone, Hal reached out and took the sheet of gibberish from the top of the stack.

"Yes," Grey said, though that much was obvious. Carruthers wrote a clear, slanted hand, with oddly curled tails on the descending letters. He came to look over Hal's shoulder, trying to see if the paper provided any clue they could have missed.

"It's laid out like verse," he observed, and, with the observation, something fluttered uneasily at the back of his mind. But what? He tried to catch a glimpse of it, but the thought skittered away like a spider under a stone.

"Yes." Hal drew a finger down the page, slowly. "But look at how these words are repeated. I think it might be a cipher, after all—if that were the case, you might be picking a different set of letters out of each line, even though the lines look much the same in themselves." He straightened up, shaking his head. "I don't know. It could be a cipher that Carruthers stumbled onto in Siverly's papers but to which he hadn't the key—and so he merely copied it and passed it on in hopes that you might discover the key yourself."

"That makes some sense." John rocked back on his heels, narrowing his eyes at his brother. "How do you come to know so much about ciphers and secret writings?"

Hal hesitated, but then smiled. Hal smiled rarely, but it transformed his face when he did.

"Minnie," he said.

"What?" Grey said, uncomprehending. His sister-in-law was a kind, pretty woman, who managed his difficult brother with great aplomb, but what—

"My secret weapon," Hal admitted, still smiling at whatever thought amused him. "Her father was Raphael Wattiswade."

"I've never heard of Raphael Wattiswade."

"You weren't meant to," his brother assured him, "and neither was anyone else. Wattiswade was a dealer in rare books—traveled to and from the Continent regularly, under the name Andrew Rennie. He was also a dealer in intelligence. A spymaster . . . who had no sons."

Grey looked at his brother for a moment.

"Tell me," he begged, "that her father did not employ Minnie as a spy."

"He did, the scrofulous old bugger," Hal replied briefly. "I caught her in my study one night during a party, magicking the locked drawer of my desk. That's how I met her."

Grey didn't bother asking what had been in the drawer. He smiled himself and picked up the decanter of sherry from the tea tray, unstoppering it.

"I gather you did not immediately have her arrested and taken before a magistrate?"

Hal took a sherry glass and held it out.

"No. I had her on the hearth rug."

The decanter slipped from Grey's fingers, and he caught it again by pure luck, splashing only a little.

"Did you, indeed?" he managed.

"Give me that, butterfingers." Hal took the decanter from him, and poured carefully, eyes fixed on the rising amber liquid. "And, yes, I did."

Grey wondered, reeling, whether Minnie had been a virgin and decided instantly not to ask.

"Then I put her into a coach, made her tell me her address, and said I would call on her in the morning, to ask after her welfare," Hal said offhandedly, and passed John a glass. "Here. Hang on to it this time. You look as though you need it."

He did, and drank off the sherry—which wasn't bad—in a couple of gulps.

"She didn't . . . actually give you her address, did she?" he asked, and cleared his throat, trying not to glance at the hearth rug. It had been there for years and years, a very worn small carpet with the family crest woven into it, much pocked with burn marks and the edge of it scorched. He thought it had been a wedding present from Hal's first wife, Esmé, to her husband.

Hal laughed.

"No, of course not. Neither did she tell it to the coachman—persuaded him to let her out at Kettrick's Eel-Pye House, then legged it down the alley and disappeared. Took me nearly six months to find her."

Hal disposed of his own sherry with dispatch, then plucked the questionable sheet off the desk again.

"Let me show her this. She's not had much opportunity to practice of late, but she might be able at least to tell us if it is encoded."

Left alone with the decanter and the hearth rug, Grey poured another drink and went back to the balcony. The garden was quiet now; the sky had clouded over and the boys had gone in for their tea—he could hear them rumpusing in the nursery overhead. Dottie and her nurse were both sound asleep on the grass by the fish pool, Dottie's gown still firmly in the nurse's grasp.

He wasn't quite sure whether Hal's story had shocked him or not. Hal made his own rules; John had long been aware of that. And if he'd temporarily had the upper hand of Minerva Wattiswade, he'd long since lost it—Hal himself knew that.

He glanced up at the ceiling, the recipient of a loud crash as a chair was overturned, shrill voices rising in the aftermath. How old was his nephew Benjamin? He glanced at the hearth rug. He'd been abroad when Benjamin was born, but his mother had written to apprise him of the event—he remembered reading the letter in a tent, with rain pattering on the canvas overhead. He'd lost three men the day before and was suffering some depression of spirit; news of the child's birth had comforted him.

He imagined it had comforted Hal, too. Grey had learned—recently, and quite by accident—that Hal's first wife, Esmé, who had died in childbirth and the child with her, had been seduced by one of Hal's friends, Nathaniel Twelvetrees, and that Hal had subsequently killed Twelvetrees in a duel. He thought that his brother had likely been quite insane at the time. How long after that had he met Minnie?

A flash of white showed at the door of the conservatory, on the far side of the garden. Minnie herself, and he drew back instinctively, though she couldn't see him. She looked up calculatingly at the sky, then glanced at the house. It wasn't raining yet, though, and she went back into the conservatory. A moment later, Hal appeared from the kitchen door and went in after her, paper in hand.

He was deeply startled at what Hal had told him—but not, on consideration, all that surprised that Hal *had* told him. His brother was secretive and self-controlled to a fault, but a tight-closed kettle will spurt steam when it reaches the boiling point. To Grey's knowledge, Hal had only three people in whom he would confide—his own mother not being among them.

The three were Grey himself, Harry Quarry—one of the regimental colonels—and Minnie.

So what, he wondered, was presently boiling under Hal? Something to do with Minnie? But Grey had spoken to her when he came in, and she'd given no indication that anything was wrong.

A spatter of rain on the window and shrieks from below made him look; a sudden shower had floated over the garden, and the nursemaid was dashing for the house, Dottie crowing in delight at the raindrops and waving her arms. He put his head out, to feel the rain himself, and smiled at the fragrant freshness of the air and the splash of rain on his skin. He closed his eyes, abandoning all thought, speculation, and worry in the momentary pleasure of breathing.

"What the devil are you doing, John?"

He withdrew his head reluctantly, drew the window to, and blinked water from his lashes. Hal was staring at him in disapproval, page in hand. There was a dark pink camellia in his buttonhole, leaning drunkenly.

"Enjoying the rain." He wiped a hand over his face and shook himself a little; his hair was damp, as was his collar and the shoulders of his coat. "Was Minnie able to be of help?"

"Yes." Hal sounded surprised at the admission. "She says it's neither a code nor a cipher."

"That's helpful? What is it, if it's neither code nor cipher?"

"She says it's Erse."

ERSE. THE WORD GAVE Grey a very odd sensation. Erse was what folk spoke in the Scottish Highlands. It sounded like no other language he'd ever heard—and, barbarous as it was, he was rather surprised to learn that it existed in a written form.

Hal was looking at him speculatively. "You must have heard it fairly often, at Ardsmuir?"

"Heard it, yes. Almost all the prisoners spoke it." Grey had been governor of Ardsmuir prison for a brief period; as much exile as appointment, in the wake of a near scandal. He disliked thinking about that period of his life, for assorted reasons.

"Did Fraser speak it?"

Oh, God, Grey thought. *Not that. Anything but that.*

"Yes," he said, though. He had often overheard James Fraser speaking in his native tongue to the other prisoners, the words mysterious and flowing.

"When did you see him last?"

"Not for some time." Grey spoke briefly, his voice careful. He hadn't spoken to the man in more than a year.

Not careful enough; Hal came round in front of him, examining him at close range, as though he might be an unusual sort of Chinese jug.

"He is still at Helwater, is he not? Will you go and ask him about Siverly?" Hal said mildly.

"No."

"No?"

"I would not piss on him was he burning in the flames of hell," Grey said politely.

One of Hal's brows flicked upward, but only momentarily.

"Just so," he said dryly. "The question, though, is whether Fraser might be inclined to perform a similar service for you."

Grey placed his cup carefully in the center of the desk.

"Only if he thought I might drown," he said, and went out.

3

An Irishman, a Gentleman

Helwater
April 2

JAMIE DRESSED AND WENT DOWN TO FORK HAY FOR THE horses, disregarding the dark and the chill in his hands and feet as he worked. *An Irishman. A gentleman.*

Who the devil could that be? And—if the Irishman existed—what had he to do with Betty? He kent some Irishmen. Such Irish gentlemen as he knew, though, were Jacobites, who'd come to Scotland with Charles Stuart. That thought froze what small parts of him weren't chilled already.

The Jacobite Cause was dead, and so was the part of his life connected with it.

Have sense, though. What would such a man want with him? He was a paroled prisoner of war, held in menial servitude, not even allowed to use his own notorious name. He was no better than a black slave, save that he couldn't be sold and no one beat him. He occasionally wished that someone would try, to give him the excuse of violence, but he recognized the desire as idle fantasy and pushed the thought aside.

Beyond that . . . how did anyone, Jacobite, Irishman, or Hottentot, know where he was? He'd had a letter from his sister in the Highlands only a week before, and she'd certainly have mentioned anyone inquiring after him, let alone an Irishman.

The air of the stable was changing, gray light seeping in through the chinks of the walls. The dark was growing thin and with it the nightly illusion of space and freedom, as the grimy boards of his prison faded into view.

At the end of the row, he put down his pitchfork and, with a hasty glance over his shoulder to be sure neither Hanks nor Crusoe had come down yet, he ducked into the empty loose box.

He let out his breath slow, as he would when hunting, and drew it in again slower, nostrils flaring to catch a scent. Nothing but the dry smell of last August's hay in the stall; behind him, the tang of fresh manure and the sweetness of mash and horses' breath. The hay was tumbled, trampled in spots. He could see where he had lain last night—and a slow flush rose in his cheeks—and another spot, perhaps, where someone might have stood, in the far corner.

Little wonder the man hadn't spoken to him, in the circumstances. He coughed. *If* he'd been there, and Jamie rather hoped he hadn't.

Irishman. An Irish gentleman. The only connection he could think of . . . His fists curled tight as the thought came to him, and he felt the echo of impact in the bones of his knuckles. Lord John Grey. He'd found an Irishman—or the hint of one—for John Grey, but surely this could have nothing to do with Grey's matter.

He hadn't seen Grey in over a year and, with luck, might never see him again. Grey had been governor of Ardsmuir prison during Jamie's imprisonment there and had arranged his parole at Helwater, the Dunsany family being longtime friends. Grey had been in the habit of visiting quarterly to inspect his prisoner, and their relations had gradually become civil, if no more.

Then Grey had offered him a bargain: if Jamie would write letters making inquiries among those Jacobites he knew living abroad regarding a matter of interest to Grey, Lord John would instruct Lord Dunsany to allow Jamie also to write openly to his family in the Highlands and to receive letters from them. Jamie had accepted this bargain, had made the desired inquiries, and had received certain information, carefully worded, that indicated that the man Lord John sought might be an Irish Jacobite—one of those followers of the Stuarts who had called themselves Wild Geese.

He didn't know what use—if any—Grey had made of the information. Things had been said at their last meeting that— He choked the memory of it off and picked up his fork, driving it into the pile of hay with some force. Whoever Betty's Irishman might be, he could have nothing to do with John Grey.

WITH THE USUAL VAGARIES of spring, the day had not so much dawned as it had merely stopped being night. Fog lay on the fells above Helwater in huge dirty banks, and the cold sky was the color of lead. Jamie's right hand ached. It had been broken once in a dozen places, and every one of them now informed him in a piercing whinge that it was going to rain.

Not that he needed telling; the steel-gray light aside, he could feel the heavy damp in his lungs and his sweat chilled on him, never drying. He worked like an automaton, his mind in two places, and neither of those where his body was.

Part of his thoughts dwelled on Betty. He needed to talk with that wee besom, preferably in a place where she couldn't get away from him easily.

The lady's maids usually took their meals with the housekeeper in her sitting room, rather than joining the lower servants in the kitchen. He couldn't go beyond the kitchen into the house—not openly. He paused for an instant, hayfork in hand, to wonder just what would happen if he entered surreptitiously and was caught? What could Lord Dunsany do to him? He couldn't be dismissed, after all.

That ludicrous thought made him laugh, and he went back to his work and his thinking in a better humor.

Well, there was church. The Dunsanys were Anglican and usually attended St. Margaret's, the village church in Ellesmere. They traveled by coach, and Betty normally went with Lady Dunsany and Lady Isobel, her mistress. He was under parole as a prisoner of war; he couldn't set foot off the estate at Helwater without leave from Lord Dunsany—but the big coach required a team of four, which meant two drivers, and Jamie was the only groom who could drive more than a gig.

Aye, that might work; he'd see. If he could get within reach of Betty, he could perhaps slip her a note that would bring her out to talk to him. God knew what he'd say, but he'd think of something.

He could of course entrust such a note to one of the kitchen maids when he had his breakfast, but the fewer people who had to do with this business, the better. He'd try it alone first.

That much tentatively decided, he stopped to wipe his face with the grubby towel that hung on a hook over the bran tub and turned his mind again toward Betty's Irish gentleman.

Did he exist at all? If he did, what the devil did he want with Alex MacKenzie? Unless, of course, it *wasn't* Alex MacKenzie but instead Jamie Fraser whom he—

This embryonic train of thought was severed by a skittering

thud and the appearance of Hanks at the foot of the ladder, yellow-jowled and smelling rancid.

"Here, Mac," he said, trying to sound jovial. "Do me a favor?"

"Aye. What?"

Hanks managed a ghastly half smile.

"Doncher want to know what it is?"

"No." What he wanted was for Hanks to leave, and now. The man stank as though he were dead inside, and the horses near him were whuffling and snorting in disgust.

"Oh." Hanks rubbed a trembling hand over his face. " 'S not much. Just . . . can you take my string out? I'm not . . ." The hand fell limp in sweeping illustration of all the things that Hanks was not.

A gust of wind came in cold beneath the stable door, smelling of the coming rain, whirling chaff and straw along the bricks between the boxes. He hesitated. It would be pouring within the hour. He could feel the storm brooding up there on the fells, dark with its gathering.

Rain wouldn't trouble the horses; they loved it. And the fog would go when the rain fell; no great danger of getting lost.

"Meet him on the fells," Betty had said. *"Where the old shepherd's hut is."*

"Aye, fine." He turned his back and began to measure out the bran and flaxseed for the mash. After a moment, he heard Hanks stumble toward the ladder and he half-turned, watching in idle curiosity to see whether the man might fall and break his neck. He didn't, though.

April 3

In the event, it had rained too hard to get high up on the fells. Jamie had taken his string of horses pounding through the mud of the lakeshore road, then walked them through the shallows of Glassmere to get the worst of it off, then back to be rubbed down and dried. He'd glanced up toward the fells once, but the rain hid the heights where the ruins of the old shepherd's hut lay.

It was cold on the fells today but bright, and he had no string to fash with. Augustus's coat steamed from the effort of the climb, and Jamie reined up at the crest of the rocky path to reconnoiter and to let the horse breathe. This high up, the landscape was still patched with winter, rags of frozen snow in the lee of the rocks and dripping icicles still hanging under ledges, but he felt the sun's warmth on his shoulders and there was a faint haze of green over White Moss, just visible in the distance below.

He'd come up this way, approaching the ruined shepherd's cottage from behind and above, to give himself an opportunity to look things over. There was no reason to suspect ambush or trap, but instinct had kept him alive so far and he seldom ignored its grim mutterings in his ear.

He'd not been up here in months, but very little changed on the fells, save the weather. There was a small tarn below, rimmed with a crescent of thin ice, last year's dry reeds poking black through it, not yet supplanted by new growth. The shepherd's hut was just beyond the tarn. So ruined was it that from the water's level you'd never see it, taking it for no more than another heap of lichened stones. From above, though, the square foundation was clearly visible—and, in one corner, something flapped in the wind. Canvas, maybe? There was a bundle of some kind there, he was almost sure.

Nothing moved below save the flapping canvas and the wind in the last of winter's grass. He slid off Augustus and hobbled him, leaving the gelding to nose among the rocks for what might be found there. He walked a short way along the ridge for a better view and, emerging from behind a jutting outcrop, saw the man sitting on a rock, thirty feet below him, also watching the ruined hut.

He was thin; Jamie could see the bones of his shoulders stark under his coat. He wore a slouched hat, but as Jamie watched him, he removed this to scratch his scalp, revealing a head of brown curls streaked with gray. He seemed familiar, and Jamie was racking his memory in search of the man's name when his foot dislodged a small rock. It made a tiny sound, but enough. The man turned and stood up, thin face lighting. He'd lost an eyetooth, Jamie saw, but it didn't impair the charm of his smile.

"Well, and is it not Himself? Well met, Jamie dear, well met!"

"Quinn?" he said, disbelieving. "Is it you?"

The Irishman glanced quizzically down at his body, patted his chest, and looked up again.

"Well, what's left of me. There's none of us is all we once were, after all—though I must say ye're lookin' well in yourself." He looked Jamie up and down with approval. "The air up here must agree with ye. And ye've filled out a bit since last I saw ye."

"I daresay," Jamie replied, rather dryly. When last he'd seen Tobias Quinn, in 1746, he had been twenty-five and starving along with the rest of the Jacobite army. Quinn was a year younger than himself, and Jamie saw the lines in the Irishman's face and the gray in his hair with a sense of dismay. If Quinn felt any similar emotion at sight of Jamie, he kept it to himself.

"Ye might have told Betty your name," Jamie said, making his way down. He held out a hand to the Irishman, but Quinn stood and flung his arms round Jamie, embracing him. Jamie was startled and embarrassed to feel tears come to his eyes at the touch, and he hugged Quinn tight for a minute, to blink them back.

"She knows my name. But I wasn't sure ye'd come, if ye knew 'twas me." Quinn stood back, brushed an unashamed knuckle under his own eyes, and laughed. "By the Blessed Mother, Jamie, it's glad I am to see ye!"

"And I you." That much was true; Jamie left alone the question of whether he would have come, knowing it was Quinn who waited on the fells. He sat down slowly on a rock, to gain a moment.

It wasn't that he disliked the man; quite the opposite. But to see this bit of the past rise up before him like a ghost from blood-soaked ground roused feelings he'd gone to great trouble to bury—and memories were stirring that he didn't want back. Beyond that . . . instinct had given over muttering in his ear and was talking plain and clear. Quinn had been one of Charles Stuart's intimates, but never a soldier. He'd fled to France after Culloden, or so Jamie had heard. What the devil was he doing here now?

"Ah, sure that Betty's a fine girl, and her with those snapping black eyes," Quinn was saying. He eyed Jamie, head on one side. "She's a bit of a fondness for *you,* my lad, I can tell."

Jamie repressed the urge to cross himself at the thought.

"Ye've a clear field there," he assured Quinn. "Dinna fash yourself that I'd queer your pitch."

Quinn blinked at him, and it struck him of a sudden that "queer your pitch" was one of Claire's expressions; maybe it was not merely English but from her own time?

Whether Quinn was puzzled or not, though, he plainly took Jamie's meaning.

"Well, I might, too—save that Betty's me late wife's sister. I'm sure there's a thing or two in the Bible about not doing the deed with your late wife's sister."

Jamie had read the Bible cover to cover several times—from necessity, it being his only book at the time—and recalled no such proscription, but he merely said, "I'm sorry to hear about your wife, man. Was it lang since that she died?"

Quinn pursed his lips and tilted his head from side to side.

"Well, when I say 'late,' I don't mean necessarily that the woman's *deceased,* if ye take my meaning."

Jamie raised one brow, and Quinn sighed.

"When it all went to smash after Culloden, and I had to scarper to France, she took a hard look at my future prospects, so to speak, and decided her fortunes lay elsewhere. My Tess always did have a sound head on her shoulders," he said, shaking his own head in admiration. "She was in Leeds, the last I heard. Inherited a tavern from her last husband. Well, by 'last,' mind, I mean the latest one, because I don't for a moment think she means to stop."

"Oh, aye?"

"But that's what I wanted to speak with ye about, conveniently enough," Quinn went on, waving an airy hand in dismissal of the erstwhile Tess.

"About Leeds? Or taverns?" Jamie prayed that the man didn't mean wives. He'd not mentioned Claire to anyone in several years and would rather have his toenails pulled out with horsenail pliers than be forced to talk about her.

"Culloden," Quinn said, causing equal amounts of relief and dismay in the bosom of his hearer. Culloden came about fourth on Jamie's list of things he didn't want to talk about, preceded only by his wife, Claire; his son, William; and Jack Randall.

Jamie got off the rock, feeling obscurely that he'd rather be on his feet just now, though not knowing whether it was needing to feel ready to meet whatever was coming or an incipient urge to flee. Either way, he felt better standing.

"Or rather," Quinn amended, "not Culloden so much as the Cause, if ye take my meaning."

"I should think the two are much the same," Jamie said, not trying to keep the edge out of his voice. "Dead."

"Ah, well, now there ye're wrong," Quinn said, waggling a bony finger at him. "Though of course ye'll have been out of touch."

"I have, aye."

Quinn continued to ignore the edge.

"The Cause may have suffered some reverses in Scotland—"

"Reverses!" Jamie exclaimed. "Ye call what happened at Drumossie *reverses*?"

"—but it's alive and thrivin' in Ireland."

Jamie stared at him for a moment of blank incomprehension, then realized what he was saying.

"Jesus!"

"Ah, thought that would gladden yer heart, lad," said Quinn, choosing to interpret Jamie's cry as one of hallelujah rather than horror. He smiled, the tip of his tongue poking briefly through the hole left by his missing eyetooth.

"There's a group of us, see. Did Betty not pass on what I said about the green branch?"

"She did, aye, but I didna ken what she meant by it."

Quinn waved a hand, dismissing this.

"Well, it took some time to pull things together after Culloden, but it's all moving a treat now. I'll not give the details just yet, if ye don't mind—"

"I dinna mind a bit."

"—but I *will* say that there's an invasion planned, maybe as soon as next year—ha-ha! Would ye look at your face now? Flabbergasted, aye? Well, I was, too, first I heard of it. But there's more!"

"Oh, God."

Quinn leaned forward conspiratorially, lowering his voice—though there was no one near enough to hear save a soaring peregrine overhead.

"And this is where *you* come into it."

"Me?!" Jamie had begun to sink back onto his rock, but this brought him up all standing at once. "Are ye mad?"

He hadn't meant it as a rhetorical question, but neither did he expect an affirmative answer, and it was just as well, because he didn't get one.

"Have ye ever heard"—and here Quinn paused to dart his eyes one way and then the other, looking out for invisible watchers—"of the *Cupán Druid riogh*?"

"I have not. A cup . . . ?"

"The cup o' the Druid king, the very thing!"

Jamie rubbed a hand over his face, feeling very tired. "Quinn, I'm pleased to see ye well, but I've work to do and—"

"Oh, indeed ye have, lad!" Quinn reached out and fastened an earnest hand to Jamie's forearm. "Let me explain."

He didn't wait for permission.

"It's the ancient possession o' the kings of Ireland, the *Cupán* is. Given to the king of kings by the chief Druid himself, so far back folk have forgotten the time of it."

"Oh, aye?"

"But the people know it still; it's spoken of in the legends, and 'tis a powerful symbol of kingship." The hand on Jamie's forearm tightened. "Think, now. How would it be, Prince *Tearlach* riding into Dublin, standin' in the courtyard o' Dublin Castle, between the Gates of Fortitude and Justice, with the *Cupán* raised high as he claims all of Ireland for his father?"

"Well, since ye ask . . ."

"Why, man, the people would rise from the *bailes* and the bogs in their thousands! We should take England with scarce a shot fired, there'd be so many!"

"Ye have *seen* the English army . . ." Jamie began, but he might as well have tried to stop the tide coming into the River Ness.

"And that's where *you* come in!" Quinn let go of his arm at last, but only in order to prod him enthusiastically in the chest.

Jamie recoiled slightly. "Me?"

"See, the thing is, we've found the *Cupán*—lost for two hundred years it's been, and legends saying the faeries took it, the Druids reclaimed it, all manner of tosh, but we—well, I myself, in fact"—here he tried to look modest, with indifferent results—"discovered it, in the hands of the monks at the monastery of Inchcleraun."

"But—"

"Now, the monks are keepin' the precious thing close and quiet, to be sure. But the thing is, the abbot at Inchcleraun is one Michael FitzGibbons." He stood back a bit, looking expectant.

Jamie raised the brow again. Quinn sighed at such obtuseness but obliged with more information.

"Mi-chael Fitz-Gib-bons," he repeated, prodding Jamie's chest anew with each syllable. Jamie moved back out of reach.

"FitzGibbons," Quinn repeated, "and the man first cousin to your godfather, Murtagh FitzGibbons Fraser, is he not? To say nothing of having grown up in the house of your uncle Alexander Fraser, and the two of them thick as thieves? Though perhaps that's not quite the figure of speech to be using for a pair of priests, but what I mean to say is, they might be brothers, so close as they are, and the two writing back and forth from month to month. So—"

Finally, Quinn was obliged to draw breath, giving Jamie the chance to stick a word in edgewise.

"No," he said definitely. "Not for all the tea in China."

Quinn's long face creased in puzzlement. "China? What's China got to do with it, for all love?"

Ah. Another of Claire's sayings, then. He tried again. "I mean I will not try to persuade my uncle Alexander to pry this thing out of FitzGibbons's hands."

"Oh, no, that's not what I had in mind, at all."

"Good, because—"

"I want ye to go to Inchcleraun yourself. Oh, now, there's that look on your face again!" Quinn laughed in amusement, rocking back, then planted his hands on his knees and leaned forward.

Jamie leaned forward, too, to forestall him.

"Quinn, I'm a prisoner of war. I've given my parole. Surely to goodness Betty told ye as much?"

"Sure and I didn't think ye were here for your health," Quinn said, with a glance round at the bleak fells and the desolate ruins of the shepherd's hut. "But that's of no moment."

"It's not?"

Quinn waved this aside as a mere quibble.

"No. It's got to be someone Father Michael trusts and at the same time someone known to be at the right hand o' the Stuarts, who can swear that the *Cupán* won't be misused but put to its right and sacred purpose in restoring a Catholic monarch to the throne of Ireland. *And* a man who can raise and lead an army. People trust you, ye know," he said earnestly, tilting his head up and examining Jamie's face. "They listen when ye speak, and men will follow ye without question. It's known of ye."

"No longer," Jamie said, and found he was clenching his fists; his throat was dried by the wind, so the words came hoarse. "No. No longer."

Quinn's fizzy manner had calmed somewhat. He clasped Jamie's hand in both his own.

"Man, dear," he said, almost gently. "Kings have their destiny about them—but so do those who serve them. This is yours. God's chosen ye for the task."

Jamie closed his eyes briefly, drew a deep breath, and pulled his hand free.

"I think God had best look elsewhere, Quinn," he said. "The blessing of Bride and Michael be on you. Goodbye."

He turned and walked away, finding Augustus where he'd been left, peacefully cropping the tufts of wiry grass that grew between the rocks. He removed the hobbles, swung up into the saddle, and turned the horse's head toward the trail. He hadn't meant to look back but at the last minute glanced down toward the shepherd's hut.

Quinn stood there in dark silhouette against the late-afternoon sun, a stick-jointed marionette with a nimbus of curls. He lifted a long-fingered hand and waved in farewell.

"See ye in Dublin town!" he called. "Stuart *go bragh*!" and his merry laugh followed Jamie down the steep track toward Helwater.

HE RODE DOWN from the fells, prey to an unsettling mix of emotions. Incredulity and impatience at Quinn's fat-heided scheme, a weary dismay at the realization that the Jacobite Cause was still alive, if only faintly squirming, and irritation at Quinn's attempt to inveigle him back into it. More than a bit of fear, if he was honest. And notwithstanding all that . . . joy at seeing

Quinn again. It had been a long time since he'd seen the face of a friend.

"Bloody Irishman," he muttered, but smiled nonetheless.

Would Quinn go away now? he wondered. The Irishman was as bullet-headed as most of his race and not likely to give up his scheme only because Jamie refused to help him with it. But he might well go and have a try at some other feckless candidate. Half of Jamie hoped to God that was the case. The other half wouldn't mind talking to the man again, hearing what news he had about the others who'd left Culloden alive.

The muscle of his leg contracted suddenly, and a chill shivered over his skin as though a ghost paced by his stirrup. Augustus snorted, sensing his tension.

He clicked his tongue in reassurance, letting the horse pick his own way through the tricky footing of the trail. His heart was racing, and he tried to breathe deep and slow to calm it. Damn Quinn for bringing it back. He'd dream tonight, and a mixed feeling of dread and hope rose in him at the knowledge. Whose face would he see?

MUCH TO HIS ANNOYANCE, he dreamed of Charles Stuart. Drunk as usual, amiable as always, the prince reeled down a dark street somewhere at Jamie's side, poking him now and then, blethering of this and that, grabbing his arm and giggling as he pointed out a row of heads mounted on spikes along a wall.

"Coimhead," the man kept saying. *"A Dhia coimhead am fear ud' seall an dealbh a th'air aodann!"* Look at that one, God, the look on its face.

"What are ye about?" Jamie demanded irritably. "Ye ken ye havena got the *Gàidhlig.*"

"Bheil e gu diofair," replied Prince *Tearlach.* Does it matter?

Quinn, who had suddenly appeared from somewhere, seized Jamie's arm with great strength, compelling him to stop.

"Coimhead nach ann oirre tha a ghruag aluinn?" Look—does she not have lovely hair?

Jamie had been trying not to look but did now and, surprised, saw that all the heads were women's. He was holding a torch and raised it to see Geneva Dunsany's face looking back at him, pale and composed, with black and empty eye sockets. From the corner of his eye, he could see that the next head had a wealth of curling light-brown hair; he dashed the torch onto the wet cobbles at his feet in order not to see and woke, heart pounding, to the sound of Charles's drunken laughter.

It wasn't, though. It was Hanks, laughing in his sleep, the sharp smell of beer and urine hanging in a cloud over his pallet; he'd pissed himself again. The moon was up, and the mice who lived in the loft were stirring; moonlight always made them venturesome. Hanks subsided into heavy breathing and Jamie could hear the tiny scratch of nails on the floor, the rustle of straw.

He threw back his blanket, determined not to go to sleep again until the dream had faded. But it had been a long day, and in spite of the cold, he dozed again.

Sleeping cold always gave him bad dreams. The new one had to do with Betty, and he woke from that in a cold sweat. Fumbling in the box that held his possessions, he found his rosary and sank back into the matted straw of his pallet, clinging to the wooden beads as though to a raft that might keep him afloat.

4

Not Good

Regimental Offices of the 46th Foot
London

MR. BEASLEY WAS DISTURBED ABOUT SOMETHING. THE AGE of Hal's regimental clerk was an unknowable secret; he had looked just the same—ancient—ever since John Grey had first set eyes on him, a quarter century before. But those who knew him well could detect small fluctuations in his gray, peering countenance in times of stress, and Grey was seeing more and more of these subtle tremors of the jaw, the subterranean quiverings of eyelid, as Mr. Beasley turned over the pages of Charles Carruthers's combustible packet with tidy, ink-stained fingers.

The elderly clerk was supposed to be making a list of the men indicted in the documents, those men whom Carruthers had known or suspected to have had dealings, financial or otherwise, with Major Gerald Siverly. Grey was supposed to be joining Hal and Harry Quarry—one of the regimental colonels and Hal's oldest friend—for a discussion of strategy, but neither one had arrived yet, and Grey had wandered into Mr. Beasley's clerk's hole to borrow a book; the old man had a remarkable collection of French novels squirreled discreetly away in one of his cabinets.

Grey took down a copy of Abbé Prévost's *Manon Lescaut,* and thumbed casually through the pages, watching Beasley covertly as he did so. He knew better than to ask; Mr. Beasley was the soul of discretion, that being only one of the attributes that made him invaluable to Hal, as he had been to the first earl of Melton, their father and the founder of the regiment.

The disturbance was growing worse. Mr. Beasley made to dip his pen but instead allowed it to hover above the ink-stand and then slowly set it down. He had turned over a page; now he turned it back and studied something upon it, thin lips compressed almost into invisibility.

"Lord John," he said at last, and removed his spectacles to blink nearsightedly up at Grey.

"Yes, Mr. Beasley." He put down *Manon Lescaut* at once and looked expectant.

"You have read these documents, I collect?"

"I have," Grey said cautiously. "Perhaps not with the greatest attention to detail, but . . ."

"And His Grace has read them. What—if I may inquire—was his state of mind upon reading them?"

Grey considered. "Well, he didn't break anything. He swore quite a bit in German, though."

"Ah." Mr. Beasley appreciated the significance of this point. He tapped spatulate fingertips upon his desk; he *was* perturbed. "Do you—would you describe him as having flown into a horrid passion?"

"I would," Grey said promptly.

"But he did not mention anything . . . *specific* . . . with regard to these documents?" He glanced at the neat stack beside him.

"No . . ." Grey said slowly. Hal had certainly noted the Erse poem, if that's what it was, but that sheet had not been given to Mr. Beasley; that couldn't be what was disturbing the elderly clerk. He risked a question. "Have you noticed something?"

Mr. Beasley grimaced and turned the sheet around, facing Grey.

"There," he said, placing a precise finger in the middle of the page. "Read that list of Major Siverly's known associates, if you would be so kind."

Grey obligingly sat down and bent his head over the sheet. Three seconds later his head snapped up and he stared at the clerk. "Jesus!"

"Yes," said Mr. Beasley mildly. "I thought that, too. You don't think he's seen it?"

"I'm sure he hasn't."

They stared at each other for a moment, hearing the sound of footsteps coming down the corridor. Grey swallowed.

"Let me do it," he said, and, taking the sheet, folded it hastily into his pocket, then rose to greet his brother.

HAL HAD A CARRIAGE waiting outside.

"We're meeting Harry at Almack's," he said.

"What for? He's not a member there, is he?" Harry was a clubbable man, but he was largely to be found at White's Chocolate House, Hal's own particular haunt in terms of coffeehouses, or at the Society for the Appreciation of the English Beefsteak, which was Grey's favorite—a gentlemen's club rather than a coffeehouse. There were occasional clashes between the patrons of White's and those of Boodle's or Almack's; London coffeehouses inspired considerable loyalty.

"He's not," Hal said tersely. "But Bartholomew Halloran is."

"And Bartholomew Halloran is . . . ?"

"The adjutant of the Thirty-fifth."

"Ah. And thus a source of information on Major Gerald Siverly, also of that regiment."

"Quite. He's a casual acquaintance of Harry's; they play cards now and then."

"I hope Harry's wily enough to lose convincingly." The carriage hit a pothole and lurched, flinging them heavily to the side. Hal saved himself by thrusting a foot hard into the opposite seat, between his brother's legs. John, with equally good reflexes, grabbed the foot.

The coach swayed precariously for an instant but then righted itself, and they resumed their original positions.

"We should have walked," Hal said, and made to stick his head out the window to call to the coachman. Grey seized him by the sleeve, though, and he looked at his brother in surprise.

"No. Just—no. Wait."

Hal stared at him for a moment, but then lowered himself back to the seat.

"What is it?" he said. He looked wary but keen.

"This," said Grey simply, and, reaching into his pocket, handed over the folded sheet. "Read the list of names in the middle."

Hal took the sheet, frowning, and began to read. Grey counted in his head. Hal didn't read quite as fast as he did.

Five . . . four . . . three . . . two . . . one . . .

"Jesus!"

"Well, yes."

They looked at each other in silence for the length of several heartbeats.

"Of *all* the men Siverly could have had dealings with—" Hal said, and shook his head violently, like a man trying to rid himself of flies.

"It has to be, of course," Grey said. "I mean, there aren't two of them, surely."

"Would that there were. But I doubt it. Edward Twelvetrees is not that common a name."

"Once upon a time, there were three brothers," Grey said, half under his breath. Hal had closed his eyes and was breathing heavily. "Reginald, Nathaniel . . . and Edward."

Hal opened his eyes. "It's always the youngest who gets the princess, isn't it?" He gave John a lopsided smile. "Younger brothers are the very devil."

AT THIS HOUR of the morning, Almack's public rooms were bustling. Harry Quarry was chatting amiably with a thin, worried-looking man whom Grey recognized as a stockbroker. On seeing them, Harry took his leave with a word and stood up, coming to meet them.

"I've bespoke a private cardroom," Harry said, shaking hands with Grey and nodding to Hal. "Symington, Clifford, and Bingham will be joining us shortly."

Grey nodded cordially, wondering what on earth Harry was about, but Hal gave no sign of surprise.

"Didn't want it to get about that inquiries were being made," Harry explained, peering out in the larger room before shutting the door to the cardroom. "We'll have a few minutes to talk, then, once the others have come, we'll have a few hands of picquet, you lot leave for another engagement, and I'll stay on. No one will notice you've even been here."

Harry looked so pleased at this stratagem for deflecting suspicion that Grey hadn't the heart to point out that Harry might simply have come to Argus House to share whatever news he'd gained from Halloran. Hal didn't look at John but nodded gravely at Harry.

"Very clever," he said. "But if we've not much time—"

He was interrupted by a servant bringing in a tray of coffee dishes, a plate of biscuits, and several decks of cards, already separated into the *talons* required for picquet.

"If we've not much time," Hal repeated, with an edge in his voice, once the servant had departed, "perhaps you'd best tell us what Halloran had to say."

"A fair amount," Harry said, sitting down. "Coffee?"

Harry's bluff, craggy face inspired confidence in men and a remarkable degree of sensual abandonment in women, which Grey considered one of the great mysteries of nature. On the other hand, he didn't presume to know what women thought attractive. In the present instance, though, Adjutant Halloran appeared to have been taken in by Harry's casual charm as easily as any society lady.

"Lot of talk, regimental gossip," Harry said, dismissing all of this with a wave of one broad hand. He spilled coffee into his saucer and blew on it, making wisps of aromatic steam rise from the dark brew. "Got him round to Siverly eventually, though. He respects Siverly, doesn't much like him. Reputation as a good soldier, good commander. Doesn't waste men. . . . What?"

Both the Greys had made noises. Hal waved a hand at Harry.

"Tell you later. Go on. Did he say anything about the mutiny in Canada?"

"No." Harry arched a brow. "But he wouldn't, would he? It wasn't brought to a general court-martial, and if it was a regimental affair . . ."

Grey nodded; regimental courts-martial were usually kept private, no regiment wanting to wash its dirty linen in public. For that matter, the public wouldn't be interested in such affairs, which dealt with the daily crimes and trespasses of common soldiers, for the most part: drunkenness, theft, fighting, insubordination, lying out of barracks without leave, and selling their uniforms. General courts-martial were different, though Grey was unsure of just what the differences were, having never been involved in one. He thought there had to be a judge advocate involved.

"He hasn't been brought before a general court-martial *yet*," Hal said grimly.

Harry's eyes narrowed, lips pursed as he sipped his coffee. It smelled good, and Grey reached for the pot.

"Really?" Harry said. "That's what we have in mind, is it?" Hal had informed Harry, by note, of their interest in Siverly, asking him to find out what he could of the man's particulars—but knowing Hal's way with letters, Grey thought there had probably not been much detail given.

"Certainly," Hal said. "So, what else?" He picked up one of the biscuits and examined it critically before popping it into his mouth.

"Siverly's not wildly popular in the regiment, but not disliked," Harry said. "Sociable, but not active. Invited in society, accepts occasionally. Has a wife, but doesn't live with her. She brought him some money, not a great deal, but no great connections."

"Has he any of his own?" Grey asked, mouth half full. The biscuits were ginger-nuts, and fresh, still warm from the kitchen. "Any family?"

"Ah," said Harry, and glanced briefly at Hal. "No family connections to speak of. Father was a captain in the Eleventh Dragoons, killed at Culloden. Mother was the daughter of a wealthy Irish family, but from the country, no influence."

"But?" Hal said sharply, having caught the glance. "He has important friends?"

Harry took a breath that swelled his waistcoat and leaned back.

"Oh, yes," he said. "The Duke of Cumberland important enough for you?"

"He'll do to be going on with," Hal said, brows raised. "What's the connection there?"

"Hunting. Siverly has an estate in Ireland and has entertained His Grace there on occasion. Together with a few of the duke's intimates."

"An estate? Inherited?" Grey asked.

"No, bought. Fairly recently."

Hal made a low humming noise that indicated satisfaction. Obviously Siverly hadn't bought a large estate, even in Ireland, on his pay. From Carruthers's accounts, Siverly's ventures in Canada had netted him something in excess of thirty thousand pounds.

"Very good," he said. "That would impress the board of a court-martial."

"Well, it might," Harry said, flicking crumbs off his stomach. "If you can get him in front of one."

"If necessary, I'll have him arrested and dragged there by force."

Harry made a hmmphing noise, one implying doubt, which made Hal give him a narrow look.

"You don't think I'd do it? This blackguard disgraces the name of his profession, as well as damaging the whole army by his gross behavior. Besides," he added, as an afterthought, "John's bound to see justice done, by his word of honor."

"Oh, I think you'd do it," Harry assured him. "And so would Grey. It's just that Siverly's in Ireland. Might complicate matters, eh?"

"Oh," said Hal, looking rather blank.

"Why?" asked Grey, stopped in the act of pouring more coffee. "What's he doing there?"

"Damned if I know. All Halloran said was that Siverly had asked for—and been granted—six months' leave to attend to personal matters."

"He didn't resign his commission, though?" Grey leaned forward, anxious. He wasn't sure but thought a court-martial couldn't try someone who was not in the army. And going after Siverly in the civil courts would be a much more laborious undertaking.

Harry shrugged. "Don't think so. Halloran only said he'd taken leave."

"Well, then." Hal put down his dish in a decided manner and turned to his brother. "You'll just have to go to Ireland and bring him back."

❦

THE ARRIVAL OF the picquet party put paid to further discussion, and Grey found himself paired with Leo Clifford, a pleasant young captain who had recently joined the regiment. Clifford was no particular hand at cards, though, which left a good bit of Grey's mind free to brood on the recent conversation.

"Go to Ireland and bring him back." He supposed he should be flattered that Hal trusted him to do such a thing, but he knew his brother well enough to know it was merely expectation and not compliment.

Could you court-martial someone *in absentia*? he wondered. He'd have to ask Minnie. She had ferreted out records of courts-martial for the crime of sodomy when their stepbrother, Percy Wainwright, had been arrested. The army had shipped Percy back to England from Germany to stand trial, so perhaps you *couldn't* try someone not physically present.

"Repique," he said absently. Clifford sighed and wrote down the score.

He'd got over Percy. Or at least he thought so, most of the time. Every now and then, though, he'd catch sight of a slender young man with dark curly hair, and his heart would jerk.

It jerked now, a tiny bump at the sudden thought that it was the mention of Ireland, more than courts-martial, that had made him think of Percy. He'd arranged for Percy to escape to Ireland, though his erstwhile lover had made his way eventually to Rome. Surely he would have no reason to go back to Ireland . . . ?

"Sixième!" Clifford said, his voice full of joy. Grey smiled, despite the loss of points, gave the proper reply of "Not good," meaning his own hand could not beat that, and put Percy firmly out of mind.

Harry had suggested that Grey and Hal might leave after the first game, but Grey was entirely aware that Harry knew this wouldn't happen. Hal was a cutthroat cardplayer, and once his blood was up, there was no dragging him away from the table. As picquet was a game for two hands, obviously Grey couldn't leave until Hal did, or the numbers would be unbalanced.

They therefore played in pairs, changing partners after each game, the two men with the highest scores to play the final game. Grey did his best to put everything out of his mind but the play. He succeeded to such an extent that he was startled when his brother—now opposing him—stiffened in his seat, head turning sharply toward the door.

There were voices raised in greeting in the outer room and the noise of several people coming in. In the midst of it, he caught the high, oddly prim voice of the Duke of Cumberland. He stared at Hal, who compressed his lips. Hal cordially disliked Cumberland—and vice versa—and the revelation that the duke was an intimate of Siverly's was unlikely to have improved this animus.

Hal's eye met his, and Grey knew what his brother was thinking: it would be necessary to proceed with the utmost secrecy. If Cumberland caught wind of the matter before the court-martial could be organized, he might well plant his fat arse right in the middle of it.

Then Grey caught the sound of another voice, deeper, gruff with age and tobacco, replying to something Cumberland had said.

"Scheisse!" Hal said, making everyone look at him curiously.

"Don't you say *carte blanche* if you have a hand with no points?" Clifford whispered, leaning over to Grey.

"Yes, you do," Grey replied, narrowing his eyes at Hal. He felt like saying something much worse himself, but it wouldn't do to attract attention. Harry, on the other side of the room, had heard that voice, too, and pursed his lips, eyes fixed on his cards.

Grey hadn't heard Reginald Twelvetrees's voice in some time, but he had vivid memories of it. Colonel Reginald Twelvetrees had headed a board of inquiry into the explosion of a cannon, two years before, and had come uncomfortably close to ruining Grey's career over it, out of the long-standing hostility that had existed between the Greys and the Twelvetrees family since Hal's duel with Nathaniel, the colonel's younger brother.

"When do you say *scheisse*?" Clifford whispered.

"When something untoward occurs," Grey whispered back, repressing an urge to laugh. *"Septième,"* he said aloud to his brother.

"Not good," Hal growled, and tossed in his hand.

5

Why Am Not I at Peace?

Helwater

IT HADN'T BEEN A GOOD NIGHT. IT WASN'T GOING TO BE A good day.

Hanks and Crusoe didn't look at him when they all made their way up to the house for breakfast. He'd been screaming in his sleep, then. A dull red flush burned up from his belly, radiating from a core of hot lead somewhere deep inside. He felt as though he'd swallowed a two-pound shot, fresh from the cannon's mouth.

He'd dreamed, he knew that much. Had wakened before dawn, shaking and drenched with sweat. It had been a dream of Culloden, because all he recalled was the sickening feel of a sword driven into flesh, the momentary toughness just before the skin split, the yielding drive into muscle and the grate and jar of bone. The feeling still quivered in his left arm; he kept flexing his hand and wiping it against his thigh.

He ate nothing but managed a mug of scalding tea the color of dirt. That soothed him, and so did the walk out to the farthest paddock, bridle in hand. The air was still chilly, but the lingering snow on the fells was melting; he could hear the voice of running water, coming down through the rocks. The bogs in the low ground—"mosses," the locals called them: White Moss, Threapland Moss, Leighton Moss—would all be greening now, the ground growing softer and more treacherous by the day.

There was a long slender switch of fresh elder floating in the horse trough in the far paddock, though there were no trees of any kind within a quarter mile and no elders nearer than the manor house. Jamie muttered, "Christ," under his breath, and plucked the stem out, dripping. The dark resinous buds had begun to split, and crumpled leaves of a vivid light green keeked out.

"He says to tell you the green branch will flower." He flung the branch over the fence. It wasn't the first. He'd found one laid across his path three days ago, when he'd brought his string in from exercise, and another yesterday, wedged into a cleft in the fence of the riding arena.

He put his hands to his mouth and shouted, "NO!" in a voice that rang off the tumbled stones at the foot of the nearest fell. He didn't expect to be heard, let alone obeyed, but it relieved his feelings. Shaking his head, he caught the horse he'd come for and made his way back to the stable.

Life had gone back to its accustomed rhythm since his meeting with Quinn, but the Irishman's pernicious influence lingered, in the form of bad dreams, as well as the mocking greenery.

And then there was Betty. Coming up to the house for his tea—much needed, he having had neither breakfast nor elevenses—he saw the lass loitering about the gate to the kitchen garden. A lady's maid had no business to be there, but the flower beds were nearby, and she had a bouquet of daffodils in one hand. She raised these to her nose and gave him a provocative look over them. He meant to go by without acknowledgment, but she stepped into his path, playfully brushing the flowers across his chest.

"They havena got any smell, have they?" he said, fending them off.

"No, but they're so pretty, aren't they?"

"If ye canna eat them, I'm no particularly inclined to admire them. Now, if ye—" He stopped abruptly, for she had pressed into his hand a sprig of willow, with its long, fuzzy yellow catkins. A note was wrapped about the stem, secured with string.

He handed it back to her without hesitation and walked up the path.

"MacKenzie!"

He knew it was a mistake to turn around, but ingrained courtesy had turned him before he could resist. "Mistress Betty?"

"I'll tell." Her black eyes glittered, and her chin thrust out pugnaciously.

"Aye, do," he said. "And I hope ye've a fine day for it." He turned his back on her but, on second thought, turned again.

"Tell who what?" he demanded.

She blinked at that. But then a sly look came into her eyes.

"What do you *think*?" she said, and turned away in a flounce of skirts.

He shook his head, trying to shake his wits into some semblance of order. Was the bloody woman talking about what he'd thought she was talking about?

He'd assumed that she meant she'd tell Lord Dunsany that he'd been secretly meeting an Irish Jacobite on the fells. But looked at logically . . . would she?

Quinn was, after all, her brother-in-law. And presumably she liked the man well enough, or why carry his messages? Would she risk having him arrested?

Was the note she had tried to give him from Quinn, in fact? He'd thought so, seeing the willow branchlet, but perhaps it was her own silly attempt at further seduction, in which case he'd just mortally offended her. He breathed heavily through his nose.

Putting that aside . . . it might cause Jamie a bit of bother if she mentioned his meeting Quinn, but if you came right down to it, the one advantage of his present position was that there really wasn't much anyone could do to make it worse. He was not Dunsany's prisoner; the baronet couldn't lock him up, put him in irons, feed him on bread and water, or flog him. The most Dunsany could do was to inform Lord John Grey.

He snorted at the thought. He doubted that wee pervert could face him, after what had been said during their last meeting, let alone take issue with him over Quinn. Still, he felt a cramping in his middle at the thought of seeing Grey again and didn't want to think too much about why.

At least there was cake for the servants' tea. He could smell its aroma, warm and yeasty, and his step quickened.

IF HE DREAMED that night, he had the mercy of not remembering it. He kept a wary eye out, but no green branches lay across his path or fell from his clothes as he dressed. Perhaps Betty had told Quinn about his ungracious response to the proffered note and the man had given up.

"Aye, that'll be the day," he muttered. He knew a number of Irishmen, and most of them persistent as saddle burrs. He also knew Quinn.

Still, the day looked like an improvement over the last—at least until word came down from the house that Lady Isobel required a groom to drive her into the town. Hanks had fallen down the ladder this morning and broken his arm—or at least he said it was broken and retired, groaning, to the loft to await the attentions of the local horse leech—and Crusoe avoided the town, he having gotten into an altercation with a blacksmith's apprentice on his last visit that had left him with a flattened nose and two black eyes.

"You go, MacKenzie," Crusoe said, pretending to be busy with a piece of harness in need of mending. "I'll take your string."

"Aye, thanks." He felt pleased at the thought of getting off Helwater for a bit. Large as the estate was, the feeling that he could not leave if he wanted to chafed him. And it had been some months since he'd been to town; he looked forward to the journey, even if it involved Lady Isobel.

Isobel Dunsany was not the horsewoman her sister, Geneva, had been. She was not precisely timid with horses, but she didn't like them, and the horses knew it. She didn't like Jamie, either, and he knew that fine well; she didn't hide it.

Nay wonder about that, he thought, handing her up into the pony trap. *If Geneva told her, she likely thinks I killed her sister.* He rather thought Geneva *had* told Isobel about his visit to Geneva's room; the sisters had been close. Almost certainly she hadn't told Isobel that she'd brought him to her bed by means of blackmail, though.

Isobel didn't look at him and jerked her elbow free of his grip the instant her foot touched the boards. That was nothing unusual—but today she turned her head suddenly, fixing him with an odd, piercing look before turning away, biting her lip.

He got up beside her and twitched the reins over the pony's back, but was aware of her eyes burning a hole in his right shoulder.

What burr's got under her saddle? he wondered. Had bloody Betty said something to her? Accused him, maybe, of interfering with her? Was that what the little besom had meant by "I'll tell"?

The lines came to him suddenly, from a play by Congreve: *Heav'n has no Rage, like Love to Hatred turn'd, / Nor Hell a Fury, like a Woman scorn'd.* Damm it, he thought irritably. Was it not possible to refuse a woman's bed without her feeling scorned? Well . . . possibly not. He had a sudden distant memory of Laoghaire MacKenzie and an ill wish, a bundle of herbs tied with colored thread. He shoved it aside.

He'd read the Congreve play in Ardsmuir prison, over the course of several weekly dinners with Lord John Grey. Could still hear Grey declaim those lines, very dramatic.

> *As you'll answer it, take heed*
> *This Slave commit no Violence upon*
> *Himself. I've been deceiv'd. The Publick Safety*
> *Requires he should be more confin'd; and none,*
> *No not the Princes self, permitted to*
> *Confer with him. I'll quit you to the King.*
> *Vile and ingrate! too late thou shalt repent*
> *The base Injustice thou hast done my Love:*
> *Yes, thou shalt know, spite of thy past Distress,*
> *And all those Ills which thou so long hast mourn'd;*
> *Heav'n has no Rage, like Love to Hatred turn'd,*
> *Nor Hell a Fury, like a Woman scorn'd.*

"What?" said Lady Isobel, rather rudely.

"I beg your pardon, my lady?"

"You snorted."

"I beg your pardon, my lady."

"Hmmph."

Musick has Charms to sooth a savage Breast,
To soften Rocks, or bend a knotted Oak.
I've read, that things inanimate have mov'd,
And, as with living Souls, have been inform'd,
By Magick Numbers and persuasive Sound.
What then am I? Am I more senseless grown
Than Trees, or Flint? O force of constant Woe!
'Tis not in Harmony to calm my Griefs.
Anselmo sleeps, and is at Peace; last Night
The silent Tomb receiv'd the good Old King;
He and his Sorrows now are safely lodg'd
Within its cold, but hospitable Bosom.
Why am not I at Peace?

He wondered whether music really did help. He could not himself distinguish one tune from another. Still, he was pleased to know that he could recall so much of the play and passed the rest of the journey pleasantly in reciting lines to himself, being careful not to snort.

AT LADY ISOBEL'S DIRECTION, he deposited her at an imposing stone house, with instructions to come back in three hours. He nodded—she glowered at him; she thought him insolent, because he never tugged his forelock in the manner she thought proper deference (*Be damned to her for a high-heided wee baggage,* he thought, smiling pleasantly)—and drove to the square, where he could unhitch and water the pony.

People looked at him, startled by his size and coloring, but then went about their own business and left him to his. He hadn't any money but enjoyed himself in strolling through the narrow streets, luxuriating in the feeling that—for however short a time—no one in the world knew exactly where he was. The day was bright, though cold, and the gardens had begun to bloom with snowdrops, tulips, and daffodils, blowing in the wind. The daffodils reminded him of Betty, but he was too much at peace with himself just now to be bothered.

It was a small town, and he'd passed the house where he'd left Isobel several times. On the fourth passage, though, he glimpsed the wind-tossed feathers of her hat through a screen of thinly leaved bushes in the back garden. Surprised, he walked to the end of the street and went round the corner. From here, he had a clear view of the back garden, neat behind a black iron fence—and a very clear view of Lady Isobel, locked in passionate embrace with a gentleman.

He ducked hastily out of sight before either of them should look up and made his way back to the square, nonplussed. Carefully casual inquiry among the loungers near the horse trough elicited the information that the house on Houghton Street with the black iron fence belonged to Mr. Wilberforce, a lawyer—and from the description of Mr. Wilberforce, it was indeed this gentleman who had been making love to Lady Isobel in his gazebo.

That explained Isobel's manner, he thought: excited, but wary lest he discover her secret. She'd had a parcel under her arm, a taped packet of documents; no doubt she'd brought them to the lawyer, her father being ill. Lord Dunsany had had a bad winter, having taken a chill that turned to pleurisy, and Isobel had come often to the town during his sickness, presumably on the family's business. Whereupon . . .

Aye, well. Perhaps I'm none so worrit by what Betty might say to her ladyship.

Whistling tunelessly through his teeth, he began leisurely to hitch up the pony.

THERE WAS A NOTABLE LACK of green branches for the next few days, nay a squeak out of Betty, and he began to relax. Then on Thursday, a warm bright day, Lord Dunsany came down to the paddock where Jamie was shoveling manure, accompanied by old Nanny Elspeth with William in her arms.

Lord Dunsany beckoned to the deeply suspicious nursemaid and waved to Jamie to approach. He did, his chest feeling tight, as though the air had suddenly grown too thick to breathe.

"My lord," he said. He didn't bob his head, let alone knuckle his forehead or make any other physical sign of subservience, and he saw the nurse's mouth purse in disapproval. He gave her a straight, hard look and was pleased to see her rear back and glance away, sallow cheeks flushing.

He was prey to the most extraordinary array of emotions. For the most part, he succeeded in keeping his thoughts of William strictly confined, though he thought of him every day. He seldom saw the child, and when he did, it was only as a glimpse of a woolly bundle in the arms of Nanny Elspeth or Peggy, the nursemaid, taking the air on one of the balconies. He had accustomed himself to thinking of William as a sort of small, glowing light in his mind, something like the flame of a wax candle lit before a saint's statue in a dark chapel. He couldn't afford such a candle, and wouldn't be allowed into the Helwater chapel, but liked to imagine himself lighting one when he said his prayers at night. He would watch the flame catch and swell, wavering a bit and then growing tall and still. He would go to sleep then and feel it burn, a peaceful watch fire in his heart.

"MacKenzie!" Dunsany said, beaming at him and waving at the child. "I thought it time my grandson became acquainted with the horses. Will you fetch out Bella?"

"Of course, my lord."

Bella was a fine old mare, long past breeding but kept by Dunsany for the sake of their long association; she was the first broodmare he had acquired when he established the Helwater stables. She had a kind eye and a good heart, and Jamie could not have chosen better for the purpose.

He had a burning in his chest now, but this was drowned by a wash of panic, guilt, and a ferocious cramp that knotted his belly as though he'd eaten bad meat.

The old nurse eyed him suspiciously, looking slowly up from his sandaled feet to his stubbled face. Plainly she was reluctant to surrender her charge to anything that looked like that. He smiled broadly at her, and she flinched, as though menaced by a savage. *Aye, fine,* he thought. He felt savage.

He plucked the little boy neatly out of her arms, though, scarcely ruffling his gown. The boy gave a small yelp of startlement and turned his head round like an owl in amazement at being suddenly up so high.

Relief washed through him, as the wide eyes stared into his face. His guilty conscience had convinced him that William was an exact small replica of himself, whose resemblance would be noted at once by anyone who saw them together. But William's round face and snub nose bore not the slightest likeness to his own features.While the child's eyes could be called blue, they were pale, an indeterminate shade between gray and blue, the color of a clouded sky.

That was all he had time to take in, as he turned without hesitation to settle the little boy on the horse's back. As he guided the chubby hands to grasp the saddle's edge, though, talking in a conversational tone that soothed horse and child together, he saw that William's hair was—thank God!—not at all red. A soft middling brown, cut in a pudding-bowl style like one of Cromwell's Roundhead soldiers. True, there was a reddish cast to it in the sunlight, but, after all, Geneva's hair had been a rich chestnut.

He looks like his mother, he thought, and sent a heartfelt prayer of thanksgiving toward the Blessed Virgin.

"Now, then, Willie," said Lord Dunsany, patting the boy's back. "Just you hold on tight. MacKenzie will take you round the paddock."

Willie looked very dubious at this proposal, and his chin drew back into the neck of his smock. "Mo!" he said, and, letting go the saddle, swung his fat little leg awkwardly to the rear, plainly intending to get off, though the ground was some feet below him.

Jamie grabbed him before he could fall.

"Mo!" Willie repeated, struggling to get down. "Momomomomo!"

"He means 'no,'" the nurse murmured, not displeased, and reached for the boy. "I said he was too young. Here, poppet, you come to Nanny Elspeth. We'll go back to the nursery and have our nice tea."

"Mo!" Willie said shrilly, and capriciously flung himself round, burrowing into Jamie's chest.

"Now, now," his grandfather soothed, reaching for him. "Come to me, lad, we'll go and—"

"MOMOMOMOMO . . ."

Jamie put a hand over the child's mouth, stilling the racket momentarily.

"We'll go and speak to the horses, aye?" he said firmly, and hoisted the child up onto his shoulders before Willie could make up his mind to shriek some more. Diverted by this splendid new perch, Willie crowed and grabbed Jamie's hair. Not waiting to hear any objections, Jamie took hold of the chubby knees wrapped round his ears and headed for the stable.

"Now, this sweet auld lad is Deacon," he said, squatting down to bring Willie to eye level with the old gelding, who lifted his nose, nostrils flaring with interest. "We call him Deke. Can ye say that? Deke?"

Willie squealed and pulled on Jamie's hair but didn't jerk away, and after a moment, urged on by his grandfather, put out a hand and ventured a hasty pat. "Deke," he said, and laughed, charmed. "Deke!"

Jamie was careful to visit only those horses of age and temperament to deal well with a two-year-old child, but he was pleased—as was Lord Dunsany—to see that William wasn't afraid of the enormous animals. Jamie kept as careful an eye on the old man as he did on the child; his lordship's color was bad, his hands skeletal, and Jamie could hear the air whistle in his lungs when he breathed. In spite of everything, he rather liked Dunsany and hoped the baronet wasn't about to die in the stable aisle.

"Oh, there's my lovely Phil," said Dunsany, breaking into a smile as they came up to one of the loose boxes. At his voice, Philemon, a beautiful eight-year-old dark bay, lifted his head and gazed at them for a moment with a soft-lashed, open look before putting his head down again, nibbling up some spilled oats from the floor.

Dunsany fumbled with the latch, and Jamie hastily reached to open the door. The horse didn't object to their coming into the box, merely shifting his huge rump a bit to one side, tail swishing.

"Now, ye must never go behind a horse," Jamie told William. "If ye startle them, they might kick, aye?" The little boy's soft chestnut hair whorled up in a cowlick at his crown. He nodded solemnly but then struggled to get down.

Jamie glanced at Dunsany, who nodded, then he set William carefully on the floor, ready to snatch him up again if he shrieked or made a rumpus. But William stood stock still, mouth a little open, watching in fascination as the huge head came close to him, soft lips nibbling at the grain, and with the oddest sense of dislocation, Jamie suddenly felt *himself* on the floor of a stable, hearing the deep slobbering crunch of a horse's chewing just beside him, seeing the huge, glassy hooves, smelling hay and oats and the wonderful pungent scent of the horse's warm hide. There had been the feeling of someone behind him, he'd been aware of the man's big legs in their woolen hose and he heard his father laugh and say something above him, but all he'd had eyes for was the horse, that massive, beautiful, gentle creature, so amazing that he'd wanted to embrace it.

William *did* embrace it. Entranced, he toddled forward and hugged Philemon's head in an access of pure love. The horse's long-lashed eyes widened in surprise and he blew out air through his nose, ruffling the child's clothes, but did no more than bob his head a bit, lifting Willie a few inches into the air, then setting him gently down as he resumed his eating.

William laughed, a giggle of pure delight, and Jamie and Lord Dunsany looked at each other and smiled, then glanced aside, each embarrassed.

Later, Jamie watched them go, William insisting upon walking, his grandfather limping behind the sturdy little form like an aged black crane, leaning heavily on his walking stick, the two of them washed in the pale gold of the soft spring sun.

Does Dunsany know? he wondered. He was nearly sure that

Lady Isobel did. Betty, quite possibly. If Lady Dunsany knew, though, she kept her own counsel, and he doubted that she would tell her husband, not wishing to shock or grieve him.

Still, the auld gentleman's no a fool. And Dunsany had been in that drawing room at Ellesmere, the day after his grandson's birth and his daughter's death, when Geneva's husband, the old Earl of Ellesmere, had raged that the child was a bastard—and Geneva Dunsany a whore—and had threatened to drop tiny William from a window onto the paving stones thirty feet below.

Jamie had seized a loaded pistol from Jeffries—the coachman, summoned with Jamie to help calm the earl—and had shot Ellesmere. *Aye, well. It did calm the auld fiend, and may he burn in hell.*

Nothing had been said to Jamie. Nothing. In the aftermath of the explosion, when Jamie had stood shaking on the hearth rug, the rescued infant in his arms—his shot had gone through the baby's draperies, missing William by an inch—Lord Dunsany had bent calmly over Ellesmere's body, pressing his fingers to the slack, fleshy throat. Then, satisfied, had come and taken the boy from Jamie's arms and told Jeffries to take Jamie to the kitchen and get him some brandy.

In the staggeringly practical way of the English, Lord Dunsany had then sent word to the local coroner that Lord Ellesmere had suffered a sad accident, to which Jeffries testified. Jamie had neither been named nor called. A few days later, the old earl and his very young wife, Geneva, had been buried together, and a week after that, Jeffries took his leave, pensioned off to County Sligo.

All the servants knew what had happened, of course. If anything, it made them even more afraid of Jamie, but they said nothing to him—or to anyone else—about the matter. It was the business of the family, and no one else. There would be no scandal.

Lord Dunsany had never said a word to Jamie, and presumably never would. Yet there was an odd sense of . . . not friendship—it could never be anything like that—but of regard between them.

Jamie toyed for an instant with the notion of telling Dunsany about Isobel and the lawyer Wilberforce. Were it his daughter, he should certainly want to know. He dismissed it, though, and turned back to his work. It was the business of the family, and no one else.

JAMIE WAS STILL IN a good humor as he bridled the horses for exercise the next morning, mind filled with a pleasant muddle of memories past and of present content. There was a fuzzy bank of cloud above the fells, betokening later rain, but no wind, and for the moment the air was cold but still and the horses bright but not frenetic, tossing their heads with anticipation of a gallop.

"MacKenzie." He hadn't heard the man's footsteps on the sawdust of the paddock, and turned, a little startled. More startled to see George Roberts, one of the footmen. It was usually Sam Morgan who came to tell him to saddle a horse or hitch up the carriage; Roberts was a senior footman, and such errands were beneath him.

"I want to talk to you." Roberts was in his livery breeches but wore a shapeless loose jacket over his shirt. His hands hung half curled at his sides, and something in his face and voice made Jamie draw himself up a little.

"I'm about my work now," Jamie said, courteous. He gestured at the four horses he had on leading reins and at Augustus, still waiting to be saddled. "Come just after dinner, if ye like. I'll have time then."

"You'll have time now," said Roberts, in an odd, half-strangled voice. "It won't take long."

Jamie nearly took the punch, not expecting it. But the man gave clear notice, falling back on his heel and pulling back his fist as though he meant to hurl a stone, and Jamie dodged by reflex. Roberts shot past, unbalanced, and came up with a thud, catching himself on the fence. The horses who were tied to it all shied, stamping and snorting, not liking this kind of nonsense so early in the day.

"What the devil d'ye think you're doing?" Jamie asked, more in a tone of curiosity than hostility. "Or, more to the point, what d'ye think *I've* done?"

Roberts pushed away from the fence, his face congested. He was not quite as tall as Jamie but heavier in the body.

"You know damned well what you've done, you Scotch bugger!"

Jamie eyed the man and lifted one brow.

"A guessing game, is it? Aye, well, then. Someone pissed in your shoes this morning, and the bootboy said it was me?"

Surprise lifted Roberts's scowl for an instant.

"What?"

"Or someone's gone off wi' his lordship's sealing wax?" He reached into the pocket of his breeches and drew out the stub of black wax. "He gave it to me; ye can ask him."

Fresh blood crimsoned Roberts's cheeks; the household staff objected very much to Jamie being allowed to write letters and did as much as they dared to obstruct him. To Roberts's credit, though, he swallowed his choler and, after breathing heavily for a moment, said, "Betty. That name ring a bell?"

It rang a whole carillon. What had the gagging wee bitch been saying?

"I ken the woman, aye." He spoke warily, keeping an eye on Roberts's feet and a hand on Augustus's bridle.

Roberts's lip curled. He was good-looking, in a heavy-featured way, but the sneer didn't flatter him.

"You *ken* the woman, do you, cully? You've bloody interfered with her!"

"I'll tell," she'd said, thrusting out her chin at him. She hadn't said *who* she'd tell—nor that she'd tell the truth.

"No," he said calmly, and, wrapping Augustus's rein neatly round the fence rail, he stepped away from the horses and turned to face Roberts squarely. "I haven't. Did ye ask her where and when? For I'm reasonably sure I havena been out of sight o' the stables in a month, save for takin' the horses out." He nodded toward the waiting string, not taking his eyes off the footman. "And she canna have left the house to meet me on the fells."

Roberts hesitated, and Jamie took the chance to press back.

"Ye might ask yourself, man, why she'd say such a thing to *you.*"

"What? Why shouldn't she say it to me?" The footman drew his chin into his heavy neck, the better to glower.

"If she wanted me arrested or whipped or gaoled, she'd ha' complained to his lordship or the constable," Jamie pointed out, his tone still civil. "If she wanted me beaten to a pudding, she'd have told Morgan and Billings, as well, because—meaning nay disrespect—I dinna think ye can manage that on your own."

The beginnings of doubt were flickering over Roberts's heavy countenance.

"But she—"

"So either she thought she'd put a flea in your ear about me and there'd be a punch-up that would do neither of us any good—or she didna think ye'd come to me but that ye'd maybe be roused on her behalf."

"Roused?" Roberts sounded confused.

Jamie drew breath, aware for the first time that his heart was pounding.

"Aye," he said. "The lass didna say I'd raped her, now, did she? No, of course not."

"Noo . . ." Roberts had gone from confusion to open doubt now. "She said you'd been a-cupping of her, toying with her breasts and the like."

"Well, there ye are," Jamie said, with a small wave toward the house. "She was only meaning to make ye jealous, in hopes that ye'd be moved to do something o' the kind yourself. That," he added helpfully, "or she meant to get ye into trouble. I hope the lass hasna got anything against ye."

Roberts's brow darkened, but with an inward thought. He glanced up at Jamie.

"I hadn't had it in mind to strike you," he said, with a certain formality. "I only meant to tell you to keep away from her."

"Verra reasonable," Jamie assured him. His shirt was damp with sweat, despite the cold day. "I dinna mean to have anything to do with the lass. Ye can tell her she's safe from me," he added, as solemnly as he could manage.

Roberts inclined his head in a professional way and offered his hand. Jamie shook it, feeling very odd, and watched the man go off toward the house, straightening his shoulders as he went.

JAMIE HEARD at breakfast next day that his lordship was ill again and had taken to his bed. He felt a stab of disappointment at the news; he had hoped the old man would bring William to the stable again.

To his surprise, he did see William at the stable again, proud as Lucifer in his first pair of breeches and this time in the company of the under-nursemaid, Peggy. The young, stout woman told him that Nanny Elspeth and Lord and Lady Dunsany were all suffering from *la grippe* (which she pronounced in the local way, as "lah gerp") but that William had made such a nuisance of himself, wanting to see the horses again, that Lady Isobel told Peggy to bring him.

"Are ye quite well yourself, ma'am?" He could see that she wasn't. She was pale as green cheese, with much the same clammy look to her skin, and hunched a little, as though she wanted to clutch her belly.

"I . . . yes. Of course," she said, a little faintly. Then she took a grip on herself and straightened. "Willie, I think we must go back to the house."

"Mo!" Willie at once ran down the aisle, tiny boots clattering on the bricks.

"William!"

"MO!" Willie screamed, turning to face her, his face going red. "Mo, mo, mo!"

Peggy breathed heavily, clearly torn between her own illness and the need to chase the wee reprobate. A drop of sweat ran down her plump throat and made a small dark spot on her kerchief.

"Ma'am," Jamie said respectfully. "Had ye not best go and sit down for a bit? Perhaps put cold water on your wrists? I can watch the lad; he'll come to nay harm."

Without waiting for an answer, he turned and called to Willie. "Ye'll come with me, lad. Ye can help me with the mash."

Willie's small face went instantly from a stubborn clench to a radiant joy, and he clattered back, beaming. Jamie bent and scooped him up, setting him on his shoulders. Willie shrieked with pleasure and grabbed Jamie's hair. Jamie smiled at Mrs. Peggy.

"We'll do."

"I . . . I really . . . well . . . all right," she said weakly. "Just . . . just for a bit." Turning, she shuffled hastily off.

Looking after her, he murmured, "Poor woman." At the same time, he hoped that her difficulties would detain her for some while, and asked a quick forgiveness from God for the thought.

"Poo ooman," Willie echoed solemnly, and pressed his knees to Jamie's ears. "Go!"

They went. The mash tub was in the tack room, and he parked William on a stool and reached down a bridle with a snaffle for the boy to play with, clicking the jointed bit to make a noise.

"D'ye remember the names of the horses, then?" he asked, measuring out the grain into the tub with the wooden scoop. William frowned, pausing in his clicking.

"Mo."

"Oh, aye, ye do. Bella? Ye ken Bella fine; ye rode on her back."

"Bella!"

"Aye, see? And what about Phil—he's the sweet lad that let ye hug his nose."

"Pill!"

"That's right. And next to Phil, there's . . ." They worked their way verbally down both sides of the aisle, stall by stall, Jamie saying the names and William repeating them, while Jamie poured the molasses, thick and black as tar and nearly as pungent, into the grain.

"I'm going to fetch the hot water," he told Willie. "You stay just there—dinna move about—and I'll be with ye in a moment."

Willie, engaged in an unsuccessful effort to get the bit into his own mouth, ignored this but made no move to follow him.

Jamie took a bucket and put his head into the factor's office, where Mr. Grieves was talking to Mr. Lowens, a farmer whose land abutted that of Dunsany's estate. Grieves nodded to him, and he came in, going to dip hot water from the cauldron kept simmering in the back of the hearth. The factor's office was the only warm place in the stable block, so was often a gathering place for visitors.

He made his way back, careful with the heavy, steaming bucket, and found Willie still sitting on his stool but having now succeeded in entangling his head and arms in the bridle, which he'd evidently tried to put on.

"Elp!" Willie said, thrashing wildly. "Elp, elp, elp!"

"Aye, I'll help ye, ye wee gomerel. Here, then." Jamie set down the bucket and went to assist, thanking his guardian angel that Willie hadn't managed to strangle himself. No wonder the little fiend required two nursemaids to watch him.

He patiently untangled the bridle—how could a child who couldn't dress himself tie knots like that?—and hung it up, then, with an admonition to Willie to keep well back, poured the hot water into the bran tub.

"Ye want to help stir?" He held out the big worn paddle—which was roughly as tall as Willie—and they stirred the mash, Willie clinging earnestly to the lower part of the handle, Jamie to the upper. The mix was stiff, though, and Willie gave up after a moment, leaving Jamie to finish the job.

He'd just about finished ladling the mash into buckets for distribution to the mangers when he noticed that William had something in his mouth.

"What's that ye've got in your mouth?"

Willie opened his mouth and picked out a wet horseshoe nail, which he regarded with interest. Jamie imagined in a split second what would have happened if the lad had swallowed it, and panic made him speak more roughly than he might have.

"Give it here!"

"Mo!" Willie jerked his hand away and glowered at Jamie under wispy brows that nonetheless were well marked.

"Nnnnn," Jamie said, leaning down close and glowering in his turn. "Nnnnno."

Willie looked suspicious and uncertain.

"Mo," he repeated, but with less surety.

"It's 'no,' believe me," Jamie assured him, straightening up and pulling the bucket of mash closer. "Ye've heard your auntie Isobel say it, have ye not?" He *hoped* Isobel—or someone—said it to Willie on occasion. Not often enough, he was sure of that.

Willie appeared to be thinking this over and, in the process, absently raised the nail to his mouth again and began licking it. Jamie cast a wary look toward the door, but no one was watching.

"Does it taste well?" he asked casually. The question of taste appeared not to have occurred to Willie, who looked startled and frowned at the nail, as though wondering where it had come from.

"Es," he said, but uncertainly.

"Give me a taste, then." He leaned toward the child, putting out his tongue, and Willie blinked once, then obligingly reached the nail up. Jamie folded his hand very gently around Willie's fist and drew his tongue delicately up the length of the nail. It tasted, naturally enough, of iron and horse hoof, but he had to admit that it wasn't a bad taste at all.

"It's no bad," he said, drawing back—but keeping his hand round Willie's. "Think it would break your teeth, though, if ye chewed it."

Willie giggled at the idea.

"It would break the horses' teeth, too, see? That's why we dinna leave such things lyin' about in the stable." He gestured through the open door of the tack room toward the row of stalls, where two or three equine heads were poking out, inquisitive as to the whereabouts of their dinner.

"Horsie," Willie said, very clearly.

"Horse, indeed," Jamie said, and smiled at him.

"Horsie eat dis?" Willie leaned curiously over the mash tub, sniffing loudly.

"Aye, they do. That's good food—not like nails. No one eats nails."

Willie had clearly forgotten the nail, though he was still holding it. He glanced at it and dropped it, whereupon Jamie picked it up and tucked it into his breeches. Willie promptly stuck a small hand into the mash and, liking the sticky feel of it, laughed and slapped his hand a couple of times on the quivering surface of the molasses-laced grain. Jamie reached out and took him by the wrist.

"Now, then," he said. "Ye wouldna like it if Deke put his hoof into *your* dinner, would ye?"

"Heeheeheeheehee."

"Well, then. Here, wipe your hand and ye can help me put the mash out." He pulled a relatively clean handkerchief from his shirtsleeve, but Willie ignored it, instead licking the sweet, sticky stuff from his fingers with every evidence of enjoyment.

Well, he had told the lad it was food, and it was wholesome enough—though he sincerely hoped Mrs. Peggy wasn't about to reappear, or they'd both be for it.

Peggy didn't reappear, and they spent a companionable quarter hour pouring mash, then forking fresh hay from the stack outside into a wheelbarrow and trundling it into the stable. On the way back, they met Mr. Lowens, looking satisfied. Whatever haggling he'd been doing with Grieves, he thought he'd got the best of it.

"MacKenzie," he said, with a cordial nod. He smiled at William, who, Jamie noticed with some dismay, had molasses down his shirt and a good deal of hay sticking out of his hair. "That your lad, is it?"

For an instant, he thought his heart would leap straight out of his mouth. He took a quick gulp of air, though, and answered calmly, "No, sir. This would be the young earl. The Earl of Ellesmere."

"Oh, aye?" Lowens laughed and squatted down to speak to Willie directly. "Knew your father, I did. Randy old bugger," he remarked to Jamie. "But he knew his horses, old Earl did. Going to be a good horseman, too, are you?" he said, returning his attention to Willie.

"Es!"

"Good lad, good lad." He reached out and ruffled Willie's hair. Willie glowered at him. "Breeched already? You're young for that." He affected to sniff deeply. "Smell a bit ripe. You've not shit yourself, have you, my lord?" He chuckled fatly, amused at his own wit.

William's eyes narrowed, in a way that reminded Jamie vividly of his own sister about to go berserk. He thanked God again that the boy's features were rounded and snub, and prepared to grab him if he tried to kick Mr. Lowens in the shins.

Instead, though, the young earl merely glared up at the farmer and said loudly and distinctly, "NNNNNNO!"

"Oh!" said Lowens, laughing. "My mistake. My apologies, my lord."

"We must be going, sir," Jamie said hastily, before William could execute any of the thoughts that were clearly going through his mind. He swung the boy off his feet and held him upside down by the ankles. "It's time for his lordship's tea."

6

Summoning

PEGGY NEVER DID COME BACK. JAMIE CARRIED WILLIAM—now right side up—back to the house and delivered him to one of the kitchen maids, who told him that Peggy was "took bad" but that she would bring his little lordship along to Lady Isobel.

Willie objected vociferously to this proposal—so vociferously that Isobel herself appeared—and was pacified only by the promise that he could visit the stable again tomorrow. Jamie carefully avoided Isobel's hard eye and absented himself as quickly as he could.

He wondered whether William *would* come back. Isobel wouldn't bring him, he was sure of that. But if Peggy felt better, and if William insisted—William struck him as being singularly stubborn, even for a child of two. He smiled at the thought.

Can't think where he gets that, he thought, and quite suddenly wondered whether his other son was the same. Claire's son.

Lord, he thought automatically, as he did whenever thought of them came to his mind, *that she might be safe. She and the child.*

How old would his first child be now? He swallowed a thickness in his throat but continued doggedly in his train of thought. Claire had been two months gone with child when she'd stepped through the stones and back to Frank.

"God bless you, ye bloody English bastard," he said through his teeth. It was his customary prayer when Frank Randall came to his mind—something he tried to avoid happening, but now and then . . . "Mind them well!"

Two months gone, and that had been April the 16, *Anno Domini* 1746. Now it was April again, and 1760. If time went on in a normal fashion—and he saw no reason why it should not—then the child would be almost fourteen.

"Christ, he's nearly a man," he whispered, and his hand closed tight on the fence rail, so tight he felt the grain of the wood.

As with Frank Randall, Jamie tried to keep from thinking too much or too specifically of Claire or of the unknown child. It hurt too much, brought home to him too vividly what he had had, and what he had lost.

He hadn't been able to avoid thinking of them, living in the cave on his own estate at Lallybroch, during the first years after Culloden. There was too little to occupy his mind, and they had crept in, his family, glimmering in the smoke when he sat by his wee fire—when he'd felt safe enough to have one—shining in the starlight when he sat outside the cave at night watching the heavens, seeing the same stars that they must see, taking comfort in the everlasting light that lay softly on him and his.

Then he'd imagined his son and holding a small, solid body on his knee, the child's heart beating against his own—and his hands curved without his willing it, remembering now what Willie felt like in his arms.

HE WAS CARRYING a huge basket of rotted manure up to the kitchen garden next morning when Morgan, one of the footmen, appeared from behind a wall and hailed him.

"Hoy, MacKenzie! You're wanted!"

He was surprised; it was mid-morning, not a usual time for visiting or errands. He'd have to catch that wee bitch Venus, presently enjoying herself in the back pasture. And the thought of driving the pony trap, with Lady Isobel's slitted eyes burning holes in his flesh, was less than appealing. It wasn't as though he had a choice, though, and he set the basket down, safely off the path, then straightened up, dusting his hands against his thighs.

"Aye, I'll have the trap round in a quarter hour."

"Not the trap," Morgan said, impatient. "I said *you're* wanted."

He glanced at the man, startled.

"Who wants me?"

"Not me, I assure you." Morgan had a long nose, and he wrinkled it ostentatiously, looking at the greenish-brown crumbles and smears on Jamie's clothes. "If there was time, I'd make you change your shirt, but there's not. He said at once, and he meant it."

"Lord Dunsany?" Jamie asked, ignoring the footman's barb.

"Who else?" Morgan was already turning away. He looked back over his shoulder and jerked his head. "Come on, then!"

HE FELT STRANGE. The polished wood floor echoed under his tread and the air smelled of hearth ash, books, and flowers. He smelled of horses, horseshit, and his own bitter sweat. Since the day he'd come to Helwater, he'd only twice been farther into the house than the kitchen where he took his meals.

Lord Dunsany had received John Grey and him in the study on that first day, and now the butler—back stiff with disapproval—

led him down the corridor to the same door. The wooden panels were carved with small rosettes; he had noticed them so intensely on his first visit that seeing them again recalled his emotions on that day—and gave him now a feeling as though he had missed the bottom step of a flight of stairs.

His immediate assumption on hearing the summons was that Isobel had seen him outside Wilberforce's house and decided to eliminate the possibility of his telling on her by informing her father of the truth of William's paternity, and his heart was in his throat, his mind filled with half-formed notions between outright panic and . . . something else. Would Dunsany cast the boy out? If he did. . . . A faint, breathtaking vision of himself walking away from Helwater, his son in his arms, came to him—but vanished at once as the door opened.

There were three men in Lord Dunsany's study. Soldiers, in uniform. A lieutenant and two private soldiers, he thought, though it had been a long time since he'd troubled with the distinctions of English uniform.

"This is MacKenzie," Lord Dunsany said, with a small nod at him. "Or rather . . . Fraser."

The officer looked him up and down, assessing, but his face gave nothing away. A middle-aged man, with a sour look. He didn't offer his name.

"You're to go with these men, Fraser," Dunsany said. His face was old, his expression remote. "Do as they tell you."

He stood mute. Damned if he'd say, "Yes, sir," and double-damned if he'd knuckle his forehead like a servant. The officer looked sharply at him, then at Dunsany, to see whether this insubordination was to be punished, but, finding nothing but weariness in the old man's face, shrugged slightly and nodded to the privates.

They moved purposefully toward him, one taking him by

each arm. He couldn't avoid it but felt the urge to jerk himself free. They led him into the hall and out the front door; he could see the butler smirking from his pantry and two of the maids hanging wide-eyed and openmouthed out of the upper windows as the men emerged onto the drive, where a coach stood waiting.

"Where are ye taking me?" he asked, with what calmness he could.

The men glanced at each other; one shrugged.

"You're going to London," he said.

"To visit the Queen," the other said, and sniggered.

He had to duck to enter the carriage and, in doing so, turned his head. Lady Isobel stood in the window, mouth open in shock. William was in her arms, small head laid in sleep on her shoulder. Behind them, Betty smiled at him, maliciously pleased.

SECTION II

Force Majeure

7

When a Man Is Tired of London, He Is Tired of Life

THE SOLDIERS GAVE HIM A SERVICEABLE CLOAK TO WEAR AND food at the taverns and inns, shoving it indifferently across the table toward him, ignoring him while they talked, save an occasional sharp glance to be sure he wasn't getting up to something. What, exactly, did they think he might do? he wondered. If he'd ever meant to escape, he could have done it much more easily from Helwater.

He gathered nothing from their conversation, which seemed mostly regimental gossip, bawdy remarks about women, and low jokes. Not a word as to their destination.

At the second stop, there was wine—decent wine. He drank it cautiously; he hadn't tasted anything stronger than small beer in years, and the lush flavor clung to his palate and rose like smoke inside his head. The soldiers shared three bottles—and so did he, welcoming the slowing of his racing thoughts as the alcohol seeped into his blood. It would do him no good to think, until he knew what to think about.

He tried to keep his mind off their unknown destination and

what might await him there, but it was like trying not to think of a—

> *"Rhinoceros," Claire said, with a muffled snort of amusement that stirred the hairs on his chest. "Have you ever seen one?"*
>
> *"I have," he said, shifting her weight so she rested more comfortably in the hollow of his shoulder. "In Louis's zoo. Aye, that would stick in the mind."*

Abruptly, she vanished and left him sitting there, blinking stupidly into his wine cup.

Had it really happened, that memory? Or was it only his desire that now and then brought her so vividly to life, in snatched moments that left him desperate with longing but strangely comforted, as though she had in fact touched him briefly?

He became aware that the soldiers had all stopped talking and were staring at him. And that he was smiling. He looked back at them over his cup, not altering his expression.

They looked away, uneasy, and he went back to his wife, for the moment tranquil in his mind.

THEY DID TAKE HIM to London.

He tried not to gawk; he was aware of the soldiers casting covert glances at him, sly smiles. They expected him to be impressed, and he declined to give them the satisfaction—but he was impressed, nonetheless.

So this was London. It had the stink of any city, the narrow alleys, the smell of slops and chimney smoke. But any large city has its own soul, and London was quite different from either Paris or Edinburgh. Paris was secretive, self-satisfied; Edinburgh solidly busy, a merchants' town. But this . . . It was rowdy, churning like an anthill, and gave off a sense of pushing, as though the energy of the place would burst its bonds and spill out over the countryside, spill out into the world at large. His blood stirred, despite his fears and the tooth-jolting ride.

The Jacobite soldiers would talk about London, early in the campaign, when they were victorious and London seemed a plum within their grasp. Wild tales—almost none of them had ever seen a city, before they came to Edinburgh. Talk of gold plates in the taverns, streets with gilded carriages thick as lice . . .

He remembered Murdo Lindsay, bug-eyed at the description of boozing kens, where the poor clustered in dark cellars, drowning the misery of life in Holland gin.

"Whole families!" Murdo exclaimed. "All of them, dead drunk! If even the poor folk can afford to stay drunk for days at a time, what must the rich ones be like?"

He'd smiled then, amused. He smiled now, bitter.

As the campaign had turned, withering in the cold, when the army camped at Derby, shivering while the commanders argued whether to push on or not, the soldiers had still talked of London. But they talked in whispers then, and not of gold plates and Holland gin. They talked of the gallows, of the famous Bridge, where the heads of traitors were displayed. Of the Tower.

That thought sent a qualm through him. Christ, could they be taking him there? He was a convicted traitor, though paroled these past four years. And he was the grandson of Lord Lovat, who had met his death on the block at that same Tower. He hadn't been fond of his grandfather, but crossed himself and murmured *"Fois air Anam . . ."* under his breath. Peace on his soul.

He wondered what the devil the Tower of London looked like.

He'd imagined it, of course, but God only knew what the reality was. It was big, though; it had to be big. So he'd have a bit of warning, seeing it. He'd be prepared.

Aye, prepared for prison? he thought. The idea of it, of cold stone and small spaces, endless days, months, and years in a cage as life and body dwindled inexorably away, shriveled his heart. *And William.* He would never see William again. But they might kill him instead. At the moment, that was his only hope.

But why? Had his parole been revoked? That last, disastrous conversation with John Grey . . . His fists curled up without thought, and one of the soldiers started, looking at him hard. With an effort, he unclenched his hands and pulled them inside his cloak, gripping his thighs under its cover hard enough to leave bruises.

He hadn't seen—or heard from—Grey since that day. Had the man been nursing a grudge all this time and finally decided to put paid to Jamie Fraser's account, once and for all? It was the most likely explanation—and unforgivable things had been said on both sides. Worse, both of them had meant the things they said, and both of them knew it. No excuse of hot blood speaking—though, in all justice, his own blood had boiled, and . . .

There it was. He gasped, couldn't help it, though it made all the soldiers look at him, conversation interrupted.

It had to be. He knew the look of a prison well enough. Huge round towers set in a grim high wall, and the filthy brown water of a broad river flowing past, flowing under an iron-barred gate. The Traitors' Gate? He'd heard of it.

All of them were grinning at him, maliciously enjoying his shock. He swallowed hard and tensed his belly muscles. They wouldn't see him cower. His pride was all he had left—but he had enough of that.

But the carriage didn't leave the road. They bowled past the grim bulk of the moated tower, the horses' hooves ringing on cobbles, and he blessed the sound because it drowned the wrenching gasp when he realized he'd stopped breathing and started again.

It wasn't a warm day, but he was drenched in sudden sweat and saw the private behind him wrinkle his nose and glance sideways at him. He reeked of fear, could smell himself.

Could ha' been worse, a bhalaich, he thought, coldly meeting the man's eye and staring 'til he looked away. *I might have shit myself and ye'd have to ride into London smelling* that.

WHAT WITH THE TANGLE of foot traffic, barrows, carriages, and horses that thronged the narrow streets, it was more than an hour before the coach finally pulled up outside a massive house that stood in its own walled grounds at the edge of a huge open park. He stared at it in astonishment. If not the tower, he'd certainly expected to be taken to a gaol of some kind. Who the devil lived here, and what did whoever it was want of him?

The soldiers didn't tell him, and he wouldn't ask.

To his amazement, they took him up the marble steps to the front door, where they made him wait while the lieutenant banged at the knocker, then spoke to the butler who answered it. The butler was a small, neat man, who blinked in disbelief at sight of Jamie, then turned to the lieutenant, plainly about to remonstrate.

"His Grace said bring him, and I've brought him," said the lieutenant impatiently. "Show us in!"

His Grace? A duke? What the devil might a duke want with him? The only duke he knew of was . . . God . . . Cumberland? His heart had already been in his throat; now his wame tried to follow it. He'd seen the Duke of Cumberland only once. When he'd left the battlefield at Culloden, wounded, hidden under a load of hay in a wagon. The wagon had passed through the edge of the government lines, just at evening, and he'd seen the big tent, a squat, vigorous figure outside it irritably waving away clouds of smoke with a gold-laced hat. The smoke of burning bodies—the smoke of the Jacobite dead.

He felt the soldiers jerk and glance at him, startled. He froze, fists at his side, but the chill and the fear were gone, burned away by the sense of rage that rose abruptly, drawing him upright with it.

His heart beat painfully, eager, for all at once the future had a shape to it. No more long days of mere survival. He had purpose, and the glow of it lit his soul.

The butler was falling back, reluctant, but unable to resist. Aye, fine. All he need do was behave circumspectly until he got within grip of the duke. He flexed his left hand briefly. There might be a knife, a letter opener, something . . . but it didn't matter.

The lieutenant jerked his head, and he moved, just in time to keep the privates from grasping his arms. He saw the butler's eyes fix on his feet, mouth twisted in a sneer of contempt. A door opened in the hallway and a woman's face appeared for a moment. She caught sight of him, gasped, and closed the door.

He would in fact have wiped his sandals, had they given him time; he'd no desire either to foul the house nor to look like the barbarian they plainly thought him. The men hastened him along, though, one on either side, and he had even less wish to give them an excuse to lay their hands on him, so he went, leaving dusty prints crumbled with dry mud and caked manure along the polished floor of the hallway.

The door to the room was open, and they propelled him inside without ceremony. He was looking everywhere at once, gauging distances, estimating the possibilities of objects as weapons, and it was a long instant before his eyes met those of the man seated at the desk.

For a moment longer, his mind refused to grasp the reality, and he blinked. No, it wasn't Cumberland. Not even the passage of years could have transformed a stout German prince into the slender, fine-featured man frowning at him across the polished wood.

"Mr. Fraser." It wasn't quite a question, nor was it quite a greeting, though the man inclined his head courteously.

Jamie was breathing as though he'd run a mile, hands shaking slightly as his body tried to burn away anger that now had no outlet.

"Who are you?" he asked rudely.

The man shot a sharp glance at the lieutenant.

"Did you not tell him, Mr. Gaskins?"

Gaskins. It was a minor relief to know the bugger's name. And a distinct pleasure to see him go red and then white.

"I . . . er . . . I . . . no, sir."

"Leave us, Lieutenant." The man didn't raise his voice, but it cut like a razor. *He's a soldier,* Jamie thought, and then, *I ken him.* But where . . . ?

The man stood up, ignoring Lieutenant Gaskins's hasty departure.

"My apologies, Mr. Fraser," he said. "Were you mistreated on your journey?"

"No," he replied automatically, scrutinizing the face before him. It was remarkably familiar, and yet he would swear he didn't . . . "Why am I here?"

The man drew a deep breath, the frown easing, and as it did,

Jamie saw the shape of the man's face, fine-boned and beautiful, though showing the marks of a hard life. He felt as though someone had punched him in the chest.

"Jesus," he said. "Ye're John Grey's brother." He groped madly for the name and found it. "Lord . . . Melton. Jesus Christ."

"Well, yes," the man said. "Though I don't use that title any longer. I've become the Duke of Pardloe since we last met." He smiled wryly. "It has been some time. Please sit down, Mr. Fraser."

8

Debts of Honor

HE WAS SO SHOCKED THAT HE WENT ON STANDING THERE, gaping like a loon at the man. Melton—Pardloe, rather—looked him up and down, brows slightly knit in concentration.

Recovering himself, Jamie sat down abruptly, the gilded chair feeling flimsy and strange under his buttocks. Pardloe sat, too, and without taking his eyes off Jamie's face shouted, "Pilcock! I want you!"

This produced a footman—Jamie didn't turn to look at the man but heard the deferential tread, the murmured "Your Grace?" behind him.

"Bring us some whisky, Pilcock," Pardloe said, still eyeing Jamie. "And biscuits—no, not biscuits, something more substantial."

Pilcock made a questioning noise, causing the duke to glance over Jamie's shoulder at him, features creasing in irritation.

"How should I know? Meat pies. Leftover joint. Roast peacock, for God's sake. Go ask Cook; go ask your mistress!"

"Yes, Your Grace!"

Pardloe shook his head, then looked at Jamie again.

"Got your bearings now?" he inquired in a perfectly normal

tone of voice, as though resuming an interrupted conversation. "I mean—you recall me?"

"I do."

He did, and the recollection jarred him almost as much as finding Pardloe instead of the Duke of Cumberland. He clutched the seat of the chair, steadying himself against the memory.

Two days past the battle, and the smoke of burning bodies swirled thick over the moor, a greasy fog that seeped into the cottage where the wounded Jacobite officers had taken refuge. They'd crossed the carnage of the field together, bleeding, frozen, stumbling . . . helping one another, dragging one another to a temporary—and totally illusory—safety.

He'd felt the whole of it an illusion. Had waked on the field, convinced he was dead, relieved it was over, the pain, the heartbreak, the struggle. Then had truly waked, to find Jack Randall lying dead on top of him, the captain's dead weight having cut off circulation to his wounded leg and saved him from bleeding to death—one final ill turn, one last indignity.

His friends had found him, forced him to his feet, brought him to the cottage. He hadn't protested; he'd seen what was left of his leg and knew it wouldn't be long.

Longer than he'd thought; it had been two days of pain and fever. Then Melton had come, and his friends had been taken out and shot, one by one. He'd been sent home, to Lallybroch.

He looked at Harold, Lord Melton—now Duke of Pardloe—with no great friendliness.

"I mind ye."

PARDLOE ROSE FROM the desk and, with a twitch of the shoulder, summoned him to a pair of wing chairs near the hearth, motioning him into one. Jamie lowered himself gingerly onto the pink-striped satin damask, but the thing was sturdily built and bore his weight without creaking.

The duke turned toward the open door to the library and bellowed, "Pilcock! Where the devil are you?"

It wasn't a footman or butler who appeared, though. The woman whose face he had glimpsed in the hall downstairs came in, skirts whispering. He had a much better look at her face now and thought his heart might stop.

"Pilcock's busy," she told the duke. "What do you want?" She was visibly older but still pretty, with a soft flush to her cheeks.

"Busy? Doing what?"

"I sent him up to the attics," the woman replied composedly. "If you're sending poor John to Ireland, he'll need a portmanteau, at least." She gave Jamie the briefest of glances before her gaze flicked back to the duke, and Jamie saw one neat eyebrow arch in question.

Jesus. They're married, then, he thought, seeing the instant communication in the gesture and the duke's grimace of acknowledgment. *She's his wife.* The green-printed wallpaper behind the duke suddenly began to flicker, and the sides of his jaws went cold. With a remote sense of shock, he realized that he was about to faint.

The duke uttered an exclamation and the woman swung round toward him. Spots flickered and grew thick before his eyes, but not thick enough that he failed to see the expression on her face. Alarm—and warning.

"Are you quite well, Mr. Fraser?" The duke's cool voice penetrated through the buzzing in his ears, and he felt a hand on the back of his neck, forcing his head down. "Put your head between your knees. Minnie, my dear—"

"I've got it. Here." The woman's voice was breathless, and he heard the clink of glass, smelled the hot scent of brandy.

"Not that, not yet. My snuffbox—it's on the mantelpiece." The duke was holding him by the shoulders, he realized, bracing him to keep him from falling. The blood was slowly coming back into his head, but his vision was still dark and his face and fingers cold.

The sound of quick light footsteps came to him—hearing was always the last sense to go, he thought dimly—clicking on the parquet, muffled on the rug, a pause, then coming swiftly back. An urgent murmur from the duke, another click, a small, soft *pop!* and the stinging rush of ammonia shot up his nose.

He gasped and jerked, trying to turn away, but a firm hand held his head, obliging him to breathe, then finally let go and allowed him to sit up, coughing and spluttering, eyes watering so badly that he could barely make out the woman's form hovering over him, the vial of smelling salts in her hand.

"Poor man," she said. "You must be half dead with travel, and hungry, to boot—it's past teatime, and I'll wager you've not had a bite in hours. Really, Hal—"

"I sent for food. I was just about to send again when he turned white and keeled over," the duke protested, indignant.

"Well, go and tell Cook, then," his wife ordered. "I'll give Mr. . . ." She turned toward Jamie, expectant.

"Fraser," Jamie managed, wiping his streaming face on his sleeve. "James Fraser." The name felt strange on his lips; he hadn't spoken it in years.

"Yes, of course. I'll give Mr. Fraser some brandy. Tell Cook we want sandwiches and cake and a pot of strong hot tea, and we want it quickly."

The duke said something vulgar in French, but went. The woman had a cup of brandy ready and held it to his lips. He took it from her, though, and looked at her over the rim.

The soft flush had gone from her cheeks. She was pale, and her gentle lips were pressed in a grim line.

"For the sake of the cause we once shared," she said very quietly, "I pray you, say nothing. Not yet."

HE WAS DEEPLY EMBARRASSED—and even more deeply unsettled. He'd fainted before, from pain or shock. But not often, and not in front of an enemy. Now here he sat, drinking tea from a porcelain cup with a gold rim, sharing sandwiches and cakes from a similarly adorned platter, with that very enemy. He was confused, annoyed, and at a considerable disadvantage. He didn't like it.

On the other hand, the food was excellent and he was, in fact, starved. His wame had been clenched in a ball since they came in sight of London, so he'd taken no breakfast.

To his credit, Pardloe made no move to take advantage of his guest's weakness. He said nothing beyond an occasional "More ham?" or "Pass the mustard, if you please," and ate in the businesslike manner of a soldier, not seeking Jamie's eye but not avoiding it, either.

The woman had left without another word and hadn't come back. That was one thing to be thankful for.

He'd known her as Mina Rennie; God knew what her real name was. She'd been the seventeen-year-old daughter of a bookseller in Paris who dealt in information and more than once had carried messages between her father and Jamie, during his days of intrigue there before the Rising. Paris seemed as distant as the planet Jupiter. The distance between a young spy and a duchess seemed even greater.

"For the sake of the cause we once shared." Had they? He'd been

under no illusions about old Rennie; his only loyalty had been to gold. Had his daughter really considered herself a Jacobite? He ate a slice of cake, absently enjoying the crunch of walnuts and the richly exotic taste of cocoa. He hadn't tasted chocolate since Paris.

He supposed it was possible. The Cause had attracted people of romantic temperament; doomed causes usually did. That made him think abruptly of Quinn, and the thought raised the hairs on his forearms. Christ. He'd nearly forgotten the bloody Irishman and his harebrained schemes, in the alarms of the last few days. What would Quinn think, hearing he'd been dragged off by English soldiers?

Well, he could do nothing about either Quinn or the Duchess of Pardloe just now. One thing at a time. He drained his cup, leaned forward, and set it on its saucer with a deliberate clink that indicated he was now ready to talk.

The duke likewise put down his cup, wiped his mouth with a napkin, and said without preamble, "Do you consider yourself in my debt, Mr. Fraser?"

"No," he said, without hesitation. "I didna ask ye to save my life."

"No, you didn't," Pardloe said dryly. "In fact, you demanded that I shoot you, if my recollection is correct."

"It is."

"Do you hold it against me that I didn't?" It was asked seriously, and Jamie answered it the same way.

"I did. But I don't now, no."

Pardloe nodded.

"Well, then." He held up both hands and folded down one thumb. "You spared my brother's life." The other thumb folded. "I spared yours." An index finger. "You objected to this action."

The other index finger. "But have upon consideration withdrawn your objection?" He raised both eyebrows, and Jamie quelled a reluctant impulse to smile. He inclined his head half an inch instead, and Pardloe nodded, lowering his hands.

"So you agree that there is no debt between us? No lingering sense of injury?"

"I wouldna go that far," Jamie replied, very dry indeed. "Ye've got three fingers left. But there's nay debt, no. Not between us."

The man was sharp; he caught the faint emphasis on "us."

"Whatever disagreements you may have with my brother do not concern me," Pardloe said. "So long as they don't interfere with the business I am about to lay before you."

Jamie wondered just what John Grey had told his brother concerning the disagreements between them—but if it wasn't Pardloe's concern, it wasn't his, either.

"Speak, then," he said, and felt a sudden knotting in his belly. They were the same words he'd said to John Grey, which had unleashed that final disastrous conversation. He had a strong foreboding that this one wasn't going to end well, either.

Pardloe took a deep breath, as though readying himself for something, then stood up.

"Come with me."

THEY WENT TO A small study down the hall. Unlike the gracious library they had just left, the study was dark, cramped, and littered with books, papers, small random objects, and a scatter of ratty quills that looked as if they'd been chewed. Clearly, this was the duke's personal lair, and no servant's intrusion was often tolerated. Tidy himself by default rather than inclination, Jamie found the place oddly appealing.

Pardloe gestured briefly at a chair, then bent to unlock the lower drawer of the desk. What could be sufficiently delicate or important that it required such precautions?

The duke withdrew a bundle of papers bound with ribbon, untied it, and, pushing things impatiently aside to make a clear space, laid a single sheet of paper on the desk in front of Jamie.

He frowned a bit, picked up the sheet, and, tilting it toward the small window for a better light, read slowly through it.

"Can you read it?" The duke was looking at him, intent.

"More or less, aye." He set it down, baffled, and looked at the duke. "Ye want to know what it says, is that it?"

"It is. Is it Erse? The speech of the Scottish Highlands?"

Jamie shook his head.

"Nay, though something close. It's *Gaeilge.* Irish. Some call that Erse, too," he added, with a tinge of contempt for ignorance.

"Irish! You're sure?" The duke stood up, his lean face positively eager.

"Yes. I wouldna claim to be fluent, but it's close enough to the *Gàidhlig*—that would be my own tongue," he said pointedly, "that I can follow it. It's a poem—or part o' one."

Pardloe's face went blank for an instant but then resumed its expression of concentration.

"What poem? What does it say?"

Jamie rubbed a forefinger slowly down the bridge of his nose, scanning the page.

"It's no a particular poem—not a proper one, wi' a name to it, I mean—or not one I know. But it's a tale o' the Wild Hunt. Ken that, do ye?"

The duke's face was a study.

"The Wild Hunt?" he said carefully. "I . . . have heard of it. In Germany. Not Ireland."

Jamie shrugged, and pushed the page away. The little study

had a faintly familiar smell to it—a sweet fuggy aroma that made him want to cough.

"Do ye not find ghost stories everywhere? Or faerie tales?"

"Ghosts?" Pardloe glanced at the page, frowning, then picked it up, scowling as though he'd force it to talk to him.

Jamie waited, wondering whether this sheet of Irish poetry had aught to do with what the woman had said. *"If you're sending poor John to Ireland . . ."* John Grey might go to the devil with his blessing, let alone Ireland, but what with the memory of Quinn and his schemes lurking in his mind, the repeated mention of the place was beginning to give Jamie Fraser the creeps.

Pardloe suddenly crumpled the paper in his hand and threw the resulting ball at the wall with a rude exclamation in Greek.

"And what has that to do with Siverly?" he demanded, glaring at Jamie.

"Siverly?" he replied, startled. "Who, Gerald Siverly?" Then could have bitten his tongue, as he saw the duke's face change yet again.

"You do know him," Pardloe said. He spoke quietly, as a hunter might do to a companion, sighting game.

There was little point in denying it. Jamie lifted one shoulder. "I kent a man by that name once, aye. What of it?"

The duke leaned back, eyeing Jamie."What, indeed. Will you tell me the circumstances in which you knew a Gerald Siverly?"

Jamie considered whether to answer or not. But he owed Siverly nothing, and it was perhaps over-early to be obstructive, given that he had no idea why Pardloe had brought him here. He might need to be offensive later, but no point in it now. And the duke *had* fed him.

As though the duke had picked up this thought, he reached into a cupboard and withdrew a stout brown bottle and a couple of worn pewter cups.

"It's not a bribe," he said, setting these on the desk with a fleeting smile. "I can't keep my temper about Siverly without the aid of a drink, and drinking in front of someone who's not makes me feel like a sot."

Recalling the effect of wine after long abstinence, Jamie had some reservations regarding whisky—he could smell it, the instant the bottle was uncorked—but nodded, nonetheless.

"Siverly," he said slowly, picking up the cup. *And how did ye ken I knew him, I wonder?* The answer to that came as quickly as the question. Mina Rennie, otherwise known as the Duchess of Pardloe. He pushed the thought aside for the moment, slowly inhaling the sweet fierce fumes of the drink.

"The man I kent wasna a real Irishman, though he'd some land in Ireland, and I think his mother was maybe Irish. He was a friend of O'Sullivan, him who was later quartermaster for . . . Charles Stuart."

Pardloe looked sharply at him, having caught the hesitation—he'd nearly said "Prince Charles"—but nodded at him to continue. "Jacobite connections," Pardloe observed. "Yet not a Jacobite himself?"

Jamie shook his head and took a cautious sip. It burned the back of his throat and sent tendrils swirling down through his body like a drop of ink in water. Oh, God. Maybe this was worth being dragged off like a convict. Then again . . .

"He dabbled. Dined at Stuart's table in Paris quite often, and ye'd see him out with O'Sullivan or one o' the prince's other Irish friends—but that's as far as it went. I met him once in Lord George Murray's company at a salon, but he kept well apart from Mar or Tullibardine." He had a moment's pang at thought of the small, cheerful Earl of Tullibardine, who, like his own grandfather, had been executed on Tower Hill after the Rising.

He lifted his cup in silent salute and drank before going on. "But then he was gone. Frightened off, thought better, saw nay profit—I hadn't enough to do wi' him myself to say why. But he wasna with Charles Stuart at Glenfinnan, nor after."

He took another sip. He wasn't liking this; the memories of the Rising were too vivid. He felt Claire there by his elbow, was afraid to turn his head and look.

"Saw no profit," the duke echoed. "No, I daresay he didn't." He sounded bitter. He sat looking into his cup for a moment, then tossed the rest back, made a houghing noise, set it down, and reached for the bundle of papers.

"Read that. If you will," he added, the courtesy clearly an afterthought.

Jamie glanced at the papers, feeling an obscure sense of unease. But again, there was no reason to refuse, and, despite his reluctance, he picked up the top few sheets and began to read.

The duke wasn't a man who seemed comfortable sitting still. He twitched, coughed, got up and lit the candle, sat down again . . . coughed harder. Jamie sighed, concentrating against the distraction.

Siverly seemed to have made the most of his army career in Canada. While Jamie disapproved of the man's behavior on general principles and admired the eloquent passion displayed by the man who had written about it, he felt no personal animus. When he came to the part about the pillaging and terrorizing of the *habitant* villages, though, he felt the blood begin to rise behind his eyes. Siverly might be a proper villain, but this wasn't personal villainy.

This was the Crown's way. The way of dealing with resistant natives. Theft, rape, murder . . . and fire.

Cumberland had done it, "cleansing" the Highlands after

Culloden. And James Wolfe had done it, too—to deprive the Citadel at Quebec of support from the countryside. Taken livestock, killed the men, burned houses . . . and left the women to starve and freeze.

God, that she might be safe! he thought in sudden agony, closing his eyes for an instant. *And the child with her.*

He glanced up from the paper. The duke was still coughing but had now dug a pipe out of the midden and was packing it with tobacco. Lord Melton had commanded troops at Culloden. Those troops—and the man who sat before him—had very likely remained to take part in the cleansing of the Highlands.

"No lingering sense of injury," he'd said. Jamie muttered something very rude under his breath in the *Gàidhlig* and went on reading, though he found his attention still distracted.

Blood pressure. That's what Claire called it. To do with how hard your heart beat and the force with which it drove the blood round your body. When your heart failed you and blood no longer reached the brain, that's what caused fainting, she said. And when it beat hard, in the grip of fear or passion, that was when you felt the blood beat in your temples and swell in your chest, ready for bed or battle.

His own blood pressure was rising like a rocket, and he'd no desire to bed Pardloe.

The duke took a spill from a pottery dish and put it to the candle flame, then used it to light his pipe. It had grown dark outside, and the smell of oncoming rain came in through the half-open window, mingling with the musky sweet scent of the tobacco. Pardloe's lean cheeks hollowed as he sucked at the pipe, the orbits of his eyes shadowed by the light that fell on brow and nose. He looked like a skull.

Abruptly, Jamie set down the papers.

"What do you want of me?" he demanded.

Pardloe took the pipe from his mouth and exhaled slow wisps of smoke.

"I want you to translate that bit of Irish. And to tell me more—whatever you know or recall of Gerald Siverly's background and connections. Beyond that . . ." The pipe was in danger of going out, and the duke took a long pull at it.

"And ye think I'll do it, for the asking?"

Pardloe gave him a level look, smoke purling from his lips.

"Yes, I do. Why not?" He raised the middle finger of one hand. "I would consider it a debt, to be paid."

"Put that bloody finger back down before I ram it up your backside."

The duke's mouth twitched, but he put the finger down without comment.

"I also wished to see you, to determine whether you might be of assistance in bringing Major Siverly to justice. I think that you can be. And what I want above all is justice."

Justice.

Jamie drew a breath and held it for a moment, to ensure against hasty speech.

"What assistance?"

The duke blew a thoughtful cloud of blue-tinged smoke, and Jamie realized suddenly what the sweet, pungent odor was. It wasn't tobacco; the duke was drinking hemp smoke. He'd smelled it once or twice before; a doctor in Paris had prescribed it to an acquaintance who suffered from a lung complaint. Was the duke ill? He didn't look it.

He didn't sound like it, either.

"Siverly has taken leave from his regiment and disappeared. We think he has gone to his estate in Ireland. I want him found and brought back." Pardloe's voice was level, and so was his gaze. "My brother is going to Ireland on this mission, but he will require help. He—"

"Did he bloody tell you to fetch me here?" Jamie's fists had doubled. "Does he think that I—"

"I don't know what he thinks, and, no, he has no idea that I've brought you here," Pardloe said. "I doubt he'll be pleased," he added thoughtfully, "but as I said—whatever disagreements you and he may have do not concern me." He laid the pipe aside and folded his hands, looking at Jamie straight on.

"I dislike doing this," he said. "And I regret the necessity."

Jamie stared at Pardloe, feeling his chest tighten. "I've been fucked up the arse by an Englishman before," he said flatly. "Spare me the kiss, aye?"

Pardloe drew breath through his nose and laid both hands flat on the desk.

"You will accompany Lieutenant-Colonel Grey to Ireland and there render him every assistance in locating Major Siverly and compelling his return to England, as well as obtaining evidence to aid in his prosecution."

Jamie sat like stone. He could hear the rasp of his own breath.

"Or your parole will be revoked. You will be taken to the Tower—today—and there committed to imprisonment at His Majesty's pleasure." The duke paused. "Do you require a moment to consider the situation?" he asked politely.

Jamie stood up abruptly. Pardloe stiffened, barely saving himself from jerking backward.

"When?" Jamie asked, and was surprised at the calmness in his voice.

Pardloe's shoulders relaxed, almost imperceptibly.

"In a few days." For the first time, his eyes left Jamie's face, surveying him from head to toe. "You'll need clothes. You'll travel as the gentleman you are. Under parole, of course." He paused, gaze returning to Jamie's face. "And I *will* consider myself in your debt, Mr. Fraser."

Jamie looked at him with contempt and turned on his heel.

"Where are you going?" Pardloe said. He sounded startled.

"Out," Jamie said, and reached for the doorknob. He glared back over his shoulder. "Under parole. Of course." He jerked the door open.

"Supper's at eight," said the duke's voice behind him. "Don't be late, will you? It puts Cook out."

9

Eros Rising

IT HAD COME ON TO RAIN, AND THE GUTTERS WERE STREAMing. John Grey was soaked to the skin and was steaming. He stamped down Monmouth Street, oblivious to pelting rain, ankle-deep puddles, and the soggy skirts of his coat flapping about his thighs.

He'd been walking for what seemed hours, thinking that the exercise would burn away his anger, make it possible for him to speak to his brother without striking him. It hadn't. If anything, he grew more infuriated with each step.

Even for Hal, to whom high-handedness was as natural as breathing, this was raw. Not only to have ignored John's plainly stated position with regard to Jamie Fraser but to have decided without a word or a by-your-leave to have Fraser brought to London—and to have bloody done it without a word to him, overriding his authority as Fraser's legal parole officer . . . and then—then!—to have compounded the crime by informing John—not asking him, oh, no, commanding him!—to go to Ireland in Fraser's company. . . . He wanted urgently to wring Hal's neck.

The only thing stopping him was the presence of James Fraser at Argus House.

He couldn't in justice blame Fraser for the present situation. He doubted the man was any happier about it than he was. Justice, however, had nothing to do with his feelings, which were exigent.

The rain turned briefly to hail, tiny balls of ice bouncing off his head and shoulders, and a covey of orange-girls scuttled past him, squealing in a mix of consternation and exhilaration, leaving a delicious scent of chilled oranges in their wake. One of them had dropped a fruit from her box; it rolled at his feet, vivid on the pavement, and he picked it up and turned to call after her, but the girls had gone.

The cold globular feel of the orange was pleasant in his hand, and the slackening hail had cooled his blood a little. He tossed the fruit in the air and caught it again.

He hadn't tried to strike Hal in anger since he was fifteen. It hadn't gone well. He could probably do it now, though. Hal was still quick and an excellent swordsman, but he was nearly forty now, and the years of campaigning had told on him. Still, what would be the point of hammering his brother, or even pegging him with an orange at short range? The situation would still be what it was. He put the orange in his pocket and sloshed moodily across a flooded street, kicking floating cabbage leaves out of the way.

"Lord John!" The shrill hail made him look up, in time to be deluged by a massive wave of filthy water thrown up by the wheels of a carriage. Spluttering, he wiped mud and offal from his face and saw a young woman in the window of the coach, her own face convulsed with laughter.

"Oh, your lordship—how wet ye are!" she managed through her giggles, shielding the red velvet flowers on her very stylish hat from the blowing rain with a spread fan.

"Yes. I am wet," he said, giving Nessie a marked look. Agnes, she was called; a young Scottish whore he'd met three years before. Apparently, she'd come up in the world considerably since. "Is that your coach?"

"Och, no," she said with regret. "If it was, I'd offer ye a ride. I'm on my way to see a new swell; he sent it for me."

"Well, I shouldn't like to spoil your client's upholstery," he said, with exquisite politeness.

"Ye'll catch your death standin' there," she advised him, ignoring this. "But ye're no far from my new house. The end o' Brydges Street. If ye go there, Mrs. Donoghue will gie ye a wee dram against the chill. And maybe a towel," she added, surveying him critically.

"I thank you for the suggestion, madam."

She flashed him a brilliant smile and waggled her fan.

"Nay charge. Get on wi' ye, then, ye stocious bugger, before I'm drowned!" she shouted toward the coachman, and, withdrawing her head, promptly snapped the window shut.

He leapt back but not quite in time to avoid receiving another discharge of cold water and wet manure across his legs as the coach surged into motion.

He stood still, dripping and breathing heavily, but then realized that there was some virtue in Nessie's suggestion. He should seek shelter, if he didn't want to die of pleurisy or come down with *la grippe.* And the only thing worse than going to Ireland in Jamie Fraser's company would be doing it with a bad head cold.

Not at a brothel, where the dram and towel would doubtless be provided at extortionate charge, and unwanted female companionship urged upon him, as well. His encounter with Nessie had jolted him out of his bad temper and into an awareness of his surroundings, though; he was no more than a few streets away from the Beefsteak, his favorite club. He could get a room there—dry clothes, perhaps a bath. And certainly a drink.

He turned and set off up Coptic Street with determination, trickles of water running down his back.

AN HOUR LATER, bathed, dressed in dry—if slightly too large—clothing, and having ingested two large brandies, he found himself in a slightly more philosophical frame of mind.

The important thing was to find Siverly and bring him back. His own honor was at stake in that venture, both because of his promise to Charlie Carruthers and because of his duty as an officer of His Majesty's army. He'd done unpleasant things before in pursuit of that duty. This would be one more, that's all.

And it was somewhat reassuring to realize that Fraser would be as uncomfortable as himself. No doubt that discomfort would prevent anything awkward being said.

He thought the philosophical frame of mind was coming along fairly well but might be further assisted by food; agitated by his conversation with Hal, he'd missed his tea and was feeling the effects of brandy on an empty stomach. Glancing at himself in the looking glass to be sure he'd got all the manure flakes out of his still-damp hair, he twitched the ill-fitting gray coat into better adjustment and made his way downstairs.

It was early evening, and the Beefsteak was quiet. Supper was not being served quite yet; there was no one in the smoking room and only one member in the library, sprawled asleep in a chair with a newspaper over his face.

Someone was in the writing room, though, shoulders hunched in thought, quill twiddling in one hand in search of inspiration.

To Grey's surprise, the hunched back proved to belong to Harry Quarry, senior colonel of the 46th. Quarry, straightening up with an unfocused look in his eye, suddenly caught sight of

Grey in the corridor and, alarmed, hastily slapped a sheet of blotting paper over the paper on the desk before him.

"A new poem, Harry?" Grey asked pleasantly, stepping into the writing room.

"What?" Harry tried—and failed utterly—to look innocently bewildered. "Poetry? Me? Letter to a lady."

"Oh, yes?"

Grey made as though to lift the blotting paper, and Quarry snatched both sheets away, pressing them to his chest.

"How dare you, sir?" he said, with what dignity he could muster. "A man's private correspondence is sacred!"

"Nothing is sacred to a man who would rhyme 'sanguineous' and 'cunnilingus,' I assure you."

He likely wouldn't have said it had the brandy warming his blood not loosened his tongue, as well. Seeing Harry's eyes bulge, though, he wanted to laugh, in spite of his regret.

Harry leapt to his feet and, going to the door, glanced wildly up and down the corridor, before turning to glare at Grey.

"I should like to see you do better. Who the devil told you?"

"How many people know?" Grey countered. "I guessed. You gave me that book for Diderot, after all." He hadn't guessed but didn't want to reveal the source of his information, that being his mother.

"You read it?" The color was beginning to come back into Harry's normally florid face.

"Well, no," Grey admitted. "Monsieur Diderot read a number of selections from it aloud, though." He grinned involuntarily at the recollection of M. Diderot—very intoxicated—declaiming poetry from Harry's anonymously published *Certain Verses Upon the Subject of Eros* while urinating behind a screen in Lady Jonas's salon.

Harry was examining him, narrow-eyed.

"Hmmph," he said. "You wouldn't know a dactyl from your left thumb. Benedicta told you."

Grey's eyebrows shot up. Not in offense at Harry's impugning of his literary judgment—which was more or less true—but in surprise. For Harry to have referred to Grey's mother by her Christian name—while revealing that she knew about the poetry—was a shocking revelation as to the intimacy of their acquaintance.

He had wondered how his mother had come to know that Harry wrote erotic poetry. He returned the narrow look, with interest.

Harry, belatedly realizing what he'd given away, looked as innocent as it was possible for a thirty-eight-year-old colonel of expansive habit, lecherous appetite, and considerable experience to look. Grey debated briefly whether to make something of that look, but, after all, his mother was safely married now to General Stanley, and neither she nor the general would thank him for causing scandal—and he really didn't want to call Harry out, anyway.

He settled for saying repressively, "The lady *is* my mother, sir," and Harry had the grace to look abashed.

Before more could be said, though, the front door opened and a cold draft swirled down the hall, lifting the papers on the desk and scattering them at Grey's feet. He stooped swiftly to pick them up before Harry could reach them.

"Christ, Harry!" His eye flickered hastily over the careful script.

"Give that back!" Harry growled, making a snatch at the paper.

Holding Harry off with one hand, he read further, out loud: "*With thighs bedew'd and foaming cunt*—Jesus, Harry, *foaming*?"

"It's a bloody rough draft!"

"Oh, it's rough, all right!" He stepped nimbly backward into the hall, evading Harry's grasp, and collided heavily with a gentleman who had just come in.

"Lord John! I do beg your pardon most humbly! Are you injured?"

Grey blinked stupidly for a moment at the enormous fair man looming solicitously over him, then straightened up from his ignominious collapse against the paneling.

"Von Namtzen!" He clasped the big Hanoverian's hand, absurdly delighted to see him again. "What brings you to London? What brings you here? Come and have supper with me, can you?"

Captain von Namtzen's sternly handsome face was wreathed in smiles, though Grey saw that it bore the marks of some recent difficulty, the lines between nose and mouth harsher than they had been, hollows beneath the broad cheekbones and the deep-set eyes. He squeezed Grey's hand to express his pleasure at their reacquaintance, and Grey felt a few bones give, though nothing actually cracked.

"I should be so pleased," von Namtzen said. "But I am engaged . . ." He turned, looking vaguely behind him and gesturing toward a well-dressed gentleman who had been standing out of range. "You know Mr. Frobisher? His lordship John Grey," he explained to Frobisher, who bowed.

"Certainly," the gentleman replied courteously. "It would give me great pleasure, Lord John, was you to join us. I have two brace of partridge ordered, a fresh-caught salmon, and a vast great trifle to follow—Captain von Namtzen and I will be quite unequal to the occasion, I am sure."

Grey, with some experience of von Namtzen's capacities, rather thought that the Hanoverian was likely to engulf the entire meal single-handedly and then require a quick snack before retiring, but before he could excuse himself, Harry snatched the kidnapped papers from his hand, thus requiring an introduction to Frobisher and von Namtzen, and in the social muddle that ensued, all four found themselves going in to supper together, with a salmagundi and a few bottles of good Burgundy hastily ordered to augment the meal.

CHRIST, IT WAS CATCHING. He'd led the conversation over the soup to the subject of poetry, meaning only to chaff Harry, but it had led to an enthusiastic declamation of a poem from Brockes's *Irdisches Vergnügen in Gott*—in German—by Mr. Frobisher, and then a heated discussion between von Namtzen and Frobisher regarding the structure of a particular German verse form and whether this was or was not the parent of the English sonnet.

Harry, asked for his opinion, grinned at Grey over his soup spoon.

"Me?" he said blandly. "Oh, I'm certainly not qualified to give an opinion. 'Mary had a little lamb' is about as far as I go in that direction. Grey, now, he's the lad for rhymes; best ask him."

Grey had hurriedly disclaimed any such knowledge, but it had set the table to the game of finding rhymes, going in turn until one man should not be able to find a rhyming word, whereat the next would choose a new one.

They'd got from the simple things like moon/June/spoon/spittoon/poltroon onto the more delicate issue of whether "porringer" could be legitimately rhymed with "oranger," the latter being arguably a real word. The worst of it was that the conversation—coupled with the sight of von Namtzen sitting opposite him, his broad face lightened a little by the wordplay, his soft fair hair curling gently round the back of his ears—had caused him to start rhyming things privately. Only rude words, to start with, but then a little couplet—he thought that was the right term for it—had begun to chant itself.

He was startled by it. Was this how Harry did it? Just have words show up and start something, all by themselves?

The words that had shown up in his own mind had fallen into an irritating bit of doggerel: *You cannot master me / but shall I your master be?*

This unsettled him, as there was nothing in his relationship—or feelings—regarding von Namtzen to which this could apply, and he realized quite well that it had to do with the presence of Jamie Fraser at Argus House.

Will you bloody go away? he thought fiercely. *I'm not ready.*

The room seemed very warm, and sweat gathered round his hairline. Luckily, the arrival of the salmagundi and the kerfuffle of serving it diverted the company's attention from verse, and he lost himself thankfully in the glories of short-crust pastry and the luscious mingled juices of game, duck, and truffles.

"WHAT'S BROUGHT YOU to London, sir?" Harry asked von Namtzen over the salad. It was plainly meant merely to break the digestive silence caused by the salmagundi, but the Hanoverian's face became shadowed, and he looked down into the plate of greens and vinegar.

"I am purchasing some properties for the captain," Mr. Frobisher put in hurriedly, with a glance at von Namtzen. "Papers to sign, you know . . ." He waved a hand, indicating vast reams of legal requirement.

Grey looked curiously at von Namtzen—who was not only captain of his own regiment but the Graf von Erdberg, as well. He knew perfectly well that the graf had a man of business in

England; all wealthy foreigners did, and he had in fact met von Namtzen's property agent once.

Whether von Namtzen had noticed his curiosity or merely felt that more explanation was necessary, he raised his head and expelled an explosive breath.

"My wife died," he said, and paused to swallow. "Last month. I—my sister is in London." Another swallow. "I have brought the . . . my children . . . to her."

"Oh, my dear sir," said Harry, putting a hand on von Namtzen's arm and speaking with the deepest sympathy. "I am so sorry."

"Danke," von Namtzen muttered, and then suddenly rose to his feet and blundered out of the room, with what might have been a word of excuse or a muffled sob.

"Oh, dear," said Frobisher, dismayed. "Poor fellow. I'd no idea he felt it so deeply."

Neither had Grey.

After an awkward pause, they resumed eating their salads, Grey gesturing to the steward to remove von Namtzen's plate. Frobisher had no details regarding the captain's sad loss, and the conversation switched to a desultory discussion of politics.

Grey, having less than no interest in the subject, was left to consider Stephan von Namtzen and supply automatic noises of interest or agreement as the rhythm of the talk demanded.

He did spare a thought for Louisa von Lowenstein, the extremely vivacious—not that he couldn't think of better words, but the woman *was* dead—Saxon princess who had married von Namtzen three years before. *God rest her soul,* he thought, and meant it—but his real concern was for Stephan.

If asked, he would have sworn that the marriage had been one of mutual convenience. He would also have sworn that Stephan's tastes lay in other directions. There had been passages between himself and von Namtzen that . . . well, true, there had been nothing explicit, no declarations—not that sort of declaration, at least—and yet he couldn't have been altogether mistaken. The sense of feeling between them . . .

He recalled the evening in Germany when he had helped Stephan to remove his shirt outdoors, had examined—and kissed—the stump of his recently amputated left arm, and how the man's skin had glowed in the magic of the dusky light. His face grew hot and he bent his head over his plate.

Still. Stephan might have been sincerely attached to Louisa, no matter what the true nature of their marriage had been. And there were men who enjoyed the physical attractions of both sexes. For that matter, Grey himself knew several women whose deaths would distress him greatly, though he had no relation with them beyond that of friendship.

Von Namtzen reappeared as the cheese plates were being taken away, his normal equanimity seeming quite restored, though his eyes were red-rimmed. The conversation over port and brandy changed smoothly to a discussion of horse racing, thence to the breeding of horses—von Namtzen had a remarkable stud at Waldesruh—and remained on purely neutral matters until they rose at last.

"Shall I see you home?" Grey said quietly to von Namtzen as they waited in the hall for the steward to bring their cloaks. His heart was thumping audibly in his ears.

Stephan's eyes flicked toward Frobisher, but the man was in close conversation with Harry about something.

"I should appreciate your company very much, Lord John," he said, and though the words were formal, his bloodshot eyes were warm.

They didn't speak in the coach. The rain had ceased and they left the windows down, the air cold and fresh on their faces. Grey's thoughts were disordered by the amount of wine drunk with dinner, more so by the tumultuous emotions of the day—and, most of all, by Stephan's close presence. He was a large man, and his knee vibrated with the coach's movement, no more than an inch from Grey's.

As he followed Stephan from the coach, he caught the scent of von Namtzen's cologne, something faint and spicy—cloves, he thought, and was absurdly reminded of Christmas, and oranges studded thick with cloves, the smell festive in the house.

His hand closed on the orange, cool and round in his pocket, and he thought of other rounded things that might fit in his hand, these warm.

"Fool," he said to himself, under his breath. "Don't even think about it."

It was, of course, impossible not to think about it.

Dismissing the yawning butler who let them in, Stephan led Grey to a small sitting room where a banked fire smoldered in the hearth. He waved Grey to a comfortable chair and took up the poker himself to stir the embers into life.

"You will have something to drink?" he asked, with a nod over his shoulder to a sideboard on which glasses and bottles stood in orderly ranks, graded by size. Grey smiled at the Germanic neatness of the array, but poured a small brandy for himself and—with a glance at Stephan's broad back—a slightly larger one for his friend.

Several of the bottles were half empty, and he wondered how long Stephan had been in London.

Seated before the fire, they sipped at their drinks in a companionable silence, watching the flames.

"It was kind of you to come with me," Stephan said at last. "I did not want to be alone tonight."

Grey lifted one shoulder in dismissal. "I am only sorry that it should be tragedy that brings us together again," he said, and meant it. He hesitated. "You . . . miss your wife greatly?"

Stephan pursed his lips a little. "I—well . . . of course I mourn Louisa," he said, with more formality than Grey would have expected. "She was a fine woman. Very good at managing things." A faint, sad smile touched his lips. "No, it is my poor children for whom I am sorrowful."

The shadow Grey had noted before clouded the broad face, clean-limned as a Teutonic saint's. "Elise and Alexander . . . They lost their own mother when they were quite small, and they loved Louisa very much; she was a wonderful mother, as kind to them as to our little Baerbel or to her own son."

"Ah," Grey said. "Siggy?" He'd met young Siegfried, Louisa's son by her first marriage, and smiled at the memory.

"Siggy," von Namtzen agreed, and smiled a little, too, but the smile soon faded. "He must remain in Lowenstein, of course; he is the heir. And that also is too bad for Lise and Sascha—they are very fond of him, and now he is gone from them, too. Baerbel is too young to know really, but it's better for them to be with my sister. I could not leave them at Lowenstein, but their faces when I had to say farewell to them this afternoon . . ."

His own face crumpled for a moment, and Grey felt by reflex in his pocket for a handkerchief, but von Namtzen buried his grief in his glass for a moment and got control of himself again.

Grey rose and turned his back tactfully as he refreshed his drink, saying something casual about his cousin Olivia's child, Cromwell, now aged almost two and the terror of the household.

"Cromwell?" von Namtzen said, clearing his throat and sounding bemused. "This is an English name?"

"Couldn't be more so." An explanation of the history of the

lord protector carried them into safe waters—though Grey suffered a slight private pang; he couldn't think of young Cromwell without remembering Percy, the stepbrother who had also been his lover. They had both been present—inadvertently—at young Cromwell's birth, and his description of this hair-raising occasion made Stephan laugh.

The house was quiet, and the small room seemed removed from everything, a warm refuge in the depths of the night. He felt as though the two of them were castaways, thrown up together on some island by the storms of life, passing uncharted time by exchanging their stories.

It wasn't the first time. When he had been wounded after Crefeld, he had been taken to Stephan's hunting lodge at Waldesruh to recover, and once he was able to carry on a conversation that lasted more than two sentences, they had often talked like this, late into the night.

"You are feeling well?" Stephan asked suddenly, picking up his train of thought in the way that close friends sometimes do. "Your wounds—do they still pain you?"

"No," he said. He had wounds that still did, but not physical ones. *"Und dein Arm?"*

Stephan laughed with pleasure at hearing him speak German and lifted the stump of his left arm a little.

"Nein. Eine Unannehmlichkeit, mehr nicht." A nuisance, no more.

He watched Stephan as they talked, now in both languages, seeing the light move on his face, as it went from humor to seriousness and back again, expressions flickering like fire shadow over his broad Teutonic bones. Grey had been startled, as well as moved, by the depth of Stephan's feeling for his children—though, on consideration, he shouldn't have been. He'd long been struck by the apparent contradiction in the Teutonic character, swinging from cold logic and ferocity in battle to the deepest romanticism and sentimentality.

Passion, he supposed you'd call it. Weirdly enough, it reminded him of the Scots, who were emotionally much the same, though less disciplined about it.

Master me, he thought. *Or shall I your master be?*

And with that casual thought, something moved viscerally in him. Well, it had been moving for some time, in all honesty. But with that particular thought, his attraction to Stephan suddenly merged with the things he had been deliberately not thinking—or feeling—with regard to Jamie Fraser, and he found himself grow flushed, discomfited.

Did he want Stephan only because of the physical similarities between him and Fraser? They were both big men, tall and commanding, both the sort that made people turn to look at them. And to look at either of them stirred him, deeply.

It was quite different, though. Stephan was his friend, his good friend, and Jamie Fraser never would be. Fraser, though, was something that Stephan never could be.

"You are hungry?" Without waiting for an answer, Stephan rose and rummaged in a cupboard, coming out with a plate of biscuits and a pot of orange marmalade.

Grey smiled, remembering his earlier prediction regarding von Namtzen's appetite. He took an almond biscuit from politeness rather than hunger and, with a feeling of affection, watched Stephan devour biscuits spread with marmalade.

The affection was tinged with doubt, though. There was a sense of deep closeness between them, here in the night, quite alone—no doubt at all of that. But what sort of closeness . . . ?

Stephan's hand brushed his, reaching for a biscuit, and von Namtzen squeezed his fingers lightly, smiling, before letting go and taking up the marmalade spoon. The touch ran up Grey's arm and straight down his spine, raising hairs in its wake.

No, he thought, struggling for logic, for decency. *I can't.*

It wouldn't be right. Not right to use Stephan, to try to slake his physical need with Stephan, perhaps risk their friendship by trying. And yet the temptation was there, no doubt of that, either. Not only the immediate desire—which was bloody strong—but the ignoble thought that he might by such means exorcise, or at least temper, the hold Fraser had upon him. It would be far easier to face Fraser, to deal with him calmly, if the sense of physical desire was at least muted, if not gone entirely.

But . . . he looked at Stephan, the kindness and the sadness in his broad face, and knew he couldn't.

"I must go," he said abruptly, and stood up, brushing crumbs from his shirt ruffle. "It's very late."

"Must you go?" Stephan sounded surprised, but rose, too.

"I—yes. Stephan—I'm so glad we met this evening," he said on impulse, and held out a hand.

Stephan took it, but rather than shake it, drew him close, and the taste of oranges was suddenly in his mouth.

"WHAT ARE YOU THINKING?" he asked at last, not sure whether he wanted to hear the answer but needing to hear Stephan speak.

To his relief, Stephan smiled, his eyes still closed, and drew his large, warm fingers gently down the slope of Grey's shoulder and over the curve of his forearm, where they curled round his wrist.

"I am wondering what is the risk that I will die before St. Catherine's Day."

"What? Why? And when is St. Catherine's Day?"

"In three weeks. That is when Father Gehring returns from Salzburg."

"Oh, yes?"

Stephan let go of his wrist and opened his eyes.

"If I go back to Hanover and confess this to Father Fenstermacher, I will probably have to hear Mass every day for a year or undertake a pilgrimage to Trier. Father Gehring is somewhat . . . less exacting."

"I see. And if you die before making your confession—"

"I will go to hell, of course," Stephan said matter-of-factly. "But I think it is worth the risk. It's a long walk to Trier." He coughed and cleared his throat.

"That—what you did. To me." He wouldn't meet Grey's eye, and a deep color rose across his broad cheekbones.

"I did a lot of things to you, Stephan." Grey struggled to keep the laughter out of his voice, but without much success. "Which one? This one?" He leaned forward on his elbow and kissed von Namtzen's mouth, enjoying the little start von Namtzen gave at the touch of his lips.

Stephan kissed men frequently, in that exuberant German way of his. But he didn't kiss them this way.

To feel the strength of those broad shoulders rise under his palm, then feel them give way, the powerful flesh melting slowly as Stephan's mouth softened, yielding to him . . .

"Better than your hundred-year-old brandy," Grey whispered.

Stephan sighed deeply. "I want to give you pleasure," he said simply, meeting Grey's eyes for the first time. "What would you like?"

Grey was speechless. Not so much at the declaration, moving as it was—but at the multitude of images that one sentence conjured. What would he *like*?

"Everything, Stephan," he said, his voice husky. "Anything. It—I mean—to touch you—just to *watch* you gives me pleasure."

Stephan's mouth curled up at that.

"You can watch," he assured Grey. "You will let me touch you, though?"

Grey nodded. "Oh, yes," he said.

"Good. What I wish to know, though—how best?" He reached out and took hold of Grey's half-hard prick, inspecting it critically.

"How?" Grey croaked. All the blood had left his head, very suddenly.

"*Ja.* Shall I put my mouth upon this? I am not sure what to do then, you see, how this is done correctly. I see there is some skill in this, which I do not have. And you are not quite ready yet, I think?"

Grey opened his mouth to observe that this condition was rapidly adjusting itself, but Stephan went on, squeezing gently.

"It is more straightforward if I put my member into your bottom and use you in that fashion. I am ready, and I am confident I can do that; it is much like what I do with my—with women."

"I—yes, I'm sure you can," Grey said rather faintly.

"But I think if I do that, I might hurt you." Stephan let go of Grey's prick and took hold of his own, frowning at the comparison. "It hurt, at first, when you did this to me. Not later—I liked it very much," he assured Grey hastily. "But at first. And I am . . . somewhat large."

Grey's mouth was so dry that it was an effort to speak. "Some . . . what," he managed. He glanced at Stephan's prick, freshly erect, then away. Then, slowly, back again, eyes drawn like iron to a magnet.

It *would* hurt. A lot. At least . . . at first . . .

He swallowed audibly. "If . . . I mean . . . if you . . ."

"I will do it very slowly, *ja.*" Stephan smiled, sudden as the sun coming from behind clouds, and reached for the large cushion they had used earlier. He threw it down and patted it. "Come then, and bend over. I will oil you."

He had taken Stephan from behind, thinking that Stephan would be less self-conscious that way, he himself loving the sight of the broad, smooth back beneath him, the powerful waist and muscular buttocks, surrendered so completely to him. He felt his own clench a little at the memory.

"Not—that way." He pushed the cushion back against the headboard and scrambled up, bracing his shoulders securely against it. "You said I could watch." And the position would give him some control—and at least a chance to avoid serious injury, should Stephan's enthusiasm outrun his caution.

Are you insane? he asked himself, wiping sweating palms against the counterpane. *You haven't got to do this, you know. You don't even like to . . . God, you'll feel it for a week, even if he doesn't . . .*

"Oh, Jesus!"

Stephan paused, surprised, in the act of pouring oil into the dish. "I have not even begun. You are all right?" A small frown drew his brows together. "You *have* . . . done this before?"

"Yes. Yes, I . . . I'm fine. I . . . just . . . anticipation."

Stephan leaned forward, very gently, and kissed him. He learned quickly, Stephan did. When he drew back after some time, he looked at Grey's body, visibly trembling despite his efforts to control it, and shook his head, smiling a little. Then he clicked his tongue softly and passed his hand over Grey's hair, once, twice, stroking him. Gentling him.

It was true that Stephan had limited experience, no artifice, and not much natural skill. But Grey had forgotten that Stephan was a horseman, and a breeder and trainer of dogs. He didn't need words to understand what an animal—or a person—was feeling. And he knew what "slowly" meant.

10

Punch and Judy

Next day

JAMIE'S CHEST FELT AS THOUGH HE'D A LEATHER STRAP around it. He hadn't drawn a proper breath since the soldiers had taken him from Helwater, but just this moment he could barely remember how lungs were meant to work. It was a conscious effort to draw breath, and he counted—*one, two, in, out, one, two*—as he walked. He had a sudden flash of memory, Claire's face, intent, as she knelt by a wee lad—was it Rabbie? aye, Rabbie MacNab—who'd fallen from the hayloft at Lallybroch.

She'd spoken to the lad, calm, one hand on his belly and the other feeling quickly down his limbs for broken bones. "Relax; your breath will come back. Yes, you see? Breathe slowly now, push out as much as you can. . . . Yes, now in . . . one . . . two. In . . . out . . ."

He caught the rhythm of it from the memory of her voice, and within a few steps he was breathing easier, though the back of his neck was wet with cold sweat and gooseflesh still rippled over his shoulders. What was the matter with him?

The duke had summoned him, and he'd walked into the

drawing room and found himself face-to-face with Colonel Quarry, looking just as he had when last seen, as the governor of Ardsmuir prison. Whereupon he'd turned on his heel and walked straight out again, through the front door and into the park, his heart hammering and his face going hot and cold and hot again.

He wiped sweating palms on his breeks and felt the slight roughness of a patch. Someone had taken away his clothes in the night, laundered and mended them.

He wasn't afraid of Quarry; he never had been. But one keek at the man and he'd felt his wame clench and spots dance before his eyes and he'd known it was get out right then or measure his length on the hearth rug at Quarry's feet.

There were trees dotted here and there; he found one and sat down on the grass, leaning back against its trunk. His hands still trembled, but he felt better with something solid at his back. He didn't want to but couldn't keep from rubbing his wrists, first one and then the other, as if to assure himself of what he knew fine—that the fetters were gone.

One of the footmen from Argus House had followed him; he recognized the dark-gray livery. The man hung back, just within the edge of the park, trying to pretend he was watching the carriages and riders that went past on the road that skirted the park. He'd done the same thing the evening before, when Jamie had come out to walk off his anger at the duke.

He hadn't troubled Jamie then and obviously didn't mean to drag him back to the house now; he'd only been sent to watch. It occurred to Jamie to wonder what yon footman would do, should he stand up and run. He had a momentary urge to do just that, and did in fact stand up. He should have run, too, because no sooner had he got to his feet than Tobias Quinn came slithering out of a bush like a toad.

"Well, and there's luck for ye," Quinn remarked, looking pleased. "I thought I should have to lurk about for days, and here Himself walks straight up to me, and me not at the watching for more than half a day!"

"Dinna bloody call me Himself," Jamie said irritably. "What the devil are ye doing here? And why are ye hiding in a bush wearing that?"

Quinn lifted a brow and dusted the yellow of spring catkins fastidiously from the sleeve of his checkered coat. It was pink and black silk, and everyone who passed within twenty yards stared at it.

"Not the greeting one might expect of a friend," he said, reproving. "And I wasn't hiding, not in the least. I was just comin' across the park when I saw ye come out, and I sidled round the bush as being quickest, since I perceived ye were about to fly and I'd have no chance of catching ye if ye did, you with the legs of a veritable stallion, so ye have. As for me plumage"—here he spread his arms and revolved, the skirts of his coat flaring out—"is it not the fine thing of the world?"

"Go away," Jamie said, repressing an urge to shove Quinn back into the bush. He turned and began to walk away. The Irishman came along.

Jamie glanced over his shoulder, but the footman was still turned away, absorbed in an entertainingly profane argument between the drivers of two carriages whose wheels had clashed and locked together as they passed each other too closely.

"The splendid thing about this coat," Quinn said chattily, pulling it off, "is that ye can wear it both ways. Inside out, like, I mean. Should ye want to avoid notice for some reason." He shook the garment, showing off the inner lining, which was a fine wool, seamed smooth and sober black. He reassumed the coat, pulled off his wig, and rubbed a hand through his poll of short curls, making them stand on end. He might have been a lawyer's clerk now, or a Quaker of moderate means.

Jamie didn't know whether it was only the man's love of the dramatic or whether there was some need of such hasty disguise. He didn't want to know.

"I've told ye," he said, struggling for civility. "I'm no the man for your job."

"Why, because of this small little complication?" Quinn waved a hand carelessly toward the bulk of Argus House, looming gray through the scrim of trees. "It's nothing, sure. I'll have ye in Ireland by the end of next week."

"What?" Jamie stared at him, uncomprehending.

"Well, you'll not want to linger in such company as that, will ye?" Quinn half-turned his head toward Argus House. He turned back, passing a critical eye over Jamie's worn clothes.

"Aye, thus, very well thus. We've to move briskly for a bit, but once into the Rookery, no one would glance twice at you. Ah . . . perhaps twice," he amended, squinting up at Jamie's height. "But not three times, surely."

It occurred belatedly to Jamie that Quinn was suggesting that they abscond. Right now.

"I canna do that!"

Quinn looked surprised.

"Why not?"

Jamie's mouth opened but without the slightest notion what might come out.

"We wouldna make it to the edge of the park, for one thing. See yon fellow in the gray? He's watching me."

Quinn squinted in the direction indicated. "He's not watchin' ye just this minute," he pointed out. He took Jamie by the hand, pulling. "Come on, then. Walk fast!"

"No!" He jerked loose and cast a wild glance at the footman, willing the man to turn round. He didn't, and Jamie turned back to Quinn, speaking firm again.

"I've told ye once, and I'll say it again. I'll have nothing to do wi' any such crack-brained notion. The Cause is dead, and I've no intent to follow it into the grave. Aye?"

Quinn affected not to have heard this, instead looking thoughtfully at Argus House.

"That's the Duke of Pardloe's house, they say," he remarked, scratching his head. "Why did the sojers bring ye here, I wonder?"

"I dinna ken. They didna tell me." This had the virtue of being half true, and he had no compunction about lying to the Irishman in any case.

"Hmm. Well, I'll tell ye, sir, was it me in the hands of the English, I'd not wait to find out."

Jamie had no wish to see Quinn in English hands, either, annoying as the man was.

"Ye should go, Quinn," he said. "It's dangerous."

"Odd, is it not?" Quinn said meditatively, as usual taking no heed. "On the one hand, they snatch ye from Helwater under armed guard and take ye to London without a word. On the other . . . they let ye wander about outside? Even with a watcher, that seems unusually trusting. Does it not strike ye that way?"

Why would the bloody footman not turn round?

"I've no idea," he said, unwilling to stand about discussing Pardloe and that gentleman's very individual convictions as to honor. For lack of anything to add to that, he walked away down the nearest path, pursued by the Irishman. At least if the footman ever did turn round, he'd see Jamie gone and start looking for him. At this point, any interruption whatever would be welcome, even if it meant being dragged back in chains.

That casual thought flickered through his mind like sheet lightning, illuminating dark corners. Chains. A dream of chains.

He was paying no attention, either to where he went or to what Quinn was saying, yammering at his side. There was a crowd ahead; he made for it. Surely even Quinn, talkative as a parrot, wouldn't be scheming out loud in the midst of a crowd. He had to shut the man up long enough to figure how to get rid of him.

The dreams. He'd pushed the thought from his mind the instant he saw it. It pushed back, though, strong. That was it. The dreams that took him back to dreadful places, the ones he only half-remembered. He'd had one last night. That was why seeing Quarry suddenly, without warning, had made him like to faint.

Chains, he thought, and knew that if he lingered on that thought for more than an instant, he'd find himself in the dream again, sweating and ill, crouched against a stone wall, unable to lift his hand to wipe the vomit from his beard, the fetters too heavy, the metal hot from his fever, inescapable, eternal captivity . . .

"No," he said fiercely, and turned abruptly off the path, coming to a halt in front of a puppet show, surrounded by people, all calling out and laughing. Noise. Color. Anything to fill his senses, to keep the clank of chains at bay.

Quinn was still talking, but Jamie ignored him, affecting to watch the play before them. He'd seen things like this in Paris, often. Wee puppets posturing and squeaking. These were long-nosed, ugly ones, shouting in shrill insult and hitting one another with sticks.

He was breathing easier now, dizziness and fear leaving him as the sheer ordinariness of the day closed round him like warm water. Punchinello—that was the man-puppet's name—and his wife was Judy. She had a stick, Judy did, and tried to strike Punch on the head with it, but he seized the stick. She whipped it up, and Punch, clinging to it, sailed across the tiny stage with a long drawn-out "Shiiiiiit!" to crash against the wall. The crowd shrieked with delight.

Willie would like it, and at thought of the boy he felt at once much better and much worse.

He could get rid of Quinn without much trouble; the man couldn't force him to go to Inchcleraun, after all. The Duke of Pardloe was another matter. He could force Jamie to go to Ireland, but at least that venture didn't involve risking his neck or the possibility of lifelong imprisonment. He could do it, finish the job as quickly as possible, and then go back. To Helwater and Willie.

He missed the boy with a sudden pang, wishing he had Willie perched on his shoulders now, grabbing at his ears and giggling at the puppets. Would Willie remember him if he was gone for months?

Well, he'd just have to find Siverly fast. Because he *was* going back to Helwater.

He could feel the child's imagined weight on his shoulders, warm and heavy, smelling faintly of wee and strawberry jam. There were some chains you wore because you wanted to.

"WHERE THE BLOODY HELL have *you* been?" Hal demanded without preamble. "And what in God's name happened to you?" His eye roamed over Grey's clothes, retrieved from the Beefsteak. The club's steward had done his best, but the overall effect was shrunken, stained, faded, and generally far from fashionable.

"Not that it's any of your business, but I got soaked in the rain and stopped the night with a friend," Grey replied equably. He felt cheerful. Relaxed and solidly at peace. Not even Hal's bad temper or the imminent prospect of meeting Jamie Fraser could disturb him. "And where is our guest?"

Hal drew in a long, exasperated breath.

"He's sitting under a tree in the park."

"What on earth for?"

"I haven't the slightest idea. Harry Quarry came for tea—I was expecting you to be here, by the way"—Hal gave him an eyeball, which he ignored—"and when Fraser came in, he took one look at Harry and walked straight out of the house without a by-your-leave. I only know where he is because I'd told one of the footmen to follow him if he went out."

"He'll like that, I'm sure," Grey said. "For God's sake, Hal. Harry was governor at Ardsmuir before me; surely you knew that?"

Hal looked irritably blank. "Possibly. So?"

"He put Fraser in irons. For eighteen months—and left him that way when he came back to London."

"Oh." Hal considered that, frowning. "I see. How was I meant to know that, for heaven's sake?"

"Well, you would have," Grey replied crushingly, "if you'd had the common sense to tell me what the devil you were doing, rather than—oh, hallo, Harry. Didn't know you were still here."

"So I gathered. Where did Fraser go?"

Harry looked rather grim, Grey saw. And he was in full uniform. No bloody wonder Fraser had left; he'd likely seen Harry's presence as a calculated insult, an attempt to further impress his own helplessness upon him.

This realization appeared to be dawning on Hal, too.

"Damn, Harry," he said. "I'm sorry. I didn't know you had a history with Fraser."

History, Grey thought. One way of putting it. Just as well he *hadn't* arrived in time for tea. He'd no idea what James Fraser might have done—confronted simultaneously and without warning by the man who'd put him in fetters, *and* by the one who'd had him flogged, in addition to the man who was currently blackmailing him—but whatever he might have done, Grey wouldn't have blamed him for doing it.

"I'd asked Harry to come so that we might discuss the Siverly affair and so that Harry could tell you what—and who—he knows in Ireland," Hal went on, turning to Grey. "But I didn't think to tell Harry about Fraser ahead of time."

"Not your fault, old man," Harry said, gruff. He squared his shoulders and straightened his lapels. "I'd best go and talk to him, hadn't I?"

"And say what, exactly?" Grey asked, out of sheer inability to imagine what could be said in the circumstances.

Harry shrugged. "Offer him satisfaction, if he likes. Don't see that there's much else to be done."

The Grey brothers exchanged a look of perfect comprehension and suppressed horror. The implications of a duel between a regimental colonel and a paroled prisoner in the custody of the colonel of the regiment, putting aside the complete illegality of the proceedings, *and* the very real possibility that one of them might well kill or maim the other . . .

"Harry—" Hal began, in measured tones, but John interrupted him.

"I'll be your second, Harry," he said hastily. "If it's necessary. I'll go and . . . er . . . inquire about the arrangements, shall I?"

Not waiting for an answer, he pulled open the front door and ran down the steps, too fast for any following shouts to reach him. He dodged across Kensington Road, ducking under the nose of an oncoming horse and being roundly cursed by its rider, and stepped into the open precincts of Hyde Park, where he paused, heart hammering, to look around.

Fraser wasn't immediately visible. After yesterday's savage downpour, today had dawned soft and clear, with the kind of pale bright sky that made one long to be a bird. Consequently, there were large numbers of people in the park, families lounging and eating under the trees, couples strolling on the paths, and pickpockets hanging about the fringes of the crowds round the Speakers' Corner and the Punch and Judy in hopes of an unguarded purse.

Ought he to go back and ask which footman had been following Fraser and where he'd last been seen? No, he decided, striding firmly into the park. He wasn't about to give Harry or Hal a chance to interfere; they'd caused quite enough trouble already.

Given Fraser's height and appearance, Grey had no doubt of his ability to pick the Scot out of any crowd. If he'd been sitting under a tree to begin with, he wasn't doing it now. Where would *he* go, he wondered, if he were Fraser? If he'd been living for several years on a horse farm in the Lake District and, prior to that, in a remote Scottish prison?

Right. He turned at once in the direction of the Punch and Judy show and was gratified as he came in sight of it to see a tall, red-haired man at the back of the crowd, easily able to see over the sea of heads and plainly absorbed in the play before him.

He didn't want to pull Fraser away from the entertainment, so kept a short distance away. Perhaps the play would put the Scot in better temper—though, hearing the shrieks from the crowd as Judy beat Punch into a cocked hat, he began to feel that the influence of the proceedings might not have quite the calmative effect he'd hoped for. He would himself pay considerable money for the privilege of seeing Fraser beat Hal into a cocked hat, though it would cause complications.

He kept one eye on Fraser, the other on the play. The puppet master, an Irishman, was both adroit with his puppets and inventive with his epithets, and Grey felt an unexpected flash of pleasure at seeing Fraser smile.

He leaned against a tree, a little distance away, enjoying the sense of temporary invisibility. He'd wondered how he'd feel, seeing Jamie Fraser in the flesh again, and was relieved to find that the episode in the stable at Helwater now seemed sufficiently distant that he could put it aside. Not forget it, unfortunately, but not have it be uppermost in his mind, either.

Now Fraser bent his head to one side, listening to something said to him by a thin, curly-headed man beside him, though without taking his eyes off the stage. The sight of the curls brought Percy briefly to mind, but Percy, too, was in the past, and he shoved the thought firmly down.

He hadn't consciously thought what he'd say or how he might start the conversation, but when the play ended, he found himself upright and walking fast, so as to come onto the path slightly in front of Fraser as he turned back toward the edge of the park.

He had no notion what had led him to do this, to let the Scot make the first move, but it seemed natural, and he heard Fraser snort behind him, a small sound with which he was familiar; it signified something between derision and amusement.

"Good afternoon, Colonel," Fraser said, sounding resigned as he swung into step beside Grey.

"Good afternoon, Captain Fraser," he replied politely, and felt rather than saw Fraser's startled glance at him. "Did you enjoy the show?"

"I thought I'd gauge how long my chain is," Fraser said, ignoring the question. "Within sight o' the house, is it?"

"For the moment," Grey said honestly. "But I did not come to retrieve you. I have a message from Colonel Quarry."

Fraser's wide mouth tightened involuntarily. "Oh, aye?"

"He wishes to offer you satisfaction."

"What?" Fraser stared at him blankly.

"Satisfaction for what injury you may have received at his hands," Grey elaborated. "If you wish to call him out—he'll come."

Fraser stopped dead.

"He's offering to fight a duel with me. Is that what ye're saying?"

"Yes," Grey said patiently. "I am."

"Jesus God." The big Scot stood still, ignoring the flow of pedestrians—all of whom gave him a wide, side-glancing berth—and rubbing a finger up and down the bridge of his nose. He stopped doing this and shook his head, in the manner of one dislodging flies.

"Quarry canna think ye'd let me. You and His Grace, I mean."

Grey's heart gave a slight jerk; Christ, he was thinking about it. Seriously.

"I personally have nothing to say regarding the matter," he said politely. "As for my brother, he said nothing to me that indicated he would interfere." Since he hadn't had a chance. Christ, what would Hal do if Fraser did call Harry out? Besides kill Grey himself for not preventing it, that is.

Fraser made a thoroughly Scotch sort of noise in his throat. Not quite a growl, but it lifted the hairs on Grey's neck, and for the first time he began to worry that Fraser just might send back a challenge. He hadn't thought—he'd thought Fraser would be startled by the notion, but then . . . He swallowed and blurted, "Should you wish to call him out, I will second you."

Whatever Fraser had thought of Quarry's original offer, Grey's startled him a good deal more. He stared at Grey, blue eyes narrowed, looking to see whether this was an ill-timed joke.

Grey's heart was thumping hard enough to cause small sparks

of pain on the left side of his chest, even though the wounds there were long since healed. Fraser's hands had curled into fists, and Grey had a sudden, vivid recollection of their last meeting, when Fraser had come within a literal inch of smashing in his face with one of those massive fists.

"Have you ever been out—fought a duel, I mean—before?"

"I have," Fraser said shortly.

The color had risen in the Scot's face. He was outwardly immobile, but whatever was going on inside his head was moving fast. Grey watched, fascinated.

That process reached its conclusion, though, and the big fists relaxed—consciously—and Fraser uttered a short, humorless laugh, his eyes focusing again on Grey.

"Why?" he said.

"Why, what? Why does Colonel Quarry offer you satisfaction? Because his sense of honor demands it, I suppose."

Fraser said something under his breath in what Grey supposed to be Erse. He further supposed it to be a comment on Quarry's honor but didn't inquire. The blue eyes were boring into his.

"Why offer to second me? D'ye dislike Quarry?"

"No," Grey said, startled. "Harry Quarry's one of my best friends."

One thick, ruddy brow went up. "Why would ye not be *his* second, then?"

Grey took a deep breath.

"Well . . . actually . . . I am. There's nothing in the rules of duello preventing it," he added. "Though I admit it's not usual."

Fraser closed his eyes for an instant, frowning, then opened them again.

"I see," he said, very dry. "So was I to kill him, ye'd be obliged to fight me? And if he killed me, ye'd fight *him*? And should we kill each other, what then?"

"I suppose I'd call a surgeon to dispose of your bodies and then commit suicide," Grey said, a little testily. "But let us not be rhetorical. You have no intent of calling him out, do you?"

"I'll admit the prospect has its attractions," Fraser said evenly. "But ye may tell Colonel Quarry I decline his offer."

"Do you wish to tell him that yourself? He's still at the house."

Fraser had begun to walk again, but stopped dead at this. His gaze shifted toward Grey in a most uncomfortable way, rather like a large cat making a decision regarding the edibility of some small animal in its vicinity.

"Um . . . if you do not choose to meet him," Grey said carefully, "I will leave you here for a quarter of an hour and make sure that he is gone before you return to the house."

Fraser turned on him with such sudden violence as to make Grey steel himself not to step backward.

"And let the gobshite think I am afraid of him? Damn you, Englishman! Dare ye to suggest such a thing? Were I to call someone out, it would be you, *mhic a diabhail*—and ye know it."

He whirled on his heel and stalked toward the house, scattering loungers like pigeons before him.

THEY SAW HIM COMING; the door opened before Jamie reached the top step, and he walked past the butler with a curt nod. The man looked apprehensive. Surely to God he must be familiar with an atmosphere of violence, Jamie thought, working in this nest of vipers.

He had an overwhelming urge to smash his fist through something and refrained from punching the walnut paneling in the foyer only because he realized just how much it would hurt—and realized also the futility of such action. He also didn't mean to meet Colonel Quarry again dripping blood or otherwise at a social disadvantage.

Where would they be? The library, almost certainly. He stalked round the corner of the hallway and nearly trod on the duchess, who gave a startled squeak.

"Your pardon, Your Grace," he said, with a creditable bow for a man still dressed like a groom.

"Captain Fraser," she said, a hand pressed winsomely to her bosom.

"Christ, you, too?" he said. It was rude, but he'd no patience left.

"Me, too, what?" she asked, puzzled.

"Why have ye all begun calling me 'Captain' Fraser?" he asked. "Ye weren't yesterday. Did His Grace tell ye to?"

She dropped the winsome hand and gave him a smile—which he distrusted just as much.

"Why, no. I suggested it." A slight dimple appeared in one cheek. "Or would you prefer to be called Broch Tuarach? It is your proper title, is it not?"

"It was—a thousand years ago. Mr. Fraser will do. Your Grace," he added as an afterthought, and made to pass. She reached out, though, and laid a hand on his sleeve.

"I wish to talk to you," she said, low-voiced. "You do remember me?"

"That was a thousand years ago, as well," he said, with a deliberate look that ran over her from upswept hair to dainty shoe, recalling exactly how he remembered her. "And I have business with Colonel Quarry just the now, if ye please."

She flushed a little but didn't otherwise betray any sign of discomposure. She held both his eyes and her smile and squeezed his arm lightly before removing her hand.

"I'll find you."

THE BRIEF INTERRUPTION had served to take the edge off his inclination to hit things, and he strode into the library with a decent sense of himself. Rage would not serve him.

Quarry was standing by the fire, talking to Pardloe; both of them turned round, hearing him come in. Quarry's face was set; wary, but not afraid. Jamie hadn't expected him to be; he knew Quarry.

Jamie walked up to Pardloe—just close enough to make the little shit look up at him—and said, "I must beg pardon, Your Grace, for taking my leave so abruptly. I felt the need of air."

Pardloe's lips twitched. "I trust you feel yourself recovered, Captain Fraser?"

"Quite, I thank ye. Colonel Quarry—your servant, sir." He'd turned to Quarry without a pause and gave him a bow correct to the inch. Quarry returned it, murmuring, "Your very obedient, sir." But Jamie had seen the tension go out of Quarry's shoulders and felt a little slackening of the tightness in his own chest.

He felt Pardloe look beyond him and knew John Grey had come in. The tightness came back.

"Do sit down, gentlemen," the duke said, with great courtesy, gesturing at the chairs near the hearth. "John, would you tell Pilcock to bring us some brandy?"

"WE WANT TO BRING HIM to court-martial, I think," Hal said, putting down his glass. "Rather than pursue a civil case in the courts, I mean. On the one hand, a civil case—if we won—would allow us to recover whatever money the bastard hasn't yet spent, and it would give us scope to blacken his name in the press, hound him relentlessly, and generally ruin his life. However—"

"However, the reverse is true, as well," Grey said dryly. He'd fortunately never been sued but had been threatened by lawsuits now and then, escaping by the hair of his teeth, and had a very good idea of the chancy and dangerous nature of the law. "He presumably has the money to employ good lawyers. Could—and quite likely would, if half what Carruthers said is true—countersue us for defamation, drag *us* through the courts, and make our lives a misery for years."

"Well, yes," Hal agreed. "There's that."

"Whereas in a court-martial, the custom of the army is the basis of procedure, not statute," Harry put in. "Offers summat more flexibility. In terms of what's evidence, I mean."

This was true; essentially, anyone who liked could give testimony at a court-martial, and everything anyone said was considered evidence, though the court-martial board might dismiss or consider any of it, giving what weight they liked to the matter.

"And if he's found guilty at a court-martial, ye could, I suppose, have him shot?"

All three Englishmen looked at Fraser, startled. The Scot had sat quietly through most of their deliberations, and they'd almost forgotten he was there.

"I think it might be hanging," Hal said, after a brief pause. "Generally, we shoot men only for desertion or mutiny."

"An attractive thought, though." Quarry lifted his glass to Fraser in acknowledgment, before turning to the others. "Do we want him dead, do you think?"

Grey considered that. The notion of bringing Siverly to justice and making him account for what were very serious crimes was one thing. The notion of hunting him deliberately to his death, though . . .

"I don't know," Grey said slowly. "But perhaps I ought not to take part in such considerations. Siverly did save my life at Quebec, and while that wouldn't stop me pursuing a case against him . . . I think—no. I don't want him dead."

Grey didn't look at Fraser, unsure whether the Scot might consider this reluctance to exterminate Siverly as pusillanimous.

"Much better to have him cashiered and imprisoned, held up as an example," Hal said. "Besides, being executed is over too quickly. I want the bugger to suffer."

There was a faint sound from the corner where Fraser sat, a little apart. Grey glanced over and saw to his surprise that the man was laughing, in that odd Highland manner that convulsed the face while making very little sound.

"And here I thought it was mercy ye offered when ye declined to shoot me," Fraser said to Hal. "A debt of honor, did ye say?" He lifted his glass, ironical.

A deep flush rose in Hal's face. Grey didn't think he'd ever seen his brother at a total loss for words before. Hal looked at Fraser for several moments, then finally nodded.

"*Touché, Captain* Fraser," he said, and without a pause turned back to Grey.

"Court-martial it is, then. Harry and I will start the business here, while you and the captain go to retrieve Major Siverly. Now, Harry—who do you know in Ireland who might be of help?"

11

Vulgar Curiosity

EDWARD TWELVETREES WAS IN GREY'S MIND WHEN HE awoke in the morning from a disturbing dream in which he faced a man in duello, at pistols drawn. His opponent had no face, but somehow he knew it was Edward Twelvetrees.

The roots of the dream were clear to him; he would never hear the name Twelvetrees without some thought of the duel in which Hal had killed Nathaniel Twelvetrees, after Nathaniel's seduction of Hal's first wife. Grey had known nothing about the duel at the time—let alone its cause—he being both too young and not present, having been sent away to Aberdeen after the death of his father.

The sense of the dream stayed with him through breakfast, and he went out into the garden, in hopes that fresh air would clear his head. He had not walked up and down for more than a few minutes, though, when his sister-in-law came out of the house, a basket with a pair of secateurs in it over her arm. She greeted him with pleasure, and they strolled up and down, talking idly of the boys, the play he'd seen earlier in the week, the state of Hal's head—his brother suffered periodically from the megrims and had had a sick headache the night before. But the thought of that duel would not leave him.

"Has Hal ever told you very much about Esmé?" he asked suddenly, on impulse. Minnie looked surprised but answered without hesitation.

"Yes, everything. Or so I suppose," she added, with a half smile. "Why?"

"Vulgar curiosity," John admitted. "I was quite young when they married and didn't really know her. I do remember the wedding—huge affair, white lace and diamonds, St. James's, hundreds of guests . . ." He trailed off, seeing her face. "I'm sorry I wasn't here for your wedding," he said hastily, trying to make amends.

"So am I," she said, dimpling on one side. "You would have doubled the guest list. Though it wasn't here. Not in England, I mean."

"A, um, private affair, I take it?"

"Rather. Hal had Harry Quarry to stand up with him, and he got the landlady of the pub to be the other witness. It was in Amsterdam. She didn't speak English and had no idea who we were."

Grey was fascinated but afraid of giving offense by being too inquisitive.

"I see."

"No, you don't." She was openly laughing at him now. "I hadn't the slightest intention of marrying him, despite a six-month belly. He paid absolutely no attention to my objections, though."

"Desp—oh. Er . . . Benjamin?"

"Yes." A flicker of what Grey thought of as maternal contentment touched her face, softening her mouth for an instant. She glanced at him, a glint in her eye. "I could have managed well enough."

"I daresay you could," he murmured. "How did you come to

meet Hal again in Amsterdam?" What was it Hal had said? *"It took me nearly six months to find her."*

"He came looking for me," she said frankly. "Strode into my father's bookshop one day with fire in his eye. I nearly fainted. So did he, when he saw I was with child."

She smiled, but it was an inward smile now, one of reminiscence.

"He took the most enormous breath, shook his head, then walked round the counter, picked me up, and carried me straight out of the shop and into a coach Harry had waiting outside. I was most impressed; I must have weighed eleven stone, at least." She glanced sideways at him. The dimple was back. "Are you dreadfully scandalized, John?"

"Dreadfully." What he was really thinking was that it was a mercy that Benjamin so strongly resembled Hal. He took her hand and tucked it comfortably into the crook of his elbow.

"Why are you thinking of poor Esmé?" she asked.

"Oh . . . just thinking that it wasn't like Hal to marry a boring woman."

"I am reasonably sure that she wasn't boring," Minnie said dryly. "Though I thank you for the implied compliment."

"Well, I know she was beautiful—quite beautiful—but as to her character . . ."

"Self-loving, narcissistic, and anxious," Minnie said concisely. "Not happy unless she was the center of attention—but very talented at getting said attention. Not stupid, by any means."

"Really." He absorbed that for a moment. "Getting attention. Do you suppose—I mean, if Hal's told you that much, I imagine you know about Nathaniel Twelvetrees?"

"I do," she said tersely, and her hand tightened a little on his arm. "Do I think she had an affair with him for his own sake, you mean? Or in order to regain Hal's attention? The latter."

He looked at her, surprised.

"You seem very sure. Is that what Hal says?"

She shook her head, and a lock of hair fell loose and drooped beside her ear. She thrust it back without ceremony. "I told him so, but I don't think he believes it.

"She loved him, you know," she said, and her mouth tightened a little. "He loved her to distraction, but it wasn't enough for her—she was one of those spoilt girls for whom no amount of devotion is ever enough. But she did love him. I read her letters." She looked up at him. "He doesn't know that, by the way."

So Hal had kept Esmé's letters, and Minnie had found them. He wondered if Hal still had them. He squeezed her hand lightly and let it go.

"He won't hear it from me."

"I know that," she said, "or I wouldn't have told you. I don't suppose you're any more anxious to see him fight another duel than I am."

"I didn't see him fight the first one. But what—why ought he—oh. Never mind." There must be something in Esmé's letters, some clue regarding yet another admirer, that Hal hadn't noticed but Minnie had.

She didn't say anything, but paused, taking her hand from his arm, and squinted balefully at a bush of some sort, turning back the rusty new leaves with one finger.

"Greenfly," she said, in a tone boding no good for either the greenflies or the gardener. Grey made an obliging noise indicating concern, and after a further glower, Minnie snorted and returned to the path.

"This Mr. Fraser of yours," she said, after they'd walked a few moments in silence.

"He's not actually *mine,*" he said. He'd intended to speak

lightly, and thought he had, but she shot him a glance that made him wonder.

"You know him, though," she said. "Is he . . . dependable, do you think?"

"I suppose that would depend upon what one expected of him," Grey replied cautiously. "If you mean, is he a man of honor, then, yes, he is. Certainly a man of his word. Beyond that . . ." He shrugged. "He is Scotch, and a Highlander, to boot."

"Meaning what?" She was interested; one brow arched upward. "Is he such a savage as people say Highlanders are? Because if so, he apes the gentleman to an amazing degree."

"James Fraser apes nothing," he assured her, feeling an obscure sense of offense on Fraser's behalf. "He is—or was—a landed gentleman, and one of breeding, with substantial property and tenants. What I meant is that he has . . ." He hesitated, not quite sure how to put it into words. ". . . a sense of himself that is quite separate from what society demands. He is inclined to make his own rules."

She laughed at that. "No wonder Hal likes him!"

"Does he?" Grey said, feeling absurdly pleased to hear it.

"Oh, yes," she assured Grey. "He was quite surprised—but very pleased. I think he feels slightly guilty, too," she added thoughtfully. "At making use of him, I mean."

"So do I."

She smiled at him with great affection. "Yes, you would. Mr. Fraser is fortunate to have you for a friend, John."

"I doubt he recognizes his good fortune," Grey said dryly.

"Well, he needn't worry—and neither need you, John. Hal won't let him come to any harm."

"No, of course not." Still, the feeling of unease at the back of his neck did not go away.

"And if your venture should be successful, I'm sure Hal would see about getting him pardoned. He could be a free man then. He could go back to his home."

Grey felt a sudden stricture in his throat, as though his valet, Tom Byrd, had tied his stock too tightly.

"Yes. Why did you ask about him—about Fraser, I mean—being dependable?"

She lifted one shoulder and let it fall.

"Oh—Hal showed me the translation Mr. Fraser made of that page of Erse. I only wondered how faithful it might be."

"Have you any reason to suppose it isn't?" he asked curiously. "I mean—why shouldn't it be?"

"No particular reason." She chewed her lower lip, though, in a thoughtful sort of way. "I don't speak Erse myself, of course, but I recognize a few words. I, um, don't know *quite* how much Hal told you about my father . . . ?"

"A bit," Grey said, and smiled at her. She smiled back.

"Well, then. I saw the occasional Jacobite document, and while most were in French or Latin, there were a few in English, and even fewer in Erse. But they all tended to have some internal clue, some casual mention of something that would assure the recipient that what they were holding wasn't merely an order for wine or a merchant's inquiry about the contents of his warehouse. And one of the code things you saw mentioned quite often was a white rose. For the Stuarts, you know?"

"I do." For a vertiginous instant, he saw—as clearly as though the scene had sprung from the earth at his feet—the face of the man he had shot on Culloden Moor, his eyes dark and the white cockade in his bonnet stark in the dying light of evening.

Minnie paid no attention to his momentary distraction, though, and went on talking.

"Well, this bit you brought Hal has the words *róisíní bhán* in it. It's not *quite* the same, but it's very similar to the Scottish words for 'white rose'—I saw them often enough to know those. And Mr. Fraser put the word 'rose' into his translation, all right—but he left out the 'white.' If it's there to begin with, I mean," she added. "And perhaps the Irish is sufficiently different that he didn't see it, if it *is* there."

They turned, as though some signal had been given, and started back toward the house. Grey swallowed, trying to quiet the thumping of his heart.

It was clear enough what she meant. The poem about the Wild Hunt might be a coded Jacobite document of some sort. And *if* it was, Fraser might have recognized that fact and deliberately suppressed it, perhaps to protect friends affiliated with the Stuart cause. If that were the case, it raised two questions, both of them disturbing.

To wit: had Siverly a Jacobite connection, and . . . what else might Jamie Fraser have left out?

"Only one way to find out," he said. "I'll ask him. Carefully."

12

The Belly of a Flea

THE ICE HAD BEEN BROKEN BETWEEN GREY AND JAMES FRAser, but Grey still felt considerable delicacy about the resumption of what might be called normal relations. He hadn't forgotten that conversation in the stables at Helwater, and he was damned sure Fraser hadn't, either.

True, they would be in close company in Ireland and must find a way to ignore the past for the sake of working together—but no need to force the matter before time.

Still, he remained acutely aware of Fraser's presence in the house. Everyone did. Half the servants were afraid of him, the others simply unsure what to do with him. Hal dealt with him courteously, but with a sense of wary formality; Grey thought that Hal might be having the occasional doubt about the wisdom of his decision to conscript Fraser, and smiled grimly at the thought. Minnie seemed the only member of the household able to talk to him with any sense of normality.

Tom Byrd had been terrified of the big Scot, having had an unsettling experience with him at Helwater—though Grey thought that was more a matter of Tom, who was quite sensitive to social nuance, picking up the violent vibrations occurring between himself and Fraser, than of personal interaction.

When informed that he would be attending to Captain Fraser's valeting, in addition to Grey's, though, Tom had grasped the nettle manfully and been very helpful in compiling the tailor's list. He was passionate in the matter of male clothing and had lost quite a bit of his nervousness in the discussion of what might be suitable.

To Grey's surprise, Tom Byrd was in the parlor when he came down in the morning, and the valet stuck his head out into the hall to hail him.

"The captain's new clothes have come, me lord! Come see!"

Tom turned a beaming face on Grey as he entered the parlor. The furniture was draped with muslin-wrapped shapes, like small Egyptian mummies. Tom had unwrapped one of these and now laid out a bottle-green coat with gilt buttons, spreading the skirts lovingly over the settee.

"That bundle on the pianoforte is shirts," he informed Grey. "I didn't like to take them up, in case the captain was asleep."

Grey glanced out the window, which showed the sun well up; it must be eight o'clock, at least. The notion that Fraser might be having a lie-in was ludicrous; he doubted the man had ever slept past dawn in his life, and he certainly hadn't done it any time in the last fifteen years. But Tom's remark indicated that the Scot hadn't either appeared for breakfast or sent for a tray. Could he be ill?

He was not. The sound of the front door opening and closing turned Grey toward the hall in time to see Fraser stride past, face flushed fresh with the morning's air.

"Mr. Fraser!" he called, and Fraser swung round, surprised but not disturbed. He came in, ducking automatically beneath the lintel. One brow was arched in inquiry, but there was no hint in his face of disquiet or of that closed expression that hid anger, fear, or calculation.

He's only been for a walk; he hasn't seen anyone, Grey thought, and was slightly ashamed of the thought. Who, after all, would he see in London?

"Behold," Grey said, smiling, and gestured toward the muslin parcels. Tom had unwrapped a suit of an odd purplish brown and was stroking the pile.

"Would you look at this, sir?" Tom said, so pleased with the garments that he momentarily overcame his nervousness of Fraser. "I've never seen such a color in me life—but it'll suit you prime!"

To Grey's surprise, Fraser smiled back, almost shyly.

"I've seen it before," he said, and put out a hand to stroke the fabric. "In France. *Couleur puce,* it was called. The Duc d'Orleans had a suit made of it, and verra proud of it he was, too."

Tom's eyes were round. He looked quickly at Grey—had his employer known that his prisoner hobnobbed with French dukes?—then back at Fraser.

"Pee-yuse?" he said, trying out the word. "Color of a . . . what's a peeyuse, then?"

Fraser actually laughed at that, and Grey felt a startled small burst of pleasure at the sound.

"A flea," Fraser told Tom. "The whole of the name means 'the color of the belly of a flea,' but that's a bit much, even for the French."

Tom squinted at the coat one-eyed, evidently comparing it to fleas he had known. "It's not like that word pew-cell, is it? Would that be like a little-bitty flea?"

Fraser's mouth twitched, and his eyes darted toward Grey.

"Pucelle?" he said, pronouncing it in good French. "I, erm, don't think so, though I might of course be mistaken."

Grey felt his ribs creak slightly but managed to speak casually. "Where did you come across the word *pucelle,* Tom?"

Tom considered for a moment.

"Oh. Colonel Quarry, when he was here last week. He asked me could I think of anything that rhymed with pew-cell. 'Usual' was all I could think of, and he didn't think much o' that, I could tell, though he wrote it down in his notebook, just in case, he said."

"Colonel Quarry writes poetry," Grey explained to Fraser, getting another lifted brow in return. "Very . . . um . . . individual style of verse."

"I know," Fraser said, to Grey's utter astonishment. "He asked me once if I could think of a suitable rhyme for 'virgin.' "

"He did? When?"

"At Ardsmuir," Fraser said, with no apparent emotion, from which Grey concluded that Harry hadn't actually shown the Scot any of his poetry. "Over dinner. I couldna bring anything to mind save 'sturgeon,' though. He didna bother writing that one down," he added, turning to Tom. "There was a good deal of brandy drunk."

"Though for what the observation is worth, *pucelle* is the French word for 'virgin,' " Grey told Tom. He glanced at Fraser. "Perhaps he couldn't manage the verse in English, abandoned it, and later decided to try it in French?"

Fraser made a small sound of amusement, but Tom was still frowning.

"Have French virgins got fleas, do you think?"

"I never met a Frenchwoman I felt I could ask," Grey said. "But I have met a good many fleas, and they tend not to be respecters of persons, let alone of purity."

Tom shook his head, dismissing this bit of natural philosophy as beyond him, and returned with an air of relief to his natural sphere of competence.

"Well, then. There's the pee-yuse velvet suit, the blue silk, the brown worsted, and two coats for everyday, bottle-green and sapphire, and three waistcoats, two plain and a yellow one with fancy-work. Dark breeches, white breeches, stockings, shirts, small-clothes . . ." He pointed at various parcels here and there about the room, consulting the list in his head. "Now, the shoes haven't come yet, nor the riding boots. Will those do for the Beefsteak, do you think, me lord?" He squinted doubtfully at the shoes on Jamie's feet, these being the sturdy objects he'd borrowed from Lady Joffrey's chairman. They had been buffed and polished to the limits of the bootboy's capability but were not intrinsically fashionable.

Grey joined Tom's scrutiny and lifted one shoulder in a shrug.

"Change the buckles, and they'll do. Take the silver-gilt ones from my brown calfskin court shoes. Mr. Fraser?" He motioned delicately at Jamie's feet, and Jamie obligingly stepped out of the objects in question, allowing Tom to take them away.

Fraser waited until Tom was safely out of hearing before inquiring, "The Beefsteak?"

"My club. The Society for the Appreciation of the English Beefsteak. We are taking dinner there today, with Captain von Namtzen." He felt a small warmth at thought of Stephan. "I've acquainted him with the Siverly matter, and he is bringing someone he knows who might be helpful. He may have some information, but I also wish him to look at that fragment of Erse poetry you translated. He knows a good deal about verse and has encountered several variations on the Wild Hunt."

"Aye? What sort of establishment is this club?" A slight crease showed between Fraser's heavy brows.

"It's not a bawdy house," Grey assured him, with an edge. "Just an ordinary gentleman's club." It occurred to him that perhaps Fraser had never *been* in a gentleman's club? Certainly he'd never been in London, but . . .

Fraser gave him a marked look. "I meant, what is the nature of the gentlemen who are members of this particular club? You say we are to meet Captain von Namtzen; is it a club patronized largely by soldiers?"

"Yes, it is," Grey said, somewhat puzzled. "Why?"

Fraser's lips compressed for an instant.

"If there is a possibility of my encountering men whom I knew during the Rising, I should like to know it."

"Ah." That possibility had not struck Grey. "I think it is not likely," he said slowly. "But it would be as well, perhaps, to arrange a . . . er . . ."

"A fiction?" Fraser said, an edge in his voice. "To account for my recent whereabouts and current situation?"

"Yes," Grey said, ignoring both the edge and the return of that simmering air of resentment. He bowed politely. "I will leave that to you, Mr. Fraser. You can inform me of the details on our way to the Beefsteak."

JAMIE FOLLOWED GREY into the Beefsteak with a sense of wary curiosity. He'd never been in a London gentleman's club, though he'd experienced a wide range of such establishments in Paris. Given the basic differences of personality and outlook between Frenchmen and Englishmen, though, he supposed that their social behavior might be different, as well. The food was certain to be.

"Von Namtzen!" Grey had caught sight of a tall, fair-haired man in a German uniform coming out of a room down the hall, and hurried toward him. This must be Stephan von Namtzen, the Graf von Erdberg, and the gentleman they had come to see.

The big man's face lighted at sight of Grey, whom he greeted with a warm kiss on both cheeks, in the continental style. Grey appeared used to this and smiled, though he did not return the embrace, stepping back to introduce Jamie.

The graf was missing one arm, the sleeve of his coat pinned up across his chest, but shook Jamie's hand warmly with his remaining one. He had shrewd gray eyes, the graf, and struck Jamie at once as both affable and competent—a good soldier. He relaxed a little; the graf presumably knew both who and what he was; there would be no need for fictions.

"Come," said von Namtzen, with a cordial inclination of his head. "I have a private room reserved for us." He led the way down the hall with Grey beside him, Jamie following more slowly, glancing aside into the various rooms they passed. The club was old and had an atmosphere of discreet, comfortable wealth. The dining room was laid with white napery and gleaming heavy silver, the smoking room furnished with well-aged leather chairs, sagging slightly in the seat and redolent of good tobacco. The runner under his feet was an aged Turkey carpet, worn nearly to the threads in the middle, but a good one, with medallions of scarlet and gold.

There was a low hum about the place, of conversation and service; he could hear the clinking of pots and spoons and crockery from a distant kitchen, and the scent of roasting meat perfumed the air. He could see why Grey liked the place; if you belonged here, it would embrace you. He himself did not belong here but, for a moment, rather wished he did.

Grey and von Namtzen had paused to exchange greetings with a friend; Jamie took the opportunity for a discreet inquiry of the steward.

"Turn right at the end of the hallway, sir, and you'll find it just to your left," the man said, with a courteous inclination of the head.

"Thank you," he said, and gave Grey a brief lift of the chin, indicating his destination. God knew what might happen over dinner. An empty bladder and clean hands were as much preparation as it lay within his power to make.

GREY NODDED at Fraser's mute gesture, and continued his conversation with Mordecai Weston, a Captain in the Buffs, who knew von Namtzen as well. He expected Fraser to return momentarily, but after five minutes began to wonder whether something was wrong and excused himself.

He came round the corner in time to see Fraser just outside the privy closet, in conversation with Edward Twelvetrees. Yes, it *was* bloody Twelvetrees. No mistaking that pale, long-nosed face, the beady little ferret-black eyes. The surprise stopped him dead, but close enough to hear Twelvetrees demand to know what Grey's business was with Fraser—and to hear Fraser decline to say.

Fraser disappeared into the privy closet with a firm shutting of the door; Grey took advantage of the sound to walk quietly up behind Twelvetrees, who was glaring at the closed door, evidently waiting for Fraser to come out and face further interrogation. Grey tapped Twelvetrees on the shoulder, and was immensely gratified when the man gave a cry of alarm and flung himself round, hands raised.

"I am so sorry to startle you, sir," he said, with extreme politeness. "Did I hear you asking after me?"

Twelvetrees's startlement changed in an instant to rage, and his hand slapped his side, reaching for the sword he fortunately wasn't wearing.

"You bloody meddler!"

Grey felt blood swell in his temples, but kept his voice light and civil.

"If you have business with me, sir, I suggest that you speak to me directly, rather than seek to harass my friends."

Twelvetrees's lip curled, but he'd got control of himself.

"Friends," he repeated, in a tone indicating astonishment that Grey should think he had any. "I suppose I should not be amazed that you make a friend of traitors. But I wonder, sir, that you should so far forget yourself as to bring such a man as that into this place."

Grey's heart had given a bump at the word "traitors," but he replied coolly, "You are fortunate that you did not use that word to the gentleman in question. While I take the liberty of offense on his behalf, he might be inclined to take action, whereas I would not sully my sword with your blood."

Twelvetrees's eyes grew brighter and blacker.

"Wouldn't you?" he said, and gave a short laugh. "Believe me, *sir*, I await your pleasure. In the meantime, I shall complain to the Committee regarding your choice of guests."

He shouldered his way past Grey, pushing him roughly aside, and walked down the hallway to the back stair, head held high.

Grey made his way back toward the dining-room, wondering how the devil Twelvetrees happened to know Jamie Fraser. *But perhaps he didn't*, he thought. If he'd inquired Fraser's name, Fraser would have told him it, as well as informing him that he was Grey's guest. And he supposed it wasn't beyond the stretch of reason that Twelvetrees should recall Fraser's name from the Rising—particularly when linked with his Scottish accent.

Yes, that might be mere chance. He was somewhat more concerned that Twelvetrees had exhibited interest in his own actions—and that Twelvetrees had called him a meddler. Meddling in what? Surely Twelvetrees couldn't know that he appeared in Carruthers's document, let alone that the Greys were in pursuit of Gerald Siverly. He hesitated for a moment, but this was not the time nor the place to speak with Twelvetrees. He shrugged and went back to von Namtzen.

"I HAVE BROUGHT a . . . gentleman of my acquaintance," the graf was saying, with a half-apologetic glance at Grey. "Since you tell me it is a matter of Irish." Lowering his voice, he said in rapid German, "I have of course said nothing to him of your matter; only that there is a poem written in his tongue and you want to know if the translation you have is accurate."

Jamie had neither spoken nor heard German in many years but was reasonably sure he'd gathered the sense of this correctly. He tried to recall whether he had ever told Grey that German was among his languages—he didn't think so, and Grey didn't glance at him when von Namtzen spoke but replied in the same language, thanking the German. Grey called him *"Du,"* Jamie noticed, using the familiar form of address—but he could have seen easily that the graf was an intimate friend by the way in which he touched Grey's sleeve.

He supposed it was reasonable that the Greys would want to check his translation of the poem—he'd told them that the *Gaidhlig* and the *Gaeilge* were different and that he did not certify his translation as completely accurate, though he could give them the overall sense of what it said. Still, there was the one small thing that he had deliberately omitted, and it gave him a minor qualm. If the graf had brought an Irish-speaker to give a new translation, the line about the Wild Hunt strewing white roses to mark the victorious path of their queen was sure to show up in contrast to his version, which had merely mentioned the faeries strewing roses.

He'd recognized it as a coded Jacobite document at once; he'd seen any number of such things during his spying days in Paris. But having no idea who had written it or what the code said, he had chosen not to mention that aspect; if there were hidden Jacobites operating in Ireland—and Tobias Quinn had told him there were—it was not his business to expose them to the interest of the English. But if—

His thoughts stopped abruptly as he followed the graf and Grey into the private room, and the gentleman already there rose to greet them.

He wasn't shocked. Or rather, he thought, it was simply that he didn't believe what he was seeing. Whichever it was, he took Thomas Lally's proffered hand with a feeling of total calm.

"Broch Tuarach," Lally said, in that clipped way of his, formal as a topiary bush at Versailles.

"Monsieur le Comte," Jamie said, shaking Lally's hand. *"Comment ça va?"*

Thomas Lally had been one of Charles Stuart's aides-de-camp. Half Irish and born in Ireland but half French, he had fled Scotland after Falkirk and promptly taken up a commission with the French army, where he had been courageous but unpopular.

How the devil did he come to be here?

Jamie hadn't voiced that thought, but it must have shown on his face, for Lally smiled sourly.

"I am, like you, a prisoner of the English," he said in French. "I was captured at Pondicherry. Though my captors are sufficiently generous as to maintain my parole in London."

"Ah, I see you are acquainted," said von Namtzen, who undoubtedly spoke French fluently but diplomatically pretended that he didn't. He beamed cordially. "How nice! Shall we eat first?"

They did, enjoying a solid dinner in the English style—Lally ate his way ravenously through three courses, and Jamie thought that while the English might be maintaining him, they weren't doing it lavishly. Lally was twenty years Jamie's senior but looked even older, deeply weathered from the Indian sun and half toothless, with hollowed cheeks that made his prominent nose and chin even more prominent than they would otherwise be and a deeply furrowed brow that gave him an air of suppressed fury rather than worry. He didn't wear a uniform, and his suit was old-fashioned, very worn at cuff and elbow, though his linen was clean.

In the course of the meal, Jamie learned that Lally's case was somewhat more complicated than his own: while the Comte de Lally was a prisoner of the English Crown, the French had charged him with treason, and Lally was agitating to be returned to France on parole, demanding a court martial there, by which he might clear his name.

The graf did not say so, but Jamie got the impression that von Namtzen had promised to put in a good word for Lally in this endeavor and thus secured his presence and—presumably—his cooperation.

He was aware that Lally was studying him as closely as he was observing Lally—and doubtless for the same reasons, wondering just what Jamie's relations were with his captors, and what was the nature of his cooperation with them.

The conversation over dinner was general in nature and conducted mostly in English. It was not until the table had been cleared and a copy of the Wild Hunt poem produced by Grey that Jamie heard Lally speak Irish, holding the sheet of paper at arm's length and reading it slowly aloud.

It gave him an odd feeling. He hadn't heard or spoken the *Gàidhlig* in many years, save in the privacy of his own mind, and hearing words with such a homely, familiar sound made him momentarily feel that he might weep. He swallowed, though, and the moment passed.

"*Herr Graf* tells me that you've done a translation of this," Lally said, putting down the paper and looking sharply at Jamie. *"An bhfuil Gaeilge agat?"* Do you have the Irish, then?

Jamie shook his head. "*Chan-eil. Ach tuigidh mi gu leor dha na faclan. Bheil thu g'am thuigsinn sa?"* he said in *Gàidhlig*. No, though I could make out many of the words. Do you understand me?

Lally smiled, his harsh expression softening wonderfully, and Jamie thought that it was long since that Lally had heard anything like the language of his birth.

"Your tongue blooms with flowers," Lally said—or Jamie thought that was what he said, and smiled back.

"You understand each the other's tongue?" von Namtzen said, interested. "It sounds very much the same to me."

"It's . . . rather like an Italian speaking wi' a Spaniard," Jamie said, still smiling at Lally. "But we might make shift."

"I should be very grateful for your assistance in this matter, *Monsieur le Comte*," Grey said formally. "As would my brother."

Oh, so that's it, Jamie thought. Pardloe would put his not inconsiderable influence to work on Lally's behalf, in return for this. The English might get an accurate translation after all. *Or maybe not,* he thought, seeing Lally's polite smile in return.

Ink, paper, and quill were brought, and the graf and Grey retired to the far side of the room, talking commonplaces in German, in order to leave Lally to his work. He read the poem through two or three times, asking Jamie brief questions, and then took up his quill.

They spoke mostly in English but dropped more and more into their respective forms of Gaelic, heads together—and eyes on the sheet, conscious of the presence of John Grey watching them.

"Did you leave out anything *machnaigh*?" Lally asked casually.

Jamie struggled with *machnaigh* but thought it meant "deliberately."

"Se an fhirinn a bh-agam. Ach a' seo—" I spoke faithfully. But here . . . He put his finger on the line about the white roses. *"Bha e . . . goirid."* I spoke . . . short.

Lally's eyes flicked to his, then back to the sheet, but the comte didn't change expression.

"Yes, I think you were right about that one," he said casually in English. He took a fresh sheet of paper, pulled another quill from the jar, and handed it to Jamie. "Here. Write down your translation. That will make it easier."

It took some time; they conferred over the sheets, Lally stabbing at Jamie's translation with his quill and leaving ink blots on the page as he asked questions—sometimes in Irish, sometimes in French or English—then scribbling on his own sheet, crossing things out and adding notes in the margin. No mention of white roses.

At last, though, he made a clean copy, writing slowly—he had rheumatism badly in his hands; his knuckles were knobbed and his fingers twisted with it—and gave this to Lord John.

"There you are, my lord," he said, and leaned back, groaning a little. "I hope it may be of help in whatever your venture may be."

"I thank you," Grey said, scanning the sheet. He looked up at Lally, one brow raised. "If you would be so kind, Monsieur—have you ever seen a thing like this before?"

"Oh—often, my lord." Lally looked surprised. "Though not written down. It is a common thing in Ireland, though—tales like that."

"You have not seen it in any other context?"

Lally shook his head, definite.

"No, my lord."

Grey sighed and folded the sheet carefully into his pocket, thanking Lally once again, and, with a brief glance at Jamie, rose to leave.

The day was fine, and they walked back to Argus House. Grey had decided, upon reflection, to make no reference to Edward Twelvetrees—not until he'd spoken to Hal. They therefore spoke very little, but as they reached the Alexandra Gate, Grey turned and said to Jamie, seriously, "Do you think he made a fair translation?"

"I am quite sure he did it to the best of his ability, my lord."

13

By Darkness Met

JAMIE ROUSED ABRUPTLY AND SAT UP IN BED, HAND GOING automatically beneath his pillow for his dirk before his mind made sense of where he was. The door closed almost silently, and he was on the verge of diving out of bed, ready to throw himself at the intruder's legs, but he smelled perfume and stopped short, completely bewildered, tangled between thoughts of prison, Jared's house in Paris, inn rooms, Claire's bed . . . but Claire had never worn a scent like that.

The woman's weight pressed down the mattress beside him, and a hand touched his arm. A light touch, and he felt the hairs bristle in response.

"Forgive me for calling upon you so unceremoniously," the duchess said, and he could hear the humor in her low voice. "I thought it better to be discreet."

"Ye think this is discreet?" he said, barely remembering to lower his own voice. "Holy God!"

"You would prefer that I pretend to encounter you by accident at a Punch and Judy show in the park?" she asked, and his heart nearly stopped. "I doubt we should have enough time."

His heart was still pounding like a drum, but he'd got control of his breath, at least.

"A long story, is it?" he asked, as evenly as possible. "Perhaps ye'd be more comfortable sitting in the chair, then."

She rose, with a small sound that might have been amusement, and he heard the muffled scrape of chair legs over the Turkey carpet. He took advantage of her movement to get out of bed—talk of being taken at a disadvantage—and sit down in the window seat, tucking the nightshirt primly round his legs.

What had she meant by that remark about the Punch and Judy show? Had his encounter with Quinn been noticed and reported? Or was it merely a chance remark?

She paused by the chair, an amorphous shape in the dark.

"Shall I light the candle?"

"No. Your Grace," he added, with a certain sardonic emphasis.

The sky was overcast, but there was a waxing moon tonight, and he'd drawn back the curtains when he went to bed, not liking the feeling of enclosure. There was a soft, bright glow through the window behind him. He wouldn't have a distinct view of her face—but she wouldn't see his at all.

She sat down, her garments whispering, and sighed briefly but said nothing immediately. It was an old trick, and one he knew well. He didn't speak, either, though his mind was churning with questions. The most important one being, did the duke know?

"Yes, he does," she said. He nearly bit his tongue.

"Oh, aye?" he managed. "And may I ask just *what* your husband knows?"

"About me, of course." The faint note of amusement was back. "He knew what my . . . mode of life . . . was when he married me."

"A man of blood and iron, then."

She laughed outright at that, though softly.

"And does he know that ye kent me back then?"

"He does. He does *not* know what I came to talk with you about."

He wondered whether the duke knew *that* she had come to talk to him in his bedroom, but merely made a polite sound of invitation, and the duchess's robe rustled softly as she settled herself.

"Do you know a man named Edward Twelvetrees?"

"I saw him briefly today," he said. "At the Beefsteak club. Who is he, and why do I care?"

"Edward Twelvetrees," she said, with a note of grimness in her voice, "is an estimable soldier, an honorable gentleman—and the younger brother of Nathaniel Twelvetrees, whom my husband killed in a duel many years ago."

"A duel over . . . ?"

"Not important," she said tersely. "The point is that the entire Twelvetrees family harbors feelings of the deepest hatred for my husband—well, for all the Greys, but particularly Pardloe—and would do anything possible to damage him.

"The second point," she went on, cutting off his next question, "is that Edward Twelvetrees is an intimate of Gerald Siverly. Very intimate. And the third is that for the last year, Edward Twelvetrees has been moving fairly large sums of money—far more than would normally pass through his hands; he's a younger brother, and has no more than his pay and his winnings at cards."

He leaned forward a little, intent now.

"Moving them where? And where do they come from?"

"They're going to Ireland. I don't know where they're coming from."

He turned that over in his mind for a moment.

"Why are ye telling me this?"

She hesitated, and he could feel her calculation but didn't know the exact nature of it. Not how much to trust him, he didn't think—only a fool would trust him with dangerous information, and he was sure the duchess was no fool. How much to tell him, though . . .

"I love my husband, Mr. Fraser," she said at last, softly. "I don't want him—or John, for that matter—to find himself in a position where the Twelvetrees family might do him harm.

"I want you, if at all possible, to see that that doesn't happen. If your inquiries in Ireland should lead you into contact with Edward Twelvetrees, I implore you, Mr. Fraser: try to keep him away from John, and try to see that whatever he's doing with Major Siverly doesn't intrude into the matter you're dealing with."

He'd followed her train of thought reasonably well, he thought, and ventured a question to check.

"Ye mean, whatever the money's about—even if it's going to, or through, Major Siverly—it's not to do wi' the matters covered by the court-martial your husband wants. And, therefore, ye want me to try to keep Lord John from following up any such trail, should he stumble over it?"

She gave a little sigh.

"Thank you, Mr. Fraser. I assure you, any entanglement with Edward Twelvetrees cannot help but lead to disaster."

"For your husband, his brother—or your father?" he asked softly, and heard the sharp intake of her breath. After the briefest instant, though, the low gurgle of her laughter came again.

"Father always said you were the best of the Jacobite agents," she said approvingly. "Are you still . . . in touch?"

"I am not," he said definitely. "But it had to be your father who told ye about the money. If either Pardloe or Grey knew that, they would have mentioned it when we were making plans with Colonel Quarry."

There was a small puff of amusement, and the duchess rose, a white blur against the darkness. She brushed down her robe and turned to go, but paused at the door.

"If you keep my secrets, Mr. Fraser, I will keep yours."

HE RESUMED HIS BED cautiously; it smelt of her scent—and her body—and while not at all unpleasant, both were unsettling to him. So was her last remark—though upon due contemplation, he thought it had been mere persiflage. He *had* no secrets that needed keeping anymore—save the one, and there was little chance that she even knew of William's existence, still less that she knew the truth of his paternity.

He could hear a church bell in the distance, striking the hour—a single, mellow *bong.* One o'clock, and the solitude of the deep night began to settle around him.

He thought briefly about what the duchess had told him about the money Twelvetrees was moving into Ireland, but there was nothing he could do with the information, and he was worn out with the strain of being constantly on his guard in this nest of English. His thoughts stretched and frayed, tangled and dissolved, and before the clock struck the half hour, he was asleep.

JOHN GREY HEARD THE BELL of St. Mary Abbot strike one and put down his book, rubbing his eyes. There were several more in an untidy pile beside him, along with the muddy dregs of the coffee that had been keeping him awake during his researches. Even coffee had its limits, though.

He had been reading through several versions of the Wild Hunt tale, as collected and recounted by various authorities. While undeniably fascinating, none of these matched with either the language or the events given in Carruthers's version, nor did they shed any particular light upon it.

If he hadn't known Charlie, hadn't seen the passion and precision with which he had prepared his complaint against Siverly, he would have been tempted to discard the document, concluding that it had been mixed in with the others by mistake. But he *did* know Charlie.

The only possibility he had been able to deduce was that Charlie himself did not know the import of the Wild Hunt poem but did know that it had to do with Siverly—and that it was important in some way. And there, for the moment, the matter rested. There was, in all justice, plenty of incriminating material with which to be going on.

With thoughts of wild faerie hordes, dark woods, and the wail of hunting horns echoing in the reaches of the night, he took his candle and went up to bed, pausing to blow out the lighted sconces that had been left burning for him in the foyer. One of the little boys had wakened earlier with stomachache or nightmare, but the nursery was quiet now. There was no light in the second-floor corridor, but he paused, hearing a sound. Soft footfalls toward the far end of the hallway, and a door opened, spilling candlelight. He caught a glimpse of Minnie, pale in flowing white muslin, stepping through the door into Hal's arms, and heard the whisper of Hal's voice.

Not wishing them to see him, he hurried quickly up the stairs to the next floor, to hide his candle, and stood there in the dark for a moment, to give them time to retire.

One of the boys must have been taken sick again. He couldn't think what else Minnie would be doing up at such an hour.

He listened carefully; the night nursery was one more floor up, but he heard no outcries, no movement in the peaceful dark. Nor was there any noise from the floor below. Evidently, the whole household was now wrapped in slumber—save him.

He rather liked the feeling of solitude, like this, he alone wakeful, lord of the sleeping world.

Not *quite* the lord of the sleeping world. A brief, sharp cry sliced through the dark, and he started as though it had been a drawing pin run into his leg.

The cry was not repeated but hadn't come from the nursery above. It had definitely come from down the corridor to his left, where the guest rooms lay. And, to his knowledge, no one slept at that end of the corridor save Jamie Fraser. Walking very quietly, he made his way toward Fraser's door.

He could hear heavy breathing, as of a man wakened from nightmare. Ought he go in? *No, you ought not,* he thought promptly. *If he's awake, he's free of the dream already.*

He was turning to creep back toward the stairs, when he heard Fraser's voice.

"Could I but lay my head in your lap, lass," Fraser's voice came softly through the door. "Feel your hand on me, and sleep wi' the scent of you about me."

Grey's mouth was dry, his limbs frozen. He should not be hearing this, was suffused with shame to hear it, but dared not move for fear of making a sound.

There came a rustling, as of a large body turning violently in the bed, and then a muffled sound—a gasp, a sob?—and silence. He stood still, listening to his own heart, to the ticking of the longcase clock in the hall below, to the distant sounds of the house, settling for night. A minute, by counted seconds. Two. Three, and he lifted a foot, stepping quietly back. One more step, and then heard a final murmur, a whisper so strangled that only the acuteness of his attention brought him the words.

"Christ, Sassenach. I need ye."

He would in that moment have sold his soul to be able to offer comfort. But there was no comfort he could give, and he made his way silently down the stairs, missing the last step in the dark and coming down hard.

14

Fridstool

BY THE NEXT AFTERNOON, THE INSIDE OF JAMIE'S HEAD WAS buzzing like a hive of bees, one thought vanishing up the arse of the next before he could get hold of it. He badly needed peace to sort through it all, but the house was nearly as busy as his mind. There were servants *everywhere.* It was as bad as Versailles, he thought. Chambermaids, wee smudgit maids called tweenies who seemed to spend all their time trudging up and down the back stairs with buckets and brushes, footmen, bootboys, butlers . . . He'd nearly run down John Grey's young valet in the hallway a minute ago, turning a corner and finding Byrd under his feet, the lad so buried under a heap of dirty linen he was carrying that he could barely see over it.

Jamie couldn't even sit quietly in his room. If someone wasn't coming in to air the sheets, someone else was coming in to build the fire or take away the rug to be beaten or bring fresh candles or ask whether his stockings needed darning. They did, but still.

What he needed, he thought suddenly, was a fridstool. As though the thought had released him in some way, he got up and set off with determination to find one, narrowly avoiding embranglement with two footmen who were carrying an enormous settee up the front stair, it being too wide for the back.

Not the park. Aside from the possibility of lurking Quinns, the place teemed with people. And while none of them would likely trouble him, the essence of a fridstool was solitude. He turned toward the hall that led toward the back of the house and the garden.

It was an elderly Anglican nun who'd told him what a fridstool was, just last year. Sister Eudoxia was a distant connection of Lady Dunsany's, who'd come to Helwater to recuperate from what Cook said was the dropsical dispersion.

Glimpsing Sister Eudoxia sitting in a wicker elbow chair on the lawn, wrinkled eyelids closed against the sun like a lizard's, he'd wondered what Claire would have said of the lady's condition. She wouldn't have called it a dropsical dispersion, he supposed, and smiled involuntarily at the thought, recalling his wife's outspokenness on the matter of such complaints as iliac passions, confined bowels, or what one practitioner called "the universal relaxation of the solids."

The sister *did* have the dropsy, though. He'd learned that when he came upon her one evening, quite unexpectedly, leaning on the paddock fence, wheezing, her lips blue.

"Shall I fetch ye someone, Sister?" he said, alarmed at her appearance. "A maid—shall I send for Lady Dunsany?"

She didn't answer at once but turned toward him, struggling for breath, and lost her grip on the fence. He seized her as she began to fall and, from sheer necessity, picked her up in his arms. He apologized profusely, much alarmed—what if she were about to die?—looking wildly round for help, but then realized that she was not in fact expiring. She was laughing. Barely able to catch breath but laughing, bony shoulders shaking slightly under the dark cloak she wore.

"No . . . young . . . man," she managed at last, and coughed a bit. "I'll be all . . . right. Take me—" She ran out of air but pointed a trembling finger toward the little folly that roosted among the trees beyond the stable.

He was disconcerted but did what she wanted. She relaxed quite naturally against him, and he was moved at sight of the neat parting in her gray hair, just visible at the edge of her veil. She was frail but heavier than he'd thought, and as he lowered her carefully onto the little bench in the folly, he saw that her lower legs and feet were grossly swollen, the flesh puffing over the straps of the sandals she wore. She smiled up at him.

"Do you know, I believe that is the first time I've found myself in a young man's arms? Quite a pleasant experience; perhaps if I'd had it earlier, I should not have been a nun."

Dark eyes twinkled up at him from a network of deep wrinkles, and he couldn't help smiling back.

"I shouldna like to think myself a threat to your vow o' chastity, Sister."

She laughed outright at that, wheezing gently, then coughed, pounding her chest with one hand.

"I dinna want to be responsible for your death, either, Sister," he said, eyeing her with concern. Her lips were faintly blue. "Should I not fetch someone for ye? Or at least tell someone to bring ye a bit of brandy?"

"You should not," she said definitely, and reached into a capacious pocket at her waist, withdrawing a small bottle. "I haven't drunk spirits in more than fifty years, but the doctor says I must have a drop for the sake of my health, and who am I to say him nay? Sit down, young man." She motioned him to the bench beside her with such a firmly authoritative air that he obeyed, after a furtive look round to see that they were not observed.

She sipped from the bottle, then offered it to him, to his surprise. He shook his head, but she pushed it into his hand.

"I insist, young man—what is your name? I cannot go on calling you 'young man.'"

"Alex MacKenzie, Sister," he said, and took a token sip of what was clearly excellent brandy, before handing back the bottle. "Sister, I must go back to my work. Let me fetch someone—"

"No," she said firmly. "You've done me a service, Mr. MacKenzie, in seeing me to my fridstool, but you will do me a much greater service by not informing the people in the house that I am here." She saw his puzzlement and smiled, exposing three or four very worn and yellowed teeth. It was an engaging smile, for all that.

"Are you not familiar with the term? Ah. I see. You are Scotch, and yet you knew to call me 'Sister,' from which I deduce that you are a Papist. Perhaps Papists do not have fridstools in their churches?"

"Perhaps not in Scottish kirks, Sister," he said cautiously. He'd thought at first it might be a sort of closestool or private privy, but probably not if you found them in churches.

"Well, everyone should have one," she said firmly, "whether Papist or not. A fridstool is a seat of refuge, of sanctuary. Churches—*English* churches—often have one, for the use of persons seeking sanctuary, though I must say, they aren't used as often these days as in former centuries." She waved a hand knobbed with rheumatism and took another drink.

"As I no longer have my cell as a place of private retirement, I was obliged to find a fridstool. And I think I have chosen well," she added, with a look of complacency about the folly.

She had, if privacy was what she wanted. The folly, a miniature Greek temple, had been erected by some forgotten architect, and while the site had much to recommend it in summer, being surrounded by copper beeches and with a view of the lake, it was an inconvenient distance from the house, and no one had visited it in months. Dead leaves lay in drifts in the corners, one of the wooden lattices hung from a corner nail, having been torn loose in a winter storm, and the white pillars that framed the opening were thick with abandoned cobwebs and spattered with dirt.

"It's a bit chilly, Sister," he said, as tactfully as possible. The place was cold as a tomb, and he didn't want her death on his conscience—let alone laid at his door.

"At my age, Mr. MacKenzie, cold is the natural state of being," she said tranquilly. "Perhaps it is nature's way of easing us toward the final chill of the grave. Nor would dying of pleurisy be that much more unpleasant—nor much faster—than dying of the dropsy, as I am. But I did bring a warm cloak, as well as the brandy."

He gave up arguing; he'd known enough strong-minded women to recognize futility when he met it. But he did wish Claire were here, to give her opinion on the old sister's health, perhaps to give her a helpful draught of something. He felt helpless himself—and surprised at the strength of his desire to help the old nun.

"You may go now, Mr. MacKenzie," she said, quite gently, and laid a hand on his, light as a moth's touch. "I won't tell anyone you brought me here."

Reluctantly, he rose.

"I'll come back for ye, how's that?" he said. He didn't want her trying to stagger back to the house by herself. She'd likely fall into the ha-ha and break her neck, if she didn't freeze to death out here.

She'd pursed her lips and narrowed her eyes at him, but he'd folded his arms and loomed over her, looking stern, and she laughed.

"Very well, then. Just before teatime, if you can manage it conveniently. Now go away, Alex MacKenzie, and may God bless you and help you find peace."

He crossed himself now, thinking of her—and caught a look

of horror from one of the kitchen maids, coming through the back gate of Argus House with a long paper-wrapped parcel that undoubtedly contained fish. Not only a Hielandman in the house, but a Papist, too! He smiled at her, gave her a tranquil "Good day," and turned to the left. There were a couple of small sheds near the big glasshouse, probably for the gardeners' use, but it was late enough in the day that the gardeners had gone off for their tea. It *might* do . . .

He paused for an instant outside the shed, but heard nothing from within and boldly pushed open the door.

A wave of disappointment passed through him. No, not here. There was a pile of burlap sacks stacked in one corner, the imprint of a body clear upon them, and a jug of beer standing beside it. This was someone's refuge already. He stepped out and closed the door, then on impulse went round behind the shed.

There was a space about two feet wide between the back wall of the shed and the garden wall. Discarded bits of rubbish, broken rakes and hoes, burlap bags of manure filled most of the space—but just within the shelter of the shed, just out of sight of the garden, was an upturned bucket. He sat down on it and let his shoulders slump, feeling truly and blessedly alone for the first time in a week. He'd found his fridstool.

He spent a moment in mindless relief, then said a brief prayer for the repose of Sister Eudoxia's soul. He thought she would not mind a Papist prayer.

She'd died two days after his conversation with her, and he'd spent a wretched night after hearing the news, convinced she'd taken a chill from the cold marble of the folly. He was infinitely relieved to learn from the kitchen gossip next day that she'd died peacefully in her sleep, and he tried to remember her in his regular prayers. It had been some time since he had, though, and he was soothed now to imagine her presence near him. Her peaceful spirit didn't intrude upon his necessary solitude.

Would it be all right, he wondered suddenly, to ask her to look after Willie while he was gone from Helwater?

It seemed a mildly heretical thought. And yet the thought felt answered at once; it gave him a feeling of . . . what? Trust? Confidence? Relief at the sharing of his burden?

He shook his head, half in dismay. Here he sat in an Englishman's rubbish, talking to a dead Protestant nun with whom he'd had two minutes' real conversation, asking her to look after a child who had grandparents, an aunt, and servants by the score, all anxious to keep him from the slightest harm. He himself couldn't have done a thing for William had he been still at Helwater. And yet he felt absurdly better at the notion that someone else knew about William and would help to watch over him.

He sat a few moments, letting his mind relax, and slowly it dawned upon him that the only truly important thing in this imbroglio *was* William. The complications and suspicions and possible dangers of the present situation mattered only insofar as they might prevent his returning to Helwater—no further.

He took a deep breath, feeling better. Aye, with that made clear, it became possible to think logically about the rest. Well, then.

Major Siverly was the ostensible root of this tangle. He was a wicked man, if half what Captain Carruthers had written about him was true, but wicked men of that sort were far from unusual, he thought. Why did the Greys want so badly to get at the man?

John Grey, by his own words, because he felt a sense of obligation to his dead friend Carruthers. Jamie might have doubted that, but given his own conversations with the dead, he was obliged to admit that John Grey might hear his own voices and have his own debts to pay.

What about Pardloe, though? It wasn't Lord John who'd dragged Jamie to London and was forcing him to go to Ireland after Siverly. Did Pardloe feel such impersonal outrage at Siverly's corruption as to explain his actions? Was it part of his ideal of the army, of his own profession, that he could not bear such a man to be tolerated in it? Or was he doing it primarily to support his brother's quixotic quest?

Jamie admitted reluctantly that it might be all these things. He didn't pretend to understand the complexities of Pardloe's character, but he had strong evidence of the man's sense of family honor. He himself was alive only because of it.

But why him? Why did the Greys need *him*?

For the poem, first. The Wild Hunt, in Erse. That much, he could see. For while the Greys might have found someone among the Scottish or Irish regiments who had the *Gàidhlig,* it would be indiscreet—and possibly dangerous, given that they hadn't known what the document contained—to put knowledge of it in the hands of someone they couldn't control as they did Lally and him.

He grimaced at the thought of their control but put it aside.

So. Having brought him to London to translate the verse, was it then merely economical to make further use of him? That made sense only if Lord John actually required assistance to apprehend Siverly, and Jamie was not sure that he did. Whatever else you liked to say about the man, he was a competent soldier.

If it was a straight matter of showing Siverly the order to appear at a court-martial and escorting him there, John Grey could plainly do that without Jamie Fraser's help. Likewise, if it were a matter of arresting the man, a detachment of soldiers would accomplish it fine.

Ergo, it wasn't a straightforward matter. What the devil did they expect to happen? He closed his eyes and breathed slowly, letting the warm sweet fumes of well-rotted manure help to focus his mind.

Siverly might well simply refuse to come back with Lord John to England. Rather than face a court-martial, he might resign his commission and either stay in Ireland or depart—as so many had—to take service with a foreign army or to live abroad; peculation on the scale Pardloe had shown him must have given Siverly the means for that.

Should he so refuse—or hear of the matter beforehand and escape—then Jamie might be of use in finding or taking the man, yes. With a bit of practice, he'd likely get along in the *Gaeilge* well enough; he could make inquiries—and his way—in places where the Greys couldn't. And then there was the matter of connections. There were Jacobites in Ireland and in France who would show him courtesy for the sake of the Stuarts, as well as his own name, but who would turn a closed face and a deaf ear to the Greys, no matter what the virtue of their quest. Despite himself, his brain began to compile a list of names, and he shook his head violently to stop it.

Yes, he *might* be useful. But was the possibility of Siverly's flight enough?

He remembered what Lord John had said about Quebec. Siverly had saved John Grey's life during the battle there. He supposed Lord John might find it an embarrassment to arrest Siverly and thus prefer Jamie to haul him back to England. He would have thought that notion funny, had he not had firsthand experience with the Grey family's sense of honor.

Even that . . . but there was a third possibility, wasn't there?

Siverly might fight. And Siverly might be killed.

"Jesus, Lord," he said softly.

What if Pardloe *wanted* Siverly killed? The possibility once named seemed as sure to him as if he'd seen it written down in rhymed couplets. Whatever the duchess had seemed to be saying to him in her nocturnal visit, there was something in the Siverly affair that touched her deeply—and what touched her, touched the duke.

He'd no idea what the connection was between the duchess and Edward Twelvetrees, but he was sure it was there. And the duchess had told him that Edward Twelvetrees was an intimate of Siverly's. Something moved in the web surrounding him, and he could feel the warning twitch of the sticky strand wrapped round his foot.

He took a long breath and let it out slowly.

In the cold light of logic, the answer was obvious—one answer, at least. Jamie was here because he was expendable. Better: because he could be made not to exist.

No one cared what became of a prisoner of war, especially not one held for so long, in such remote circumstances. The Dunsanys would not complain if he never came back, nor ask what had happened to him. His sister and Ian might—well, they *would*—make inquiries, but it would be a simple matter merely to inform them that he'd died of the flux or something, and leave it at that. They'd have no way of pursuing the matter or discovering the truth, even if they suspected they'd been lied to.

And if he *were* obliged to kill Siverly—or if it could be made to look as though he had—he shivered. He could be tried and hanged for it, if they cared to make the matter public; what would his word count for? Or John Grey could simply cut his throat and leave him sunk in an Irish bog, once he'd served his purpose, and tell the world what he liked.

He felt hot and cold together and found that he must make a conscious effort to keep breathing.

He'd thought that it would be a simple if annoying matter: do what Pardloe demanded, and be then returned to Helwater and William. But if it came to this . . .

Some sound made him open his eyes, to see John Grey standing in front of him, openmouthed.

"I . . . beg your pardon," Grey said, recovering himself with some effort. "I did not mean to disturb—"

"What the bloody hell are ye doing here!?" Without intent, he found himself on his feet, his fist bunched in Grey's shirtfront. Grey smartly jerked his forearm up, breaking Jamie's hold, and stepped back, stuffing his rumpled shirt back into his waistcoat.

"You are without doubt the touchiest son of a bitch I have ever encountered," Grey said, his face flushed. "And I include in that roster such men as my brother and the King of Prussia. Can you not behave like a civil being for more than ten minutes together?"

"Touchy, is it?" The blood was pounding in Jamie's temples, and it took some effort to keep his fists curled at his sides.

"I grant you, your situation is invidious," Grey said, making an obvious effort at conciliation. "I admit the provocation. However—"

"Invidious. Is that what ye call it? I am to be your cat's-paw. To preserve what ye're pleased to call your honor." He felt so far beyond fury that he spoke with perfect calm. "And ye call it provoking?"

"What?" Grey seized Jamie's sleeve as he made to turn away, and withstood the look of contempt directed at him. "What the *devil* do you mean by that?"

He jerked his sleeve out of Grey's hand.

"I speak English as well as you do, ye bloody coward, and ye take my meaning fine!"

Grey drew breath, and Jamie could see the thoughts cross the Englishman's face in rapid succession: the urge to lunge at him, the urge to make it more formal and call him out, a rush of unnameable calculation, and, finally—all within the space of a moment—a sudden clamping down, a forcible cooling of fury.

"Sit," Grey said through his teeth, jerking his head at the bucket.

"I am not a dog!"

Grey rubbed a hand over his face. "A casual observer might argue the point," he said. "But, no. I apologize for the implication. Come with me." He turned away, adding over his shoulder, "If you please, Mr. Fraser."

After a moment's hesitation, Jamie followed the man. There was no point in remaining with the garden rubbish, after all.

Grey pushed open the door of the glasshouse and beckoned him inside. It was near twilight, but the place glowed like a king's treasure, reds and pinks and whites and yellows glimmering in an emerald jungle in the dusk, and the air flooded in upon him, moist and caressing, filled with the scents of flowers and leaves, herbs and vegetables. For an instant, he smelled his wife's hair among them and gulped air as though he'd been shot in the lung.

Pulsing with agitation, he followed Grey past a group of palms and gigantic things with leaves like the ragged ears of elephants. Round a corner, a group of wicker furniture stood beneath an enormous arbor covered with grapevines. Grey stopped short here and turned to him.

"I've had a bloody long day, and I want to sit down," he said. "You can suit yourself." He promptly collapsed into a basket chair and leaned back, thrust out his booted feet, and closed his eyes with a little sigh.

Jamie hesitated, not knowing whether to turn on his heel and leave, sit down in his turn, or pull John Grey out of the chair by his collar and punch him.

"We'll have a half hour or so of privacy here," Grey said, not opening his eyes. "The cook's already come for the vegetables and Minerva's hearing Benjamin's recitation of Caesar. She won't come for the table flowers 'til he's done, and he's doing *D*

Bello Gallico; he never gets past *Fere libenter homines id quod volunt credunt* without losing his place and having to start over."

Jamie recognized the passage without difficulty: *Men always believe what they wish to believe.* He pressed his lips tight together and sat down in the other basket chair, wicker creaking under his weight. Grey opened his eyes.

"Now. What exactly do you mean," he said, sitting up straight, "about cat's-paws and my so-called honor?"

The brief walk through the glasshouse and Grey's unexpected equanimity had defused something of Jamie's rage, but nothing had changed the conclusions he'd come to.

He considered it for a moment, but, after all, what was to be gained by keeping those conclusions to himself? Forewarned was forearmed, after all, and it might be no bad thing for the Greys to know he *was* forewarned.

He told Grey, shortly, what he'd been thinking and the conclusions to which he'd come, leaving out only the duchess's visit to his room—and William.

Grey listened, sitting quite still, with no change of expression until Jamie had finished. Then he rubbed a hand hard over his face and said, "Damn Hal!" under his breath.

The grapevines had been cut back for winter, but the new spring growth was well sprouted, delicate rusty leaves deckling the rough-knuckled vines that roped through the arbor. A faint draft moved through the rich air of the glasshouse, ruffling the leaves.

"Right," Grey said, dropping his hand. "You aren't a cat's-paw, to begin with. A stalking horse, perhaps. And for what the assurance is worth, I had nothing to do with your presence here, let alone the notion that you should accompany me to Ireland." He paused. "Do you believe that?" he asked, looking intently at Jamie.

"I do," Jamie said, after a brief silence.

"Good. I am, however, probably to blame for the fact that you *are* involved in this situation. My brother wished me to take that blasted poem to Helwater and request you to translate it. I refused, whereupon he took matters into his own hands." He made a small gesture, indicating exasperated resignation.

"My interest in the matter is exactly what Hal told you. My friend Carruthers entrusted me with the job of bringing Major Siverly to a court-martial, and I *will* do that." He paused once more. "Do you believe me?"

"Aye, I do," Jamie said reluctantly. "But His Grace . . ."

"My brother does not let go of things," Grey observed. "You may have noticed that."

"I have."

"But he is not, to the best of my knowledge, either a murderer or an unprincipled knave."

"I'm obliged to take your word for it, Colonel."

"You may," Grey said politely. "He can—and will, I'm afraid—use you to accomplish his ends regarding Siverly, but those ends do not include either kidnapping or murder, and he intends you no harm. In fact"—he hesitated for a moment, but then firmed his jaw and went on, eyes fixed on the hands that hung between his knees—"should this venture end in success, I think I can promise you that you will . . . benefit from it."

"In what way?" Jamie asked sharply.

"As to that . . . I cannot make specific promises without consulting my brother and . . . perhaps other people. But I do promise that you will not be harmed by the . . . association."

Jamie made a noise in his throat, on the verge of rudeness, indicating what he thought of the Greys' promises, and Grey's head snapped up, his eyes direct, their pale blue darkened by the fading light.

"Either you take me at my word, Mr. Fraser," he said, "or you don't. Which is it?"

Jamie met his eyes and didn't look away. The light had dimmed to a sea of gray-green dusk, but the flush that rose now in Grey's face was still visible. It was the same dim light that had lain between them in the stable at Helwater, the last time they had spoken privately.

The last time he had taken Grey at his word. He had come within an inch of killing the man then—and both of them recalled that moment vividly.

Grey had said on that occasion, his voice barely audible with his passion, *"I tell you, sir—were I to take you to my bed—I could make you scream. And by God, I would do it."*

Jamie had swung with all his force, by simple reflex—not so much at Grey, but at the memory of Jack Randall that Grey's words unleashed in him—and had, by a miracle, missed. He sat without moving now, every muscle in his body hard as rock and aching with the memory of violence, of Jack Randall, and of what had happened in the dungeon of Wentworth prison.

Neither one of them would—or could—look away. There were sounds in the garden, people moving to and fro, the door to the house slamming, a distant treble of children's voices.

"Why did ye follow me?" Jamie asked at last. The words didn't seemed to be shaped right; they felt strange in his mouth. "This afternoon."

He saw the look of surprise bloom on Grey's face, pale in the gloom of the grape arbor. And remembered the same look on the man's face when he had opened his eyes half an hour earlier, to see Grey standing in front of him.

"I didn't," Grey said simply. "I was looking for a place to be alone for a bit. And you were there."

Jamie breathed deep and, with an effort that felt like lifting a cannon, rose to his feet.

"I'll take ye at your word," he said, and went out.

IT *HAD* BEEN a long day. Grey dressed for the evening meal, feeling tired but at peace, as though he had climbed some arduous peak and found himself now safe upon its summit. There might be more mountains to climb tomorrow, but for the moment the sun had gone down, the campfire had been lit, and he could eat his supper with an easy mind.

Tom Byrd was packing; they would leave in the morning for Dublin, and the room was strewn with stockings, hairbrushes, powder, shirts, and whatever else Tom considered essential to the credit of his employer's public appearance. Grey never would have believed that all of these items would fit into one trunk and a couple of portmanteaux, had he not seen Tom accomplish the feat repeatedly.

"Have you packed up Captain Fraser already?" he asked, pulling on his stockings.

"Oh, yes, me lord," Tom assured him. "Everything save what he's wearing—and his nightshirt, to be sure," he added as an afterthought. "I did *try* to make him wear powder for supper," he said, with an air of reproach. "He says it makes him sneeze."

Grey laughed and went down, meeting Hal on the stairs. His brother brandished a small book at him.

"Look what I've got!"

"Let me see . . . No! Where did you get it?"

"It" was a copy of Harry Quarry's book of poetry, entitled *Certain Verses Upon the Subject of Eros.* The original, which Grey had presented to Denis Diderot, had been bound in calfskin whereas this copy was a much cheaper version, done with plain buckram covers, and selling—according to the cover—at half a shilling a copy.

"Mr. Beasley had it. He says he bought it at Stubbs's print-shop, in Fleet Street. I recognized it instantly from the title and sent him off to get me a copy. Have you read it?"

"No, I hadn't the chance—only heard a few choice bits that Diderot read out over the piss pot . . . Oh, Christ!" He'd flipped the book open at random and now read out, *"Bent upon scratching his unseemly itch / This self-fellating son of a bitch . . ."*

Hal gave a strangled whoop and laughed so hard that he had to lean momentarily against the wall for support. "*Self*-fellating? Is that even possible?"

"You're asking *me*? I certainly can't do it," said Grey.

"I havena any personal experience in that regard myself," said a dry Scottish voice behind him, "but dogs dinna seem to find it difficult."

Both Greys swung round, startled; they hadn't heard him approach. He looked well, John thought, with a slight sense of pride. Upon Fraser's arrival, Minnie had sent hastily to the Pettigrews, who kept a pair of immense blackamoor servants to carry their sedan chair, and borrowed a fairly new suit of livery. The shirt had been washed, starched, and ironed and the plain coat and waistcoat well brushed, and while neither the color—a deep navy blue—nor style were what a fashionable gentleman would wear, it suited Fraser's own vivid coloring amazing well.

"It *is* possible, though," Fraser added, coming even with them. "For a man, I mean."

Hal had straightened up at Fraser's arrival but didn't abandon his own amusement, smiling broadly at Fraser's remark.

"Really? Dare I ask how you come by this knowledge, Captain?"

Fraser's mouth twitched slightly, and he shot a glance at Grey. He answered Hal readily, though.

"On one memorable evening in Paris, some years ago, I was the guest of the Duc di Castellotti, a gentleman with . . . individual tastes. He took a number of his dinner guests on a tour of some of the city's more interesting establishments, one of which featured a pair of acrobats. Extremely"—he paused—"flexible."

Hal laughed and turned to his brother.

"D'you think Harry's writing from personal experience, John?"

"It's my impression that Colonel Quarry has considerable experience of various kinds upon which to draw," Fraser said, before John could answer. "Though I shouldna have taken him for a man of letters. D'ye mean to say that he composed that remarkable bit o' verse?"

"Astonishingly enough, yes," Hal said. "And quite a lot more of a similar nature, if I am to believe the reports. Wouldn't think it to look at him, would you?"

Hal had turned, quite naturally, with a lift of the shoulder that invited Fraser to walk beside him, and they now went down the corridor, conversing in a pleasant manner, leaving Grey to follow, book in hand.

Minnie had gone out to the theater with a friend, and the men dined alone, in a surprising atmosphere of friendliness. There was no sign of wariness or resentment in Fraser's manner; he behaved with immense civility, as though the Greys were cordial acquaintances. Grey felt a sense of grateful astonishment; evidently Fraser had meant it when he said he would take Grey at his word.

Master me. Or let me your master be.

He thought he would settle for mutual respect—and, for the first time since Hal had put this scheme in hand, began to look forward to Ireland.

SECTION III

Beast in View

15

The Return of Tobias Quinn

"IS HE ALL RIGHT, ME LORD?" TOM ASKED IN LOWERED VOICE, nodding toward the dock. Turning, Grey saw Fraser standing there like a great rock in the middle of a stream, obliging hands and passengers to flow around him. Despite his immobility, there was something in his face that reminded Grey irresistibly of a horse about to bolt, and by instinct he fought his way down the gangway and laid a hand on Fraser's sleeve before he could think about it.

"It will be all right," he said. "Come, it will be all right."

Fraser glanced at him, torn from whatever dark thought had possessed him.

"I doubt it," he said, but absently, as though to himself. He didn't pull away from John's hand on his arm, but rather walked out from under it without noticing and trudged up the gangway like a man going to his execution.

The one good thing, Grey reflected a few hours later, was that Tom had quite lost his fear of the big Scot. It wasn't possible to be afraid of someone you had seen rendered so utterly helpless, so reduced by physical misery—and placed in so undignified a position.

"He did tell me once that he was prone to *mal de mer,*" Grey said to Tom, as they stood by the rail for a grateful moment of fresh air, despite the lashing of rain that stung their faces.

"I haven't seen a cove that sick since me uncle Morris what was a sailor in a merchant man come down with the hocko-grockle," said Tom, shaking his head. "And *he* died of it."

"I am reliably informed that no one actually dies of seasickness," Grey said, trying to sound authoritative and reassuring. The sea was rough, white froth flying from the tops of the surging billows, and the small craft lurched sickeningly from moment to moment, plunging nose down into troughs, only to be hurled abruptly upward by a rising wave. He was a good sailor himself—and smug about it—but if he thought about it for more than a few seconds . . .

"Wish I'd a-known," Tom said, his round face creased with worry. "Me old gran says a sour pickle's the thing for seasickness. She made me uncle Morris take a jar of 'em, put up special with dill weed, whenever he set to sea. And he never had seasickness to start with." He looked at Grey, his expression under the wet seeming to accuse his employer of gross negligence in the provisioning of pickles.

Grey felt himself falling under some kind of horrid trance, as he watched the surface of the ocean rise and fall, rise and fall . . .

"Yes," he said faintly. "What a good idea. But perhaps . . ."

"Your pardon, your honor," said a voice at his elbow. "Would ye be by way of being friends of the gentleman downstairs what's sick as a dog, and a tremenjous big dog, too?"

Grateful for the distraction, Grey turned his back on the roiling sea and blinked water from his lashes. The Irishman was a few inches taller than himself, but painfully thin. Despite that sailing seemed to agree with him; his face was ruddy with cold and wind, pale eyes sparkling, and water gleamed in his spray-soaked curls.

"Yes," Grey said. "Is he worse?" He made to go past the man, but his new acquaintance put out a hand, reaching with the other into a capacious cloak that billowed round him like a cloud.

"If he was any the worse for it, he'd be dead," the Irishman said, bringing out a small, square black bottle. "I only wondered, would ye maybe accept a bit o' medicine for him? I offered it to him meself, only he was too far gone to answer."

"I thank you, sir," Grey said, accepting the bottle. "Er . . . what is it, if you please?"

"Mostly bad whisky," the Irishman said frankly. "But with the ginger-root and a small little spoon of powdered opium stirred into it, as well." He smiled, showing a missing eyetooth. "Works wonders, it does. But do shake it first."

"What have we got to lose?" Tom said practically. He gestured at the deck, now thronged with passengers who had emerged from the companionway, driven upward by the insalubrious conditions in the cramped space below. Many of them were hanging over the rail themselves; the rest glared at Grey, plainly holding him responsible.

"If we don't do something about him prompt-like, one of that lot's a-going to knock him on the head. *And* us."

JAMIE HEARD FOOTSTEPS approaching and hoped fervently that whoever it was intended to shoot him; he'd heard a few such intentions expressed within his hearing recently. He was all for it but lacked the strength to say so.

"A bit under the weather, are ye, now?" He cracked one eye

open, to see Toby Quinn's beaming face bending over him, surrounded by crazily fluttering shadows cast by the swinging lanterns. He closed the eye and curled himself into a tighter ball.

"Go away," he managed, before the next wrench of nausea seized him. Quinn leapt nimbly back, just in time, but came forward again, cautiously skirting the fetid little pool surrounding Jamie.

"Now, then, good sir," Quinn said soothingly. "I've a draught here will help."

The word "draught," with its implication of swallowing something, made Jamie's stomach writhe afresh. He clapped a hand to his mouth and breathed through his nose, though it hurt to do so, as spewing bile had seared the sensitive membranes of his nasal passages. He closed his eyes against the horrible rhythmic sway of the shadows. Each one seemed to take his mind swinging with it, leaving his belly poised over some hideous sheer drop.

It won't stop, itwonteverstopohGod . . .

"Mr. Fraser." There was a hand on his shoulder. He twitched feebly, trying to get rid of it. If they wouldn't have the decency to kill him, could they not just let him die in peace?

The sense of alarm at Quinn's presence, which would in other circumstances have been pronounced, was so faint as barely to register on the blank slate of his mind. But it wasn't Quinn touching him; it was John Grey. *"Take your hand off me,"* he wanted to say, but couldn't. *"Kill you. Take your hand . . . kill you . . ."*

A general chorus of blasphemy greeted the results when he opened his mouth in an attempt to utter the threat. It was followed by more varied response, including a shocked female voice: "Dear bleedin' heart o' Mairy, the poor man's spittin' blood!"

He curled up again, knees clasped as tight to his belly as he could get them. He'd heard himself whimpering and, shocked at the sound, had bitten the inside of his cheek hard to stop it.

The chorus were saying something about the draught, all of them urging him to take it. An uncorked bottle of something hot-smelling and sickly-sweet was waved under his nose. Opium. The word flared a warning in his mind. He'd had opium before, in France. He still remembered the dreams, a nasty mix of lust and nightmare. And he remembered being told that he'd raved in the midst of them, too, talking wildly of the naked demons that he saw. Again, on the crossing to France: he'd been wounded then, and had suffered all those wounds again—and worse—in opium dreams. And what had happened later, at the abbey, when he'd fought the shade of Black Jack Randall in fire and shadow, had done something terrible to him against a stone wall . . . that was opium, too.

The whole cabin shot into the air and then fell with shocking violence, flinging people into the bulkheads like birds smashing into windowpanes. Jamie rolled off the bench on which he'd been lying, crashed into several bodies, and ended entangled with one of them, both wedged between the bulkhead and a large sliding crate of chickens that no one had thought to secure.

"Bloody get off me!" A strangled English voice came from somewhere under him and, realizing that it was John Grey he lay on, he rose like a rocket, cracking his head on the low beam above. Clutching his head—obviously shattered—he sank to his knees and fell half upon the crate, to the great consternation of the chickens. Shrieks and squawks and an explosion of down feathers and bits of chicken shit erupted through the slats, in an ammoniac reek that stabbed right through his nose and into what was left of his brain.

He subsided slowly onto the floor, not caring what he lay in.

More squawking, this human. Hands. They hauled him half sitting, though he hung like a bag of laundry, unable to help.

"Christ, he's a heavy motherfucker!" said a rough voice in his ear.

"Open your mouth," said another voice, breathless but determined.

Grey, he thought dimly.

Fingers seized his raw nose and squeezed and he yelped, only to choke as a cascade of vile liquid poured into his mouth. Someone cupped his chin and slammed his jaw shut.

"Swallow, for God's sake!"

The whisky burned down his throat and into his chest and, for one brief moment, cleared his mind of the omnipresent nausea. He opened his eyes and caught sight of Quinn, staring at him with an expression of intense concern.

I mustn't speak of him. Mustn't risk it, being muddled. Mustn't speak.

He worked his tongue, gasping for breath, gathering his strength. Then snatched the bottle from John Grey and drained it.

❧

JAMIE WOKE IN A rather pleasant state of mind; he couldn't remember who he was, let alone where, but it didn't seem to matter. He was lying on a bed and it wasn't moving. The light in the room flickered like sunlight on waves, but this was in fact the work of a large tree he could see, standing outside the window, fluttering its leaves in a lackadaisical manner. He thought there were not any trees in the ocean but couldn't swear to it, what with the peculiar images still floating languidly now and then across the back of his eyes.

He closed his eyes, the better to examine one of these, which seemed to be a mermaid with three breasts, one of which she was pointing at him in an enticing sort of way.

"Will you be havin' a pot of coffee, sir?" she said. Her breast began to stream black coffee, and her other hand held a dish beneath to catch it.

"Does one o' the other ones squirt whisky?" he asked. There was a sudden gasp in his ear, and he managed to open one eye a crack, squeezing the other closed in order to keep the mermaid in sight, lest she swim off with his coffee.

He was looking at a spindly girl in a cap and apron, who was staring at him with her mouth open. She had a long, bony nose, red at the tip. She had a dish of coffee in her hand, too, that was strange. Nay teats at all, though.

"No hope o' cream, then, I suppose," he murmured, and shut the eye.

"You'd best leave him to us, miss," said an English voice, sounding rather self-important.

"Yes," said another, also English, but testy. "Leave the coffee, too, for God's sake."

There was a soft green light about the mermaid, and a small striped fish swam out of her hair, nosing its way down between her breasts. Lucky fish.

"What do you think, me lord?" said the first voice, now dubious. "Cold water down his neck, maybe?"

"Splendid idea," said the second voice, now cordial. "You do it."

"Oh, I shouldn't want to presume, me lord."

"I'm sure he isn't violent, Tom."

"Just as you say, me lord. But he might turn nasty, mightn't he? Gentlemen do, sometimes, after a hard night."

"I trust you do not speak from personal experience, Tom?"

"Certainly not, me lord!"

"Opium doesn't take you like that, anyway," said the second voice, coming nearer. It sounded distracted. "It does give you the most peculiar dreams, though."

"Is he still asleep, do you think?" The first voice was coming nearer, too. He could feel someone's breath on his face. The mermaid took offense at this familiarity and vanished. He opened his eyes, and Tom Byrd, who had been hovering over him with a wet sponge, let out a small shriek and dropped it on his chest.

With a detached sense of interest, he watched his own hand rise into the air and pluck the sponge off his shirt, where it was making a wet patch. He had no particular idea what to do with it next, though, and dropped it on the floor.

"Good morning." John Grey's face came into view behind Tom, wearing an expression of cautious amusement. "Are you feeling somewhat more human this morning?"

He wasn't sure but nodded nonetheless and sat up, swinging his legs over the side of the bed. He didn't feel badly, but very strange. There was a wicked taste in his mouth, though, and he held out a hand to Tom Byrd, who was advancing on him slowly, coffee held before him like a flag of truce.

The cup Tom put in his hand was warm, and he sat for a moment, regaining his senses. The air smelled of peat smoke, cooking meat, and something vaguely nasty of a vegetable nature—scorched cabbage. His slow mind located the word.

He took a grateful mouthful of coffee and found a few more words.

"We're in Ireland, then, are we?"

"Yes, thank God. Are you always—" Grey cut himself off.

"I am."

"Jesus." Grey shook his head in disbelief. "Rather fortunate that you were not transported after Culloden, then. I doubt you would have survived the voyage."

Jamie gave him a narrow look—it was owing to Grey's personal intervention that he had not been transported, and he hadn't been at all pleased at the time—but evidently Grey meant nothing now beyond the obvious, and he merely nodded, sipping coffee.

A soft knock came at the door, which stood half open, and Quinn's long face came poking round the jamb. Had Jamie's reflexes been halfway normal, he might have dropped the coffee. As it was, he merely sat there, staring stupidly at the Irishman, whose existence he'd forgotten in the maze of opium dreams.

"Beggin' your pardon, good sirs," Quinn said, with an engaging smile round the room. "I hoped to inquire after the gentleman's welfare, but I see he's quite himself again, may God set a flower on his head."

Quinn advanced into the room, uninvited, but Grey recovered his manners instantly and offered him coffee, then sent Tom down to order up some breakfast, as well.

"It's pleased I am to see ye so far recovered, sir," Quinn said to Jamie, and reached into his pocket, coming out with a corked bottle. He pulled the cork and poured a thin stream of pungent whiskey into Jamie's coffee. "Perhaps this will aid in your complete return to the land o' the living?"

Jamie's sense of self-preservation was jumping up and down somewhere in the back of his mind, trying to attract his attention, but the whiskey was much more immediate. He raised his cup briefly to Quinn, said, *"Moran taing,"* and took a deep gulp, shuddering slightly.

Quinn was chatting easily to John Grey, telling him things about Dublin, asking after Grey's plans, offering to recommend him to the best livery stable in the town.

"Will it be a coach ye'll be needin', sir, or are you after takin' the post chaise?"

"How far is it to Athlone?" Grey asked. Siverly's estate was, by report, within ten miles of Castle Athlone.

"Oh, maybe two days' ride, with the blessing and a good horse. Slower by coach, of course. The post chaise would be one and a bit, but that's if it doesn't rain." Quinn made a quick sign of the horns against this evil thought.

Grey tapped his chin thoughtfully, looking at Jamie.

"I can ride," Jamie assured him, scratching his ribs. He felt fine now—extremely hungry, in fact.

"But there's the baggage to consider, me lord." Tom had popped back into the room, armed with a mug of shaving soap, a folding razor, and a strop.

"Well, yes. You'll have to go by coach with the baggage, Tom. I'm thinking, though, that Captain Fraser and myself might travel by horseback. Quicker, and less chance of being held up by bad roads."

He glanced at Jamie, one eyebrow raised in question.

"Aye, fine." Jamie set aside the empty cup. Now that he was fully awake, his attention was focused more on Quinn than on Grey. He narrowed his eyes at the Irishman, who sedulously ignored him.

"And a fine day for the riding it is, too," said Quinn approvingly. "My own road lies toward Athlone—if you gentleman might find it convenient, you're more than welcome to travel with me, so far as ye like."

Jamie jerked, startling Tom, who was about to apply a brushful of soap to his face.

"I should think we can find our own path," he said, putting up a hand to ward off Tom. "Athlone's not out of the way, from what I understand. Though we thank you for your kindness, sir," he added to Quinn, not wanting to seem churlish. He was in fact strongly inclined to pick Quinn up and decant him swiftly out of the window. The last thing he needed was to have a pixilated Irishman along on this expedition, breathing traitorous suggestions down his neck and distracting his attention while he dealt with Grey and Siverly and whatever else Ireland might have in store for him in the way of trouble.

"Oh, not at all, at all," Quinn said, waving an airy hand. "I'll be setting off just after the Angelus bell—at noon, I mean—should that suit your honors. I'll meet you in the courtyard, aye?"

He moved swiftly out the door before anyone could say anything, then popped his head suddenly back in.

"Darcy's, in the High Street. Tell Hugh Darcy that it's Toby Quinn as sent ye, and he'll see ye mounted on his best."

GREY THOUGHT THAT Quinn had been as good as his word. The horses provided by Mr. Darcy were sound, well shod, and as well tempered as a livery horse was likely to be. Mr. Quinn himself had turned up at the stable to give advice and had successfully bargained for a decent price. Jamie had given Quinn a narrowed eye, but the man seemed merely kind, if a trifle familiar, and besides, there was no way of preventing his riding out of Dublin along with them—it was a public road, after all.

There was a bit of small talk, as was common among strangers traveling together—Mr. Quinn was bent on business in County Roscommon, he said; an inheritance from a cousin that required the personal touch.

"Are you familiar with County Roscommon, sir?" Grey asked. "Do you perhaps know a gentleman named Siverly? Gerald Siverly."

Quinn looked interested but shook his head.

"Sure, I've heard the name. He's got the fine estate, he has, over near Ballybonaggin. But he wouldn't be knowing the likes of me," he said, with a deprecating grin.

"What is your trade, sir?" Grey asked, though worried that the man might be a gentleman—there was something in his manner that suggested it, though not his dress—and thus might be insulted. Quinn seemed not to take the question amiss, though, and replied equably.

"Oh, a bit of this and a bit o' that, sir—though I make most of my living from the printing of sermons and philosophical works of what ye might call a spiritual nature."

"Did you say something, Mr. Fraser?" Grey turned round in his saddle to look at Fraser, who was following them at the moment.

"I swallowed a gnat," Fraser replied shortly.

"Ah, better that than to be chokin' on a camel, so they say," said Quinn, and laughed at his own wit, though Grey smiled as well.

After a bit, though, conversation ceased, and they went on at a good pace. Grey sank into his own thoughts, these concerned mostly with the impending interview with Gerald Siverly. Always assuming Siverly was in fact in Ireland and hadn't buggered off to Sweden or India with his ill-gotten gains.

He knew Siverly, very slightly. Had sought him out after the Battle of Quebec to thank him for saving his life, which he'd done by deflecting the blow of a tomahawk that would have brained Grey. Siverly had been quite gracious, and they had shared the necessary glass of wine, but that was the sum total of their relations to date.

That made the current situation a trifle awkward, but Grey had no real scruples over what he was about to do. If Siverly was by some chance innocent—and he didn't see how he could be—then he should be pleased at the chance to clear his name by coming back and answering the charges at a court-martial. Grey had discussed his plans—some of them—with Hal, and they had thought that this was the best tack to take, perhaps: an apparent assumption on his part of Siverly's innocence, with earnest representations as to the desirability of facing down these infamous accusations.

Siverly might find it awkward to refuse to accompany Grey, under those circumstances. If he did have the brass neck to refuse, though, Grey had pointed out to his brother that it would be as well to have another plan—or two—in place. Was there anything useful with which he could threaten Siverly?

Yes, he could point out that Siverly risked expulsion from his regiment if the charges went unanswered—to say nothing of expulsion from his clubs, if he belonged to any, and from society in general. Hal made a decent threat, himself; Grey could suggest—with complete truth—that his brother, the duke, was upset by the seriousness of the charges and might bring a question in the House of Lords, but being a reasonable man (he grinned to himself at that) would certainly be willing to meet with Major Siverly. Grey might delicately suggest that in that case, a court-martial might be avoided.

Not bad, he thought judiciously, reliving the conversation with Hal. If neither personal appeal to honor nor threat to reputation worked, he could then turn to official channels; the Justiciar of Athlone Castle was the highest authority within easy reach of Siverly's estate, and Grey had provided himself with a letter of introduction from Hal, as well as a copy of Carruthers's packet of evidence. The justiciar might be persuaded that the charges were sufficiently serious as to arrest Siverly and commit him to Grey's authority. And if all else failed, there was Plan C, which involved a certain amount of physical intimidation and would require the services of Jamie Fraser.

It didn't seem useful to plan in further detail until he actually saw Siverly, though, and could judge better how he might respond. He therefore let his mind relax, enjoying the soft, moist air and the beautiful green of the countryside. Behind him, he heard Jamie ask Mr. Quinn, in tones of earnest inquiry, what he thought the most interesting sermon he had printed, but being himself uninterested in sermons, spurred up and left them to it.

16

Tower House

IT WAS A SOFT NIGHT, TOO, AND DAMP, WITH THE LITHE chill of spring moving in the air. Grey lay wrapped in his cloak in a shallow declivity, his rustic couch lined thick with grass and tiny star-shaped flowers, wondering whether he was about to die.

Night had come upon them in open country, and while debating the wisdom of pressing on to the next hamlet or turning back to the last crossroads, in hope of finding shelter for the night at a cottage, Quinn had suggested that as it was not raining, they might do worse than take shelter by a *túrtheach* he knew.

They'd passed two or three of these ruined tower houses on the journey from Dublin, tall bleak remnants of the Middle Ages. No more than shells now, crumbling, roofless, and black with damp, the tenacious dark ivy that crawled up their walls the only sign of life. This tower was much the same—though it had a well, this being Quinn's chief reason for recommending it, they having finished the ale Tom had packed for them.

They found the well, marked by a rough circle of stones, just within the tower's walls. Jamie Fraser had tied a string to his canteen and dropped it down to the dark water six feet below, then brought it up and sniffed at it with a long, suspicious nose before taking a cautious sip.

"I think nothing's died in it lately."

"Well and good," said Quinn. "We'll say a prayer, then, and slake our thirst, shall we?"

To Grey's surprise, both his companions promptly bowed their heads over the crude well coping and murmured something. The words weren't the same—they appeared each to be speaking his own language—but the rhythm was similar. Grey was unsure whether this was a prayer of thanksgiving for the provision of water or some ceremonial invocation against being poisoned by it, but he obligingly fixed his eyes on the ground and waited in silence until it was done.

They'd hobbled the horses and set them to graze on the lush grass, then supped themselves, decently if not luxuriously, on bread and cheese and dried apples. There hadn't been much talk over the food; it had been a long day in the saddle, and they sought their beds soon after.

He'd fallen promptly asleep; the ability to sleep anywhere, instantly, was a soldier's talent, and one he'd acquired very early in his career. And then had wakened some unknown time later, heart thumping and hairs erect, clutching for the dagger in his belt.

He had no idea what had wakened him and lay quite still, listening for all he was worth. Then there was a rustling of the grass nearby, quite loud, and he tensed himself to roll away and spring to his feet. Before he could move, though, there came the swish of moving feet and the hiss of a Scottish whisper.

"Are ye mad? Drop it, or I break your arm."

There was a startled huff of air and the faint thump of something hitting the ground. Grey lay frozen, waiting.

"Hush, man." Quinn's voice came to him, barely louder than the sigh of the wind. "Ye don't want to wake him."

"Oh, that I do, if ye were doing what I think ye were."

"Not here. Come away, for God's sake!"

The sound of breathing, hesitance, then the quiet sough of feet through thick grass as they moved off.

Very quietly, Grey rolled onto his knees, shucking off his cloak. He took the pistol from the bag he'd been using for a pillow, rose, and followed, matching the rhythm of his movements to theirs. The moon had set, but he could see them by starlight, twenty yards ahead: Fraser a looming mass against the paler ground, Quinn so close beside him that he thought Fraser might be grasping the Irishman by the arm, pulling him along.

They went around the ruined tower and essentially disappeared, no longer visible against the dark bulk of its stone. He stood still, not breathing, until he heard them again.

"Now, then." Fraser's voice came clearly to him, soft but with the anger clear in it. "What the devil d'ye mean by this?"

"We don't need him." Grey noted with interest that Quinn didn't sound frightened—merely persuasive. "*You* don't need him, *Mo chara.*"

"There are a good many folk in the world I don't need, including you, ye wee gomerel. If I thought it right to kill them on that account, I'd have done awa' wi' you before we left London."

Grey blinked at that and felt a cold finger down his back. So Quinn had been in touch with Jamie in London? How? Had Jamie sought him out? What had Fraser told him—and why had he joined their company? And why had Fraser not told Grey that he knew Quinn before? He swallowed bile and moved a little closer, fingering the pistol. It was loaded but not primed, because of the damp.

"If he's dead, ye could disappear, *Mac Dubh.* Nothing easier. Ye're safe out of England now; I've more than one place in Ireland where ye could lie hidden for a bit, or ye could go across to France should ye feel the need—but who would hunt ye?"

"That man's brother, for one," Fraser said coldly. "Ye've not had the benefit of meeting His Grace the Duke of Pardloe, but I'd sooner be hunted by the fiend himself. Did it never occur to you to ask if I thought it a good idea to kill the Englishman?"

"Thought I'd save ye the trouble, *Mac Dubh.*" Quinn sounded amused, damn him!

"Dinna be calling me *Mac Dubh.*"

"I know ye've a tender conscience, so ye have. Another minute and I'd have had him taken care of and tucked away safe down the well. Ye'd have no call to worry yourself."

"Oh, aye? And what then? Did ye mean to tell me, or just give it out that he'd changed his mind and gone off on foot?"

"Oh, I'd have told you, sure. What d'ye take me for, *Mac Dubh*?"

There was a moment of marked silence.

"What d'ye owe him?" Quinn demanded, breaking it. "Him *or* his brother? The swarthy-johns have imprisoned ye, enslaved ye! Taken your land, killed your kin and your comrades—"

"After saving my life, aye." Fraser's voice had grown dry; he was losing the edge of his anger, Grey thought, and wondered whether that was a good thing.

He wasn't really concerned that Quinn would talk Fraser round; he knew Fraser's innate stubbornness much too well. He was a trifle worried that Fraser might not talk the Irishman round, though—he didn't fancy lying sleepless night after night, expecting a knife in the back or his throat cut at any moment. He felt in the pocket of his coat for the small brass powder horn he carried . . . just in case.

Fraser gave a deep, exasperated sigh.

"Look ye," he said, in a low, firm voice. "I've given my word in this. If ye dare to dishonor me by killing the Englishman, I tell ye flat, Quinn—it'll be you joining him at the bottom of a well."

Well, that was some relief. Fraser might or might not want him dead—certainly he *had,* at various points of their acquaintance with each other—but he wasn't willing to have him assassinated. Grey supposed he should be affronted by the implication that it was only Fraser's fear of dishonor or Hal that was keeping Grey alive, but under the circumstances . . .

Quinn muttered something sulky that Grey didn't catch, but his submission was clear. Grey didn't let go of the powder horn but didn't take it out of his pocket, either; his thumb rubbed back and forth, restless on the line of engraving round the rim.

Acta non verba, it said: action, not words. The breeze had changed direction, and he could no longer hear clearly. Mumbling, disconnected words, and he edged a little closer, pressing near the dank stones of the wall.

". . . he's in the way of our business." Those words came clear, and Grey stopped abruptly. He was still clutching the powder horn in his pocket.

"You and I have nay business. I've told ye that a dozen times."

"Ye think so, do ye?" Quinn's voice was rising; he was striving for the effect of anger, Grey thought with interest, but was not truly angry. "It's the business of every true Catholic, every true man!"

"Ye'll gang your own way, Quinn, and I shallna hinder ye. But I've my own business to see to, and ye'll not stand in my way, either. D'ye hear me?"

Quinn snorted, but had obviously heard.

"Oidhche mhath," Fraser said quietly, and Grey heard footsteps come in his direction. He pressed flat against the tower, hoping

that the Scot would not pass downwind of him; he harbored a sudden irrational conviction that Fraser could smell his sweat—for despite the cool of the night, drops ran tickling down his ribs and matted the hair to the back of his neck—and would hunt him like a Highland stag.

But Fraser sheered off and went into the tower, muttering under his breath in the Scottish sort of Gaelic, and a moment later Grey heard splashing sounds. Presumably Fraser dashing water in his face to cool his anger.

He heard nothing from the other direction and could not see Quinn among the shadows. Perhaps the man had gone off to settle his own pique or was simply sitting there brooding. In any case, he seized the opportunity to peel himself off the wall and make his way back to his sleeping place, lest either of the irascible Gaels come looking for him.

Only as he approached the dark puddle of his discarded cloak did he become aware that he was still clutching the pistol in one hand, the other still clenched, aching, round the powder horn in his pocket. Letting go, he put away the pistol and sat down, rubbing his thumb across the palm of his hand, where he could clearly feel the word *"Acta"* embossed in the flesh.

HE LAY AWAKE until dawn, watching the hazy stars fade from the sky, but no one disturbed him. His thoughts, though, were another matter.

He clung to the minor reassurance provided by his recollection that Jamie Fraser had tried to prevent Quinn from accompanying them—and that he, Grey, had airily overridden his objections. That meant that whatever Quinn had in mind, Fraser presumably was not part of it.

But he knows what it is. And had refrained from telling Grey about it. But that might be innocent, if Fraser hadn't expected Quinn to attack Grey.

"He's in the way of our business," the Irishman had said, apparently meaning Grey himself. What the devil was the "business," and how was his presence an interference with it?

Well, there were clues. Quinn's reference to *"every true Catholic, every true man,"* for instance. That had the smell of Jacobitism about it. And while the Stuarts' cause had been decisively crushed in the Highlands fifteen years before, Grey did know that there were sputtering plots still smoldering in Ireland—all over the Continent, for that matter: France, Italy, Spain . . . One of them now and then erupted into brief flame before being stamped out, but it had been a year or two since he'd heard of anything active.

Thomas Lally came suddenly to mind, as did what Minnie had said about that bloody verse. A white rose, the Jacobite symbol. Fraser hadn't mentioned the white rose, nor had Lally. And Lally had been one of Charles Stuart's officers before going off to involve himself with the French. What had Lally and Fraser said to each other in those brief sentences of stilted Erse?

Grey closed his eyes briefly in dismay. More bloody Jacobites? Would they never give up?

By what Fraser said, he had met Quinn in London. So much for Hal's insistence that Fraser be treated as a gentleman and not a prisoner, allowed to walk out freely as he liked!

"Serve you right if that Irish blackguard had cut my throat," he muttered to his absent brother.

Still, this was beside the point. The important thing, he reminded himself, was that Jamie didn't want him dead—a warming thought—and had stopped Quinn from killing him.

Would that continue to be the case, if he spoke directly to Fraser about the matter?

As he saw it, he had only two alternatives: say nothing, watch them, and do his best never to sleep . . . or talk to Jamie Fraser. He scratched his chest meditatively. He could go one night without sleep, possibly two. That would bring them within reach of Siverly. But he didn't wish to face Gerald Siverly exhausted and fuzzy-minded.

While Fraser's reasons for not allowing Quinn to kill him were neither personal nor flattering, another point was that he plainly wanted nothing to do with what Quinn intended—but Quinn needed or wanted Fraser to be involved with it.

The air about him was still black-dark, but it had shifted, rising in some way, the night beginning to lift, restless to depart. At some distance, he heard the small sounds of a man waking: a cough, the clearing of a throat, a soft groan as gravity made its fresh demands. He couldn't tell which man it was, but both of them would doubtless make their presence known as soon as it was light, looking for breakfast.

If Quinn suspected anything, he might well try to kill Grey regardless of Jamie's threat. Just how well did the Irishman know Jamie? Grey wondered. Anyone who knew him well would take him at his word—but someone who didn't might not.

Quinn did know him, though. He'd called him *"Mac Dubh."* That's what the prisoners at Ardsmuir had called Fraser; Grey had heard it often enough that he'd asked one of the Gaelic-speaking orderlies what it meant. *"Son of the Black One,"* he'd been told, in a matter-of-fact way. He'd wondered at the time whether this was a satanic reference of some sort, but it didn't seem so, from his informant's attitude. Perhaps it was a literal reference to some aspect of Fraser's father's character or appearance, and he spared an instant to wonder what Fraser's father had been like.

The horses were drowsing under the tower wall; one of them released a long, rumbling fart and another shook its head, mane flapping. Now the birds were at it, tentative chirps from the distant hedgerows.

He'd talk to Fraser.

AFTER SOME THOUGHT, Grey decided that directness was the simplest way of obtaining privacy.

"Mr. Quinn," he said pleasantly, when the Irishman came back from his morning ablutions, water droplets shining in his curls. "I need to discuss various aspects of our business with Mr. Fraser before we arrive at Athlone. Would you do me the favor of riding on? We shall follow shortly and catch you up before noon."

The Irishman looked startled and glanced quickly at Jamie, who gave no indication that this was an out-of-the-way request, then looked back to Grey and nodded awkwardly.

"Certainly."

Grey thought that Quinn was not a particularly experienced *intrigant* and hoped he had even less experience as an assassin. On the other hand, it wasn't necessarily a job requiring skill. More, of course, if your victim was forewarned. He smiled at Quinn, who looked taken aback.

Breakfast was even more cursory than supper had been, though Jamie toasted two pieces of bread with cheese between, so that the cheese melted, something Grey hadn't seen before but thought very tasty. Quinn mounted up without comment afterward and headed back to the road.

Grey sat on a moss-covered rock, watching until the Irishman had got well away, then swiveled back to face Fraser, who was tidily rolling up a pair of stockings into a ball.

"I woke up last night," he said without preamble.

Fraser stuffed the stockings into his portmanteau and reached for the heel of bread, which followed the stockings.

"Did you," he said, not looking up.

"Yes. One question—does Mr. Quinn know the nature of our business with Siverly?"

Fraser hesitated a moment before answering.

"Probably not." He looked up, eyes a startlingly deep blue. "If he does, he didna hear it from me."

"Where the devil else might he have heard it?" Grey demanded, and Fraser glared at him.

"From your brother's servants, I imagine. That's where he learned that ye had business in Ireland and that I was to go with ye."

Grey blinked, but it was all too likely. He'd sent Tom Byrd often enough to extract information from other people's servants.

"How did he come to be in London?"

Fraser's eyes narrowed, but he answered.

"He followed me, when your brother had me taken from Helwater. And if ye want to know how he came to be at Helwater, ye'll need to ask him, because I don't know."

Grey raised one brow; if Fraser didn't know, he probably could make a damned good guess, but it wasn't necessary to go into that. Not now, at least.

Fraser stood up suddenly and, picking up the portmanteau, went to saddle his horse. Grey followed.

They made their way back to the road; Quinn was well out of sight. It was a beautiful morning, with the birds whose tentative chirpings had greeted the dawn now gone mad, swooping to and fro overhead and whooping out of the meadows in riotous flocks, flushed by their passage. The road was wide enough to ride side by side, and they continued in that fashion for a quarter of an hour or so before Grey spoke again.

"Will you swear to me that Quinn's matter does not threaten either our intent with regard to Major Siverly or the safety of England?"

Fraser gave him a sidelong glance. "No," he said bluntly.

Grey wouldn't have believed any other answer, but the bluntness—and its implications—gave him a mild shock. "Which is it?" he asked after a moment. "Or is it both?"

Fraser inhaled strongly through his nose, like a man much tried.

"Quinn's affairs are his own, Colonel. If he has secrets, they are not mine to share."

Grey gave a short laugh. "That's nicely phrased," he said. "Do you imply that you are in ignorance of Quinn's aims? Or that you know what he's up to but your sense of honor prevents your telling me?"

"Take your choice." Fraser's lips thinned, and his eyes stayed fixed on the road ahead.

They rode in silence for a bit. The lush green of the countryside was monotonous and soothing but was having little effect on Grey's temper.

"I suppose it is frivolous to point out that assisting the king's enemies—even by inaction—is treason," he remarked eventually.

"It is not frivolous to point out that I am a convicted traitor," Fraser replied evenly. "Are there judicial degrees of that crime? Is it additive? Because when they tried me, all they said was 'treason' before putting a rope around my neck."

"A rope . . . but you were not sentenced to hanging, were you?" It was certainly possible; a good many Jacobites had been executed, but a good many more had had their sentences commuted to transportation or imprisonment.

"No." Fraser's color was already high, from sun and wind. It became noticeably deeper. For a moment, Grey thought that was all he meant to say on the matter, but after another moment the words burst out of him, as though he could not contain them.

"They marched me—us—from Inverness to Ardsmuir. With ropes about our necks, to show that our lives were forfeit, given back to us only by the generosity"—he choked, actually choked, on the word, and shook his head, clearing his throat with violence—"the generosity of the king."

He kicked his horse suddenly; it snorted and jolted a little way ahead, then, lacking further stimulus from its rider, lapsed back into a trot, looking curiously over its shoulder at Grey and his mount, as though wondering how they'd got so far behind.

Grey rode for a bit, turning half a dozen things over in his mind at once, then nudged his horse, which was already attempting to catch up with its fellow, not liking to be left.

"Thank you," he said, coming even with Fraser again. "For not allowing the Irishman to kill me."

Fraser nodded, not turning his head. "You're welcome."

"May I expect this courtesy to continue?"

He could have sworn that the corner of Fraser's mouth twitched. "You may."

Quinn was visible now, a quarter mile ahead. He had turned aside to wait for them, and was leaning on a stile, chatting to a cottager who was holding a small white pig, by his gestures evidently displaying the animal's finer points.

They had almost reached Quinn when Fraser spoke again, turning this time to look at him, his face now cool-skinned and sober.

"Ye'll do what ye have to, Colonel. And so shall I."

17

Castle Athlone

ATHLONE CASTLE WAS BLACK AND SQUAT. IT REMINDED GREY vaguely of an oasthouse, those cone-shaped structures in Kent where hops were dried. Much bigger, though.

"Something of a family seat," he said to Jamie, joking. "One of my ancestors built it, back in the thirteenth century. Justiciar John de Gray, he was called."

"Oh, aye? Was your family Irish, then?"

"No," Grey admitted. "English back to the Conquest, largely Normans before that. Though I do have that one disreputable Scottish connection, of course." His mother's father had been Scottish, from one of the powerful Border families.

Fraser snorted. He didn't think much more of Lowlanders than of Englishmen.

Quinn had gracefully taken leave of them once in Athlone and gone off with vague murmurs of looking up a friend—and the assurance that he would rejoin them in the morning, to see them along their way. Grey rather resented the implication that, lacking such assistance, they would wander helplessly about the countryside like a pack of boobies, but swallowed his annoyance and thanked Quinn tersely for his help—though in fact he proposed to learn where Siverly's estate was from the justiciar, rather than depend on an Irishman who would happily assassinate him were it not for Fraser's threatening presence.

The guard who admitted them to the castle led them up the curving walkway into the center of the fortress, past a series of arrow slits set into the immense outer wall. These were narrow in their outer aspect but much wider on the inside, to allow an archer to draw a longbow, Grey supposed, and wondered idly if he could fit his head through one.

It was an ancient construction, originally a motte and bailey, and remnants of this were still evident, the central donjon rising like a twelve-sided pepperpot from the old bailey, now a paved courtyard ringed with smaller structures that crowded up against the huge surrounding wall.

The present justiciar was a man named Sir Melchior Williamson, also English, and while neither Grey nor Hal knew him, Harry did, and a note from the brother of the Duke of Pardloe had been enough to secure an invitation to dine at the castle.

"Is it wise to advertise your presence?" Jamie had asked, frowning, when Grey had written the note, enclosing Harry's introduction. "If we need to take Siverly by force, best if no one knows who ye are, surely."

"It's a thought," Grey agreed, folding and stamping the note. "But force should be our last resort. And I want to know whatever the justiciar can tell us about Siverly before I go to see him. Best to know the terrain before a battle." The terrain in this case included Sir Melchior's disposition and potential to be of assistance, should Plan B need to be invoked—but that judgment would have to wait until he saw the man.

Fraser snorted a little but seemed resigned.

"Aye. I'll tell wee Byrd to lay hold of a couple of burlap bags, then."

"What for?"

"To wear over our heads when we break in to Siverly's house."

Grey had stopped in the act of putting his signet back on and eyed Fraser.

"Haven't much faith in my powers of diplomacy, have you?"

"No, and neither has your brother, or I wouldna be here."

That stung.

"My brother prefers to have all contingencies covered," Grey said, with exquisite politeness. "And with that in mind . . . I'll mention the bags to Tom."

Sir Melchior Williamson proved to be a short, thick-bodied man with the mournful eyes of a bloodhound—these belying a cordial, if wary, nature. He greeted them with pleasure and showed them the facilities of the castle, such as they were.

"Cold as charity," he said, ushering them afterward into the small dining room in his quarters. "And nearly as cramped. Damp as a sieve, too, with the Shannon running past within bow shot of the walls." He sneezed, sniffed, and wiped his nose on his sleeve. "I've had a cold in the head since I came here, two years ago. Going to France day after tomorrow, thank God—though I'm glad you came before I left." *So much for Plan B,* Grey thought.

The dinner was simple but well cooked, and there was sufficient wine as to allow for comfortable conversation, during which Grey was able to inquire about Major Siverly without making his interest too obvious.

"Glastuig, his place is called," Sir Melchior said, leaning back in his chair and unbuttoning the lower buttons of his waistcoat with an absentmindedness born of long practice. "I've been there just the once, soon after I came. Beautiful house. That was when Mrs. Siverly was in residence, though."

Grey made an encouraging sound.

"She went back to her father's house, when the major went

off to Canada. From what I hear, husband and wife never had agreed very well, though, and she declined to come back when he returned."

"The major lives quietly now, does he?" Fraser asked. He'd not taken the lead in conversation but had been useful in leading it back in the desired direction whenever Sir Melchior, who had a tendency to ramble, made off in some unprofitable direction.

"Very quietly. Though I hear he's done the place over lately. Perhaps he proposes to lure his wife back with damask wall-paper." Sir Melchior laughed, the bloodhound wrinkles of his face all turning up.

The conversation moved on to speculation as to what amenities might best please a woman. Sir Melchior was not married but had hopes in that direction; hence his journey to France—though he feared his intended would find the castle less than appealing.

"She's half English, half French," he explained. "Hates Irish food, thinks the Irish even more barbarous than the Scots—meaning no offense, Captain Fraser."

"None taken, sir," Jamie murmured, refilling his glass.

"And I do not know that I can count upon the appeal of my person to overcome such objections." Sir Melchior looked over the rounded slope of his belly and shook his head, resigned.

Conversation became general at that point, and while Grey and Fraser prodded gently from time to time, they learned little more about Gerald Siverly, save for the interesting fact that his father had been a Jacobite.

"Marcus Siverly was one of the Wild Geese," Sir Melchior said. "Know about them, do you?"

Grey did, but shook his head obligingly.

"That's what they called themselves, the Irish brigades who fought for the Stuarts at the end of the last century.

"The castle was rather important then," Sir Melchior explained, beckoning the steward to bring more wine, "because of the river ford. The bridge—you saw the bridge? Of course you did—it leads into Connaught Province, a Jacobite stronghold in the last war. The last war here, I mean," he added, with a courteous inclination of the head toward Jamie.

"The Williamites assaulted Athlone on the west, the Connaught side, but the Jacobites destroyed the bridge over the Shannon and managed to hold them off. So the Williamites bombarded the town—according to the castle records, more than sixty thousand shots were fired into the town over a ten-day period. They never did take the town, but the Williamite general, a Dutchman named Ginkel, cleverly went downriver a bit—the Shannon's navigable for most of its length—crossed there, and came round behind the Jacobites, flushing them out.

"The Jacobites were crushed at Aughrim then, of course—but the survivors made it to Limerick, and there took ship to Spain. The flight of the Wild Geese, they called it." Sir Melchior took a meditative mouthful of wine and held it for a moment before swallowing; it was good wine.

"So Major Siverly's father left for Spain, did he?" said Grey, taking up his own glass casually. "When did he come back?"

"Oh, he never did. Fought in Spain, some years later. The son came back about six years ago, bought Glastuig, which had fallen into disrepair, and began to build it back up. I hear he's come into quite a bit of money lately," Sir Melchior added. "Inheritance from some distant relative, I heard."

"Has he? How fortunate," Grey murmured, and met Jamie's eye across the table.

Jamie gave the shadow of a nod and put his hand into his coat.

"I wonder, sir—as ye seem to know so much regarding the

history of these parts—might ye ever have seen a poem such as this?" He handed across a folded copy of the fragment of the Wild Hunt, translated into English.

Sir Melchior looked interested and sat up, fumbling for his spectacles. Placing these on his nose, he read the lines slowly out loud, following the words with a blunt fingertip.

Listen, you men of the three lands.
Listen for the sound of the horns that wail in the wind,
that come out of the night.

She is coming. The Queen is coming
and they come following, her great train, her retinue
wild of hair and eye,
the volunteers who follow the Queen.

They search out blood, they seek its heat. They echo the voice
of the king under the hill.

"Deuced odd thing, that," he said, looking up from the page and blinking owlishly through his spectacles at them. "I've heard of the Wild Hunt but can't say I've ever seen an account quite like this one. Where'd you get it?"

"From a soldier," Jamie said, with perfect truth. "As ye see, it's not complete. I should like to find out the rest of it, and maybe who wrote it." He gave Sir Melchior a look of convincingly scholarly earnestness, quite surprising Grey. He hadn't known Fraser capable of acting. "I have it in mind to publish a wee book one day, with some of the auld tales. This would be a fine addition, if it were complete. Might ye be acquainted with anyone familiar wi' such things?"

"Why . . . yes. Yes, I think perhaps I do know someone." Sir Melchior beckoned to his steward to fetch a fresh decanter of port. "Do you know Inchcleraun?"

Both Grey and Fraser shook their heads, but Grey felt his heart pick up its pace a bit.

"It's a Catholic monastery," Sir Melchior said. "A glass with you, Lord John? Yes, yes." He drank deep and set down the glass to be refilled, belching contentedly. "It's on an island—the island's called Inchcleraun, too—up toward the north end of Lough Ree. Only about ten miles from here by water. The abbot—Michael FitzGibbons, he's called—is quite a collector of old things: parchments, oddments, all-sorts. I met him once; decent sort, for a priest. I think if anyone could tell you where to find the rest of your poem, it might be him."

Grey saw Jamie's face change suddenly. The change was transient, like the ripple of wine in the glass the steward set down before him, but definitely there. Perhaps he took exception to that "decent for a priest" remark? Surely not; such remarks were commonplace, and it hadn't been said with any particular tone of derogation.

"I thank ye," Jamie said, and smiled, nodding over his lifted glass. "A glass with ye, sir? It's a verra nice make of wine, to be sure."

18

Fireside Tales

GREY HAD HOPED TO BE RID OF QUINN ONCE THEY REACHED Athlone, but the Irishman clung like a burr, popping up wherever he and Jamie went in the city, cheerful as a grig, and giving no indication that he viewed John as anything but an esteemed acquaintance.

"Can't you get rid of him?" he'd snapped at Jamie finally, discovering Quinn lounging in the yard of the stable where they'd gone to hire a mule cart for the larger baggage—for Tom had arrived by coach that morning.

"D'ye want me to shoot him?" Fraser inquired. "You've got the pistols, aye?"

"What does he bloody want?" Grey demanded in exasperation, but Fraser merely shrugged and looked stubborn—or, rather, more stubborn than usual, if such a thing were possible.

"He says he has business near Inchcleraun, and I've nay grounds to call him a liar. Have you? Or do ye ken the way, for that matter?"

Grey had given up, having no choice, and suffered Quinn to ride along with them. With Tom and the baggage-cart and with

Jamie Fraser's inclination to seasickness in mind, they had determined to go by road up the coast of Lough Ree, then find a boat to ferry Jamie across to Inchcleraun, where he would see the abbot and make inquiries regarding the Wild Hunt poem, before they made their assault upon Siverly's estate near the village of Ballybonaggin, this being only a few miles from the end of Lough Ree, where the island of Inchcleraun lay.

Quinn had promptly declared that he knew Lough Ree well, would guide them safely and find them transport to Inchcleraun. "For sure, I'm after having my own small bit of business nearby, am I not?"

It was roughly twenty miles from Athlone to the far end of Lough Ree, but a torrential downpour that turned the road to liquid mud, bogged the horses, and sank the cart to its axles marooned them four miles short of their goal.

At this point, Grey was not precisely grateful but at least not displeased that Quinn had come with them, for the Irishman did apparently know the countryside and found them shelter in a tumbledown structure that had once been a cow byre. True, the roof leaked and there was a lingering scent of the building's former inhabitants, but it was substantially drier than the open air, and there was enough dung and a few damp peats to scrape together for a meager fire.

Grey admitted to a reluctant admiration for Quinn's sangfroid. He behaved precisely as though they were all jolly companions, joking and telling stories, and such was his skill that in fact the atmosphere in the dank little shelter was relaxed and pleasant, in spite of what Grey either knew or suspected of the Irishman.

"And what of you, lad?" Quinn was saying to Tom. "D'ye have a tale to tell, to pass the time?"

Tom blushed visibly, despite the darkness.

"I'm no hand with a tale, sir," he said, deprecating. "I, um, could maybe read a bit, though?"

Tom had, for reasons best known to himself, brought along as light recreational reading for the journey a shabby volume borrowed from Hal's library, entitled *The Gentleman Instructed.* This was a treatise on deportment, etiquette, and general behavior, dating roughly from the year of Grey's birth, and, while extremely entertaining in spots, was perhaps a trifle obsolete in its advice.

"Oh, by all means, Tom," Grey said. "I'm sure all profit from a bit of elevating discourse."

Tom looked pleased and, after a bit of thumbing, cleared his throat and read:

"Dueling is a Great Evil, which a Christian Gentleman should strive always to avoid. Should appeal to Reason fail to resolve Conflict and Honor prevent gracious Capitulation, a Gentleman should then seek the Assistance of Friends, who by dint of Persuasion may bring your Opponent to a sense of Christian Obligation and Responsibility. However . . ."

Someone must have given it to Grey's father—his name was inscribed on the flyleaf—but Grey couldn't imagine his father having actually purchased such a book himself.

Still, Grey reflected, he'd take *The Gentleman Instructed* any day in preference to Tom's usual favorite, *Arbuthnot's Ailments,* from which he was accustomed to regale Grey, in tones of gloomy relish, with descriptions of exactly what happened to persons so reckless as to neglect the proper balance of their humors. Allowing one's phlegm to get the upper hand was particularly dire, he understood, and cleared his throat in reflex at the thought, spitting neatly into the fire, which hissed and sizzled at the insult.

"Should Armed Conflict prove unavoidable, the Gentleman should give his Opponent every Opportunity for Withdrawal without loss of

Reputation. To this end, such Epithets as 'Coward,' 'Seducer,' 'Fop,' or most particularly 'Dog' are strongly discouraged to be used."

Grey was beginning to wonder whether perhaps his mother had given the book to his father as a joke. It would be quite like her.

He relaxed against the backstop of his portmanteau and, with belly pleasantly full and lulled by Tom's reading, fell into a half dream in which he called Siverly out. A duel would be so much more straightforward, he reflected drowsily. *"Have at you, sir!"* And a straight thrust through the heart . . . Well, no, better through the guts; the poltroon didn't deserve a clean, uncomplicated death.

He'd been out a few times, mostly with swords. Inconsequential encounters—both parties drunk, hasty words, perhaps a blow—that neither one could find enough coherence to apologize for while preserving any countenance.

The advantage to dueling while drunk, he'd found, was that there wasn't any sense of fear or urgency about it; it was an elevated sort of feeling, literally—he felt as though he stood a little above himself, living at a faster pace, so that he saw every move, every thrust, as though performed in exquisite slow motion. The grunt of effort, the tickle of sweat, and the smell of his opponent's body were vivid punctuations of their dance, and the sense of being intensely alive was intoxicating in itself.

He always won; it didn't occur to him that he might not. A decent fight, a simple stab, a quick slash that drew a little blood, honor satisfied, and they stood together, chests heaving, often laughing and leaning on each other, still drunk. He hadn't had that sort of duel in years, though.

"Ye've been out now and then yourself, haven't ye, Jamie?"

Distracted by memory, Grey hadn't noticed that Tom had stopped reading, but was pulled from his thoughts by Quinn's interjection. Grey looked up and caught a most peculiar expression on Jamie's face.

"Once or twice," Jamie muttered, averting his eyes. He picked up a stick and poked the fire unnecessarily, making the peats crumble and glow.

"In the Bois de Boulogne, wasn't it? With some Englishman. I recall hearing about it—a famous fight! And did ye not end in the Bastille for it?" Quinn laughed.

Fraser glanced round with a truly awful look in his eyes, and had Quinn been watching him, he would either have been turned to stone on the spot or leapt up and run for his life.

John himself leapt in, wanting above all to disrupt the conversation.

"I once killed a man by accident during a duel—or thought I had. It was the last duel I fought; I think it might be the last altogether. A most distressing experience."

That duel had been with pistols. He hadn't been drunk then. He'd been suffering the aftereffects of being electrocuted by an electric eel, and the entire experience had been so unreal that he still didn't trust his memories of it. He had no idea how it had begun, still less how it had finished.

His opponent had died, and he regretted that—though not very much, he admitted to himself; Nicholls had been a boor and a waste to society, and, besides, he'd asked for it. Still, his death had been an accident, and Grey really preferred to kill on purpose, when it was necessary.

Interrupted, but not offended, Tom shut the book with his finger in it to hold his place and leaned forward, face wary. That duel had sent him and Lord John to Canada; he hadn't been there when Grey killed Nicholls but certainly remembered the occasion, and it occurred to Grey to wonder whether Tom had chosen the *Gentleman*'s admonition against dueling on purpose.

Quinn's interest had shifted from Fraser to Grey, though, which was what Grey had intended, so he answered when Quinn inquired what he meant by saying he thought he'd killed the man by accident.

"I meant to delope—to fire up into the air?" Quinn nodded impatiently, familiar with the term. "But my man fell and sat bleeding on the grass—he was quite alive, though, and didn't seem much hurt. The bullet had gone up and more or less fallen on him from a height but hadn't struck him on the head or anything. He walked off, in fact, in the company of a surgeon who happened to be there—it was following a party. I was therefore entirely shocked to hear the next morning that he'd died."

"An accident, sure. But are ye saying that really wasn't the way of it, at all?"

"I am, indeed. It was months later that I received a letter from the surgeon, informing me that the man had had a congenital weakness of the heart—an aneurysm, he called it—that had burst as a result of the shock. It wasn't my shot at all that had killed him—or only indirectly—and Dr. Hunter said that he might have died at any time."

"Dr. Hunter?" Quinn sat up straight and crossed himself. "John Hunter, is it—him they call the Body-Snatcher?"

"Dr. John Hunter, yes," Grey said warily, suddenly on dicey ground. He hadn't meant to mention Hunter by name—and hadn't expected either of the men to know that name, either. Hunter did indeed have a most unsavory reputation, being rapacious in the collection of bodies for dissection. And the question as to just how Dr. Hunter knew of Nicholls's aneurysm . . .

"God between us and evil," Quinn said, shuddering visibly. His usual breezy manner had quite vanished. "Think of it! To be taken off and anatomized like a criminal, skinned like an animal and your flesh cut into bloody bits . . . God and all angels preserve me from such a fate!"

Grey coughed and, glancing to the side, caught Tom's eye. He hadn't shown Tom Dr. Hunter's letter, but Tom was his valet and knew things. Tom coughed, too, and neatly closed his book.

"It's a nightmare I have sometimes," Quinn confided, rubbing his hands together as though he were cold. "The anatomists have got me, and they've boiled up me bones and strung me up as a skellington, left hanging there grinning in some medical bugger's surgery for all eternity. Wake from that in a cold sweat, I tell ye truly."

"I shall keep a lookout, Quinn," Jamie said, making a decent attempt at a grin. "Should I see a skeleton wi' a missing eyetooth, I promise I'll buy it and see it given decent burial, just in case."

Quinn reached for his cup and raised it to Jamie.

"It's a bargain, Jamie dear," he said. "And I shall do the same for you, shall I? Though I'm not sure I should be able to tell the difference between your skeleton and that of a gorilla, now."

"And where would ye ever have seen a gorilla, Quinn?" Jamie leaned forward to pour himself another mug of ale.

"In Paris, of course. King Louis's zoo. The King of France is most generous to his subjects," Quinn explained to Tom, who had come to put more fuel on the fire. "On certain days, his collection of outrageous animals is open to the public—and a boggling sight they are, to be sure. Ever seen an ostrich, have ye, lad?"

Grey drew breath, relaxing slightly as the conversation turned safely away from dangerous topics. He wondered briefly about the famous duel in the Bois de Bologne and who the Englishman had been that Fraser fought. That would have been before the

Rising; Fraser had mentioned being in Paris then, during a conversation about French novels that they had had at Ardsmuir.

Quite suddenly—and with a yearning that astonished him with its strength—he thought of those rare evenings of friendship, for they had been friends, in spite of their uneasy relationship as prisoner and gaoler; had shared conversation, humor, experience, a commonality of mind that was rare indeed. If he had only had more control, had not made his feelings known . . . Well, a good many regrettable things wouldn't have happened, and he had cursed himself on many occasions since, for his bad judgment. And yet . . .

He watched Fraser through his lashes, the glow of the burning peat shining red along the long, straight bridge of the Scotsman's nose and across the broad cheekbones, the light molten bronze in the loose tail of hair pulled back with a leather thong and dripping wet down his back. *And yet* . . . he thought.

He had sacrificed their easiness together, and that was a great loss. Fraser, in his turn, had reacted with such revulsion to the revelation of Grey's nature as had led to terrible exchanges between them—and Grey still didn't wish to think about the revelation that had come to him regarding just why—but in the final analysis, he had not lost everything. Fraser knew. And that was in itself a remarkable thing.

There was not easiness between them any longer—but there *was* honesty. And that was a thing he had had—ever would have—with precious few men.

Quinn was telling some tale now, but Grey paid no great attention.

Tom had been humming under his breath as he went about the business of supper and now escalated to whistling. Absorbed in his own thoughts, Grey hadn't noticed what he was whistling but suddenly caught a phrase that echoed in his head with its words: *Down among the dead men, let him lie!*

He jerked, with a quick, reflexive glance at Fraser. "Down Among the Dead Men" was a popular song, originally from Queen Anne's time, but, in the way of popular songs, with words often adapted to current feeling. The patrons of this afternoon's pub had been singing a blatantly anti-Catholic version, and while Fraser had given little outward sign of offense, Grey was well enough accustomed to his facial expressions—or lack of them—as to have detected the attention to his ale cup that hid the smolder of his eyes.

Surely he would not think Tom's absentminded whistling a reference to—

"Sure, he'll not be troubled," said Quinn casually. "He doesn't hear music, the creature, only words. Now, when it came time to—"

Grey smiled and pretended courteous attention to the rest of Quinn's tale, but was deaf to its details. He was startled not only by the Irishman's acuity—as to have noticed both his wary glance at Fraser and to have deduced the cause of it—but by the casual revelation that Quinn knew that Fraser was tone-deaf.

Grey himself knew that, though he had momentarily forgotten it. In the time at Ardsmuir when he and Fraser had dined together regularly, Fraser had told him—as the result of a question regarding which was his favorite composer—that in consequence of an ax blow to the head some years before, he had quite lost the ability to distinguish one note from another.

True, Jamie might have mentioned this disability to Quinn in passing sometime during the last two days—but Grey doubted it extremely. Jamie was an extraordinarily private man, and while capable of extreme civility when he wanted to be, his cordiality was often used as a shield to keep his conversant at arm's length.

Grey flattered himself that he knew Fraser better than most people did—and paused for an instant to ask himself whether he was perhaps only discomfited to think that Fraser might have shared this personal bit of information with a stranger. But he dismissed that possibility at once. Which left the logical, if equally discomfiting, conclusion that Quinn had known Fraser before he joined their company. Long before London. With a sudden jolt, he recalled Quinn's remark about ostriches and the King of France's zoo. He, too, had been in France. And by the mathematical principle of equality, if A equaled B . . . then B equaled A. Fraser had known Quinn before—intimately. And had said nothing.

19

Quagmire

THE MONASTERY OF INCHCLERAUN STOOD ON THE EDGE OF A small lake, a cluster of small stone buildings surrounding the church. There had once been a surrounding wall and a tall, circular tower, but these had crumbled—or been knocked down—and the stones lay tumbled, half sunk in the soft soil and mottled with lichens and moss.

Despite the signs of past depredation, the monastery was unquestionably inhabited and lively. Jamie had heard the bell from the far side of the lake and now saw the monks coming out of the church, scattering to their labors. There was a fenced pasture behind the buildings, where a small flock of sheep was grazing, and a stone archway showed the ordered rows of a vegetable garden, where two lay brothers hoed weeds in the resigned manner of men who had long since accepted their Sisyphean lot.

One of these directed him to the largest of the stone buildings, where a long-nosed clerk took his particulars, then left him in an anteroom. The atmosphere of the place was peaceful, but Jamie wasn't. Besides the conflict between Grey and Quinn—

one more remark from either one, and he was seriously tempted to crack their heads together—there was the looming confrontation with Siverly to be thought about, and the duchess's cryptic warnings about Twelvetrees . . . and, somewhere far down underneath the more pressing concerns, an uneasy awareness that Quinn's Druid cup was presumably here, and he had not quite made up his mind whether to ask about it or not. And if it was here, what then?

Despite these agitations, his first sight of the abbot made him break into a smile. Michael FitzGibbons was a leprechaun. Jamie recognized him at once from Quinn's description of the race.

The man came up perhaps to Jamie's elbow but stood straight as a sawn-off arrow, a stiff white beard bristling pugnaciously from the edges of his jaw and with a pair of green eyes, bright with curiosity.

These eyes had fixed upon Jamie at once, and lit with cordiality when he introduced himself and mentioned his uncle by way of bona fides.

"Alexander's nephew!" Abbot Michael exclaimed, in good English. "Aye, I mind you, boy. I heard a good deal of your adventures, years agone—you and your English wife." He grinned in his beard, displaying small, even white teeth.

"She turned St. Anne's finely upon its ear, from what I heard. Is she with you now, by chance? In Ireland, I mean."

Jamie could tell from the sudden look of awareness and horror on the abbot's face what his own must look like. He felt the abbot's hand on his forearm, amazingly strong for its size.

"No, Father," he heard his own voice say, calm and remote. "I lost her. In the Rising."

The abbot drew a breath of audible pain, clicked his tongue three times, and drew Jamie toward a chair.

"May God rest her soul, poor dear lady. Come, lad, sit. You'll have a tint of whiskey."

This wasn't phrased as an invitation, and Jamie made no argument when a sizable dram was poured and shoved into his hand. He lifted the glass mechanically toward the abbot in acknowledgment, but didn't speak; he was too busy repeating over and over within himself, *Lord, that she might be safe! She and the child!* as though fearing the abbot's words had indeed sent her to heaven.

The shock of it waned quickly, though, and soon enough the icy ball in his wame began to thaw under the gentle flame of the whiskey. There were immediate things to be dealt with; grief must be put away.

Abbot Michael was talking of neutral things: the weather (unusually good and a blessing for the lambs), the state of the chapel roof (holes so big it looked as though a pig had walked across the roof, and a full-grown pig, too), the day (so fortunate that it was Thursday and not Friday, as there would be meat for dinner, and of course Jamie would be joining them; he would enjoy Brother Bertram's version of a sauce; it had no particular name and was of an indistinct color—purple, the abbot would have called it, but it was well known he had no sense of color and had to ask the sacristan which cope to wear in ordinary time, as he could not tell red from green and took it only on faith that there were such colors in the world, but Brother Daniel—he'd have met Brother Daniel, the clerk outside?—assured him it was so, and surely a man with a face like that would never lie, you had only to look at the size of his nose to know that), and other things to which Jamie could nod or smile or make a noise. And all the time, the green eyes searched his face—kind but penetrating.

The abbot saw the moment when Jamie felt once more in

command of himself and sat back a little, inviting him by posture more than words to state his business.

"If I might ask a moment of your time, Father . . ." He drew the folded sheet of paper out of his bosom and handed it across. "I know ye've a reputation for learning and history, and I ken my uncle said ye've a rare collection of tales of the Auld Ones. I should value your opinion of this bit of verse."

Abbot Michael's brows were thick and white, with long hairs curling wildly in the manner of old men. These perked up, vibrating with interest, and he bent his attention to the paper, eyes flicking from line to line like a hummingbird in a flower patch.

Jamie's own eyes had been traveling round the room as Abbot Michael talked. It was an interesting place—any place where work was done interested him—and he stood up with a murmured excuse and went to the bookshelves, leaving the abbot to his close inspection of the poem.

The room was as big as the Duke of Pardloe's library and had at least as many books, and yet the feeling of it was more akin to the small cluttered hole in which Pardloe clearly did his thinking.

You could tell from the books whether a library was meant for show or not. Books that were used had an open, interested feel to them, even if closed and neatly lined up on a shelf in strict order with their fellows. You felt as though the book took as much interest in you as you did in it and was willing to help when you reached for it.

The abbot's books were even more overt. A dozen volumes—at least—lay open on the big table by the window, half of them lying on top of one another, all open, and leaves of scribbled notes sticking out of the pile, wavering—beckoning—in the draft from the window.

Jamie felt a strong desire to go across and see what the open books were, to go to the shelves and run his knuckles gently over the leather and wood and buckram of the bindings until a book should speak to him and come willingly into his hand.

It had been a long time since he'd owned a book.

The abbot had read through the sheet several times, with interest, then frowning in concentration, soft lips moving silently over the words. Now he sat back with a small, explosive 'hmmph!' and looked over it at Jamie.

"Well, now, there's a piece of work," he said. "Would you know who wrote it?"

"I would not, Father. It was given into my hand by an Englishman, but it wasn't him who wrote it. He'd been sent it and wanted me to translate it for him. Which I did but poorly, I'm afraid, me not having the Irish close to my tongue."

"Mmm-hmm, mmm-hmm." The abbot's childlike fingers tapped gently on the page, as though he might feel out the truth of the words.

"I've never seen a thing like it," he said at last, sitting back in his little chair. "There are a deal of stories about the Wild Hunt—you'll know that, maybe?"

"I ken 'Tam Lin,' though it's nay a Highland tale. A man from the Lowlands told it, when we were in prison together."

"Aye," the abbot said thoughtfully. "Aye, that's right; it's from the Borders. And this wee sheet doesn't mention anything from Tam Lin's tale—save maybe for this reference to the *teind.* Ye'll know that word, will you?"

Jamie hadn't much noticed the word when doing his own translation, but at the speaking of it felt a prickling of the hairs across his shoulders, like a dog putting up its hackles at a scent.

"A tithe?" he said.

The abbot nodded, tapping his fingers now against his chin as he thought.

"A tithe to hell. Some versions of the tale have it, and some don't. But the notion is that the faeries owe a tithe to hell, for their long lives—and that tithe is one of their number, given over once every seven years."

His lips pursed, pink and clean in the neat frame of his beard. "But I'll swear this isn't truly old, as you might think. I couldn't be saying, now, without a good bit more thought, what it is exactly about this"—he rubbed his fingers softly over the lines—"that makes me think it was a man of this century who wrote it, but I do think that."

Father Michael rose abruptly from his desk. "D'you find that you think better on your feet? I do, and a wearisome thing it is in the chapter meetings, the brothers going on at length and me wanting to leap from my seat and dance a jig in the middle of the room to clear my mind but pinned in my chair like that small little fellow there."

He gestured toward a glass case on one of the shelves, in which a gigantic beetle with a huge horny protuberance on its head was pinned to a sheet of thin wood. The sight of its thorny legs and tiny, nasty clawed feet gave Jamie a strong crawling sensation down his back.

"A grand specimen, Father," he said, eyeing it warily.

"Do you like it? 'Twas sent me by a friend from Westphalia, a Jew. A most philosophical sort of Jew," he assured Jamie, "a man of rare parts named Stern. Look, he sent me this, as well."

He plucked a discolored chunk of what looked like ivory out of the clutter on the shelf and put it into Jamie's hand. It proved to be an enormous tooth, long and curving to a blunt point.

"Recognize that, do you?"

"It's the tooth of something verra large that eats flesh, Father," Jamie said, smiling slightly. "But I couldna tell ye is it a lion or a bear, having not had the advantage of bein' bitten by either one. Yet," he added, with a discreet sign against evil. "But as I havena heard that there are lions in Germany . . ."

The abbot laughed.

"Most observant, *mo mhic,* a bear is just what it is. A cave bear. You'll have heard of them?"

"I have not," Jamie said obligingly, recognizing that this apparently idle chat was in fact the abbot's means of walking up and down while turning over the question of the poem in his head. Besides, he was in no hurry to return to his companions. With luck, one of them would have killed the other before he came back, thus simplifying his life. At the moment, he didn't much mind which one survived.

"These would be the massive things, sure. Stern gave me the measurements he'd taken of the thing's skull, and I tell you, man, 'twould be as long as the distance from your elbow to the tip of your longest finger—and I do mean yours, and not mine," he added, twinkling and flexing his wee arm in demonstration.

"All gone now, though, alas," he said, and shook his head regretfully. "There are bears still in the German forests, the creatures, but nothing on the lines of the fellow that bore that tooth. Stern thinks it's some thousands of years old."

"Oh, aye?" Jamie said, not knowing quite what to say to that.

His eye had caught the glint of metal on the shelf, and he squinted, trying to make it out. It was a glass box, with something dark inside, and the gleam of gold within that. But what—

"Oh, you've spotted our hand!" said the abbot, delighted at the chance to show another of his curiosities. "Now, there's a thing!"

He stood on his tiptoes to reach down the box and beckoned Jamie over to the broad table, washed in sunlight from the open window. There was a flowering vine of some kind twining round the window, and the monastery's herb garden was visible outside. The fine spring day washed in on a tide of sweet scent—all of these overpowered when the abbot opened the box.

"Peat?" Jamie said, though there could be no doubt about it. The curled black object—which was indeed a human hand, broken off at the wrist and dried in some way—gave off the same acrid tang as the peat bricks that graced every hearth in Ireland.

The abbot nodded, moving the hand delicately so the ring wedded to the skin of one bony finger showed more clearly.

"One of the brothers found it in a bog. We didn't know whose it was, but clearly 'twas no peasant. Well, we poked about a bit more and found butter, of course—"

"Butter? In the bog?"

"*Beannachtaí m' mhic,* everyone puts their butter into the bog in summer to keep cool. Now and then, the woman o' the house forgets just where she put it—or maybe dies, poor creature—and there it sits in its wee bucket. We often find butter when the lay brothers cut peats for the fire. Not often edible," he added, with regret. "But recognizable, even after a great long while. Peat preserves things." He nodded at the hand. "And as I was saying, we went back and prodded and cut a bit, and eventually we found the rest of him."

Jamie had a sudden odd feeling that someone was standing just behind his shoulder, but fought back the urge to turn round.

"He was lying on his back, as though he'd been laid out dead, and he had on rough breeks and a cloak with a small gold brooch to fasten it at the throat. Speaking of throats, someone had cut his for him, and had bashed in his head for good measure." The abbot smiled, though without his usual humor. "And to make quite sure of the thing, there was a thin rope wrapped tight round his neck."

The feeling of someone behind him was so strong that Jamie

shifted his position, as though to relieve some stiffness, and took the opportunity for a quick glance. No one there, of course.

"You've not the Irish, you say—so I suppose you'll not know the *Aided Diarnmata meic Cerbaill*? Or *Aided Muirchertaig meic Erca*?"

"Ah . . . no. Though . . . does *aided* mean, perhaps, 'death'?" It was nothing like the *Gàidhlig* word for it, but he thought he'd maybe heard it from Quinn, muttering about Grey.

The abbot nodded, as though this ignorance was forgivable, if regrettable.

"Aye, it does. Both those poems tell of men who suffered the threefold death—that being a procedure usually reserved for gods or heroes, but, in the case of *Diarnmata* and *Muirchertaig meic Erca,* was imposed for crimes committed against the Church."

Jamie backed a little away from the table and leaned against the wall, folding his arms in what he hoped was a casual manner. The hair still prickled under the clubbed queue at his neck, but he felt somewhat better.

"And ye're thinking that this"—he nodded at the hand—"gentleman had done something o' the sort?"

"I shouldn't think so," the abbot said, "but the sorry fact is, we don't know." He put down the lid of the glass box with gentle fingers and left them resting there.

"We dug quite a bit and harvested three months' worth of peats for our trouble, which was quite enough reward in itself, as I told the brothers who did the work, but we found near the body the gold hilt of a sword—I'm afraid peat does not preserve baser metals at all well—and a cup, inlaid with jewels. And some little distance away—those." He gestured toward the far wall of the study, where two large curving bits of metal gleamed in the shadow.

"What are they?" Jamie was loath to leave the shelter of his wall, but curiosity drove him toward the objects, which upon inspection proved to be a sort of primitive trumpet, though with a curved long stalk and a flattened end rather than a bell.

"A very old woman who lives near the bog told me that they're called *lir,* but I've no notion how she knows, and neither did she. Obviously there was more ceremony than murder about this man's death, though."

The abbot rubbed a knuckle absently across his upper lip.

"Word got about, of course," he said. "And the talk! The folk of the country thought he might be everything from the High King of the Druids—assuming there ever to have been such a creature—to Fionn MacCumhaill, though why he should be lying in a bog and not having it away with the female denizens of Tír na nÓg, I don't know—to St. Hugelphus."

"St. Hugelphus? Is there a St. Hugelphus?"

The abbot's hand dragged down over his chin and he shook his head, defeated by the perversity of his flock.

"No, but not a whit of good does it do for me to tell them so. They were after building a special chapel and putting the poor fellow's body in it in a glass case, with beeswax candles burning at the head and foot." He glanced at Jamie, one brow lifted. "You say you're newly come to Ireland, so you'll maybe not know how it is with the Catholics here, since the penal laws."

"I could maybe guess," Jamie said, and the abbot smiled in wry response.

"Maybe you could, at that. Leave it that the monastery once owned as much land as a man could walk over in half a day. Now we've the buildings left, barely the ground to grow a few heads of cabbage, and lucky to have it. As to dealings with the government and the Protestant landowners, especially the Anglo-Irish settlers . . ." His lips tightened. "The very last thing I need is to have flocks of pilgrims making their way here to venerate a false saint covered in gold."

"How did ye stop it?"

"We put the poor fellow back in the bog," the abbot said frankly. "I doubt he was a Christian, but I said a proper Mass for him, and we buried him with the words. I let it be known that I'd taken his jewels off and sent them to Dublin—I did send the brooch and the sword hilt—to discourage anyone looking to dig him up again. We mustn't put folk in the way of temptation, now, must we? D'you want to see the cup?"

Jamie's heart gave an unexpected thump, but he nodded, keeping an expression of mild interest on his face.

The abbot stretched up on his tiptoes to reach down a bunch of keys that hung from a hook by the door and beckoned Jamie to come along.

Outside in the cloister walk, the day was fine, and fat bees buzzed over the herb garden that lay within the square of the cloister, dusted thick with the yellow pollen. The air was mild, but Jamie could not get rid of the sense of chill that had struck him at sight of that clawed black hand with its gold ring.

"Father," he blurted, "why did you keep his hand?"

The abbot had reached a carved wooden door and was groping through his ring of keys, but looked up at that.

"The ring," he said. "There are runes upon it, and I think them maybe done in the old Ogham way of writing. I didn't like to take the thing off, for it's plain to see that you couldn't do it without pulling the finger to pieces. So I kept the hand, in order to make a drawing of the ring and its markings, meaning to send it to a fellow I know who claims to have some notion of Ogham. I was meaning to bury the hand with the rest of the body—and still am," he added, finding the key he wanted. "I just haven't found the time to do it. Here, now—" The door swung open, silent on leather hinges, revealing a set of steps, and a smell of onions and potatoes floated up from the depths of a dark cellar.

For an instant, Jamie wondered why one would lock a root cellar but then realized that, with the famine Quinn had spoken of still green in the memory of Ireland, food might be the most valuable thing the monastery had.

There was a lantern and a tinderbox standing on the top step; Jamie lighted the lantern for the abbot, then followed him down, privately amused at the abbot's practicality in finding a hiding place for a valuable thing, shoved casually behind a row of last winter's apples wizened by now into wrinkled things the size of a cow's eyeball.

It was valuable, too; a glance was enough to show him that. The cup was about the size of a small quaich and fit in the palm of his hand when the Abbot gave it to him.

It was made of a polished wood, to his surprise, rather than gold. Stained and darkened by immersion in the peat, but still beautifully made. There was a carving in the bottom of the bowl, and gemstones—uncut, but polished—were set round the rim, each one sunk into a small carved depression and apparently fastened there with some sort of resin.

The cup gave him the same feeling he'd had in the abbot's study: the sense that someone—or something—was standing close behind him. He didn't like it at all, and the abbot saw that.

"What is it, *mo mhic*?" he asked quietly. "Does this speak to you?"

"Aye, it does," he said, trying for a smile. "And I think it's saying, '*Put me back.*'" He handed the cup to the abbot, repressing a strong urge to wipe his hand on his breeks.

"Is it an evil thing, do you think?"

"I canna say that, Father. Only that it gives me the cold grue to touch it. But"—he clasped his hands behind his back and leaned forward—"what is the thing carved into the bottom there?"

"A *carraig mór,* or so I think. A long stone." The abbot turned the bowl, holding it sideways so that the lantern light illumined the dish. The cold grue slid right down the backs of Jamie's legs, and he shuddered. The carving showed what was plainly a standing stone—cleft down the center.

"Father," he said abruptly, making up his mind on the moment. "I've a thing or two to tell ye. Might ye hear my confession?"

THEY STOPPED BRIEFLY for Father Michael to fetch his stola, then walked out across the sheep field and into a small apple orchard, thick with scent and the humming of bees. There they found a couple of stones to sit upon, and he told the abbot, as simply as he could, about Quinn, the notion of a fresh Jacobite rising from Ireland, and the idea of using the Druid king's *Cupán* to legitimize the Stuarts' last bid for the throne of three kingdoms.

The abbot sat clutching the ends of the purple stola that hung round his neck, head down, listening. He didn't move or make any response while Jamie laid out for him Quinn's plan. When Jamie had finished, though, Father Michael looked up at him.

"Did you come to steal the cup for this purpose yourself?" the abbot asked, quite casually.

"No!" He spoke from astonishment rather than resentment; the abbot saw it and smiled faintly.

"No, of course not." He was sitting on a rock, the cup itself perched on his knee. He looked down at it, contemplating. "Put it back, you said."

"It's no my place to say, Father. But I—" The presence that had hovered near him earlier had vanished, but the memory of it was cold in his mind. "It—he—he wants it back, Father," he blurted. "The man ye found in the bog."

The abbot's green eyes went wide, and he studied Jamie closely. "He spoke to you, did he?"

"Not in words, no. I—I feel him. Felt him. He's gone now."

The abbot picked up the cup and peered into it, his thumb stroking the ancient wood. Then he put it down on his knee and, looking at Jamie, said quietly, "There's more, is there not? Tell me."

Jamie hesitated. Grey's business was not his to share—and it had nothing to do with the bog-man, the cup, nor anything that was the abbot's concern. But the priest's green eyes were on him, kind but firm.

"It's under the seal, you know, *mo mhic,*" he said, conversationally. "And I can see you've a burden on your soul."

Jamie closed his eyes, the breath going out of him in a long, long sigh.

"I have, Father," he said. He got up from the stone where he'd sat and knelt down at the abbot's feet.

"It's not a sin, Father," he said. "Or most of it's not. But it troubles me."

"Tell God, and let him ease you, man," the abbot said, and, taking Jamie's hands, placed them on his bony knees and laid his own hand gently on Jamie's head.

He told it all. Slowly, with many hesitations. Then faster, the words beginning to find themselves. What the Greys wanted of him, and how they had made him come to Ireland. How it was, caught between the loyalty of his old friendship to Quinn and his present forced obligation to John Grey. Swallowing, face burning and hands tight on the black cloth of the abbot's habit, he told about Grey's feeling for him and what had passed between them in the stable at Helwater. And finally—with the feeling of jumping from a high cliff into a roaring sea—he told about Willie. And Geneva.

There were tears running down his face before he had finished. When Jamie had come to the end of it, the abbot drew his hand softly down Jamie's cheek before dipping his hand into his robe and coming out with a large, worn, mostly clean black handkerchief, which he handed him.

"Sit, man," he said. "Bide for a bit, and rest while I think."

Jamie got up and sat on the flat stone again, blowing his nose and wiping his face. He felt emptied of turmoil, purged. And more at peace than he'd been since the days before Culloden.

His mind was blank, and he made no effort to inscribe anything on it. He breathed freely, no tightness in his chest. That was enough. There was more, though: the spring sun came out from behind the clouds and warmed him, a bee lighted briefly on his sleeve, spilling grains of yellow pollen when it rose, and the bruised grass where he'd knelt smelled of rest and comfort.

He had no idea how long he'd sat in this pleasant state of exhausted mindlessness. But Father Michael stirred at last, stretched his old back with a muffled groan, and smiled at him.

"Well, now," he said. "Let's begin with the easy bits. You're not in the habit of fornicating regularly with young women, I hope? Good. Don't start. If you feel you—no." He shook his head. "No. I was going to recommend that you find a good girl and marry her, but I saw how it is with you; your wife's still with you." He spoke in an entirely matter-of-fact tone of voice.

"It wouldn't be fair on a young woman, were you to marry

while that's the case. At the same time, you mustn't cling over-long to the memory of your wife; she's safe with God now, and you must deal with your life. Soon . . . but you'll know when it's right. Meanwhile, avoid the occasion of sin, aye?"

"Aye, Father," Jamie said obediently, thinking briefly of Betty. He'd avoided her so far, and certainly meant to keep doing so.

"Cold baths help. That and reading. Now, your son . . ." These words were equally matter-of-fact but gave Jamie a breathless feeling, a small bubble of happiness beneath his ribs—one that popped with the abbot's next words.

"You must do nothing to endanger him." The abbot looked at him seriously. "You've no claim on him, and from what you say, he's well settled. Might it not be better—for the both of you—for you to leave this place where he is?"

"I—" Jamie began, hardly knowing where to begin for the rush of words and feelings that flooded his brain, but the abbot raised a hand.

"Aye, I know you said you're a paroled prisoner—but from what you say regarding the service these English require of you, I think there is an excellent chance that you might win your freedom as a result."

Jamie thought so, too, and the thought filled him with a violent confusion. To be free was one thing—to leave his son was another. Two months ago, he might have been able to leave, knowing William well looked after. Not now.

He forced down the sense of violent refusal the abbot's words had roused in him.

"Father—I hear what ye say. But . . . the boy has no father, no man to . . . to show him the way of being a man. His grandfather's a worthy gentleman, but very old, and the man who was legally his father is . . . is dead." He drew a deep breath; need he confess that he had killed the old earl? No. He'd done it to save

William's life, and that could be no sin. "If I thought for an instant that my presence there was danger to him, rather than benefit—I would go at once. But I do not think I delude myself in thinking that . . . he needs me."

The last words came hoarsely, and the abbot regarded him closely for a moment, before nodding.

"You must pray for the strength to do the right thing—God will give it to you."

He nodded mutely. He'd prayed for strength like that twice before, and it had been granted. He hadn't thought he'd survive, either time, but he had. He hoped if it came to a third time, he wouldn't.

"I thought ye said this was the easy bits," Jamie said, forcing a smile.

The abbot grimaced, not without sympathy.

"Easy to see what's to do, I meant. Not necessarily easy to do it." He stood up and brushed a fuzzy catkin from the shoulder of his robe. "Come, let's be walking a bit. A man could turn to stone sitting too long."

They paced slowly through the orchard and out into a stretch of fields, some left in meadow for a few sheep and the odd cow, some sowed and already sprouting, a green haze covering the furrows. They kept to the edges, not to trample the young neeps and tattie-vines, and eventually emerged on the edge of a bog.

This was a proper bog, not merely the soggy clay or spongy footing common everywhere in Ireland. A treeless gray-green bumpy landscape, it stretched a good half mile before them to a tiny hillock of rock in the far distance, from which a stunted pine tree sprouted, flaglike in the wind. For once out of the shelter of the trees, the wind had come up and sang about their ears, flapping the ends of Father Michael's stola and tugging at the skirts of their clothing.

Father Michael beckoned to him, and, following, he found a wooden trackway, half sunk between the hummocks of moss-choked grass that rose up among a thousand tiny channels and pools.

"I don't know who made these tracks to begin with," the abbot remarked, setting a sandaled foot on the thin planks. "They've been here longer than any man remembers. We keep them up, though; it's the only safe way across the moss."

Jamie nodded; the planks gave slightly when stepped upon, water oozing through the cracks between. But they bore his weight, though the vibration of his step made the bog beside the trackway tremble, the antennae of moss quivering in curiosity as he passed.

"The Old Ones thought the number three holy, just as we do." Father Michael's words, half-shouted above the wind, drifted back to him. "They had the three gods—the god of thunder, him they called Taranis. Then Esus, the god of the underworld—mind, they didn't see the underworld quite the same way we think of hell, but it wasn't a pleasant place, nonetheless."

"And the third?" Jamie was still clutching the abbot's handkerchief. He wiped his nose with it; the chill wind made it stream.

"Ah, now, that would be . . ." The abbot didn't stop walking but tapped his fingers briskly on his skull, to assist thought. "Now, who in creation . . . Oh, of course. The third is the god of the particular tribe, so they'd all have different names."

"Oh, aye." Was the abbot telling him this only to pass the time? He wondered. Obviously they weren't out walking for their health, and he knew of only one reason they might be traversing a bog.

He was right.

"Now, a proper god requires sacrifice, does he not? And the old gods wanted blood."

He'd drawn close to the abbot now and could hear him clearly, despite the whine of the wind. There were birds in the moss, too; he heard the call of a snipe, thin and high.

"They would take prisoners of war and burn them in great wicker cages, for Taranis." The abbot turned his head to look back at Jamie, showing a smile. "A good thing for you the English are more civilized now?" The ironic question at the end of this remark was evidently meant to convey the abbot's doubt regarding the level of English civilization, and Jamie gave him back a wry smile, acknowledging it. Being burned alive . . . well, they'd done that, too, the English. Fired crofts and fields, without regard to the women and children they condemned—either by the fire itself, or by cold and slow starvation.

"I'm fortunate, to be sure, Father."

"They do still hang men—the English," the abbot said thoughtfully. It wasn't a question, but Jamie gave an obliging grunt.

"That was the means of dispatch preferred by Esus—hanging or stabbing. Sometimes both!"

"Well, the hanging doesna always answer," Jamie replied, a little tersely. "Sometimes a man will live, in spite of it. Which," he added, in hopes of leading the abbot on to the point he seemed to be tending toward, "is why whoever did in your bogman wrapped the rope around his neck instead. Though I should have thought the bashing and throat-cutting and drowning—assuming he had any breath left to drown with—would have made it certain enough in any case."

The abbot nodded, unperturbed. The wind was pulling wisps of his white hair loose and causing them to wave about his tonsure, much like the wisps of bog-cotton that grew near the track.

"Teutates," he said triumphantly. "That's the name of one of the old tribal gods, at least. Aye, he took his victims into his embrace in the water—drowning in sacred wells and the like. This way." He had come to a spot where the trackway forked, half of it going off toward the little hillock, the other toward a gaping hole in the bog. That would be where the monks were in the habit of cutting their peats, Jamie supposed—and where they'd found the bog-man, whose grave they were almost certainly heading for.

Why? he wondered uneasily. The abbot's conversation had implied that this wee expedition had something to do with Jamie's confession—and, whatever it was, it wasn't meant to be easy.

But he hadn't yet been absolved of his sins. And so he followed, as the abbot turned toward the hill.

"I didn't think I should put him straight back where he came from," Father Michael explained, flattening the flying wisps of hair with his palm. "Someone cutting peats would just be digging him up again, and the whole wearisome business to do again."

"So ye put him under the hill," Jamie said, and a sudden chill went up his back at the phrase. That was in the poem "The King from Under the Hill"—and, to his knowledge, the folk "under the hill" were the Auld Ones, the faerie folk. His mouth was dry from the wind, and he had to swallow before speaking further. Before he could ask his question, though, the abbot bent to take off his sandals and, hiking up the skirts of his robe, skipped on ahead.

"This way," he called back over his shoulder. "We'll need to wade the last little bit!"

Muttering—but carefully avoiding blasphemy—Jamie stripped off shoes and stockings and followed the abbot's footsteps carefully. He was twice the abbot's size; there was no chance the priest would be able to pull him free, should he strike a shaking quagmire and sink.

The dark water purled up between his toes, cold but not unpleasant on his bare feet. He could feel the springy peat beneath it, spongy, slightly prickling. He sank ankle-deep at each step, but no further, and came ashore on the little hillock with no more damage than a few splashes to his breeks.

"Well, then," Father Michael said, turning to him. "The difficult part."

FATHER MICHAEL LED HIM to the top of the little hillock, and there beneath the pine tree was a crude seat, carved out of the native stone. It was blotched with blue and green and yellow lichens and had plainly stood there for centuries.

"This is the High Seat—the *árd chnoc*—where the kings of this place were confirmed before the old gods," the priest said, and crossed himself. Jamie did likewise, impressed despite himself. It was a very old place, and the stone seemed to hold a deep silence; even the wind over the bog had died, and he could hear his heart beating in his chest, slow and steady.

Father Michael reached into the leather pouch he wore at his belt and, to Jamie's disquiet, drew out the gem-studded wooden cup, which he placed gently on the ancient seat.

"I know what you once were," he said to Jamie, in a conversational tone of voice. "Your uncle Alex would write to me with news of you, during the Rising. You were a great warrior for the king. The rightful king."

"That was a long time ago, Father." He was beginning to have an uneasy feeling, and not only because of the cup, though the sight of it was making the hair prickle on his neck again.

The abbot straightened up and eyed him appraisingly.

"You're in the prime of your manhood, *Shéamais Mac Bhrian,*" he said. "Is it right that you should waste the strength and the gift you have for leading men?" *Jesus God, he wants me to do it,* Jamie thought, appalled. *Take that cursed thing and do as Quinn wants.*

"Is it right for me to lead men to their deaths, for the sake of a vain cause?" he asked, sharply enough that the abbot blinked.

"Vain? The cause of the Church, of God? To restore the anointed king and remove the foot of the English from the neck of your people and mine?"

"Vain, Father," he said, striving for calmness, though the mere thought of the Rising in Scotland tightened every muscle he had. "Ye know what I was, ye say. But ye dinna ken what I saw, what happened there. Ye havena seen what happened after, when the clans were crushed—crushed, Father! When they—" He stopped abruptly and closed his eyes, mouth pressed tight shut 'til he should recover himself.

"I hid," Jamie said, after a moment. "On my own land. Hid in a cave for seven years, for fear of the English." He took a deep breath and felt the scars tight on his back, burning. He opened his eyes and fixed the priest's gaze with his own.

"I came down one night to hunt, perhaps a year past the time of Culloden. I passed a burnt-out croft, one I'd passed a hundred times. But rain had washed out the path and I stepped aside—and I stepped on her." He swallowed, remembering the heart-stopping snap of the bone under his foot. The terrible delicacy of the tiny ribs, the sprinkle of bones that had once been hands, strewn careless as pebbles.

"A wee lass. She'd been there months. . . . The foxes and corbies . . . I didna ken which one she was. There were three of them lived there, three wee lassies, near in age, and their hair brown—it was all that was left of her, her hair—so I couldna say was she Mairi or Beathag or wee Cairistiona—I—" He stopped speaking, abruptly.

"I said it would be difficult." The priest spoke quietly, not looking away. His eyes were dark, the brightness of them shadowed but steady. "Do you think I've not seen such things here?"

"Do ye want to see them again?" His hands had curled into fists without his knowledge.

"Will they stop?" the priest snapped. "Will ye condemn your countrymen and mine to such cruelties, to the rule of the yellow-johns, for lack of will? I'd not thought from Alexander's letters that ye lacked courage, but perhaps he was wrong in what he thought of you."

"Oh, no, Father," he said, and his voice dropped low in his throat. "Dinna be trying that one on me. Aye, I ken what it is to lead men, and how it's done. I'll not be led."

Father Michael gave a brief snort, half amused, but his eyes stayed dark.

"Is it the boy?" he asked. "You'd turn aside from your duty—from the thing God has called you to do!—to be a lickspittle to the English, to wear their chains, to go and tend a child who does not need you, who will never bear your name?"

"No," Jamie said between his teeth. "I have left home and family before, for the sake of duty. I lost my wife to it. And I saw what that duty led to. Mind me, Father—if it comes to war, it will not be different this time. It. Will. Not. Be. Different!"

"Not if men like you will not chance it! Mind what I say—there are sins of omission, as well as those of commission. And remember the parable of the talents, will you now. Do you mean to stand before God, come the Last Day, and tell Him you spurned the gifts He gave you?"

It came to Jamie quite suddenly that Father Michael knew.

Knew what, or how much, Jamie couldn't say—but the news of Quinn's machinations perhaps fitted in with other things Father Michael knew, of the Irish Jacobites. This was not the first inkling he'd had of what was afoot, Jamie would swear to it.

He gathered himself, pushing down his temper. The man was doing his own duty—as he saw it.

"Is there a lang stone like that one somewhere nearby?" he asked, lifting his chin toward the cup. The cleft stone carved into its bowl wasn't visible from where he stood, but there was a feeling on the back of his neck like a cool wind blowing—and the boughs of the little pine tree were still.

Father Michael was disconcerted by this sudden change of subject.

"I—why . . . Aye, there is." He turned his head toward the west, where the sun was slowly sinking behind a scrim of cloud, red as a fresh-fired cannonball, and pointed beyond the edge of the bog. "A mile or so that way. There's a wee circle of stones, standing in a field. One of them is cleft like that." He turned back, looking curiously at Jamie. "Why?"

Why, indeed. Jamie's mouth was dry and he swallowed, but without much effect. Must he tell the priest exactly why he was certain that this effort to restore the Stuarts would not succeed, any more than the Rising in Scotland had?

No, he decided. He wouldn't. Claire was his, alone. There was nothing sinful in his love for her, nothing that concerned Father Michael, and he meant to keep her to himself.

Beyond that, he thought wryly, *if I told him, he'd be convinced I'd lost my wits—or was trying to feign madness to wriggle out of this foolish coil.*

"Why did ye bring that here?" he asked, ignoring the priest's question and nodding at the cup.

Father Michael looked at him for a time without answering, then lifted one shoulder.

"If you should be the man that God has chosen for the task, then I meant to give it to you, to use as you thought best. If you are not . . ." He squared his shoulders under the black broadcloth of his habit. "Then I shall give it back to its original owner."

"I am not, Father," Jamie said. "I canna touch the thing. Perhaps it's a sign that I am not the man."

The look of curiosity returned. "Do you . . . feel his presence? The bog-man? Now?"

"I do." He did, too; the sense of someone standing behind him was back and had about it something of . . . eagerness? Desperation? He could not say what it was exactly, but it was bloody unsettling.

Was the dead man one like Claire? Was that the meaning of the carving in the bowl? If so, what fate had come upon him, to leave him here, in this place of desolation, far from wherever he had come?

Doubt seized him suddenly in jaws of iron. What if she had not made it back through the stones, back to safety? What if she, like the man who lay beneath the black waters here, had gone astray? Horror clenched his fists so tightly that the nails cut into his palms, and he kept them so, clung to the realness of the physical pain with stubborn force, so that he might dismiss the much more painful thought as something unreal, insubstantial.

Lord, that she might be safe! he prayed in agony. *She and the child!*

"Absolve me, Father," he whispered. "I would go now."

The abbot's lips pressed tight, reluctant, and the hair trigger of Jamie's temper went off.

"Do you think to blackmail me by withholding absolution? Ye blackguard priest! You would betray your vows and your office for the sake of—"

Father Michael stopped him with an upraised hand. He glared

at Jamie for a moment, unmoving, then traced the sign of the cross in the air, in sharp, precise movements.

"Ego te absolvo, in nomine Patris—"

"I'm sorry, Father," Jamie blurted. "I shouldna have spoken to ye like that. I—"

"We'll count that as part of your confession, shall we?" murmured Father Michael. "Say the rosary every day for a month; there's your penance." The shadow of a wry smile crossed his face, and he finished, *"et Filii, et Spiritus Sancti, Amen."* He lowered his hand and spoke normally.

"I didn't think to ask how long it had been since your last confession. D'you remember how the Act of Contrition goes, or had I best help you?" It was said seriously, but Jamie saw the trace of the leprechaun lurking in those bright green eyes. Father Michael folded his hands and bowed his head, as much to hide a smile as for piety.

"Mon Dieu, je regrette . . ." He said it in French, as he always had. And as it always had, a sense of peace came upon him with the saying.

He stopped speaking, and the air of the evening was still.

For the first time, he saw what he had not seen before: the mound of slightly darker rock and soil, speckled with the sprouting green blades of fresh grass, spangled with the tiny jewels of wildflowers. And a small wooden cross at the head of it, just under the pine tree.

Dust to dust. This was the stranger's grave, then; they had given him burial in the Christian way, letting the unseemly jumble of bones and leather, so long preserved in dark water, crumble at last in peaceful anonymity. Here, by the seat of kings.

The sun was still above the horizon, but the light came low, and shadows lay dark upon the bog, ready to rise and join the coming night.

"Wait for a bit, *mo mhic,*" Father Michael said, reaching to retrieve the cup. "Let me put this away safe, and I'll see ye back."

In the distance, Jamie could see the dark gash of the pit where the peat-cutters had been at work. They called that sort of place a moss-hag in Scotland, he thought, and wondered briefly what—or who?—might lie in other bogs.

"Dinna fash yourself, Father," he said, looking out across the tumps and hummocks, the shallow pools glinting in the last of the sun. "I'll find my own way."

20

Stalking Horse

QUINN HAD GONE, PRESUMABLY TO TEND TO HIS OWN BUSIness. Jamie found his absence soothing but not reassuring; Quinn hadn't gone far. Jamie told Grey what the abbot had said regarding the Wild Hunt poem, and after some discussion it was decided that Jamie should make the first approach to Siverly.

"Show him the Wild Hunt poem," Grey had suggested. "I want to know if he seems to recognize it. If not, there's at least the possibility that it has nothing to do with him and was somehow included with Carruthers's packet by mistake. If he *does* recognize it, though, I want to know what he says about it." He'd smiled at Jamie, eyes alight with the imminence of action. "And once you've spied out the land for me, I'll have a better notion of which tack to take when I see him."

A stalking horse, Jamie noted dourly. At least Grey had been honest about that.

On Tom Byrd's advice, Jamie wore the brown worsted suit, as being more suitable to a day call in the country—the puce velvet was much too fine for such an occasion. There had been an argument between Tom and Lord John as to whether the yellow silk waistcoat with the blackwork was preferable to the plain cream-colored one, as indicating Jamie's presumed wealth, or not, as possibly being thought vulgar.

"I dinna mind if he thinks I'm common," Jamie assured Tom. "It will put him at his ease if he feels himself my superior. And the one thing we know of him for sure is that he likes money; so much the better if he thinks me a rich vulgarian."

Lord John made a noise that he hastily converted to a sneeze, causing both Jamie and Tom to look at him austerely.

Jamie was not sure how much—if at all—Siverly might recall him. He had seen Siverly only now and then in Paris, and only for a few weeks. He thought they might have exchanged words once in the course of a dinner, but that was the extent of their interaction. Still . . . Jamie recalled Siverly; it was not unthinkable that the man would remember him, particularly given Jamie's noticeable appearance.

In Paris, he had worked in his cousin Jared's wine business; he might reasonably have continued in trade, after the Rising. There would be no reason for Siverly either to have heard of his actions, nor to have followed his movements after Culloden.

Jamie hadn't bothered noting that his English speech would likely cause Siverly to regard him as a social inferior, no matter what he wore, and thus when he gave his horse to the gatekeeper who came out of the lodge to meet him, he broadened his accent slightly.

"What's the name of this place, lad?"

"Glastuig," the man said. "Will it be the place ye're lookin' for, then?"

"The verra place. Will your master be at home the day?"

"Himself's in the house," the gatekeeper said dubiously. "As for bein' at home . . . I'll send and see, if ye like, sir."

"Much obliged to ye, lad. Here, then, give him this—and that wee bawbee's for yourself." He handed over the note he'd prepared, enclosing the introduction from Sir Melchior and asking for an interview, along with a lavish thrupenny bit.

His role as a rich vulgarian thus promisingly begun, he furthered it by openly gaping at the imposing house and its extensive grounds as he walked slowly up the drive after the servant. It was an old house—he hadn't yet seen a newly built one in Ireland—but well kept up, its dark stonework freshly pointed and the chimneys—fourteen, he counted them—all alight and drawing well. Six good horses in the far pasture, including one that he wouldn't have minded seeing closer to—a big dark bay with a white blaze and a nice arse end; good muscle, he thought approvingly. A good-sized lawn spread out before the house, a gardener pushing a heavy roller over it with no perceptible enthusiasm, and the gardens themselves had a dull, prosperous gleam to their leaves, wet with the drizzling rain.

He was in no great doubt that he'd be admitted, and by the time he'd reached the door, there was a butler standing in it to take his hat and cloak and show him to a drawing room. Like the house itself, it was richly appointed—there was a huge silver candlestick, with six beeswax tapers shedding a gracious light—but lacking any great sense of style. He wandered slowly around the room, fingering the ornaments: a Meissen figurine of a woman, a dove perched on her hand, taking a comfit from her lips; a longcase clock with three dials, showing the time, the barometric pressure, and the phase of the moon; a tobacco humidor made of a dark, unfamiliar kind of wood that he thought might be African; a footed silver bowl full of sugared violets, jumbled and broken among a handful of ginger-nut biscuits; a vicious-looking club with a peculiar knob at the end; a curious piece of something . . . He picked it up to examine closer. It was a rectangular strip, perhaps ten inches by five (he measured it automatically, using the joints of his left middle finger as gauge), made of small, odd beads—what were they made of? Not glass . . . Shell?—strung on a woven thread in an interesting pattern of blue and white and black.

Surely no woman had assembled these things. He wondered just what the owner of such a magpie collection would be like. For all their delving into the man's antecedents, the Greys had given Jamie no coherent picture of Siverly's personality. Carruthers had painted a vivid portrait of the man—but his record was concerned only with the man's crimes and did little to reveal the man himself.

"A man may smile, and smile, and be a villain," he thought to himself. He had himself met personable villains. And amiable fools whose actions did more damage than deliberately wicked men. His mouth set at the memory of Charles Edward Stuart. He had no doubt that this Siverly was a villain—but what kind of villain?

A heavy, limping step came down the hall, and Major Siverly came in. He was still an imposing man, nearly as tall as Jamie himself, though a good deal older now and going to paunch. His face was slab-sided, the skin faintly gray, as though he'd been cut from the same rock as his house, and while he had adopted an expression of welcome, this was unable to conceal the clear lines of harshness and open cruelty in his face.

Jamie offered his hand and a cordial greeting, thinking to himself that any soldier unlucky enough to draw Siverly as a commander would have known at once what he was in for. "Failure to suppress a mutiny" was one of the charges against him.

"Your servant, sir," Siverly said politely, offering his hand in return. He looked Jamie over with a practiced glance—*nay a fool, no,* Jamie thought, as he made his own courtesies—but if he recalled Jamie, there was no hint of it in his manner.

"So Melchior Williamson says that you've something in

which I might have an interest," Siverly said abruptly. No offer of refreshment, nor even a seat, Jamie noted. Evidently he was not sufficiently interesting in himself as to merit much of the man's time.

"Aye, sir, I have," he answered, reaching into his bosom for the copy of the Wild Hunt poem he'd brought. "Sir Melchior said that you'd some expertise in matters of antiquity—as I see ye have." He nodded at the silver bowl, which he knew from its hallmark to have been made no more than fifty years prior and could plainly see was the work of a mediocre silversmith. Siverly's lip twitched, not quite curling, and he took the paper from Jamie, jerking his head at the settee in what was not quite an invitation to sit down.

Jamie sat, nonetheless. Siverly glanced briefly at the paper, clearly not expecting anything of interest—and then stiffened, looked at Jamie with a brief, piercing glare, then returned to the sheet. He read it through twice, turned the paper over to examine the back, then set it down carefully on the mantelpiece.

He walked over and stood in front of Jamie, looking down. Jamie gave him a bland look, keeping his feet under him in case the man went for his throat—from the look of him, it was in his mind.

"Who the bloody hell are you?" Siverly demanded. His voice was pitched low and was meant to sound dangerous.

Jamie smiled up at him. "Who do ye think I am?" he asked softly.

That gave Siverly pause. He stood looking at Jamie, his eyes narrowed, for quite a long time.

"Who gave you that paper?"

"A friend," Jamie replied, with complete truth. "His name is not mine to share." *Can I go further? "Is deonach é."* He is a volunteer.

That stopped Siverly as surely as if he had received a bullet in the heart. Very slowly, he lowered himself to a chair opposite, not taking his eyes from Jamie's face. Did a flicker of recognition stir in those eyes, or only at last suspicion?

Jamie's heart was beating fast and he felt the prickle of excitement down his forearms.

"No," Siverly said at last, and his voice had changed. It was casual now, dismissive. "I've no idea how your friend came by that paper, but it doesn't matter. The subject of the poem is ancient, to be sure. But the verse itself is no more ancient than you yourself are, Mr. Fraser. Anyone who's read Irish verse in a scholarly way could tell you that." He smiled, an expression that didn't reach his deep-set eyes, the color of rainwater on slate.

"What is your interest in such a thing, Mr. Fraser?" he asked, becoming overtly cordial. "If you are in the way to collect antiquities and curios, I should be pleased to give you an introduction to one or two dealers in Dublin."

"I should be most obliged to ye, sir," Jamie said pleasantly. "I did think of going to Dublin; I ken a man at the great university there to whom I thought of showing this. Perhaps your dealers might have an interest in it, too."

A spark of alarm flickered in the deep-set eyes. At what? Jamie wondered, but the answer came immediately. *He doesna want a great many people to see it—lest the wrong person hear about it. And who might that be, I wonder?*

"Really," Siverly said, pretending doubt. "What is the name of your university man? Perhaps I know him."

Jamie's mind went blank for an instant. He fumbled among the names of his Irish acquaintance for anyone he'd known who might conceivably be or have been at Trinity—but then caught sight of the tenseness of Siverly's shoulders. The man was trying it on as much as he was.

"O'Hanlon," he said carelessly, choosing a name at random. "Peter O'Hanlon. D'ye ken him?"

"No, I'm afraid not."

"Well, nay matter. I'll thank ye for your time, sir." Jamie leaned forward, preparatory to rising. He'd accomplished what he came for. He'd learned that the Irish poem was connected to Siverly and had some secret meaning—and he'd successfully fixed Siverly's attention on him as a person of interest, that was certain. The man was looking at him like a wolf with a prey in view.

"Where are you staying, Mr. Fraser?" he asked. "Perhaps I might discover some further information that would be helpful to you. If, that is, you are still interested in learning more regarding your verse?"

"Oh, aye, sir, that I am. I'm in the village, at Beckett's public house. Much obliged to ye, sir."

He stood and bowed to Siverly, then crossed the room to take the paper from the mantelpiece. He heard Siverly rise behind him, saying, "Not at all, Mr. Fraser."

The reflexes bred from a lifetime of people trying to kill him saved him. Jamie heard the man's sharp intake of breath and dodged aside, as the knob of the club slashed through the spot where his head had been and crashed down on the wooden mantel, making splinters fly.

Siverly was between him and the door. Jamie lowered his head and charged the man, butting him in the chest. Siverly stumbled back, hit a small table, and sent it flying in a shower of sugared violets, its collection of small ornaments bouncing and ringing off the floor.

Jamie made for the door, then by impulse doubled back, seized the paper, which had floated to the floor, and shoved the settee into Siverly's way as the man lunged for him, murder in his eye. He'd got hold of the club again and swung it as Jamie danced back, catching him a glancing blow on the point of the shoulder that numbed his arm to the fingers.

Jamie grabbed the candlestick and flung it at Siverly's head, the candles falling in a clatter of beeswax and smoke as they went out. There were running footsteps in the hall—servants coming.

Without the slightest hesitation, Jamie leapt onto a glove table by the window, kicked out the lights, and hurled himself through the resultant hole, catching a final ignominious blow across the arse as he did so.

He half-ran, half-hobbled straight through the formal garden, trampling roses and flower beds. Where was his horse? Had the gatekeeper taken it to the stable?

He had not. It was tied by the rein to a rail outside the lodge. Stuffing the crumpled paper into his coat, he undid the knot one-handed, blessing the Virgin Mother that Siverly had struck him on the right side. The numbness was fading, but tingling jolts buzzed down his right arm, jarring his fingers so they fumbled and twitched, all but useless. His clever left was all right, though, and before the gatekeeper had realized something was amiss and come out to see, he had flung himself onto the startled horse and was trotting down the road toward the village.

His left buttock was knotted tight, bruised from the blow, and he leaned in his saddle like a drunk, unable to put weight on it. He looked back over his shoulder, but there was no pursuit. *And why should there be?* he thought, breathing heavily. Siverly knew where to find him. And find him he would; the verse was only a copy, but Siverly didn't know that. Jamie touched the pocket of his coat, and the paper crackled reassuringly.

It was raining harder now, and water ran down his face. He'd left his hat and cloak; Tom Byrd would be annoyed. He smiled a little at the thought and, trembling with reaction, wiped his face on his sleeve.

He'd done his part. Now it was John Grey's turn.

21

A Poultice for Bruising

IN ORDER TO KEEP FROM GOING OUTSIDE EVERY FEW MINutes, Grey had accepted the invitation of two local men to join them at darts. One of his opponents had only one eye—or at least wore a patch over the problematic socket—but seemed little incommoded on that account, and Grey strongly suspected that the patch was mere gauze, doubled and dyed black, but no true obstacle to aim.

No stranger to sharp practice, his answer to this stratagem was the proposal that they play for pints rather than coin. This agreeable arrangement ensured that, regardless of skill or artifice, any man who won repeatedly would soon lose. The beer was good, and Grey managed for the most part not to think about what might be happening at Glastuig, but as the day drew down and the landlord began to light rush dips, he was unable to keep his thoughts at bay and thus excused himself from the game on grounds that he could no longer see to aim and stepped outside for a breath of air.

Outside, the rain had finally ceased, though the plants all bore such a burden of water that merely brushing the grass by the path soaked his stockings.

Quinn had gone off on unstated business of his own—and Grey would not have made a confidant of the Irishman in any case. Tom also had disappeared; Mr. Beckett had a comely daughter who served in the public room, but she had vanished, replaced by her mother. Grey didn't mind, but he would have liked to have someone with whom to share his worry over Jamie Fraser's prolonged absence.

There were of course excellent possible reasons for it. Siverly might have been intrigued by the poem, or by Fraser, and thus invited him to stay for supper in order to carry on their conversation. That would be the best possibility, Grey supposed.

Less good, but still acceptable, was the possibility—well, call it likelihood, given the state of the roads—that Fraser's horse had thrown a shoe or gone lame on the way back and had had to be walked, taken to a farrier, or, at worst, shot. They had sent back the livery's horses; Fraser was riding a nag borrowed from Mr. Beckett.

Running down the list of increasingly dire possibilities, Grey thought of highwaymen, who were attracted by the horse (surely not; the thing looked like a cow, and an elderly cow at that) and had then noticed the gaudy vest and shot Fraser when he was unable to produce any money. (He should have insisted Jamie have money; it wasn't right to keep him penniless.) A larger than usual mudhole that had forced him off the road, there to fall into a quaking bog, which had promptly swallowed him and the horse. A sudden apoplexy—Fraser had once mentioned that his father had died of an apoplexy. Were such things hereditary?

"Or perhaps a goose fell dead out of the sky and hit him on the head," he muttered, kicking viciously at a stone on the path. It shot into the air, struck a fence post, and ricocheted back, striking him smartly on the shin.

"Me lord?"

Clutching his shin, he looked up to see Tom hovering in the gloaming. At first assuming that his valet had been attracted by his cry of pain, he straightened up, dismissing it—but then saw the agitation of Tom's countenance.

"What—"

"Come with me, me lord," Tom said, low-voiced, and, glancing over his shoulder, led the way through a thick growth of weeds and brambles that put paid altogether to Grey's stockings.

Behind the pub, Tom led the way around a ramshackle chicken run and beckoned Grey toward an overgrown hedge.

"He's in here," he whispered, holding up a swath of branches.

Grey crouched down and beheld an extremely cross-looking James Fraser, ribbon lost, hair coming out of its plait, and a good bit of his face obscured by dried blood. He was hunched to one side and held one shoulder stiffly, higher than the other. The light under the hedge was dim, but there was sufficient left to make out the glare in the slanted blue eyes.

"Why are you sitting in the hedge, Mr. Fraser?" he inquired, having rapidly considered and discarded several other inquiries as being perhaps impolitic.

"Because if I go inside the pub at suppertime looking like this, the whole countryside is going to be talkin' about it by dawn, speculating about who did it. And everyone in said public house kens perfectly well that I'm wi' you. Meaning that Major Siverly will ken it's you on his trail by the time he's finished his coffee tomorrow morning." He shifted slightly and drew in his breath.

"Are you badly hurt?"

"I am not," Fraser said testily. "It's only bruises."

"Er . . . your face is covered with blood, sir," Tom said helpfully, in a tone suggesting that Fraser might not have noticed this, and then added, in substantially more horrified tones, "It's got onto your waistcoat!"

Fraser shot Tom a dark look suggesting that he meant to say something cutting about waistcoats, but whatever it was, he swallowed it, turning back to Grey.

"A wee shard o' glass cut my head, is all. It stopped bleeding some while ago. All I need is a wet cloth."

From the slow difficulty with which Fraser wormed his way out of the hedge, Grey rather thought a bit more than a wet cloth might be needed but forbore saying so.

"What happened?" he asked instead. "Was it an accident?"

"No." Fraser rolled clumsily onto hands and knees, got one knee up, foot braced—and then stopped, clearly contemplating the mechanical considerations involved in getting to his feet. Without comment, Grey stooped, got him under the left arm, and levered him into a standing position, this operation being accompanied by a muffled groan.

"I showed the poem to Siverly," Fraser said, jerking his coat straight. "He pretended not to know me, but he did. He read it, asked me who I was, then tried to dismiss it as a fraud of some sort, a faked antiquity. Then I turned my back to take my leave, and he tried to kill me." Despite obvious pain, he gave Grey a lopsided smile. "I suppose ye'd call that evidence, aye?"

"I would, yes." Grey gave him back the smile. "Thank you, Mr. Fraser."

"Ye're most welcome," Fraser said politely.

Tom arrived at this point with a bowl of water, a cloth, and an anxious-looking young woman.

"Oh, sir," she cried, seeing Fraser. "Mr. Tom said ye'd been thrown off your horse, the wicked creature, and into a ditch on your head! Are ye damaged at all?"

Fraser looked utterly outraged at the notion that he might

have been thrown by an aged mare—plainly this excuse for his appearance would never have occurred to him—but he luckily refrained from speaking his mind and submitted with grimaces to having his face swabbed clean. With ill grace and to the accompaniment of much sympathetic—and some derisive—comment from the taproom, he allowed Grey and Tom to assist him up the stairs, it having become obvious that he could not raise his left knee more than an inch or two. They lowered him upon the bed, whereat he gave an agonized cry and rolled onto one side.

"What's the matter?" Tom asked anxiously. "Have you injured your spine, Captain? Ye could be paralyzed, if it's your spine. Can ye wiggle your toes?"

"It's no my spine," Fraser said through his teeth. "It's my arse."

It would have seemed odd to leave the room, so Grey remained, but in deference to what he assumed to be Fraser's sensibilities, he stood back and allowed Tom to help Fraser remove his breeches, averting his own gaze without being obvious about it.

A shocked exclamation from Tom made him look, though, and he echoed it with his own.

"Jesus Christ! What the devil did he do to you?" Fraser half-lay on the bed, shirt rucked up to display the damage. Nearly the whole of Fraser's left buttock was an ugly purplish-blue, surrounding a swollen contusion that was almost black.

"I told ye," Fraser said grouchily, "he tried to cave my heid in. With a sort of club wi' a knob on one end."

"He's got the devil of a bad aim."

Fraser didn't actually laugh, but his scowl relaxed a little.

"What you want," Tom informed him, "is a poultice for bruising. Me mam would make one out of brick dust and egg and a bit of pounded milk thistle, when me and me brothers would get a black eye or summat of the kind."

"I believe there is a distinct shortage of brick dust in the neighborhood," Grey said. "But you might see what your *inamorata* recommends in the nature of a poultice, Tom."

"Likely a handful of manure," Fraser muttered.

In the event, Tom returned with the landlord's wife, bearing a moist cloth full of sliced, charred onions, which she applied, with many expressions of sympathetic horror (punctuated by loud expressions of astonishment as to how such a kind, sweet horse as our Bedelia, and her so gentle a soul as could have given our Lord a ride into Jerusalem, might ever have come to give the gentleman such a cruel toss, which made Fraser grind his teeth audibly), to the sufferer's shoulder, leaving the more delicate application to Tom.

Owing to the nature of his injuries, Fraser could not lie comfortably on his back, or on either side, and was obliged to lie on his stomach, the bad shoulder cradled by a pillow and the air of the chamber perfumed with the eye-watering fragrance of hot onions.

Grey lounged against the wall by the window, now and then looking out, just in case Siverly might have organized some sort of pursuit, but the darkening road remained empty.

From the corner of his eye, he could see the woman completing her ministrations. She went and came again with a second poultice, then climbed the stairs once more, puffing slightly, with a dram of whiskey, which she held carefully with one hand, lifting Fraser's head with the other to help him drink, though he resisted this assistance.

The movement had disarranged the first poultice, and she pulled back the neck of Fraser's shirt to replace it. The firelight glinted across the white scars, clearly visible across his shoulder blade, and she gave a single, shocked click of the tongue when she saw them. She gave Grey a hard, straight look, then, with great gentleness but a tight mouth, she straightened the shirt, unplaited Jamie's hair and combed it, then braided it loosely and bound it with a bit of string.

Grey was conscious of a sudden lurch within, watching sparks of copper glint from the thick dark-red strands that slid through the woman's fingers. A sharp spurt of what began as simple jealousy ended as a sense of baffled longing as he saw Fraser, eyes closed, relax and turn his cheek into the pillow, his body yielding, unthinking, compliant to the woman's touch.

When she had done, she went out, glancing sidelong at Tom. He looked at Grey and, receiving a nod of assent, went downstairs after her.

Grey himself poked up the fire and then sat down on a stool beside the bed.

"Do you need to sleep?" he inquired, rather gruffly.

The slanted blue eyes opened at once.

"No." Fraser raised himself gingerly, weight resting on his left forearm. "Jesus, that hurts!"

Grey reached into his portmanteau and withdrew his flask, which he handed over.

"Brandy," he said.

"Thank you," Fraser said fervently, and uncorked it. Grey sat down again, with a small glow of gratification.

"Tell me, if you will, exactly what happened."

Fraser obliged, pausing periodically to swallow brandy, wipe his eyes, or blow his nose, as the onion fumes made these run profusely.

"So, plainly he recognized the poem," Grey said. "Which is

reasonable; it confirms our original assumption that it had something to do with Siverly, as Carruthers had made a point of including it. What is more interesting is his question to you: 'Who are you?' That implies that the answer was something other than your name, does it not? Particularly if, as you say, he recognized you."

Fraser nodded. "Aye, it does. It also implies that there are people he doesna ken personally, but who might be expected to recognize that poem—and to seek out others o' the same ilk, using the poem as a signal. In other words—"

"A conspiracy," Grey said, with a feeling between dread and excitement settling in his stomach.

Fraser gave a small grunt of assent and, handing back the half-empty flask, eased himself down, grimacing.

"What sort of conspiracy do you think it is, Mr. Fraser?" Grey asked, watching him closely. The Scot's mouth tightened for a moment, but he'd plainly already done his thinking on the matter, for he answered without hesitation.

"Politics. There's a wee reference in the poem to a white rose. That canna mean anything but Jacobites." He spoke in a tone of absolute conviction.

"Ah." Grey paused, then, striving for casualness, said, "I don't believe you mentioned the white rose in your original translation."

Fraser blew his nose with a vicious honk. "No," he said calmly, sniffing, "nor after I showed it to Captain Lally. Neither did he."

"And yet you tell me now," Grey observed.

Fraser gave him a sideways look, put out a hand for the flask, and drank more brandy, as though considering his answer, though Grey was reasonably sure he'd considered it extensively already.

"Now it's real," he said finally, putting down the flask. He shifted a little, grimacing. "Ye wouldna ken, but in the time before the Rising in Scotland, and to nay little extent after, there were dozens—nay, hundreds—of tiny conspiracies. Plots, suggestions o' plots, hints of plots—any man who could hold a pen writing coded letters, talking of money, praising his own connections, and blackening the names of others—and nearly all of it nothing but wind."

He wiped his eyes, sneezed, and wiped his nose.

"Jesus, I may never eat onions again."

"Does it help? With the pain, I mean."

Fraser looked surprised, as though it had never occurred to him to wonder.

"Aye, it does; it warms the sore parts." His mouth twitched. "That, or maybe it's the brandy." He cleared his throat. "Anyway. I saw hundreds of things like that, in Paris. For a time, it was my business to look for such things. That's where I made the acquaintance of your sister-in-law."

Jamie spoke casually, but Grey saw the Scot's sidelong look and manfully concealed his own surprise.

"Yes, Hal said her father was a . . . dealer in documents."

"That's a verra tactful way to put it." He sniffed and looked up, one eyebrow raised. "I'm surprised that she didna tell ye about the white rose herself," he said. "She must ha' seen it." And then his gaze sharpened. "Oh," he said, with a half smile. "Of course, she did. I should have kent that."

"You should," Grey agreed dryly. "But you said, 'Now it's real.' Why? Only because Siverly is involved in some way?"

Jamie nodded and shifted himself, looking for a more comfortable way to lie. He settled for resting his forehead on his crossed forearms.

"Because Siverly's rich," he said, his voice a little muffled. "Whether he stole his money or made it, we ken he's got it, do we not?"

"We do," Grey said, a little grimly. "Or at least he had it at one point. For all I know, he's spent it all on whores and horses. Or that monstrous great house."

Fraser made a motion of the head that might have been agreement.

"Either way, he has something to lose," he said. "And there's the minor consideration that he tried, verra seriously, to kill me." He raised his head from the pillow, squinting at Grey. "He'll try again, aye?" he observed, though without much concern. "Ye havena got much more than tomorrow morning before he turns up here."

"I mean to call upon Major Siverly in the morning," Grey assured him. "But you have not completely answered my question, Mr. Fraser. You said, 'Now it's real,' and I understand that. But should not the possibility of a substantial conspiracy, well funded and decently managed, increase your loyalty to the Stuart cause?"

Fraser laid his head on his arms, but turned his face toward Grey and studied him for some time, eyes narrowed.

"I shall never fight in that cause again," he said at last, softly, and Grey thought he spoke with a sense of true regret. "Not from cowardice, but from the sure knowledge of its futility. Major Siverly's nay friend to me. And should there be men I know involved in this . . . I will do them nay service to let it go further."

He turned his face away again and lay quiet.

Grey picked up the flask and shook it. There was very little left in it, but he drank this, slowly, watching the play of fire through the tangled strands of the peat bricks in the hearth.

Was Fraser telling the truth? He thought so. If so—was his assessment of that one phrase in the poem sufficient as to conjure up a complete Jacobite conspiracy? But that wasn't the only evidence, he reminded himself. Minnie had said the same—and, above all, Siverly's attempt on Fraser's life argued that the poem itself was dangerous in some way. How else if not, as Fraser said, a signal of recognition? But a signal to whom?

He fell to thinking of how his meeting with Siverly might go, knowing what he now did. Ought he, too, present a copy of the same poem, to see what response it drew? He had made a point of seeking out Siverly after the Battle of Quebec, to thank him for his service in saving Grey from being brained by a tomahawk. Siverly had modestly dismissed the matter—but it would plainly be foremost in his mind at sight of Grey.

Grey grimaced. Yes, he owed Siverly a debt of honor. But if Siverly had done half what Carruthers claimed, he had forfeited his right to such consideration.

The room was warm. He loosened his neckcloth, which made him think of his dress uniform, its leather stock and silver gorget. Tom had packed it with great care, preserving it from loss and damage on the journey, for the sole purpose of being worn to arrest Gerald Siverly, if necessary.

Had the time come for that? He thought not yet. He'd take with him not only the poem but a few selected sheets from Carruthers's packet and, depending upon Siverly's reception of him, would decide whether—and which—to show him. Showing the poem would link him immediately with Jamie Fraser, and thus perhaps threaten Siverly. If he could persuade Siverly to go back to England voluntarily, that was by far the best result. But if not . . . He brooded for a bit, but he was sick of thinking of Siverly, and his mind wandered. The scent of onions had subsided to a pleasant odor that conjured thoughts of supper. It was very late. Perhaps he should go down; he could have the girl bring something up for Fraser. . . .

Once more he saw the woman's hands, gentle on Fraser's face and body, and the big Scot turning at once to her touch, a stranger's touch. Only because she was a woman. If he himself had ventured to touch the man . . .

But I have. If not directly. The open neck of the shirt had slipped back, and the faint glimmer of the scars showed once more.

Jamie's head turned, and his eyes opened, as though he had felt the pressure of Grey's gaze. He didn't speak but lay quiet, meeting John's eyes. Grey was conscious all at once of the silence; the pub's customers had all gone home, the landlord and his family retired for the night.

"I'm sorry," he said, very softly.

"Ego te absolvo," Fraser murmured, and shut his eyes.

22

Glastuig

THE BAY GELDING WAS LAME IN THE RIGHT FORE, AND JOHN Grey had declined to ride the unfortunate Bedelia, on grounds that she would be instantly recognized, thus establishing a link between himself and Jamie Fraser and causing Major Siverly to smell a rat. He therefore walked the two miles from Beckett's inn to Siverly's estate, Glastuig, reciting Latin poetry as a means of keeping his thoughts off the impending meeting.

He'd done what planning was possible. Once the strategy and tactics of a battle were decided, you put it out of your mind until you came to the field and saw what was what. Trying to fight a battle in your head was pointless and did nothing but fret the nerves and exhaust the energies.

He'd had a hearty breakfast of black pudding and buttered eggs with toasted soda bread, washed down with Mr. Beckett's very good beer. Thus internally fortified, and dressed in a country gentleman's good wool suit—complete with gaiters to save his lisle stockings from the mud—and with several documents carefully stowed in separate pockets, he was armed and ready.

Qui nunc it per iter tenebricosum
illuc, unde negant redire quemquam.

Now he goes along the dark road, thither whence they say no man returns.

It was a very beautiful morning, and a small group of pigs were enjoying it to the maximum, snorting and rooting under a tumbled stone wall. Aside from these, the landscape seemed entirely empty, until after a mile or so a woman in a shawl came past him in the lane, leading an ass with a small boy sitting on it. He lifted his hat politely to the woman and wished her good morning. All of them stared at him, the woman and the boy turning round in order to keep staring after they'd passed him. Possibly strangers were not common in the neighborhood, he thought.

This conclusion was borne out when he rapped his walking stick on the door of Siverly's manor, and a weedy-looking young butler with astonishingly vivid ginger hair and a large quantity of freckles blinked at him as though he'd sprung out from behind a mushroom.

"I've come to call upon Major Siverly," Grey said politely. "My name is Grey."

"Is it?" said the butler uncertainly. "You're an Englishman, I daresay?"

"Yes, it is," Grey assured him. "And, yes, I am. Is your master at home?"

"Well, he is, then, but—" The man glanced over his shoulder at a closed door on the far side of a spacious foyer. "Oh!" A thought seemed to strike him, and he looked back at Grey with the air of one who has successfully put two and two together to make four.

"You'll be after being a friend of the other Englishman, sure!"

"The . . . other Englishman?"

"Why, the one what rode over this morning from Brampton Court!" the butler exclaimed happily. "He's in the library with the master, and them talking away sixteen to the dozen. They'll be expecting you, then, won't they?"

"Oh, to be sure," Grey said cordially, wondering what the devil he was about to walk in to but walking after the butler, nonetheless.

The butler pulled open the beautifully carved door to the library and bowed with an extravagant gesture, ushering Grey in.

He was looking for Siverly and therefore saw him at once, the major looking up with surprise from what looked like a pair of account books.

"Major Siverly—" he began, infusing his voice with warmth. But then he caught sight of the major's companion, seated across the desk from Siverly, and the words stuck in his throat.

"What on earth—Bulstrode, what the devil are you at?" Siverly barked at the butler, who blinked, bewildered. "Haven't I told you not to bring visitors in unannounced?"

"I—I thought—" The hapless butler was stuttering, glancing wildly back and forth between Grey and Edward Twelvetrees, who was staring at Lord John with a look somewhere between astonishment and outrage.

"Oh, go away, you clot," Siverly said irritably, getting up and shooing the butler off. "Colonel Grey! What a pleasant surprise. You must forgive the . . . er . . . unorthodox welcome." He smiled, though with considerable reservation in his eyes. "Allow me to make you acquainted with Captain—"

"We've met." Twelvetrees's words were as clipped as bits of wire. He stood up slowly, keeping his eyes fixed on Grey as he closed the ledger in front of him. Not before Grey had time to see that it contained a listing of what looked like fairly large sums.

And speaking of sums—there was an ironbound chest sitting on the desk, its lid open, more than half filled with a quantity of small wash-leather bags, each tied round with string. Under the bay window, the lid of a blanket chest stood open. A depression in the blankets showed where the ironbound chest had rested. Siverly's eyes darted toward this, and his hand twitched, but he stayed it, evidently not wanting to draw attention to the chest by closing it.

"What are you doing here?" Twelvetrees asked coldly.

Grey took a deep breath. Nothing for it but charge straight in.

"I came to pay a call on Major Siverly," he said mildly. "And you?"

Twelvetrees's mouth pursed a little. "Just happened to be in the neighborhood, eh?"

"No, I came particularly to speak with the major about a matter of some importance. But of course I have no wish to intrude," Grey said, with a brief bow to Siverly. "Perhaps I might come again at some more convenient occasion?"

Siverly was looking back and forth between Grey and Twelvetrees, plainly trying to fathom what was going on.

"No, no, do stay," he said. "I must confess—a matter of importance, you said?" His face was not particularly mobile, but he wasn't a good cardplayer, and wariness and calculation flickered over his slab-sided features.

"A private matter," Grey said, smiling pleasantly at Twelvetrees, who was surveying him through narrowed eyes. "As I say, a more convenient—"

"I'm sure Captain Twelvetrees will excuse us for a few moments," Siverly interrupted. "Edward?"

Christian names, is it? Grey thought. *Well, well.*

"Certainly." Twelvetrees moved slowly toward the door, eyes like a pair of pistol barrels fixed on Grey.

"No, no," Siverly said, gesturing him back to his seat. "You stay here, Edward; Bulstrode will bring some tea. Colonel Grey and I will just take a stroll down to the summerhouse and back."

Grey bowed to Twelvetrees, keeping a charming smile on his face, and followed Siverly out of the library, feeling Twelvetrees's eyes burning holes between his shoulder blades.

Hastily, he reviewed his strategy as he followed Siverly's broad back across the freshly rolled lawn. At least he wasn't going to have to carry out his inquisition in front of Twelvetrees, but he'd have to assume that anything he said might well be conveyed to "Edward."

"What a beautiful property," he said, as they rounded the corner of the house. It was true; the lawns spread a stately distance before and behind, and edging the back lawn were terraces of roses and other flowering bushes, with a walled garden to the left that was likely the kitchen garden; Grey saw what looked like espaliered fruit trees poking up above the plastered wall. In the distance, beyond the formal terraces, was a charming small white summerhouse, standing on the edge of an ornamental wood, and, beyond that, the stables.

"Thank you," Siverly said, a note of pride in his voice. "I've been improving it, these last few years." But he was not a man to be distracted by compliments. "You did say . . . ?" He turned to Grey, one steel-gray eyebrow raised.

"Yes." In for a penny, in for a pound. Grey felt something of the giddy recklessness he experienced when plunging into a fight. "Do you by chance recall an adjutant named Charles Carruthers? He was with one of your companies in Quebec."

"Carruthers," Siverly said, a mildly questioning tone in his voice—but it was plain from his face that the name was familiar to him.

"He had a deformed hand," Grey said. He disliked reducing Charlie to such a description, but it was the quickest and surest way forward.

"Oh, yes. Of course." Siverly's broad, pockmarked brow lowered a bit. "But he's dead. I'm sure I heard that he was dead. Measles, was it? Some sort of ague?"

"He is dead, I'm afraid." Grey's hand dipped into his coat, hoping he remembered which pocket he'd put the folded paper in. He pulled it out but held it in his hand, not offering it yet to Siverly.

"Do you know my brother, by chance?"

"Your brother?" Siverly now looked frankly puzzled, "The duke? Yes, of course. I know of him, I mean; we aren't personally acquainted."

"Yes. Well, he has come into possession of a rather curious set of documents, compiled by Captain Carruthers. Concerning you."

"Concerning me? What the devil—" Siverly snatched the paper from Grey's hand, anger flaring so suddenly in his eyes that Grey had an instant apprehension of how some of the incidents Charlie had described had come about. The violence in the man was simmering just below the skin; he saw only too well how Siverly had come so close to killing Jamie Fraser.

Siverly read the page quickly, crushed it in his hand, and threw it to the ground. A vein stood out on his temple, pulsing blue under his skin, which had gone an unpleasant purplish color.

"What balderdash is this?" he said, his voice thick with rage. "How dare you come bringing me such whinging, blithering—"

"Do you deny that there is any truth in Captain Carruthers's account?" The page was one regarding the events leading to the mutiny in Canada. There were more damning pages—many of them—but Grey had thought to start with something clear-cut.

"I deny that Pardloe has any right to question me in the slightest particular! And as for you, sir—" Siverly loomed suddenly over Grey, fists clenched. "Damn you for an interfering, busybodying fool! Get out of my sight."

Before Grey could move or speak, Siverly had whirled on his heel and stamped off, moving like an ox with its tail on fire.

Grey blinked, belatedly realized that he was holding his breath, and exhaled. The summerhouse was twenty feet away; he went and sat on the steps to collect himself.

"So much for gentle persuasion," he said under his breath. Siverly had already reached the lawn and was forging up it to the house, making the occasional furious gesture en route.

Plainly an alternative plan would have to be put in train. But in the meantime, there was a good deal to think about. Edward Twelvetrees, for one. That ironbound chest, for another.

Grey had been in the army in one capacity or another since the age of sixteen. He knew what a paymaster's books looked like—and, likewise, a paymaster's chest. Clearly Twelvetrees and Siverly were involved in something together that involved the disbursement of funds—and fairly considerable funds—to a number of individuals.

Siverly had disappeared into the house. Grey continued to sit for a little, thinking, but could come to no firm conclusions. Obviously, Siverly wasn't going to tell him anything about the paymaster's chest. Perhaps it would be worth riding over to Brampton Court—that's where the butler had said Twelvetrees was staying—and trying to inveigle information out of the other conspirator. At least he was reasonably sure that Twelvetrees wouldn't try to kill him out of hand. Though it might be as well to bring his dagger.

Just as Grey rose to his feet, Twelvetrees himself came out of the house and, looking out across the lawn, saw Grey at the summerhouse. He lowered his head and came down, looking bitter and determined.

Grey waited.

Twelvetrees was slightly flushed when he arrived but had himself well in hand. None of Siverly's volcanic passion showed in that lean, long-nosed face. There was hostility, to be sure, and considerable dislike.

"You should leave, Colonel Grey," he said without preamble. "And do not come back. I tell you this for your own good; there is no profit in pestering Major Siverly, no matter what your motive—and I confess I cannot make that out. No, don't tell me—" He held up a minatory hand. "I don't care. Neither do you need to know what my motives are. Suffice it to say that you meddle in matters that you do not understand, and if you continue to do so, you will regret it."

He made to turn on his heel, but Grey, moved by impulse, put out a hand and grasped his sleeve.

"A moment, Captain, if you please." He groped with his free hand for his waistcoat pocket and pulled out another sheet of paper—one of the copies of the Wild Hunt verse. "Look at this."

Twelvetrees looked as though he meant to jerk away, but instead seized the paper impatiently and opened it.

He didn't even read it but turned pale at sight of the words.

"Where did you get this?" he said, his voice nearly a whisper.

"From Charlie Carruthers," Grey said. "I see you recognize it. Do you—"

He never got to complete the sentence. Twelvetrees shoved

the paper into his chest so hard that he took a step backward to avoid falling. He caught his balance, but Twelvetrees was already striding away across the little flagstone walk. Grey caught sight of a snail on the stone. Twelvetrees's shoe came down upon the animal with an audible crunch. He paid no attention but forged blindly on, leaving a small, wet stain glimmering on the flags.

23

Plan B

THE NEXT DAY DAWNED SULLEN AND OVERCAST BUT NOT actually raining. Yet. Grey dressed carefully in his uniform, Tom Byrd assisting him with the same sense of solemn ceremony as though preparing Grey for battle. Leather stock, gorget, polished boots . . . Grey hesitated for a moment over wearing his dagger, but in the end, thinking of Siverly's attack on Jamie Fraser, put it in his belt.

Fraser leaned against the window frame, half-sitting on the sill, watching the preparations with a small frown. He'd offered to go with Grey, but John had declined, thinking that his presence could not but inflame Siverly. It was going to be a sufficiently sticky interview without introducing further complications.

"If I don't come back," he told Fraser at the door, "you have my explicit permission to do whatever you like to Siverly." He'd meant it as a joke, but the Scotsman nodded soberly.

"I'll take your body home to your brother."

Tom Byrd made a horrified noise, but Grey smiled, affecting to think this a witty riposte to his own feeble jest.

"Yes, you do that," he said, and went downstairs, bootheels thumping.

The butler at Glastuig opened the door to him, eyes wide at seeing him in his uniform.

"I will see your master, if you please," Grey informed him, stepping inside without invitation. "Where is he?"

The butler gave way, flustered.

"The master's not in the house, sir!"

"Where is he, then?"

The man's mouth worked for a moment and he glanced from side to side, looking for a suitable answer, but he was too discomposed by the uniform to lie.

"Why . . . he's out in the summerhouse, to be sure. He often sits out there of a morning. But he—"

Grey nodded and turned on his heel, leaving the butler dithering behind him.

He walked across the lawn toward the folly, rehearsing what to say—and thinking what to do next if his reasoning did not move Siverly. He had very little expectation that it would, but he owed it to his own sense of fairness to give the man a chance to come back voluntarily.

If not . . . then he'd come back under arrest. The slightly sticky part being that Grey had no formal authority in Ireland, still less the authority to arrest anyone, and Siverly almost certainly knew that. Grey could do it legally, by requesting the justiciar at Athlone to send a party of soldiers to bring Siverly to the castle—if the justiciar saw the matter in the same light—there to be formally handed over to Grey, who would then serve as a military escort to see Siverly into the custody of the British army.

This supposed, though, that Siverly would remain in situ while Grey rode to Athlone and back, that the justiciar's deputy (the justiciar being presumably a-wooing in France at the moment) would be moved by the force of Grey's argument to arrest an obviously wealthy and locally esteemed man and then submit him to the mercies of a foreign government, and that Siverly would in turn meekly submit to the justiciar's men. Frankly, Grey thought the odds low on all three fronts.

The alternative was summary arrest—well, kidnapping, if you wanted to be blunt about it—carried out by Grey and Jamie Fraser, with Tom Byrd holding the horses. Grey was strongly inclined to favor this line of action, and he knew that Fraser would be only too pleased to assist him.

While it had the appeal of directness—plus the additional charming possibility of collateral damage sustained by Siverly in the course of resisting arrest—he didn't delude himself that it would be simple. They'd have to get Siverly across half of Ireland and onto a ship without attracting undue attention—in a country where he spoke the local language and they didn't.

"Needs must when the devil drives," he muttered, and stamped heavily up the steps of the folly, in order to give Siverly fair warning of his advent. He thought he heard movement inside, but as his head came above the top of the steps, the folly appeared to be empty.

He'd been a soldier for a long time, though, and the sense of danger struck him so acutely that he ducked before realizing consciously that anything was wrong. Crouched on the steps with his heart hammering, he grasped his dagger and listened for all he was worth. He heard a loud rustling of the shrubbery behind the folly and instantly leapt up, ran down the steps and round the folly.

Siverly had made it into the ornamental wood; Grey couldn't see the man, but he heard the snap and crunch of a body forcing its way through undergrowth in a hurry. Follow, or go round?

He hesitated for no more than an instant, then ran to the left. The man must be heading for the stables; he could cut him off.

He vaguely saw servants in the distance, pointing at him and shouting, but paid them no mind. He'd lost his hat, but that didn't matter, either. He galloped through the kitchen garden, leaping a basket of turnip greens set dead in the middle of the walk, and dodging the openmouthed cook who'd set it there.

The gate was shut, and he didn't bother fumbling for the latch but seized it with both hands and vaulted over, feeling an absurd rush of fierce pleasure in the feat. A short, destructive dash through a terrace of rosebushes, and the stables loomed ahead of him. The big sliding door was closed; Siverly hadn't got out yet. He wrenched the door open and charged into the dim-lit stable, where his tumultuous advent startled a number of horses, who snorted and whinnied, dancing and curvetting in their stalls. He ignored them all and stood panting in the center of the aisle, facing the door at the opposite end.

The guilty flee where no man pursueth. The words came to him and he would have laughed, if he'd had breath. He hadn't wanted any more proof of Siverly's guilt, but this open admission by flight would give Grey the excuse to make an immediate arrest.

It occurred to him vaguely that Siverly outweighed him by at least three stone and might be armed, but he dismissed the thought. He had the advantage of surprise here, and meant to use it. He took up a position to the side of the sliding door and stepped into a narrow alcove used for storing tack.

The horses had calmed down, still snorting and bobbing their heads but now beginning to munch hay again. He heard the rumbling as the sliding door opened—but it was the wrong door, the one he'd come in by. He risked a quick glance out of his hiding place but saw only a groom, pitchfork and manure shovel in hand. He ducked back, muttering, "Shit," under his breath. He didn't need a witness, let alone one armed with a pitchfork, who would likely come to his master's aid.

The groom's eyes flicked from side to side, though, instantly sensing something amiss among the horses. He dropped the shovel with a clang and advanced toward Grey's end of the stable, fork held menacingly before him.

"Come on! Let's be havin' ye out of there!"

Not much help for it. Grey tucked his dagger out of sight and stepped out into the aisle.

"Good morning," he said pleasantly. "Is your master about?"

The groom halted, blinking at this crimson-clad apparition.

"And who the divil are you? Sir," he added uncertainly.

"An acquaintance of Major Siverly's. Grey is my name," he added helpfully.

The man, middle-aged and possessed of a head like a cannonball, paused, blinking suspiciously. Grey wondered whether he'd ever met an Englishman—but of course he must have; Edward Twelvetrees had visited here.

"How does your honor come to be in the stable, eh?" The pitchfork stayed steady. Surely the idiot didn't take him for a horse thief?

"The butler told me Major Siverly was here, of course." Grey allowed a certain impatience to creep into his tone, all too aware that Siverly himself might come in at any moment. So much for his ambush! He'd just have to put the best face on it he could and inveigle Siverly into walking back to the house with him. Once out of pitchfork reach . . .

"Himself's not here."

"Yes, I noticed that. I'll . . . um . . . look for him outside." Before he could be forcibly escorted out with a pitchfork aimed at the seat of his breeches, he whirled on his heel and strode briskly toward the door. The groom came after him, but slowly.

He was mentally cursing his luck and trying to think how best to deal with Siverly—but was saved the effort, as Siverly was not in fact advancing on the stable. A paddock and a field lay between the stable and the little wood where the folly stood, and both were empty.

Grey said a bad word.

"Your honor?" said the groom, startled.

"Are all the horses in the stable?" he demanded, turning on the groom. The man eyed him narrowly, but the pitchfork was now resting tines on the ground, thank God. The groom scratched his head slowly.

"What would they be doing there, for all love? There's Bessie and Clover out with the big wagon, and the gray mare and her colt with the others in the upper field, and—"

"Saddle horses, for God's sake!"

"Oh, saddle horses, is it?" The groom was at last beginning to be moved by his urgency, and wrinkled his brow. He squinted off to the left, where Grey perceived several horses switching their tails in a distant field. "Well, there's the four up there—that's Richard Lionheart, and Istanbul, and Marco, and—"

"Will you just for God's sake tell me if any are missing?" Grey's urgency was taking on a sense of nightmare, the sort of dream where one strove to make progress through some sucking bog, only to encounter the walls of an endless maze.

"No, your honor." Before the words were fully out of the groom's mouth, Grey was striding back toward the folly, the sense of nightmare growing.

It wasn't Siverly's alarm at his presence that he'd sensed on the steps of the folly. It was acute, impending danger, a sense of harm. He was running now, ignoring the groom's shout behind him.

He took the steps of the folly in two great strides, smelling it before he saw it, what he must have smelled faintly before, but so much stronger now, and his foot came down in the blood and slid out from under him. He waved his arms, staggering to keep his balance, and fetched up hard against the railing of the folly, breathless and choked with the smell of it, the whiff of death now full-blown and reeking at his feet.

24

Clishmaclaver

AMIE HAD BORROWED A BOOK FROM PARDLOE'S LIBRARY, A ocket edition of Homer's *Iliad,* in Greek. He'd not read Greek n some years, and thought perhaps to renew his acquaintance vith the language, but distraction of mind was interfering with is concentration.

> *Not thus the lion glories in his might,*
> *Nor panther braves his spotted foe in fight,*
> *Nor thus the boar (those terrors of the plain;)*
> *Man only vaunts his force, and vaunts in vain.*

He'd last spoken Greek in Ardsmuir prison, trading bits of ristophanes with Lord John over a makeshift supper of poridge and sliced ham, the rations being short even in the goveror's quarters, owing to a storm that had kept regular supplies rom being delivered. There had been claret to wash it down vith, though, and it had been a cordial evening. He'd taken care f the bits of business that needed to be done on behalf of the risoners, and then they'd played chess, a long, drawn-out duel hat had lasted nearly 'til dawn. Grey had won, at last, and had hesitated, glancing at the battered sofa in his office, clearly wondering whether he might offer Jamie the use of it, rather than send him back to the cells for an hour's sleep before the prisoners rose.

Jamie had appreciated the thought, but it wouldn't do, and he'd set his face impassively, bowed correctly, and bade Lord John good night, himself rapping on the doorframe to summon the dozing guard.

"Merde," he said under his breath. He'd been sitting on the bench outside the inn, gazing down the road with the book open on his knee, for God knew how long. Now it had come on to rain and wee drops stippled the page, brushing soft against his face.

He wiped the page hastily with his sleeve and went inside putting the book in his pocket. Tom Byrd was sitting by the hearth, helping young Moira Beckett wind her fresh-dyed yarn. He'd been making sheep's eyes at Moira, but at the sound of Jamie's entrance, his head swiveled round like a compass needle.

Jamie shook his head slightly, and Tom grimaced, but then turned back to Moira.

"D'you know what time it is, Miss Beckett?" Tom asked politely.

"About half-three, so it is," she replied, looking a little startled. Jamie suppressed a smile. She'd turned her head to look out the window at the light, just as Jamie had when Tom asked the question. The notion that anyone would not be able to know what time it was by the light was clearly foreign to her, but Tom was a Londoner bred and born, and thus never out of hearing of the bells of one church or another.

"I s'pose his lordship must be having a good visit with his friend," Tom offered, looking to Jamie for confirmation.

"Aye, well, I hope he had a more cordial reception than I did." Grey had left for Glastuig just after ten; it was no more than a half hour's ride. Five hours was surely a portent of something, but whether it might be good news or bad . . .

He shook his head and went upstairs. He sat by the window and opened his book again, but could not bend either eye or mind to the tragedy of Hector's ignominious death.

If it came to him having to go back to England with Grey's body and deliver him to Pardloe . . . he might just take Quinn at his offer and run, he thought. But surely the wee fool would have been on his guard, knowing what had happened to him? After all—

He sat up straight, his eye catching the flicker of movement far down the road. It wasn't Grey, though; it was a man on foot, half-running, with the hitching, lolloping gait of one forcing himself past his bodily limits.

He was down the stairs and out the door, Tom Byrd on his heels, by the time the runner came within hailing distance, and they rushed to him, supporting him.

Quinn was deathly pale, drenched in sweat, and gasping for breath.

"I think ye'd best come, Jamie. Your friend's killed Major Siverly, and the constable's after arresting him."

THERE WAS A KNOT of people standing on the lawn, most of them gesticulating. There was a man in a sober cloth coat and good cocked hat who seemed to be in charge of the proceedings—Jamie supposed this must be the constable. Most of the other folk there were obviously the servants of the house, all talking at once and waving their arms. And in the midst of it all stood John Grey, looking vastly irritated.

He was disheveled, his hair coming out of its plait, and there were smears of mud on his uniform—*Tom Byrd willna care for that,*

Jamie thought automatically. He was right; beside him, Tom gave a small squeak of outrage, and Jamie put his hand on the lad's arm to keep him quiet.

Making his way cautiously toward the little knot of people, he kept out of sight as much as he might, until he should determine how best to be of help. From twenty feet away, he saw that Grey's wrists were bound together in front of him and that the dark smears on his boots and breeks were blood, not dirt.

Grey was saying something, his voice pitched loud to be heard over the clishmaclaver, but Jamie couldn't make out what he said. Grey turned away from the constable, shaking his head in disgust—and his eye caught Jamie's. His face went from anger to calculation in an instant, and he made a brief, violent shooing gesture with one hand. *"Go away,"* it said, clear as day.

"What are they going to do with him?" Tom whispered urgently in Jamie's ear.

"I dinna ken." Jamie faded back a step or two into the shrubbery. "They've arrested him, Quinn said. Maybe they'll take him to the local gaol."

"They can't do that!"

He glanced at Tom, whose round face was set in indignation, fists clenched at his sides.

"Aye, well, wait and see." Thoughts were running through his mind, trying to make out what it was Grey wanted him to do.

"Go out where he can see ye, wee Byrd," he said, narrowing his eyes at the scene. "They'll let ye near him, I think, as ye're his servant."

Tom gave him a wild look, but then drew himself up and nodded manfully. He stepped out of the shrubbery and walked toward the group, and Jamie saw Grey's expression of annoyance and anxiety ease a little. His own eased, as well; he'd guessed right, then.

There was a good bit of palaver and some shoving, the servants trying to keep Tom Byrd away from Grey. The young valet stood his ground, though, and Grey added his own insistence, scowling and gesturing at the constable with his bound hands. The constable looked slow and suspicious, but he had an air about him of authority; when he lifted a hand for silence, the magpie chatter ceased.

"You're this man's valet, ye say?" Jamie could just hear, above the patter of rain on the leaves and the servants' muttering.

"I am, sir." Tom Byrd bowed deeply. "Will you let me talk to him, please?"

The constable glanced from Tom Byrd to Grey, then back. He stood in thought for some moments, but then nodded.

"Aye, go ahead. You lot!" He lifted his chin imperiously at the servants. "I want to speak to the person who found the body."

There was a general shifting and glancing to and fro, but then a maid stepped out of the throng, pushed by two of her fellow servants. She looked wild, her eyes showing white like a spooked horse, and her hands wrapped in her apron, strangling it.

"Was it you found your master, then? Go on, now, there's naught to fear," the constable said, in a tone that he probably thought was reassuring. He might as well have said that he proposed to take her straight to the hangman, for the maid wailed in terror and threw the mangled apron over her head.

One of the men with her appeared to be her husband, for he put an arm around her and stuck out his chin—trembling, but out, Jamie noted with approval—at the constable.

"She did, then, your honor, and it's quite put her out of her wits with the shock, as ye see."

"I see," the constable said rather brusquely. "Well, who the fook else saw what happened? You?"

"Oh, not me, oh, no, your honor," said the husband, turning

white and stepping back, making a sign against evil. His wife shrieked, feeling his sheltering arm depart, and cowered. Her friends among the servants obligingly set up a companionable keening to keep her company, and the constable set his jaw like a bulldog against the racket, lower teeth set hard in his upper lip.

While the constable conducted his laborious investigations, and the rain began to fall more heavily, Jamie saw Grey draw Tom Byrd aside with a jerk of his head, then bend close to his ear, clearly giving instructions, glancing now and then as he did so at the shrubbery where Jamie stood hidden.

He thought he made out from the incoherent babblings of the maid that she'd found the master in the summerhouse, and as the constable seemed indisposed to go and look for himself, Jamie eased out of the shrubbery and went quietly round the back of the little wood.

More than one person had run through it; he could see that from the fresh-broken twigs and trampled ferns. He skirted the damage delicately and stole quietly up to the rear of the summerhouse. It was made with latticed panels, these interspersed with open sections, which were barred with an ornamental railing, with latticework below. Tall as he was, he could just manage to peer through this latticework by standing on his toes.

The first thing he saw was not Siverly's body, but the weapon. It was the same odd, knob-headed club with which Siverly had attacked him, and he crossed himself at the sight, with a peculiar feeling that was not satisfaction but more awe at God's sense of justice.

Grey had recognized the thing from his description; had told him it was a war club, a weapon made by the Iroquois. Hardwood, and, in the right hands, a very deadly thing. Evidently, Siverly had run into someone who knew how to employ it—the knob at the end was thick with blood and hair, and . . . His eye tracked across the wide swath of blood that lay smeared over the floor of the summerhouse and came to rest on an object that he knew must be Siverly's head, only because it could be nothing else.

The man was lying with his head toward Jamie, the rest of his body largely invisible. The blow had caved in his skull to a shocking extent; white bone showed, and rimming the wound was a pinkish ooze that he knew to be brain. He felt his gorge rise and turned round hastily, shutting his eyes and trying not to breathe, for the smell of blood and death was thick in his nose.

There was little to be learned here, and sooner or later someone would come; he couldn't be found lurking near the body. He stole quietly out through the wood, turned right, and circled round the house, coming out of the gardens near the drive, just in time to see Lord John being taken away. The constable had commandeered a wagon from the estate and rode his mule alongside, keeping a sharp eye on his prisoner. The prisoner himself sat straight as a ramrod on the wagon's seat, looking extremely cross but self-possessed. Jamie saw him say something to the constable that made the latter rear back, blinking, but then glower at Lord John and make an abrupt gesture to the wagon's driver, who clicked his tongue to the horses and set off at a trot that nearly toppled John Grey off his perch, unable to catch himself with his hands bound.

Jamie felt an angry spasm of kinship at the sight; he'd known such small cruelties when he'd worn fetters. He murmured a deliberate curse toward the constable and walked out onto the drive, where the servants were clustered accusingly round Tom Byrd.

They all fell silent at sight of Jamie, falling back a little. He ignored the lot of them and jerked his head at Tom, saying merely, "Come with me, Mr. Byrd," as he turned away down the drive.

Tom followed promptly, and while there was a hostile muttering behind them, no one hindered their departure.

"I'm that glad you come up when you did, sir," Tom said, hurrying a little to come even with him and glancing back over his shoulder. "I thought they were a-going to take me to pieces—and so did they."

"Aye, well, they're like dogs whose master's died," Jamie said, not unkindly. "They dinna ken what to do, so they howl and snap at one another. What did his lordship tell ye, wee Byrd?"

Tom was pale and excited but had control of himself. He rubbed his sleeve across his face to wipe away the rain and settled himself to recite Lord John's message.

"Right, sir. To begin with, the constable—that was the constable, the loud fat man—is taking his lordship to Castle Athlone."

"Aye? Well, that's good—it's not?" Jamie asked, seeing Tom shake his head.

"No, sir. He says the justiciar has gone to France, and whoever's in charge will either keep him locked up or make him give his parole, and that won't do."

"It won't? Did he say why not?"

"No, sir, there wasn't time. He says you must come and get him out, quick as ever you can."

Jamie rubbed a hand over his face, brushing water out of his eyebrows.

"Does he, then," he said dryly. "Did he suggest how I was to do that?"

Tom half-smiled, despite his worry.

"No, sir. He says to tell you that he trusts in your native wit and ferocity to accomplish this. I'm to help you," he added modestly, with a sideways look up at Jamie. He put a hand to his middle, looking portentous. "His lordship gave me his dagger to keep for him."

"That will be a great help," Jamie assured him gravely. "Dinna stick anyone with it unless I tell ye, though, aye? I dinna want to have to save ye both from the hangman."

The rain was coming down harder now, but as they were already wet through, there was little point in hurry, and they strode along without talking, the rain pattering on their heads and shoulders.

25

Escape from Athlone

QUINN HAD NOT GONE BACK TO GLASTUIG WITH THEM; they found him crouched by the fire with a glass of arrack in his hands, still shivering. He got up when he saw Jamie, though, and came outside at the jerk of Jamie's head.

The rain had stopped, at least for a bit, and Jamie led the way down the road so they might talk unheard. In a few words, he acquainted Quinn with the news of John Grey's arrest, which caused Quinn to cross himself piously—though Jamie could see from his face that he did not regard this as particularly unwelcome news.

He'd known pretty much what Quinn's reaction was likely to be and had decided what to do about it.

"Ye still want that cup, aye?" Jamie asked Quinn abruptly. "The *Cupán Druid riogh*?"

Quinn looked at him, wide-eyed, and grasped him by the arm.

"Ye'll never mean ye've got it, man?"

"No, I have not." Jamie detached his arm, though without violence.

"But ye know where it is." Quinn's restless eyes had stilled, fixed intently on his, and it wasn't a question.

"Aye, I know. It's well beyond anyone's reach, is where it is. I told the abbot to put it back where it came from, and to the best of my knowledge"—*which is considerable,* he added silently to himself—"he did."

Quinn's lips pursed in thought. "Someone will know," he said. "All the monks had to know when they dug the poor fella up—they'll remember where he was planted, too."

"Aye. Well, ye want to go and ask them, do that—but ye're no going until we get John Grey out of Athlone."

Quinn's strange light eyes bulged a bit.

"Out of Athlone Castle? Man, are ye demented?"

"Aye, I am," Jamie said crossly. "But I mean to do it, anyway."

"Why? The man's not only English, not only your captor—he's a fecking murderer!"

"No, that he's not," Jamie said, with decision. "He may be a good many disagreeable things, but not that."

"But they found him standin' over Siverly's body, and the blood fresh on his boots!"

"I saw, aye?"

Quinn fumed visibly. "Why the devil d'ye think he didn't do the man in, then? Ye heard what he had to say about him and all his talk about bringin' the fellow to justice. Ye don't get more justice than a bullet through the head!"

There was no point in telling Quinn that Siverly's death—however administered—wouldn't have been justice in John Grey's book, save it had been preceded by a court-martial.

"He didn't," Jamie repeated stubbornly.

There was also no way to explain to Quinn what he knew to be true of John Grey. That being that the only circumstance in which Grey might possibly have killed Siverly was if he was in fear of his own life—and had that been the case, he would have said so. To Jamie, at least, via Tom Byrd.

He wasn't going to argue the point, though, and not only because it would be futile. There was also the consideration that if Grey hadn't killed Siverly, someone else had. And there were relatively few persons known to have been nearby, one of whom was Quinn. He couldn't think why Quinn might have done such a thing, but thought it wiser not to point that out, given that he proposed to continue in company with Quinn for the next wee while.

"I'm going to Athlone, and ye're goin' with me."

"What? Why?" Quinn cried, indignant. "Where d'ye get off, dragging me into it?"

"Where did you get off, dragging me into your bloody crackbrained scheme? You go with me, and I'll take ye to Abbot Michael—ye can make your own case to him about the *Cupán.*"

"Crackbrained?!" Quinn went pale with indignation; his curls stood on end, nearly crackling with it.

"Aye, crackbrained. And ye're goin' with me to Athlone because ye can sail a boat, and I can't."

"A boat?" Quinn said, momentarily distracted from his affront. "What boat?"

"How do I know what boat?" Jamie said, very irritated. "We'll find one when we get there."

"But—"

"If ye think I'm going to abscond from an English prison with his lordship and try to escape through a countryside that's nay more than a monstrous bog with the occasional pig to stumble over—think again," he advised Quinn briefly.

"But—"

"Athlone Castle is nearby the River Shannon, and the justiciar said the Shannon's navigable. So we'll bloody navigate it. Come on!"

HE'D GIVEN HIS INSTRUCTIONS to Tom Byrd on the way back from Glastuig, and the valet had managed accordingly, not packing up all their belongings, as Jamie wished to cause no more stir than there was already, but acquiring what he could for an instant journey.

They found Tom Byrd waiting impatiently by the road with horses, a little way from the ordinary. Tom gave both men a narrow look, glancing from face to face, but said nothing. He had procured a cabbage, and a few potatoes, which he modestly displayed.

"That'll do us fine for a supper," Quinn said, patting Tom approvingly on the shoulder. He looked to the sky. "It's going to rain again," he said in resigned tones. "We'd best find a spot and cook it while we can."

Peat fires burned hot but gave little light. The fire at their feet was not much more than a sullen glow, as though the earth itself was burning from within, but it had cooked their food and warmed their feet. Some of their food—lacking a pot, they ate the cabbage raw, despite Quinn's dire predictions of unparalleled flatulence.

"It's nay as though there's anyone to hear, is there?" Jamie said, nibbling gingerly at a thick, waxy leaf. It squeaked between his teeth like a live mouse and was bitter as he imagined wormwood and gall to be, but it helped to kill his hunger. He'd eaten worse than raw cabbage, often.

Tom scrabbled a half dozen blackened knobs out of the embers and speared one with Lord John's dagger. It hadn't left his person since his employer had entrusted him with the knife upon his arrest.

"It's a bit hard in the middle," he said, gingerly poking at the potato. "But I don't know as more roasting would help it any."

"Nay bother," Jamie assured him. "I've got all my teeth, and none of them loose." Lacking a dirk, he stabbed two of the measly things neatly with his rapier and waved them gently in the air to cool.

"Show-away," said Quinn, but without rancor. The Irishman had sulked on their way back to collect Tom but seemed to have recovered his spirits since, despite the fact that the rain he had predicted was now falling. He'd been for finding supper and refuge for the night with a cottager, but Jamie had preferred to camp briefly, then go on as soon as they were rested. News of their presence would spread like butter on hot toast—his wame gurgled at thought of butter, but he sternly ignored it—and they could not afford to be picked up by a curious constable. There were enough people already who knew Lord John had had companions. Edward Twelvetrees, for one.

Did Twelvetrees know about Siverly yet? He wondered.

He tilted his head to spill the rain from the brim of his hat and blew on the hot potatoes.

Tom gathered the remaining potatoes in a fold of his cloak, deposited two in front of Quinn without remark, and came to sit down beside Jamie to eat his own share. Jamie hadn't yet told him about his plan—if his intentions could be dignified by such a word—let alone about Quinn's desire to abandon Grey, but was interested to see that Tom plainly didn't trust the Irishman.

Good lad, he thought.

Rain hissed and sputtered as it struck the fire. It wouldn't last much longer.

"How far is it to Athlone?" he asked, licking his fingers.

Quinn grimaced in thought. "From here? Maybe two hours."

Jamie felt, rather than saw, Tom perk up a bit at that, and turned his head to smile at the young valet.

"We'll get him back," he said, and was surprised at how gratified he was to see relief and trust flood Tom's round face.

"A-course we will," Tom said stoutly. "Sir," he added hastily. He didn't ask for details, which was just as well, Jamie thought.

"Sleep a bit," he said to Tom, when the fire showed signs of being finally extinguished. "I'll wake ye later, when it's time to go."

Quinn gave a small snort at this, but Jamie ignored it. Quinn knew fine that Jamie didn't trust him, and plainly Tom knew, too. It didn't need saying.

Jamie wrapped the borrowed cloak tighter round his body, wishing for a plaid and thick Highland stockings. The cloak was wool and would hold his heat, even if wet—but nothing shed water like the waulked wool of a Highland plaid. He sighed and found a place to sit where his arse wouldn't be in a puddle and there was a stone at his back to lean on.

His mind kept nagging at him, wanting to think, to make plans. But plans were pointless, until they reached Athlone and saw how things lay. As for thinking . . . he needed to let matters rest and sort themselves. He was bone-tired, and knew it. He patted his breeches and found the pleasantly bumpy little bundle of his rosary. And there was the matter of his penance, after all.

The smooth wooden beads were a comfort to his fingers, as the repetition of the *Aves* was to his mind, and he felt his shoulders finally begin to relax, the counterpoint of the pattering rain on his hat and the distant gurgling of his wame a peaceful background to his prayers.

"It's not a crackbrained scheme."

"Eh?" Quinn had spoken so quietly that Jamie had only half-heard him, such was his state of mind.

"I said, it's not a crackbrained scheme." Quinn swiveled on his rock to look at Jamie directly, his eyes dark holes in his face. "The plan."

"Aye?" Jamie's brain was slow to focus on this. *What plan?* He thought dimly. "Perhaps I spoke too hasty, Quinn. I'll ask your pardon."

Quinn's attitude changed at once from hostility to forgiveness; he straightened and, with a glance at Tom curled in a sodden lump some distance away, got up and came to crouch beside Jamie.

"Not a bit of it, *mo chara,*" he said, patting Jamie's shoulder. "I hadn't told ye the meat of it—doubtless it sounded fanciful."

Jamie made a sound meant to indicate cordial dismissal of this notion, privately wondering what in the name of God himself . . . oh, Jesus.

"The cup?" he asked. "Because I told ye, when—"

"No," Quinn replied. "I mean, that's a part of it, sure, but what I hadn't told ye yet was how the invasion is to work."

"The invasion . . ." Jamie's mind was coming hastily back from its peaceful bourne of prayer, and the knotting of his belly was not due to raw cabbage alone. "Ye'd mentioned raising an army. I recall that." And he recalled fine that Quinn had wanted him to raise it.

"Aye, but there's more." He saw Quinn's head turn as he looked over his shoulder, the picture of stealth. Then the Irishman leaned closer, close enough that Jamie could smell the man's sour breath. "The Irish Brigade," Quinn whispered in his ear.

"Aye?" He must have sounded as baffled as he felt, for Quinn gave a brief sigh of exasperation.

"Ye'll have heard of the Irish Brigade, at least?"

"I have, aye." He glanced at Tom, regretting that he hadn't let the lad take first watch; Quinn wouldn't be telling him this sort of thing. The Irishman's next words drove vain regrets from his mind, though.

"There are three regiments of the Irish Brigade in London," Quinn whispered, eyes alight with suppressed glee. "The officers of two of them are with us. When the word comes that all is in hand here in Ireland, they'll seize the king and hold St. James's Palace!"

Jamie was struck dumb, and a good thing, too, for Quinn went on:

"We've loyal men in brigade regiments posted in Italy and France, too. Not all the officers—but once the thing is in motion, the rest will fall in. Or if they don't—" He lifted one shoulder, a fatalist's shrug.

"If they don't . . . what?" Jamie knew what that shrug meant, but he wanted it spelled out, if only to give himself a moment's time to think. His scalp was prickling, and his wame had curled itself up into a quivering ball beneath his ribs.

Quinn pursed his lips. "Why, then . . . those loyal to the Cause will take command, of course."

"Ye mean they'll kill those who don't go along with it."

"Now, then. Ye know as well as I do, ye can't make wine without squeezin'—"

"Don't bloody say it!" Jamie had the obscure feeling that cliché on top of treasonous insanity was more than anyone should be obliged to put up with. He rubbed a wet hand over his wet face, the bristles of his beard harsh under his palm.

"Each regiment has at least two volunteers among the officers. When the signal comes . . ." But Quinn hadn't said "volunteers" in English, though he was speaking English. He'd used the Irish term, *"Deonaigh."*

In Jamie's experience, excluding clergy and peasants, Irishmen seemed to consist of two sorts: rabid fighters and maniac poets. These traits weren't often combined in the same man, though.

That word, *"Deonach."* It was in the Wild Hunt poem; he wouldn't have taken notice, save that there was a popular soldier's song, a sentimental, maudlin thing in Irish, called "The Volunteer." There'd been several Irishmen in the group of mercenaries with whom he'd fought in France, much given to singing it when in liquor. That was almost the last song he recalled, before the blow of an ax had severed him forever from music.

"Sé an fuil á lorgadh, is é a teas á lorgadh," he said abruptly, his heart beating quicker, and Quinn's face turned sharply toward him. *They search out blood, they seek its heat.*

A moment's silence, save for the rain. The fire was drowned now, even the black mark it left on the earth quite drowned in darkness. The cabbage was making its presence felt and Jamie clenched his buttocks, silently easing himself.

"Where did ye hear that, now?" Quinn said, his voice mild, and Jamie realized with a small shock that his life might depend upon his answer.

"Thomas Lally said it to me," he replied, his voice as mild as Quinn's. "When I met him in London." Quinn might know that he'd met Lally—and it was true that Lally had said those words to him, reading them from the written sheet, a puzzled expression on his face.

"He did?" Quinn sounded blank, perhaps a little frightened, and Jamie expelled his breath, only then realizing that he'd been holding it. So. Lally maybe wasn't part of the plot. But Quinn was fearful lest he knew about it?

"Tell me more about this, will ye?" Jamie said quickly. "Is there a date set for it?"

Quinn hesitated, still suspicious, but eagerness to talk and desire to win Jamie over got the better of him.

"Well, there is, then. All I can say is, it'll be a day when the streets will be crowded, the beer flowing from the taverns, the squares all hoaching like weevils in a sack of grain. All the regiments will parade down Pall Mall and then go off to barracks. One of the Irish Brigade regiments will come at the last of the procession, and instead of heading back to their quarters, they'll go round behind the palace. Once His Majesty's gone inside, they'll move into the grounds, overpower any guards at the back, and take the palace. The guards in the front will be taken up with the crowds and won't know a thing's afoot until it's too late—and then the second regiment sweeps in to secure the place. All the other regiments will be busy stripping off and putting away their tack—even if word comes as to what's happening, they'll never pull themselves together in time to stop it. And once the king is in hand, messengers will go out to our supporters in Wales and Scotland, ready to march and take London entire!"

It might conceivably work. God knew, much madder schemes had.

"But they canna hold out for very long, even wi' the king's person to bargain with," Jamie pointed out. "What if there's some delay in Charles Stuart coming wi' the new army from Ireland?" *Some delay,* he thought, remembering all too well what it took to assemble even an ill-equipped rabble, let alone feed and transport them. And that was reckoning without the Bonnie Prince himself—a weak reed for a revolution to lean upon, and surely to God Quinn must know that much. Or was that what the conspiracy counted upon?

"We thought of that," Quinn said importantly, and Jamie wondered just who "we" were. Could he get Quinn to tell him names? "There are fallbacks. The regiments in London don't stir a step until they've heard the word."

"Oh, aye? And what word is that?"

Quinn grinned at him and shook his head.

"Never you mind that, laddie. It's a mark of the great trust I bear ye that I've told ye what I have—but 'tis more than my life's worth to say more just yet." He leaned back and a loud fart ripped the air beneath him, surprising him.

"Jesus, Mary, and Joseph!"

Despite the recent hair-raising revelations, Jamie laughed. Tom stirred at the sound, and a popping noise like distant gunfire emerged from the mound of wet blankets. Quinn glanced at Jamie, eyebrow raised.

"Three's a lucky number, so it is."

JOHN GREY HAD SOME experience of prisons but had never been a guest of one. As such establishments went, the cell to which he'd been shown was fairly reasonable: there was no one else in the tiny room, the slop bucket was empty and dry, and there was a small, barred window. The walls oozed damp—why not, everything else in Ireland did—but there were no puddles on the floor, and while there was neither bed nor pallet, there was a wadded blanket in one corner of the room. He was glad to see it; the cell was bloody cold and his clothes were damp, his linen clammy; the heavens had opened on them an hour before they reached Athlone.

He paced the dimensions of the cell: eight feet by ten. If he were to walk seven hundred lengths of the cell, that would be approximately a mile. He shook out the blanket, dislodging a dead cricket, two live moths, and the broken fragments of what had once been a cockroach. What the devil had eaten it? he wondered. Rats?

Suddenly very tired, he sat down on the floor and pulled the blanket round his shoulders, shivering. He'd had time to think, riding to Athlone. He thought he'd have quite a bit more now but didn't expect it to do him much good.

It was both good luck and bad that Sir Melchior was gone. Bad, as it meant that the sergeant of the garrison had locked Grey up, because the deputy justiciar had not yet arrived, and the sergeant refused to summon the magistrate from the town until the morning. Good, as Sir Melchior or his deputy would very likely have questioned Grey—rather awkward—and then either put him under guard or demanded his parole, either of which would have kept him from getting back to Siverly's house or making his own investigation into Siverly's death.

His main concern was for Edward Twelvetrees. There had been no sign of the man, and none of the servants had mentioned his being there. Had he been at Glastuig, he could not but have noticed the uproar and come out to inquire. Ergo, he wasn't there—presumably because he had fled in the wake of the murder.

It had to have been Twelvetrees that Grey had heard in precipitate flight from the summerhouse after the murder. And as the man plainly had not gone to the stable, he must have returned—however briefly—to the main house. Why?

Either to fetch away something, or because he was cool enough to have realized that open flight would be an admission of guilt. Or possibly both, Grey thought. It was a substantial chest; it would have taken two footmen to carry it. Twelvetrees couldn't merely have scooped it up and ridden off with it under his arm.

It had been nearly noon when Grey found Siverly's body. Had Twelvetrees ridden up to the property, left his horse, then crept up to the summerhouse and bashed in Siverly's head with what Grey recognized as an Iroquois war club—doubtless the weapon with which Siverly had attacked Jamie Fraser?

Or had Twelvetrees never come back at all? It was possible, Grey supposed, that Siverly had enemies—given his record, it would be strange if he did not. And his possession of an Iroquois war club argued some fear of his life, did it not? Though the man did collect things; his room showed the normal accretions of a military man.

He sighed, closed his eyes, and tried to find a comfortable position, resting his head on an outstretched elbow.

Bloody hell. He simply didn't know enough. But he did know that he had to get out of here, and he had to go back to Glastuig, as soon as possible. There was nothing he could do but wait for Jamie Fraser.

THE SOUND OF FEET on the paving stones outside waked him. He blinked and squinted at the barred window, in an attempt to judge the time. The sky was overcast, but from the feel of things, he thought it was well past midnight—and the footsteps he heard weren't those of the regular midnight guard, in any case. There were several men.

He was on his feet, shod, and buttoning his waistcoat before the key grated in the lock. The door swung open, revealing the sergeant of the guard, lantern in one hand and a look of apoplectic fury on his face. Behind him loomed Jamie Fraser.

"I see ye were expecting us." Fraser sounded mildly amused. "Have ye got something to quiet this gentleman's humors?" He prodded the sergeant, a small, rawboned man, in the back with a large horse pistol, sending him stumbling into the cell.

"You filthy cur!" the sergeant exclaimed, the aubergine hue of his face deepening in the lantern light. "Your soul to the devil, ye wicked Scotch dog! And you—" He turned toward Grey, only to be interrupted by Grey's handkerchief, balled up and stuffed into his mouth.

Tom Byrd darted into the cell, seized the blanket, and, with a huge grin at Grey, drew Grey's dagger from his own belt and efficiently ripped off several strips, these being used at once to secure the sergeant. Tom then thrust the dagger into his employer's hand, and with a hoarsely whispered "Good to see you looking well, me lord!" he darted out again, presumably to scout for wandering guards.

"Thank you, Mr. Fraser," Grey murmured, shrugging into his coat as he headed for the door in his turn. In truth, he hadn't expected rescue, had only half-hoped for it, and his chest filled with a breathless excitement.

Fraser handed Grey the lantern, then waved the pistol, ushering him out. With a cordial nod at the sergeant, he pulled the door softly to behind them and locked it. He took back the lantern then and turned to the left. Near the corner, he paused, considering which way to go.

"I shouldn't have addressed you by name," Grey said, low-voiced. "I'm sorry."

Fraser shrugged, eyes squinted against the gloom that cloaked the courtyard. It was not quite drizzling, but the slates gleamed dully with wet where the lantern light reached them.

"Nay bother. There're none sae many redheided Scotsmen o' my size abroad in County Roscommon. It wouldna take them long to learn my name—and they wouldna require one to shoot me, in any case. Come on, wee Byrd," he said under his breath, "where are ye?"

As though the remark had conjured him, a dim figure appeared suddenly on the far side of the old bailey, waving. They walked—at a normal pace, lantern swinging low at Fraser's side—to the archway where Tom was waiting, his round face pale with excitement.

"This way," he breathed, and directed them to a set of shallow stone steps leading up to the walkway lined with arrow slits. "There's another stair at the far end, as goes down to the river gate," he whispered to John as he passed. "I didn't see any guards, but I hear voices."

John nodded, taking hold of his dagger. He hoped, for assorted reasons, that they weren't going to have to fight their way out.

"Should you leave the lantern?" he whispered, climbing close behind Jamie. Jamie shook his head.

"Better not," he said. "I may need it." Jamie stepped out onto the walkway and strode at what Grey considered an agonizingly slow pace. Grey and Tom Byrd followed like goslings. As they approached the bend of the wall, Grey heard voices from somewhere below and half-halted, only to be prodded on by Tom.

"Go on, me lord! We daren't stop," he whispered.

Feeling desperately exposed, Grey matched his step to Fraser's slow stride. He glanced quickly down and saw an open doorway across the courtyard, light spilling from it. The guardroom, it must be; he glimpsed several soldiers and could tell from the sudden hush, followed by laughter, groans, and exclamations, that they were dicing.

Just let someone throw a double six, he prayed.

Around another bend, out of sight, and he breathed again,

blood hammering in his ears. The dark below was silent, though he could still hear the guards behind them.

Fraser's plait hung down his back, unclubbed. It swung gently between his shoulder blades, a snakelet of gold light from the lantern vanishing up the smooth auburn strands into darkness. Suddenly Fraser stopped, and Grey nearly ran into him.

He heard the Scot draw a long, deep breath and saw him cross himself. Jamie turned toward Grey, bending to bring his mouth near Grey's ear.

"There's someone below, at the gate," he said very quietly, his breath warm on Grey's cheek. "We'll have to take him. Try not to kill him, aye?"

And with that, he threw the lantern into the courtyard. It landed with a loud clank and went out.

"Fumble-fingers," said a sarcastic voice from below. "That you, Ferguson? Drop something, didja?" A man came out from the niche at the foot of the stair; Grey saw him as a squat, thick shape against the dark stones. Fraser took in a great lungful of air, vaulted the low wall, and leapt feetfirst from the walkway, startling Grey so badly that he nearly followed inadvertently.

Fraser had struck the man a glancing blow in falling on him but enough to stop his wind for a moment; the two of them writhed on the stones, no more than gasps and grunts to mark their struggle. Grey rushed down the steps, heedless of the clatter.

"Tom, get the gate!" He rushed to the struggling figures and, seeing that the shorter man had momentarily got astride Fraser and was punching him vigorously in the head, picked his moment as well as he might in the dark and kicked the short figure with great force in the balls from behind.

The man rolled off Fraser with a horrible noise, and the Scot got to his knees, breathing like a grampus. Grey was already on his own knees, groping the guard's clothing for anything usable. The man had neither pistol nor shot but sported a sort of short sword, rather like a Roman gladius. Grey wondered at this unorthodox choice of weapon but took it anyway, pausing to administer a silencing kick in the belly before following Fraser into the niche.

Tom had got the gate unbolted. The Shannon lay just within bow shot, its sullen waters dark as pitch.

Fraser was limping badly; the fall hadn't done his bruised arse any good. He was also cursing roundly under his breath in *Gàidhlig,* by which Grey deduced the object of his wrath.

"Bloody hell," said Tom, moved either by excitement or example. "Where is he? He's not left us, has he?"

"If he has, he's a dead man," Fraser muttered briefly, and vanished into the dark, casting upstream. Grey deduced that "he" was likely Quinn and that Fraser had gone to find him.

"Are we waiting for a boat?" Grey asked Tom, keeping one eye on the bulk of the castle above them. They were no more than twenty yards from the wall, and every instinct urged him to leg it as fast as possible.

"Yes, me lord. Quinn said he could find a boat, and he was to meet us here at"—he glanced round, helpless—"well, at whatever time it was Mr. Fraser said. Which I think it's just now." He, too, glanced back at the castle, his face a pale splotch in the darkness. There was no light in the town nearby, not even a watchman's lantern in the streets.

Grey clutched the gladius in one hand, his dagger in the other—and precious little use either one would be to him if they were fired upon from the ramparts. Not much if the whole garrison suddenly poured out of the gate, eith—

"Hold these!" He shoved the weapons into Tom's startled

hands and, crouching, moved fast along the riverbank, scrabbling his hands through the edge of the water, searching for an appropriate bit of flotsam. He stubbed toes and fingers, floundering in the dark, but found what he wanted: a chunk of wood—a shattered plank. He tugged it free of the mud and ran back to the river gate, where he thrust his prize beneath the edge of the door. It slid under easily; no good, he needed—

Tom, bless him, had divined his need and was just behind him, his arms full of rubbish, sticks, and stones. Grey rummaged feverishly through this pile of dripping rejecta and crammed as much as he could beneath the free end of the plank, driving the wad in with his foot. His toes were going to be as blue as Fraser's arse, he thought, giving his improvised door jam a final, vicious kick.

Final, because there was no time to do more. There were shouts coming from inside the castle. Seizing Tom by the arm, Grey ran up the bank in the direction Fraser had gone.

The ground was muddy and uneven, and they lurched and stumbled, gasping as they went. Grey's foot skidded in the mud, then shot suddenly downward, and he fell sideways with a tremendous splash; he'd stepped into a reedbed. Gasping, he surfaced on his back, waving arms and legs in a vain attempt to stand up and catch his breath at the same time.

"Me lord!" Tom splashed in after him, though more carefully, wading out knee-deep, the reeds creaking and rasping as he pushed his way through them.

There was a sudden rattle, like pebbles thrown against glass. Shots, Grey thought, and flung himself over in a heavy swash of awkward, sopping clothes, able at last to get a purchase and crawl toward shore on hands and knees.

Single shots now, an irregular *pop-pop! Pop!* Could they see Tom and him, or were they firing at random to make a show? He thought suddenly of the arrow slits, and his shoulders hunched instinctively. Tom got him by the arm and hoisted him onto the shore like a harpooned turtle.

"Let's—" Tom said, and stopped suddenly, with a choked grunt of surprise.

"What—Tom!" Tom's knees were buckling. Grey caught him halfway down and eased him to the ground. "Where?" he said. "Where are you hit?" He'd heard that sound before: sheer astonishment—and, all too often, a man's final comment on life.

"Arm," Tom said, quite breathless but still more astonished than alarmed. "Something hit my arm. Like a hammer."

It was dark as the inside of a coal mine, but Grey could make out a black smudge on the left arm of Tom's coat. Spreading fast. He swore under his breath, scrabbled through the wet mass of his hair, and came away with a mangled ribbon between his fingers.

"Above the elbow? Below?" he asked rapidly, prodding the arm.

"Ow! Just there—ow!" A little above. He wrapped the ribbon round Tom's arm, regretting the loss of his handkerchief, and pulled it tight. It snapped.

A moment's panic, when the night blurred round him and the sound of shots hitting water sounded harmless, like the early drops of rain from a passing cloud. Then things clicked back into focus, and he found—to his vague surprise—that some part of his mind had kept on working; he was sitting on the ground, one shoe off, pulling the sopping stocking off his foot.

This, with the other balled up to use as a wad, made an admirable tourniquet.

"I shall have something to say to the coves at Jennings and Brown," Tom said, in a voice that quavered only a little. "That's where I bought that ribbon."

"You do that, Tom," Grey said, smiling in spite of himself as he shoved his bare feet back into wet shoes. His mind was working through the possibilities. If Tom was seriously hurt, then he needed care at once. And the only place to get it was the castle. If it was no more than a flesh wound, though . . . "Do you think you can walk? Can you sit up?"

"Oh, yes, me . . . ohhh . . ." Tom, halfway up, suddenly sagged and subsided onto the ground. "Oh," he murmured. "Me head's not half spinnnn . . ." His voice trailed off into silence. Grey felt frantically for a heartbeat, ripping Tom's shirt out of his breeches and rummaging up under it, feeling here and there on the cold, wet skin of his chest. He found one, thank God, and, with a gasp of relief, pulled his hand out of Tom's shirt and looked round.

The river gate was opening, in slow jerks as men hit it from behind, forcing loose his improvised jam. He could see the light of their lanterns, rimming the door in a fiery nimbus.

"Shit," he said, and, seizing Tom under the arms, waded back into the reeds, dragging his senseless valet.

THE BOAT BOBBED as Jamie shifted his weight, bringing his heart into his mouth.

"Be still, ye great galoot." Quinn's voice came from behind, just audible over the lapping of the water against the sides, and the water uneasily close to the top of the boat, if you asked Jamie. "Ye'll have us over, if ye don't give over your squirming, and you like a tiger in a sack. Are ye like to be sick again?"

"Dinna even mention it," Jamie said, and swallowed, closing his eyes. He'd tried convincing himself that if he couldn't see the water, his stomach would be oblivious, but he was morbidly aware that less than an inch of wood separated his cringing buttocks from the cold black water of the Shannon, and that wood leaking like a sieve. His feet were wet, and as for squirming, he was convinced that the wicked wee boat was doing just that, even drifting down the current as they were.

"Should we not row?" he whispered back over his shoulder—having been warned that sound travels over water.

"We shall not," Quinn said decidedly. "It's a bloody flat calm, so it is, and if ye think I mean to go splashing past Castle Athlone, hallooing and cryin' out for your friends . . . Hist!"

Jamie jerked his head round to see the bulk of the castle rise up on his right, black as hell against the drizzling sky. The intimation of hell was the more pronounced as he saw the river gate from which they had escaped now burst open, spilling red light and black, shouting figures that capered, demonlike, on the bank of the river.

"Hail Mary, Mother of God . . ." he whispered, and took firm hold of the edge of the boat to steady himself. Where were Grey and Tom Byrd? He shut his eyes tight to accustom them to dark and looked away from the castle before opening them again. But what he could see of the bank was featureless, dark blobs that might be boats or sea monsters bobbing near the shore, the black patches of what Quinn said were reedbeds like tar against the dull shimmer of the water. Nothing seemed to move. Nothing that looked like two men running, at least. And, by God, they *should* be running, he thought, with that lot after them.

For now the whole garrison was roused, and the shore near the castle was aglow with lanterns, their swinging lights shooting beams up and down the riverbank, the bawling of the sergeant—Jamie grinned despite the situation, recognizing the furious voice of the man he'd taken prisoner—echoing across the water.

A quiet splash made him turn his head. Quinn had put an oar in the water and was sculling, very gently, to slow their progress. The boat's head turned inward in a slow, meditative circle.

"What if they're not here?" Quinn said very quietly.

"They're here. I left them on the bank, just by the castle."

"They're not there now," Quinn observed, an edge to his voice, low as it was.

"They saw me go upstream. They'll have followed me. We'll need to turn round. They'll not have seen us, coming down so quiet."

He spoke with a great deal more confidence than he felt, but Quinn said no more than a muttered "God and Mary and Padraic be with us" before putting the other oar in the water and settling himself to it. The boat turned, the current hissing past its sides, and with as little splashing as could be managed, they began slowly to retrace their progress, Jamie leaning out as far as he dared to scan the shore.

Nothing. He caught a flicker of movement, but it disappeared between two sheds. A dog, likely—too small to be a man, let alone two.

Where would they go, with the soldiers about to erupt into the night? Into the town was the logical answer. The castle was surrounded by a labyrinth of narrow, winding streets.

"How far d'ye want to go?" Quinn grunted. He was breathing hard with the effort of rowing against the current.

"This is far enough. Turn round again," Jamie said abruptly. They were perhaps a furlong upstream of the castle; if Grey and the lad had been on the bank, they would have found them by now. They must have gone into the town, and the soldiers would doubtless be coming to that conclusion, too.

Jamie started praying again. How was he to find them in the town? He was as noticeable himself as either of the Englishmen. It would have to be Quinn searching the town, and he doubted that the Irishman would be enthused at the prospect.

Aye, well, he'd just have to—

A heavy *clunk!* struck the hull of the boat near his hand, and he jerked with such violence that the little vessel rocked wildly. Quinn cursed and backed his oars.

"What in the name of the Holy Ghost did we hit?"

Clunk! Clunk! Clunk! The sound was repeated, a frenzied demand, and Jamie leaned over the side and nearly let out a skelloch at the sight that greeted him: a wild-eyed head like Medusa protruding from the water a few inches from his hand, snaky hair in all directions and teeth bared in a ferocious grimace. This startling figure held what looked to be a large bundle in one arm, a sort of sword in the other hand, and as Jamie gaped at it, openmouthed, the figure gritted its teeth and swung the weapon once more against the side of the boat with a peremptory *clunk!*

"Get us in!" said the figure. "I can't hold him much longer."

26

Opium Dreams

GREY HUDDLED IN A SODDEN HEAP IN THE BOTTOM OF THE boat, dully aware of Fraser's back in front of him. The Scot's long arms stretched and pulled, shoulders bunching as he rowed steadily upstream, and the black bulk of the castle slowly, slowly diminished behind them. He heard peremptory shouts from the shore and Quinn, standing up in the boat, clinging to the mast and shouting back in Irish, but Grey was too dazed with cold and exhaustion to worry much about what he was saying.

"That'll hold 'em," Quinn muttered, sitting down on the tiny slatted seat behind Grey. He put a hand on Grey's shoulder to steady himself and leaned forward. "How are ye, boy?" Tom was curled next to Grey, his head on Grey's knee, shivering convulsively. They both were, in spite of the cloaks Quinn had hastily wrapped round them.

"F-f-f-fine," Tom said. His body was tight with pain; Grey could feel the bulge of Tom's cheek against his leg as Tom clenched his teeth, and he laid a hand on his valet's head, hoping to comfort him a little. He fumbled with his other hand under the cloak covering Tom, but his fingers were clumsy with cold, unable to deal with the makeshift tourniquet.

"We n-need to loosen the t-t-tourniquet," he managed, hating his awkward helplessness, the chattering of his own teeth.

Quinn bent swiftly to help, his curls brushing Grey's face; the Irishman smelled of peat smoke, sweat, and sausage grease, a strangely comforting, warm aroma.

"Let me have a bit of a look, now," he said, his tone friendly, soothing. "Ah, there I have it, the sorrow and the woe! Now, ye'll be holding quite still, Mr. Byrd, and I'll just . . ." His voice trailed off in absorption as he felt his way. Grey felt the warmth of Quinn's body, was soothed himself as much by the physical presences of Quinn and Fraser, close by, as by the knowledge of escape.

Tom was making small whimpering noises. Grey curled his fingers into his valet's tangled damp hair, rubbing a little behind the cold ear, as he would to distract a dog while a tick was removed.

"Ah, now," Quinn murmured, fingers working busily in the dark. "Almost there. Aye, that's got it."

Tom gave a great gasp and gulped air, and dug the fingers of his good hand hard into Grey's leg. Grey deduced that the tourniquet was now loosed, letting a rush of blood flow into the wounded arm, waking the numbed nerves. He knew exactly what that felt like and clasped his own free hand over Tom's, squeezing hard.

"Is the bleeding bad?" he asked quietly.

"Bad enough," Quinn replied absently, still feeling about beneath the cloak. "Not spurtin', though. A little bandage will do, with the blessing." He rose up, shaking his head a little, and reached into his coat, coming out with a familiar square black bottle.

"It's as well I brought the tonic, thinkin' Jamie might need it

r when the provisional government moved to London. In
tler said that 'after final victory, we must effect a reconcili-
King must go – in his place the Duke of Windsor. With him
permanent treaty of friendship instead of a peace treaty.' The
commander of Britain would be Franz Six, with Mosley acting
in this fantasy world, Amery saw himself as the future foreign

ld Courlander an anti-Jewish committee in England had offered
o fund the Legion. He cited Domvile, Fuller, the Duke of Hamilton
s associated with the Link, the Anglo-German Fellowship, the Right
'Cliveden set' and other pre-war pro-German groups. Few picked
urlander's fantastical revelations. What is interesting is the similarity
ommittee to Haushofer's view of the 'peace party'. Was Amery a victim
British deception operation sprung in 1941?

Following a German Foreign Office directive, in September 1943 the British
Legion was placed in the hands of Waffen-SS recruiter Gottlob Berger. He had 'no great belief in this unit' but within three months the SS possessed a British Free Corps (BFC), largely made up of former BU personnel. 'In our barracks', wrote Alfred Minchin, 'we had a photograph of the Duke of Windsor, whom we all admired as he was also a rebel. We all recognised him as the King of England.' The BFC never fought on the Eastern Front, though Cooper boasted 'he had taken part in atrocities against the Jews'. After the war these renegades were tried and imprisoned.

Excluded from the BFC, Amery travelled to Vichy France and met with BU member Mariette Smart. Daughter of a German mother, she worked as an interpreter in interrogations and accompanied the Gestapo on arrests of Jews, whose deportation she directed. She delighted in betraying her French neighbours and after the war was arrested and sentenced to death by a Court in
Smart had been recruited as an *Abwehr* agent for missions in Switzer-
Italy, where she met Theodore Schurch, the BU member working for
s. When Mussolini was ousted and Italy changed sides in September
urch was handed over to the *Abwehr* as a 'going concern' for
in southern France and northern Italy. Captured in Rome in April
n a mission to report on Vatican attitudes towards the Allies, he
Swiss and his defence lawyer pleaded he had been misled by
e. 'Many more illustrious people than himself held these views,'
The court, however, was unmoved and condemned him to be

mmer of 1943 Diana recalled that she and Mosley stripped
the prison yard. A priest told a warden it was 'like the
here – Lady Mosley in her little knickers'. Mosley could

75 and 76. Mosley returned to street politics in May 1948 with the formation of the Union Movement

77. Mosley seen here with his main officials and supporters in the UM, Jeffrey Hamm, Commandant Mary Allen, Raven Thomson, Victor Burgess and Tommy Moran

78. A key collaborator was former South African Defence Minister, Oswald Pirow, with whom he constructed the apartheid-minded Euro-Africa policy

79. Mosley's rival in influencing the post-war neo-Nazi networks was a young and deranged American lawyer at the Nuremberg War trials, Francis Parker Yockey

80. Exiling himself to Europe and Ireland for much of the fifties, Mosley returned to the fray following the outbreak of the Notting Hill riots

81. The Mosleys visited Venice with their sons in 1954

(Right) 82. Max seen here with his mother in August 1962, leaving Old Street Magistrates Court, after a hearing held into disturbances in Dalston

'devastating effect' on British domest
without the unpredictable Amer
Foreign Press Club, he was 'abs
a conversation'. He was 'plagued
no way out for himself'.

John Brown was one PoW the En
Royal Artillery sergeant captured on t
manager at Truman's Brewery in Surrey an
to fall into German hands. BU colleagues sai
house on the streets of Whitechapel and Bethnal
and of course their Jewish co-conspirators'. In fact,
who learnt the codes to communicate with London f
escape and evasion organization MI9. British Intelligenc
February 1943 – the remnants of the German 6th Army ha
in Stalingrad – of plans for a 'British anti-Bolshevik Legion'.

In April, Amery launched his book *England Faces Europe*. In a p
state and drunk, on the 8th he mistakenly gave his wife, who re
headache pill, a poison ampoule which he carried with him to ensure
death in the event of being abducted. When the following morning he tr
rouse her she was dead. On 21 April he entered St Denis PoW camp on be
of a 'committee in England' and appealed to Britons 'to answer this call
arms in defence of our homes . . . against Asiatic and Jewish bestiality. Within the limits of military possibilities, the Legion of St George will fight at the junction of the German and Finnish troops.' He found no support but in Paris told Antonia Hunt, a Briton detained by the SS, that 'when the Germans win the war, we will have the Duke of Windsor as King of occupied England'. An alternative government would be used to enhance peace elem within England.

The England Committee did recruit twenty pro-German
to be imprisoned alongside Jews and regarded Wi
Mosley as their Leader. They were led by Thom
German. Working for a firm of oil importer
BU's Hammersmith branch in 1938. Joh
and sent the information he collected v
Also recruited was Roy Courlander
tion, who had seen at first hand t
would win the war.

Arrested at the end of the
Nazi blueprint for Britain pres
Committee that if the British legion
ance the formation of a 'provisional
territory – the German-held Channel Islan

be 'so naughty', Diana remembered, in what was still a women's prison. 'He does tease – he lies around sunbathing with all those poor girls all screaming out of their windows.' Nicholas, during periods of leave from his regiment, and Vivien, who was working as a machine-tool operator in an armaments factory, visited their father. In London their lives revolved round Aunt Irene, who did relief work in the East End. She had moved in permanently to the Dorchester, 'a rallying-place for many of the influential and once-beautiful people of the kind who had used to gravitate around' the Mosleys and who were now running the war.

Mosley felt closest to Nicholas and tried in letters 'to show affection, and to interest him in books and ideas which filled his own mind at that time'. Mosley was forty-five and might have been expected to be reaching the peak of his political life but it was ending prematurely in isolation. However, just as with his period of convalescence in hospital during the First World War, he used his forced confinement to educate himself and to reconsider his career and the path he had chosen.

'Plato's requirement of withdrawal from life for a considerable period of study and reflection before entering on the final phase of action', Mosley wrote, 'was fulfilled in my case, though not by my own volition.' He set himself the task of 'learning to think and feel as a European', with a philosophy that went 'beyond both fascism and democracy' to a synthesis at a higher level. There were numerous Germans in Brixton and by the time he joined Diana in Holloway he knew enough to be able to read Goethe, Schiller and Nietzsche, and was soon able to recite his favourite passages by heart and quote extensively from *Faust* and *Also Sprach Zarathustra*.

Mosley was influenced by Nietzsche and Spengler but knew that behind them 'stood the shadowy but towering figure of Goethe, whom alone both recognised as their master'. *Faust* made the most profound impression on him – a book 'transcending almost every other imaginative work' – and he later published an English translation with his own introduction. *Faust* rested upon the premise that man was placed on earth for a definite purpose, to bring about higher forms of life. Goethe, Mosley told Gerard Mignard, had overcome 'the age-old antithesis between man's lower and higher self, between egoism and altruism by showing how the lower is in fact an instrument of the higher'. He denied identifying his own destiny with Faust, except 'in the belief in always striving'. He referred to Shaw's reference: 'perhaps in Nature that only things survive if they are striving'. In this sense, life's purpose is 'the development of the self in Achievement, as an artist in action and life, who creates, also, for humanity'. 'Whoever strives will be redeemed' was the motto for his higher form philosophy.

Diana said Mosley's view of life was 'dramatically influenced by Goethe's philosophy and his Hellenism, as well as his pantheism'. He initially explored the Greek world through the writings of eighteenth-century German neo-Hellenists such as Winckelmann, Wieland and Schiller. He read in translation the tragedians Aeschylus, Sophocles and his favourite, Euripides, and Plato and Aristotle with their aristocratic philosophy of heroic pessimism. These were for pleasure, recalled Diana. For work, despite his professed antipathy to psychoanlysis, he read Freud, Jung and Adler.

Completion of his imagined synthesis of democracy and fascism required 'a healing synthesis' – 'a union of Hellenism, calm but radiant embrace of the beauty and wonder of life with the Gothic impulse of new discoveries urging men to reach beyond their present precarious balance'. With his tendency to self-importance, he claimed his doctrine was derived from Euryclites and owed much to sciences. 'Modern statesmen should live and work with scientists as the Medicis lived with the artists. This doctrine is a synthesis between Sciences and Philosophy.' He admitted his approach was 'Lamarckian'. 'Life is a steady movement from simple to higher forms. From the simple amoeba, the primitive organism, to where we stand today and furthermore in the future.' He was aware of giving offence by suggesting 'a higher and a lower civilization can exist in cultural achievement or even in Nature, but to follow that opinion to its logical end, we have to affirm that Isaac Newton was in no way a higher type than the inmate of a lunatic asylum'.

Mosley argued that if society retained 'its evolutionary urge' towards higher forms, then a father figure was 'necessary to break through the force of inertia'. He hated puritanism, which 'represses for the sake of repressing, particularly in the Left' – where 'small souls are urged by their subconscious instinct to hate the Father Figure of the man of action'. Dictatorship was wrong but leadership was required.

Fascism had 'too much paganism and not enough Christianity'. Assisting the emergence of higher forms of life also served the purpose of God. Mosley wrote in his composite of his wartime reading, *The Alternative*, that 'no mechanism of Society or of Government can function unless we can produce more such men: they are the lights of humanity'. His synthesis of the 'democratic camel and the fascist lion of Nietzsche's Three Metamorphoses' must give way to something higher – the innocence and new beginning encapsulated in the child. An old interned BU member claimed Mosley was already stating that 'the old fascism had gone and that we would have to unite Europe'. Europe was that new beginning. At least, that was what Mosley would claim, though when it came to action the vision looked much the same as the old. A change was an emphasis on individual rights, which reflected his anger at imprisonment without trial, but also a concession that Fascism had destroyed such rights.

24

'Lucifer Fallen'

In the summer of 1943 friends feared for Mosley's well-being. Lady Redesdale visited Mrs Churchill, who had been one of her bridesmaids, to ensure the facts of his condition – the worsening of the congestion of the blood in his lower limbs – were known to her husband. Clementine, however, infuriated her by suggesting prison was at least protecting her family 'from the fury of mobs outside'. Mosley was seen by his physician, Dr Geoffrey Evans, and the King's doctor, Lord Dawson, who warned if there was no improvement in his confinement – temperatures dropped to freezing point during the night – there was a 'substantial risk' of the phlebitis 'producing permanent danger to health and even to life'. Based on their report, Mosley's solicitor asked for his detention order to be suspended.

The Home Office was not especially worried when Prison Medical Officer Dr Jameson noted that the forty-six-year-old, six foot two inch Mosley weighed only 157 pounds, though 'the average weight for a man of his age and height is 197 pounds'. This was blamed on 'a mild anxiety state arising from a deep sense of frustration and consequent depression'. This may have been true. Mosley was an isolated figure; during August Admiral Domvile and Robert Gordon-Canning were released, leaving few senior figures in confinement. Jameson, however, did not support Dr Evans's view that 'confinement and isolation are breaking Sir Oswald's nerve', so the request to suspend his order was refused.

Herbert Morrison criticized Mosley's 'class friends', in particular 'a fashionable lady ... "fluttering about" trying to use her influence in important quarters' on his behalf. Baba Metcalfe pressurized friends such as Walter Monckton (who had secretly visited Mosley – the purpose of which remains unknown) and Lord Halifax, ambassador in Washington, to appeal to the Home Secretary to seek his release. On 4 September Halifax informed Morrison that 'a clot of blood that was in his leg has shifted up into his stomach . . . he might well die . . . and that if it happened it would be a scandal and that nobody could defend it after warnings received'. Morrison suggested that all Mosley needed was fresh air and exercise.

On 5 October Evans and Dawson re-examined Mosley and found his phlebitis was 'clearly progressive'. Churchill asked for an update on the state of health of Mosley, who wrote to the prison governor on 17 October, blaming his condition on the failure to heat the annexe at Holloway during the winter of 1942–3, the long-term effects of imprisonment and worry about his wife's health. Morrison again refused his release.

On 22 October Churchill told *Manchester Guardian* editor W. P. Crozier that he worried about Mosley.

I think no good of him, but he's been in prison all this time and he's likely to die in prison this winter, and he has never been accused and never tried – a frightful thing to anyone concerned about English liberties. I did it because the country was in danger of destruction and we could run no risk, we had to do it and we were right to do it, but now the great emergency has passed and the necessity is no longer there.

As head of a coalition, Churchill was still constrained by the informal alliance between the Labour Party and MI5. Diana decided they needed the PM's Private Secretary, Brendan Bracken, to get to 'the big man'. On 3 November Baba appealed for his help on Mosley. 'There is no time to lose. In his present condition he is a prey to flu or pneumonia and then, as his doctor said, nothing can save him . . . Today he looked like a dying man to me.'

A conference on Mosley's health on 9 November was attended by Dawson and Evans, and doctors Mathieson (Governor of Holloway), Fenton (Brixton's doctor) and Methuen, the Medical Commissioner for prisons; all agreed it would be wise to release him. The public, however, were resentful that people less important than Mosley did not have such a galaxy of medical talent at their disposal. Someone, discovering that it could cure phlebitis, sent a bottle of rat poison to the Home Office.

Morrison faced a dilemma. To free Mosley would anger Labour supporters but to keep him in prison would run the risk of elevating him into a martyr. The danger, one MP said, was of Fascism becoming 'a permanent factor in the political issues of this country'. Nicholas was in Taranto, Italy. 'Away from my sophisticated friends of the Rifle Brigade, the name of Mosley suddenly became a difficulty . . . people to whom I had to introduce myself were apt to say – "Not any relation of that bastard?" ' On 16 November he hoped his father 'never does anything rash politically again. It is terrible to think how he bungled things earlier . . . They are obviously still very frightened of him . . . he is still a force to be reckoned with in the political world.'

Prison doctors recommended Mosley be released and on 17 November Morrison informed the Cabinet he intended to do so on 'humanitarian grounds'. Minister of Labour Ernest Bevin, who loathed Morrison, said it would 'weaken morale'. Mosley, however, was no longer considered a danger but news of his release heralded the biggest storm of Morrison's career. He was in trouble with his party and there was a risk he might have to resign. He did, however, receive the support of Beaverbrook, who hailed him as a future prime minister. While other newspapers hurled abuse, the *Express* gave 'staunch support of his policy of freedom'. Told he could advocate Mosley's release, editor Christiansen mistakenly assumed he was equally entitled not to do so. He recalled the 'disastrous effect which support of Mosley had had on sales of the *Mail* in the 1930s'. Beaverbook was furious and only the pleadings by managers saved Christiansen from dismissal. Against his will, Michael Foot had to write a grudging article of endorsement.

Sackloads of letters arrived at the Home Office, protesting against the release of the 'Number One Traitor'. Home Intelligence reports noted a 'storm of indignation' across the country. 'A feeling lingers that Mosley represents in this country all those things against which we are fighting.' Working-class comment was blunt: 'Mosley is a traitor and a symbol of fascism.' The Communist Party organized protests, especially in factories on war production, and deputations of workers marched into Whitehall.

The CP's Harry Pollitt warned on 20 November that Mosley's release was a 'betrayal of the anti-Fascist war' and had done more to harm national unity 'than Goebbels could ever have hoped to achieve'. The *Jewish Chronicle* asserted that 'Morrison's Folly' raised doubts as to whether government leaders were 'really heart and soul in the war against the monstrosity Fascism'. George Bernard Shaw, however, regarded their response as shameful. 'Even if Mosley were in rude health, it was high time to release him with apologies for having let him frighten us into scrapping the Habeas Corpus Act . . . We have produced the ridiculous situation in which we may buy Hitler's *Mein Kampf* in any bookshop in Britain, but may not buy ten lines written by Mosley. The whole affair has become too silly for words.' The *Völkischer Beobachter* claimed Mosley had been set free out of fear that he might die in gaol and 'raise a tornado of popular indignation'.

Mosley and his wife were released at 7 a.m. on the morning of Saturday 20 November. Press photographers were waiting outside the main gate but the couple were taken out through Holloway's murderess gate. Placed under house arrest, Mosley had to report monthly to the police, undertake no political activities, make no attempt to contact former followers and not travel more than seven miles from his residence.

The Jacksons agreed to the Mosleys staying with them at Rignell House near Banbury. A well-known figure in government circles, Derek was employed in secret work on 'window', the strips of metal paper which interfered with enemy radar. He welcomed a 'dead pale and frighteningly thin' Mosley with a feast. The press soon guessed their location and reporters besieged the house. The Home Office then woke up to the fact that they were 'living at the house of a famous Air Ministry scientist who was privy to the most secret information'.

Mosley's presence was considered risky and to forestall a question in the Commons, Morrison telephoned Derek and said the couple must go elsewhere. Derek swore at Morrison for 'presuming to tell him whom he could or could not receive in his house'.

On 21 November the PM telegraphed Morrison from Cairo: 'I HIGHLY APPROVE YOUR ACTIONS.' Churchill had received a critical report on MI5 condemning the lack of ministerial control and its abuse of powers. He was convinced 18B should be abolished, 'as the national emergency no longer justifies abrogation of individual rights of habeas corpus and trial by jury on definite charges'. He added that 'the power of the Executive to cast a man into prison without formulating any charge known to the law, and particularly to deny him the judgement of his peers, is in the highest degree odious and is the foundation of all totalitarian government whether Nazi or Communist . . . Extraordinary powers assumed by the Executive with the consent of Parliament in emergencies should be yielded up when and as the emergency declines.' The Home Office vetoed circulation of his comments. Morrison was nervous of the 'shock to public opinion' but the PM replied that 'any unpopularity you have incurred through correct and humane exercise of your functions will be repaid in a few months by public respect'.

Morrison made a statement to MPs on 23 November and assured a packed Commons that, although the government would continue to oppose the 'evil cancer' of Fascism, Mosley no longer posed 'any undue risk to national security'. Chips Channon suggested arguments about Mosley's release had been 'whipped up by Communists and Jewish elements'. A crowd of 2,000 people blocked the St Stephen's entrance and were removed by police using batons. The public lobby was crowded with 'young factory workers indignantly protesting at his release'. Morrison made a fighting speech, declaring he would not 'bow to the dictates of the mob. If you say I am to keep this man in because I hate him or disagree with him but I am to let another man out because I have sympathy with him, then the House must frame a law under which that could be done.' He said 'the extraordinary powers of detention without trial must not be used except in so far as they are essential for national security'. He was 'not prepared to let anyone die in detention unnecessarily'.

Press observers said it was 'a great personal triumph' with the heat taken out of the issue. Channon, however, 'rather enjoyed the ironical scene of the Labour Party so enraged by the release of one of their ex-Ministers by a Labour Home Secretary! Their indignation seemed great.' He had known Mosley but considered him 'an unscrupulous but not unattractive fellow, dominated by an urge for power and publicity'.

Mosley was the most detested man in Britain. On 23 November Durham miners resolved to strike if he was not put back in jail. Hugh Dalton, who 'hated Mosley worse than any other man in public life – and I don't really hate many of them', wrote that the following day's National Executive meeting was 'bloody awful!'. Ellen Wilkinson made 'an impassioned defence, with sobs in her throat, but it really isn't very convincing, except to the purists for civil liberty, who like to think that 18B is being administered leniently'. He realized that Morrison 'will get away with it after all', despite having 'made a thorough mess of it', after being advised by a 'clever Australian Jew'. Dalton admitted he 'would not have been at all sorry to let [Mosley] die, provided there was not too sharp a comeback from anywhere that mattered. When so many millions are dying, including so many who are so worthwhile, it is revolting to me that any step, however small, should have been taken to prolong the life of this filthy blackguard, who was clearly marked out to be Gauleiter of this country had the Huns got ashore.'

In a letter to the *San Francisco Chronicle* Diana's sister Jessica complained that the Mosleys' release was 'a slap in the face of anti-fascists in every country and a direct betrayal of those who have died for the cause of anti-fascism. They should be kept in jail, where they belong.' Diana received letters from her 'waggish sister' sealed with stickers reading 'Put MOSLEY back in GAOL!'. Although he had only been out a week, Lady Redesdale was able to tell Nancy on 27 November that Mosley's health was 'already improved'. Morrison later noted that 'whatever doubts may persist about the medical advice on Mosley – that gentleman's survival into a healthy old age can hardly diminish them'. On 28 November a huge crowd marched to Trafalgar Square demanding Mosley's reinternment. On the following day Harold Nicolson, at lunch at the Ritz, told Liberal MP Violet Bonham-Carter he feared the affair had 'widened the class breach' providing 'a nasty reminder of the prejudice and passion of the proletariat'.

Ernest Bevin's animosity towards Morrison boiled up and he threatened to resign over Mosley. Morrison defended his action to a party meeting and an official resolution, broadly supporting him, was passed, but only after a critical amendment had been narrowly defeated. The Labour Party was, therefore, split. Hannen Swaffer wrote in the *People* on 28 November that 'it would be almost a disaster to the working class cause if his decision over Mosley ended the career of Morrison, the ablest and most outspoken of all the Socialist leaders'. Two days later Churchill's doctor Lord Moran recorded the PM saying that 'the government may go over Mosley. Bevin is kicking.' On the eve of a Commons debate, Bracken wrote to Bevin that the PM regarded him as 'a rock of strength'. His resignation 'would add a great deal to [his] burdens . . . It would indeed be an awful piece of irony if the contemptible Mosley became the cause of splitting the only government which can see this country through its perils and lay the foundation for a better England.' Bevin withdrew his threat.

In the debate on 1 December George Woods moved a resolution regretting Mosley's release as a decision 'calculated to retard the war effort and lead to misunderstanding at home and abroad'. Sydney Silverman claimed he had seen the medical reports and none contained anything serious until 9 November, when high-level intervention persuaded the doctors to change their opinion. He called for the reports to be published. Morrison angrily refused. Irene went to listen and was sickened by the venom of many MPs. In the end the government was able easily to defeat the resolution, 327 to 62.

'Morrison's authority over Parliament is second only to that wielded by the Prime Minister,' claimed the *Evening Standard*. But in the country he was continually heckled at meetings. Albert Worral at Vickers Manchester factory shouted 'Down with Mosley' on a BBC *Works Wonders* programme but the broadcast was cut off and he was sacked. During Question Time on 10 December Commander Locker-Lampson summed up the sentiments of many when he told Morrison, 'Mosley has got off, and so will Mussolini and Hitler.' Beaverbrook wrote to Sir Samuel Hoare that it had all been 'a small political comedy'. The

> roles of hero and villain were both filled by Herbert Morrison. He played them with equal vigour and aplomb, being cheered as hero from the stalls and hooted as villain from the gallery. It is true that the comedy nearly turned into drama. This was because another, and unauthorized, set of producers took a hand. Citrine mistook the TUC for the Committee of Public Safety. And the Communist Party with its genius for crowd scenes brought a series of well-disciplined processions into Whitehall.

By Christmas, the TUC, NCCL and Labour's NEC had dropped campaigns to have Mosley reinterned.

Mosley was weak and desperately thin but newspapers were hostile. The *Daily Worker* said he should be put back in prison because he was 'in rude and vigorous health'. Once it was realized Jackson was engaged on secret war work, the Mosleys were made to leave. The house was surrounded at 3 a.m. by police with dogs and the Mosleys were taken away to a disused hotel, the Shaven Crown, in Shipton-under-Wychwood in the Cotswolds. They were joined by Nanny Higgs, Alexander and Max. It was six miles from Swinbrook and occasionally Unity would be driven over to see them. The siege by the press continued. Fearing trouble, MI5's Roger Hollis drew up a list of Communists living within thirty miles and Scotland Yard sent a detective called Shipton to keep an eye on the Mosleys. He told them crime stories. The hotel's manager later showed visitors the rooms where the Mosleys had stayed. He said there had been two attempts on their life by angry locals, and the scars left by a hand grenade could still be seen on the front wall. It was the nearest that Mosley came to action during the war.

Mosley decided to settle down as a country gentleman. With Savehay Farm still requisitioned, he bought the 'pretty, rather bourgeois' Crux Easton, near Newbury, with views of the Hampshire countryside for £35,000 (£735,000). When his father was rector of the Georgian church, the inventor and aviator Sir Geoffrey de Havilland spent his childhood there and, in the grounds of the estate, designed his first aircraft, the Tiger Moth, later flying it from nearby Beacon Hill. With the opening of the Second Front in June 1944 the danger of invasion was past but the house arrest remained in force until the end of the war. A policeman, Detective Sergeant Buswell, nicknamed by the children 'bugger-shit Buswell', was assigned to keep an eye on Mosley but he was not even billeted in the village.

Mosley's health quickly improved and after six months he recovered much of his old vigour. While Allied troops were fighting to free Europe, the Mosleys walked a great deal in the local countryside. Diana's brother Tom had been fighting in North Africa and Italy, and returned to England in July 1944 to the Staff College. Bill Deedes claimed Tom 'did not share the political passions of Unity, Jessica or Diana'. However, in a diary entry for 27 August 1944 James Lees-Milne recorded a conversation in which Tom affirmed that 'all the best Germans are Nazis and if I were a German I would be one'. Tom visited the Mosleys and they discussed philosophy and politics. He had, Diana recalled, 'decided that the imminent invasion of Germany was something he would prefer not to take part in'.

Prison affected Diana more deeply than her husband, though being reunited with the four children was a huge boost. Mosley was not a demonstrative father but loved to see Alexander and Max enjoying the countryside. He had a big temper, which he kept under control but 'just once or twice there was a faint suggestion that it might be a good idea if people didn't make too much noise' when he was reading. Nicholas visited when on leave – he had won a Military Cross in the Italian campaign. His father wished him well on a career as a novelist, though, Diana noted, 'he did not go so far as to read his books'.

Diana organized things so that Mosley was happy. He had no visits from friends – he had spurned or affronted most of them. He blamed Churchill for the continuance of the war and regarded the entire Churchill family as arch-enemies. Osbert Sitwell was one of the few to stay loyal. Diana's friends – John Betjeman, Robert Swann, Gerald Berners and Daisy Fellowes – often came to stay. Mosley was, Diana said, 'tremendously easy to talk to because he was never condescending; I noticed exactly the same thing when he talked to farm labourers. He might occasionally talk over our heads about philosophy but even that was flattering as it assumed we were frightfully well-read.' With a low-boredom threshold, he loved fun and jokes.

Despite restrictions on political activity, Mosley was in contact with former colleagues such as George Dunlop, the main force behind the 18B groups, and

Charlie Watts, who laid the basis for the Mosleyite revival. The Jewish Defence Committee reported reunions among former BU detainees and anti-Semitic street meetings. A fund-raising concert attended by 500 people was held at the Kingsway Hall for the 18B Detainees Fund. The 18B Publicity Council staged a number of socials and dances, with up to 1,000 Fascists and their supporters in attendance. The 18B campaign was a link between the pre-war BU and the new Fascist groups that would spring up after 1945. In considering why the post-war Fascist revival happened so quickly, Douglas Hyde pointed out that the Fascist groups never went out of existence. Most were feeble enterprises with limited funds and only a few dozen members but they kept alive a Fascist and anti-Semitic tradition. There were over fifty groups with several thousand individual members. Hyde was visited by Special Branch officers, who admitted they had 'no worthwhile information on the neo-fascists and neither had MI5'.

One such group was the National Front after Victory, which aimed to co-ordinate the activities of anti-Jewish groups. It had been founded by A. K. Chesterton who, after serving in East Africa and being invalided out of the army in 1944, was appointed assistant editor of *Truth*. At an 18B Detainees Aid Fund meeting an SB agent heard former BU member Mr Valeriani remark that Mosley 'had paid a lot of money for special medical attention to AKC in Germany, and they hoped they would get a return for their money'. They were, however, disappointed. His estrangement from the Mosleyites was total.

The British League of Ex-Servicemen and Women, led by Jeffrey Hamm, an ex-BU member and 18B detainee, was at the forefront of the Fascist revival. Hamm had been detained in the Falkland Islands, where he was a school-teacher, and then moved to a camp in South Africa. Returning to England in 1941, he volunteered for the Royal Tank Regiment, but was discharged, detained and again put on restricted release in 1944. Hamm was typical of those Fascists whose detention forged a bond of martyrdom and strengthened their commitment to Mosley. He organized the League to defend the interests of ex-service men returning home and to advance policies based on Mosley's writings.

On 5 November 1944 the League's first meeting in Hyde Park was met by a hostile crowd. Despite the stipulation that they refrain from political activity, Hamm promoted the message 'Britain for the British', as well as Mosleyite attacks on 'international finance'. The crowd responded with 'Here we go again. Here's where the Jew baiting begins.' The identification of 18B as a Jewish regulation was a constant feature of the propaganda. Hamm's propaganda director, Victor Burgess, confirmed the League was Fascist and that those not '100 per cent British by race' would be disqualified from voting.

The League came to represent the Fascist revival on the streets in violent public meetings. George Dunlop was disturbed by its stance as it contradicted

Mosley's instruction to emphasize its non-political status. This disagreement eventually led to the first split in the post-18B world of British Fascism. However, as the League's activities intensified it became the main contributor in terms of members to Mosley's own crusade.

In the new year Mosley decided the most useful thing he could do would be to farm. There was, however, no land at Crux Easton so in February 1945 he asked the Public Trustees Department, which had looked after Mosley's family business, to seek a suitable country estate. He bought unseen for £35,293,161, a 1,100 acre farm and a Queen Anne house at Crowood, near Ramsbury in Wiltshire, a few miles from Faringdon, stately home of Diana's old friend Lord Berners. Mosley planned to manage it by travelling to it each day from Crux Easton but the government decided that he could not himself employ labour and the estate was run by the Trust.

Diana received a telegram informing her that Tom, second in command of the Devonshire Regiment, had been shot in Burma by a Japanese sniper. He died of his wounds on 30 March 1945 aged thirty-six. 'His loss', Diana wrote, 'was something from which I never recovered for the rest of my life.' Shortly afterwards James Lees-Milne was at the Redesdales' when she unexpectedly arrived, having not seen her father, who had snubbed her marriage to Mosley, for seven years. Diana, who was still under house arrest, motored up in a Daimler accompanied by policemen. Nancy recalled her sailing in 'unabashed, and at once, like the old Diana, held the stage and became the centre of them all'. To her surprise, her father greeted her affectionately even when she explained that 'the Man Mosley', who feared he would still be *persona non grata*, was waiting in the car.

Osbert Sitwell wrote to Mosley on 15 April that 'to have been unjustly deprived, as you have been, of a period of time, is beyond bearing. The only comfort for you must be that it is impossible to blame you for anything that happened in those years.' The war was nearing its end in Europe but Hitler still clung to hopes of a 'national awakening' and a rise in anti-Semitism among the young in England. Goebbels tried to dispel Hitler's gloom by reading extracts from the Führer's favourite book: Carlyle's *Frederick the Great*. A passage described the moment in the Seven Years War when Frederick was saved from disaster by a miracle. But there was to be no miracle and Hitler's path 'led to the grave, to the final catastrophe which had long haunted his mind, to the twilight of the gods'. Fascism had begun with the march on Rome in 1922 and ended in a Berlin bunker in 1945.

Three days before she killed her six children before taking a cyanide capsule herself, Magda Goebbels wrote to her son that 'our magnificent idea is finished – and with it everything beautiful, admirable, noble and good that I have known in my life. The world that will come after the Führer and National Socialism is not worth living in, and for that reason I have brought the children here as well.' Diana, who was fond of Magda, thought it 'just too awful to dwell on what she did, it makes one ill. She was caught up in a ghastly situation.' But she was 'not sure that she was altogether wrong. The Russians would have got the children and they'd have put them all in different labour camps where they would have a ghastly time. One can't put a hand on one's heart and say one would have done differently. I think she was very brave.'

William Joyce made his last broadcast on 30 April. 'Germany is sorely wounded', but her people 'understand the European position with a clarity which is, unfortunately, denied to the people of Britain, and they realize that the great alternative lies between civilization and Bolshevisation'. It was a theme central to Mosley's thinking.

The day the Second World War ended the forty-one-year-old Mosley said to Diana, 'Fascism is dead. Now we must make Europe.' She believed

> everything turned out according to [his] predictions. He had always said that if outside powers were drawn into Europe's quarrels they would end the war paramount in our continent. England counted for nothing at Yalta or at Potsdam. Russia, with the compliance of ignorant America, drew new frontiers. With the enthusiastic connivance of America the British Empire began to be liquidated . . . Not only was half Europe occupied by Russia and subjected to compulsory communism but England was gradually shrunk from a great power to its present little measure.

Mosley was engaged in political plans for the future. He wrote to Nicholas on 11 May that he had been 'suffering early stirrings of a book: what are the pains of women in childbirth compared to such a moment!'

The remaining thirty-nine BU member internees, detained to near the end because of their strong pro-Nazi sympathies, were released, including Audrey Hepburn's father Anthony Hepburn-Ruston, who disappeared to Ireland. The massive wartime expansion of MI5's power troubled Churchill and MI6 Chief Stewart Menzies, who expressed fears of a Gestapo. After VE Day, Churchill ensured Regulation 18B was abolished by Order in Council, though he was aware that Special Branch and MI5 wanted to retain it permanently. For the rest of his political life Churchill had 'a jaundiced view of the Security Service'.

Colin Cross argued 'British fascism ended in May 1940, and has not been revived under that name'. Fascism was a phenomenon born out of the particular circumstances that arose from the catastrophe of the First World War. History was not to repeat itself and the havoc that Fascism wreaked across Europe, which revealed the black core of its ideology, ensured there would be no significant post-Second World War revival. Racist, anti-Semitic and neo-Nazi groupings would emerge for short periods, but none would offer a real challenge to the State or construct a coherent Fascist ideology as strong as the inter-war variant. However, that was not how it looked in spring 1945.

'Staggering as it may seem,' Douglas Hyde wrote in the *Daily Worker* on 5 May, 'former Fascists are more active in Britain today than they have been for the last five years. They play an active part in newly-created organisations and old ones that are being resurrected.' MI5 decided Fascism was not 'a transient phenomenon. It goes back, for instance, to Hobbes and in its modern form it has not been killed by the circumstances of the war.' There were 'British people of National Socialist mentality who looked upon Adolf Hitler as a great and inspiring leader. They looked on the defeat of Germany as the defeat of all their hopes. The problem of Fascism is therefore one which, as far as can be foreseen, seems likely to engage the attention of the Security Service in the coming peace as it did in the inter-war period, but in very different circumstances.' MI5 expected Fascists to continue in Europe and that, 'as happened before the war, there will be continued association between them and people of a similar mentality in this country'.

Mosley was keen to compare himself with Chatham and the younger Pitt, who had been 'proved right by events, and were able to stamp their influence on British history'. He admitted that 'directly the war was over and I was free to move anywhere in Britain I began the organisation of a political movement'. In fact, he began planning before the war was over. In prison he secretly communicated with followers and following his release made meticulous plans with George Dunlop for his comeback, which included putting up candidates, who were not suspected of pro-Fascist or anti-Jewish sympathies, at the first post-war general election. A key figure in these moves was an insurance agent, Dick Sayer, an activist in the BU Central Hackney branch who helped Dunlop raise money for the 18B Detainees Aid Fund.

Mosley covertly created a front of Independent Nationalists under the slogan 'Freedom, Equity and Authority'. His plans were known only to a few but the Board of Deputies of British Jews had reactivated a pre-war agent, former Special Branch Inspector Pavey. He reported on 2 June that Mosleyites were 'seething with revolt' and threatened 'to split into separate factions, each formulating a policy of its own to be pursued with the reckless abandon of men who say that, having lost everything, they have nothing now to lose'. They despised milk and water policies and blamed 'the Jews as the cause of all the trouble' but wondered 'what was Mosley doing about it'.

A week later at the 18B Detainees Aid Fund committee George Dunlop – supported by John Jones, Edward Conner and Alfred Flockhart – spoke with 'Mosley's authority' and admitted he had 'run the "Fund" with a dual purpose'. They had discussed with the Leader 'many proposals and counter-proposals, each designed to further the cause of the British Union. We worked for the day when it would be possible to come out again into the open and we hoped at the same time to be prepared for the inevitable general election with many candidates to take the field.' However, 'several things have militated against this course. Germany collapsed much earlier than we had anticipated. Details of the policy on which we had been working leaked out with the result that the press confused the minds of the people, heralding the Independent Nationalists as the old British Union with a new name.' Moreover, there had been a disappointing response. 'Financially we are not embarrassed, but numerically we are.' Mosley had spent £100,000 (£3.4m) of his own money on the BU and his resources had been drained, but he had restored this amount by speculating on the stock market and had the funds. The problem was that 'we can do nothing without the support of the people – and here is where the snag lies'.

Dunlop revealed that Mosley had written a book – 'And what a book!' – and would come out into the open with its publication. 'But in the meantime our best men are clamouring for immediate action and immediate leadership. If they don't get it from Mosley they will appoint local leaders.' In Stoke Newington Mick Clarke had already opposed the idea of Independent Nationalists and wanted the BU 'in name and character – or nothing' to fight the Jews. To Dunlop this was unacceptable. He would take a 'six months holiday from politics and await a leader. A National Leader will emerge as is the way of leaders – they are not appointed. I intend to tell Mosley this.'

Dunlop hoped that after meeting with Mosley, a directive would be issued revealing the whole scheme. A booklet was prepared, which was 'the real thing. When the boys see this booklet, together with "Warnings to a Warrior" (possibly the title of Mosley's book!) they will sing a different tune. You have to remember that they are not only Jew-wise, but politically minded. Never in actual fact were they so keyed-up for action, or more conscious of the power which would slip from their grasp with disunity.' Dunlop explained to those 'jealous of my position with the Leader' that he had simply stepped into the breach when others had been interned. He hoped they 'would all respond to the Leader's call once he decides to make it'.

At a hurried meeting on 14 June of the 18B Detainees committee at his flat in Dolphin Square, Mosley said 'recent events had . . . rendered obsolete much of the painstaking work which had been prepared'. The sudden general election had 'placed them at a great disadvantage, and now they must wait'. He intended to retire to the country and for twelve months would 'write books and breed cattle', but would be back 'at the appropriate time'. He then departed, leaving Dunlop to speak with 'brutal frankness'. It was 'thanks to some of you fellows' that the project was 'indefinitely suspended'. He had had to tolerate Flockhart, Franklin, Spicer, who 'all worked against me. The movement was killed by publicity and innuendo, and by your blah-blahs and petty jealousies, before it had a chance of survival.' Dunlop said the Fund would be wound up. There was no challenge to his sweeping denunciations.

The decision was confirmed on 27 June when Mosley told the *Mirror* he was 'not interested in active politics. My only interests are books and farming.'

Despite Mosley's absence, the Fascist revival continued, aided by the emergence of Zionist terrorism in Palestine as Jews, fleeing from a devastated Europe, fought Arabs and British troops to create their own state. The British League of Ex-Servicemen said its street meetings 'were designed as protests against terrorism in Palestine'. Working as a bookkeeper to a firm of milliners, Hamm moved his meetings to the traditional Fascist stamping ground in East London, with the aim of creating publicity. However, he was so depressed by Mosley's statement that he considered giving up and joining the Colonial Office. Mick Clarke did give up. He could not find a job and was for a time, along with other internees, employed by Mosley on his farm. 'For the majority of fascist internees,' Thurlow notes, 'their experiences in the Second World War terminated their interest in extremist politics.' For others the memory of internment became the main driving force in their re-emergence. Richard Bellamy said 'some ex-18Bers and other former Blackshirts, mostly ex-servicemen recently demobilised, banded together, more with the object of forming an association of old companions than for the promotion of political ideas'.

With the end of hostilities in Europe the National Front After Victory held its first secret meeting in June as it sought contact among a spectrum of organizations. Closest links were achieved with the Duke of Bedford's reformed British People's Party (BPP), which included extremists such as Aubrey Lees. Support was given to Hamm and John Beckett spread the message among the disparate groups of the need for unity against Communism. It attracted the interest of Lord Nuffield. Lord Vansittart suggested that what was remarkable about it was the membership, which included Pepler of the *Weekly Review*, H. T. Mills of the *Patriot*, Henry Williamson, Major-General Fuller, Ben Greene, Lord Portsmouth (formerly Lord Sydenham) and Collin Brooks, editor of *Truth*. An anti-Semitic nationalist movement in revisionist clothing, it represented a cross-section of the anti-Semitic, but mainly non-Mosleyite, radical Right.

The NF After V proved to be largely stillborn. Based on intelligence derived from the BoD mole, Vansittart made a speech in the Lords condemning the revival of Fascism and exposing the group as a Fascist front run by ex-internees. In doing so, he effectively prevented a merger between it and the BPP, the result of which was to destroy the organization. News that Chesterton told members he had a letter from the Imperial Fascist League proposing the creation of an armed underground movement, with strict discipline enforceable by death, added to the view that it was an extremist group.

At the July general election the Labour Party swept to power with a massive majority and a mandate to ensure there was no return to the conditions and mass unemployment of the thirties. Clement Attlee, the man who replaced Mosley in the second Labour government, was Prime Minister of a government that might have been headed by Mosley, had he stayed the course and not resigned from the party in 1931. On election night John Warburton, a journalist and BU member, was at Labour's victory party at the Savoy Hotel. He heard one of Aneurin Bevan's 'idolisers' raise the question of Mosley. Bevan said that 'if we hadn't forced Churchill to imprison Mosley – who knows what he might have achieved? He was getting dangerous. People were beginning to listen to him and agree. He might have forced a quick end to the war and become the alternative force to capitalism. Now he's discredited, but I warn all of you – don't rely on it. Mosley is a man who will never be finished.'

During August the Mosleys were still living temporarily at Crux Easton, where one of the few visitors was Irene, who saw Diana for the first time since 1940. Irene remained jealous of Baba, an emotion which to a large extent ruined the latter part of her life. She sought psychiatric help, but it brought little relief. In general, the Mosleys were ostracized and few people would meet the notorious couple.

'This was a time', Nicholas recalled, 'when the worst stories of German atrocities had not yet come out: there was not much news of the extermination camps, which were in territory overrun by Russia: the news was of Belsen and Dachau, the horrors of which could just conceivably and to some extent be explained by the disease and starvation resulting from the chaos and bombing of the last stages of the war.' George Bernard Shaw argued in his preface to *Geneva* (1945) that any deaths were caused by 'overcrowding and lack of food'. The atrocities were the result of the 'natural percentage of callous toughs' among the guards and occurred in every war. When the subject was mentioned to Mosley, there was 'just a flash from my father's eyes: a guillotine look from Diana's bright blue ones'.

Diana said Hitler might have given the Jews 'Morocco or some other emptyish place. And then they would have been told "either go, or stay at your own risk".' David Herbert wrote that she possessed a degree of heartlessness that could find her saying of two friends: 'They had such a lovely evening last night, let's put them in the gas oven today.' When a difficult question arose in conversation it was hard to pin her down. She would lower her eyes and employ her charm to full effect. Diana told Anne de Courcy that 'knowing about the Holocaust absolutely did not change my perspective of Hitler. I don't think of him as the man who did that, I think of him as the man I knew, who wouldn't have been capable of that.'

In September, with their release from house arrest, the Mosleys went to live at Crowood House, where Nicholas spent most of the time getting in the harvest. Within a year his father was the proud owner of the first combine harvester in Wiltshire. He was proud, 'as his grandfather had been, of his herd of shorthorn cattle'. It was an idyllic time, even if Mosley was something of a taboo figure and few locals came to shoot. Ironically, his gamekeeper was a black West Indian, who organized pheasant and partridge shoots. He said Mosley 'was almost the only white Englishman he knew who did not seem to notice his colour'. Friends nearby – Gerald Berners at Faringdon, Daisy Fellowes, the daughter of a French duke and an American mother, at Donnington, the Betjemans at Wantage – were guests at the weekend. Nicholas, however, recognized that the couple were largely marooned. There was little serious intellectual challenge to Mosley's flights of oratory at the dinner table.

Mosley found it impossible to ignore the lure of the political stage. He kept a watch on Hampstead, where in October a popular 'anti-alien' petition was launched. Under the pretext of securing homes for returning ex-servicemen, Jewish refugees were targeted. Headed by the local Conservative MP, Charles Challen, the petition owed much to the extreme right-wing Fighting Fund for Freedom, led by eccentric Tory MP Sir Waldron Smithers. The petition intersected with a similar national campaign being waged by Allied Newspapers against Jewish refugees. The campaign was led by the Britons' Vigilantes Action League (BVAL), run by former BU activist John Preen, who compiled lists of Hampstead houses used by Jewish refugees. The BVAL was funded by Lord Kemsley, who was advised by Henry Newnham, former editor of *Truth*. The anti-alien petition, with its emphasis on housing shortages, was 'a local issue that could be channelled into its assault on the Labour government and its nationalisation programme'.

Although it is difficult to conceive of him rejoining the political mainstream, according to Mosley, friends tried to attract him back into the Tory fold. There was limited convergence around an anti-socialist/Communist and anti-nationalization agenda. This had been signposted by Chesterton's role in the National Front After Victory and his employment by Beaverbrook and Conservative Central Office, and the propaganda activities of the National Citizens Union, which included Tories such as the Duke of Wellington and veteran Fascists such as Sir Alliott Verdon Roe and Commandant Mary Allen. Verbal support was given to the anti-nationalization campaign but Mosley's name was too controversial and his ego too big to be accommodated by another's campaign.

Under fierce opposition, the petition issue died down but its supporters sought out allies unconcerned by adverse publicity. A meeting was arranged between Conservative candidate Eleonora Tennant and Jeffrey Hamm of the British League of Ex-Servicemen. For their 21 November meeting Hamm removed a portrait of Mosley but he need not have worried as Tennant wanted to go 'all out against the Jew', though she cautioned against using the word Jew, preferring in public the term 'alien'. Their relationship floundered but

Hamm realized Hampstead was 'a good stamping ground' for anti-Semitism. Far from being put off by the violence of the petition issue, he saw it as 'a good advertisement' as the East End was producing 'lacklustre results'. Fascists campaigned in Hampstead on a platform identical to that of the petitioners with handbills declaring the area had been deluged by a 'Flood of Alien Jewish Immigrants' who 'live in mansions while you live in slums'. Mosley was impressed by Hamm's provocative campaigning.

On 1 December Mosley told the *Sunday Pictorial* he had not changed his ideas 'one inch. I do not retract anything that I have either said or stood for in the past.' Asked if he was a Fascist and National Socialist, he said, 'Yes, but you and I have always meant different things by those words.' It was claimed Mosley was planning a big comeback. On the same day Charlie Watts promised former BU members that a new movement would soon be launched but insisted they discard the 'Heil Hitler Brigade', so that 'when British Union is again reconstituted, we can start off with a decent, clean British organisation to which the British people can give their full confidence'.

There was mass excitement among the 800 ex-Fascists and former detainees when, on 16 December, Mosley made a comeback at a 18B reunion dinner at the Royal Court Hotel. In a stage-managed entrance, he entered through a backstage fire escape. According to the *Daily Worker*, hundreds of hands shot up in the Fascist salute. They chanted 'M-o-s-l-e-y, Mosley' for nearly five minutes. Outside, journalists were roughly handled by Fascist thugs, which led to questions in Parliament.

Inside, Special Branch noted the measures taken to prevent the collection of signatures for an appeal for the commutation of William Joyce's death sentence. Mosley was not prepared to provide the State with an excuse to suppress his views. He said he 'did not intend to start as the Leader of any named political party'; his object was 'to put his own particular thoughts and ideas on paper so that they can be read and understood by whoever wishes to read and understand them'. At the end of his speech, Mosley was 'the centre of a surging mob of hero-worshippers many of whom were on the edge of hysteria'. The SB noted the religious veneration in which he was held by supporters. Throughout the evening, the crowd pressed round him for a word or an autograph from 'The Leader'; some burst into tears after touching his clothes. John Warburton recalled Raven Thomson 'rubbing his hands, full of enthusiasm: "When do we start?".' The proceedings finally broke up to the accompaniment of Fascist salutes and 'Hail Mosley' as fur-coated women and elegantly dressed men, including Captain Archibald Ramsay of the Right Club and Admiral Sir Barry Domvile of the Link, got into the long line of expensive cars waiting outside.

Ramsay was one of the last to leave prison. Willie Gallacher MP asked Morrison whether mothers, whose sons were at war, were to be informed 'that their sacrifice has enabled him to release this unspeakable blackguard'. One of his last acts as a Member of Parliament was to table a Commons motion calling for the reintroduction of the medieval Statute of Jewry. The *Daily Worker* spoke of the 'Streicher-like obsession' of 'Britain's No. 1 Jew baiter'. Ramsay soon left public life and spent his money funding Britons Publishing with Arnold Leese.

Anna Wolkoff tried to mount an appeal and wanted McGuirk Hughes to testify, but according to Lord Jowitt's summary of the trial published in 1954, the man who had handed her the incriminating letter 'was never identified [and] could not be called as a witness'. Hughes is believed to have left for South America on an intelligence assignment. Home Office files disclose that Wolkoff, contrary to reports that said she had been killed in 1969, was still alive in 1973. Tyler Kent's release and return to the United States in 1945, and a request for a transcript of his trial, created ripples within the British State. It disturbed MI5 since it risked exposing the identity of undercover agents now active in the Communist Party. Harald Kurtz worked for the BBC and then at the Nuremberg trials, where he recorded the dying words of Nazi war criminals. The assignment 'did not improve his drink habit'. After much agonizing the transcript was released. Though not made public, Kent deposited a copy in the Yale University Library.

Irene and Baba were distressed by Mosley's appearance at the 18B event. 'Why cannot the man keep quiet?' Having just defeated Nazism and Fascism, they wondered why there should be any supporters left to listen to him, 'especially when the meeting clashed with the announcement of the death sentences for Lord Haw Haw and John Amery'. Following Mosley's address, Labour MPs, critical of the failure to act against domestic Fascism, questioned Home Secretary Chuter Ede as to what he was going to do about this 'strutting peacock'.

In Cabinet, Ministers for Labour (Isaacs), Health (Bevan) and Fuel and Power (Shinwell) wanted a ban on Fascism but were opposed by Chuter Ede, who adopted the classic Home Office line that a ban would only drive it underground and make it more difficult to control. He was guided by MI5 reports of growing divisions between Fascists, lack of impact and numerical insignificance, and legal advice about the difficulties in defining Fascism. However, the Foreign Office argued that leaving Mosley free was bad for Britain's image in those countries where Fascism had taken root, which were seeking to establish a democratic system. Public opinion in those countries would be influenced by the attitude taken towards the re-emergence of Fascism. The Cabinet did establish a Committee on Fascism, chaired by the Lord Chancellor Lord Jowitt.

Gordon-Canning sent a telegram wishing the Mosleys the best for the new year: 'For you both the Oak survived the Gale.' The last link with the old life was severed on 1 January 1946 when Savehay Farm was sold for £25,499 (£530,000) followed by a sale of its furniture. Mosley was liquidating assets and raising cash. The family jewels he had given Diana on marriage were now returned and sold at auction.

Douglas Hyde noted 'a tremendous amount of coming and going in ex-fascist circles today. Former Mosleyites are being contacted and sounded as to where they stand.' They had 'the leading cadres, the framework of a national organisation, the basis of a rank-and-file of some thousands, a number of friendly bookshops in existence with more planned, and the prospect of a flow of new material from the proposed Mosley press'. The reappearance of Mosley would be 'quickly followed by mergers with a number of kindred organisations'. There were fifty Fascist, neo-Fascist and crypto-Fascist groups led by 'would-be Führers trying to cash in on the enforced inactivity of the big fascist leaders'. The idea was to 'create a multitude of small bodies whose importance and numbers would appear to be too small to bother with but which in fact would in time add up to something of some significance'.

A major problem for Mosley's ambitions was that the traitorous activities of former followers were still fresh in the public's mind. The National Council for Civil Liberties published a 'Roll of Honour' listing ex-BU members who had aided the enemy by committing radio treason, co-operating with German or Italian intelligence, or joined the SS's British Free Corps, such as Francis McLardy, and Benson Freeman and Gerald Hewitt who worked in Goebbels's Propaganda Department. This included two (William Joyce and Theodore Schurch) sentenced to death and two (Thomas Cooper and Roy Purdy) whose death sentences were commuted. MI5 listed ten BU members who infringed the Defence Regulations. These 'bad apples' were acknowledged by Mosley, who expelled members found guilty of dubious behaviour.

Joyce had been arrested by British troops and brought to London for trial on a charge of treason. His trial was presided over by Justice Tucker who, Joyce noted, had in the course of the Wolkoff trial 'described me as a "traitor". But we are not making this significant fact a ground of appeal . . . Nonetheless, it is reassuring to find that . . . old 'Ucker did not approach the trial in a state of what might be called, for lack of a better phrase, "mental virginity".' Gordon-Canning, who disappears from *Who's Who* at this point, helped to defray the legal costs. He achieved notoriety for purchasing a bust of Hitler at the sale of the contents of the German embassy. He bought it 'to prevent a historical work of art falling into the hands of iconoclasts'. He told a reporter that, like Christ, Hitler would come into his own again.

The hanging of Joyce at Wandsworth Prison on 3 January 1946 for treason and, on the following day, at Pentonville of Schurch, created a public perception of Mosley also being guilty by association. Dr Margaret Vivian wrote to fellow Mosleyite Robert Saunders that 'we are covered with mud to such an extent that I doubt whether we could ever be successful, and when the next war comes, we might all end in jail'. Ralph Jebb told him, 'If there was anything to save I would risk that but there isn't.' Many thought the Fascists had learnt nothing. Before long there were disturbances at meetings of the League of Ex-Servicemen. When A. R. Hilliard, a member of its executive, asked why the League devoted its energies to anti-Semitism, Hamm replied that if they dropped it, the Communists would be entitled to say they had defeated them. Writer Rebecca West correctly asserted that Hamm's aim was to lure Mosley back into politics, though she found it hard to believe he would fall for this. It would be 'indeed as if the proposition that Queen Anne is dead were disputed by Queen Anne herself'.

The negative reaction to Fascist activity meant that Mosley was careful about going public. Fascists were under stricter surveillance than in the 1930s and he was hampered by the need to do nothing that would call into question the legality of his actions. There was pressure from anti-Fascists, 5,000 of whom rallied in Hyde Park against Hamm's campaign in Hampstead. In mid-January someone located the Mosleys' flat and plastered 'shit and things on the door'. Diana responded to Nancy that 'of course they think the busy little housewife will clean it off, but really darling I can't be bothered'. Mosley was forced to write to the Home Office with details of private meetings in order to seek police protection. The first serious conflict between Fascists and Jewish anti-Fascists took place at Whitestone Pond, near Hampstead Heath, in February.

According to Irish documents, during 1946 Mosley 'expressed an intention of coming to live in Ireland', away from the press and State surveillance. Sean Nunan at the Department of External Affairs recalled that after consultation with the Taoiseach, Eamon de Valera, Mosley's solicitor was told 'that the time was perhaps not opportune for him to take up permanent residence and that he might delay his decision for some time until international tempers were quieter'.

The Committee on Fascism's report was accepted by the Cabinet, which decided not to ban Fascism but agreed to keep it under surveillance. In April Chuter Ede insisted the law was 'fully adequate to enable action to be taken against all really dangerous activities'. Mosley was having planning meetings with Fuller and Raven Thomson, the only former colleague invited to stay at Crowood, who acted as his personal liaison at the private meetings of his re-emerging followers. Mosley was writing the main post-war explanation of his ideas, *The Alternative*. When no publisher would print and distribute his books, he formed his own publishling company.

In August Mosley's *My Answer* appeared, with a 20,000-word foreword, which defended his opposition to the war, and a reprint of 1938's *Tomorrow We Live*. His purpose was 'to justify our position in the past', not to 'provide a policy for the present or the future'. It was a past which he recognized constituted a major barrier to future action. However, he was unwilling to retract anything as he rebutted the allegations of treason, opportunism and anti-Semitism. On the first page he used Lloyd George's statement: 'Is every man or politician who opposes a war during the progress of necessity a traitor? If so, Chatham was a traitor and Burke and Fox especially and, in later times, Cobden and Bright and even Mister Chamberlain, all these were traitors.' He delivered a scathing attack on the internment of BU members, signalling to supporters that he had kept the faith. Booksellers refused to stock it.

Mosley's potential audience was fragmented into 'Book Clubs' and the 'Modern Thought' groups, which had been set up to provide a forum to discuss the Leader's ideas and a means of recruiting a generation of respectable Fascists. Those such as the Spengler Book Club in Winchester, the Phoenix Book Club (Manchester, Bristol and Croydon) and the Corporate Club in Oxford, were reminders of the main themes of the BU and had pronounced links to the past. Thomson's Club for Fascists in Chelsea claimed 500 members. Even these activities were carried out with difficulty and Mosley failed to break the publicity boycott. Irate proprietors of halls cancelled meetings of the Modern Thought groups when they learnt of the speaker's identity. Some meetings were planning cells organized by Raven Thomson. The Home Office was aware from BoD mole Inspector Pavey that the long-term plan was to amalgamate the Clubs with populist street corner groups in a 'spontaneous' demonstration to coax Mosley back. He was only 'rumbled' when Hamm fed him false information about the location of the book clubs. His exposure, however, made little difference, since the Home Office learnt that the response to 'all Mosley's melodramatic comings and goings' was 'negligible'.

Following a complaint from Mosley after anti-Fascists attempted to disrupt a book club, the Home Office instructed Metropolitan Police Commissioner Sir Harold Scott that 'if a group of Communists approached the place where a private meeting of this "book club" was to be held with the obvious intention of preventing or breaking it up they would constitute an unlawful assembly and it would be the duty of the police to disperse them'. Further, 'if they succeeded in entering such a meeting and assault any of those taking part, the police, if they are called in, should take the names of those concerned and, if no proceedings are taken by the victims of the assault, should prosecute the offenders'. Such instructions led anti-Fascists to accuse the authorities of treating the Fascists with kid gloves while using the full range of powers against them.

The government was under pressure from the foreign press over its perceived failure to deal with Fascism. The Russians were angry that British Fascist material was available in Germany. In September Piers Dixon, Private Secretary to Foreign Secretary Ernest Bevin, wrote to the Home Office, advocating laws against Fascists publishing material abroad. However, it decided against stopping Mosley sending propaganda to aid resurgent German neo-Nazi groups. The Home Office replied that 'to tamper with the principle of freedom of expression would weaken our position with democratic opinion abroad' and that 'to prohibit the publication of Fascist literature would have equally serious disadvantages at home'. The Cabinet rejected withholding paper from Fascist book publishers on the grounds that they would claim political discrimination.

When it came to newsprint the situation was different. Diana wrote on 14 October to her father that Mosley wanted to start a newspaper. 'Somebody ought to have a crack at those unspeakable swine.' His ambition, however, was curtailed by the lack of a paper quota. Diana added that she often saw 'the newsreel at the cinema and it makes me sick with rage and misery every single time'. She found the Nuremberg trials and executions of Nazi war criminals, over which her old acquaintance Norman Birkett was helping to preside, 'a cynical farce'.

Rudolf Hess's behaviour during the trials exasperated his lawyers and embarrassed his fellow-Nazis. He suffered, or pretended to suffer, from lost memory – which he would then recover. He spoke of a mysterious revelation – revealed to him in England – which he was going to make and, on 30 August 1946, tried to make it. However, he never completed his speech. Instead, he determined in October that the full text should be sent secretly to the only man who could be trusted to publish it. At the head of the forty-nine pages he wrote, in English and German, 'To be transmitted in the most secret way to Sir Oswald Mosley in London. A very high gratification will be granted later on.' His testament never reached Mosley. It was intercepted by the American deputy commandant. Eventually it came into the possession of the *Sunday Times*, where it was assessed by former MI5 officer Hugh Trevor-Roper.

'It proves', wrote Trevor-Roper, 'that Hitler was speaking conservatively when he said that Hess was only half-sane.' Hess wrote that his captors in England determined to kill him by 'unimaginable sufferings'. He did not deny the atrocities in the concentration camps but 'the SS must have been bewitched'. In interpreting inter-war European history, he said all the troubles were 'deliberately fomented by the Jews who, by bewitching the statesmen and peoples of Europe, engineered two world wars for the weakening of the Nordic race'. This was why the Nuremberg trials were irrelevant: the real authors of 'crimes against humanity' were not the defendants. His revelation triumphantly unmasked them as 'the Jews'.

Mosley had met Hess and the deputy Führer had received regular reports on the BU during the thirties. Why Hess should choose him as the recipient of his testament is not clear. However, the mystery is deepened by a typed wartime message on a scrap of paper found in the archives of the Wiener Library. Undated and unsourced, the message reads: 'Sir OM and Hess conferred last week under the auspices of British Intelligence. Danton Walker in the News.' If true, it sounds as though Mosley was taken to see Hess while they were both in prison.

An indication of Mosley's real intentions was the publication of his first *News Letter* on 15 November 1946, edited by long-serving secretary George Sutton. A monthly publication with a pseudo-academic approach to current political problems, it ran for fifteen issues until December 1947. Mosley wrote that it was 'in the interest of America to have a partner rather than a pensioner. It is in the interest of the world for a power to arise which can render hopeless the Russian design for the subjection of Europe to communism. We shall thus combine in an enduring union the undying tradition of Europe and the profound revolution of modern science.' Print unions disrupted printing of the *News Letter*. It failed to reach beyond the converted but was a means of keeping in touch with the book clubs.

Mosley suffered a setback when, in December, he was refused a new passport on the grounds that it was undesirable he be allowed to travel abroad. There was also a more mundane reason. Following his arrest, his passport was lost in transit and the Home Office had no idea as to where it might be. Ex-detainees could be stopped from going abroad under the New Emergency Laws Act of 1946. The Lord Chancellor, disclosing the ban to the Lords on 12 December, explained that there was 'a reasonable chance' that Mosley might make mischief abroad. 'It is only too true that fascism and Nazism have not been rooted out . . . They are dormant at this present time, but it is possible that they might once more be fanned into flame. If I were a Jew living in Europe today I could imagine that I should feel deeply annoyed at the visit to the country where I was living of a man who had, rightly or wrongly, been identified as being very anti-Jew in this country.' Mosleyite street corner speakers were spewing out a torrent of anti-Semitic abuse. Special Branch reported that Victor Burgess of the Union of British Freedom had called for Palestinian Jews to be publicly flogged.

Just before Christmas Mosley was given a 'Welcome Home' party by BU members in an East End pub. Nicholas drove his father and Diana to 'a street corner rendezvous – they had arranged to be picked up by a guide – and then suddenly there were two motor bikes in front of us and we were being escorted through streets like VIPs'. When they reached the venue his father 'became urgent, with his chin up, striding'; the act took over. 'People clapped and cheered; as he walked between them from the door to the bar they . . . touched the hem of his garment, they wanted to get some magic from him.' He said there was a 'stirring again in England and in the world some of those things we felt so deeply together. I have always regarded the East End as the birthplace of those ideas . . . They did their best to throw us in gaols, into concentration camps but they never shook the faith within us and they never will.' Nicholas feared he had 'gone back like an old alcoholic to his old haunts!'

Cynthia Jebb, wife of the Foreign Office official, ran into the Mosleys at a bookshop. 'He had that look in his eye (they both had) that people no doubt acquire when they are accustomed to being shunned – a kind of studied indifference. Both Oswald and Diana Mosley are evil characters, Lucifer fallen from heaven, and he in particular has a sinister and almost hypnotic power.' Mosley decided the time had come to use that power. The book clubs were growing and the Cabinet agreed to grant him a paper licence. Diana admitted a principal reason for his decision to resurrect the BU was 'the steadfast loyalty of his political companions who had suffered for their beliefs'. She claimed 'his own dreams were shattered'. For former BU members there was, according to John Warburton, 'unfinished business'. In retrospect Michael Quill agreed that Mosley 'felt that he was being loyal to the members'. He 'perhaps didn't want to come back but didn't want to let us down. He didn't think he would get power again. Not in the serious political business.'

The starting point of Mosley's thinking was the recurring notion that capitalism was on the verge of its final crisis. 'We still live in an economic crisis which threatens the life of Britain.' The Jewish question, however, still loomed large. Skidelsky argued Mosley encouraged anti-Semitism 'to die away by refusing to recognise a Jewish question [which] meant that anti-semites sought other pastures'. That was true during 1944–6 when he attempted a more respectable movement but the old antagonism was revived by events in Palestine. During 1945–8 80,000 British troops policed the territory, where 338 British subjects were killed. Following bomb attacks on the King David Hotel and the killing of two sergeants at Natanya, anti-Jewish outbursts resurfaced in August 1947 after publicity given to the activities of Irgun Zvai Leumi. Riots in Salford, Liverpool and Manchester, and smaller incidents around the country, lasted a week. Police and Jewish sources agreed that 'although fascist groups were willing to capitalise on the violence, they were not generally the instigators of the disturbances.'

However, it helped feed their anti-Jewish campaign. A British League speaker claimed Britain was being run by a 'lying rotten Jewish dictatorship'. On synagogues hostile scrawlings appeared: 'Hang all the Jews'. BU-like anti-Semitism seemed to be on the rise again. In the light of the Hampstead experience, both Mosley and Hamm agreed upon this fact. Their tactics did not change. The objective was to create publicity and hope to gain recruits by stirring up trouble with rallies in sensitive areas where Jews lived. The aim was 'to create a sense of insecurity – necessary ingredients in any possible fascist revival'. A colleague admitted that the anti-Semitism was overdone and it 'did attract some thuggish, anti-Jewish types, especially in the East End'.

Opposing the revival was the Association of Jewish Ex-Servicemen (AJEX), organized by Lionel Rose. Claiming to have 10,000 members, it attempted to combine the politics of the Board of Deputies with the drive of Jewish Communists. At street meetings ex-army speakers defended Zionism and the role of Jews in the war. The idea, notes David Renton, 'was to put forward a positive message of religious toleration and thus to undermine anti-semitism through education'. The militant 43 Group was quick to oppose the re-emergence of Mosley's henchmen, such as Jeffrey Hamm and Alf Flockhart. At its peak it had 2,000 members, its own paper, *On Guard*, distributed petitions and daubed anti-Fascist slogans on walls. Members – Doris Kaye, James Cotter and Wendy Turner – infiltrated the book clubs and the British League. By summer 1947 they uncovered Mosley's plans to create a new movement by linking together all the Fascist groups. The 43 Goup sent anti-Fascist ex-paratroopers and commandos to heckle Fascist speakers and turn over Fascist platforms in an effort 'to physically out-violence the fascists'. The resultant public order problems delayed the lifting of the embargo on political marches, which had been renewed every three months since 1937.

The public was horrified to find Mosleyites parading on the streets and wondered how this had happened. Douglas Hyde in the July edition of *On Guard* explained that during the war 'the fascist organisations never went out of existence'. Mosleyites founded their greatest support within a narrow area between Hackney and East London. The British League had its strongest base in the area between Shoreditch and Bethnal Green, and around Dalston Junction. 'A thousand working class men and women cheered wildly and hysterically as one fascist speaker after another paid homage to Mosley,' reported the *Sunday Pictorial* on 17 August. Large crowds opposed Fascist speakers, which often led to disturbances, which were broken up by mobile police units. Starting in the summer, confrontations regularly took place between Fascists and anti-Fascists at Ridley Road, in disturbances similar to those of the pre-war years. Rebecca West, reporting on the phenomenon in the *Evening Standard*, described a Communist street meeting broken up by 'boys and girls between sixteen and twenty, adolescents who were children during the war ... and now miss the excitement ... singing and shouting about a Mosley whom none of them has ever seen'.

Anti-Fascists felt the Fascists were on an upward curve with 'more outdoor meetings at both regular and new pitches, while the many new faces at these meetings confirmed ... the success of their recruitment drive'. The police recorded twenty-two British League meetings in the first half of August, thirty in the second. By concentrating their resources, the Fascists could bring together 2,000–3,000 Mosleyites. The size of the meetings suggested there might be as many as 6,000–7,000 people nationally who looked to Mosley for leadership. This was, however, a serious overestimate: the same hardcore

Mosleyites were turning up to the meetings; apart from them, he had little or no support.

Hackney Trades Council could mobilize 2,000 people for anti-Fascist counter-demonstrations, which effectively closed down most Fascist meetings. Hamm told his League executive he had contacted the Home Office to ask for protection from the 43 Group, while Raven Thomson was alleged to have said that 'if we don't find a way to finish off those bastards, they'll do for us'. Mosleyites found it difficult to expand the support base. After one meeting a Fascist told journalist Tom Pocock, 'Don't get us wrong . . . We only appeal to the "caff boys" in these street meetings. It's no good talking to them about policy.'

Speakers such as Hamm, Duke Pile, Mike Ryan and Jock Holliwell prepared the way for Mosley's return. Lionel Rose noted that the Fascist speakers were 'brazenly' pro-Mosley and anti-Semitic. The meetings were inevitably attended by large numbers of police and plain-clothes (SB) officers who took shorthand notes of the proceedings. However, few prosecutions followed. Interestingly, he also noticed the presence of German PoWs in conversation with the speakers. The Mosleys were visited at Crowood by ex-PoWs who had stayed in the countryside as agricultural labourers. Thomson acted as the confidential liaison with the Nazi and *Wehrmacht* PoWs, careful to avoid Security Service surveillance of meetings.

MI5 hoped a blow had been dealt to Mosley's cause when in March, following a trial at the Old Bailey, Arnold Leese and six Imperial Fascist Leaguers were jailed for a year for helping two Dutch Waffen-SS soldiers escape from Epsom Downs PoW camp. Gerhard Meijer and Hendrik Tiechen made contact with Leese after reading his letter in the magazine *John Bull*. They escaped in June 1946 and made for Leese's Guildford home, where they were passed down a line of 'safe houses' in the East End. Leese arranged for them to see the Argentine chargé d'affaires to negotiate a passage. The fugitive Dutchmen were eventually picked up by Special Branch in December and deported to Holland. MI5 found that the Mosleyites' 'reactions towards Leese and company were uncompromisingly hostile. They have done great harm to the Fascist cause.'

It did not, however, dissuade Mosley from using a PoW as his foreign adviser. His 'chief German collaborator' was an officer who 'had been strongly opposed to the Nazi Party; he had then been a man of the army, and later of agriculture, rather than of politics'. US Army Counter-Intelligence files identify him as Dr Alfred Franke-Gricksch who, the FBI found, belonged to the Bruderschaft (Brotherhood), an elite underground society of ex-SS officers. The Americans claimed Mosley was involved in its creation. He certainly offered assistance and may have provided finance. Franke-Gricksch, a former SS officer and the Bruderschaft's chief ideologist, was an avid proponent of the 'Europe as a third force' concept and influenced Mosley's thinking.

Skidelsky acknowledged that Mosley's thinking on Europe had its origins in the kind of Fascist solidarity which led Joyce to Berlin and which had thrown up collaborators all over Europe. As Roger Eatwell suggests, the more intellectual Fascists had shown a greater tendency to some form of Europeanism than insular nationalism. There was much in common with Nazi 'New Order' propaganda and the attempt to shape the destiny of Europe was, in however perverted a manifestation, seen as a form of European unity. This manifested itself in the need to protect Europe from invasion by the Soviet Union's 'Asiatic hordes' and the international Communist Fifth Column.

Mosley's ideas also developed out of his pre-war thinking. In *The World Alternative* (1936) he advised: 'We must return to the fundamental concept of a European Nation which animated the war generation of 1918.' The article had impressed the Nazis, particularly the geopolitics hierarchy, including a prominent Nazi ideologue of Scottish extraction known to Mosley, Colin Ross, who had recommended the article for publication in Germany. In 1940, in Paris, Ross lectured on 'The Coming of a New Europe Within the Framework of a New World Order'. He argued that 'the European peoples find themselves obliged to constitute together a greater community. And thus the first step to take henceforth is the creation of Europe.'

To propagate these ideas Le Groupe 'Collaboration' (Grouping of Energies for European Unity) was founded in September 1940 by an aristocratic Hitler admirer, Alphonse de Chateaubriand. Its members included not only Henrik de Man and Marcel Déat but other Front Generation socialists who turned to Fascism and reunited around the European ideal. Friedrich Grimm, in charge of Nazi propaganda in France, called for a 'new European order' to combat 'Jewish Bolshevism'. Le Groupe promoted Franco-German reconciliation, European solidarity and sponsored the 'Jeunesse de l'Europe Nouvelle' (Youth of the New Europe). Ross told them that he believed in 'the New Europe, which will be the great common Fatherland of the French and the Germans'.

Mosley's ideas were foreshadowed in Déat's proclamation of a community of European nations ranged against the evils of Bolshevism and capitalism. Hitler's 'Secret Book' raised the spectre of a future conflict with the United States – the epitome of capitalist decadence. Europe would have a socio-economic as well as a geopolitical aspect, in a 'third way' vision of organization, in which Italy would contribute through its exploitation of its African colonies.

Axis defeats in 1943 only served to intensify Europeanism as the new order's last line of defence was entrusted to the younger generation 'still chasing an absurd mirage'. The last-stand Salo Republic was 'to start its existence without a history, and unburdened by all the errors of the previous regime'. When British traitor John Amery travelled to Lake Garda, Mussolini said he had made a mistake in compromising with the monarchy and in not carrying through a 'Social Republic'. The stress on Fascism's 'social' aspect regarding workers' welfare impressed itself on Mosley's thinking. On 14 November 1944 Mussolini proposed in the Verona programme 'a European Community, with a federation of all nations' and the development of Africa's natural resources.

Mosleyite poet Ezra Pound hoped Salo would help construct 'a world-wide monetary system that is honest'. The 'agreement between Mosley and the Social Creditors arose from this knowledge, that is, that fascism was the only movement . . . of action, capable of putting into effect monetary justice'. He recognized in a letter on 28 November 1944 that Fascism had been ill-served by its 'lack of habeas corpus (few cases, but enough to serve as a scandal and the fulcrum of enemy propaganda)'. It was a theme also picked up by Mosley.

The Eastern Front was transformed into the 'European Front' as Europe's defence became a supra-national moral obligation. The Waffen SS assumed the role of Europe's army and its struggle to hold back the Bolsheviks from overrunning the West invoked an embryonic Europeanism, which became a central myth of post-war Fascism. Neo-Fascist thinker Maurice Bardeche wrote that 'the Defence of the West has remained in the memory, and this is still the chief meaning of fascist ideas'.

In Brussels in early March 1944, Léon Degrelle and his Rexists were 'concerned not with immediate military problems facing the Axis, but visionary aspirations. Namely the forthcoming European federation.' Degrelle, the commander of the Waffen SS Viking brigade, said they were 'preparing the political cadres of the post-war world in the great seminary of the front line'. With the world collapsing around them, in late 1944 the Nazis organized a New European conference in Prague, chaired by the SS's Franz Six. It presented an alternative to the Atlantic Charter, the Grande Concerte Européenne.

Six had helped plan the invasion of Britain. Head of the German Foreign Policy Institute, he promoted the united Europe concept in his book *Europe's Civil Wars and the Present War of Unification*. His poster propaganda in the occupied territories depicted an idealized post-war federal Europe, which included Britain. The British Free Corps was part of SS plans to bring together Europe on racial lines. A Nazi sympathizer would be restored to the British throne, with a pro-Fascist government and the BFC's fighting men leading the reconstruction.

In April 1945 Mosley's adviser Alfred Franke-Gricksch had been head of the Personnel Section of Himmler's Reich Security Head Office preparing a blueprint for Europe. Developing Six's ideas, his twelve-point pan-European peace settlement included the creation of a European Community of peoples who would retain their rights to form their own political organization, in allegiance to a Germanic Reich, which would drop claims to sole leadership. Franke-Gricksch envisioned a post-Hitler Europe freed from the biological exaltation of the German race. The Bruderschaft promoted Franke-Gricksch's pan-European ideas, but it also had an important role organizing ratlines for escaping Nazis.

The Bruderschaft had contacts among SS, *Wehrmacht* and *Luftwaffe* officers; the most celebrated being Colonel Hans-Ulrich Rudel, Hitler's ace fighter pilot, who founded the Kamaradenwerk to aid imprisoned comrades. This brought him in contact with the 'mutual aid society', ODESSA (Organisation der ehemaligen SS-Angehörigen), created by ex-SS Colonel Otto Skorzeny. The two Third Reich 'heroes' became close friends and acquaintances of Mosley. The Bruderschaft had been formed during 1945–6 in a PoW camp in Germany, where a staff officer of the Grossdeutschland Division, Major Helmut Beck-Broichsitter, discussed with like-minded prisoners ways to salvage the future. It could be done, he argued, by bringing together the leadership elites. He was joined by Franke-Gricksch, who had been a faithful follower of Otto Strasser before entering the SS. Strasserite ideas on the 'third way' were at the core of Mosley's own thinking.

Franke-Gricksch's plans were interrupted when he was transferred to a camp in Colchester. He is said to have been recruited by British Intelligence and allowed to circumvent denazification procedures. He remained a PoW until the autumn of 1948 but during his detention made contact with British Fascists. Kevin Coogan makes the point that Franke-Gricksch's SD role had included accumulating lists of potential British collaborators. Therefore he already knew about Mosley and the BU. He remained a leading figure inside the Bruderschaft and after his return to Germany became its 'ideological spiritus rector'. Mosleyites admit that 'a number of them did meet him in London with great difficulty. The Establishment in England were doing all they could do to prevent it.' One thing is certain, 'the Bruderschaft was thoroughly infiltrated by the intelligence services of all the occupying powers'.

The Bruderschaft's mission, Franke-Gricksch argued, was to create a new elite now that the era of the masses had passed. They would fight the 'moral vacuum' and once 'a materialistic, mechanistic view of society had been vanquished, a new elite-led organismic German socialism would overcome social alienation'. They would recapture power through 'slow, methodical insinuation into governmental and party positions, under cover of such secrecy or camouflage as might be necessary for the success of the venture'. In the knowledge that he was not going to lead a mass movement, Mosley's strategy was based on similar lines and may have developed from joint discussions. Certainly, he adopted the strategy of 'permeation', though with poor results.

In December 1946 Salo Republic members formed the neo-Fascist Movimento Sociale Italiano (MSI), which promised to cleanse the 'stinking' atmosphere of Italy. It opened a European Study Centre, published *Europa Unità* and created a network of neo-Fascist leaders who were invited to Rome. They included Nazis, Rexists, Quislings, Dutch Mussert partisans, Spanish Falanga and Fascists who had fled to South America. At the same time the Swedish Fascist Per Engdahl expanded operations into Norway and Denmark, and merged their Fascist groups into the 'National Scandinavian Reform Movement'. It is in this context that Mosley's decision to revive his own movement should be seen. Without a political base, he would be denied entry into the exclusive club of neo-Fascist pro-Europeans.

The problem was that they were operating against the backdrop of the Holocaust. In *London Tidings* on 6 September 1947, A. K. Chesterton rejected Mosley's route out of the Fascist ghetto. Fascism 'was too narrowly nationalistic. He will not repeat the mistake. He will, instead, unite Europe and exploit Africa, that he may succeed where Fascism failed: "Hail Mosley!" shout his followers in ecstatic agreement.' But Fascism failed 'so disastrously it is impossible even to mention the word without invoking, not what its adherents meant when they used it, but what its deadliest enemies intended people to believe it to have meant. And that is defeat indeed!'

Around this time emerged Mosley's only real rival as a Fascist philosopher. Francis Parker Yockey was a shadowy intellectual and mysterious American with many aliases, who was rumoured to be half-Jewish. A bohemian figure, he had a brilliant mind but was also 'high-strung, erratic, unpredictable and dictatorial'. As a twenty-two-year-old he had addressed a pre-war meeting of the pro-Nazi Silver Shirts. Joining the army, in 1943 he was medically discharged 'by reason of disability due to dementia praecox, paranoid type'. His discharge and anti-Semitism did not prevent him from being employed from 1946 in the US legal team at Nuremberg, where he worked for the 7708 War Crimes Group, investigating and prosecuting low-level war criminals and evaluating clemency petitions. On 26 November Yockey was fired. Officials came to believe he was a mole for the Nazi defendants, seeking to subvert the Allies' case. Shortly after, Counter-Intelligence-Corps raided his home, but he managed to stay one step ahead of his pursuers.

Yockey visited England in autumn 1947 with the aim of meeting Mosley. He was introduced to Anthony Gannon, a former BU district leader in Manchester, who ran the Imperial Defence League, by Raven Thomson with the comment that he would find him interesting. Yockey said he had 'come to Europe to meet others in the service of the Idea, in particular, Mosley, before writing a book'. He tried to solicit aid for condemned German officers but Mosley, not wanting to run foul of the authorities, was wary of 'a young man of some ability, who had an indiscreet obsession with the Jewish Question'.

Mosley publicly denounced the trials and the 'pursuit of vengeance against a whole people'. He resented the treatment of soldiers 'whose only crime was to obey orders' and expressed sympathy for the Waffen SS. They were 'passionately European and entirely supported my advanced European ideas.

I had heard from many of them long before I was free to travel and had an insight into what they were then thinking, which is perhaps almost unique.' He believed they were natural leaders of a post-Hitler Fascism freed from the 'old nationalism'.

Abandoning his wife and children, on 18 September – his thirtieth birthday – Yockey fled to Brittas Bay, County Wicklow, Ireland. Working without notes, he began writing on an old typewriter – 'the devil machine' – a 600-page, two-volume Spenglerian magnum opus, *Imperium*. A few miles away was the pro-Nazi philosopher Martin Heidegger, working on his own epic undertaking *Philosophical Investigations*.

On 1 October Mosley published his long-awaited book *The Alternative* – 'Chaos looms and the people of Europe seek the alternative'. He had begun writing his political treatise on 2 February in an old diary and finished it at the end of May, having abandoned an earlier effort for being too nationalistic. His second version was, in fact, little different from his BUF policy except that he expanded it to the international stage rather than limiting it exclusively to Britain. 'Our creed was brought to dust because the Fascist outlook in each land was too national, we had no sense of European union.' In the third issue of his *News Letter* (January–February 1947) Mosley had argued for an 'extension of patriotism' to 'embrace all of like kind'. The book was based on his prison readings and the distillation of a series of lost letters to Nicholas. The second version was also the result of discussions with German advisers, particularly Franke-Gricksch.

The Alternative is a pretentious book, full of phrases such as 'transcending the diurnal politics of normality'. The 'Analysis of Failure' collates his *News Letter* pieces, dealing with day-to-day politics. The rest is a curious work overladen with psychoanalysis, a discipline that Mosley supposedly despised. He pondered how dynamism and action could be harnessed for the benefit of all without causing harm to individuals. He reveals his fascination with Jung – 'the most outstanding and comprehensive intellect that the new science has yet produced' – but shows no insight into his own character. Predictably, there is no apology for the past. It was 'one of the tear-laden paradoxes of history', Mosley wrote, 'that the man whom the mass of the English learnt to regard as their greatest enemy cherished a sentimental feeling towards a "sister nation" which, in the eyes of historic realism, must border on the irrational and, in the test of fact, was pregnant with the doom of all he loved'. It seemed to Nicholas that his father 'had no comprehension of what had occurred and was intent on denying the reality of the catastrophe that Hitler had unleashed'. In some ways his thought appeared more Fascist as he attempted to readjust National Socialism to the post-war world.

Building on Spenglerian fantasies, he now envisioned his task as defending Europe from Bolshevik 'barbarians'. His strategy would be based on 'Europe

A Nation'. In *The European Situation: The Third Force* (1948), Mosley said he proposed it because 'it seemed to be both the deep desire of the European and the practical necessity of the present situation'. New Europe would be 'a great unity imbued with a sense of high mission, not a market state of jealous battling interests'. It would 'insure that Europeans shall never be slaves either of West or East; either of finance or of bolshevism. We shall neither be bought by Wall Street nor conquered by the Kremlin.'

Mosley's vision was similar to that of French writer and Vichy supporter Maurice Bardeche, who acquired a position of respect in neo-Fascist circles after his own imprisonment. Those who 'carry on the Fascist idea are men who feel, more deeply and more desperately than other men, that it is a means of salvation. In all these men without exception – there was a nostalgia for what Fascism had failed to achieve – Socialism and European unity.' They approved of the Verona programme and a 'third force' Europe. This 'imaginary island lying between two hostile continents was conceived', he wrote, 'by doctrinaire Fascists between 1946 and 1948'. They included those of the German underground nationalist groups, which adapted the fantasies of Salo and Otto Strasser's ideas for European confederation and 'Eurafrika'. These were transmitted by the Strasserite Franke-Gricksch to Mosley who now promoted an 'extension of patriotism' from the mythic core of the 'Greater Britain' to the Utopian 'Euro-Africa'.

Europe a Nation would be protected by tariffs and take its wealth from an Africa ruled under apartheid conditions of extreme exploitation. Mosley argued in his *News Letter* (March–April 1947) that 'instead of playing the fool by pretending that we can educate negroes in a few years into running Africa, let us face realities. Let us develop Africa as a great estate of the European and give the negro an assured and guaranteed place in that new economy. He will thus enjoy . . . a far higher standard of life than he will obtain for generations by the unaided exertions of his own brains.' Mosley's purpose, noted Mervyn Jones, 'was to make each eager youngster envisage himself, suitably clad in khaki shorts and carrying a whip or revolver, striding magisterially across a vast plantation where countless black backs bend in rhythm'. Mosley was not alone in his absurd vision. Former Labour colleague Ernest Bevin, now Foreign Secretary, proposed a Third Force Euro-Africa bloc, which would exploit the 'invisible empire' of the Sterling Area. The difference was that Mosley's version was explicitly racist. He said, 'Have we a "sacred trust" to keep jungles fit for negroes to live in?'

A new (white) Faustian 'Thought-Deed' man would be required to live in Euro-Africa. In *The Alternative* Mosley argued that only through constant striving could mankind evolve in the modern era. 'The mass of the people can only share in the benefits which modern science can bring through the devoted service of those whom they entrust with the task of government . . . to secure that system they must . . . an altogether new and higher type of man who is dedicated in whole life and purpose to the service of the people and the State.' Using political soldier rhetoric, he said 'the prime necessity of our age is to accelerate evolution. This generation must play the midwife to Destiny in hastening a new birth.'

This higher type would be produced by a programme of 'breeding, selection and environment'. Mosley wanted to 'deliberately accelerate evolution: it is no longer a matter of volition but of necessity. Is it a sin to strive in union with the revealed purpose of God?' He provided no blueprint for the training he envisioned for this new type, whose 'mighty shadow has already appeared on Earth'. Hitler was still seen as an example of a successful leader but it was Mosley himself who was the prototype. Only he could save Europe from the 'architects of chaos'. 'I must give myself to this task . . . because no other can.' He had refrained from 'forming again a political movement in Britain in order to serve a new European idea – "beyond both Fascism and Democracy"'. He believed that his ideas would win because 'the power of God in nature is now with us'. Mosley had simply lost all touch with reality.

Henry Williamson, whose loyalty never faltered, considered *The Alternative* Mosley's best book, though it was largely ignored. The *Manchester Guardian* on 1 October thought 'the most remarkable thing about Sir Oswald is his entire consistency . . . His programme of 1947 is in essentials his programme of the thirties – with one verbal difference, the dropping of the word "Fascist".'

Mosley had listened to his supporters and, finally, met their needs. On 15 November 1947 he held a private meeting at the Memorial Hall, Farringdon Street where, fifteen years earlier, the New Party had held its inaugural meeting. Attending were the 'Big Four' pro-Fascist organizations – Gannon's Imperial Defence League, Horace Gowing's Sons of St George in Derby, Victor Burgess's Union for British Freedom, Hamm's British League of ex-Servicemen – and fifty smaller groups such as the book clubs. Mosley said that by 'linking the union of Europe with the development of Africa, a new civilization will appear which will surpass any power in this world'. He was considering re-entering politics with the 'Union Movement'. Tommy Moran, co-founder of the Order of the Sons of St George, Michael Ryan, a shop steward of the Transport and General Workers' Union, and Alfred Flockhart, Mosley's closest associate, pledged themselves to it. Hamm wrote in the *British League Review* that Mosley had 'given us The Idea, and it is for us to build The Movement that will propagate that idea'.

John Warburton was at the meeting and knew Mosley fairly intimately. 'I and others thought of him as a god. As I grew older I realised that he was human but he was the most god-like human I have known. When he walked into a room, there was a presence. When he was in small groups he was electric.' Although he was 'The Leader' and there was no vote, he 'listened to what people' such as Hamm ('a secretive sort of bloke'), Flockhart ('a real live wire'), Hector McKechnie and Robert Row 'had to say'. Michael Quill judged that the best people around him remained Raven Thomson and Francis Hawkins. However, outside the circle of committed colleagues, 'some of them didn't seem one hundred per cent genuine. Some were there just to be paid. Many were not intrinsically political. They didn't organise like parties and involve themselves in political activity such as canvassing.' Raven Thomson, editor of *Union*, expressed surprise at the growth of street corner Fascism and the ease of 'getting away with it.'

A week later Louis Hydleman, Chairman of the Jewish Board of Deputies' Defence Committee, reported that they had succeeded 'in insulating increasing numbers against the poison of anti-semitic propaganda'. Well-organized opposition prevented Mosley from launching the respectable movement he planned. Instead, he was mired in the realm of street violence:

Mosley had hoped that the numerous book-clubs and discussion groups would have provided cover for his re-appearance on a higher plane and in better company, than his former attempt; he hoped that the Jeffrey Hamms would succeed in stirring passions and feelings in the streets of London without Mosley himself being connected with this rabble-rousing. Instead, I believe we have succeeded in making sure Mosley is treated as part and parcel of this rabble-rousing.

Following the pre-launch meeting, on 28 November Mosley gave an interview in which he said Jews would not be allowed to join and that a Fascist government would deport them from Britain. When journalists referred to the Nazi concentration camps, he said 'history will record to what extent the ruin in Germany was brought about by our bombing and to what extent by the policy of the Government. If you have typhus outbreaks you are bound to have a situation where you have to use the gas ovens to get rid of the bodies. If we had been bombed here in prisons and concentration camps, there would have been a few of us going into the gas ovens.' He claimed Buchenwald and Belsen were 'completely unproved' and that 'pictorial evidence proves nothing at all. We have no impartial evidence. I don't know the facts and nobody does until an impartial court inquires into the whole thing.' However, he condemned the Nuremberg hangings. 'Anybody can assassinate their opponents when they win a war. It is a contemptible thing to do.'

In January 1948 Robert Saunders in Dorchester began writing to former BU colleagues in the south-west, urging them to join Mosley's new crusade. He wrote to Rafe Temple-Cotton promising that the UM would be different and not a duplicate of the BU. The East End meetings might be the same but he blamed any violence on Hamm's British League, which was 'without doubt little more than 1939 BU operating in 1947'. He added that 'we all know that a part of BU's support came from people who were crudely anti-Jewish and nothing more', and recognized Temple-Cotton's fear that the UM 'will be dominated by the same type of people'. Saunders saw the danger but 'the important thing is to see that UM's leadership, locally as well as nationally, is in the right hands'. Temple-Cotton decided not to join because of the pre-war associations. The 43 Group's *On Guard* listed those BU-Fascists now involved in Mosley's UM. 'The prevalence of the "old guard"', notes Skidelsky, 'soon gave it a depressingly familiar look. Like the Bourbons, the Fascists seemed to have learnt nothing and forgotten nothing.'

25

The Union Movement

The Union Movement was officially launched at Wilfred Street School, Victoria, on 8 February 1948. In attendance were 250 delegates from fifty street-corner organizations, provincial groups and book clubs. The UM, Mosley argued, would 'build where the old parties have destroyed . . . we will create a third empire after they have lost two empires'. Several hundred police – the largest number yet used for such an occasion – protected the meeting. Walter Grunfeld, writing in the *New Republic*, noted that the UM was 'scarcely different from its pre-war model. It boasts the same anti-Semitism, the same violent, anti-alien chauvinism, and the same dream of a one-party totalitarian state blindly following its "leader".'

Certainly, street meetings were little different. A meeting at Clapham Common on 2 February organized by Michael Ryan was closed by police after forty anti-Fascists tried to turn over the platform. The 43 Group sometimes resorted to violent methods to make up for lack of numbers. 'Our commandos', Morris Beckman recalled, 'would form three solid wedges of very hard men. At a given signal, they would start to move slowly towards the fascist platform. And then they would pick up speed . . . When the platform went over, the meeting was finished.' In turn, Fascists fought like street thugs with some carrying knuckledusters. In Romford, a gang of Maltese was hired to repel the 43 Group and threw potatoes embedded with razors.

The 43 Group aimed to kick the Fascists off the streets and deny them a base from which to organize. UM member John Bean believed the attacks were counter-productive and 'acted as recruiting agents for Mosley'. Anti-Fascist Chanie Rosenberg disagreed. 'If we had left them alone, Mosley would have had some brief blossoming of sorts, and he would have kept a nucleus there . . . The anti-fascist activity more or less eliminated any possibilities they had.' The British League was forced to stop holding regular meetings at Ridley Road.

Former Common Wealth member J. C. Banks agrees this was the case. 'Far from attempting to debate with [the Mosleyites] Common Wealth was their main opponent particularly in Hackney and Stoke Newington, and over a number of week-ends throughout the winter of 1947/8 denied the fascists the use of their prime site in Dalston Road . . . the Communists were nowhere to be seen.' One of the 43 Group founders acknowledged to Laurens Otter that 'the only people who were there to stand with us and fight the fascists and the police were Common Wealth, the ILP, the Anarchists and the Trots'. The Labour people were an ex-Common Wealth faction around Commander Millington MP, who had been expelled from Labour for 'his unruly behaviour in fighting the fascists' and had joined the ILP.

Hamm blamed the retreat on the severe winter. Whatever the real reason, the Home Office was concerned about potential violence and asked chief constables to report to MI5 on UM meetings in their area. In spring 1948 Home Secretary Chuter Ede imposed a ban preventing all political marches in East London.

On the foundation of the UM, the American FBI began to take an interest in Mosley. On 7 February J. Edgar Hoover received a report that the Bureau's files had failed 'to disclose any information relating to [name blacked out]' who was alleged to have 'recently had several interviews' with the UM leader and was 'acting on behalf of a group of Americans who are anxious to support Mosley'. Mosley displayed his characteristic lack of political judgement by entrusting negotiations to a confidence trickster who was also a possible MI5 informer. In March Mosley sent Gerald Hamilton to New York to negotiate $250,000 (£2m) from a range of right-wing American luminaries including Colonel Robert McCormick, owner of the *Chicago Tribune*. Hamilton, who had been interned during the war, was a 'renowned con man and spy, whose reputation for intrigue and mendacity was already well known'. Following a stormy interview on his return, Mosley discovered Hamilton had pocketed the money.

Questions over Mosley's pre-war funding and links to Italian Fascism and German Nazis were raised in the Commons on 25 February and again on 3 March. John Platts-Mills, the Labour MP for Finsbury, asked the Foreign Secretary 'if he will publish all those documents captured by the Allied Forces which relate to the relations between' the BU and the Nazis. Ernest Bevin claimed none had been 'found among the captured German Foreign Ministry documents'. A year later, Communist MP Philip Piratin again raised the matter but Bevin's deputy, Hector McNeil, stated 'the position has not changed'. Amid calls of 'crypto-Communist' from the Tories, Platts-Mills asked Bevin why Mosley's propagandist, Bill Allen, was employed as a Counsellor at the British embassy in Ankara. According to James Fox, Allen was in reality working for MI6 and was friendly with Kim Philby. In 1948 Allen received an OBE – 'as a form of polite whitewash', according to his wife – for his work 'passing on disinformation' in Turkey. Bevin told the Commons: 'I understand this man owes no allegiance to any other country.' Mosley had not seen Allen since 1940, when they parted on bitter terms over money matters. When, during 1948, they happened to meet in a restaurant such feelings had dissolved and the two were seen exchanging pleasantries.

After six months, Francis Yockey had finished writing *Imperium* and returned to London to find a publisher. Very much under Spengler's spell, Yockey glorified the West and bemoaned its decay in a sweeping historial tour de force which promoted the concept of a pro-Russian Europe standing up to the US and China, as 'the first blow in the gigantic war for the liberation of Europe'. He contrasted his conception of Europe as a single, integrated entity with 'the miserable plans of retarded souls to "unite" Europe as an economic area for purposes of exploitation by and defense of the Imperialism of extra-European forces'. These souls were the United States and the Soviet Union which, in Yockey's view, had conquered the Continent and turned it into a spiritual swamp.

In an upbeat message, Yockey summoned beleaguered Nazis to engage in a 'world-historical struggle'. He believed in a philosophy of cultural vitalism in which a heroic sense of purpose emanating from an elite 'culture-bearing stratum' would trickle down to the masses, thereby ushering in a quasi-religious Age of Authority, in contrast to the decadent 'Rule of Money'. The Jews were blamed for plotting the war as a counter-force to the 'European Revolution of 1933'. Yockey was one of the first to claim that the Final Solution was a myth. He argued that photographs of 'gas chambers' were forgeries.

On 6 February Yockey contacted Major-General Fuller and military historian Basil Liddell Hart, both of whom would later write glowing reviews of *Imperium*. He also began working as a paid official in the UM's European Contact Section with Guy Chesham, which enabled him to cultivate ties to the European-wide neo-Fascist network, which included Alfred Franke-Gricksch. Yockey gathered around him a group of extremists influenced by his plan to create anti-American hostility by establishing links with the Soviet Union for funding propaganda.

Yockey continued his secret campaign against the war crimes tribunal. Maurice Bardeche's book, *Nuremberg ou la Terre Promise* (1948), was an early attempt to deny the Holocaust. It, too, claimed that evidence had been falsified and, like Mosley, attributed the genocide to illness and starvation. Bardeche was in receipt of archive documents from 'Ulick Varange' – the pseudonym Yockey affixed to *Imperium*. In his memoir *Souvenirs* (1993), Bardeche acknowledged these were used to aid the defence of SS war criminal Lieutenant-General Otto Ohlendorf, who commanded an Einsatzgruppe in Ukraine, which murdered 90,000 people. Yockey was active in the defence of Lieutenant-Colonel Fritz Knoechlein, commander of the 2nd Totenkopf (Death's Head) unit, which machine-gunned a hundred British troops holed up in a French farm. Mosley unsuccessfully intervened on behalf of Knoechlein, who was convicted on 25 October 1948 and later hanged.

Mosley's claim in *Union* that races were the 'First Reality of European Union' brought him perilously close to Nazi ideas. He considered our nearest kindred to be the Germans, the northern French and the Scandinavians. However, his contacts extended to neo-Fascists in South Africa and Argentina, where he supplied propaganda to Dr Walter Schilling, who had a wide network of Nazi correspondents. He found the fliers 'terrific. Put together so skilfully. I will do my utmost to make propaganda in German and English circles.' A letter to Mosley ended: 'Perhaps you will get through to him some day that he, Churchill, was the grave digger of Europe.'

At the end of the previous year Mosley had entered into friendly relations with Oswald Pirow, South African leader of the extreme right-wing New Order. In April 1948 Mosley put forward his colonial proposals in association with the former South African Minister of Defence. In joining with Pirow, Mosley revived pre-war links with South Africa and the extremists of Osserwabrandlag. The New Order had split during the war from the majority Malan Afrikaner Party, because it refused to join in the war against Germany but also with the aim of creating a Christian National Socialist system, based on the ideas of the Portuguese dictator Salazar. It rejected 'British-Jewish imperialism and capitalism', and wanted independence from the Empire. Pirow's growing contempt for democracy, however, effectively destroyed his political career. Post-war, he mostly devoted himself to his legal practice, though he continued to publish a newsletter until the fifties.

Mosley denied that his joint plan with Pirow was a revival of the Empire. It called for the division of Africa into black and white. As a Lamarckian, Mosley believed culture rather than race was the main factor behind evolution. He derived from Spengler 'a belief that different cultures should be separated from each other because contact brought decay'. At a London press conference, Mosley and Pirow advocated allocating two-thirds of sub-Saharan Africa to black states and one-third to white because 'equal rights between black majority and white minority in the same state must inevitably lead to the disappearance of Western civilization'. Pirow presented the policy as 'equality, coupled with separation. In other words, it concedes to the Black Man complete equality of status and opportunity but in his own areas . . . it means a segregation, not of the Native but of the White Man.' He said the 'solution proposed is necessary to safeguard the future of the White Man, but it is imperative if we want to do justice to the Black Man to-day'. They never made clear how they would separate the two.

Mosley tried to make a distinction between their proposals and South

Africa's apartheid policy, which he nevertheless thought might develop into something better.

> A genuine apartheid, a real separation of the two peoples into two nations which enjoy equal opportunity and status . . . is a strong contradiction to the bogus apartheid which seeks to keep the negro within white territory but segregated into black ghettos which are reserves of sweated labour living in wretched conditions . . . Hysterical propaganda has made the term apartheid cover both concepts, although they are entirely opposed.

In mid April 1948 a Special Branch investigation of Fascist and Communist organizations by Deputy Commander Len Burt reported there was serious danger of violence in London. Mosley was planning to celebrate May Day by staging the UM's first march from Dalston to the East End. This was going to be the 'big one'. For weeks the area had been flooded with posters announcing the 'Leader' would speak in Hereford Street. The event was intended to be a showcase for recruitment and indicate that the UM was a force to be reckoned with. On 29 April Sir Harold Scott, the Metropolitan Police Commissioner, warned the Home Office that his powers were inadequate 'to prevent serious public disorder'. The Home Secretary responded by prohibiting it through the East End and forcing Mosley to reroute it.

Jonathan and Desmond were doing their National Service and, dressed as 'conspicuously unmilitary Privates', escorted Diana to Hereford Road, where mounted police drove back the assembled crowd and attempts by the 43 Group to break up the meeting. She thought Mosley 'gallant' but Maurice Beckman said he 'resembled nothing more than a middle-aged weary civilian, puffy of cheek and eye with a drooping shoulder . . . the charismatic orations that once inflamed his supporters into ecstasies of loyalty had now gone'. Four hundred UM supporters then made their way to Highbury Corner, where they formed into a larger procession, which tried to march to Camden Town. There were, however, 1,500 anti-Fascists in their way and there was fighting along the route, forcing the march to end early outside Holloway Prison. In trying to keep the two sides apart, the 800 police made thirty-two arrests. The parade was a 'damp squib' and the expected new recruits failed to materialize. Active UM membership in 1948 probably totalled less than 3,750.

Lionel Rose of AJEX claimed Mosley had been 'forced into the open before his movement has any sound organisational structure or support. There is a considerable gap, almost wholly empty, between Mosley and his backers and entourage at the top, and the street corner gangs at the bottom.' With the ban on marches extended to cover all of London, Mosley began to feel there was 'a barrier between him and the British People'. Meetings and street-corner speeches took place but were met with continued opposition, and many halls were closed to him. He informed Union readers that the ban meant Fascists were back to the harsh times of 1940 and 'the end of real free speech'. It was no longer possible to build a mass movement and, instead, they would have to try new methods, including 'permeation'.

UM members, wrote Mosley, should infiltrate 'athletic clubs, boxing and cycling teams'. More seriously, he advocated joining existing political parties in order to take them over from within. Permeation was a long-term tactic, whose chief instigator was Charlie Watts. In a circular written by a 'skilled and experienced observer', the UM was viewed as a cadre training ground for an elite, who were to convert leading members of other organizations to Mosley's ideas. Senior figures recognized Fascism could not yet be revived, but believed there would come a time when the movement would grow. When this stage was reached, covert Fascists would be able to come out into the open. The reality was that permeation had negligible results. However, the transformation to a cadre elite suited Mosley's ambitions as he increasingly used the UM as an entré to the Continental networks he had been cultivating through his Contacts Section. Europe, not the domestic scene, became the focus of his activities.

Yockey had extensive discussions with Raven Thomson on Europe and in particular American culture. He remembered 'a brilliant young intellectual American expatriate with a strong anti-American phobia, taking the view that the present American influence in Europe is more damaging to European culture than the direct but alien threat of communism from the East'. Yockey was the lover of a mysterious Baroness Alice von Pflugl, an older woman who lived in a mansion near Regent's Park, who influenced his thinking along the lines of the pro-Strasserite 'National Bolshevist' faction of the Bruderschaft, of which Franke-Gricksch, who visited London to spread his gospel, was the most vocal advocate. They believed the way to resurrect German nationalism and stem the Americanization of Europe was by aligning themselves with the Soviet Union, which was judged to be National Socialist and anti-Semitic. Stalin's military repression of Eastern Europe, Yockey wrote, was less harmful in the long run because it did not corrupt the Western soul as American capitalism did.

Yockey's views put him at odds with Mosley, whose more moderate crusade included coming to terms with American hegemony over Western Europe. During the Berlin blockade he called for Russia's withdrawal from Europe and disarmament subject to Western verification. 'If the Bolsheviks refuse to accept this ultimatum, they should be assailed with the atom bomb and with all other weapons of modern science which the Western nations possess, but which the Soviets do not yet possess.' In *The European Situation: The Third Force* Mosley argued that 'under Russia, European freedom is killed, and under America, European freedom can still exist and even grow. That is the basic difference which must determine the question of attitude.' As Kevin

Coogan notes, 'The more Mosley tilted West, the more Yockey tilted East.' The latter wrote to a friend that when he discovered Mosley was 'pro-Churchill and pro-American and anti-Russian, even to the extent of mobilizing Europe to fight for American-Jewish victory over Russia, I left him'.

Raven Thomson believed Yockey joined the UM 'in the hope of getting our chief to finance his book'. Elsa Dewette remembered Yockey begging for an interview with Mosley, and when 'his Grandeur' deigned to see him, he treated him offhandedly. The American left the manuscript with Mosley but when he returned after a few days, he had the impression Mosley 'had only glanced at a few pages, and certainly not read it through' because, Raven Thomson recalled, 'it was full of Spenglerian pessimism and was unnecessarily offensive to America'. Hamm thought *Imperium* was just 'an imitation of OM's *The Alternative*'. At this point Yockey was so desperate that he suggested Mosley 'sign his name under it, as the author'. He refused and from then on treated Yockey 'with disdain and irony. He never at any moment took him seriously.' Thereafter, Dewette added, 'Yockey hated Mosley.' Raven Thomson found him to be 'so conceited and unstable in personal relations that it is almost impossible to work with him'. The 'neo-*Mein Kampf* for neo-Nazis' is rambling and largely incomprehensible, which is probably why it has an enduring reputation among American neo-Fascists and anti-Semites.

Mosley's Oxford-educated lieutenant, Guy Chesham, sent him a 'Memorandum of Dissociation' over Yockey's treatment and lashed out at him for 'not even reviewing this significant book, contrary to your promise'. In the margin Mosley wrote, 'Absurd falsehood: Why should we?' A 'philosophical quibble on some difference between Goebbels and Spengler was', Chesham recollected, 'your official excuse. How ironical that your group should set itself up as the keeper of the National Socialist conscience! It has no point of contact whatsoever with the Nazi Movement, spiritual, ideological, organizational, traditional or cultural.' He charged that 'your treatment of the author underlined your well-known inability to tolerate men of intellect and imagination about you, but it was your failure to adopt the ideology of the book which displayed the full extent of your purely social-economic activity and your incredible delusions of grandeur. You hated *Imperium* because it was a summons to action, because it demanded a shattering of illusion and a manly facing of political facts.' In the margin Mosley wrote that it was 'a very dull re-hash of Spengler'.

Diana acknowledged her husband did not read *Imperium*. 'Yockey came to stay at Crowood and had talks. He was a talkative American, a very neurotic man.' They thought him 'a bit mad'. Mosley 'suffered neither fools nor madmen gladly and being accused by Yockey of being an American agent and tool of Churchill placed him in that category'. He put any material on Yockey in his 'crackpots' file, which included other deranged individuals such as Joyce.

Mosley dropped Yockey and warned supporters to avoid him. In May, he left the UM when Mosley allegedly punched him on the nose during a dispute in Hyde Park. Shortly afterwards he fell in with a group of disillusioned Mosleyites, who embraced him as a Fascist guru.

Thanks to the wealthy Baroness von Pflugl, 1,000 copies of volume one and 200 of volume two of *Imperium* were published by Westropa Press, and agreement was reached with Franke-Gricksch to publish a German translation. Chesham warned Mosley that 'acceptance of *Imperium* among political and intellectual circles at home and abroad is now a political fact'. At this point there developed deep divisions within British Fascism, as Mosley's faults, both real and imagined, notes Thurlow, 'increasingly became the scapegoat for British fascist political failure. Non-Mosleyite fascists, ex-BU followers and a new generation of British "Nationalists" and neo-Nazis, either blamed Mosley for the personal and political disaster of British fascism, or railed against the new ideas of the Mosley movement.'

Anthony Gannon thought Mosley had suffered a loss of nerve and was sceptical as to the UM's prospects of ever being a real political force. 'Whereas Hitler's imprisonment in Landsberg forged the steel of personal resolution and dedication, Mosley's sojourn in Holloway gaol proved to be the opposite. His confidence had been shaken, he was older, less decisive, more opportunistic.' Peter Huxley-Blythe also had misgivings. As a student in a right-wing family in the late 1930s, he became interested in Mosley. After serving in the Royal Navy, he returned to the north of England, where he met Gannon, who introduced him to Yockey at a UM conference. He found the UM divided between those who remembered Mosley with nostalgia and 'younger ones like myself who wanted more dynamic leadership. We didn't want to have to apologise for the past.' Mosley, however, 'was not the man of action that he was and, upon reflection, he may never have been'.

Chesham claimed the movement was 'non-existent'. There was an 'irreducible minimum of 2–300, all of whom are of the lowest intellectual and political calibre'. Rebecca West had already noted the 'low intellectual level' of speakers such as Michael Ryan, which was 'common to them all'. Chesham said officials preserved the 'squalid status quo of the payroll and the political small-time. Reliable only in flattery . . . trustworthy only in self-interest', they rejoiced in 'womanish gossip and petty, amateurish spying'. An insider agreed that the UM was 'riven like the BUF had been by petty jealousies. Hamm and Burgess would not talk to each other because of affairs. The whole thing was seedy.' Outside London, Chesham added, 'there is nothing'. He blamed this on Mosley's obsession with European contacts, absences abroad, poorly produced crude propaganda and his description of disasters as 'temporary setbacks'.

*

Mid 1948 was an unsettling period for the Mosleys. At Inch Kenneth, Diana's mother wrote to her on 27 May that 'Bobo is much less well and I feel greatly worried'. Next day she died from meningitis. The Mosleys attended Unity's funeral at Swinbrook. A few weeks later Mosley's mother died. She had often stayed at Crowood and for her last years she had lived near her son John in Norfolk. The three Mosley brothers attended the funeral, the first time they had been together for many years. Edward had been in the army in Syria and Palestine, and retired to Chad, Somerset. John despaired that his brother had revived his movement: 'Why is he doing it again, for goodness sake. It is a waste.' They did visit Crowood but the relationship between the brothers remained distant.

Mosley organized several projects to recruit the children of the bourgeoisie, including the student Corporate Club at Oxford University, run by Desmond Stewart and P. Thomas. Simon Mosley recalled seeing his uncle and 'his acolytes around him' at New College, Oxford. 'Diana gracefully joined us on our chaise. She had so many adoring her.' A former don was appalled by the 'insidious respectability which undergraduate Fascism has begun to acquire'. There were those who said 'Hitler delivered the goods' and 'those who are more "intellectual" who take themselves seriously as "political theorists"'.

Surviving 43 Group members claim credit for disrupting Mosley's plans. Its intelligence section scored a coup when in June 1948 Michael Maclean, UM organizer in Birmingham, left, claiming the UM was a 'gangster organisation', and set up an Anti-Fascist League, recruiting former Mosleyites who had rejected Fascism. When Mosley's power began to slip, 'even his own men started to desert him. You could see that he was a very beaten man. He knew that we had finished him off.' Mosley, however, was faced with a bleak political future in England and turned towards developing his European strategy.

The FBI in London forwarded to Hoover intelligence that Mosley was planning a Fascist International. On 30 July 1948 the *Daily Worker* announced MOSLEY: LINK UP WITH GERMAN NAZIS. He had arranged distribution of 10,000 copies of a British-printed broadsheet, *Deutsches Flugblatt*, in the British and American zones in Germany. Headed by his portrait, the broadsheet promoted Europe a Nation. Its publication caused uproar and provoked questions in the Commons. Although not illegal, this was a time of paper shortages and such literature was viewed by the Allied Control Commission as 'subversive' and in breach of rules regarding the importation of such material.

Two weeks later the FBI in Madrid sent reports from the Spanish newspaper *Arriba* that 'Oswald Pirow Comes to Spain' and plans to set up with Mosley 'a new political party – The Enemies of the Soviet Union'. Britain's Foreign

Office heard that Mosley proposed to visit the United States and the FBI reported that he was 'expected to arrive shortly at unknown port to attend Gerald K. Smith Party Convention, St Louis, August 21'. Smith's anti-Semitic and anti-Communist Christian Nationalist Crusade called for the deportation of Zionists and the expulsion of Blacks to Africa. With no passport, a visit from Mosley was unlikely, though US authorities remained 'very much interested' in Mosley with 'a view toward excluding him from the United States'.

On 16 October Mosley proposed that 'every European be able to vote for any other European' for a European assembly. His Europe a Nation was 'fundamentally different from all the weak compromises which grope and hesitate somewhere between a new league of nations and some form of old fashioned federalism. This idea overcomes many problems which more timid policies merely aggravate. Questions of frontiers and the old national sovereignties do not arise within a new and greater nation, which has only one sovereignty and only one frontier.'

Although a core group of ex-18B internees developed a Freikorps spirit and were dedicated to the concept of a 'new Europe arising phoenix like from the ashes of the old', UM canvassers found that such dreams made no impact on potential recruits. John Warburton thought they were 'too far advanced for people to understand. Mosley was interested in tomorrow. People aren't visionaries. They're captured on bread-and-butter politics. He was always twenty years advanced in his thinking. It was very hard for members to grasp what he was advocating.' In the East End Michael Quill found 'big support' for the old-style BU. The European idea 'did not touch their hearts as did the "Britain First" policy'. Most 'didn't realise the full extent of what was going on in Europe. The BU people were patriotic "Britain" and didn't believe in Europe. They couldn't accept the French, Germans etc.' They were dismayed by the discarding of the Empire and not enthused by his vision of Africa.

John Tyndall, who later led the National Front, was interested in Mosley but on hearing of Europe a Nation was immediately put off. It 'was, and is, out of the question, being wholly undesirable and not remotely possible. He attempted to justify the change by explaining that the British Empire now no longer existed, having been destroyed by that war.' This justification for joining Europe was 'complete nonsense'. The dominions were 'really vital elements of the Empire, the members of which, by reason of their white and largely British populations, and their primary-producing resources and consequent complementary economies, provided the basis for the self-sufficient economic area advocated in Mosley's pre-war policy'. Thoughts of support for Mosley were 'killed at birth'.

Quill claimed that some recruits embraced the Europe idea but more Mosley's analysis that rearmament had prevented a pre-war crisis. The British elite would be incapable of preventing a peacetime crisis of 'Old Gang' capitalism, which would lead to mass unemployment. The economist Roy Harrod talked to him about these issues and tried to persuade him to write a book setting out his ideas but, 'unfortunately', Diana noted, 'he never did so'. Speakers were told that Labour had made such a mess of the economy – there was bread rationing and the banning of luxuries – that they had no need to be defensive about Fascism, since the long predicted crisis was imminent. However, Quill found that with the 'improvement in economic circumstances as wartime shortages were overcome and consumer goods became available, it became hard to build a zeal equal to pre-war'.

There was a short recession in late 1947 with wage freezes and ration cuts. However, by spring 1948 there were signs of an upturn with unemployment limited to 3 per cent. Living standards improved, and if there was resentment of rationing and 'bureaucratization', Renton notes that the benefits were reaped by the Conservative Party, which exercised a 'total hegemony over the right' on matters such as denationalization, so much so that 'fascism was not even a potential rival'. John Warburton admitted that 'at the top of the UM they had not thought it out. It was a different world.' While 'the First World War had touched everyone of that generation, after the Second, it was never again', though attacks on immigration gave the UM limited impetus in East London.

From autumn 1948 the UM attacked immigrants from the West Indies but anti-Semitism remained at the core of its agitation. Such anti-Semitism was boosted when Sidney Stanley, an East End spiv, appeared before the Lynskey Tribunal, accused of bribing a Board of Trade minister. Newspapers made anti-Semitic jokes at his expense and demanded his deportation. Articles in *Union* – headlined LIFE BLOOD FLOWS OUT, SEWAGE FLOWS IN – claimed every 'spiv and shark' was determined to get into Britain. UM agitators revived the chant 'the yids, the yids, we've got to get rid of the yids'. In November a UM speaker at Lewisham asked the crowd to 'imagine what a stink they made, all that number of Yids together'. In West Green Jews were described as 'filthy, parasitic vermin, feeding on the political body of the country. The sooner we get rid of this lot the better. Hitler closed the doors of his gas chambers too soon.' Mosley was more careful with language but his followers knew exactly to whom he was referring when he criticized 'American capitalists'.

Special Branch shorthand writers took down every word at these meetings. 'We had a mutual understanding', Hamm recalled, 'that if I was carried away as the adrenalin flowed, and started to speak too fast for them, they would signal me to slow down, and I would do so.' Despite this, prosecutions for incitement were rare, although Woodrow Wyatt witnessed police removing hecklers who had 'the temerity to shout: "Down with fascism"'. Even resurrecting anti-Semitism could not halt the slide in support.

At the end of January 1949 Mosley spoke at Kensington Town Hall, in order 'to ignite a resurgence of Union power'. Whereas she had attended no BUF meetings, Diana now insisted on being at Mosley's meetings, despite the violence, which had become a regular feature. This time 700 Fascists attended but outside an estimated 2,000 anti-Fascists demonstrated behind six divisions of London police. The meeting was brought to a chaotic end with the release of tear-gas canisters. On the platform above the fumes, Mosley 'wondered why his audience was coughing and sneezing'. Finally, with streaming eyes, they were forced to leave the building. The ensuing mêlée outside was dealt with by mounted police, who made seventeen arrests.

In March, 5,000 people opposed 150 UM members at Ridley Road. There were thirty-four arrests. On 11 March Harold Pinter and Jewish friends were attacked after a meeting. They had previously encountered Fascist gangs who used bicycle chains and broken bottles. Because the books they were carrying were by foreign authors, the Fascists said they must be Communists. They were saved from serious injury by running on to the open platform of a passing bus. The teenagers' account of the attack, which left Pinter beaten and bruised, was rubbished by the investigating officers at Dalston police station. A report was passed to the Home Secretary, who had been asked by MPs and the National Council for Civil Liberties to investigate the activities of the Fascists. However, the authorities were more concerned about Communist influence over the NCCL. Metropolitan Police claimed there had been 'no organised attacks on citizens by Fascist or any other group. During the past twelve months there have been numerous political meetings in the Dalston area but no serious assaults have been reported to police.'

'We were not alone', Pinter later wrote, 'in wondering what the Home Secretary was doing by not banning these groups and why the police were not getting to grips with the problem. Under the banner of free speech, they were allowing these stupid and pathetic, but dangerous people to do serious physical harm to others.' Within weeks, more Jewish teenagers were attacked, one suffering a fractured skull. This time the culprits were caught and one, described by the judge at the trial as the leader of a 'Dalston strong arm squad', was jailed. The ban on marches was reimposed after Mosley tried to hold one in the East End.

In April the UM put up three candidates for the London County Council, led by Victor Burgess in Kensington. They polled 600 votes apiece, but twelve candidates in the local elections obtained fewer than 2,000 votes in total. *Union* sales were down by three-quarters and key supporters such as Tommy Moran had left. Quill acknowledged that 'as the UM was very much based on the comradeship of shared experiences when one man went others soon followed'. A bitter Moran told *Reynolds News* that Mosley's concept of leadership was 'dictatorship and his idea of service is slavery'. Peter Huxley-

Blythe also departed. 'One expected more of Mosley than he could give.' He was among the radicals who wanted action, but came to believe that Mosley had not given his all like others 'who had decided to have a go'.

Mosley's political failure, his vanity and Europeanism, notes Thurlow, 'made him anathema to all but those captivated by his personal charisma'. Potentially a figure of the first rank, he found himself 'baying in the backwaters of British politics'. The UM was even more marginal to British politics than the BU had been. It was a sideshow to keep loyalists involved.

That Mosley had given up on the UM as a mass popular movement became evident in the summer of 1949 when he left for a four-month trip around Fascist haunts in the Mediterranean. He wrote to Brendan Bracken requesting help in retrieving his passport. An old Labour colleague, Hugh Sherwood, raised the matter in the Lords, where the Lord Chancellor reminded peers that Mosley had never been charged with any offence. He knew that by right Britons could in peacetime leave the country and return at will, with or without a passport. Raven Thomson had made contact with friends in Franco's Spain and Salazar's Portugal to ask whether Mosley might enter without a passport. Major de Laessoe, who had worked in Portugal, visited Spain on Mosley's behalf. On release from internment he farmed a smallholding in Norfolk with a group of ex-detainees and, despite his advanced years, helped establish UM branches in East Anglia. He died soon afterwards as a result of the strain of imprisonment. Mosley received assurances that he would be accepted without a passport.

In May the Cabinet agreed to return Mosley's passport – which he said he needed in order to go to France for the sake of his health – after word reached the Foreign Office that they were about to be made to look like fools. 'Curiously enough,' Diana recalled, 'on the eve of our departure, we were given our passports. We were free at last.' They had bought a sixty-ton ketch, the *Alianora*, which could withstand Atlantic storms, and on 11 June set sail from Southampton with Alexander and Max, two seamen and a butler. 'Our happiness was boundless,' Diana wrote. In a leisurely cruise, they called at Bordeaux and made for Corunna. MI5 gave details of the trip to France's Direction de la Surveillance du Territoire, which began tracking the Mosleys. The DST's Roger Wybot reported that Mosley 'wants to restart his political career. He has abandoned anti-semitism, an unwelcome view to hold after the war, and advocates a Europe of nations . . . He wishes to meet several big shots of the French extreme right wing who escaped the purge.'

On 17 June, with Portuguese friends in Lisbon, Diana celebrated her thirty-ninth birthday. The objective was Spain and they took a train to Madrid for an arranged meeting with the former Foreign Minister and Fascist ideologue Serrano Suner and his wife Zita, General Franco's sister-in-law. Suner had been the Caudillo's right-hand man and his pronounced Nazi sympathies led the Axis powers to hope Spain might join in the war. He was a carbon-copy Nazi and imagined he was 'going to play Hitler or Mussolini', having, like Franco, anticipated a German victory. Franco dismissed him in 1942 and he spent his remaining years rewriting his past. Suner resumed his profession as a lawyer and avowed a discreet loyalty to the Generalissimo. He amassed a fortune through business operations smoothed by his family connections. Suner obtained a Spanish passport for Mosley.

The Mosleys paid homage at the tomb of José Antonio Primo de Rivera, who had met Mosley in London in the thirties. The Falange founder had made a deep impression on Mosley, and 'his assassination seemed to me always one of the saddest of the individual tragedies of Europe'. The Caudillo's only concern with the Falange was to keep it quiet. Franco's regime lived wholly within its own little world; internal opposition was impotent and it remained aloof to foreigners. Suner acted as Mosley's sponsor but the government officially distanced itself from the British Fascist, as he met political figures such as Gaston Bergery, ex-leader of the French Radical Party who had opposed the war. Acquitted of collaboration after spending time in detention, he had resumed his vocation as a lawyer. Diana corresponded with her sister Nancy, who in turn wrote to Evelyn Waugh on 30 July that the Mosleys were having a 'whizz of a time with special bull fights, official dinners and a minister to take them round'. They sailed on to Majorca and met Mussolini's Foreign Minister Filipo Anfuso, in exile after being condemned to death but later amnestied and elected as a deputy to the Italian parliament for his native Sicily.

It was a summer and autumn of harbour hopping from Tangier, Antibes and Monte Carlo, down the Italian coast to Rome, where they met members of the Italian Social Movement (MSI). More powerful than the UM, it had made a fresh start in the hope of winning over at least part of the electorate, and officially played the democratic game, winning 2 per cent of the vote and six seats in the 1948 election. It rapidly became divided between radical neo-Fascist and conservative anti-Communist factions, but remained the most significant post-war link with the Fascist tradition. This was symbolized by the election as leader of Giorgio Almirante, a junior functionary in the Salo Republic. Mosley already had contact with the MSI through Tuli Abeilli, who had visited London, and met Ernesto Massi, its Secretary General, who claimed the European Community was born on the Eastern front, Fabio Lonciari, editor of *Europa Unità*, and General Costa, head of foreign contacts.

When the Mosleys moved on to France, the DST worried that they might settle on the Côte d'Azur. Maurice Lacarrière set in motion 'discreet surveillance' but it led to 'the discovery of nothing of interest to our service. The guests, acompanied by Mosley, visited the normal picturesque areas.' In

Cannes they were joined by a figure from the past, Brian Howard. Speaking fluent French and German, Mosley told an interviewer that for the first time he 'felt European'.

In Germany, by the summer of 1949, preparatory work for Franke-Gricksch's and Beck's secret organization was complete. At a founding meeting in Hamburg on 22 July, chaired by former Gauleiter of Hamburg Karl Kaufman, participants 'swore to remain loyal to the principles of National Socialism' but committed themselves to 'an elastic ideological framework', which 'could encompass all the various strands of nationalist opposition'. However, a fierce internal rivalry between the Franke-Gricksch and Beck factions, over their respective support for the Soviet or American positions on Europe, limited its capacity to carry through its plans. US Army Intelligence intercepted a letter from a 'Hamburg addressee unknown to source', to Der Deutsche Block's headquarters, confirming that Raven Thomson, as Mosley's representative, intended to visit Munich in order to meet Karl Meissner, DDB's 'Reichsführer'.

The Mosleys moved on to Paris, where Diana renewed relations with Nancy, unaware of her part in her arrest in 1940. Nancy believed Diana's life had been ruined by Mosley, who in turn considered her to be a silly woman: 'I've suffered from that type all my life.' Nancy wrote to a friend on 27 August that Colonel Gaston Palewski, with whom she was having an affair, 'met them (a great secret) and was much taken aback at being talked to as if he were a fellow fascist!' He thought Mosley 'charming but a little mad'. Nancy wrote to Waugh on 26 September that Diana and Mosley, in no hurry to return home, were 'in a whirl of traitors. I suspect they are up to no good.'

Mosley was considering living in France, where there would be more opportunity to propagate his European ideas. 'If you are trying to shift a load of manure,' he mused to Diana, 'you don't start by putting yourself underneath it.' She was in entire agreement with him. 'The loss of the Empire was a great blow to M. and his supporters . . . My own predilection had always been for Europe.' He wanted 'to become a European, in a way that is hardly possible for somebody living in England'. His propaganda for Europe a Nation, however, was dwarfed by Churchill's more respectable United Europe Movement. They ended their four-month trip and left the boat in Cannes for the winter.

Mosley returned in October to find the UM in a poor state. Alf Flockhart told journalist Dudley Barker they had 108 branches with up to thirty-eight members in each, but it was a lie. There were no more than 2,000 members, mostly concentrated in East London. Mosley redoubled his efforts and spoke at Kensington Town Hall on 17 October to an audience, Mervyn Jones noted, of 'sentimental old ladies, retired colonels, flash young men bored with their jobs and ordinary people of the small shopkeepers'. His appeal was in 'restoring the psychological outlet which India for 150 years provided for the spirited young sons of the British middle classes'. He was 'a bitter, disappointed, frustrated man. He deeply resents his rejection by his country and reacts by self-praise and hatred.'

Mosley presented a picture of Europe as 'a great power able to defy Bolshevism and reject American aid', and a 'Faustian vision of Africa'. Heroic technicians would open up the continent, 'reclaiming marshes and deserts for the uses of man, cutting tunnels, canals, railways and highways through natural obstacles. Just think what could be done.' Jones acknowledged that Mosley did not favour sweated labour but he had made clear his contempt for Africans. An appeal to racial fears was embodied in claims that the old parties are 'waiting till the juju-men are ready to take over'.

Mosley's policies were met with such indifference that the 43 Group had ceased attacking UM meetings. 'This was', John Bean remembered, 'a greater blow to Mosleyites than all the bans on their marches . . . For it was only when a fight broke out at a meeting that they received any mention in the press.' AJEX was similarly convinced that 'with very rare exceptions, the most effective way to combat Mosley was to ignore both their marches and their meetings'. To stem the tide, Bean recalled, Mosley resorted to provocative marches through areas that were 'either notorious as a Red stronghold, or had a large Jewish population'. When he realized he was 'wasting his sweetness on the desert air' to a handful of supporters, 'some uniformed police, two Special Branch officers and a few stray dogs' at Ridley Road, he gave up.

Germany assumed increasing importance. The Frankfurt newspaper *Abend Post* noted on 28 November that Mosley books and pamphlets 'overflow West Germany'. They were being sent to 'former Hitler Youth leaders', with a strong pro-Mosley presence among 'former members of the office VI (6th HQ) of the chief command headquarters of the Waffen SS staff'. The courier service Mosley ran was 'taken care of by English people visiting and vacationing in Germany', which was the 'essential basis' of his Europe a Nation and Euro-Africa policy. *Union* stated on 10 December that in Africa, 'Germany will find the Lebensraum of which she has been temporarily deprived in the East'.

A prophet without honour in his own country, *The Alternative* gave Mosley a certain cachet among what Bardeche termed 'these bands of lost soldiers who recognized each other in the murk of injustice and hatred'. He openly sought the 'good will' of German admirers and dedicated the German edition 'to his German comrades in unshakeable belief in European brotherhood by an Englishman who has become a European'. In a new foreword he said 'their enemy was not so much the English people but much more the small authoritative clique in England whose politics has defeated all great projects and powerful performances for so long a time, not only in Europe but also in

England'. The Americans, the English and the French are accused in newspaper reports of

> the burning of living opposers at the martyr stake, whipping and other torture methods, rape and other violations of women and children . . . whilst the Germans were molested with accusations before a court and a judge instated by the allies which are still too fresh, too well known and too extensive that they demand or permit a repetition here. The Germans will surely receive the opportunity to prove before history whether the terrible conditions in their concentration camps during the war were evoked mostly through the bombardments of the allies and the epidemics which followed.

US CIC reports noted the positive reviews of the book in Germany.

The volume of propaganda Mosley was sending to Germany led newspapers to conclude that he viewed 'the national socialistic elements in West Germany as the most suitable partners at the organising of a fascist concentration movement in Europe'. He was 'continuing the tradition of a Fascist International which Hitler was forced to abandon. He has hit on a stratagem which gives him the air of a progressive spirit.' The Austrian neo-Nazi paper *Alpenruf* suggested on 31 December that 'the spiritual centre of a cleansed Fascism is today neither in Germany nor in Austria, but – strange though it may seem – in England'. The Swedish Fascist paper *Vaegen Framat* claimed the European underground movements were growing but needed to be brought together to preserve everything that had been valuable in the past. The war had weakened their position and co-operation was essential, even for racial policies. Nations were not strong enough 'to enforce the unity of Europe (which the Fascists want on an anti-democratic basis)', and which was now smaller on account of the Iron Curtain, but enough nationalism would remain to justify a Fascist International.

With the absence of a crisis and the lack of a mass base, the permeation strategy became Mosley's only real option. Charlie Watts wrote to Robert Saunders that 'when the crack-up comes, and you and I know just how inevitable that is; when the masses of the people find that they want a strong lead, these [covert Fascists] will be in the best position to come out into the open and join forces with the active movement'. One of the few successes was John Charnley of the Lancashire Chamber of Commerce, who joined the Conservatives and within two years was Chairman of the Burscough branch. Raven Thomson was responsible for external contacts and held talks with Welsh Nationalist leaders to persuade them to join in a United Europe. He argued that smaller nations working together would enjoy more power than by being just an attachment to England. He was involved with the very first signs of the 'Green Movement'.

The BU's agricultural adviser Jorian Jenks had during the war made contact with Montague Fordham and the Rural Reconstruction Association. In reaction to overuse of chemicals in farming, Jenks helped form the Soil Association to facilitate organic farming. Robert Saunders, however, believed genetic adjustment of crops was the answer to food shortages. Raven Thomson attempted to reconcile their views. Saunders joined the Dorchester Agricultural Society and the Rural Reconstruction Association. He stood as an 'independent' in local elections and in the early sixties came within one vote of beating Henry Plumb in the contest for the vice-presidency of the National Farmers Union. Links had already been made with respectable animal rights groups, through M. Dudley Ward, who had connections with the RSPCA and the Animal Defence Society. In the end, attempts at permeation were small scale and those who achieved positions of authority often left a movement they recognized was in serious decline.

In the spring of 1950, in looking at propaganda themes for the summer, Raven Thomson warned Mosley that interest in the UM 'is dying away in the most serious manner. It is my considered opinion that there is a grave danger of the British Movement folding up as a serious political force in this country, unless some stimulus is given.' Mosley, however, turned his attention to creating a European neo-Fascist International.

Mosley had talks with MSI leaders Giorgio Almirante, Alvise Loredan and naval hero Prince Junio Valerio Borghese; Maurice Bardeche of the Comité Français National; 'passionately pro-European' SS survivors and *Wehrmacht Partizankrieg* expert Arthur Ehrhardt, later the publisher of *Nation Europa*; Mussolini's rescuer Otto Skorzeny; air ace Hans-Ulrich Rudel; as well as First World War intellectual Ernst Junger, one of the first to advocate the union of Europe. Mosley's travels were monitored by US Army 430th CIC, which observed his renewed relationship with Johannes K. Bernhardt, who had been involved in the pre-war radio project as Goering's representative. The monitoring of these 'close contacts' was part of an investigation into a 'possible espionage ring in Vienna'. During February Mosley arranged for his representative in Hamburg, Karl Meissner, to confer with other Nazi figures, though the files do not reveal the nature of the discussions.

As a practical means of realizing a post-war Fascist new order, the MSI held a preparatory conference in Rome in March 1950, which was attended by Mosley; Anna Maria Mussolini, daughter of the late Duce; delegates from the Spanish Falange; associates of Swiss neo-Nazi Guy Amaudruz; Bruderschaft organizers; French collaborationists such as Georges Albertini, former ADC of Marcel Déat, Bardeche and Guy Lemonnier; and Sweden's Per Engdahl, leader of the Nysvenska Rorelsen who had been financed by Carl Carlberg, an anti-Semitic millionaire who bankrolled European Fascists, though he had repudiated the creed by 1950. Delegates agreed to organize a gathering in the autumn.

Over the Whitsun weekend the UM held a camp at Lymington in the New Forest. Late on Sunday Mosley made a brief visit, after flying in to London from Madrid. In search of allies, he then left for Argentina to meet Perón. With his strength in the trade unions, the Argentine leader considered himself a social radical, combining dictatorship and (anti-American) nationalism with a fight against the landowners. He was attacked by both Conservatives and Liberals. Just as Mosley wanted to unite Europe, Perón wanted to unite Latin America.

On the return journey Mosley stopped off at Madrid for a pre-arranged meeting with Oswald Pirow, who had suggested that 'our contact must become close'. He told Mosley 'the New Order has latterly made more progress than at any time since the end of hostilities'. *The Alternative* was 'making a great impression in Germany'.

Only Mosley's closest colleagues, principally Raven Thomson, were privy to the nature of his international travels, even Jeffrey Hamm and Robert Row did not really know what was happening. When Nicholas asked Hamm, 'What did you think when my father was supposed to be head of UM, he was hardly ever here, he was always in France, he was always going to Venice?' he replied, 'I did wonder about that, but then he'd say all these people were lined up and ready to back him.' When nothing happened Hamm would say, 'Oh, I used to wonder about that, too.' John Warburton recalled Mosley disappearing off for mysterious telephone calls to Europe and meetings whose purpose was never explained. There was a 'most strange atmosphere'.

CIC files reveal that Mosley frequently exchanged letters with Franke-Gricksch, who during the summer established lines of communication to the Soviet Military Administration and to the East Zonal authorities. The Bruderschaft's hitherto uniform policy line showed increasing diversity. At one in anti-Western resentment, Franke-Gricksch and Beck disagreed on aims and became leaders of rival factions. Representing the SS, Hitler Youth and Conservative Revolutionary elements, Franke-Gricksch, with his folkish-racist jargon, led the East-orientated National Bolsheviks, while the practical Beck headed the former *Wehrmacht* officers, who 'saw their task not so much in the permanent weakening of the defensive powers of the West as in the insistence on conditions that would make West German rearmament impossible without their own well-rewarded assistance'. Franke-Gricksch still saw 'the task of German policy in constructing a uniting order for the European peoples within "Nation Europa"', though he wanted it to embrace 'the young, Slavic peoples of the East'.

Developing links between neo-Nazis and the Soviet Union, and a rising tide of anti-Americanism, to which Mosley's Europe a Nation ideas to an extent contributed, worried British Intelligence, which monitored the Nazi revival. The right-wing, nationalist German Conservative and Right Party

(DKP-DRP), founded in 1946, attracted former Nazis. Swiftly banned by the Federal Republic, the DKP-DRP's rump merged with other groups to form the Socialist Reich Party in 1949, which was a significant force for a few years before fading away. In 1947 Adolf von Thadden, former artillery officer and member of the Deutsche Rechtspartei, approached MI6. His half-sister had been a member of the White Rose student resistance group in Munich and had been tortured and executed. He subsequently developed a deep-rooted hatred of the Nazis and proved to be an extremely valuable MI6 asset as it looked at ways of 'tainting and compromising the extreme right and their Soviet friends'.

In *The European Situation* (1950) Mosley argued Russia would launch 'not a war of States but a war of politics reinforced by violence'. The age of nuclear stalemate would usher in an era of the urban guerrilla, fomenting industrial sabotage, striking against the 'nerve centres of opposing governments . . . which have been softened by internal propaganda and thoroughly permeated by highly-placed agents in the key positions of administration and defence'.

When Bruderschaft leaders made contact with Werner Naumann, a man of influence in Nazi circles, its underground activities moved from the protection of former Nazis to overt political targets. Employed in the Ministry of Propaganda in 1944, aged thirty-four, he became the youngest under-secretary in the Hitler regime. In his testament the grateful Führer appointed him to succeed Goebbels as Minister. After an amnesty was declared for former Nazis, Naumann and friends with whom he had kept in secret contact thought 'the air sufficiently clear for him to venture into the open'. They co-ordinated efforts to put Nazis in positions of influence in political parties, the press and youth organizations. Top priority was given to penetrating the three right-wing parties that formed Chancellor Adenauer's governing coalition. Naumann managed an import-export firm in Düsseldorf, where he organized talks with the Bruderschaft banker Hjalmar Schacht and Hans-Ulrich Rudel, patron saint of the radical Nazi underground. Although not charged with war crimes, Rudel joined his compatriots in Argentina as a paid adviser to Perón. Also attending the talks was Otto Skorzeny, a major figure in running 'ratlines' and gun running, as well as in the reactivation of German business contacts. Unfortunately, the Foreign Office file on Skorzeny has been destroyed, as has one on Mosley's ties to Austrian neo-Nazis.

The Naumann/Bruderschaft circle, with its conception of elite selection and nationalist revival, was effective in its underground foreign dealings and developed contacts with Bardeche, the MSI and former officials of the Nazi Party's Foreign Organization. CIC files and UM members confirm that Mosley was in contact with all these individuals. 'A highly intelligent German', wrote Mosley, Naumann 'saw clearly that the only hope for all the Europeans was the making of Europe. However, his most normal and legitimate entry into politics produced a convulsion of acute hysteria in the British occupation authority' but 'no move was made against him until he was in contact with me'. Naumann admitted he had known Mosley 'since before the war . . . as a good personal friend'.

Such associations did little to reassure those having second thoughts about supporting the UM. Dr Margaret Vivian left in 1950 because 'any chance we had was ruined by the disgraceful way we were treated in the war which makes the proletariat regard us as Quislings'. Watts, too, recognized that 'we were now being held responsible for and answerable for all the vile Nazi atrocities'. He decided he was not going to waste his life 'on people who were not worth the effort' and was 'no longer going to knock my head against a brick wall'. Mosley tried to rid the UM of anti-Semites but was realizing he was engaged in 'a sterile and unpopular revival of the BU policy'.

On 27 June 1950 the writer James Pope-Hennessy, whose lover Len Adams was a UM member, dined with the Mosleys at the Hampstead home of the poet Derek Hill. Diana was 'hopelessly Mitford – that meaningless exaggerated manner and voice', but he thought her 'very funny about prison'. She was bored when Mosley began talking politics but Pope-Hennessy thought him 'remarkably intelligent, and to the point and somehow real'. Mosley said, 'Were it not for the working people, he would leave England; they alone are worth anything here now.' That summer was spent sailing on *Alianora* to the South of France.

In July the DST wanted to know about the Mosleys' movements. It had intelligence from source 'Rose' that they were 'due to arrive in Paris on 28 July under the name of "Morley" and were thinking of travelling to Antibes in their car, registration number CHO 143, a black MG cabriolet convertible'. At Antibes they boarded the *Alianora*. Roger Wybot asked DST offices in Marseilles and Nice to keep track of Mosley, who 'will probably meet up with or will have on board people with whom he will have political contact'. The boat was expected to move on to Naples, Trieste, Venice and other Italian ports, where they were monitored by Italian security. On 17 August a report was forwarded to Wybot detailing Mosley's encounters with Italian Fascists and the French collaborationists associated with the Pétain regime, Alfred Fabre-Luce and Gaston Bergery.

Nice Commissioner Maurice Cottentin forwarded details to Paris of an unexpected development. Intelligence gathered in Marseilles and passed to the central office in Cannes revealed a plot by 'Italian anarchists' to blow up the *Alianora*. The DST was forced to keep Mosley under closer surveillance to protect him from the anarchists. In the end the plot fell apart because soon afterwards Mosley sold the boat to a British subject.

*

The MSI's second meeting took place in Rome on 22 October, organized by its Fronte Universitario di Azione Nazionale. A new addition was Karl-Heinz Priester, leader of the NPD's radical wing. A former Hitler Youth leader, Priester spoke for those who supported a united Europe as a 'third force'. A European Committee was formed and elected Engdahl as president, Bardeche and Fabio Lonciari as vice-presidents. They agreed to organize a conference in southern Sweden the following spring as the springboard for an openly pro-Fascist international. An unidentified British representative briefed the absent Mosley. US intelligence noted that he 'did not appear at public meetings of associations of international Fascism' but was 'in contact with its high-ranking personalities'.

Even larger UM meetings were now only attracting an average of 250 people. A meeting at Kensington Town Hall in the autumn of 1950 was typical in that violent opposition had more or less ceased. Mosley's propaganda policy was 'based on the assumption that any news is good news'. Consequently the greatest blow the opposition struck his cause, John Bean conceded, 'was their cessation of organised attacks on public meetings and marches. For the most part the only recruits such publicity gained were political morons looking for excitement.' The audience was the same faithful supporters with a few 'inquisitive persons, wives and girlfriends who had been dragged along to keep the peace'. There were few active supporters outside London.

To attract a crowd, Bean would masquerade as a heckler, which came easily because he had become 'aware of the fallacies, half truths, and prejudices which UM's policy was built on'. The marches were stage-managed by East London Organizer Alf Flockhart, a homosexual whose drum corps was nicknamed the 'bum corps'. In October he fell from grace amid allegations, which he denied, that he was involved in a homosexual rape. He wrote to Mosley suggesting it would be unwise to attend the court case, one 'that will have a very strong distasteful smell for a long time'. Bean realized his colleagues were 'not a band of six foot broad shouldered thugs, as the general public seem to visualise, but a rather drab looking crowd of vacant faced nondescript men and women – although not without courage'. When marches failed to attract a counter-demonstration and generate publicity, the UM looked to new stunts and the decision was taken to attack Communist meetings. 'All this, of course, in the quest for publicity, and to keep the "boys" occupied.'

Mosley was on the verge of renouncing all practical activity and had decided to leave England. The immediate cause was a tax case which he lost; after it his counsel remarked, 'I should have won that case for anyone in the country except you.' They planned to buy a house in Ireland, attracted by 'a low rate of taxation and food in abundance' and the presence of friends such as the Jacksons, who had a large house at Tullamaine, County Tipperary, where they hunted with the 'noble Tips'. Appointed Professor of Spectroscopy at

Oxford in 1947, Derek was a large shareholder in the *News of the World*, which was sent to him in a plain wrapper as it was banned by the censor in the Republic of Ireland. Deborah Mitford, whose husband had succeeded as Duke of Devonshire, was chatelaine of Lismore Castle. Diana had connections from her Guinness days. At the end of December the Mosleys were in Paris, seeking another home in Europe. In the new year Crowood was sold for £80,000 (£1.6m).

Mosley predicted in *Union* in January 1951 that when the crisis returned, 'Europe led by dedicated men from all nations, would shatter its fetters and succeed where fascism had failed'. A new movement was 'uniting these elements in defence of Europe, which have fought for a generation against the Soviet menace, and once in a disunited Europe engaged in internecine strife flung the Red Army back 600 miles into the Russian Steppes'. The new movement was centred around *Nation Europa*, founded as the journal of international Fascism by Mosley and, among a select group, Per Engdahl. An admirer of Mussolini, Engdahl's New Swedish Movement boasted 4,000 followers and promoted a corporativist, anti-Semitic, anti-Communist and fiercely nationalist doctrine, which appealed to Scandinavian Nazi collaborators. *Nation Europa*'s first issue, edited by Arthur Ehrhardt, appeared in January 1951 with the sub-title 'Monthly for European Regeneration'. Ehrhardt had been assigned to the counter-intelligence section of the High Command but switched to the Waffen SS, though he did not join the Nazi Party. In 1945 he described his aims as 'the union of Europe on a national basis' and asserted that 'Europe had already been created' within the wartime European SS organizations.

Nation Europa counted among its directors the Swedish industrialist Carl Carlberg and Arthur Kogel of Chicago. Mosley and Raven Thomson contributed articles, as did Major-General Fuller and Basil Liddell Hart, which gave it some credibility. Chief essayists were former Nazi officials and writers such as Hans Grimm, Otto Karl Dupow, Adolf von Thadden and Karl-Heinz Priester; from France, René Binet, Maurice Bardeche; from Italy, Professor J. Evola and Fabio Lonciari; and from South Africa, Oswald Pirow. *Nation Europa* claimed a steady rising circulation of 6,000 copies, which suggested its influence was not considerable. However, it was directed to an 'elite' and its content was above the heads of rank-and-file Fascists.

The elite were Skorzeny and Rudel, who set up an 'external organization' in Madrid, with subordinate roles entrusted to Himmler's principal agent in Italy SS-Colonel Eugen Dollmane; former commander of the Legion Wallonie living in exile in Spain, Léon Degrelle; and the Jew baiter, SS-Colonel Johann von Leers. From 1951 Skorzeny did not confine his activities to Germany and Spain and, acting as a commercial traveller, was able to present himself as a businessman more interested in money than an adventurous life. However, he played an important role, through Priester, former propaganda chief of the Hitler Jugend SS and Chairman of the Deutsche Soziale Bewegung, in bringing together the various groups in a neo-Nazi International. Priester stressed *Nation Europa*'s 'third force' perspective and visited London for talks with Mosley.

The Union Movement limped on until February 1951, when Mosley at Kensington Town Hall denounced Britain as 'an island prison' and went off to a self-imposed exile in Ireland. As in the 1930s, his rationalization for failure was that the economic and political crisis which he needed to succeed had unaccountably failed to happen. He told disappointed UM followers he would 'speak in England again when the efforts of our movement from without and from within have scrapped some of the bars. It is easier to break locks from outside than from inside.'

Information that Mosley intended to live in Ireland reached the Irish government. D. Costigan of the Department of Justice reminded Sean Nunan, Permanent Under-Secretary of External Affairs, that Mosley had applied to live in Ireland five years previously when the Taoiseach had suggested he 'might try at a later date'. There was 'no evidence that Sir Oswald has engaged in political activity here or that he is in any way connected with the "Black Legion"', and so it was agreed he could stay. On 19 February Costigan reported Mosley had purchased Clonfert Palace, Eyrecourt, in County Galway. The former home of Protestant bishops, dating from the seventeenth century, it stood on the edge of a bog less than a mile from the River Shannon and was in a poor state, requiring bathrooms and electricity.

Costigan reported that while renovations were undertaken, Diana's 'two sons, Alexander (13) and Max (11), are staying with their father in Dublin. They spend most of their time at a Dublin riding school.' Alexander regretted leaving Crowood and the familiar faces, but Max adored hunting and found plenty of opportunities with Derek Jackson and the Devonshires. Clonfert, recalled Mosley, was 'rambling and romantic rather than beautiful, and redolent of the usual legends of Cromwellian misbehaviour'. Diana found life there was 'something like pre-war Wootton, there was fishing and rough shooting'.

During a visit to Paris the Mosleys discovered the Temple de la Gloire, a run-down building of grand Hellenic proportions twenty miles from Paris, near the village of Orsay. Built in 1800 by the architect Vignon, it was a gift from the wife and mother-in-law of General Moreau, chief of the armies of the Rhine, who was a rival of Napoleon's until his death, to celebrate his victory at Hohenlinden. Its high-sounding name became a permanent joke for Mosley, who admitted his friends 'thought I am always a little "exalté", but now I am right round the bend'. When the Mosleys purchased the Temple in

March 1951 for £5,000 (£100,000), it was in need of restoration. They also bought a flat in central Paris so as to be in contact with friends. France, however, was the only country in which Mosley refused to be involved in politics, although it was a good base from which to travel around Europe.

In Ireland he hoped to escape the press, the anti-Fascists and State surveillance. Mosley could spend up to ninety days in England which, he said, 'were adequate to the meetings and conferences it was necessary to hold'. Within the UM, many believed he had deserted the cause and a number left. Nicholas realized his father did not take the UM 'very seriously as a political movement. I think he saw it as a way of ticking over, keeping a nucleus of supporters there, in case something happened in the great big world.' Indeed, Mosley only needed the UM as a means of entrée into the international networks on which he concentrated his energies and resources.

26

The Neo-Fascist Internationals

At the end of May 1951, at the invitation of Per Engdahl, a hundred representatives of the principal Fascist and neo-Nazi groups from across Europe assembled at Malmö, Sweden, to found a new international. Twenty West German Nazis were invited but the Swedish authorities refused them entry permits. 'Dr Franz Richter', a Nazi official who was elected a member of the Bundestag for the Socialist Reich Party (DRP), took part in the proceedings after getting across the frontier by using false papers to conceal his real name, Fritz Roessler. The MSI was represented by individual members, such as Arturo Michelini and Fabio Lonciari, because its leadership refused to be entangled with a potentially compromising international. There was a gulf between the conservatives, who wanted an international under their direction, and young radicals, who sought a manifesto to rally their foreign counterparts and simultaneously satisfy both the 'socialist' and the neo-Nazi factions. But like the DRP, they were unwilling to compromise themselves too deeply, justifying Maurice Bardeche's claim that for them, 'nationalism is still the mainspring of their doctrine'. Among those who expressed solidarity with the Malmö rally but failed to get there, having been denied visas, were its main instigators, Otto Skorzeny, Karl-Heinz Priester and Mosley.

Malmö's immediate goals were to rehabilitate Fascism, and to devise a common programme and an agreed-upon framework of action. The intention was to field candidates in the forthcoming elections for the European Parliament, so policy was moderated in order to attract popular support. Representatives refused to invoke Mussolini and Hitler as their spiritual forefathers and distanced themselves from crucial aspects of their ideology. Fascism and Nazism in general, said Bardeche, 'belong to the past'. The new movement refused 'to revive or imitate political forms that are today superseded . . . our doctrine can make use of all the experiments of the past, but our ideal is a new one which is only inspired by the present'.

Moderates rejected anti-Semitism in order to project the image of 'reasonable men who wanted the public to welcome a new "cleansed national-socialism" purged of most of the racialist excesses of the Hitler regime'. The third way 'neutralism' – 'neither Morgenthau, nor Moscow' – was of a kind with which Hitler had tried to unite Europe but, aside from its *Nation Europa* elements, the vague manifesto 'reflected the ideals of Mussolini or Salazar far more than it did those of Hitler'. However, the public announcements were, notes Jeffrey Bale, 'little more than cynical, opportunistic ploys designed to alleviate legitimate public concerns'; a view confirmed by the less diplomatic phraseology employed in their own press.

Malmö gave birth to the Mouvement Social Européen/Europäische Soziale Bewegung (MSE/ESB). Engdahl was elected head of its governing 'four-man council', which included Bardeche, Priester and moderate MSI leader Augusto de Marsanich, a Minister for Foreign Affairs under Mussolini, and prepared a candidates' list for the planned elections – later cancelled – for the European Parliament. Sixteen movements affiliated to the 'Malmö International' and a secretariat was set up in Rome. Activists tried to establish national branches for their pan-European umbrella movement. The *New York Times* claimed that one of its main objectives was 'to penetrate United States and British democratic organisations by taking advantage of the rising tide of anti-Communism'. Contacts were established with forty extremist organizations in Europe, pro-Arab friendship leagues and Association Argentina-Europa, a co-ordinating body for twenty neo-Nazi groups under the leadership of Kameradenwerk chief Hans-Ulrich Rudel.

There were no representatives of the Bruderschaft, which was in the process of splitting. The hostility between Beck's pro-Western faction and Franke-Gricksch's Russophile faction, coupled with adverse publicity about the organization's role as a Nazi secret society, led to Franke-Gricksch's formal expulsion. The role of the intelligence services in these events is unclear, but the Russians suspected Beck was working as an agent provocateur for US Intelligence. Shortly afterwards it was formally dissolved. In the end, the Bruderschaft did not 'exert any realistic behind-the-scenes influence over significant political events of the day', although a prominent member, Dr Gustav Scheel, former Gauleiter of Salzburg, continued to scheme with the elite group centred on Dr Werner Naumann.

In order to increase influence behind the scenes, Naumann's associates strengthened their ties to military circles and veterans' organizations, industrialists, youth and cultural groups, and publishers such as ex-SS man Waldemar Schutz's Pleasse-Verlag and the international backers of *Nation Europa*, which included Mosley. The most significant contact was with Dr Eberhard Taubert of the Volksbund für Frieden und Freiheit (VFF), which led to political plotting with Skorzeny, Rudel and Wilfred von Oven, Goebbels's former adjutant. Naumann claimed the circle was simply a 'discussion group', which was unjustly persecuted by the 'victors'. However, his diary and secret speeches, in which he explicitly advocated the takeover of respectable rightist parties, tell otherwise. The chief efforts were devoted to infiltrating rightist parties, especially the Deutsche Partei (DP), with a view towards penetrating the entire state apparatus, and they ended up controlling North Rhine-Westphalia and Lower Saxony, Rudel's old stamping ground.

As the brains trust of the Fascist International, *Nation Europa* – on whose editorial board was Raven Thomson – was directed by the Mouvement Social Européen (MSE). However, apart from press attempts to portray Malmö as a 'revival of Hitler's Third Reich', the MSE achieved little. It was 'a great success on the symbolic level and thus fanned the initial hopes of many participants', but it 'soon lost the support of much of its own base'. Its financial foundations were shaky and at the end of 1951 Naumann had to come to the rescue by mobilizing financial assistance. He visited Paris where he met Mosley, Bardeche, Guy Amaudruz, Jean-Maurice Bauverd, Guy Lemonnier and Georges Albertini. Mosley helped a number of Fascist groups but not always with money. The US CIC reported that 'in a letter (22 June) written by Fritz Ploetz, business manager of the DDB, a (FNU) Schmidt of the Eggenfelden Printing Co. was asked if he is interested in purchasing 200 tons of Swedish paper which the DDB has at its disposal. The DDB obtained this paper through Mosley at a low price and is selling it to obtain funds.'

Bardeche attributed the MSE's decline 'to the failure of its component groups to develop as anticipated and the repressive actions and surveillance which its members were subjected to'. There were the usual personality conflicts among the would-be Führers but it was the issue of race that proved fatal. The 'third force' Europe of the 'moderates' such as Mosley and Bardeche failed as 'an answer to the dreams of the younger generations, who demanded action and were steeped in racialist ideas'. They disliked the 'soft-pedalling' of anti-Semitism and founded, at Zurich, the Nouvel Ordre Européen (NOE), which was characterized by virulent anti-Semitism.

Frenchman René Binet and other German and Italian militants founded the European Liaison office as a rival to the MSE, and inaugurated the NOE on 28 September 1951, under his presidency and the secretaryship of the Swiss neo-Nazi leader Guy Amaudruz. Contacts were established with Falangists, the MSI's right wing and the American National Renaissance Party. The NOE supported a 'third force' Europe built around the Berlin–Rome axis with a declaration that was explicitly racist. Bardeche had harsh things to say of those who 'take refuge in memories'.

According to US CIC files on the Swiss Youth leader Ernst Schmidt, in secret attendance at Zurich were Mosley and Priester, illustrating the complexity of individual ideological positions but also Mosley's willingness to associate himself with extreme elements, while publicly aligning himself with the moderates. When CIC officers attempting to find more about the MSE interviewed Priester in Bremen, he confirmed he had 'met with Mosley during his stay in Lörrach, Switzerland, and stated that he and Mosley were in agreement about the necessity of establishing contacts and influence in South Africa'.

In October 1951 Mosley's former German adviser, Franke-Gricksch, went missing in East Berlin and 'was never heard from again'. He was soon followed by his wife. Four years later she returned to West Germany and claimed they had been tried by a Russian military court on charges of pro-Western spying and anti-Soviet propaganda activity. Franke-Gricksch had been condemned to death, while she received a twenty-five-year sentence. The Red Cross later confirmed that Franke-Gricksch had died in a camp in 1953.

Like Mussolini, Mosley reverted to his left-wing roots once Fascism had failed. In his *European Socialism* he argued that international capitalism produced conflict not harmony, but he recognized his thirties' planned economy was 'too bureaucratic' and now proposed a 'synthesis of private enterprise and syndicalism'. His new faith envisaged a form of workers' control in industry and, later, the managerial revolution extolled in *Europe: Faith and Plan*. This was an outgrowth of inter-war Fascist thought, as expressed in Raven Thomson's *The Coming Corporate State* and his own earlier guild socialism. It was to be, Mosley argued, more decentralized and would extol individual initiative. Small industrial enterprises would be allowed complete freedom under private ownership but once they reached a certain size and when the founder had retired from active control, they were to pass to the ownership of their workers. The role of the State would be reduced to pioneering new industries, initiating projects too big for private enterprise and to provide macro-planning functions. State planning functions would be considerable and coexisted uneasily with the ideas of European socialism.

These ideas, however, held little appeal for the electorate and the UM was reduced to creating publicity stunts against the Communist Party. An insider agreed that Mosley was 'to some degree a political stunt merchant'. These were organized by ex-paratrooper Peter Lesley-Jones (later a Bevanite), who led a small corps of eighteen picked men. At the 1951 October general election the CP contested seats in East London and held a march from Stepney to Stoke Newington. The UM launched an attack on the march as it passed through what they considered their territory in Dalston. Although twelve UM members, including Lesley-Jones, were arrested, three of them being jailed, Mosleyites believed it was worth it. It was thought it would generate nationwide publicity as the only movement actively opposed to Communism; in fact, John Bean recalled, 'it confirmed the general public's view that they were a party of lay-abouts lacking any political argument'. The Special Propaganda Section was also responsible for organizing election campaigns but was ineffective and the three candidates, led by Burgess, received only an average of 470 votes in the 1952 by-elections. The SPS 'fizzled out, killed by the joint jealousies of the Headquarters hierarchy and the East End mobsters'.

*

Diana was now settled near Paris and for much of 1952 was absorbed in work on the Temple de la Gloire. Her relationship with her sister Nancy blossomed and, though she disliked 'Sir Ogre' ('Why will one's sisters marry these sewers?'), Nancy became a regular guest at the Mosleys'. However, she could never overcome her suspicions of their behaviour. The Mosleys' routine was to spend summers in Venice, shooting in the autumn in Normandy on the estate of friends, winters in Ireland, Christmas in Paris with Countess Mona Bismarck and New Year's Eve with the Duke and Duchess of Windsor, who lived nearby in the Moulin de la Tuilerie ('the Mill'). Max would then rush back to Ireland for the hunting.

Like the Mosleys, the Windsors were exiled, cut off from the society they craved. The couples dined together at the Mill twice a week and as frequently at the Temple. The Duke liked to indulge in genealogical gossip. 'He would say: "Now let me see. Lady so-and-so was Lord so-and-so's great-aunt. Recto?",' recalled Diana. 'I loved the Duke and have seldom met his like for charm. He was always ready to laugh and be amused and . . . his face lit up in a most engaging way. He had the almost miraculous memory that royal personages so cleverly cultivate and which everyone finds flattering.' In turn, he admired the Mosleys and talked about Germany and current affairs. He said, 'Tom would have made a first-rate Prime Minister.'

Diana was clear that the Windsors shared the Mosleys' views on politics. The Duchess was 'politically sophisticated and knew exactly what she was saying'. They all felt that if a separate peace had been made with Germany in 1939 and Hitler had been given a free hand against the Soviet Union, it would have saved the world from Communism and the British Empire from collapse. If Hitler 'had been allowed to deport the Jews, if Britain and America had accepted them, there would have been no need for a holocaust. There was of course no room in Palestine for them.' The two couples 'could not exonerate Hitler for being impatient and provoking World War Two' but with 'two egos like Churchill and Hitler, there was little chance for peace in the world . . . if the right people had been in power in England, particularly Lloyd George, there could have been a negotiated peace'. They agreed 'Allied forces should have occupied what were now the satellite countries of the Soviets before the Russians got to them, and should have proceeded to conquer the Soviet Union itself'. Nancy said the friendship between the two couples was based on nostalgia for the days of the Third Reich: 'I believe their wickedness knows no bounds.'

Back in Ireland there was concern about whether Mosley was engaged in political activities in the country after reports on 8 February from the Department of Defence that 'a good many of the people with whom he was prominently associated in England are again showing evidence of interest in a revival of their old activities'. The Director of Intelligence, Dan Bryan, told Sean Nunan on the 28th that he had 'no information' Mosley was 'taking any interest in political or other activities here'. Government officials were informed that while he was 'still politically active, he probably works from his residence outside Paris'. Bryan said, 'He seems more or less to have lost interest in the remnants of his Union Movement.'

Even anti-Semitism had lost its appeal. A study by J. H. Robb found that anti-Semites had little faith in the UM and 'most of them reject it vigorously', partly because of the 'very strong disfavour in which Fascism is held'. The UM's street politics reinforced the image of illegitimacy, the result of the heavy preponderance of adolescent youths at its meetings. Bean, who had wanted a 'modern' UM, was dismayed that 'with several other notable exceptions Mosley's followers post-war contained a higher percentage of degenerates and the socially dysfunctional than they did pre-war in the BUF'.

Mosley turned to immigration as the issue to garner support. *Union* regaled readers with tales of 'dope-pedlars, molesters of white women, and black crime' and demanded a 'white Brixton'. Growth of immigration from Commonwealth countries grew rapidly during the decade. With cheap passage, most came from the West Indies, but increasingly from India and Pakistan. The numbers of Indians, Pakistanis and West Indians in Britain stood in 1951 at 30,800, 5,000 and 15,300 respectively, and apart from at arrival ports, black or Asian people were few and far between. The UM argued it was 'high time that some public protest should be made about this influx of coloured work-shys. Obviously the great difference between the standard of life of the African negroes and of the British people is such that work-shy negroes are perfectly prepared to exist in idleness and in slum conditions on the dole and what they can scrounge from the public assistance authorities.'

In a statement on 27 February 1952 Mosley defined his attitude to the trickle of West Indian immigration: 'I am strongly against any offensive abuse of Negroes.' We must live with them as 'friendly neighbours' but not in an 'ad-mixture of races' but in an apartheid system as in Africa. 'The same principle must apply to Britain. Therefore we must prevent the residence of Negroes in Britain.' He wanted those immigrants already here involuntarily repatriated with some compensation. Diana said, 'He had thought it all out, you know, even repatriation.'

'There were mounting pressures within the Movement', John Charnley recalled, 'to renew the initiative for a series of meetings in the major towns and cities, and through it, build up mass support for our policies. I was very encouraged to receive an invitation to spend a weekend of discussion in Dublin with OM.' The Mosleys' presence in Ireland intrigued the British and a diplomat in the Dublin embassy maintained contact with Nunan. 'We should always be interested to have any further knowledge of their eventual return to Ireland.'

In September the British Foreign Office informed Dublin that Mosley was to hold 'a forthcoming meeting with his principal UK lieutenants in the Russell Hotel' and asked the Irish to keep it under surveillance. Reports sent to the Irish government said the expected arrivals were 'E. J. Hamm, Robert Row and John Charnley. A. Raven Thomson, the Secretary of the Union Movement, would also be present. Our authorities comment that the Union Movement has made no progress whatever since Mosley left England, and that it is only kept going by subsidies from the leader himself, who is still a wealthy man. It is thought in London that Mosley today is a spent force politically and that he has little security interest.' His money kept the headquarters going in Vauxhall Bridge Road, the paper *Union*, which proved difficult to sell on street corners, and the wages of its editor, Raven Thomson, and those of Hamm. On 27 September Mosley met his colleagues in Dublin.

The primary purpose of the meeting was to discuss the launch of a monthly journal, *The European*. Hamm was to be in charge of the business side, with Diana its editor. Row recalled that Mosley said 'he was deliberately recruiting two writers who opposed our pre-war stance but now firmly agreed over Europe. He would write a column every month, advancing his idea of "Europe a Nation". The journal would also carry major economic articles and features on the ideological clash with Soviet communism; the "cold war" was very much on at the time.' In addition, the meeting agreed to test the views and interest of pre- and post-war members in a possible series of meetings. A private meeting restricted to supporters of a United Europe was arranged in Manchester, attended by the leading pre-war East End figure Mick Clarke. But not much came of the initiative. The Dublin conclave had been monitored by Ireland's G2 Military Intelligence, but had little to report to officials, who passed on information to Chadwick in the British embassy.

New Fascist internationals cropped up every few months. The European People's Movement was an attempt to heal the rift between moderates and extremists. In early January 1953 it aimed to 'unite all forces fighting to save Christian civilization from Judaism, Communism and Freemasonry' and to create a united Europe in accordance with the old concept of Hitler and Mussolini. The Congress Hall in Paris was decorated with streamers proclaiming 'the Jews are a plague' and 'Let us carry on the racial policy in Europe'. Sixty delegates from Europe, the US, the Middle East and Argentina 'sang their Nazi songs, shouted their fascist war-cries and agreed to stand together', although the Malmö International and the ELO continued their separate existences. Mosley sent a telegram supporting the new venture, which established headquarters in Strassbourg-Neudorf. The Movement's first chairman was Bardeche, who said that 'as France was so vulnerable, leadership had to be passed on to Germany. Only under German leadership could Europe be protected against Communism. The only solution would be the armed but neutral United States of Europe.'

In March, *The European*, a 'journal of opposition', was launched which Diana edited for six years, as well as writing a diary and reviewing political memoirs. Self-consciously highbrow, it attracted serious writers, with fiction from Desmond Stewart, one-time Professor of English at the College of Arts and Sciences, Baghdad, who dealt with Arab and Palestinian affairs; poets and writers Roy Campbell, Henry Williamson and Hugo Charteris. A group of young writers were interested in Ezra Pound, who contributed, including Noel Stock, Peter Whigham, Denis Goacher and Alan Neame, who had the look of an SS officer but treated everything to do with Mosley as a big joke. They gravitated to *Agenda*, a Poundian poetry-cum-criticism magazine. A. James Gregor, who made his name in political science, wrote essays on syndicalism and Nazi racial theories. According to Row, Gregor believed Fascism was a viable creed in the contemporary world. From France came the translator Jacques Brousse, Henri Gilbert and Michel Mohrt, novelist and literary critic for *Le Figaro*. *The European* also published the work of old Nazis and Vichyites. From Germany there were political exchanges from Henrich Sanden, editor of *Nation Europa*, about disarmament and Russia, while Dr Otto Strasser wrote on Europe, amid articles with titles such as 'Eugenics for Europe'. In practice the majority of contributors were sympathetic to neo-Fascist ideas.

Mosley wrote essays under his own name and contributed a regular commentary on world affairs under the pen-name 'European'. He produced his best non-political essays for *The European*, in particular, literary essays such as 'Wagner and Shaw: A Synthesis', which argued against Shaw's negative interpretation in *The Perfect Wagnerite* of Wagner's *Ring*. Mosley thought that 'what was required before there could be super-human achievement was the emergence of the being "who weeps because he has killed a swan rather than exults because he can kill a dragon; who holds the all-powerful spear on condition that he does not use it"'. His work was republished in *Nation Europa* and in Buenos Aires by *Dinamico Social*, which noted that 'contrary to the general belief that Asia is the key to the world', Mosley was 'convinced that Europe, together with Africa and Latin America, holds the key to the future'.

Some of Mosley's friends thought he should have given up the UM and concentrated on *The European*, as it was the most dignified of his activities. Some Mosleyites, however, resented Diana's 'entertainers'. 'She surrounds herself with people like that. They all go across to have meetings about *The European* and they always turn into parties. They're not serious.' While Row and Hamm were desperate for the lowly wages, Alan Neame and others had no difficulty in collecting the cheques for their articles. *The European* was not, however, a financial success and was restricted to limited circles. The aim had been to start a forum of debate of Mosley's position but his isolation and reputation meant that it was met with a deafening silence.

Mosley's ties to the Werner Naumann circle put his name on the front pages of newspapers across Europe, though it was not the kind of publicity he sought. Naumann had tried to create 'a leadership cadre dedicated to a moderate, modified national socialism' which he could insert 'inconspicuously into existing licensed parties'. This was frustrated by High Commissioner Sir Ivone Kirkpatrick, who ordered the arrest on 14 January 1953 of Naumann, the former SS General Paul Zimmermann, and F. K. Bornemann, the Bruderschaft's liaison man. British Intelligence took a serious view of Naumann's clandestine activities and believed he was making progress and the threat needed to be curtailed. He exerted influence on the Deutsche Reichspartei (DRP) led by Adolf von Thadden which, despite never having more than 16,000 members, was deemed a success.

Von Thadden's political career took off at a time of crisis for German neo-Nazis. Hitler's personal bodyguard, Major-General Otto Remer, who formed the Socialist Reich Party in the British zone, had been arrested and imprisoned. He was entered on a 'watch list' of fanatical Nazis as 'a very dangerous man and potential Werewolf leader'. Facing another term of imprisonment, Remer fled to the Middle East to serve a series of Arab dictators and terror groups. Von Thadden stepped in and formed the DRP, which was careful not to attack Dr Adenauer's West German government. He managed to win a parliamentary seat, which showed that there was support for National Socialism.

In response to the arrest of Naumann, who was 'assailed with a shower of ridiculous charges', Mosley employed his own solicitor to act on his behalf for his friend. Kirkpatrick 'then quickly learnt that British law still existed even within the arbitrary dictatorship of the occupation authority'. On 31 March, Chancellor Adenauer claimed documents provided by Kirkpatrick showed that 'not inconsiderable' financial aid was given to Naumann by British, Belgian and French sources. He named Belgian Fascist Léon Degrelle and Mosley, who immediately dismissed the accusation as 'quite untrue'. In the Commons the Labour MP James Hoy asked the Chancellor of the Exchequer 'if he is aware that British citizens have transferred sterling for the financial assistance of Naumann'. He wanted to know if there was 'any information as to where this money is coming from'. The Treasury Secretary, Reginald Maudling, replied that he understood Mosley was 'a resident of Eire, and therefore not subject to our exchange control'.

On 22 April the Irish government's Department of External Affairs informed the Finance Department that 'the Naumann group are being defended by London solicitor and counsel. Obviously Sir O could help to defray these legal expenses by cheque to London without help or hindrance from the Exchange Control.' On the following day the Finance Minister, Sean MacEntee, replied that 'no exchange control approval for the transfer of funds to the Federal Republic of Germany for the purpose stated in the Deputy's question had been sought by, or granted to, Mosley'. He told the Dáil that in May 1952 Mosley's Dublin accountants had informed the Department that he held

a contract under which he gives a portion of his time to a Swiss publishing firm for a remuneration (including expenses) of 7,200 Swiss francs per annum. This sum, however, is barely sufficient to cover his expenses during his visits to Europe on the Swiss firm's business and that of his own firm. In view of the latest developments it cannot be overlooked that the Swiss funds at his disposal during the past two years might have been used by him to aid political friends in Germany, but if such occurred the transfers were made without our knowledge or consent.

The Swiss firm turned out to be that of François Genoud, Agent Litteraire, Lausanne, a shadowy Swiss neo-Nazi banker who was a financier of Fascism and used his contacts to help the networks known as ODESSA, and to manage the hidden Swiss treasure of the Third Reich, most of which had been stolen from Jews in the concentration camps. Genoud was a member of the Swiss Nazi Party and worked for German military intelligence during the war. Somehow he secured the posthumous rights to the writings of Hitler, Goebbels and Bormann. 'He knew everybody,' said his close friend Otto Remer. Genoud dedicated his life to Arab nationalism because he saw it as a natural extension of his anti-Semitism. He was involved with Remer in the shipment of arms to the Algerian National Liberation Front at the height of the Algerian War and managed FLN funds through his Geneva-based Arab Commercial Bank, which had as its consultant Dr Hjalmar Schacht. Genoud supported the ultra left-wing anti-Israeli terrorists from Western Europe linked to the Carlos network during the 1970s. He committed suicide in 1996. An insider also admits that Mosley invested funds with Genoud.

Mosley's legal team went to Germany and instituted libel proceedings against the German Chancellor. On 7 May, referring to a statement by Dr Dehler, Minister of Justice, that he 'had sent a great deal of his writings to Germany so that they could be sold and the proceeds credited to the Naumann movement', Mosley stated that the allegation 'was as untrue as was the former statement by Dr Adenauer that he had sent money to Naumann'. Adenauer backtracked and 'came across with a handsome apology, published to the world'. In the end, all charges against Naumann were quashed in the Supreme Court, which seemed to Mosley to be 'a fair reading of the facts that British officials were directly responsible for this whole trouble. They had no love for me because for years I had attacked their policies in my own country in terms which were vehement.'

Did Mosley finance Naumann? Probably not, since he needed his limited funds for his own activities. However, he did provide valuable newsprint and contributed to the legal funds. UM members admit he was in contact with Naumann, who visited him in Paris, despite his denials.

John Bean recalled that at the beginning, 'adulation of Adolf Hitler was only heard in the private conversations of some members'. But then 'both Mosley and Raven Thomson began to come out in the open again in support of certain aspects of the Nazi past'. By March 1953 'this Nazi apologia had reached such a peak over the Naumann business' that he decided to quit.

Mosley provided funds for *Nation Europa*. During the summer of 1953 a corporation was formed and readers of the monthly were invited to buy shares. Ehrhardt had no great difficulty in raising DM 39,000. In September it produced a special issue on Britain and Europe, with contributions from Mosley, Raven Thomson and Major-General Fuller, who demanded that 'the German army must once again become the most powerful in Europe'. This was at a time when Mosley was working with Genoud, who acted as a 'middleman' between Nazi generals, former Paratroop Commander Bernhard Ramcke and the Panzer Army Commander Heinz Guderian, and Western government advisers over opposition to the European Defence Community, a Cold War alliance. Mosley proclaimed that 'a European creed existed before the war which could and did defeat Communism' and that 'the victors in the war have failed in the seven subsequent years to produce any creed to answer Communism'. These contributions were a token of what *Union* called 'the close cooperation which now exists between all those who stand for the Union of Europe and the restoration of our continent to a leading position in world affairs'.

With Mosley in exile, reinvigorating the UM was left in the hands of a small headquarters coterie that included Robert Row. Hamm was dispatched to organize non-existent forces in Manchester. Before he quit, Bean attended the UM's Annual Conference in the East End – 'one of the biggest farces it has been my lot to witness'. Members were 'persuaded, bribed, or blackmailed to come along to make a presentable show of numbers', which was not easy, as there were so few members. Now fat, bald and increasingly a sick man, Raven Thomson as General Secretary spoke from the platform for two hours. Then four drummers marched round the room loudly beating their drums, after which Raven Thomson announced that the 'Leader' had recorded a speech for them on a tape recorder. He said he had not deserted them and hinted that he was in close contact with like thinkers on the European mainland. The recorded speech finished to loud cheers and 'Mosley' chants from the 'delegates'.

The UM was an irrelevance and, as Thurlow suggests, 'the further 1945 receded into history, the less significant the Mosleyite tradition became' as a new generation of anti-Mosley Fascists coalesced around 'a motley entourage of ex-Mosleyites (Yockeyistes), neo-Nazis, neo-fascists, racial populists, and radical and reactionary right Conservatives, grouping and regrouping across the far right'. This was ironic, because Mosley's post-war ideas were more interesting than his inter-war Fascism. The first significant anti-Mosleyite grouping, the League of Empire Loyalists, was founded in 1953 by A. K. Chesterton, a former Blackshirt and author of a Mosley hagiography. The League's manifesto was remarkably similar to Mosley's pre-war 'Greater Britain' with its idealization of the Empire, though its conspiratorial tone was not Mosleyite.

In Paris, Mosley dined with Bob Boothby and James Lees-Milne, who found Diana 'as beautiful as she was at 17 and more so than when first married in her early twenties'. Mosley was 'fatter, rather greyer. He is well-mannered and attentive . . . when he gets talking he is on the verge of delivering . . . a benevolent dictator's harangue. He talks of England as though it were a foreign country and the English as "they".' On 10 September Lees-Milne decided his cousin was 'no longer extreme; whether to hoodwink or through bitter resolve who can tell. He said only amateur politicians in England harboured bitterness against each other; the professional ones . . . did not.' Despite opposing him on all matters of principle, Boothby and Beaverbrook had 'remained the closest friends' and Mosley was still in correspondence with the latter. Not everyone was as accommodating of the Mosleys. Bridget Parsons refused to meet them. 'She was sure that Diana would as willingly shovel us all into a gas oven as smile on us.' Marcel Proust's god-daughter Priscilla Bibesco was among the Mosleys' friends. When over lunch Diana, indulging her love of the Nazis, said 'Goebbels had the most beautiful blue eyes', Priscilla responded, 'Such a pity, then, he had to murder all those children.'

On a cold night in Ireland in December 1953 disaster struck. Diana was in London, having put off her journey back to Clonfert to see her father. In the middle of the night Alexander was woken by the whinnying of a horse and discovered that the room next to his was on fire; its origin was ultimately traced to the kitchen chimney, which contained inflammable resin from the centuries-old burning of wood. Alexander woke his father and the chauffeur, and a French maid, Mademoiselle Cerrecoundo. The maid, who returned to her room to save clothes and was trapped by the flames, was injured when she jumped from a second-floor window on to a blanket held by Mosley and the others.

Unfortunately, the fire brigade was fourteen miles away at Ballinasloe. Because there was no telephone, it took a long time to get word to it and the fire was out of control when it arrived. They managed to check the fire before it reached the end wing, where some of the Mosley family pictures were hung, but the house remained an uninhabitable shell. Diana was upset that all Mosley's letters to her from Brixton and three family portraits by Pavel Tchelichew were lost to the flames, as were Mosley's papers and many BUF and UM internal documents.

Within days they heard of a house for sale. In the Regency style, Ileclash, famous for its salmon fishing, was situated on the cliff above the Blackwater near Fermoy, twenty miles north of Cork and about fifteen miles from Lismore. They bought it at once and took on a butler and a cook, Jerry Lehane and his wife Emily, who stayed devoted to them to the end. Max was at school in Germany, but on his return liked Ileclash, with its opportunities to hunt with various packs, including that of their neighbour Paddy Flynn.

Bill Allen lived not far away at Whitechurch House, Cappagh, Waterford. His wife Natasha had turned the derelict mansion into a home that attracted numerous guests. James Villiers-Stuart, whose wife Emily worked for British Intelligence during the war, recalled that Kim Philby and Guy Burgess had turned up on different occasions. Bill's fourth wife said he 'knew Mosley was living close by, but no longer trusted him', though Diana recalled they dined with him at a Paris restaurant. A curious visitor to Paris was the MI5 officer Maxwell Knight – the subject of their conversation remains a mystery.

Mosley travelled to Ireland infrequently. He preferred France where, 'as a matter of courtesy', he ignored politics, 'since we were guests living in the country'. The British Foreign Office forbade diplomats to consort with the Mosleys. The Paris ambassador, Sir Gladwyn Jebb, ruled that if diplomats found themselves at a table with Mosley they had to make an excuse and leave. At one dinner the Duchess of Windsor asked Christopher Phillpotts, officially a counsellor but, in fact, an MI6 officer, 'What would you have done if you had found Sir Oswald here?' He said, 'You are clearly familiar with the instructions in the Embassy circular. You know very well what I'd have done.' The Duchess laughed. Such snubs wounded Diana, who claimed, 'As a rule, it mattered not at all'.

At luncheons at the Temple, Diana 'would fall silent if Mosley spoke, her eyes fixed upon him, listening to a story she had heard again and again, adding the same coos of delight, expressions of surprise or peals of laughter'. She supported his political stance wholeheartedly. Her mild anti-Semitic prejudice, notes Anne de Courcy, 'had become a full-blown conviction that "international Jewry" was an enemy of both her country and her husband'. Hugh Purcell recalled sitting next to her when 'she asked me how many Jews I thought had perished. I answered that the accepted figure was between five and six million. "Oh really?" she replied. "Very interesting."'

This was consistent with a story John Julius Norwich heard from Nancy.

She said she loved Diana but 'I know that I mustn't get on to the subject of the last war . . . she will say something I can't bear . . . how will we keep off the subject?' When they met, Nancy had managed to do so for a couple of days. On the final day, however: 'We had the most terrible row . . . Diana was determined to get on to it somehow. She made a sort of defence of Hitler.' Nancy replied, 'Given all that but alright, seven million Jews were exterminated in the death camps.' Diana apparently looked at her and said, 'But darling, it was so much the kindest way.' Nancy walked out of the room. 'I just couldn't bear it another minute.' Diana later said her talented sister 'was the most disloyal person I ever knew'.

Except for his travelling, Diana was seldom apart from Mosley. She was, however, miserable and suffered from stress-related migraines, brought on by suspicion that he had returned to his former habits and was being unfaithful to her, despite 'their sense of joint destiny, the unique bonding of their prison experience . . . and cherishing in which she had wrapped him since', it had not been enough. He used their Paris flat and many of his conquests were drawn from their immediate circle, including Rita Luke and Lotsie Fabre-Luce, wives of writers. Equally painful for Diana was an attempted reconciliation Mosley arranged with Baba Metcalfe, who hated him for not acknowledging her efforts to help during the war and refused to speak to Diana. The meeting was 'a complete disaster'.

Mosley was a notable absentee, in January 1954, from another attempt to heal the differences between the two wings of the extreme Right with the creation of the European New Order. The MSI had become a pro-NATO party and a bridge 'between the old and the new ruling class, between the clericals of today and the Fascists of yesterday'. It believed in European unity as 'a bulwark of Western ideas against Bolshevism'. Conferences took place in Brussels and The Hague, with secret meetings in Madrid attended by Arab and Latin American representatives. Mosley sent his greetings, but deemed it prudent to avoid being associated with networks under intense surveillance. However, the resurrection of nationalism became an obstacle to an international. There were quarrels with the MSI over the bitter territorial dispute concerning South Tyrol. Karl Meissner, head of the German block, refused to attend meetings of the European Social Movement with the MSI so long as it 'encouraged the flagrant violations of the South Tyrol Convention by the Italian Government' against the German population.

A US CIC officer discovered that, on 18 September 1954, the recently released Naumann had conferred in Stuttgart with the Deutsche Reichspartei and told them Adolf von Thadden had held talks in London with Mosley and the journalist Sefton Delmer. Why was Delmer, a wartime intelligence officer running black propaganda operations against the Nazis and recently author of a series of 'exposés' on the emergence of a neo-Fascist 'fourth Reich' involved? Von Thadden had an English grandmother and 'liked coming to Britain, and liked Britain very much'. He had volunteered his services to MI6 as 'a German patriot who longed to give his country a democratic future'. Dr Hans Horchem, head of Hamburg's Verfassungsschutz (West German security service, 1969–81), held regular discussions on security with British Intelligence liaison officers, who admitted 'von Thadden was in contact with us' in the 1950s. It is likely that Delmer, just recruited as an agent by MI6's Maurice Oldfield, was acting as his 'cut-out' in a standard 'arm's-length' operation.

The Mosleys had begun travelling to the reopened Bayreuth Festival, where they renewed their acquaintance with Frau Wagner. They were friends with surviving Nazi leaders, some of whom wanted their children to visit London to meet people of their own age and study English. Travel arrangements were made by Sid Proud, an extreme anti-Semite, who gathered around him a group of UM members known as 'the fringe', neo-Nazis dismissed by Mosley as 'crackpots'. Mosleyites acted as couriers for Proud, both on legitimate business for his Spanish Travel Agency and in illegal currency transactions, often to cover legitimate holiday bills but also to do with Mosley's ties to the international neo-Nazi networks (he organized the travel arrangements of Otto Skorzeny). He turned against the Leader when Mosley's son, Alexander, who worked for his agency, broke off his relationship with his daughter Cynthia. He accused Mosley of being Jewish. UM insiders were aware Proud was 'a crook and his people bribe crooked fascists in Barcelona and Madrid but he never takes a single risk but lets other people do the dirty work'. He was also a Special Branch informant.

The man Mosley entrusted to deal with the visitors was Alf Flockhart who, appropriately, had a Hitler moustache. Mosley paid their expenses while they were in London and gave Edna and Sidney Grundy, two virulent anti-Semitic Mosleyites, money to look after them. Trevor Grundy has described his mother's adulation of Mosley: 'She used to touch him and she'd say afterwards: "That will give me strength till next year."' She later committed suicide, ending a dreadful depression. Trevor only then discovered that she was Jewish and her family could be traced back to the Sephardic Jews of Spain.

Among the visitors were Skorzeny's daughter Waltraut, who was studying languages, including Russian – she said that one day Germany would conquer the Soviet Union and interpreters would be required – Klaus Naumann, son of Werner, and Gudrun Burwitz, née Himmler. 'I got to know many fascists there,' recalled Gudrun. Sidney Proud invited her and Adolf von Ribbentrop, son of the hanged Foreign Minister, to his house and proudly showed off his portraits of Hitler. There was also a photographer present and the pictures appeared in newspapers all over the world. It was an acute embarrassment to

Gudrun and Adolf because they roused people's ire everywhere against the Nazi children. On her return to Germany Gudrun lost her job, changed her appearance and became secretary of Silent Help, which aided high-profile war criminals in procuring false passports and passage abroad. 'I see it as my mission in life to make the world see my father in a different light,' she admitted. 'My father is seen as the greatest mass murderer of all times. I want to revise this picture.' She was the guest of honour at several SS veteran reunions, where officers stood to attention in front of the daughter of their leader.

In late 1955 Mosley wrote to Nicholas that he had 'a feeling that before long the rush may begin again, though I am as usual premature. But when it does, all charm of life flies, as well as all sense, for a long season!' He missed the political stage. An insider said he was 'itching to get back. After the war, he was covered in dung and had to get out but life in France had become too comfortable. He wanted to take risks.' He told UM secretary Jeffrey Hamm, who succeeded Raven Thomson who had died of cancer, that he would return in the new year for a series of meetings on Europe. Mosley addressed his first meeting in five years on 20 March 1956, in front of 600 supporters at Kensington Town Hall. There were 1,500 at the Manchester Free Trade Hall in November, followed by university debates at Cambridge and Oxford. A *Telegraph* reporter wrote that 'none of the fizz has gone out of him'.

Curiously, the UM's headquarters in Kensington was in the home of Mary Tavener, the 'actress' Mosley had been involved with in the early thirties who had threatened him with the law over her claims that he asked her to marry him. Clearly, they had resolved their differences since she became the unofficial secretary of a non-political charity Mosley had set up. John Warburton remembered 'an attractive woman, who was socially well-connected locally'.

Mosley's most ardent pursuit was reserved for eighteen-year-old Jeannie Campbell, daughter of the Duke of Argyll and Janet Aitken. Tall, dark, with sparkling eyes, after living with her grandfather Lord Beaverbrook she had several affairs with older men. She was 'fascinated by Mosley's views, the power of his personality and the frisson of intrigue involved in such an affair'. He hoped she would further his cause with her grandfather in the expectation of publicity. In London they used chauffeur-driven Daimlers and met in a flat rented from Nicholas, who remembered his father being 'involved with a girlfriend much younger than himself; they visited us at Lyminster; his cavortings and mine would overlap in London'. Nicholas realized that Diana knew. Mosley had a theory, much admired by Randolph Churchill, that a man should 'span' at least fifty years, 'beginning with a woman 20 years older when he was 18, and then 30 years younger when he was 60'.

When Beaverbrook learnt of Jeannie's affair, he sent her off to the US to work for the *Evening Standard*. Mosley defended his action by claiming he could still remain true to loved ones. 'I so much prefer the Catholic sense that a healthy lapse can bring you nearer to a state of grace.' Naturally, it devastated Diana who, in reality, was a quite fragile person. There is no jealousy like sexual jealousy and she retaliated with 'freezing disdain . . . and wittily malicious comments on the women concerned, a technique that sometimes cowed even Mosley'.

Mosley made occasional trips back to Ireland, primarily to deal with his publishing company, Euphorian Books, whose greatest success was with Hans-Ulrich Rudel's *Stuka Pilot*, about his extraordinary feats with his dive-bomber. In 1956 he was guest of honour at a UM dinner. Mosley met Germans in secret meetings which escaped the attentions of the Irish authorities. One was with Otto Skorzeny, who enjoyed General Franco's protection and the support of the ex-dictator Perón, and on behalf of ODESSA sold at a profit weapons hidden by the SS in France, Austria and Italy. Ireland was ideal for his operations. Posing as a man about to retire with considerable funds at his disposal and interested in investing money in hotels and land, he took advantage of the tax-free provisions for foreigners and bought seventy large estates for associates, including Alexander von Dornberg and Albert Schmidt, his contact man in Dublin, who managed a coffee bar as a front. Dornberg, a former Ribbentrop staff member, was his courier between Ireland and Germany. Well-organized, Skorzeny's 'German colony' was allegedly a cover for the transfer of the 'external organisation's' headquarters from Madrid to Ireland. In the Dáil Dr Noel Brown questioned the propriety of permitting a known Nazi and still dangerous man to live in the country.

Mosley's push fizzled out as he was absent for most of spring 1957, ill with penicillin poisoning. When the European Economic Community was created that year, in a familiar call Mosley reproached the British government for its 'refusal to enter fully and completely into European life'. He advocated building a Channel tunnel and attacked anti-federalist attitudes: 'The only thing which is certain is that the Conservative Party will never stand for Europe a Nation. They will never merge British Government in European Government.' A year later he published *Europe: Faith and Plan – A Way Out from the Coming Crises*, which asked: 'Can these relatively small, isolated, individual nations of Western Europe face for fifteen years on world markets the competition of America's normal production surplus, plus the deliberate market-breaking dumping of the Soviets at below European production costs?' No, because they 'are dependent on external supplies of raw materials for their industries . . . they are forced to pay for these necessities by exports sold in open competition in world markets, under conditions where they have no influence whatever'. A closed internal free market system was necessary, though he recognized that to put the common market before common government negated 'all the real possibilities opened up by European union'.

Mosley suggested a wage-price policy as the cure to Britain's Stop-Go problems and as the instrument for equating supply and demand in his European socialist economy, in which 'it would be illegal for any man or any organisation to pay lower wages than a rival in the same sphere of industry; anyone may undercut a rival by greater efficiency, but not by paying lower wages'. Mosley argued the 'wage-price mechanism', which would fix the levels of wages and of prices to one another, would stabilize the value of goods in terms of labour. He distinguished between its 'positive' uses to secure even growth in a self-contained system and the 'negative' form of a wage-price freeze to hold down costs in order to compete on world markets.

A wage-price mechanism, planned investment and development policy would produce an environment 'in which the conditions for true freedom could be attained'. Free enterprise would operate with minimal interference from the State, and the elimination of restrictive practices and bureaucracy would result in vast tax reductions. It was, however, all highly centralized and he admitted it would be 'possible to decide which industries continued and which ceased to exist . . . The flow of labour could be controlled as directly as the flow of water by differential levels . . . It is the most potent instrument for shaping the future development of industry which could be devised.' It was almost a war economy.

Mosley's vision also advocated 'industrial self-government', because 'workers understand the problems in their own industry'. This reflected interest in syndicalism and guild socialism, and dislike of 'mandarin socialism'. Trade unions would play a role with employers' federations in administering a restructured welfare state, and in the general economy; a policy which harked back to his days in the Independent Labour Party and his support of John Wheatley, as well as reflecting wartime developments. However, resistance towards government control of wages, for instance, would result in a violent showdown with the full force of the State against them.

The picture which emerged, suggested Skidelsky, is of 'a rather sluggish, high-consumption society, with a small, fast-growing sector of advanced technology created and run by an elite of creative entrepreneurs'. It added little to the UM's appeal and Europeanism and prices and incomes policies 'alienated rather than attracted working-class opinion'. Hamm wrote to Mosley that John Charnley was 'perturbed at the lack of response he has experienced among businessmen regarding our industrial policy'. Although he regarded Mosley as 'a man of vision', because 'his ultimate goal is so obvious to him, he is inclined to be impatient with those who cannot see it with his eyes. He must therefore be made to realise that it takes time to bring others up to the acceptance of his ultimate goal.'

The Times noted the difference between official UM policy and the reasons members had for joining. 'Those immediately below the Leader look to him for political guidance and seem to have a genuine desire to see his policies instituted.' However, some followers joined 'because they are anti-semitic but the largest number, it seems, because they like fighting Communists'. UM leaders admitted these elements were 'out of the control of the party'. An insider recalled that Mosley was 'always having to get rid of crackpots. They were a permanent nuisance.'

Nicholas was present when Mosley reprimanded an official for disobeying orders that they should not become involved in breaking up opponents' meetings. 'My father shouted at him for a time; the man was saying, "Yes sir, sorry sir"; then my father said quietly, "Well don't do it again." And as he showed the man out into the passage some sort of wink seemed to pass between the man and my father – a recognition of comradeship or complicity beyond the demands of discipline.' The same thing happened when he reprimanded Peter Shaw, who had suggested getting 'hold of an immigrant and hang him upside-down from Blackfriar's Bridge with a notice around his neck saying "Coloureds go home"' as a means of generating publicity. When Nicholas talked to his father about such incidents he would half smile and say, 'one must keep the boys happy'.

It was the issue of immigration which offered the UM another opportunity to counter the decline in its fortunes. Mosley moved its operations and resources out of its traditional stamping ground in East London to the run-down areas around Notting Hill, where there were rumblings of discontent over the number of black workers from the West Indies. At the same time, as his attempts to build support in Argentina came to nought, Mosley bought up South African shares, which delivered dividends of £5,600 (£67,000) a year. A 'great schemer', an insider said Mosley now saw South Africa as 'the final redoubt for when the great collapse came'.

27

'The Coloured Invasion'

There had been a steady drip of newspaper stories, not much different from UM propaganda, focused on scapegoats and domestic threats – black marketeers and spivs – which, as Trevor and Mike Phillips point out, 'translated easily into a widespread hostility towards the immigrants'. It seemed likely something was going to happen somewhere. An affray in Nottingham – in fact, not that serious – sparked off the Notting Hill riots of 1958. The riots, the Phillipses suggest, 'might have been predictable, but they were not inevitable. Race was the trigger which set them off and kept the passions burning, but the causes were due to a number of complex elements.'

Mosley's UM did not spark off the riots, nor was it responsible for them – it had only a small branch in Kensington – but in the atmosphere of hostility which began to surround migrants it provided 'a vocabulary and a programme of action which shaped the resentments of inarticulate and disgruntled people'. The UM had been distributing leaflets on 'The Coloured Invasion' and Jeffrey Hamm addressed large street crowds, weaving together 'gossip, rumour and complaint about migrants'.

Parts of Notting Hill were 'a slum, full of multi-occupied houses, crawling with rats and rubbish'. People were generally poor as 'Poles, Irish and blacks competed for jobs and living space with the natives'. There was gang fighting, illegal drinking clubs, gambling and prostitution and 'violence between the various factions, the police and any unfortunate bystanders was endemic'. On Saturday 23 August, Teddy boys in west London began converging on the area as news of fighting spread.

On the Sunday morning police stopped groups of young white men in cars as Teds set out looking for black victims, embarrassed, suggest the Phillipses, 'by the fact that a bunch of provincial Teds in a distant town somewhere up North were hogging the sort of headlines no Ted had seen since they had trashed the cinemas during the first showings of *Rock Around the Clock*'. After assaults on black people in Ladbroke Grove, police arrested youths armed with 'iron bars, table legs, starting handles and at least one knife'. Edward Scobie in *Tribune* realized 'that these white hoodlums ... had appointed themselves a law unto themselves. Armed with daggers they issued fascist directions to coloured people. They shouted, "Don't walk in groups or you will be attacked."' Metropolitan Police files confirm that the disturbances were triggered by a 300- to 400-strong 'keep Britain White' mob intent on 'nigger-hunting'.

In one street a *Times* journalist found men 'singing "Old Man River" and "Bye Bye Blackbird" and punctuating the songs with vicious anti-Negro slogans'. They made 'all sorts of wild charges against their coloured neighbours', bitter at the Labour Party for 'letting them in'. Watching a mob of 700 men, women and children, a local reporter noted that 'in the middle of the screaming, jeering youths and adults, a speaker from the Union Movement was urging his excited audience to "get rid of them" . . . Suddenly, hundreds of leaflets were thrown over the crowd, a fierce cry rent the air and the mob rushed off in the direction of Latimer Road, shouting, "Kill the niggers!"' The mob then broke scores of windows and set upon two black men who were lucky to escape with cuts and bruises. Small groups roamed around the district, breaking into homes and attacking any West Indian they could find. PC Richard Bedford came across a mob shouting 'We will kill all black bastards. Why don't you send them home?' The first night left five black men lying unconscious on Notting Hill's pavements.

Teddy boys, including Mosley's sons Alexander (aged nineteen) and Max (eighteen), had for some time been prominent at UM events. Both Mosley boys were photographed in Notting Hill looking 'like local toughs'. Mosley described the Teds as 'fine virile types, which is what youth should be'. Mosley was abroad at the time but Max was in charge of the UM Youth Unit recruiting teenagers for its rock and roll club. Max thought the UM should appeal more to the Teds and show that it didn't go on about Hitler and Mussolini and British Fascism all the time. Alexander said Max found 'it hard to believe that a teenager living in the middle of London, surrounded by millions of girls his own age, could spend Saturdays selling *Union* newspapers'.

Alexander was arrested while distributing a leaflet near Ladbroke Grove underground station. The leaflet infuriated the TUC Congress in Bournemouth into condemning Mosley for 'fanning the flames of racial violence'. Aimed at the North Kensington MP George Rogers, and the Labour Party, who 'wanted coloured invaders settling permanently in this country', it urged people to 'Join Mosley in this fight'. *The Times* concluded the UM was 'exploiting rather than creating the disturbances. It will not condemn the violence, but is rather pointing to a target behind the one that is now being attacked.' Members were rushed to this 'hot place' to sell *Action*, which claimed its propaganda was 'directed towards diverting racial hatred to anti-government feeling rather than inciting violence'.

The disturbances continued night after night until they finally petered out on 5 September. Altogether, 108 people were charged with offences ranging from grievous bodily harm to affray and riot and possessing offensive weapons of whom seventy-two were white and thirty-six 'coloured'. The Metropolitan Police tried to play down the racial aspects to the riots in reports to the Home Secretary, Rab Butler. Detective Sergeant Walters of the Notting Hill police said the press had been wrong to portray the street disturbances as 'racial': 'Whereas there certainly was some ill feeling between white and coloured residents in this area, it is abundantly clear much of the trouble was caused by ruffians, both coloured and white, who seized on this opportunity to indulge in hooliganism.'

Statements from rank-and-file police officers make plain that 'racial prejudices were leading to serious disturbances' but these were ignored by superiors. However, as the Phillipses suggest, 'they were not exclusively about skin colour or about the number of migrants in Britain'. The reality was that they were 'as much about the feelings of exclusion and deprivation experienced by a wide swath of the English population as they were about the presence of black migrants. But for the next decade political debate about the social problems of urban life in Britain was to be distracted and dominated by race.'

Part of the reason for the scale and intensity of the riots had been inept policing. But the use of police reinforcements, the increasing number of arrests and the draconian sentences handed out to the rioters had their effect. At the Old Bailey on 16 September, Judge Salmon handed down exemplary sentences of four years each on nine mostly lower-working-class white Teds, aged sixteen to twenty-one. Salmon declared, 'You are a minute and insignificant section of the population but you have brought shame upon this district where you live and have filled the Nation with horror, indignation and disgust.' The sentences curtailed all other attempts to use racial violence.

The riots marked Nicholas Mosley's final disillusionment with his father. When he complained about the violence, Mosley admitted he was 'probably guilty in not doing enough to stop it'. He tried to rationalize it all as 'the faults of adolescence, coupled with a driving sense of urgency in desperate situations. A desperate child is capable of any horror. Movements can begin as children and then can become adult . . . We are faced here with the problem of producing a leadership and a movement which is adult; the old Platonic problem of making men fit for power.' He was, however, excited by the opportunity the riots presented and, in their aftermath, began a sustained campaign to build on the support for the UM, whose membership may temporarily have reached 1,500. However, fear of more racial disorders caused him to be banned from most indoor venues, except in Birmingham and Manchester's Free Trade Hall, where there was heckling but little disruption. He was studiously ignored by the press.

*

According to the *Johannesburg Sunday Times*, Mosley visited South Africa in January 1959 to meet 'important contacts' and promote the Europe-Africa Association, whose secretary was a British immigrant, Derek Alexander. Addressing a meeting of Dr Verwoerd's Nationalist Party, Alexander said he had given up his work as a teacher to concentrate on a nationwide campaign on behalf of his Fascist movement, an offshoot of the European National Movement. He published a version of the UM's *Action*, on sale at State-owned bookstalls, and was responsible for launching the Friends of South Africa, an 'information service to tell the truth to the people of Britain about the Nationalists in South Africa'. Alexander talked to Cabinet Ministers, stressing the similarity between apartheid and Mosley's plan for 'separate living space' for white and black in Africa. Mosley told the *Rand Daily Mail* that he was 'a believer in total apartheid. I think the plan of Dr Verwoerd to establish Bantu States in South Africa is courageous.' The PM's support for Mosley was evident in the meetings arranged with Cabinet Ministers and being introduced on the government-controlled radio as a 'leading statesman'.

On his return to Europe, Mosley decided to contest the October 1959 parliamentary election and stand in North Kensington. He closed *The European* and diverted resources into building up his following in the constituency. 'Someone should give this electorate the opportunity to express legally and peacefully by their votes what they felt about the issues involved' but realized 'my entry would be misrepresented as an attempt to exploit the situation'. Even before he officially announced his candidacy, the ground was prepared with provocative meetings and speeches. Jeffrey Hamm protested over the prison sentences imposed upon the gang of Teddy boys convicted of violence during the riots. Holding aloft a picture of the convicted criminals, he declared them to be 'some of the finest faces you could wish to see in Britain'. In April Mosley announced he was standing at a well-attended public meeting; within a week, in the same area, a white gang beat up three blacks and stabbed another. The first fatality occurred when Kelso Cochrane, a young black carpenter engaged to be married, was stabbed to death by a white gang on Whit Sunday. Locals believed the police knew who did it but let them go. It was an incident which helped turn people against Mosley.

Action editor Robert Row had written a thin book, *The Colour Question* (1959), which attacked the Labour Party for signing the 'Black Pact' with Cuba in 1951. By this treaty sugar was no longer purchased in the West Indies, their main source of wealth, resulting in the emigration of their inhabitants to Britain 'to fill the slums in the "Black belts" of the big cities'. There were 250,000 immigrants in 1959 and the danger was that 'a large number of firms today employ coloured labour at lower wages than a white man could accept'.

The government was, therefore, 'entirely responsible for this misery and unemployment'. Mosley thought the whole policy wrong. Diana suggested

> it would have been possible to reverse the decision taken by the government to import unskilled labour. If great empty countries like Canada and Australia restricted immigration, how much more so should crowded Britain? Since we had been reduced by the war to a relatively weak position in the world we depended for survival upon skill, brains and inventiveness; among the fifty-five million inhabitants there were plenty of unskilled workers without importing more.

Mosley used the rhetoric of capitalistic exploitation evident in the Mosley–Pirow proposals. He advocated 'compulsory free passage back to the West Indies for the immigrants, combined with heavy British investment to build up local West Indian employment and the purchase of all British sugar from Jamaica' on long-term contracts. He proclaimed 'Jamaica for the Jamaicans and Britain for the British. I say let the Jamaicans have their country back – and let us have ours.' Later he suggested resettling immigrants in Guyana.

Mosley's policy, Henry Vane noted, was 'a curious mixture of straightforward left-wing anti-colonialism and anti-coloured agitation'. He said he was dealing with an economic and social problem but supporters cited racial issues. Diana said he 'did not give a fig as to whether he was called a racialist because he opposed immigration and advocated paying for the blacks to be repatriated while investing in their islands so that they could find work'. He used to say 'they only come because we have neglected our colonies and they are starving'. He foresaw mass unemployment and 'the whole business added an unnecessary problem to the many we already faced, and it speedily became an irreversible problem'. Commentators noted there was 'a cynical dose of political expediency too'. Mosley promoted policies on race in those areas where he hoped they would attract controversy and publicity. Vane said the number one appeal was to 'fears of mongrelization of the British race'.

In an interview in *John Bull* magazine, Mosley described himself as 'what Goethe called the educated soldier – that is, a man capable equally of reflection and action. In my case I tend to submerge myself completely in either quality.' He admitted that 'in action, all my reflective qualities disappear'. He now submerged himself into the unreflective man of action, as the thugs, attracted by the 'reputation of violence' which clung to his name, joined a campaign directed against black immigrants. In his desperate effort to court a mass following, his decision reflected 'a Jekyll and Hyde character rather than the ever-striving Faust'. He admitted action could become a vice, for it might treat a minority unfairly: 'You can't have action by violating human decencies.'

During the election campaign a local anti-Fascist, Eddie Adams, recalled that the Teddy boys supported Mosley, with 'the old pre-war Fascist members, mainly orchestrating what was going on . . . And his son was one of the main actors in it.' He still radiated some of the aura of a major political personality. People 'would really come from everywhere and listen to Mosley', Rudy Braithwaite noticed. 'He was a very convincing speaker. He would speak and things would roll out of his mouth . . . he used to say, "Many of the people who are in high places, who are politicians, would love to say what I am saying now."' Adams heckled Mosley, who he thought was 'a bit old fashioned for that time. He used to speak from the back of a lorry and they would have arc lights on him, and he would sort of say something and pause theatrically, I suppose for applause and things like that.' He thought he was 'a man past his time really, but the trouble was that if you were opposed to him, you'd be chased up the road by some of his supporters'.

Mosley hammered away at the issue of racial discrimination, with inflammatory statements: 'Every white man in a job knows that he has got a coloured man at his elbow, ready to take that job at a cheaper rate'; 'When the white woman is going out to work in the cold dawn the blacks are coming back from their all-night parties'; 'All the places including your beautiful squares will be inhabited by the blacks'. He exploited and encouraged racial hatred. Mosleyites infiltrated the community via pubs where 'they would ingratiate themselves with local people prior to meetings by buying rounds of drinks, which tended to win trust, and then use pub gossip to disseminate the most virulent racism'. They found a receptive audience as in the eyes of many white residents the 'sight of black people living in overcrowded hovels was proof . . . that West Indians were dirty and primitive'.

Mosley responded with 'sordid tales of sexual offences by coloured men, spiced with such nasty remarks as that West Indians provided cheap labour because they could at a pinch live off a tin of Kit-E-Kat a day'. Nicholas had expected he 'at least would be putting over the aspect of his case that was reasonable; but instead there he was roaring on about such things as black men being able to live on tins of cat food, and teenage girls being kept by gangs of blacks in attics'.

The UM had been canvassing in the area since the previous summer and Mosley believed the seat was his for the taking. 'People were running out of their houses to shake him by the hand as he passed,' wrote Diana to a friend. *Action* on 17 October predicted a vote of 35 per cent for Mosley. 'It was therefore one of the chief surprises of my life when we polled only eight per cent of the votes' and he lost his deposit. He polled a mere 2,821 votes out of a total of 34,912. The surprise was so great that he asked the High Court to check the ballot papers but his case was unsuccessful. Shaken, Mosley returned to France.

*

Diana, who never voted – not even for her husband – said in mitigation that 'only a small part of the constituency was affected by the arrival of the West Indians; unfortunately the remainder took the then popular liberal line'. If he had been elected Britain would not be in the unfortunate position of being 'the sick man of Europe. At every stage of our decline he has put forward a constructive policy; had he been in Parliament his voice could not have been ignored.'

The angry young Colin Wilson, who was a darling of the media with his novel *The Outsider*, had been intrigued by Mosley, but now asked how he could 'allow his followers to use these methods? It seems to me not only a bad thing to do, but from the political standpoint, silly and incompetent. In many ways, Mosley shows a disturbing lack of insight into his own time.' A decade later Nicholas wrote that he now saw clearly 'that while the right hand dealt with grandiose ideas and glory, the left hand let the rat out of the sewer'.

Nicholas wrote to his father that the UM

> has got the general reputation, whether fairly or unfairly, of having to depend on racial hatred in order to maintain its appeal and impetus . . . One would have thought these steps would have included instructions to avoid, in speech and writing and action, all controversial racial issues like the plague; failure to take this sort of action seems only to mean that in spite of your words on paper, your intention is not seriously to eradicate from people's minds the impression of your need for racial hatred.

Mosley reluctantly agreed to a 'profoundly pessimistic' Robert Saunders that 'very direct methods may have frightened a good many people'. He had noticed that 'the method of indirect appeal and innuendo rather than direct, clear statements, rather to my surprise, are very effective'.

Nicholas was so annoyed by his father's reply that no UM meeting in Notting Hill had resulted directly in violence, that he felt it necessary to confront him. He saw him in his office. 'I spewed it all out – What he was doing was not only wrong it was squalid; he had done this before, he was doing it again, was he so crazy as not to know what he was doing?' After a time Mosley said quietly, 'I will never speak to you again.' Expecting a thunderbolt, Nicholas said, 'Well, I will always speak to you.' Then he left.

Always loyal, Diana remained silent at the meeting but had taken note of the attack on Mosley's ability as a father. She was unhappy over his unfaithfulness, which was aggravated by their quarrels over money for Alexander and Max. The older children had the Leiter money inherited from their mother and the Guinness boys had a rich family. Mosley resented spending money on his family and refused to allow Alexander to go to university, and dismissed his ambitions with the jibe that it was 'a terrible thing for a boy of twenty years and three months who is politically ambitious never to have addressed a big crowd or even had an article published'. Alexander had either to submit and just be an imitation of the father he so much resembled, or to break free and be as unlike as possible.

'I think he was jealous of Alexander, a beautiful, brilliant young man,' Nicholas recalled. 'He made his life dreadfully miserable.' He had been working for the travel agent Sid Proud, for whom he had been acting as a courier to Spain. He left the agency at his father's insistence to become an apprentice chartered accountant; it was at this time that he became seriously depressed. Encouraged by Nicholas, Alexander escaped his father's influence by moving to South America, where he supported himself by teaching English and French, and working for the British Council.

Even though he found the electoral rebuff inexplicable, in January 1960, Mosley planned yet another comeback in an attempt to win a seat in Parliament. He told supporters, 'I will be back soon. Back in the East End and in all the big cities.' One way the UM gained publicity was through its active backing for South Africa in Britain. On 28 February the UM marched against the 'Boycott Movement's Campaign against South African goods'. In front of 10,000 people in Trafalgar Square, Mosley promised to defeat the boycott and reiterated his belief that apartheid should be established over the whole African continent. 'Jeff' thought the sixty-three-year-old Mosley had lost none of his oratorical skills. 'When you listened to him you felt special, you weren't just a primary school boy from west London, you were a member of the greatest country the world had ever seen that was going on to even greater things.' Others disagreed and supporters of the boycott clashed with Mosleyites in the shadow of South Africa House.

In April 1960 a second 'Lausanne Declaration' Fascist gathering in Switzerland attended by Mosley was followed by outbreaks of anti-Semitism across Europe, which were dealt with by the police. More serious was the discontent in Belgium caused by the loss of the Congo. Jean Thiriart hoped to exploit the situation and at the same time enter into an alliance with French extremists of the Secret Army Organization (OAS) who wanted to delay settlement of the Algerian question. In his Manifesto to the European Nation, Thiriart said, 'Europe must be defended at Algiers as well as in Britain. It is the same campaign. We cannot tolerate control of the Mediterranean by the enemies of Europe. We shall remain in Algeria and help our European compatriots, who are fighting for us.' There followed a revival of neo-Fascism, galvanized by the hope that Algeria would be a repetition of Spain in 1936. Anti-parliamentarian and Poujadist-style nationalists hoped to unite ex-settlers in order to pressure the Belgian government to intervene militarily in the Congo. Thiriart and Paul Teichmann, an OAS supporter, led the Mouvement d'Action Civique (MAC).

A radical, Thiriart, like Mosley, was influenced by syndicalism and hoped to unite all extremist groups around a 'European Communitarian party', which would form the 'hard core' of a 'revolutionary centre'. Although the number of hardcore MAC militants never exceeded 350, half of whom were former colonists or paratroopers, his dynamic leadership lent it a degree of influence out of all proportion to its numerical strength. It was a model Mosley hoped to copy but he never had the seriousness of Thiriart, who used MAC to boost the Jeune Europe International, of which he was undisputed leader. MAC helped South Africa with propaganda and was violently anti-Communist. For Thiriart, the quarrel between the Flemish and the Walloon was to disappear within 'Europe a Nation'.

Mosley placed great importance on international links and arranged many gatherings of European Fascists. On 22 July 1960 one took place in Bonn, where he met with Rudel – described by the *Telegraph*'s Bonn correspondent as 'one of the most inflammatory spokesmen of the neo-Nazi German Reich Party', and Otto Skorzeny, who arrived from his estate at Curragh, Ireland.

A month later Nancy Mitford wrote to Violet Hammersley that she had seen Diana. The Mosleys were going to stay in Venice with Count Alvise Loredon, secretary of the MSI, but 'no decent Venetian will speak to him. Meanwhile Diana says Sir O has never been so busy – it makes my flesh creep. No doubt we shall all be in camps very soon.' In the autumn they moved to London, to a flat in Lowndes Court, where they planned to spend the winters and also to enable Mosley to put in place his plans for a 'Friends of Europe' rally in December. He said, 'Europe must forget and forgive and the wounds must be healed before the construction of Europe can begin.'

Mosley had delivered a number speeches in front of large audiences in Rome to prepare for the rally of his friends. Invitations went out to Rudel, the MSI's Filippo Anfuso, who after a long exile had been elected to Parliament in Italy, and representatives from France, Austria and Sweden. Unfortunately for Mosley, the Home Office refused permission for Rudel to enter the country and the Marylebone Council hurriedly banned the rally from taking place at the Seymour Hall. 'It is a clear case of political discrimination,' Mosley declared.

At the begining of 1961 Alexander returned to England, where he re-established relations with his father. He then left for the United States for Columbia University. Generously, Nicholas and Michael agreed to pay their stepbrother's £1,400-a-year fees and provide an annual covenant of £700. His father refused to support him, believing he was not bright enough, but Diana did send him an allowance. Andrea Kelsey, who knew Alexander, recalled Diana 'saying at some times that she had to go into capital to send him money and this distressed her'.

In the New Year the Mosleys holidayed in Nassau, as 'house-guest of a distinguished, retired British Foreign Service Officer, who had been head of UK information services in New York during the Second World War'. That the Governor of Bermuda attended a dinner party with them was noted by the local American consul, whose cable to Washington was dealt with by FBI Director Hoover. He said Mosley intended to visit the US but questioned the reasons for refusing entry even though he was regarded by the US authorities as a 'controversial figure' who should not be given 'latitude to travel to us at will'. The consul said that 'if Mosley's own government has apparently forgiven or forgotten, why is USG more harsh on this 70-year-old man than they are? By cancelling multiple-entry visa, we irritate Mosley, but he still gets in and I presume . . . could be source of embarrassment due to demonstrations . . . If he's really that much of an embarrassment, then he should be denied a visa and kept out (and we're quite prepared to do that, too), not just annoyed and then let in.'

In an attempt to present a moderate front before UM members stood in elections, on 15 January 1961 *Action* declared that 'we stand on clear cut principles which are equally opposed to the crackpots who want to persecute all Jews and to the cravens who treat all Jews as beyond criticism because they fear the financial power of some Jews'. They were identified as the neo-Nazis/Fascists who were vying with each other to replace Mosley as the head of British Fascism. Colin Jordan was a disciple of Arnold Leese and tried to emulate him in his extreme views on Jews; John Bean, formerly of the UM, had formed the National Labour Party; Andrew Fountain joined with Bean to lead the British National Party; John Tyndall and Martin Webster had created the anti-Semitic National Socialist Movement.

Although the UM came third in council elections at Islington in April, with a respectable 2,505 votes for its three candidates, it was still far behind Labour's 21,000 votes. Its only success was the election of Max Mosley as secretary of the Oxford Union. When Mosley was invited to the Union debate, there was an argument about whether he should be allowed to speak. Max campaigned in favour on the slogan 'Free Speech for Fascists'. As editor of the student magazine *Isis* Paul Foot asked why they should listen to a man who had stirred up racial prejudice against Jewish people. When Mosley threatened a writ for libel, *Isis*'s printers insisted on an apology. Mosley entertained the audience 'with his clever oratory and aristocratic charm', recalled Foot, who resigned as editor.

In front of the Oxford Debating Union, Mosley 'made mincemeat' of Liberal MP Jeremy Thorpe, on a motion proposing that South Africa should be expelled from the Commonwealth, despite the Union being a stronghold of liberalism. Mosley received an ovation from the packed house. Max's friend

Robert Skidelsky said his interest in Mosley 'was born at this point. I greatly admire courage and intelligence, and it had taken the one for a man as unpopular as Mosley to come to the Union at all, and the other for him to gain a triumph.' Soon afterwards Max 'whipped off Skidelsky to Paris' to see his father. Nancy Mitford met the Warden of New College Oxford, Sir William Hayter, whom she had known since he was at the embassy in Paris, and wrote to her sister the Duchess of Devonshire that he had told her 'the boys here and at Cambridge can't have enough of Sir O. – they don't agree with him but he fascinates them'.

In December 1961 the future Chancellor of the Exchequer Kenneth Clarke invited Mosley to speak at the Cambridge University Conservative Association on the basis that he was 'a serious political figure who had got to be faced'. One person resigned in protest – Michael Howard, who went on to lead the Conservative Party. In front of 1,500 students Mosley easily outwitted Clarke and another future Tory Minister John Gummer. *Varsity* noted that 'during the final minutes, the shouts of "answer the question" grew apace with the realization that Mosley sidestepped almost every important question put to him . . .'

At the beginning of 1962, worried by the slowness of the campaign for European unity, the bigger neo-Fascist parties decided to forge closer links between themselves. Mosley convened a congress in Venice on 4 March with the aim of creating a 'European National Party'. He visited Germany and Italy to invite participants, then Switzerland, where he told Amaudruz, leader of the New European Order, he was not welcome because of his open racism. By this stage Mosley was generally regarded by the extreme Right as being 'too moderate for the tough . . . and too tough for the moderate'.

The other key figure promoting the congress was Thiriart, who preached a third way 'social European revolution'. However, the congress was very much Mosley's affair. On 1 March 1962, dozens of Fascist and neo-Nazi groups assembled in Venice, including the Deutsche Reichspartei led by von Thadden and the MSI, represented by Mosley's personal friends, Giovanni Lanfree, Ponce de León and Count Alvise Loredan, who helped to organize it. The MSI leadership refused to sanction the Congress because it was unwilling to jeopardize its role as a player in Italian politics, having helped in the victory of Tambroni as Prime Minister. With almost 80,000 members, the MSI was far more significant a force than Mosley's minute UM. It had many sympathizers among trade unionists and its popular press had daily sales of 100,000. UM representatives included long-standing Mosleyites Hector McKechnie and Walter Hesketh.

For the forum a round table was used, an idea suggested by Mosley for the future government of Europe. From the symbol to the ideas, everything, *Action* later proclaimed, was his work, including the declaration – 'Europe a Nation with a common Government elected by the whole people of Europe'. It would 'free Europe from the present dominion of world finance operating from Wall Street and the disastrous alternative of Communist tyranny'. Delegates signed the 'European Protocol', which advocated creating a central European government – closed, inward-looking, a white man's club ruled by an authoritarian government opposed to the United Nations.

The Protocol repeated the tenets of Europe a Nation and the Pirow–Mosley proposals, and Mosley's advocacy of the wage-price mechanism. Those that solemnly signed it on 4 March 1962 – Lanfree, Loredan, von Thadden, Thiriart and Mosley – agreed to change their party names to the National Party of Europe (NPE). It was determined that its emblem would be that of the UM – a flash of lightning in a circle. They vowed to accept the principle of central direction by a 'European political bureau', under the principles of 'Progress . . . Solidarity . . . Unity'. In was in such a spirit that they signed a declaration to stop the incidents in Tyrol between Italians and Austrians of German stock. They would, henceforth, meet at a round table event every two or three months.

The attempt to make themselves paladins of a reunification of the 'real' Europe stretching 'from Brest to Bucharest' never got further than the signing of the Protocol. It was, Lanfree noted, 'almost impossible to find any traces of this event in the European papers. The agreement reached was not even published in Italy but only in England and Belgium.' The NPE existed only on paper; the Movimento Sociale Italiano continued to call itself the MSI, and the DRP and the UM retained their old names. UM members said after the Congress, 'This makes no difference to us.' Some of those not present, such as Bardeche, agreed the Congress was 'a relative consecration of his European ideas'; however, he 'certainly emphasised it too much'. For Mosley, Venice was a 'massive achievement'.

Immediately after the Congress Thiriart renamed his MAC organization Jeune Europe (JE) and reorganized it into a clandestine network of localized 'cells'. In seeking support for the creation of JE branches across Europe, he contacted smaller and more radical neo-Fascist groups, as well as Kameradenwerk Chief Hans-Ulrich Rudel. The JE set up branches which received Thiriart's instructions, propaganda and advice regarding organization, and a JE International centre was established at Forschhausen near Frankfurt.

It was, however, the transnational contacts that accounted for its significance as a transmitter of unconventional warfare techniques – later to be used in 'Gladio'-style operations – to new generations of European neo-Fascists who had adopted the Celtic cross as their emblem. MAC was linked to Mosley's Union Movement, which the previous September had launched the Young Britain Movement, headed by international athlete Walter Hesketh.

Other JE-linked groups included Mouvement Jeune Nation and ultras in Spain and Portugal. Thiriart forged connections with Skorzeny and Rudel, and to Jean-Marie Le Pen's pro-Algérie Française movement in France, which made MAC into a 'principal agent' of the OAS in Belgium. But this was more impressive on paper than in practice. Bardeche noted that neo-Fascism was not equal to the occasion: 'Whereas the Communists immediately transposed the Algerian problem into terms of international Communism, the Fascists never thought for a moment of expressing it in terms of a Fascist International.'

Flushed with 'success' in Venice, Mosley turned to the domestic campaign. He presented a moderate front in the face of competition from the new generation of nationalists. The *Jewish Chronicle* declared on 4 May 1962 that the UM was no longer 'pre-occupied by Jewish matters, indeed the word "Jew" is not mentioned in its latest publications'. A month later *The Times* noted, 'Mosleyites are frequently given to violently racial opinions in private but at the moment their public behaviour is respectable to a point bordering on piety.'

Mosley targeted the recent influx of Commonwealth immigrants. Little had changed since Notting Hill and race relations was a potentially explosive cauldron of prejudice and hate. The 'coloured' population had risen in ten years from 74,500 to 336,000. Many British cities had black communities concentrated in deprived inner cities, which often led 'to rampant prejudice and of discrimination in such areas as private housing and employment'. Although ethnic communities were mostly peaceful, 'there had been disturbances to remind British people of the possible powder keg of racial tension that had manifested itself in so many American cities in the past'. Mosleyites played on these fears and, partly in response to this, in 1962 the Macmillan government passed an Immigration Bill, which restricted Commonwealth immigration by way of a voucher system. It was not sufficient to satisfy the Mosleyites but it did enough to blunt any hope of electoral success.

Mosley asked Mary Tavener, who had ties to several right-wing groups, to make an approach to Colin Jordan and John Bean. She was married to a man who tried on the satire programme *TW3* to punch Bernard Levin, who had scathingly reviewed his wife's acting. She was involved in attempts to get a reprieve for an SS colonel, who had been found guilty in Italy of ordering the shooting of partisans and with whom she appeared to be in love. Mosley was willing to make Jordan and Bean his national organizers, on a par with Hamm. She outlined the advantages of unity, pointed out that Mosley still had a name to conjure with and stressed the experience of the UM in fighting elections. Not long afterwards she died, after falling down some stairs.

Jordan was too mistrustful of Mosley to agree to a meeting but Bean did so at the Eccleston Hotel, where he received 'the full Mosley hypnosis treatment, with the opening and lowering of the eyelids which made his pupils appear to dilate'. He had not realized Bean had been in the UM. 'We must make amends and see that your organising and speaking abilities are fully utilised as a senior officer within my movement.' Bean was flattered but pointed out that 'while he could go a considerable way with his views on Europe' it was 'premature to call for "Europe a Nation"'. The other problem was that Mosley had been labelled an anti-Semite and, because of this, 'he would never be able to obtain power through the ballot box'. Bean then explained his idea for co-operation in public rallies and elections in a 'National Front' but Mosley was not interested.

Jordan attempted to organize an openly Nazi movement. When the National Socialist Movement held its first rally in Trafalgar Square in July 1962, anti-Fascists disrupted the meeting and the police arrested Tyndall and Jordan for insulting words likely to cause a breach of the peace. Jordan had argued that Hitler had been right and that we should have been fighting world Jewry in the Second World War and not Germany. Tyndall said the Jew was the 'assassin of Europe' and like a 'poisonous maggot' in society. Jordan was imprisoned for two months and Tyndall six weeks. The attempts at respectability were spoilt, Mosley raged, by such 'lunatic fringe action'. Hamm declared, 'We thoroughly disapprove of Jordan. We feared all along his clowning in [Trafalgar] Square might put our next meeting in jeopardy and it turned out to be right.'

Mosley was scheduled to hold a public meeting in the square. These normally passed off with little incident. However, on 22 July there were 7,000 people present, most of them determined to stop Mosley. The rally was halted after fifteen minutes with fifty-six arrests. A week later Mosley and thirty supporters tried to march through Manchester to Belle Vue. He was knocked down three times, there were forty-seven arrests and the meeting was called off before a hostile crowd of 5,000 people.

What alarmed the Left (and the authorities) was the sign from the Venice Conference and the rise of the new nationalist groups that the Right was regrouping and hoped to become an international and domestic force. The anti-Fascist challenge came from Jewish groups, who were, the *Sunday Telegraph* reported, 'planning a nation-wide campaign . . . against Mosley's Union Movement'. Threats were made to sweep Fascism off the streets from the Yellow Star movement and a faction within it, the newly formed 62 Group – a revival of the 43 Group – supported by Jewish shopkeepers and businessmen in the East End, who supplied funds. Through intelligence gathering and guerrilla-like tactics, the 62 Group attempted to expose the true nature and activities of the UM, and to prevent Mosley from speaking. This led to many confrontations on the streets, which sometimes ended in violence.

The climax of the violence occurred on 31 July, when the sixty-five-year-old

Mosley was punched and knocked down in the 'Battle of Ridley Road', in which sixty people were arrested. Max, who had just left Oxford and was reading for the Bar, acted as his father's right-hand man and at one point saved him from a beating. Jewish ex-servicemen posing as Mosleyites had infiltrated the cordon of over 200 policemen. When Mosley stood up and tried to speak under a shower of coins and tomatoes, the police stopped the meeting. While walking back to his car, he was again assaulted and his chauffeur injured. The next day Max defended himself before the magistrates and was acquitted.

On 30 August the police banned all political marches in London for a forty-eight-hour period. Three days later they made forty arrests in Bethnal Green, and Mosley was kicked and punched. A week later he finished his speech in Bethnal Green, well guarded by ranks of police. Whether Mosley encouraged the disorder is unclear, but his top minder Danny Harmston, a Smithfield Market manager and professional boxer, paid a porter, Tony Lambrianou (later a member of the Kray gang), and his brother Jimmy, 'to create a fracas while he's talking' so as to attract publicity. 'On several occasions', admitted Lambrianou, 'we were getting £50 a time to be out there Jew-baiting.' On 29 September, in Manchester, 250 policemen kept Mosley and the Northern Council against Fascism apart, but he had had enough. He decided to stop rallies in the provinces. His activity would be limited to private meetings, door-to-door canvassing and the publication of journals. He lamented to an insider, 'I fear the character of the people has changed . . . they won't go on marches.'

The publicity generated by the violence – which the public believed belonged to another era – did not halt the decline in UM membership. Colin Cross estimated there were 1,000 members, mostly working-class activists, though the true figure was probably lower. A *Sunday Times* reporter, Michael Hamlyn, suggested 10–15,000 UM sympathizers but that probably included all who had passed through its ranks. Alan Rogers, who 'unveiled all their secrets' in the *Herald*, said 'membership subscription was about £6,000 [£72,000], with donations which fluctuate between £5,000 and £30,000 pounds in a good year. The minimum annual running of UM costs were between £15–16,000.' Mosley himself made up any deficit incurred, though some money was said to be coming from Rhodesia and South Africa.

In September Mosley sent William Webster, a former boxer, to South Africa to raise funds. In a successful tour he boasted he had collected £100,000 (£1,200,000). He approached the government for a contribution and was directed to Nationalist Party headquarters for a donation. Webster's boast was probably just that; there was some money but nowhere near as much as he claimed. Rogers concluded that the UM would put up three or four candidates at the next general election, which was 'hardly an impressive performance for a party which Mosley believes could sweep to power within five years'.

A last meeting in Tunbridge Wells broke up in disorder on 20 October. Thirty-six years of grass-roots campaigning had ended in failure. One reason for the UM's collapse was anti-Fascist activity, which the 62 Group claimed had 'swept Mosley from the streets for the last time'. It was, Martin Walker suggests, no great achievement since he had no movement of any significance which could capitalize upon the publicity. The fighting at his meetings was shown on television, though not a word of his speeches was reported. The BBC's head of talks told editorial staff that on no account was he to be invited to be interviewed for the 'exposure of extreme views'. He did do interviews with popular television presenters such as Dan Farson and Malcolm Muggeridge, but 'not one minute of the interview was shown in either case'. The Director-General, Hugh Greene, had ruled that it 'would not be right to offer a platform to Sir Oswald Mosley'. He later admitted that a report that Mosley would only 'come on the air over my dead body was not an exaggeration'.

Mosley escaped from the problems at home with an invitation in September 1962 from students at the University of Buffalo, in New York, to take part in a televised debate. Treated as a security case by Hoover, FBI agents 'conducted a discreet surveillance at the airport' when Mosley landed. His stay at the Hotel Lennox was monitored by an unidentified source and plain-clothes men were 'stationed in the hotel lobby to keep unauthorized persons away from the subject'.

An FBI agent took notes of the debate, during which Mosley characterized Fascism as '(a) Nationalism and (b) "urge to action", both of which are good things in themselves, but "led to disaster" because of being carried too far. He said that at that time there was no "Fascist International".' Fascism, he added, 'was not responsible for the atrocities committed "mostly during the war", which had no more to do with Fascism than the bombing of Hiroshima had to do with Democracy'. The agent noted that 'some of the questioners became bitter and abusive in reference to Mosley's attitude toward Hitler during the war'. He defended himself by claiming it would have been 'best for Britain to keep out of the war and let Hitler "smash East", and that Hitler had no desire to take up "a multi-racial empire" such as the British'. The agent thought there was 'much humbug in the speech as a whole. His rhetoric, however, was that of an experienced British politician, yet some of the contrived climaxes in his presentation had quite a "Fascist" tone. He repeatedly stated to hecklers that he has been slandered and accused of advocating ideas he never stood for, and that the "truth" was to be found "in the record".'

On his return to Europe, Mosley was interviewed on 22 October by the writer Angelo del Boca. He reiterated his view of Europe as a 'third block', which would rid itself of American and Russian troops, reunify Germany, reconquer lost German territories, give Italy breathing space and put an end to the United Nations' power. It was megalomania, thought Boca: 'Mosley has foreseen everything.' Europe would leave Asia to the Soviets; the US would keep its protectorate over South America, and Europe take that part of Africa inhabited by Whites. Mosley then 'fixed his steely eyes upon me' and added, 'if they then tell us to get out of the whole of Africa, we must say that we have not the slightest intention of doing so, any more than the Americans would be willing to leave their continent to the Redskins. Europe can't be separated from Africa.'

In early 1963, Mosley was in South Africa advising British immigrants to join the National Party. At home, there was little UM activity. Robert Saunders stood for the vice-presidency of the National Farmers Union but lost by one vote to Henry Plumb. He blamed his failure on making public his ties to Mosley. Saunders hoped to influence the NFU and through his tireless campaigning a policy to make Britain as self-sufficient as possible in agricultural production did take root in the early seventies, and his arguments for Britain to join the Common Market finally became NFU policy.

In the spring the Mosleys' Irish house, Ileclash, was sold. After three years in England, they decided to divide their time between the Temple near Paris and a large London flat in Lowndes Court.

British MPs began warning about the international ramifications of a revived Nazi movement. The West German Ministry of the Interior listed 450 organizations and publishing houses outside Germany associated with international Fascism. Mosley described his activities in this area in the May edition of *Action*. He had been in Bologna for a congress of Giovane Nazione, chaired by Thiriart, who had 'done splendid work in publishing the policy of the Declaration of Venice in several languages'. Mosley said 'it was a chance to meet the new men of value to the European future'. These were radical students who opposed the MSI's 'gradual trend towards bourgeois ways' and glorified OAS terrorist methods in the pages of its Turin review, *Quaderni Neri*, to which Mosley contributed. It drew readers' attention to the revolutionary upsurge in Europe, which would follow the 'path of Nietzsche's superman' and 'European Nationalism'. At Mosley's urging the extremists achieved 'partial and mediocre success' by merging into a new grouping, Giovane Europe.

Mosley was seen as a moderate on the right, yet he aligned himself with radical groups, which in the sixties and seventies engaged in shootings and bombings as part of the anti-Communist 'strategy of tension' linked to the MI6/CIA sponsored 'Gladio' stay-behind networks, which in Italy and Belgium relied on neo-Fascist 'gladiators/terrorists'. Was Mosley aware of the deeper intelligence background that surrounded his activities? Some of those close to him, such as John Warburton, did wonder what he was really up to with these extremists. Curiously, BUF member Edmund Warburton had joined the very first stay-behind network. When fighting stopped in Germany in 1945 he was recruited to a secret special forces unit to take on the Soviets.

During the summer of 1963, Jeune Europe split over the Alto Adige issue. This was discussed at a special conference, where most of the delegates belonged to the Gladio networks. The German speakers were in favour of supporting action to create an independent Tyrolese State, but Thiriart and the Italians said it would harm the cause of European unity and favoured a negotiated settlement of the controversy between Austria and Italy. The dispute led groups to abandon JE and form a new international, Europafront, under the leadership of Austrian extremist and Gladio operative Fred Borth. Thiriart accused his adversaries of 'neo-Nazism' and expelled them. Mosley was party to these discussions, which shows that he was moving in some very murky waters. UM members attended a European Easter camp in Belgium organized by MAC and Jeune Europe, where OAS personnel were present. In September 1963 George Parisy, an on-the-run OAS gunman involved in a plot to kill General de Gaulle, was arrested in a London flat with a number of passports and a loaded gun found under the pillow of a bed he was sharing with a homosexual member of the UM. Links to Thiriart had obviously been of some use.

With Mosley abroad, *Action* became irregular and subject to a permanent financial crisis until it was wound up in May 1964. When Mosley withdrew his candidates from the June general election, it was the beginning of the end for the UM, which was now conducted by a directorate of Bailey, Harmston, Moloney, Quill, Row and Hamm; the last two full-time officials. There was an active membership of no more than 200 and less than 1,000 inactive supporters in the country. When George Thayer began studying the UM he found a rank and file composed of 'young and violent racists who join the Movement as an excuse to release their anti-social attitudes'. They were 'the misfits, the dullards and the outcasts of society'. Why Mosley, Thayer wondered, 'allows his Movement to be dominated by these people has never been explained adequately'.

The fire had gone from Mosley: when he posed the question 'What are our chances?' he answered, 'None until crisis.' The years in the political wilderness had had their effect. Thayer noticed his pride was 'beginning to crack around the edges; he seems very sensitive to slights and the first glimmerings of self-doubt are noticeable. He seemed resigned to his ostracism . . . He gives the impression that he dislikes his squalid surroundings, the furtiveness of his life, and the men with whom he associates. Above all, he seemed to miss the company and confidence of great men.'

The Europe campaign enabled him to attract some of the respect he craved.

In July he gave a press conference in Milan organized by Jeune Europe and pursued contacts in West Germany, through his close friend Adolf von Thadden, who was in discussions with leaders of the disbanded Deutsche Reichspartei and several smaller groups. On 28 November, with West Germany facing an economic depression, the National Democratic Party (NPD) emerged from these discussions, held together by a common commitment to German unification and an end to occupation by foreign armies. Von Thadden was to become its 'Führer'. This was, Gerry Gable notes, 'neo-nazism in three-piece suits, with the thugs operating in the shadows'. Mosley offered his support. In a letter on 16 December to leading NPD member Wolfgang Frenz, he stressed it was 'of the greatest importance . . . to support the formation of a nationalist party for Europe'.

Von Thadden came closer than anyone to giving the far Right influence over post-war West German politics. The NPD grew rapidly and made impressive showings in regional elections. However, Mosley backed off when his friends developed a more radical agenda. Some became the founding fathers of the post-war 'Third Position', which embraced Perón in Argentina and emerging leaders in Africa. Von Thadden split the NPD and its allies across Europe by suddenly espousing a pro-Chinese and anti-Soviet line. How much this change was due to his British Intelligence masters, who were 'running' him, is not known. The NPD was infiltrated by West German security and senior members, bought by money or blackmail, were its agents. This poses the question: to what extent did counter-intelligence officers sustain the far Right in their efforts to monitor it? Von Thadden later dropped the radical ideology and the NPD lost most of its support to established conservative politicians who adopted some of its goals during the 1970s.

Mosley asked in *Action*: 'What progress was the "National Party of Europe" making after its inauguration in Venice?' He claimed 'a very great advance' had been made but complained that lack of funds was holding up progress. 'We did not at this stage get beyond a series of meetings to establish the liaison decided by the Conference.' If, against the evidence, he remained optimistic, privately he knew the problem was more than just funding. Venice had been 'the last hope of merging the old patriotisms in a wider patriotism of Europe'. He had found the most ardent Europeans among 'the young Germans fresh from the Army' – especially from the SS regiments. However, the 'increasing sense of insult, humiliation and repression among many of them' led to a frustration with the dreams of a united Europe and caused many of 'the protagonists of Venice' to be 'thrown back into nationalism, and into a wild futility'.

Giovanni Lanfree said Mosley 'tried to give life to one great party of the European Right but it was a failure because of the too narrow nationalism of the countries represented and the desire of the German for revenge'. They yearned for the Nazi era and looked towards the past and not the future. All the post-war internationals were derailed because the Germans and Italians 'had no real intention of sub-ordinating the autonomy of their own organisations to a larger entity under someone else's control'. They felt Mosley was too European and that would affect their chances to win elections in their home countries. Typically, they were riven with political rivalries between leaders, who were, Mosley claimed, 'nonentities'. There was also the Algerian problem and whether to help or not to help the OAS. Other Fascists – Bardeche, Amaudruz, Duprat, Coston – considered Mosley's European action extremely limited and said he was just a clever and opportunist demagogue.

With little success with his European project, Mosley turned again to South Africa, which he visited during 1965, and praised its 'latent power'. However, Prime Minister Verwoerd had found other less controversial outlets on the right of the Tory Party for propaganda campaigns and had little use for the UM, which had no influence on British policy. The Vice-Chairman of the Monday Club, Harold Soref, who was intensely involved with pro-South African activities, was a former Blackshirt. Mosley then sought support in Ian Smith's Rhodesia, where a Mosleyite South African propagandist, Ivor Benson, had been hired to mastermind the creation of a new image for the country.

In February 1966 Mosley's name was again current when the BBC broadcast a programme called *The Threat of Fascism* in the series *The Thirties*, during which the commentator declared that 'Mosley was trying to enforce his policy by deliberately invoking violence . . .' The UM began another campaign, centred on housing shortages and immigration. However, the immigration issue had rather fizzled out when Mosley decided to make one last attempt to enter Parliament, standing in the March 1966 general election in Shoreditch. He polled only 1,127 votes – 4.6 per cent of the total. All seven nationalist candidates who campaigned against immigration lost their deposit.

The UM contested Birmingham Handsworth, a constituency with a growing non-white population and major social problems, but it attracted only 4.1 per cent of the poll. It was a collapse of the 'racialist appeal' to the electorate. 'The people we worked with were perfect and this made it bearable for me,' wrote Diana. She dismissed Mosley's vote with a typically flippant remark: 'We did not canvass and the result was no surprise. There was a feeling of enormous apathy reflected in the high rate of abstentions.' The reality was that the exploitation of race and immigration rarely becomes a major political issue when left to fringe parties. John Brewer's study of the Handsworth election makes the point that the UM's failure was 'a product of the fact that whatever fears there were in the population were translated through the established parties. Voters reject neo-fascist movements: they have consistently rejected Mosley, Britain's closest approximation to a fascist leader.'

Mosley realized the futility of the effort. He announced his retirement from 'party warfare'. 'I detached myself from party politics in order to advocate a policy and action beyond parties.' He had been rejected by the British public but remained undaunted, with his ability for self-deception undiminished.

28

Rehabilitation

In 1966 Mosley launched his final campaign – to rehabilitate his own reputation in the eyes of the British Establishment. He issued a 'Broadsheet' dealing with political topics, took part in university debates, talked to the Tory Bow Group and spoke at the Liberal Party's *New Outlook* magazine's history seminars. He also began work on an autobiography. The media, however, remained closed to him. Constantine FitzGibbon, at the time compiling a feature on British Fascism, revealed he was told on 'no account to record the voice of Mosley who was permanently banned from the BBC'. Mosley issued a libel writ against the BBC's Director-General, Sir Hugh Greene, over a statement that he had organized violence.

When the libel was repeated, Mosley applied to the High Court to have BBC Governors committed to prison for contempt of court. The case was heard in February 1966 before Lord Chief Justice Parker, who in his summing up said he had 'considerable sympathy with the applicant . . . It is perfectly clear that the respondents will not have him on their programme. I am not criticising them for that, but it does disclose a curious system whereby someone who has the ear of the whole nation can say things and the unfortunate subject has no means of answering back in the same medium.' When Mosley applied to the European Court of Human Rights, which agreed to hear his complaint, it so alarmed the BBC that the ban was dropped.

After correspondence in the *Observer* over his 'quarrel' with Jews, on 6 June 1966 Mosley contacted the editor of the *Jewish Chronicle* William Frankel. He said 'the quarrel is over' and that it was not 'in accord with the traditional wisdom of your people to turn a past quarrel into a personal feud'. Frankel disclaimed any personal feud but said, 'Jews cannot be expected to have any great affection for one who is known to have held opinions to which you gave expression in the past, unless it was patent that there had been a sincere change of attitude.' Mosley claimed he had 'never been an anti-Semite' and the quarrel had been with 'some Jews' who desired a war between Britain and Germany. He explained his position and requested a meeting for a frank discussion.

On 3 November Mosley told Frankel he had been wrong to single out Jews. He now recognized they legitimately felt both a Jewish loyalty and a British loyalty – as he himself affirmed a loyalty to Europe and to his own country. Frankel felt Mosley 'had no concept of the depth of Jewish emotions about the Holocaust'. When he conveyed some idea of 'the still bleeding wound' it had inflicted on every Jew, Mosley agreed it was too much 'to expect Jews to welcome his offer of reconciliation'. Frankel suggested that a statement of his attitude to Jews be accompanied by a donation to an appropiate Jewish cause. Mosley said it was 'difficult for a politician to don sackcloth and ashes'. Nicholas learnt that 'the statement, if it existed outside his imagination, was never sent'. In fact, Mosley did send a letter to the *Chronicle* (on 21 December 1969) admitting atrocities were committed in Germany and seeking 'an end to this quarrel which arose from reasons long past and desire my relations with Jews perfectly normal'. That, however, was the extent of his statement. Seemingly, a charity donation was rejected. Someone privy to the correspondence recalled Mosley complaining that 'they are always raising the anti'.

Mosley had turned over the UM to a directorate of mainly older Blackshirts, with a nostalgic faith in his political judgement. He said 'Labour and the Tories have failed equally; the Liberals have no answer at all. The only way is to go above and beyond the parties to a national union of the best of our people.' He wanted a government of action with 'hard centre' ideas. He recognized that 'no government of the centre based on national unity has yet been achieved in peacetime but it may be helped by a change in the system of voting'. The UM needed 'a strong base for a rapid advance when the great economic crisis comes off; which we alone have warned the country for years past. Quite often in recent times movements with lesser votes have been in power very soon afterwards . . .'

A newspaper profile said Mosley lived 'the life of a country gentleman of around 1900 with a full staff that would certainly be unobtainable in England'. As well as a holiday in Venice, in January 1967 the Mosleys spent time in Johannesburg, where Diana experienced some respite from her frequent migraines. She had fewer worries over Alexander now but it was the warm dry climate that really helped and, henceforth, the Mosleys went to South Africa most winters. Mosley had become very possessive of Diana. It seemed that it was only when he needed to depend on her that he truly loved her. She downplayed her own personality to support him. Her loyalty was absolute and she disowned 'anyone who offered even the mildest criticism of him, and only adulation would serve from anyone writing about him'.

In February 1967 Diana informed Robert Skidelsky's literary agent there would be no conflict between Mosley's autobiography – 'the opening of negotiations for peace with the British Establishment' – and 'the authorised biography that is being written by Mr Skidelsky'. Skidelsky had known Max at Oxford and was impressed when his father spoke at the Union. As President of the Humanist Society, Skidelsky invited Mosley down to speak, which angered some dons. Max was very supportive, though Mosley, writing his autobiography, was not initially co-operative. Diana admitted she wanted 'a hagiography'.

The prevailing view of Mosley as an extremist was tempered by the creation of the National Front – a merger between A. K. Chesterton's League of Empire Loyalists, John Bean's British National Party, the Racial Preservation Society and the Greater Britain Movement of John Tyndall and Martin Webster. With his passionate anti-Nazism and pro-Empire stance, Chesterton – the BUF's former chief propagandist – was the respectable head who appealed to ultra right-wing Monday Club activists of the Tory Party. Its membership soon eclipsed that of the UM, although initially it had little more success than Mosley. Ironically, the NF came into being as a result of Mosley's attempt in the early sixties to unite the different factions of British Fascism. He was the catalyst, Martin Walker noted, 'because of the seeds he had planted in the mind of Bean', who talked of a 'National Front' of like-minded bodies. Tyndall called for the unification of non-Mosleyite groups. In 1965 *New Society* said 'the break with pre-war fascism is almost complete. The BNP has no "Leader" whom it puts forwards as a potential dictator and it avowedly works within the Parliamentary framework . . . Bean says he regards himself as "the drummer boy" awakening public opinion rather than as "the new Charlemagne".'

NF policy owed much to Mosley's vision of 'Imperial Defence' and 'Economic Integration', but the movement distanced itself from him. Tyndall criticized Mosley for aping the continental movements in respect of the external imagery adopted. 'Today the focal points of world affairs have moved elsewhere, calling for different approaches and policies, so that the question of whether we should endorse the whole of the Mosley programme of that earlier period simply does not arise.' Mosley dismissed the NF's outdated nationalism, which harked back to a non-existent empire and anti-Europeanism. He blamed this on the 'Nordic idea', a concept destructive to the idea of a United Europe. He told an insider the NF was 'funded by Jews'.

Although he put forward the most coherent ideology of any Fascist in Europe, Mosley had little influence on the extreme right in Britain in the late sixties and early seventies. He was distrusted by the little Hitlers of the neo-Fascist Right. He was too Fascist and too openly anti-Semitic for the ultras on the Tory Right, and too soft and too 'kosher' for 'real' Fascists. He failed the test as a 'revolutionary' Fascist. He led a violent movement but had been too law-abiding to take command of the streets. A Fascist of any standing would have put the Mitford family up against a wall and had them shot. He was too much of the Establishment and only really succeeded as Rothermere's militant wing of the Tory Party. He failed at almost everything; even as a Fascist agitator. He had some influence in Italy, where the younger generation of neo-Fascists read his writings. MSI leader Giorgio Pini and those young activists who went on publicly to disown the Fascist past visited Mosley in the late sixties. John Warburton said 'they couldn't get enough Mosley material'.

Mosley's absence from television screens ended in November 1967 when he appeared on ITV's *Frost Programme*. Face to face with old East End opponents such as 'Solly' Kaye, he denied the charge of anti-Semitism and claimed he had been driven to retaliate 'against Jewish rascals yelling at me and attacking my meetings with razors, bludgeons, weapons of every sort'. It was when the 1935 message of congratulations from Streicher to one of his speeches and Mosley's telegram of thanks were shown that the audience began to see through his deceptions. Frost realized he 'saw everything through the distorting mirror of his own fantasies, and was irretrievably consumed by them. He would never see himself as others saw him.'

Someone who did take Mosley seriously was Cecil King, nephew of Lord Rothermere and Chairman of the International Publishing Corporation. With *Mirror* editor Hugh Cudlipp, King regularly discussed 'what would happen, and how soon, and who in various activities in the land could be of any use when the fabric of the British way of life broke down'. In March 1968, when King met with French politicians, bankers and publishers, Cudlipp asked Paris correspondent Peter Stephens to monitor his activities. King was pushing for a United Europe. 'Dumbfounded hacks at the *Mirror*,' wrote Chris Horrie, 'were required to write article after article setting out the plan for "Nation Europa", which were then foisted on a mostly baffled *Mirror* readership.' King claimed 'that eventually there will be a dictator in Britain perhaps not next year, but it is certainly coming because parliament is totally discredited'. He wanted an independent strong man to take charge and 'turned to exactly the same "strong man" as Rothermere – Mosley'.

King suggested the *Mirror* serialize Mosley's autobiography and wanted to invite him to lunch. Cudlipp thought the idea 'abhorrent'. King wanted advice and to sound out Mosley as the head of a military-backed government. Lord Louis Mountbatten, the country's highest-ranking military officer, was his next choice. On 8 May King had his famous meeting with Mountbatten when they talked of the 'forthcoming crisis' and the likelihood of bloodshed in the streets, and the desire for a 'massive resurgence'. King thought the hour of his destiny was at hand and on 11 May the *Mirror* led with the headline ENOUGH IS ENOUGH, amid calls for the resignation of the Prime Minister, Harold Wilson. Cudlipp said that in the ensuing political chaos the list of names King had written down, including that of Mosley, would be called upon to save Britain.

Mosley's autobiography, *My Life*, was brought out in October by a reputable publisher, Nelson. There was a press conference at the Café Royal, where King talked with Mosley. A sympathetic article by Tory MP Norman St John

Stevas appeared in *The Times*, which serialized the book. Mosley was 'a man of idiosyncratic views endowed with great political courage but little political sense'. The claim that he was not an anti-Semite was convincing: 'The charge that could be levelled against him with more justification is not anti-Semitism but a callous indifference to the fate of European Jewry.' He claimed 'to be a man of action, but men of action do not wait upon the occurrence of hypothetical events. They seize them as they are and mould them to their will.' Mosley was 'a man of ideas'.

Colin Coote said it was 'the best-written volume of memoirs emanating from my generation'. It is ably written and was greatly helped by Diana's editing and the research of two assistants. It is also an unrepentant and self-deluded apologia; an unreflective account which deliberately conceals key areas of Mosley's political activities. He was an 'expert forgetter' who expunged much compromising and dubious material on the BUF. The book glosses over areas such as the radio project in order, as he admitted, to protect the identities of people still alive. Those BU members mentioned by name were already dead. Mosley argued that internment had blighted their lives to such an extent that anonymity was the best guarantee of preventing further grief for such committed individuals. In the end, he produced a sickly, overbearingly vain and narcissistic book – one of the great monuments to one person's monstrous ego. The great man Mosley is never wrong.

Bill Allen wrote to Mosley that his book was 'splendid, balanced and even kindly'. There were favourable reviews but Conservative Party historian Robert Blake, while praising its readability, warned 'the book should not delude the reader into believing that Mosleyism was other than a thoroughly evil manifestation of the human spirit'. It sold poorly; he received an advance of £5,000 and bought back 2,500 copies. *My Life*'s publication did break the BBC ban. For thirty-four years Mosley had not been allowed to say a word on the BBC. On 24 October he was interviewed on *Panorama* by James Mossman and attracted eight and a half million viewers. Mosley answered questions on anti-Semitism (he appeared to recognize that six million Jews had been killed), Fascism and his attitude to Hitler, whether he was waiting for a future call and whether he should have stayed in the Labour Party. The *Jewish Chronicle* said he looked 'moderate and reasonable', and had an answer for each point.

Nancy Mitford wrote to her sister Decca on 15 November: 'Have you noted all the carry-on about Sir O? He says he was never anti-semitic. Good Gracious! I quite love the old soul now but really!' On the previous day King lunched at the Ritz with Mosley, who tried 'to convince everybody that he was never anti-Jewish, never pro-German, and never favoured violence at his meetings. Surely he protests too much.' At seventy-one he still hoped to play a political part. 'Adenauer came to power at seventy-four and continued to be important till he was ninety-one . . . He thinks an economic breakdown here is inevitable and that then we must all be ready – but ready to do what?' King added that Mosley had talked to Enoch Powell.

Earlier in the year Powell, a member of the Conservative shadow cabinet, delivered his 'rivers of blood' speech in which he said the country was mad to allow in 50,000 dependants of immigrants. The apocalyptic speech with its reference to 'wide-eyed, grinning piccaninnies' brought 'the language of the neo-fascist political fringe into the heart of the establishment'. One of Mosley's few dynamic lieutenants, 'Big Dan' Harmston, mobilized 500 Smithfield porters in support of Powell and his anti-immigration views. Powell was able 'to cut across traditional divisions of party identification in forging his mass constituency'. However, like Mosley, he was a maverick and individualist who remained a political outcast. The UM argued Powellism was 'the last spasm of Little England' and its anti-Powell line was in sharp contrast to the NF's support. Diana said her husband belonged to the 'hard centre' while Powell was of the extreme Right. In a snobbish aside to Hugh Purcell, Mosley called him 'a middle-class Alf Garnett'. Despite this, Harmston remained a loyal Mosleyite. There were few left.

Skidelsky wrote to Mosley on 22 November that the focus of his own book 'would be the central episode of your life – the period 1929–1931 – which is not only right, but also most favourable to you'. Skidelsky later admitted he had been emotionally tied to the period of his thesis, which had been published as *Politicians and the Slump*. It added to the overly Keynesian interpretation of Mosley's thinking.

Ross McKibben criticized Skidelsky's 'neo-Keynesian critiques' of the second Labour government for overestimating the choices available to it and underestimating the social and economic structural constraints. A Keynesian solution was impossible, not because it was inherently wrong, but because too many powerful people would not have accepted the measures necessary to carry it through. McKibben argued 'the problem of who had political control of the economy had to be solved before reflationary policies could be followed. The real barrier to such reflation was thus always a political one.' It was true, as Mosley argued, that government had intervened, planned and organized during the First World War, but 'restraints to treating depression as war' remained and it was 'difficult to conceive of the then British ruling classes, however broadly or narrowly that term is interpreted, consenting to state direction of the economy'. The failure to adopt reflationary policies, therefore, was structural and not intellectual.

'Whenever coherent and integrated programmes have been presented by someone whose views have commanded public credibility,' as Geoffrey Ingham suggests in the case of Mosley in the 1920s (and Wilson in the 1960s), 'the dominant class has been merciless in its condemnation.' His contemporaries noted that his economics were 'not only an alternative to Labour's international socialism, but also to international "finance capitalism" and, not surprisingly, he also suffered rejection by the orthodox right'. Efforts to support productioneering appeared 'revolutionary' in their implications. 'The City–industry opposition', argues Ingham, 'cannot be resolved by isolated and narrowly economic adjustments. The institutional means to achieve this end do not exist, and attempts at their creation immediately mobilise the most deeply entrenched forces of tradition within British society.'

While undermining Skidelsky's argument McKibben, without obviously meaning to, made Mosley's case for him. Mosley was a radical planner who argued he had 'gone beyond' Keynes. Without articulating it, Mosley concluded that without a restructuring of the State, an alternative economic strategy could not be carried out. In one sense his decision to create a Fascist movement was logical and an inevitable consequence of his line of thinking, even if he was blind to Fascism's inherent defects. Mosley's time would have come during the Second World War when the State carried out many of the measures he advocated. It would have been interesting to have seen how he would have dealt with Labour's post-war Fabian-style nationalization programme, which was at odds with his professed syndicalist ideas. Certainly, he would have attacked New Labour economics with the same ferocity as he did Philip Snowden, whose natural heir is Gordon Brown.

Skidelsky told Mosley 'that your actions in the 1930s cannot be meaningfully discussed except against the background of your hopes and ideals in the 1920s; and that if that context is borne competely in mind, your actions in the 1930s [forming the BUF] might not be ignobly viewed even by those who consider that you set the wrong course'. The Duke of Windsor believed Mosley had set the right course. On 24 January 1969 he wrote that he hoped to discuss with him 'some of your vital and telling criticisms of the disastrous policies pursued by British political leaders in the 1930s'. There was also the question of the 'possible release of poor Rudolf Hess. It seems incredible that such inhuman cruelty can still be inflicted upon a distinguished German who at least tried to stop that senseless Second World War, and save so much death and suffering.'

On 20 March King heard Mosley say that 'the drift towards the revolution that he tried to take charge of during the thirties has resumed. He maintains that everything points to the decay of our society . . . he sees himself in charge at last. This seems to me quite fantastic, but there is so little leadership of any kind these days that even the Powells and the Mosleys are not entirely incredible.' King's diaries were carefully written; Stephens reported that he had said Mosley was 'by far the cleverest politician of the 1930s. He just chose the wrong side during the war.' Asked if he would include him in his government, King replied, 'Why not? People have forgotten about his past.' King's wife,

Ruth Railton, thought Mosley had 'moments or periods when he is a compelling influence on others, of which he is afterwards unaware. So that when he protests that his movement was not a bullying, Jew-baiting one, he sincerely believes this and does not realise the character or misdeeds of some of his followers under his influence.'

In the autumn Mosley told King a crash was coming. He expected the Americans to pull out of Europe, leaving it in 'grave danger of serious disturbance', organized so as to give the Russians an excuse to intervene. 'He is still very much the professional soldier and confident he still has a part to play.' There seemed to be, Cudlipp wrote, 'a magnetic force that draws together in the barren twilight of their lives, in their loneliness and their final rejection, the Men of Destiny upon whom inadvertently or wisely destiny did not call'.

The teenage Ivor Mosley visited his grandfather and found him a disturbing but alluring figure. 'Like a man set in stone, a sculpture come to life, he would fix one with his beady eyes and then open them saucer-wide. I remember feeling a transient discomfort at this, as if I were the honoured victim of a bird of prey. Being in his company was like being on stage in a static drama whose meaning I could not fathom.' Mosley was not an easy object of affection, although James Lees-Milne thought he had 'changed from the bombastic pseudo-Mussolini to the calm, wise, elder statesman'. Bob Boothby, however, noted that 'at seventy-seven he is still waiting for the call'.

The oil crisis and other problems of the mid-seventies provided Mosley with the opportunity to restate old themes. Inflation would be cured by mass unemployment but the unemployed could be used to rebuild new public amenities. A government drawn from politics, business and the military would rescue the country from anarchy. Lord Londonderry wrote to him that the country was 'sleepwalking into a social revolution'. James Goldsmith had asked Londonderry if he wanted his son to grow up in a country 'where sewage flowing in the streets is accepted as normal'. He was off to 'convert more useless stocks into Krugerrands'. King's last letter to Mosley on 18 February 1977 warned that it was 'too late for GB to pull itself out of its decline. A takeover of Western Europe by the Russians seems to be just a matter of time.' He now saw Mosley as the 'one major political figure to have emerged since the First World War (Lloyd George and Churchill established reputations before 1918)'.

Mosley travelled intensively, delivered speeches, recorded radio programmes, appeared on television and slowly earned a reputation as a commentator on world affairs and the economy. When Lord Longford took him to lunch at the Gay Hussar, they found themselves next to Michael Foot. 'A pleasure to see you over here, Sir Oswald,' said Foot. A delighted Mosley told Longford, 'It couldn't happen anywhere but England. Two old political enemies fraternising like that.'

The UM was active on immigration but it was the National Front which cornered the issue. The UM took part in pro-European Community activities but John Tyndall maintained that 'European union has been the graveyard of every nationalist movement, both in Britain and on the continent – for the very good reason that it is incompatible with true nationalism, and has scarcely any popular appeal.' Attacks followed on Mosley with claims that Chesterton had deserted him because of his 'foreign' ideology. Mosley banned fraternization with other groups as Mosleyites turned on the Front. In turn, the shadowy League of St George, formed by militant former supporters of Mosley, was proscribed for Front members.

John Mosley, who retired after fifty years as a member of the Stock Exchange, died in 1973 but Mosley did not attend his brother's funeral. He was at Nancy Mitford's funeral in June, where the three sisters, Diana, Debo, Pam, filed past the coffin, 'their heads covered in scarves like black crows'. It was the first time Diana had seen Jessica since the 1930s. Despite Jessica's bitter attacks on Mosley, Diana was in a forgiving mood. Though less able to overlook the past, Jessica admitted 'it wasn't dreadful – we actually got along very well'.

The seventies were not a good period for Diana. She loved her husband but wrote to Nicholas of 'the harm he does to Aly and I suffer for it'. He was generous to guests and the servants but miserly with the family. His clothes were handmade but he gave little to Diana, who was expected to dress in Parisian haute couture. He sought a reconciliation with Baba Metcalfe and invited her to the Temple but her hatred of Diana had not diminished and it was not a success. Diana suffered with migraines and Mosley could be an 'angel', but his bitterness could also come to the surface.

When the new owner of Savehay informed Mosley that Cimmie's tomb had been vandalized, Mosley responded by claiming, 'It's the Jews!' A friend told John Parker that while Mosley could be 'his normal, charming, jovial self', at the end of one meal 'his eyes began to flare just as they did when he was screaming his hateful speeches before a mass rally or leading a march against the Jews in the East End. Then he would degenerate into a tirade against the Yids and niggers.' After journalist Paul Callan interviewed Mosley and pointed out that he was Jewish, Diana confided to a mutual friend that 'had I known I wouldn't have allowed it. He certainly didn't look Jewish – but, then, they are clever and come in all shapes.'

The high point in Mosley's rehabilitation was the publication in 1975 of Skidelsky's biography. He had sent chapters to Diana, who forwarded 'furious letters about his unfair approach to my idol. Quite undaunted, he went ahead and produced an excellent book.' Nicholas thought Skidelsky was 'starry-eyed' about his father. Skidelsky admitted his sympathies were for 'outsiders', whose great merit was 'that they were not only outsize in personality, but they straddled the ground between Right and Left'. A Labour supporter, he was attracted to Mosley as an advocate of 'heroic values' and admired 'his passion for ideas, his courage, and the fact that he cared so much about the decline of his country. I was loath to admit that he had a dark side.' Critics pointed out the 'inherent defects of character' but he eschewed psychological explanations.

Skidelsky developed the idea that Mosley was 'Labour's lost leader' but it is doubtful whether he could have led a democratic party. He wanted to command a political army, not make grubby political deals. A man whose colleagues admit he was a notoriously bad judge of events and character was unlikely to be a good leader in a party system that required compromise. He lacked the imagination to assess the impact on other people of his personality or his politics. He 'never stopped to consider why so few people accepted him at his own self-evaluation, as a man of destiny'. Mosley rejected the political system and preferred to go down fighting. He was not Skidelsky's 'authoritarian moderniser' but a Don Quixote, who retired into 'a fantasy world where many of his ideas lost contact with reality'.

Skidelsky criticized writers for lacking 'that indispensable quality of sympathy' but the controversy which the book aroused had to do with, he admitted, 'my unduly benign treatment of his later Fascist phase'. Skidelsky was accused of a 'whitewash' since Fascism stood condemned on its own record. He put forward the theory that Mosley had turned to anti-Semitism because the Jews made him do so. He had a 'real' quarrel with many Jews and his reasons were 'genuine': Jews heckled him and boycotted German goods and he had to respond. The Jews 'must take some of the blame for what happened'. Skidelsky claimed 'East End fascism was not the "socialism of fools", but the kind of radicalism which easily arises when the capitalist can be identified as foreign'. It was difficult to be fascinated, as Skidelsky seemed to be, by 'Mosley grappling with the problem of satisfying black African aspirations while retaining Africa within the framework of European political economy'. He conceded his arguments 'gave the impression of special pleading on Mosley's behalf' but it took time for him to change his view. On 23 November 1977 he told James Lees-Milne he had come to respect Mosley, who 'never hated the Jews: merely thought that international Jewry was a bad thing, and that East End Jews ought to be removed'. Lees-Milne asked, 'Where to?'

Mosley's reviews for *Books and Bookmen* and articles in the *Telegraph* magazine brought a degree of acceptance. By the time Diana published her vacuous memoirs, *A Life of Contrasts*, in 1977, he was frail with Parkinson's disease. Differences of opinion within the family had faded. Alexander had left politics behind and was a publisher in France. He treated his father's activities as a huge joke with 'a typical kind of Mitford attitude'. Max had been a prospective UM candidate in the sixties. 'If I had a completely open choice in my life, I would have chosen party politics,' he admitted. 'But because of my name, that's impossible.' He entered motor sport where no one cared about his surname, though on one occasion Baron Fritz von Kanstein, who had won the Mille Miglia in 1940 and had been an SS colonel, said to him 'it's nice to meet the son of a real politician'. Max established the March racing team and became president of the Fédération Internationale de l'Automobile, the sport's governing body. He decided his father would not have made a good dictator. 'He would have been better as a conventional politician. He was more of an ideas man.'

By spring 1980 it was clear that Mosley did not expect to live long. On 3 May James Lees-Milne dined at the Temple and found him greatly changed: 'Shapeless, bent, blotched cheeks, crooked nose, no moustache, and tiny eyes in place of those luminous, dilating orbs.' The eccentric Father Brocard Sewell, a former Distributist League and BUF member, saw him at a reception for the publication of Diana's biography of the Duchess of Windsor. Sewell published a literary review at Aylesford Priory, to where Captain Brian Donovan had retired in the fifties. 'I think he sensed that we would not meet again, for he was especially affectionate in his manner when I took my leave of him.' The same process happened with a number of old colleagues.

In the autumn Nicholas visited the Temple following an invitation from Diana and told his father that 'someone should write about you. People either think you are God or the devil, but what's interesting about you is the truth.' He asked if he could have his papers. The ever-loyal Diana claimed, 'Nicholas put on a great show of affection for the occasion; I suppose this was being "crafty".' Mosley decided to give him his papers. 'It was as if', Nicholas recalled, 'he knew as part of him had always known that if anything was to survive of what he had cared about it would be to do with efforts at truth.' Mosley had been saddened by the recent death of his brother Edward.

Sir Oswald Mosley died on 3 December 1980 aged eighty-four. Of the 200 people who attended the secular funeral at the Columbarium at Père Lachaise, only three were Fascist comrades. Diana, gaunt and thin, waited in the cold in the chapel of the crematorium for the ashes to cool. His sons read favourite passages from Swinburne and Goethe between the music. Hugh Purcell, making a BBC biography that turned into an obituary, recalled Fauré's 'In Paradisum' filling the chapel. A journalist next to him whispered: 'At least he hasn't been strung up by his heels!' Purcell thought 'this juxtaposition of high culture and low ugliness was typical of Mosley's life'. Two days later the ashes were scattered by the lake near the Temple.

The Times obituary said Mosley 'has no parallel in British public life, past or present . . . His rise to fame was as meteoric as his collapse . . . Impatience with the slow processes of democratic government combined with some inherent fault of character to send him off the rails. He went Fascist . . .' The press had difficulty finding anyone to defend him; only Bob Boothby stepped forward and delivered a tribute on the radio. Diana wrote to thank him on

12 December. 'It was perfect . . . He so often spoke of you and your brillance, he admired you, but it was much more than that, it was deep affection.' Diana's grief was overwhelming and it was thought she might commit suicide. She suffered a brain tumour which, oddly, helped her deal with the loss. She talked to Nicholas 'with extraordinary openness', perhaps hoping to 'liberate some of the complexities that she felt about my father, but then when this was done she would be able to revert to a more simple form of loyalty'. In her own autobiography 'she had kept hidden almost everything of significance for the sake of so-called loyalty'.

Nicholas's *Rules of the Game* was published in 1982. Diana said she did not read the second volume, *Beyond the Pale* (1983). 'I did not expect him to include the more personal material about his mother.' *The Times* critic said, 'He has emptied a bucket of mud over his father.' Diana hated the 'unrecognizable caricature' of Mosley, who 'would have deplored the vulgarity and the insensitivity, but have been amused by such a classic example of a son trying to reduce an extraordinary father to his own level'. She cruelly added, 'I am sure Freud would have an explanation. Not as talented as his father.' The biographies were eventually used as the basis of the mini-series *Mosley*, broadcast on Channel 4 in 1999. One of its Jewish writers, Maurice Gran, believed Mosley was 'redeemable politically until about 1934', which seems about three years too late. The anti-Fascist journalist, Frederic Mullally, who opposed Mosley in the thirties and forties, said the series 'portrays him as a glamorous, highly attractive, misunderstood idealist. Surely this is dangerous?' Diana complained that the portrayal of her husband as a philanderer was 'suburban'.

Long after Hitler's death the first lady of Fascism remained unrepentant. One day she expected there to be 'statues to Hitler and Goebbels in the capitals of Europe'. Appearing on BBC Radio Four's *Desert Island Discs* in November 1989, Diana was asked if Mosley was anti-Semitic. She said, 'He did not know a Jew from a gentile but was attacked so much by Jews both in the newspapers and physically on marches . . . that he picked up the challenge.' She did not regret her friendship with Hitler: 'I admired him very much. He had extremely mesmeric blue eyes and also he had so much to say. He was so interesting and fascinating, and perfectly willing to talk.' She still found it difficult to acknowledge that the Holocaust occurred. 'I don't really, I'm afraid, believe that six million people were killed. I think this is just not conceivable. It's too many.' To a friend she said, 'Awful, awful things happened on both sides in the war and we don't really know the truth.'

Every year Diana attended the dinner organized by the Friends of Mosley on his birthday, 16 November. The FoM had been set up to trace old BUF members and run an 'Old Comrades' association. The speeches expressed the view that 'OM was the greatest man this country has ever known or will ever know'. Diana remained an icon to the faithful. On her ninetieth birthday elderly BUF members travelled to Paris to raise a glass to her.

The Temple was sold to an American for £1 million and Diana went to live in an apartment in the rue de l'Université. She was interviewed for this book in 2000. The sun streamed through the window, highlighting her silver hair, as she sat perched, dressed in a beautifully cut two-piece suit, on a pale-blue and gilded settee like a petite bird, hands on knees, doll-like. A. N. Wilson said 'her face is a blank, sad stare, eerily still, like the brave composure of someone who has decided not to flinch in front of a firing squad'. Almost deaf, she studied the German documents brought to her with interest but dismissed them with an aside in the exaggerated vowels of the pre-war upper class: 'If it is in the documents, then it must be true.' In 2003 Diana suffered a mild stroke. On 11 August she died peacefully in her Paris apartment. 'Lady Mosley will go to hell when she dies,' thought Andrew Roberts. 'It strikes me that anyone who can say that she didn't know whether Hitler was in hell or heaven is quite likely to follow him down.'

The French specialist on the extreme Right, Pierre-André Taguieff, suggests that 'neither "fascism" nor "racism" will do us the favour of returning in such a way that we can recognise them easily'. Attempts to create a modern version of Mussolini's and Hitler's 'revolutionary nationalist' movements have failed – the horror of their misdeeds has been an unsurmountable barrier to their revival. Mosley's Europe a Nation and Euro-Africa ideas were doomed attempts to forge a new synthesis to break through that barrier. All that is left are fragmentary groups, which Martin Blinkhorn dismissed as 'too tiny to mention' and too small to mount a semi-legal 'conquest of power'. Fascist ideology has evolved, spurred on by the 'alleged threats of mass immigration, the homogenisation of Europe by the Euro and the globalisation of culture and economics'. Added to which has been the attack on the corruption of the political classes; another symptom of 'decadence'. Groups led by Jean-Marie Le Pen in France and Austria's Jorg Haider (and the British National Party) have had some success, but their most significant effect has been in turning conservative and social democratic parties to the right with their crackdown on immigrants and refugees, and the introduction of draconian law-and-order and anti-terrorism policies.

Is the twenty-first century safe from Fascism? In a new form and shape, an authoritarian regime led by a charismatic leader which scapegoats outsiders will find a mass audience. Just as in the pre-First World War period, ideas that we dismiss as mad are probably floating around the Internet ready to be synthesized into a destructive ideology. Historian Norman Cohn warned that there exists 'a subterranean world where pathological fantasies disguised as ideas are churned out by crooks and half-educated fanatics for the benefit of the ignorant and superstitious. There are times when this underworld emerges from the depths and suddenly captures and dominates multitudes of usually sane and responsible people, who thereupon take leave of sanity and responsibility.' Fortunately, it takes a cataclysmic event such as a world war to turn these fantasies into nightmares.

Mosley failed, but he was the forerunner for the kind of 'manipulative self' which, James Glass suggests, has come to be valued as 'a desirable paradigm' for a political leader. Pathological narcissists are the model for the 'successful, admired, tough and calculating' politician, who excels at 'manipulation and rational organising', no matter what the content or techniques used. He resists self-reflection and sees 'all forms of human encounter in the language of utility'. These prized values, adds Glass, have been 'translated into a popular ideal and dominate modern consciousness'.

He is certainly not a Fascist but New Labour's Tony Blair is an obvious example of the narcissist leader. 'He is in thrall to the idea of the strong leader,' according to biographer John Rentoul. A devourer of biographies of Lloyd George, Churchill and Cromwell, like Mosley he is transfixed by leaders who 'force the nation on to a new path by exercise of will'. The essence of his 'third way' was synthesis as an end in itself – a concept one commentator, unaware of Mosley, claimed he had 'never before seen advocated so openly in democratic politics. It is either breathtaking, or sinisterly Orwellian.' Political actors such as Blair – synthetic and lacking genuineness – are dangerous and suffer from hubris. They lead men to war.

On the death of Pim Fortuyn – killed in May 2002 by an animal rights activist – a letter writer in the *Telegraph*, Quentin Fox, noticed the similarity between the Dutch populist and Mosley, who 'exhibited the same restless intellectual voyaging as the former Marxist'. An academic, charming and a master of self-promotion, the homosexual Fortuyn was something of a dandy figure. Matthew Parris, himself homosexual, wrote that some gay men – believers in consumerism and economic individualism – are attracted to the populist Right, with its authoritarian streak. With his anti-establishment message, people believed Fortuyn was demanding the 'truth'. He synthesized ideas from a variety of sources, including the Left's concept of grass-roots democracy, social democratic views on social care, liberal ideas on taxation and an ultra-right hatred of foreigners. Fox believed that 'Fortuyn's arguments against the narrow-minded Islam preached by farmboy imams would have followed a similar trajectory [as Mosley in the 1930s] into simple hatred and "Paki-bashing"'. Here was the potential for 'pre-Fascism' of a kind Harold Nicolson had seen in the New Party and had wanted to dress in marigold shirts.

Aldous Huxley wrote in 1937 in *Ends and Means* that 'so long as men worship the Caesars and Napoleons, Caesars and Napoleons will duly arise and make them miserable'.

Selected Notes

The following notes are intended for the general reader. While every fact and quote has been meticulously sourced, the notes are not a catalogue of each point, more a selection of the relevant and most important sources. Books referred to by the author are listed in the Bibliography. References to Oswald Mosley, A. K. Chesterton, Colin Cross, Robert Skidelsky and Nicholas Mosley are made where they do not refer to Mosley's autobiography or to their biographies of Mosley. The full set of detailed notes with appendices and a collection of documents on Mosley can be accessed on the author's website – www.rogerdog.demon.co.uk.

Chapter One: 'Tommy'

Background: Maud Mosley diary, Mosley deposit, Birmingham University (BU); interviews with Diana Mosley, Paris; Mosley interview with Peter Liddle, 1977; Drennan; Hamilton Fyfe, *Sixty Years of Fleet Street*, 1949; Forwood letter.

Manchester: Bill Williams, 'The Anti-Semitism of Tolerance: Middle-Class Manchester and the Jews 1870–1900', in Alan Kidd and K. W. Roberts (eds), *City, Class and Culture: Studies of social policy and cultural production in Victorian Manchester*, 1985; Alan Kidd, Manchester, Ryburn.

Psychology: Lasch; Chodorow; Peter Gay, *Freud for Historians*, 1985; W. F. Mandle, 'Psychology and History', *NZ Journal of History*, 2, 1968; Peter Davison (ed.), *George Orwell: Facing Unpleasant Facts 1937–39*, 2000; Ellen Cameron, *An Introduction to Graphology*, 1989.

Education: www.westdowns.com. Information from Daniel Hodson, Simon Mosley and John Mosley; Peter Parker, *The Old Lie: The Great War and the Public-School Ethos*, 1987; Denis Richard, *Portal of Hungerford: The Life of Marshal of the Royal Air Force Viscount Portal of Hungerford*, 1977; Sir Robert Bruce Lockhart, *Your England*, 1955.

Chapter Two: The First World War

Air War: Wohl; Liddle, op. cit. and *The Airmen's War 1914–18*, 1987; Michael Paris, 'The Rise of the Airmen, *c*. 1890–1918', *JCH*, 28, 1993; Mark Girouard, *The Return to Camelot: Chivalry and the English Gentleman*, 1981; Nigel Steel and Peter Hart, *Tumult in the Clouds: The British Experience of the War in the Air 1914–1918*, 1997; Colin Cook, 'A fascist memory: Oswald Mosley and the myth of the airman', *ERH*, 4, 2, 1997; Arthur Marwick, *The Deluge: British Society and the First World War*, 1965.

Military record/action: Colonel Henry Graham, *History of the Sixteenth, The Queen's Light Dragoons, 1912 to 1925*, 1926; Mosley's RFC records WO 339/15781; Tyrrel Hawker, *Hawker, VC*, Mitre Press; Stewart, *'Occuli Exercitus': No. 6 Squadron, RAF*, 1963, James McWilliams and R. James Steel, *Gas! The Battle for Ypres, 1915*, 1985; Ulrich Trumpener, 'The Road to Ypres: The Beginning of Gas Warfare in WWI', *JMH*, 47, September 1975; Lieutenant-Colonel L. A. Strange, *Recollections of an Airman*, 1989.

Reading: Liddle, op. cit.; White; Bishop; Higginbottom; Reilly, *Pitt the Younger 1759–1806*, 1978; Robert Blake, *Disraeli*; Prion; H. Edwards; Anthony Harrison, *Swinburne's Medievalism: A Study in Victorian Love Poetry*, 1979; James Webb, *The Flight from Reason: The Age of the Irrational*, 1980; Lachman; Roger Griffin, *The fascist quest to regenerate time*, 1998; Thurlow, 'The Return of Jeremiah', in Lunn/Thurlow.

Economy/MoM/FO: Ritschell; Stevenson, *British Society 1914–45*; Newton/Porter; Davenport-Hines; Marrison; Steel/Hart; Thurlow, 'Secret; Mosley: From Empire to Europe', *20th-C.S*, 1, March 1969.

War's end: Malcolm Brown, *The Imperial War Museum Book of 1918: Year of Victory*, 1999; Osbert Sitwell, *Laughter in the Next Room*, 1976; Siegfried Sassoon, *Diaries, 1915–1918*, 1983; Bellamy; Sternhell.

Chapter Three: The Patriotic Peace

Election/Social Imperialism: Mosley, 'From Tory to Labour', *Labour Magazine*, May 1929 and interview, *Huddersfield Examiner*, 4.8.75; Gamble; Searle; Semmel; Skidelsky, *Interests*; Walter L. Arnstein, *Edwardian Politics: Turbulent Spring or Indian Summer?*; Daniel Deudney, 'Greater Britain or Greater Synthesis? Seeley, Mackinder and Wells on Britain in the global industrial era', *RIS*, 2, April 2001; Geroid Tuathail, 'Putting Mackinder in his Place: Material Transformation and Myth', *PG*, 11, January 1992; Geoff Eley, 'Defining Social Imperialism: Use and Abuse of an Idea', *SH*, 2, May 1976; Gisela Lebzelter, *Anti-Semitism: a Focal Point for the British Radical Right*; Kennedy/Nicholls.

Croft: Witherell; William D. Rubenstein, 'Henry Page Croft and the Nationalist Party 1917–22', *JCH*, 9, 1.

Economy/parliament: Mark Thomas, 'An Input-Output Approach to the British

Economy, 1890–1914', *JEH*, 45, 1985; A. P. Thornton, *The Habit of Authority: Paternalism in British History*, 1966; Thurlow; K. Morgan; White; Cook, op. cit.

Social life/Astors: Cartland; John Grigg, *Nancy Astor: Portrait of a Pioneer*, 1980; Pugh, *Women*; N. Nicolson; Leonard Mosley, *Curzon: The End of an Epoch*, 1960; Marchioness Curzon of Kedleston, *Reminiscences*, 1960; Hugh David, *Heroes, Mavericks and Bounders*, 1991.

MP: Mosley, *From Tory . . .* op. cit.; Campbell, *Smith*; Skidelsky, *Interests*; K. Morgan; Sir Colin Coote, *Editorial: The Memoirs of Colin R. Coote*, 1965; Seymour-Ure.

Finances: Ingham; Newton/Porter; N. Nicolson; Ravensdale; de Courcy; *Derby Evening Telegraph*, 21.2.98.

Psychology: James Glass, 'Hobbes and Narcissism: Pathology in the State of Nature', *PT*, 8, August 1980; H. Rosenfeld, 'On the Psychopathology of Narcissism', *IJP*, 45, 1964.

Chapter Four: 'The Vision Splendid'

Ireland/government/election: K. Morgan; Martel; Margaret FitzHerbert, *The Man Who Was Greenmantle: A Biography of Aubrey Herbert*, 1983; Boyce, quoting Hammond MSS; Benewick; L. Mosley; Lord Beaverbrook, *Decline and Fall of Lloyd George*, 1960; Ravensdale; Mary Soames (ed.), *Speaking for Themselves: The Personal Letters of Winston and Clementine Churchill*, 1998; Pugh, *Women*.

Foreign Policy: *The Letters and Papers of Chaim Weizmann*, 11; Thurlow; Bellamy.

Politics: McKibben; Skidelsky, *Slump*; White; Brendon.

Labour contacts: Webb diary; Kramnick/Sheerman; Ridley.

Social life: Trzebinski; Green; William McBrien, *Cole Porter*, 1998; Artemis Cooper (ed.), *A Durable Fire: The Letters of Duff and Diana Cooper 1913–1950*, 1983; Letter, Robert Rhodes James; Barbara Cartland, *Daily Telegraph*, 27.6.98.

Chapter Five: The Underworld of Rejected Knowledge

Orage/syndicalism/guild socialism: S. Glass; Taylor, *Orage*; Steele; Finlay; Redman; Cornford; Sternhell; Holton; Webb; Booth/Pack; Thurlow and 'Return'; Townshend; Marcel van der Linden, 'Second thoughts on revolutionary syndicalism', *LHR*, 63, 2, 1998; Richard Price, 'Contextualising British Syndicalism *c.* 1907–*c.*1920', *LHR*, 63, 3, 1998; A. W. Wright, 'Fabianism and Guild Socialism', *IRSH*, 1978.

Fascist origins: H. Edwards; Sternhell; Normand; Roberts; Roger Eatwell, 'On Defining the "Fascist Minimum": The Centrality of Ideology', *JPI*, 1996.

Hulme/Lewis/Sorel: Robert Ferguson, *The Short, Sharp Life of T. E. Hulme*, 2003; Meyers; Jameson; Edward Shils, *Georges Sorel: Reflections on Violence*, Macmillan, 1961.

Anti-Semitism: Cheyette and 'Jewish stereotyping and English literature 1875–1920:

Towards a political analysis', in Kushner/Lunn; Holmes, *Anti-Semitism*; Feldman; Claire Hirschfield, 'The British Left and the "Jewish Conspiracy": A Case Study of Modern Antisemitism', *JSS*, 1981; Lebzelter.

ILP: Booth/Pack; Hollis; Pimlott; Townshend; Newman; Ritschell; Skidelsky, *Interests*; Boyce; F. Beckett; Neal Wood, *Communism and British Intellectuals*, 1959; Adrian Oldfield, 'Independent Labour Party and Planning, 1920–26', *IRSH*, 21, 1976, and 'The growth of the concept of economic planning in the doctrine of the British Labour Party, 1914–1935', Ph.D. thesis, 1973.

Chapter Six: The Labour Party

Labour Party reception: Scanlon; Wertheimer; Cline; Brockway; Boyce; F. Beckett; Webb diary; Brewer.

Birmingham: J. Johnson, 'Birmingham Labour and the New Party', April 1931; David Dilks, *Neville Chamberlain: Pioneering and Reform, 1869–1929*, 1984.

Strachey/Labour: Dowse; Brockway; Pimlott; Thompson; Thomas; Newman; Strachey, 'The Education of a Communist', *Left Review*, December 1934; Stuart Macintyre, 'John Strachey 1901–1931: The Making of an English Marxist', MA thesis, 1971; Martin Pugh, 'Women & Class traitors: Conservative recruits to Labour, 1900–30', *EHR*, February 1998; Wood; Stuart Rawnsley, *Fascism and Fascists in Britain*, Bradford, 1983.

Shaw: Mosley, *Revolution by Reason*, 1925; Bentley; Holroyd; Brian Holden Reid, 'Impressions of Mosley', 25.8.77; Aschheim, op. cit.; Hayes; Desmond MacCarthy, *Shaw: The Plays*, 1951.

Revolution by Reason/Strachey: Skidelsky, *Slump* and *Keynes*; Oldfield, op. cit.; Pimlott and *Labour*; Dowse; Newton/Porter; Ritschell; Rawnsley, Ph.D. thesis; Thurlow and 'Return'; Thompson; Macintyre, op. cit.; Newman; Thomas; Ingham; Wood; Wertheimer; Lebzelter; Mark Burrows, 'The left-wing road to Fascism: An investigation of the influence of left-wing ideas upon the political ideology of the BUF', Ph.D. thesis, 1999; Rawnsley, Ph.D.

Social: Bowra; Amabel Williams-Ellis, *All Stracheys are Cousins*, 1983; Robert Boothby, *I Fight to Live*, 1947; Thomas.

USA: Boyce; White; Charles S. Maier, 'Between Taylorism and Technocracy: European ideologies and the vision of industrial productivity in the 1920s', *JCH*, 5, 2, 1970; Ray Batchelor, *Henry Ford: Mass Production, Modernism and Design*, 1994; BBC Radio 3, *Personality and Power*, October 1970; Letters, Roosevelt archive, Washington.

High wages/policy debate/social credit: Ritschell; Boyce; Paton; Brockway, *Tomorrow*; Oldfield, op. cit.; Booth/Pack; Dowse; Wood; Webb diary; Donoughue/Jones; Snowden; J. Johnson, op. cit.; Finlay; Webb; Macintyre, op. cit.; Thompson.

Chapter Seven: 'The Coming Figure'

Views of Mosley: Webb diary; Snowden, II; Lord Elton, *Among Others*, 1938; Ellen Wilkinson, *Peeps at Politicians*, 1930.

Personality: Glass, *Hobbes*, op. cit.; Amabel Williams-Ellis, *The Wall of Glass*, 1927; Skidelsky, *Keynes*; Cannadine.

Labour: Thomas; Cline; Pimlott; Marquand; White; Wertheimer; F. Beckett; McKibben; Paton.

Social life: Gottlieb; de Courcy; Philip Ziegler, *Osbert Sitwell*, 1998; Bradford, *Sachie*; Philip Hoare, *Serious Pleasures*; Hugo Vickers, *Cecil Beaton: The Authorised Autobiography*, 1985; Michael Luke, *David Tennant and the Gargoyle Years*, 1991; Joan Wyndham, *Daily Telegraph*, 6.7.98; Anne Chisholm, *Nancy Cunard: A Biography*, 1981; C. Mosley; Holroyd, *Shaw*; James; Lees-Milne, *Nicolson*; N. Nicolson.

Reactions to Mosley: Taylor, *Beaverbrook*; Pimlott, *Dalton*; Marquand, *MacDonald*; Wertheimer; Laybourn; Skidelsky, *Keynes* and *Interests*; Kenneth Young, *Churchill and Beaverbrook: A Study in Friendship and Politics*, 1966; Webb diary; Kramnick/Sheerman; 'Janitor', *The Feet of the Young Men: Some Candid Comments on the Rising Generation*, 1928.

Cole: Neil Riddell, '"The Age of Cole?" G. D. H. Cole and the British Labour Movement 1929–1933', *HJ*, 38, 4, 1995; Skidelsky, *Slump* and *Interests*; Newton/Porter.

Election: Brewer; Wertheimer; Johnson, op. cit.; Pugh, *Women*; Anthony Sampson, *Macmillan: A Study in Ambiguity*, 1967.

Chapter Eight: 'A Young Man in a Hurry'

Office: Kingsley Martin, *Harold Laski*, 1953; K. Young; M. A. Hamilton, *Remembering My Good Friends*, 1944; Farr; Catlin; Skidelsky, *Slump*; Boyce; Marquand; K. Harris; Shinwell; Shepherd; F. Beckett; Brockway, *Tomorrow*.

Snowden and colleagues: Melville, *The Truth about the New Party*, 1932; Smart; Catlin; Laybourn; Skidelsky, *Slump*; Riddell, op. cit.; Addison; K. Young; Thomas Johnston, *Memories*, 1946; Lansbury, *My England*, 1934; Cline; Raymond Postgate, *The Life of George Lansbury*, 1951; T. Jones and Webb diaries.

Beaverbrook/Bevan/Lee: Taylor, *Beaverbrook*; Ball; Clark; Addison; A. L. Rowse, *Notebook*, 1995; Campbell, *Bevan*; Hollis; Lee; *A Kind of Exile*, ITV, 1970.

Cimmie: Skidelsky and *Slump*; Webb diary; *Lobster* 42.

Protectionism/Young Tories: MacDonald papers; Skidelsky, *Slump*; Boyce; Taylor, *Beaverbrook*; Marrison; W. R. Garside, 'Party Politics, Political Economy and British Protectionism, 1919–1932', *BU*, 83, January 1998; Newton/Porter; Ritschell; Davenport-Hines; R. Boothby et al, *Industry and the State*, 1927; Ball; Seymour-Ure; Clark.

Internal debate: Nicolson diary; Melville, *NP*; W. F. Mandle, 'Sir Oswald Mosley's

Resignation from the Labour Government', *HS*, 10, May 1963; Macintyre; Skidelsky, *Slump*; Ritschell; Marquand, *Cabinet minutes*; G. C. Peden, 'The "Treasury View" on Public Works and Employment in the Interwar Period', *EHR*, May 1984; *Sunday Telegraph*, 3.8.69; Donoughue/Jones.

MacDonald/Snowden/lack of action: Thomson; MacDonald diary and Thomas papers; Snowden, II; Skidelsky, *Keynes*; Thomson.

Cabinet meetings: Nicolson, T. Jones and MacDonald diaries.

Beckett: F. Beckett and 'The Rebel Who Lost His Cause', *History Today*, May 1994; James.

Resignation: Melville, *NP* and 'Political Upheaval: Sir Oswald Mosley', *Fortnightly Review*, May 1931; Marquand; Webb and Strauss diaries; Catlin; K. Young; Mandle, 'Resignation'; Brewer; Skidelsky, *Slump*; Shinwell; Ravensdale.

Chapter Nine: 'After Baldwin and MacDonald Comes . . . ?'

Resignation speech: Ritschell; Skidelsky, *Slump*; Mandle, 'Resignation'; Webb and MacDonald diaries; Marquand.

Backbencher: George Catlin, 'Fascist Stirrings in Britain', *Current History*, February 1934; Thomas.

Churchill/Young Tories: Addison; K. Young; Stewart; Taylor, *Beaverbrook*; Nicolson diary; E. H. H. Green, 'The Case of Arthur Steel-Maitland', in E. Green.

MacDonald affair: Laybourn; Marquand, *MacDonald*; Stephen Roskill, *Hankey: Man of Secrets, 1931–63*, 1974; Michael Quill interview.

William Morris: Adeney and *The Motor Makers: The Turbulent History of Britain's Car Industry*, 1988; Boyce; Overy; Ingham; K. Young; Headlam.

Llandudno: Brewer; Marquand, *MacDonald*; Catlin; W. F. Mandle, 'Sir Oswald Leaves the Labour Party, March 1931', *AJLH*, 12, May 1967; Foot; Brockway, *Left*.

New Labour/bitterness: Marcus Collins, 'The New Party 1931–2', thesis, 1992; Brockway, *Tomorrow*; Campbell, *Bevan*; Pugh, *Women*; Hollis; Mandle, 'Leaves'; Skidelsky, *Interests*, *Keynes* and *Slump*; Bullock; Marquand, *MacDonald*; Brown; Laybourn.

Allen: Boothby; Mandle, 'Leaves'; *The Times*, 21.9.73; Drennan; Thurlow; F. Beckett; T. Jones diary.

Young Tories/Labour conflict: Mandle, 'Leaves'; Colin Coote, *The Other Club*, 1972; Nicolson diary; Hugh Dalton, *Political Diary*, 1986.

Mosley manifesto/reaction: Davenport-Hines; Ball; Ritschell; Webb/Passfield papers; Skidelsky, *Slump* and *Keynes*; Nicolson diary; Mandle, 'Leaves'; Lees-Milne, *Nicolson*.

Planning: Ritschell; D. Winch, *Economics and Policy*; Marwick; G. D. H. Cole, *Principles of Planning*, 1935; Mandle, 'Leaves'; T. Jones diary.

Boothby: *Queen's Quarterly*, January 1931; Boothby to Mosley, 30.1.31; James.

Speech: Weir; Mandle, 'Leaves'; Nicolson diary.

Chapter Ten: The New Party

Wells: Wells Archive, University of Illinois Library; Coupland; Wells, op. cit.; *The Autocracy of Mr Pelham*; Catlin; Bishop.

Beginnings: Barry diary; Joad, 'Prolegomena to Fascism', *Political Quarterly*, 1931; Foot; Brockway, *Tomorrow*; Brittain/Holtby; Brown; Ritschell; Catlin, *History*, op. cit.; M. Collins, op. cit.; Taylor, *Beaverbrook*.

Desertion/reaction: Foot; Jennie Lee, *Tomorrow is a New Day*, 1939; Benewick; Williams-Ellis, *Stracheys*; Webb diary; Seymour-Ure; Clark.

A National Policy: Thomas; Gamble; Newman; Brewer.

Lewis/Nazis: O'Keeffe; Meyers; Sternhell; Normand; Brigitte Granzow, *A Mirror of Nazism: British Opinion and the Emergence of Hitler 1929–1933*, 1964.

Ashton: Brewer; J. Johnson, 'Birmingham Labour and the New Party', April 1931; BBC WA, PP Eckersley papers; W. F. Mandle, 'The New Party', *HS*, 12, October 1966; HO 283 series; Melville, *NP*; M. Collins, op. cit.; J. Jones; Hodge; Nicolson diary.

Result: Strachey, *Fascism*; Lewis; Thomas; Shinwell in Skidelsky; Taylor, *Beaverbrook*; Ball.

Stewarding/Howard: Joad, op. cit.; Dave Renton, *Red Shirts and Black: Fascists and Anti-Fascists in Oxford in the 1930s*, 1996; Michael Davie (ed.), *The Diaries of Evelyn Waugh*, 1995; Nicolson diary; M. Collins, op. cit.; Lees-Milne, *Nicolson*; Anne Gordon letter.

Debates: Melville, *NP*; J. Jones; Hodge; Farr; Nicolson diary.

Fencing/Beaumont/Cheyney: Sitwell diary; Richard Cohen, 'Charles-Louis de Beaumont: A short biography', in Edmund Gray, *Modern British Fencing*, Amateur Fencing Association, 1984; Farr, op. cit.; Gordon; Michael Harrison, *Peter Cheyney: Prince of Hokum*, 1955; Information from Julian Petkowski; Nicolson diary.

Morris/Duke: Adeney, *Nuffield*; Nicolson diary; Lewis; Lees-Milne, *Nicolson*.

'National Government': Martel; Brendon; Nicolson diary; Charles Edward Lysaght, *Brendan Bracken*, 1979; Addison; Stewart; John Charnley, *Churchill: The end of glory*, 1993.

Sitwells/culture: Green; John Pearson, *Façades: Edith, Osbert and Sacheverell Sitwell*, 1989; Wohl, *1914*; Blanch; Haynes; Meyers; Steele.

Crisis: Addison; Hollis; Bishop; Nicolson diary; Farr, op. cit.; Holroyd; K. Young; Brian Roberts, *Randolph: A Study of Churchill's Son*, 1984.

Bankers/economy: Leopold Amery, *My Political Life: The Unforgiving Years, 1929–40*, 1955; Skidelsky, *Keynes*.

Meetings: Smart; Nicolson diary and notes; Ritschell; Hodge.

Action: Seymour-Ure; Koss; Green; Samuel Hynes, *The Auden Generation: Literature and Politics in England in the 1930s*, 1976.

Election: Charles Stuart, *The Reith Diaries*, 1975; Nicolson diary; Hodge; Gordon; Jacobs; David Turner, *Fascism and anti-Fascism in the Medway Towns 1927–1940*, 1993; Berry/Bishop.

Violence: Harrison, *Cheyney*; J. Jones; Lees-Milne, *Self*; Smart; Stevenson/Cook; Nicolson diary; Brewer; M. Collins, op. cit.

Chapter Eleven: The New Movement

NUPA: F. Beckett; John Beckett, 'Why I joined the New Party: The New Party and the Old Toryism', *NP*, 1931; 'Mosley – Right or Wrong?', 1961; Hodge; Melville, *NP*; M. Collins, op. cit.; Nicolson diary; K. Young.

Mussolini/Italy: Brendon; R. J. B. Bosworth, 'The British Press, the Conservatives and Mussolini, 1920–34', *JCH*, 5, 2, 1970; K. Young; de Grand.

Nazis: James; N. Nicolson, *Vita*; Lees-Milne, *Nicolson*; Lebzelter; Tony Kushner, *Politics of Marginality*.

Jewish members: Sylvester letter; BBC Radio 4, *Start the Week*, 9.2.98; Lewis Morton, *Ted Kid Lewis: His Life and Times*, 1990.

Radical Right/National Party: Thurlow; G. R. Searle, 'Critics of Edwardian Society: The Case of the Radical Right', and 'The "Revolt from the Right" in Edwardian Britain', in Kennedy/Nicholls; Barbara Lee Farr, 'The Development and Impact of Right-wing Politics in England 1903–32', Ph.D thesis, 1976; John Hope, 'Fascism and the State in Britain: The Case of the British Fascists 1923–31', *AJPH*, 39, 3, 1993; Chris Wrigley, '"In the Excess of their Patriotism": The National Party and Threats of Subversion', in Wrigley, *Warfare, Diplomacy and Politics: Essays in Honour of A. J. P. Taylor*, 1986; Steven Ascheim, 'Nietzschean Socialism: Left and Right, 1890–1933', *JCH*, Vol. 23, 1988; Rubenstein, op. cit.; Henry Page Croft, *My Life and Before*, 1949.

Drummond: Richard Usborne, *Clubland Heroes: A nostalgic study of some recurrent characters in the romantic fiction of Dornford Yates, John Buchan and Sapper*, 1983.

The BF: Markku Ruotsila, 'The Antisemitism of the Eighth Duke of Northumberland's the *Patriot*, 1922–1930', *JCH*, 39, 1, 2004; Richard Gilman, *Behind World Revolution: The Strange Career of Nesta H. Webster*, 1982; Douglas; Alfio Bernabei letter; HO 45 series; Catlin, *Fascist Stirrings*, op. cit.

Ball/Makgill: John Ferris and U Bar-Joseph, 'Getting Marlowe to hold his tongue: The Conservative Party, the Intelligence Services and the Zinoviev Letter', *INS*, 8, October 1993; Gill Bennett, '"A most extraordinary and mysterious business": The Zinoviev Letter of 1924', *History Notes*, February 1999.

Hughes/Knight: Ron Bean, *Liverpool shipping employers and the anti-communist activities of J. M. Hughes, 1920–25*, 1977; John Hope, 'Fascism, The Security Service and the curious careers of Maxwell Knight and James McGuirk Hughes', *Lobster* 22 and 'British Fascism and the State, 1917–27: A Re-examination of the Documentary Evidence', *LHR*, 57, 3, 1992, and 'Surveillance or Collusion? Maxwell Knight, MI5 and the British Fascisti', *INS*, 9, October 1994; HO 283 series; D. Turner letter.

Joyce: Selwyn; KV 2/245 and HO 283 series; Martland; Cole; Kenny; Bryan Clough,

'State Secrets: The Wolkoff Files', www.state-secrets.com; West; Cole; Benewick; Selwyn; Joyce, *Twilight over England*, Berlin, 1941.

Allen: Benewick; Cabinet records; Douglas.

National Fascisti: '"Investigator", The Fascist Movement in Great Britain', SR Investigations, February 1926; Thurlow; J. Wheelwright, Pol/Marg; Benewick.

Barnes: Information from Alfio Bernabie; Farr, op. cit.; Benewick; James Strachey Barnes, *Half a Life Left*, 1937; Griffin; Bianchi.

Diana: D. Mosley, *Loved*; Dalley; de Courcy; Guinness; C. Mosley; Lovell; Lees-Milne, *Independent*, 13 August 2003.

Nicolson/Howard: Gordon; Eckersley.

IFL: Holmes; Arnold Leese, *Out of Step: Events in the Two Lives of an Anti-Jewish Camel Doctor*, 1946; Benewick; Catlin; Lebzelter; Thurlow; HO 45 series.

BFs: HO 144 and 283 series; G. C. Webber, *Intolerance and discretion: Conservatives and British fascism, 1918–1926*; Benewick; Thurlow; Lewis; Nicolson letters; Farr, op. cit.

ILP: R. P. Dutt, *Fascism and Social Revolution*, 1935; Ellen Wilkinson and Edward Conze, *Why Fascism?*, *c.* 1934; Philip M. Coupland, '"Left-wing Fascism" in Theory and Practice: The case of the British Union of Fascists', *20thCBH*, 13, 1, 2002; Philip Rees, *Changing interpretation of British Fascism: A Bibliographical Survey*; Burrows, op. cit.; W. Risdon, 'The Heritage of National Socialism', *BU Quarterly*, 1937, and 'Can a Marxist Become a Fascist?', *Action*, 10.4.37.

Churchill: Winston S. Churchill, *His Father's Son: The Life of Randolph Churchill*, 1996; Smart; Stewart; Mack Smith; Cannadine; Bosworth.

NO/Greater Britain/anti-Semitism: M. Collins, op. cit.; Nicolson letters; Linehan; Claire Hirchfield, 'The British Left and the "Jewish Conspiracy": A Case Study of Modern Antisemitism', *JSS*, Spring 1981; Colin Holmes, 'J. A. Hobson and the Jews', in Holmes (ed.), *Immigrants and Minorities in British Society*, 1978, and *Anti-Semitism*; Skidelsky, *Interests*; HO 283 series; Cheyette and *Politics of Marginality*, and 'Hilaire Belloc and the "Marconi Scandal" 1900–1914: A Re-assessment of the interactionist model of racial hatred', in Kushner/Lunn, *Politics of Marginality*; Melville, *NP*; Sternhell; Mandle, 'Anti-semitism'; D. Turner, op. cit.

Grandi: Mack Smith; Italian FO records St Antony's (NA GFM 36/141); Philip Coupland, 'H. G. Wells's "Liberal Fascism"', *JCH*, 35, 4, 2000.

Sieff/PEP: de Courcy; Ravensdale; Ritschell; Israel Sieff, *Memoirs*, 1970; Marcus Sieff, *Don't Ask the Price: The Memoirs of the President of Marks & Sparks*, 1986; Newton/Porter; Booth/Pack.

NP/BUF: Information from John Hope; Jordan manuscript, *c.* 1933–4, MSS127; 'Robert Richards', 'Geordie Recollections 1932–39'; *Comrade*, May–July 1994.

Assessment: K. Young; Taylor, *History*; *The Thirties in Britain: The Threat of Fascism*, BBC Third Programme, 10.11.65; Harold Macmillan, *Past Masters*; Bruce Coleman, 'The Conservative Party and the Frustration of the Extreme Right', in Andrew Thorne (ed.), *The failure of Political Extremism in inter-war Britain*, Exeter Studies in History, No. 21, 1989; Thurlow, *Failure*; Julian

Critchley, *A Bag of Boiled Sweets*, 1994; BBC 2, *A Fall Like Lucifer*, 1975; Leo Amery, *My Political Life, 1929–40*, 1955.

Chapter Twelve: The British Union of Fascists

Corporate State: W. Warren Wagar, 'The Steel-Gray Saviour: Technocracy as Utopia and Ideology', *AF*, 2, 2, 1979; Philip M. Coupland, 'The Blackshirted Utopians', *JCH*, April 1998; Mosley, *GB*; Ritschell; Pimlott; Rees; Nugent; Lewis.

Italy: Martel; Earl of Portsmouth, *A Knot of Roots*, 1965; D. Mosley, *Loved*.

Anti-Semitism: Mandle, 'Anti-semitism'; de Courcy.

Wells/Shaw: Kingsley Martin, *NS*, 29.10.32; Robert Row, 'Sir Oswald Mosley', *JHR*, 1984; Holroyd; Cheyette.

Violence/NUWM: Benewick, 'The Threshold of Violence', in R. Benewick and T. Smith (eds), *Direct Action and Democratic Politics*, 1972; 'The struggle against Fascism in the thirties', *NELHB*, 18, 1984; Alexander Miles, 'The Streets are still: Mosley', in Mosley, *c.* 1937; John Stevenson, 'The Politics of Violence', in Peele/Cook and 'The State and Public Order during the 1930s'; Thurlow; Hollis; R. Hayburn, 'The National Unemployed Workers Movement, 1921–36', *IRSH*, 23, 1983; McKibben.

Diana: de Courcy; Guinness; Gottlieb; Dalley; D. Mosley, *Loved*; C. Mosley; Pryce-Jones; Lovell.

Roosevelt: Letters, Franklin D. Roosevelt Library.

FUBW/Women: Coupland, 'Left-wing fascism'; William Parsons, 'What was FUBW?', *Comrade*, June–August 1991; Martin Durham in *Politics of Marginality*; Leighton; Gottlieb; George Orwell, *The Road to Wigan Pier*, 1937.

Macho/membership: Silke Hesse, 'Fascism and the Hypertrophy of Male Adolescence', in Milfull (ed.), *The Attraction of Fascism*, 1990; John Brewer, 'The BUF: Some Tentative Conclusions on its Membership', in Stein Uglvik Larsen, Bernt Hagtvet, Jan Petter Myklebust (eds), *Who were the Fascists?: Social Roots of European Fascism*, University of Bergen; Stevenson/Cook.

Violence: Benewick; Skidelsky, *Reflect* and *Interests*; Stephen Cullen, 'Political Violence: The Case of the British Union of Fascists', *JCH*, 28, 2, 1993; Stuart Rawnsley, *Fascism and Fascists in Britain in the 1930s*, Bradford, 1983; Barrett; Margaret Mullins, 'The Left and Fascism in the East End of London, 1932–39', Ph.D. thesis, 1985; John Hope, 'Blackshirts, Knuckle-dusters and Lawyers', Documentary essay on the Mosley versus Marchbanks papers; Arthur Bevan, *Mosley Black shirts*; Phillpott, May 1933, MSS 292.

Jews: Griffiths, *Right*; Sybille Bedford, *Aldous Huxley: A Biography*, 1993; Tony Kushner, 'Asylum or servitude? Refugee domestics in Britain, 1933–45', *BSSLH*, 53, 3, Winter 1988.

CP: Laybourn/Murphy; Rawnsley, *BUF* and *Fascism*; Neil Barrett, *The anti-fascist movement in south-east Lancashire, 1933–1940*.

Italy/anti-Semitism: Emilio Gentile, 'Impending Modernity: Fascism and the Ambivalent Image of the United States', *JCH*, 28, 1993; Ledeen and Ledeen, 'Fascismo

Universale: The Theory and Practice of the Fascist International 1928–1936', Ph.D. thesis, 1969; Ravensdale; Griffin; Annalisa Capristo, 'The Exclusion of Jews from the Academy of Italy', *Israel Monthly Review*, March 2002; Lebzelter; Fredericks MSS 292; Celli: *Army records*, Fort Meade; N. Mosley archive, BU; Letters Dorothy Dundas and John Warburton; Bernabie; Beverley Nichols, *A Thatched Roof*, 1933; Bianchi, op. cit.; Mack Smith; W. E. D. Allen, 'The Fascist idea in Britain', *Quarterly Review*, October 1933.

CAUR: Ledeen; Payne; Asvero Gravelli (ed.), *Il Fascismo Inglese*, 1934; Mosley, 'Le Ripercussioni del Patto a Quattro in Inghilterra', *Gerarchi*, 13, 1933.

Chapter Thirteen: Universal Fascism

Ward Price; Cudlipp; Bourne; Taylor, *Beaverbrook*; K. Young.

Grandi/funds: Archivo Vitetti; Renzo de Felice, *Mussolini il duce: 1. Gli anni del consenso 1929–1936*, 1981; Italian FO and Ministry of Popular Culture T-586 series; *Focal Point*, 30.10.81; HO 283 and 45 series.

Black House: Catlin; HO 144 series; Charnley; Miles, op. cit.; D. Mosley interview; Benewick; Bevan, *Mosley Black shirts*.

Recruits: W. F. Mandle, 'The Leadership of the British Union of Fascists', *JPH*, 12, 3, December 1966; Bellamy; R. M. White, 'Some Features of the Development of Fascism in England', *Communist International*, 10, October 1933; Coupland, 'Left-wing'.

Diana/Unity/Germany: Guinness; Dalley; Metcalfe; Hanfstaengl; Martland; Mark Amory, *Lord Berners: The Last Eccentric*, 1998.

Agriculture: Benewick; Bellamy; Brewer; *The Canterbury Tales*, Channel Four, 1996; HO 144 series; Leighton, op. cit.; Cornford; Edwards; Portsmouth; Webber, *Ideology*; Robert Speaight, *The Life of Hilaire Belloc*, 1957; Lunn in Lunn/Thurlow; Alastair Hamilton, *The Appeal of Fascism: A Study of Intellectuals and Fascism 1919–1945*, 1971.

Chesterton/Beckett/Thomson: Baker; Chesterton, *Creed of a Fascist Revolutionary*, *c.* 1937; Beckett unpublished manuscript; F. Beckett and letter; *Comrade*, July 1994; Peter Pugh, op. cit.; HO 144 series; A. Raven Thomson, *Civilisation as Divine Superman: A Superorganic Philosophy of History*, 1932; Coupland, 'Left-Wing'; Thurlow, 'Return'; Charnley; Miles, op. cit.

Nazis/Mussolini: HO 144 series; German and Italian FO documents; de Courcy; Stevenson MSS 292.

English Review Circle: Leighton, op. cit.; Webber, *Ideology*; Smart; Wrench; Yeats-Brown, *Gold Horn*, 1932; Stewart; HO 144 series; Bevan, *Mosley Black shirts*; Geoffrey Alderman, 'Dr Robert Forgan's resignation from the British Union of Fascists', *LHR*, 57, 1, Spring 1992; P. M. Luttman-Johnson interview and papers.

Anti-Semitism: C. C. Aronsfield, 'Old Fascist, Writ Large: Mosley's Memories', *PP*, 11, November–December 1968; Holmes, *Anti*; Lewis.

Nazis: C. Mosley; Hastings; Guinness; Pryce-Jones; Lovell; D. Mosley and *Contrasts*;

Chisholm/Davie; Robert Rhodes James (ed.), *Chips: The Diaries of Sir Henry Channon*, 1993; German FO documents; *Searchlight* No. 171, 1989.

Tavener: Dalley; D. Mosley interview.

IFL/Taylor: HO 144 series; Lebzelter; Arnold Spencer Leese, op. cit.; Ivan Greenberg papers; Fredericks MSS 292; *Comrade*, May–June 1987; Miles, op. cit.; Charles Dolan, *The Blackshirt Racket – Mosley Exposed*, 1934; Miscellaneous papers Tait collection, Stirling University.

Mosley/violence: Phillpott reports; Stevenson/Cook; Hope, op. cits; MEPOL 2/3069 and 3077; Treasury and Cabinet records; HO 144, 83 and 45 series; Dolan, op. cit.; John Warburton memoir; Curry; Coupland, 'Left-wing'; Andrew, *MI5*; Masters; West.

CP/Cripps: Marchbank papers MSS 127; HO 144 and 45 series; Fredericks MSS 292; Stevenson/Cook; Simon Burgess, *Stafford Cripps: A Political Life*, 1999; Skidelsky, *Interests*.

Allen: C. M. Hamilton, *Life Errant*, 1935; Douglas.

Airmen: L. Wise, in *Mosley Black shirts*; Coupland and Wagar, op. cits.

Gartner: Curry; D. C. Watt, *Personalities: Margarete Gartner, Ambassadress of good will*, 1955; German FO documents.

Chapter Fourteen: Rothermere

Ward Price/Rothermere: Gannon; S. Taylor; Cudlipp; Paul Addison, 'Patriotism under Pressure: Lord Rothermere and British Foreign Policy', in Gillian Peel and Chris Cook (eds), *The Politics of Reappraisal*, 1975; Italian FO records; HO 144 and 283 series; John Hope, 'Cable Street, the BUF and the Italian subsidy', *Searchlight*, October 1999; Mosley/Liddle, op. cit.; Bianchi; Koss; Smart; Horrie; Mandle, 'Anti-semitism'; Benewick; Eatwell; Griffin; Paxton.

Department Z: TUC and Miles, op. cit.; HO 144 series; Benewick.

Opposition: David Lewellyn, *Nye, The Beloved Patrician*, 1960; James King, *Virginia Woolf*, 1994; Hermione Lee, *Virginia Woolf*, 1996; A. J. P. Taylor (ed.), *Off the Record: Political Interviews 1933–1943*, W. P. Crozier, 1973.

Government: NA MacDonald papers; HO 144 series; Sylvia Scaffardi, *Fire Under the Carpet: Working for civil liberties in the 1930s*, 1986; Andrew Moore, 'Sir Philip Game's "Other Life": The Making of the 1936 Public Order Act in Britain', *AJP*, 36, 1, 1990.

Funding: Strachey, *Growth*; Joan Leighton, 'Power Elites and the British Union of Fascists 1932–1940', M.Phil. thesis, 1992; Thurlow; HO 45, 144 and 283 series; Adeney, *Nuffield*; Selwyn; Maitles.

Allen/Fascism/Spengler: Thurlow and 'Mod' and 'Return' and 'Destiny and doom, Spengler, Hitler and "British" Fascism', *PP*, 15, 4, October 1981; Jonathan Dollimore, *Death, Desire and Loss in Western Culture*, 1998; Roger Griffin (ed.), *Fascism*, 1995 and (ed.), *International Fascism: Theories, causes and the new consensus*, 1998; www.britishembassy.org.ge/information/roots; Louise Irvine, *Mosley's Blackshirts: The Inside Story of the British Union of Fascists 1932–*

1940, 1986; Philip Coupland, 'The Blackshirt Utopians', *JCH*, 33, 2, April 1998 and 'The Black Shirt in Britain', in Linehan/Gottlieb; Mandle, 'Anti-semitism'; Bentley; R. Gordon-Canning, *The Inward Strength of a National Socialist*, 1938; Beverley Nichols, *News of England or a Country Without a Hero*, 1937; Olive Hawks, *Time is my Debtor*; National Council of Labour, *What is this Fascism?*, 1934; Holtby.

Feminism: Kushner/Lunn, *Politics*; Douglas; Gottlieb; Hilda Kean, 'Some problems of reconstructing a suffragette's life: Mary Richardson, suffragette, socialist and fascist', *WHR*, 7, 4, 1998; Stephen Cullen, 'Four Women for Mosley: Women in the BUF, 1932–1940', *OH*, 24, 1, Spring 1986; Martin Durham, 'Women in the British Union of Fascists, 1932–1940' and 'Gender and the BUF', *JCH*, 27, 1992.

Streicher/CAUR/IUN/Pfister: Pryce-Jones; Boyce; Michaelis; Soucy; *Wiener Library Bulletin*, 'The Nationalist International'; Fritz Calusen, *Volk und Staat im Grenzland*, Zurich, 1936; Pfister, Naturalization certificate, NA Australia; H. P. Knickerbocker, *Blackshirts in England*, 1934; German FO documents; Bauerkamper; HO 144 series.

Canada/Scotland/Ireland: Lita-Rose Betcherman, *The Swastika and the Maple Leaf*, 1975; German FO documents; J. Loughlin, 'Northern Ireland and British Fascism in the Inter-War Years', *IHS*, 29, November 1995; R. M. Douglas, 'The Swastika and the Shamrock: British Fascism and the Irish Question, 1918–1940', *Albion*, 29, 1, Spring 1997; Philip Schlesinger letter; PRONI files CAB 9F.

MI5/Italy: Curry; HO 144 series; Thurlow; Italian FO documents.

Wells/Eliot: H. G. Wells, *Experiment in Autobiography*, 1934; T. S. Mathews, *Great Tom: Notes Towards the Definition of T. S. Eliot*, 1974; Coupland, 'Wells', op. cit.; Michael Foot, *H. G.: The History of Mr Wells*, 1995.

Campaigns: Tony Milligan, 'Adolf's Tartan Army: Fascists and "men of the night" in 1930s Scotland', *Cencrastus*, Spring 1995; Barrett; Martin Pugh, 'Lancashire, Cotton and Indian Reform: Conservative Controversies in the 1930s', *20th CBH*, 15, 2, 2004; G. C. Webber, 'The British Isles', in Detlef Muhlberger, *The social basis of European Fascist movements*, 1987; HO 144 series.

MI5/Nazis/Jews/Pfister: German FO documents; Guinness; Bourne.

India/Rothermere: Webber, *Ideology*; Ramsden; Taylor, *Beaverbrook*; Koss; Stanley Baldwin, *This Torch of Freedom*, 1937; HO 144 series.

Defence Force: Tait Collection, op. cit.; Cohen, op. cit.

Aristocrats: Miles, op. cit.; Benewick; Trzebinski; Ziegler.

Chapter Fifteen: Olympia

Special Branch: HO 144 series; Miles, op. cit.; Stevenson/Cook.

The event: Amory; Crowson; Addison; Catlin, *Go*; Ronald Blythe, *The Age of Illusion: England in the Twenties and Thirties 1919–1940*, 1963; Wrench; Fredericks MSS 292; Lewis; HO 144 series.

Reaction: Martin Pugh, 'The BUF and the Olympia debate', *HJ*, 41, 2, 1998; Jon

Lawrence, 'Fascist violence and the politics of public order in inter-war Britain: the Olympia debate revisited', *HR*, 76, 192, May 2003; Crowson; Smart; K. Young; MEPO 2/3073; HO 144 series; Scaffardi, op. cit.; M. Cowling, *The Impact of Hitler*, 1975; CAB 23/79.

Nazi reaction/Pfister/anti-Semitism: HO 144 series; German FO documents; Baukamper.

MI5: Leighton, op. cit.; HO 144 series.

Rothermere/anti-Semitism: German FO documents; A. K. Chesterton and Joseph Leftwich, *The Tragedy of Anti-Semitism*, 1948; Baker; Kramnick/Sheerman; *Query* 1938; Lewis; Thurlow; Stephen Cullen, 'Political Violence: The case of the British Union of Fascists', *JCH*, 28, 1993.

Rothermere break: HO 144 series; Cudlipp; Thurlow; Mosley archive Box 8; Brendon; Pugh, op. cit.; Koss; German FO documents; Peter Aldag, *Das Judentum in England*, 1943; S. Taylor; Bourne.

Forgan: Geoffrey Alderman, *The Jewish Community in British Politics*, 1983; Lees-Milne diary; Webber; Thurlow.

Fuller: Holden Reid, *Fuller* and *Studies*, and 'Impressions of Mosley', 25.8.77; Obit., *The Times*, 11.2.66; Trythall.

MI5/Ball: HO 144 series; Webber and *Ideology*; Ferris/Bar-Joseph; Taylor, *Ball*; Adeney, *Nuffield*; *Round Table*, September 1934; Skidelsky, *Interests*; Martin Blinkhorn, *Fascists and Conservatives: The radical right and the establishment in twentieth-century Europe*, 1990; Ritschell; Thurlow and 'Mod'; Policy Political Broadcasting BUF, 1934–39, BBC archives.

Economy/Cripps: H. W. Richardson, *Economic Recovery in Britain, 1932–9*, 1967; Forrest Capie and Michael Collins, 'The extent of British Economic Recovery in the 1930s', *Economy and History*, 23, 1980; Thurlow, 'Failure'; Barrett; O'Keeffe; Meyers.

Chapter Sixteen: The Nazis

European Fascists/Grégoire: HO 144 series; Paul Preston, *The Politics of Revenge: Fascism and the military in twentieth-century Spain*, 1990; Stanley G. Payne, *Falange: A History of Spanish Fascism*, 1961; Soucy; Lewis; Martin Conway, *Collaboration in Belgium: Léon Degrelle and the Rexist Movement 1940–1944*, 1993; Hans Fredrik Dahl, *Quisling: A study in treachery*, 1999; Maurice Manning, *The Blueshirts*, 1970; Douglas; PRONI CAB 4/328; Loughlin; US Department of State and Justice files; Robert Sourcy, *French Fascism: The Second Wave 1933–1939*, 1995; Eugen Weber, *The Hollow Years: France in the 1930s*, 1995; Higham; HO 144 series; Leighton, op. cit.

Italy: Ravensdale; HO 144 series; Bosworth; Michaelis; James; Richard Lamb, *Mussolini and the British*, 1997.

CP/rallies/Hyde Park: HO 45 and 144 series; Copsey, *Anti-Fascism in Britain*; Margaret Mullins, 'The Left and Fascism in the East End of London 1932–39', Ph.D. thesis, 1985; Thurlow, 'Mod'; Pugh; Kevin Morgan, *Against Fascism and*

War: Ruptures and continuities in British Communist politics, 1935–41, 1989; Laybourn/Murphy; German FO documents; www.mucjs.org/mwolf; Mandle.

Diana: D. Mosley; Pryce-Jones; Guinness; Dalley; Gottlieb; 21. HO 144 series; de Courcy.

Forgan/rebellion: Fredericks MSS 292; HO 144 series; Thurlow, 'Failure'; Mandle; Dolan/Miles/Coupland, op. cit.

Anti-Semitism: Holmes, 'Anti'; Mandle, 'Anti-Semitism'; Ravensdale; Wrench; Thurlow; HO 144 series; Bondy; German FO documents; Mack Smith; R. Farinacci (ed.), *Regime Fascista*; G. Preziosi (ed.), *La Vista Italiana*; Skidelsky, *Interests*; Brewer.

Kenya: Elspeth Huxley, *Nellie: Letters from Africa*, 1980; Trzebinski.

IUN/CAUR: Zeman; Manning; Ledeen; Michaelis; Dahl; German FO documents.

Aeroplane/NLA: David Edgerton, *England and the Aeroplane: An Essay on a Militant and Technological Nation*, 1991; Holden Reid; Colin Cook; Soames; Cannadine; Bourne; Addison; Crowson; Glyn Roberts, *The most powerful man in the world: The Life of Sir Henri Deterding*, 1938; Japanese Foreign Ministry documents; Baldwin papers.

Ribbentrop: G. T. Waddington, '"An idyllic and unruffled atmosphere of complete Anglo-German misunderstanding": Aspects of the Operations of the Dienststelle Ribbentrop in Great Britain, 1934–38', *History*, 82, 265, January 1997; Richard Spitzy, *How we squandered the Reich*, 1997; Louis Lochner Collection, Hoover Institute; Wrench; David Kahn, *Hitler's Spies: German Military Intelligence in World War II*, 1978; Baukamper; Hans-Adolf Jacobsen, *Karl Haushofer: Leben und Werk, Band I: Lebensweg 1869–1946 und ausgewählte Texte zur Geopolitik*, 1979.

Funding: *Searchlight*, No. 292, October 1999; Brewer; Benewick.

Organization/Box/Richardson: Thurlow; HO 144 and KV 2/245 series; Linehan; Beckett; Benewick; Gottlieb.

Unity/Diana/Hitler: Pryce-Jones; Brendon; Guinness; de Courcy, *DM*; Diana interview; West, *Orwell*.

Rothermere/IDL: Stewart; Crowson; Soames; HO 144 and 283 series.

Cuts/funds: HO 45 and 144 series; *Searchlight*, October 1999; Benewick; Bianchi; de Courcy; Thurlow.

Nazis/BUF: HO 45 and 144 series; Thurlow, Kushner/Lunn.

Gordon-Canning: Information from John Hope, Mary Redvers and Louise Goring; HO 144 series; Mandle; *Mosley Black shirts*, L. Irvine; Griffiths; Benewick.

NLA: Crowson; Gilbert, *Churchill*, V; Koss; Bourne; Colin Cook; Taylor; Addison.

Hitler: Baukamper; German FO documents; Lees-Milne, *Deep*; Mosley/Liddle, op. cit.; D. Mosley; Guinness; Hart-Davis; *Hitler's Henchman: Goebbels*, Channel Five, 17.12.2000; Bergmeier; Irving, *Goebbels*.

Chapter Seventeen: 1935

Hitler/Unity/Diana: Dalley; Stobl; Speer; Pryce-Jones; Guinness; Lovell; Lebzelter; German FO documents; Bondy; Hastings.

Tester/Hepburn: Walker; German FO documents; *Searchlight*, Nos 236 and 237; A. A. Tester, *England – Quo Vadis?*, 1943; Ladislas Farago, *The Game of the Foxes*, 1973.

Italy: *Searchlight*, No. 292, October 1999.

East End: *Mosley Black shirts*; Patrick O'Donegan; Brewer; Thurlow, 'Mod' and 'Re Cable Street'; Bailey and Warburton, in Morton; Robert Wistrich, *Antisemitism: The Longest Hatred*, 1992; Linehan; Holmes, 'Anti' and 'BUF'; William J. Fishman, 'A People's Journey: The Battle of Cable Street', in Frederick Krantz (ed.), *History from Below: Studies in popular ideology in honour of George Rudé*; Jacobs; H. F. Srebrnik, 'The Jewish Communist Movement in Stepney: Ideological Mobilization and Political Victories in an East London Borough, 1935–1945', Ph.D. thesis, 1984.

CP: HO 45 and 144 series; Baukamper; Morgan; Laybourn/Murphy; Thurlow, 'Re Cable Street'; Cullen.

Abyssinia: Michael Pugh, 'Peace with Italy: BUF Reactions to the Abyssinian War 1935–1936', *Wiener Library Bulletin*, 27, 32, 1974; Fuller, *Last of the League Wars*, 1936; W. J. West; BBC R51/83, *The Citizen and the Government 1935–36*; Crowson; Curry; Peter and Leni Gillman, *Collar The Lot!*, 1980; West, *Truth Betrayed*; HO 144 and 283 series; Simpson; Lewis; Thurlow; Wright; Trythall; Fuller, 'Germany: As I see it', *English Review*, 60, 1935; Mosley/Liddle, op. cit.; Beckett; F. Beckett; Daniel Waley, *British Public Opinion and the Abyssinian War 1935–6*, 1975; Mandle; FO 371 series; Italian FO documents GFM 36/39; Luigi Goglia, 'La propaganda italiana sostegno della guerra contro l'Etiopia svolta in Gran Bretagna nel 1935–36', *Storia Contemporanea*, 15, 5, October 1984.

Italy/holiday: de Courcy and *DM*; Lovell; Violet Trefusis, *Don't Look Round*, 1952.

Campbell: Leo Villa and Tony Gray, *The Record Breakers: Sir Malcolm and Donald Campbell Land and Water Speed Kings of the 20th Century*, 1969; *Comrade*, January 1991; *Automobile*, May 1985 and December 1990; US Army files, Fort Meade.

Unity/Nuremberg: Pryce-Jones; J. W. Blanch, 'Henry Williamson and the Romantic Appeal of Fascism', *Durham University Journal*, 1, 1, December 1988; Williamson; Higginbottom; Lois Lamplugh, *A Shadowed Man: Henry Williamson 1895–1977*, 1991; Alexander Prokopov letter; Dr Karl-Hans Galinksy, *British Fascism*, Verlag und Druck von B. G. Teubner, Berlin, 1935.

BBC: Paddy Scannell and David Cardiff, *A Social History of British Broadcasting, 1922–1939: Serving the Nation*, 1991; W. J. West.

Fuller/Abyssinia/propaganda/Jews: Fuller, *League Wars*; Brendon; Wright; Trythall, *'Boney' Fuller*; W. J. West; Gottlieb; Strachey Barnes; Martin Stannard, *Evelyn Waugh: The Early Years 1903–1939*; Italian FO documents GFM 36/55; Archivo de Felice; Beckett; Mandle, 'Anti-semitism'; Linehan; Thurlow, 'Re Cable Street'; Michaelis.

Italy/funds/spies: M. Pugh; HO 45 and 144 series; Andrew; Smith; *La Nuovo Antologia*; A. Gravelli, op. cit.; Archivo de Felice; Curry; Kahn.

Nazi spies: Ian Kershaw, *Making Friends with Hitler: Lord Londonderry and Britain's road to war*, 2004; Waddington; Griffiths; Jacobsen; Zeman; Wilfred von Oven, *Mit Goebbels bis zum Ende*, 1949; Angela Schwarz, 'British Visitors to National Socialist Germany: In a Familar or in a Foreign Country?', *JCH*, 28, 1993; Karlheinz Schadlich, '"Appeaser" in "Action": Hitler's British Friends in the Anglo-German Fellowship', *Historical Yearbook*, 3, 1969; Aigner; Goebbels diary; HO 144 series.

Election/Abyssinia: Smart; Bianchi; Brendon; CAB 23/82 minutes; Goglia, op. cit.; de Courcy; Smith; G. Waddington, 'Hassegener: German views of Great Britain in the Later 1930s', *H*, 81, 261, 1996; HO 144 series; Information from Alfio Bernabei and Linette Pearson; W. J. West.

Organization: HO 144 series; FO 371 series; CAB 129/8; Italian documents St A; Waley, op. cit.; West, *MI5*; Brewer; Dalley; Linehan.

Failure/economy: John Stevenson, 'Conservatism and the failure of fascism in interwar Britain', in Martin Blinkhorn, *Fascists and Conservatives: The radical right and the establishment in twentieth-century Europe*, 1990; Ramsden; Smart; Stewart; Stevenson/Cook; Harrison; H. Pelling, *The British Communist Party*, 1958; Skidelsky, *Interests*; Ingham; Peden, op. cit.; Mark Thomas; Brewer; Lebzelter; Coleman, 'Frustration', in Andrew Thorpe (ed.), *The Failure of Political Extremism in Inter-war Britain*, Exeter Studies in History, 21, 1989; G. Orwell, *England Your England, Inside the Whale and other Essays*, 1968.

Chapter Eighteen: The East End

Funds: HO 144 series; *Searchlight*, October 1999; N. Mosley archive, box 11; Lewis; Thurlow, 'Mod'; Charnley; Benewick; Cabinet minutes; BBC archives.

National socialists/Nazi funds: Sonia and Ian Angus (eds), *The Collected Essays, Journalism and Letters of George Orwell, An Age Like This 1920–1940*, 1968; Goebbels diary; Pryce-Jones; Nicolson diary and letters; Charles Higham, *Trading with the Enemy: An Exposé of the Nazi-American Money Plot 1933–1949*, 1983; Information from Scott Newton.

Drummond: Information from Ben Clingin, Philip Coupland and D. Mosley interview; Alf Goldberg, *World's End for Sir Oswald Mosley*, 1999; Griffiths.

Sanctions: Renzo de Felice, *Mussolini il duce: 1. Gli anni del consenso 1929–1936*, 1974; Rees, *Changing*; Gravelli, op. cit.; Mack Smith; Lewis; Strachey Barnes; S. Lang and E. von Schenck (eds), *Memoirs of Alfred Rosenberg*, 1949.

East End/anti-Semitism: Laybourn/Murphy; Crowson; Srebrnik; Benewick; HO 144 and 283 series; Thurlow; Mosley, *Tomorrow We Live*; Holmes, 'Anti'; Lebzelter.

Nazi funds: Goebbels diary; Irving, *Goebbels*; Curry.

Schurch: WO 76–1107; US Army records.

Diana: D. Mosley and *Loved*; de Courcy; Guinness; Lovell; Mosley/Liddle, op. cit.

Spain: Paul Preston, *Franco*, 1993; Amherst; Douglas.

Police/anti-Semitism: Moore; Thurlow, 'Failure'; Lebzelter; MEPOL 2/3043.

Magda Goebbels/Olympic Games: D. Mosley; Gottlieb; Anja Klabunde, *Magda Goebbels*, 2002; Gottfried Wagner, *He Who Does Not Howl with the Wolf: The Wagner Legacy*, 1998; Geoffrey G. Field, *Evangelist of Race: The Germanic Vision of Houston Stewart Chamberlain*, 1981; Dalley; D. Mosley.

Haushofer/geopolitics: Baukamper; Lewis; Thurlow, 'Return'; Hans-Adolf Jacobsen, *Karl Haushofer: Leben und Werk, Ausgewählter Schriftwechsel 1917–1946*, 1979; Mosley, 'Das Grosse Entweder Oder', *Zeitschrift für Geopolitik*, September 1936.

Wedding: M. Goebbels letter, BU, Mosley deposit, Louis Lochner Collection, Hoover Institute; Guinness; Goebbels diary.

Radio project: Mosley statement, BU; Pronay and Taylor; Eckersley and letter; Allen; James; Pryce-Jones.

Allen: HO 144 series; Douglas.

Cable Street: Laybourn/Murphy; Peter Catterell (ed.), 'Witness Seminar: The Battle of Cable Street', *CR*, 8, 1, Summer 1994; Thurlow, 'Mod'; Mandle; Chisholm papers, ML MSS 1246; HO 144 series; Gottlieb, 'Re Cable Street'; Lewis; Kushner/Valman; Clarkson; *Comrade*, August 1999; James Morton, *East End Gangland*, 2001; Richard Thurlow, 'British Fascism and State Surveillance', *INS*; W. F. Deedes, *Dear Bill*, 1999; Srebrnik; Stevenson/Cook; Linehan; Skidelsky, *Interests*.

Wedding/Berlin: Gottlieb, 'Re Cable Street'; Goebbels diary; German FO documents; Michael Bloch, *Ribbentrop*, 1992; D. Mosley; Pryce-Jones; Guinness; Irving, *Goebbels*; US National Archives, Ribbentrop T120; Dalley.

Post-Cable Street: MEPOL 2/3043; Linehan; 'Re Cable Street'; Cohen; Charnley; HO 144 series; *Searchlight*, October 1999; Thurlow; Kushner/Valman; Leighton; Andrew Moore, 'Sir Philip Game's "Other Life": The making of the 1936 Public Order Act in Britain', *AJP*, 36, 1, 1990; Stevenson/Cook; Morton; Mandle; Deedes, op. cit.; Laski papers; Kramnick/Sheerman; Colin Holmes, 'East End Anti-Semitism, 1936', *SSLHB*, 32, Spring 1976; Crowson, p. 174; Dietrich Aigner, *The Struggle for England*.

Chapter Nineteen: The Abdication

Lewis/Pound/Campbell: Wright, *Tank*; WO 106/1578; Holden Reid; HO 144 series; Douglas; O'Keeffe; Meyers; Normand; Joseph Pearce, *Bloomsbury and Beyond: The friends and enemies of Roy Campbell*, 2002; Bernard Bergonzi, 'Roy Campbell: Outsider on the Right', *JCH*, 2, 2, 1967.

Joyce: Thurlow; Webber; Crowson; Benewick; George Orwell, *The Road to Wigan Pier*, 1936; HO 45 and 144 series; Linehan.

Axis: Andrew Sharf, *The British Press and the Jews under Nazi Rule*, 1964; Goebbels diary; HO 144 and KV 4/1 series.

Save the King/Joyce/Beckett: Crowson; John Charnley, *Duff Cooper*, 1986; Lewis; Warburton/Quill interviews; Beckett; HO 144 series; Thurlow; Curry.

King's Party: Bryan/Murphy; Crowson; Cazalet, Amery, Reith and Goebbels diaries; German FO documents; Ziegler; West, *MI5*; Higham; J. Parker; Lees-Milne, *Peace*; Koss; Robert Rhodes James, *Memoirs of a Conservative: J. C. C. Davidson's Memoirs and Papers, 1910–37*, 1969.

Failure on crisis: Beckett; HO 144 series; Higham; Thurlow; Coleman, *Frustration*; Linehan.

POA: Thurlow; P. Cohen, 'The Police, the Home Office and the Surveillance of the British Union of Fascists', *INS*, 1, 3, September 1986; Thurlow, 'British Fascism and State Surveillance'; Benewick; John Mortimer, *Clinging to the Wreckage*, 1982; Anderson, *Fascists and Communists*, op. cit.; Webber.

Book clubs: Webber; E. H. H. Green, 'Book Clubs and Conservatism in the 1930s', in his *Ideologies of Conservatism: Conservative Political Ideas in the Twentieth Century*, 2002.

Funds: HO 144 series; Curry; Linehan; de Courcy and *DM*; Gottlieb; Goebbels diary; F. Elwyn-Jones, *The Battle for Peace*, 1938, and *In My Life*, 1983; N. Mosley, Box 12, BU; Baukamper.

East End: Beckett; Mandle; Stevenson/Cook; Lebzelter; Srebrnik; HO 144 series; C. Wegg-Prosser, *Fascism Exposed*, 1938; Joyce files KV 2/245 series; Martland; Skidelsky, *Reflect*; Thurlow; Benewick; 'Re Cable Street', Renton and Linehan; Goebbels diary.

Mussolini funds: Hope, *Searchlight*, October 1999; Beckett; HO 283 series.

Joyce: Joyce files KV 2/245; Martland; Benewick; HO 45 series; Wegg-Prosser, op. cit.

Restructuring: Linehan; Beckett; HO 144 series; Gottlieb; Benewick.

Radio/Sark/Lawton: Guinness; Goebbels diary; *History Today*, March 1990; Eckersley; D. Mosley, *Loved*; Simpson; HO 45 series; Barbara Stoney, *Sibyl, Dame of Sark*, 1978; de Courcy, *DM*; Dalley.

POA/marches: Stevenson/Cook; Benewick; Baker; Morley; MEPOL 2/3110; Laybourn/Murphy.

Radio/Gemona: Simpson; Eckersley; West; Guinness; Lovell; D. Mosley, *Loved*; Goebbels diary; Irving, *Goebbels*; Bergmeier/Lotz; Dalley.

Visits to Germany/Nazi funds: Lebzelter; Ribbentrop files; Goebbels diary; Lovell; Aigner; Irving, *Goebbels*; Lewis.

BUF spying: W. J. Brown, 'The strange case of Major Vernon', *NCCL*; *History*, February 2003; Tony Bunyan, *The History and Practice of the Political Police in Britain*, 1976; Nigel West, *The Illegals: The Double Lives of the Cold War's Most Secret Agents*, 1993; HO 45 and 283 series; Hope, 'Fascism, the Security Service'.

Hitler/Unity: Nikolaus von Below, *Als Hitlers Adjutant 1937–45*, 1980; Pryce-Jones; Ernest R. Pope, *Munich Playground*, 1941; Spitzy; Die Aufzeichnungen Heinrich Heims herausgegeben Werner Jochmann, *Adolf Hitler: Monologe im Führer-Hauptquartier 1941–1944*, 1980; Speer, *Inside the Third Reich*; Goebbels diary.

Chapter Twenty: The Radio Project

Link/Domvile: Thurlow and Kushner/Lunn; Griffiths; Aaron Goldman, 'The Link and the Anglo-German Review', *South Atlantic Quarterly*, 71, 1972; Aigner; J. B. White, *The Big Lie*, 1955; Domvile; Simpson.

Nordic League: Griffiths; Simpson; HO 45, 144 and 283 series; Thurlow; BoD of British Jews C6/10/29.

Nazi spying: Michaelis; Farago; Curry; Kahn.

Belgium/Tester: German FO documents; John Hope and David Turner, 'The Curious Case of Dr Tester', *Searchlight*, February–March 1995; Conway.

Duke of Windsor: Spitzy; Michael Thornton, *Royal Feud: The Queen Mother and the Duchess of Windsor*, 1985; Speer; Higham; Bradford; Bloch, 'Secret File'; Ziegler.

Radio: Simpson; Stoney; D. Mosley, *Loved* and Box 7 BU; de Courcy, *DM*; German FO documents.

Austria: Lewis; David Irving, *The War Path: Hitler's Germany 1933–9*, 1978; Curry; Virginia Cowles, *The Rothschilds: A Family Fortune*, 1975; Benewick; Mosley: *The Facts*.

Chesterton: Mandle; HO 144 series; A. K. Chesterton, *Why I Left Mosley*, National Socialist League, 1938; Baker; Thurlow.

Radio/Germany: de Courcy, *DM*; Sir Frederick Lawton letter; Kahn; Dalley; Lovell; N. Mosley Box 11 BU; D. Mosley, *Loved*; Guinness; Eckersley; Nicholas Pronay and Philip Taylor, 'The British Government and clandestine radio propaganda operations against Germany during the Munich Crisis and after', *JCH*, 19, 1984; West.

Allens: Allen; Mrs Allen letter; Eckersley; Andrew; Thurlow; Information from John Hope; N. Mosley Box 11 BU.

Czechs/Luxembourg: Betcherman; Joyce files KV 2/245; Martland; Taylor; Pronay/Taylor, op. cit.; West; Eckersley; John Costello and Oleg Tsarev, *Deadly Illusions*, 1993.

Contract: Dalley; de Courcy, *DM*; Granzow.

Chapter Twenty-one: The Darkening Clouds

BUF campaigns/revival: Mayall, *Politics of Maginality*; Japanese FO documents; Guinness; Harrison; T. Balogh, 'Economic Policy and Rearmament in Britain', *Manchester School*, 7, 1936; Brewer; Webber; HO 144 series; Linehan; Skidelsky, *Interests*; S. Rawnsley, 'The membership of the British Union of Fascists', in *British Fascism*, K. Lunn and R. Thurlow (eds), 1980.

Family: D. Mosley, *Loved*; Ravensdale; de Courcy and *DM*.

Pro-Nazi groups: Cornford; Benewick; Webb.

Nazi spying: Farago; Kahn; Gunter Peis, *The Mirror of Deception: How Britain turned the Nazi spy machine against itself*, 1978; N. West, *MI5: British Security Service Operations 1909–1945*, 1983 and *MI6: British Secret Intelligence Service*

Operations 1909–1945, 1985; J. C. Masterman, *The Double-Cross System in the War of 1939 to 1945*, 1972; Curry; Tester.

Knight/MI5: Thurlow; HO 144 series; Masters; Simpson; Miller.

Appeasement: Thurlow and 'Mod'; de Courcy; Linehan; Griffiths; Webber.

Ironside: Leonard Wise letter, Sheffield University; Thurlow; Trythall; Ironside diary and letter.

Pro-Nazi groups/co-operation: Thurlow, Kushner/Lunn and 'Mod'; Simpson; BoDBJ files; Benewick; 'Re Cable Street', Neil Barrett; Goldman, op. cit.; Linehan; Jeffrey; HO 45 and 144 series; Bondy; J. S. Wiggins, 'The Link', MA thesis, 1985; Maule Ramsay, *The Nameless War*, 1954; Domvile diary.

BPP/pro-Germans: F. Beckett; Thurlow; Simpson; Cornford; HO 45 and 283 series; Griffiths; Allen.

Fuller: Griffiths; Trythall, *Fuller*; Wright; Jeffrey; D. Mosley.

Right Club/Ramsay/Wolkoff: Kushner; Simpson; Ramsay, op. cit.; Griffiths, R/C; Spector Manuscript in Wiener Library; Thurlow and Kushner/Lunn; HO 45 and 144 series; BoDBJ files; Tyler Kent trial transcript; Martland; F. Beckett.

Rothschilds: HO 45 series; Eckersley; Cowles, op. cit.

Earls Court: Skidelsky, *Interests*; Guinness; Domvile diary; Griffiths; de Courcy and *DM*; Italian FO documents; Irving, *Goebbels*; Charnley; Gottlieb; Bondy; Aigner.

Radio: de Courcy, *DM*; Mosley letter 1969, DM Box 12 BU.

Unity/Diana/Hitler: de Courcy, *DM*; Amanda Smith, *Hostage to Fortune: The letters of Joseph P. Kennedy*, 2001; Aufzeichnungen Heinrich Heims op. cit.; Hildegard von Kotze, *Heeresadjutant bei Hitler, 1938–1943, Aufzeichnungen des Majors Engel*, 1974; Pryce-Jones; D. Mosley; Mosley/Liddle, op. cit.; J. Parker; Guinness; Dalley.

Radio: Eckersley; Skidelsky, *Interests*; Dalley.

Emergency powers/Joyce: HO 45 series; Simpson; Gillman; Cole, *Lord Haw Haw*; C. E. Bechoffer Roberts, *The Trial of William Joyce*, 1946; Martland; Selwyn.

Chapter Twenty-two: The Phoney War

Membership/plans: Kushner; Lewis; Linehan; Brewer; Thurlow; HO 45, 144 and 283 series; Simpson; Information from Julian Pakowski; Gottlieb.

Ironside/leaks/Peace Party: Thurlow, 'SS', 'Failure' and Kushner/Lunn; Fuller and Ironside diaries; Bryan/Murphy; Ziegler; Higham; Griffiths, Patriotism Perverted.

Meetings: HO 144 series; Thurlow, 'SS'; Griffiths, Patriotism Perverted; Domvile diary; Simpson.

Internment/Thomas: HO 45, 144 and 283 series; Thurlow; Griffiths and R/C; BoDBJ files; Bondy; German FO documents; Linehan; Simpson; DM Box 16 BU.

Collaboration/MI5/Patriotism Perverted: Thurlow, 'SS' and Kushner/Lunn; Simpson; Griffiths R/C; HO 45, 144 and 283, KV 2/840 series; Kushner; Clough; US NA memo RG 84 series; Kent transcript; Jeffrey; Crowson.

BCCSE/anti-Semitism: Treasury 27/522 series; Griffiths, *Patriotism Perverted*; Kushner; D. Mosley; HO 144 series; Thurlow.

Ironside/Fuller: R. H. Larson, *The British Army and the Theory of Armoured Warfare, 1918–1940*, 1984; War Cabinet minutes.

Berlin/Peace Party: German Foreign Policy documents, D, 8; Dr Hans-Gunther Seraphim (ed.), *Das politische Tagebuch Alfred Rosenbergs aus den Jahren 1934/35 und 1939/40: Nach der photographischen Wiedergabe der Handschrift aus den Nürnberger Akten herausgegeben und erlautet*, 1956; J. Noakes and G. Pridham, *Nazism 1919–1945*, Vol. 3, *Foreign Policy, War and Racial Extermination.*

Secret meetings/Thomas: Thurlow and Kushner/Lunn; HO 45, 144 and 283 series; Griffiths, *Patriotism Perverted*; F. Beckett; Simpson; Domvile diary.

Mrs Amor/Right Club: KV 4/227 and 2/902 series; Griffiths, *Patriotism Perverted*; Clough; Jowitt; Simpson; Bearse/Read; Thurlow Kushner/Lunn; Linehan; Ramsay, *Nameless War*; Kushner.

Allen: HO 45 and 283 series; Thurlow; David Smiley, *Irregular Soldier*, Norwich, 1994.

MI5/HO: Simpson; Jenifer Hart, *Ask me no more*, 1998; Thurlow, 'Failure'; Montgomery Hyde, *Norman Birkett.*

Hore-Belisha: Roberts; Kushner; Griffiths, *Patriotism Perverted*; Ironside diary.

Peace Party/Duke of Windsor/Ironside: Simpson; Thurlow; Griffiths, *Patriotism Perverted*; Liddell and Fuller diaries; David Dilks (ed.), *The Diaries of Sir Alexander Cadogan 1938–1945*, 1971; Bloch; Donaldson; Bradford; Higham; German Foreign Policy documents.

Raids: Hinsley/Simkins; Thurlow, 'SS'; HO 45 series; N. West, *MI5*; Liddell diary; Simpson; Kushner.

Kent/Wolkoff: Simpson; Griffiths, *Patriotism Perverted*; Crowson; 'Dr Pauline Henri', 'Verge of Treason: The Friends of Sir Oswald Mosley: Tyler Kent, Anna Wolkoff and the BUF', *Searchlight*, September–October 1989; Gillman; Berse/Read; Jowitt; Kent transcript; Clough; Masters; Thurlow and 'The Evolution of the Mythical British Fifth Column', *20th CBH*, 10, 4, 1999.

Hamilton: Gerald Hamilton, *The way it was with me*, 1969; Marie-Jacqueline Lancaster (ed.), *Brian Howard: Portrait of a failure*, 1968; SOE archives; John Costello, *Mask of Treachery*, 1990; John Warburton letter; West/Tsarov, *The Crown Jewels.*

Fifth Column: Curry; Lancaster; Brooks diary; HO 45 and 144 series; Cabinet minutes; Thurlow, Kushner/Lunn, 'Failure' and 'The Evolution'.

Wolkoff/Norway: Ironside diary; W. Schellenberg, *Memoirs*, 1956; Thurlow, Kushner/Lunn and 'Failure'; Kahn; KV 2/543 series; F. H. Hinsley et al., *British Intelligence in the Second World War*, Vol. 1, 1979; Clough; Griffiths, *Patriotism Perverted*; Jowitt; Simpson; Thurlow; Kahn, *Hitler's Spies: German Military Intelligence in World War Two*, 1978; Griffiths, *Patriotism Perverted*; Costello; Bearse/Read.

Fifth Column: Griffiths, *Patriotism Perverted*; HO 45 and 144 series; Clough.

Invasion/Ironside: Kushner; Bloch; Clark; Goebbels diary; Cornford; Higham; Malcolm Muggeridge, *Chronicles of Wasted Time: An Autobiography*, 1973; Simpson; Thurlow, 'SS' and Kushner/Lunn; Trythall; Joint Intelligence Committee/CAB minutes; HO 45 series; de Courcy.

Roosevelt: Kimball/Bartlett; Joseph P. Lash, *Roosevelt and Churchill, 1939–1941: The Partnership that Saved the West*, 1977; O. H. Bullitt (ed.), *For the President – Personal and Secret: Correspondence between Franklin D. Roosevelt and William C. Bullitt*, 1972; Costello; Kahn, *The Codebreakers*, 1966.

Kent affair/internment: Simpson; State Department #5318 documents; Warren F. Kimball and Bruce Bartlett, 'Roosevelt and pre-war commitments to Churchill', *DH*, 5, 1981; Thurlow, 'SS' and 'Mod'; PREM 7/2 and CAB 98/18 documents; Higham; Lash; Griffiths, *Patriotism Perverted*; Bearse/Read; Liddell diary; Hart.

Quislings: Mark Pottle, *Champion Redoubtable: The Diaries and Letters of Violet Bonham-Carter 1914–1945*, 1998; Cross (ed.), *Life with Lloyd George: The Diary of A. J. Sylvester 1931–45*, 1975; Liddell diary; Thurlow, 'Mod' and 'SS'; State Deptartment RG-84, Box 3; Irving, *Churchill's War*; CAB 65/7 documents; Gilbert, *Finest Hour*; Simpson; Roberts.

Arrests: HO 45 and 144 series; Simpson; D. Mosley; Dalton diary; Goebbels diary; F. Beckett; Douglas; de Courcy, *DM*; Williamson.

Wrong people: Thurlow, Kushner/Lunn; *Mosley Black shirts*, L. Wise, 'J Christian' and L. Irvine; Simpson.

Chapter Twenty-three: Prisoner Number 2202

Dunkirk/Security Executive: Irving, *Churchill's War*; Gilbert, *Finest Hour* and *War Papers*; Dalton diary and *Fateful Years*; Pimlott; HO 144 series; A. Boyle, *Trenchard*, 1962; Chiefs of Staff papers; Simpson; Hinsley/Simkins; Thurlow.

Internment: de Courcy, *DM*; Gottlieb; HO 45 and 144 series; Kushner/Lunn; Simpson; CAB minutes; TS 27/493; Thurlow 'SS' and 'Failure'; Hinsley/Simkins; Gilbert, *Finest Hour*.

Kurtz/Fifth Column: HO 45 and 283, FO 371 series; Simpson; Thurlow and 'SS'; Curry; N. West, *MI5*.

Roosevelt: FO 371 series; Lukacs; State Department documents.

Hitler/Mosley/Quislings: Engel, op. cit.; Giles MacDonogh, *A Good German: Adam von Trott zu Solz*, 1989; Kahn; Simpson; Norman Longmate, *If Britain had Fallen*, 1972; Mosley/Liddle, op. cit.; Frank Owen, *Tempestuous Journey: Lloyd George, His Life and Times*, 1954; K. Young; Higham; Kenneth Macksey, *Invasion: The German Invasion of England, July 1940*, 1980 and letter; Holden Reid; HO 45 series; Thurlow, Kushner/Lunn; M. Cowling, *The Impact of Hitler: British Politics and British Policy 1933–1940*, 1975; F. Beckett; Kushner; FO 954 series; Ziegler; Curry.

Diana: C. Mosley; de Courcy, *DM*; Gottlieb; Gilbert, *Finest Hour*; Colville diary; Simpson; D. Mosley and *Loved*; HO 144 series; Thurlow; Kushner, *Politics of Marginality*; Dalley.

Case against Mosley: N. Driver, *From the Shadows of Exile* (n.d.); Thurlow and 'Mod'; West; HO 283 series; Simpson; Hart; Row; Mosley/Liddle, op. cit.

Invasion/White List: *Sunday Pictorial*, 15/22/29.3.59 and 5/12.4.59; Schellenberg; F. Beckett; Longmate; Lukacs.

Ironside: Thurlow, 'SS' and K/L; Richard Ingrams, *Muggeridge*, 1996.

Interrogation: William Charles Crocker, *Far from Humdrum: A Lawyer's Life*, 1959; Simpson; Oliver Hoare (intro.), *Camp 020: MI5 and the Nazi Spies*, 2000; J. L. Battersby, *The Bishop said Amen*, 1947; Thurlow.

No Fifth Column: Thurlow, 'The Evolution'; Simpson; CIA records, Troy papers, Box 2; HO 45 series.

Diana: HO 144 series; Simpson; de Courcy, *DM*; Kushner; D. Mosley and *Loved*; Thurlow; Dalley.

Kent/Wolkoff trials: Kimball/Bartlett; Bearse/Read; Simpson; Thurlow and 'SS'; Addison; H. Morrison.

Prison visits: de Courcy, *DM*; Gilbert, *Finest Hour*; Thurlow, 'SS'; James; F. Beckett.

Deception/Hess: Costello papers; Miranda Carter, *Anthony Blunt: His Lives*, 2001; Oliver Harvey diary; Richard Deacon, *A History of the British Secret Service*, 1969; Holden Reid; Kenneth Benton, 'The ISOS Years: Madrid 1941–3', *JCH*, 30, 1995, and letter; FO 898 series; Martin Allen, *The Hitler/Hess Deception: British Intelligence's Best-Kept Secret of the Second World War*, 2003; Simpson; Angus Calder, *The People's War: Britain 1939–45*, 1969.

Mosleys together: D. Mosley and *Loved*; de Courcy, *DM*; CAB minutes; Simpson; Watts MS.

Hitler/England Committee/Tester: Rattan, *John Amery* (unpublished); Hugh Trevor-Roper, *Hitler's Table Talk*, 1953; German Tester file; German FO documents.

Fascist revival: Spector documents; Kushner; Gottlieb; Simpson; Wrench; HO 45 and 144 series; Peter Aldag, *Das Judentum in England*, 1943; Srebrnik.

Amery/England Committee: Rattan, op. cit.; Adrian Weale, *Patriot Traitors, Roger Casement, John Amery and the Real Meaning of Treason*, 2001, and *Renegades, Hitler's Englishmen*, 1994; USNA, T-120 and MISC-X Section; KV 2/81 and 76 series; Spitzy; Toland; Thornton; Dalton diary; Selwyn; HO 45 series; Brendan Murphy, *Turncoat: The Strange Case of Sergeant Harold Cole, 'The Worst Traitor of the War'*, 1989.

Diana/family/reading: de Courcy, *DM*; Gérard Mignard, 'Sir Oswald Mosley, Philosophy and Action after 1945', Faculté des Lettres et des Sciences Humaines, Paris, 1977; D. Mosley, *Loved*; Mosley, *The Alternative* and *Mosley – Right or Wrong?*, 1961; Warburton letter; Roger Eatwell, 'Fascism and political racism in post-war Britain'.

Chapter Twenty-four: 'Lucifer Fallen'

Illness: de Courcy, *DM*; Herbert Morrison, *An Autobiography*, 1960; Roberts, *Halifax*; Simpson; A. J. P. Taylor, *Off the Record: Political Interviews 1933–43*, W. P. Crozier, 1973; HO 45 series; Stafford, *Churchill*; CAB minutes; Koss.

Opposition to release: HO 45 and 262 series; Richard Thurlow, 'The Guardian of the "Sacred Flame": The failed political resurrection of Sir Oswald Mosley', *JCH*, 33, 2, April 1998; de Courcy, *DM*; Kushner K/L; Holroyd; James Lees-Milne, *Ancestral Voices*, 1975; Nicolson diary.

Churchill/Morrison: Pimlott; Gilbert, *Road*; Srebrnik; de Courcy; Channon diary; Thurlow, 'Mod'; Lord Moran, *Winston Churchill: The Struggle for Survival, 1940–1965*, 1966; Charles Edward Lysaght, *Brendan Bracken*, 1979; H. Morrison; Harris.

Tom/Diana: D. Mosley, *Loved*; Dalley; de Courcy; James Lees-Milne, *Prophesying Peace*, 1977; Guinness.

18B groups/NFV: Kushner K/L and Prejudice; Dave Renton, 'The Attempted Revival of British Fascism: Fascism and Anti-Fascism 1945–51', Ph.D. thesis, 1998; Mignard; Hamm; Simpson; Thurlow, 'Mod'; Srebrnik; Lees-Milne, *Peace*; Greenberg papers 110/5.

Nazi end: D. Mosley, *Loved*; Aigner; Brendon; Anja Klabunde, *Magda Goebbels*, 2002.

Fascist revival/Dunlop: Thurlow; Information John Hope; Vansittart Papers ('Independent Nationalists').

Anti-Semitism: de Courcy and *DM*; Dalley; Graham Macklin, '"A quite natural and moderate defensive feeling"? The 1945 Hampstead "anti-alien" petition', *PP*, 37, 3, 2003; Catherine Shepherd, 'Fascism in Hampstead, 1945–49', Parts 1 and 2, *AJR Journal*, 2, 4, April 2002 and 5 May 2002; Renton.

Mosley return: HO 45 series; Renton; Simpson; CAB minutes; Bondy.

Fascism ban: CAB minutes; HO 45 series; Thurlow and 'Mod'; PREM documents.

Fascist revival: Renton; Douglas Hyde, *I believed: the autobiography of a former British Communist*, 1951; Thayer.

Traitors: Thurlow, 'Mod'; BU Roll of Honour, NCCL; WO 76 and HO 45 series; Simpson; Renton.

Book clubs/newspaper letter: HO 45 series; Hamm; Renton; *History*, January 2003; Lionel S. Rose, 'Fascism in Britain', Factual Survey No. 1, February 1948; D. Mosley, *Loved*; Miles Jebb (ed.), *The Diaries of Cynthia Gladwyn*, 1995; interviews with Warburton and Quill; CAB minutes.

Hess: *Sunday Times*, 24.5.70; Lord Dacre interview; Graham Macklin letter; Box 3 *Jewish Chronicle* Library Collection.

Anti-semitism/opposition/AJEX 43 Group: Renton; Beckman; www.geocities.com/andrewjharveyl/um; Mignard, op. cit.; Tony Kushner, 'Anti-Semitism and Austerity: The August 1947 Riots' in *Racial Violence in Britain in the Nineteenth and Twentieth Centuries*, 1996, K/L; HO 45 series; Lionel Rose, 'Survey of Open-Air Meetings held by Pro-Fascist Organisations April–October 1947', Factual Survey No. 2, February 1948; BBC History, January 2004.

SS/New order/Europe: Thurlow, 'Mod'; John Laughland, *The Tainted Source: The Undemocratic Origins of the European Idea*, 1997; Coogan; Boca; Redman; Littlejohn; M. L. Smith and Peter M. R. Stirk (eds), *Making the New Europe: European Unity and the Second World War*, 1990; Weale; Rattan, op. cit.

Franke/Skorzeny/Brotherhood: Boca; H. Jaeger, *The Reappearance of the Swastika: Neo-Nazism and the Fascist International*, 1960; Lee; Tauber, 1 and 11; Coogan; Warburton interview; Eisenberg.

Yockey: Coogan and Francis Parker, 'Yockey and the Nazi International: A Preliminary Report', document in Wiener Library; Lee.

The Alternative: Thayer; Coogan; R. Griffin (ed.), *Fascism: a reader*, 1995; Boca; Thurlow, 'Mod'; Diana Mosley, 'The Politics of Henry Williamson', *HW Society Journal*, 3.5.81.

UM: Renton; Rose, op. cits; Thayer; Warburton and Quill interviews; BoDBJ files; Spector collection; T. Kushner, *The Holocaust and the Liberal Imagination: A Social and Cultural History*, 1994; Renton; Saunders collection, Sheffield University.

Chapter Twenty-five: The Union Movement

Anti-Fascists: Renton; Rose, 2; Bean; HO 45 and MEPO 3/546 series.

FBI: FBI 100–268487–4; KV 2 series; *History Today*, December 2003.

Yockey/war crimes: Lee; Thurlow; Renton; Coogan; Fuller diary; FBI files CG100–25647.

Pirow; Thurlow; Mosley, *The Alternative*; Mignard.

Meetings: Walker; Beckman; Renton; Harvey, *UM*.

Permeation: Rose, BoDBJ files; Mignard; Renton; Saunders collection.

National Bolshevism/Yockey/*Imperium*: Lee; Lewis; John George and Laird Wilcox, *American Extremists, Militias, Supremacists, Klansmen, Communists, & Others*, 1996; Thurlow, 'Mod'; D. Prowe, 'Classic Fascism and the New Radical Right in Western Europe: Comparison and Continuity', *CEH*, 3.3.94.

Anti-immigration -Semitism/violence: J. Gross. 'The Lynskey Tribunal', in Sissons and French; H. T. F. Rhodes, *The Lynskey Tribunal*, 1949; Hamm; MEPOL documents; BBC History, September 2004.

Failure: Thurlow, 'Mod'; Dalley; Guinness; D. Mosley; Bean.

Passport/abroad: CAB minutes; D. Mosley; Roger Faligot and Pascal Krop, *DST: Police Secrète*, 1999; Graham Macklin letter; Guinness; Richard Thurlow, *Fascism*, 1999; C. Mosley; Mignard, op. cit.; Tauber, 1; US CIC files; Dalley.

German propaganda: US CIC files; Jaeger.

MSI/Fascist International: Mignard, op. cit.; US CIC files; Jaeger; Jeffrey Bale, 'The "Black" Terrorist International; Fascist Paramilitary Networks and the Strategy of Tension in Italy 1968–74', Ph.D. thesis, 1995; Harvey, *UM*; Tauber, 1; Lee; Coogan.

South of France: Peter Quennell (ed.), *A Lonely Business: A Self-Portrait of James Pope-Hennessy*, 1981; de Courcy; Guinness; Faligot/Krop; DST dossier, French archives.

Nation Europa: Tauber, 1; Eisenberg; Boca; Glenn B. Infield, *Skorzeny: Hitler's Commando*, 1981.

Ireland: Irish Military Archives; Dalley; de Courcy, *DM*; D. Mosley, *Loved*; Mignard, op. cit.; Guinness; Harvey, *UM*.

Chapter Twenty-six: The Neo-Fascist Internationals

Malmö/MSE: Boca; Eisenberg; Hayes, *Fascism*; Payne; Jaeger; US CIC files.

Brotherhood: Tauber; Jeffrey Bale, 'The "Black" Terrorist International', op. cit.; 'The Naumann Plot: Evidence from the Impounded Documents', *WLB*, 8, 3–4, May–August 1953; Jaeger; US CIC files; Lee.

UM: Sir Oswald Mosley, *European Socialism*, 1951; Roger Eatwell, 'Fascism and political racism in post-war Britain'; Bean; Thurlow, 'Mod'.

Windsors: C. Mosley; Nancy Mitford letters; D. Mosley; Ziegler; Higham; Bryan/Murphy.

Immigration: Bean; Harvey, www.geocities.com/andrewjharveyl/um.

The European: de Courcy, *DM*; Mignard, op. cit.; D. Mosley.

Neo-Nazis/Genoud: Tauber; Boca; *Searchlight*, September 2002; Lee; Irish government documents.

Ireland: Irish government documents; D. Mosley; de Courcy, *DM*; Bryan/Murphy.

Anti-Semitism: de Courcy, *DM*; BBC History, December 2000; BBC 1, *Omnibus*, 7.2.2001.

Nazi visitors: Boca; US CIC files; Grundy; Hamm; Thurlow, 'Mod'; Norbert and Stephen Lebert, *My Father's Keeper*, 2004; *Searchlight*, July 2001; Mignard, op. cit.; Warburton letter.

Women: Chisholm/Davie; de Courcy, *DM*; N. Mosley, *Truth*.

Ideas: Laughland and *Sunday Telegraph*, 22.7.99; Lewis; Eatwell; DM Box 18 BU.

Chapter Twenty-seven: 'The Coloured Invasion'

Notting Hill: Phillips; *Tribune/The Times/Guardian/Mirror/Sketch/Kensington News* and *West London Times*; Harvey, *UM*; N. Mosley, *Truth*; Grundy; Mignard, op. cit.; Lewis.

South Africa: *Johannesburg Sunday Times*, 1.2.59; *Rand Daily Mail*, 3.2.59; Eisenberg.

1959 election: de Courcy, *DM*; BBC Radio Four *Timeshift: Notting Hill Riots*, 23.1.2003; Mignard, op. cit.; BBC History, December 2000; D. Mosley, *Loved*; Benewick; Phillips; Harvey, *UM*; K. Kyle, 'North Kensington', in D. E. Butler and R. Rose, *The British General Election of 1959*, 1960; N. Mosley, *Truth*.

Declaration/Thiriart: Mignard, op. cit.; Eisenberg; Harvey, *UM*; Boca; Bale, op. cit.; C. Mosley, Nancy Mitford letters; FBI files.

Oxford: *Isis/Cherwell/News Chronicle*; Robert Rhodes James letter; Paul Foot interview; Mignard, op. cit.; C. Mosley, Nancy Mitford letters; Andy McSmith, *Kenneth Clarke: A Political Biography*, 1994.

European National Party: Boca; Mignard, op. cit.; Eisenberg.

Violence: Tony Lambrianou, *Inside the Firm: The Untold Story of the Krays' Reign of Terror*, 2003; Eatwell; Harvey, *UM*, op. cit.; BBC Archives Mosley Speaker File.

USA: State Department and FBI files.

JE: Boca; *Searchlight*, July–September 2002; Thayer; Eisenberg; www.natvan.com/national-vanguard/117/ndp; Mignard, op. cit.

UM: John Brewer, 'Postscript: anti-immigration and Union Movement in Handsworth', in *Mosley's Men*, 1984.

Chapter Twenty-eight: Rehabilitation

Rehabilitation: *New Outlook*, October 1966–December 1968/April–May 1970; *Radio Times*, 16.3.66; D. Mosley, *Loved*; *The Times*, 15.6.68.

Anti-Semitism: *Jewish Chronicle*, 13.2.98; *Sunday Telegraph*, 3.11.96; Insider interview.

NF: Walker; Tyndall; Warburton/Insiders 1 and 2 interviews.

King: Horrie; S. Dorril and R. Ramsay, *Smear!: Wilson and the Secret State*, 1991; Cudlipp; King diary; Ruth Dudley Edwards, *Newspapermen, Hugh Cudlipp, Cecil Harmsworth King and the Glory Days of Fleet Street*, 2003.

Autobiography/TV: David Frost, *From Congregations to Audiences*, 1993; Thurlow, 'Mod'; Mignard, op. cit.; Allen letter DM BU; C. Mosley, Nancy Mitford letters.

Powell: Mignard, op. cit.; BBC History, December 2000; Douglas Scheon, *Enoch Powell and the Powellites*, 1977.

Skidelsky: D. Mosley files Box 12 BU; Ingham; R. McKibben, 'The Economic Policy of the Second Labour Government 1929–31', *P&P*, 68, 1975; Pimlott; Skidelsky, *Interests*.

NF: *Spearhead*, August–September 1975; www.alphalink.com.au/radnat/britfascism/chapter 2; *Searchlight*, September 1982; Ray Hill, *The Other Side of Terror: Inside Europe's Neo-Nazi Network*, 1988.

Anti-Semitism: de Courcy, *DM*; James Lees-Milne, *Ancient as the Hills, Diaries, 1973–74*, 1997; J. Parker; *Sunday Express*, 17.8.2003.

Skidelsky biography: *Times Literary Supplement*, 4.4.75; *Encounter*, June 1975; Skidelsky, *Reflect*; W. Bader, 'The Return of Mosley', *WLB*, 30, 41–2, 1977; R. Benewick, 'Interpretations of British Fascism', *PS*, 14, 3; R. Skidelsky, 'The Return of Mosley: A Reply', *WLB*, 30, 43–4, 1977; R. Thurlow, 'The black knight', *PP*, 9, 3, May–June 1975.

Death/funeral: James Lees-Milne, *Through Wood and Dale, Diaries, 1975–78*, 1998 and *Deep Romantic Chasm, Diaries, 1979–81*, 2000; D. Mosley, *Loved*; N. Mosley interview and *Truth*; Sewell obits *The Times/Telegraph* 5/4.4.2000; John Mosley letter; de Courcy, *DM*; Skidelsky, *Interests*; BBC History, December 2000; James.

Diana: D. Mosley, *Loved* and interview; N. Mosley interview; de Courcy, *DM*.

Fascism: Roger Griffin, 'A spotter's guide to fascism in the post-fascist era', *Searchlight*, November 2002.

AF Alternative Futures; *AJLH Australian Journal of Labour History*; *AJPH Australian Journal of Political History*; *BSSLH Bulletin of the Society for the Study of*

Labour History; CR *Contemporary Record*; EHR *English Historical Review*; EHRR *Economic History Review*; ERH *European Review of History*; HJ *Historical Journal*; HR *History Research*; HS *History Studies*; IHS *Irish Historical Studies*; IJP *International Journal of Psychoanalysis*; INS *Intelligence and National Security*; IRSH *International Review of Social History*; JCH *Journal of Contemporary History*; JEH *Journal of Economic History*; JHR *Journal of Historical Review*; JMH *Journal of Modern History*; JPH *Journal of Politics and History*; JPI *Journal of Political Ideologies*; JSS *Jewish Social Studies*; LHR *Labour History Review*; NELHB *North East Labour History Bulletin*; OH *Oral History*; PG *Political Geography*; PP *Patterns of Prejudice*; P&P *Past and Present*; PS *Political Studies*; PT *Political Theory*; RIS *Review of International Studies*; SH *Social History*; 20thCBH *20th Century British History*; 20thCS *Twentieth Century Studies*; WHR *Women's History Review*; WLB *Wiener Library Bulletin*.

Bibliography

Unless otherwise stated, all books were published in London.

Addison, Paul, *Churchill on the Home Front*, 1992

Adeney, Martin, *Nuffield: A Biography*, 1993

Allen, W. E. D., *David Allens: The History of a Family Firm 1857–1957*, 1975

Andrew, Christopher, *Secret Service: The Making of the British Intelligence Community*, 1985

Baker, David, *Ideology of Obsession: A. K. Chesterton and British Fascism*, 1996

Ball, Stuart, *Baldwin and the Conservative Party: The Crisis of 1929–1931*, 1988

—— *Parliament and Politics in the Age of Baldwin and MacDonald: The Headlam Diaries 1923–1935*, 1992

Bauerkamper, Arnd, *Die 'Radikale Rechte' in Grossbritannien, Nationalistische, Antisemitische und Faschistische Bewegungen vom späten Neunzehnter Jahrhundert bis 1945*, Göttingen, Van Denhoeck and Ruprecht, 1991

Bean, John, *Many Shades of Black*, 1999

Bearse, Ray and Read, Anthony, *Conspirator: The Untold Story of Churchill, Roosevelt and Tyler Kent, Spy*, 1991

Beckett, Francis, *The Rebel Who Lost His Cause: The Tragedy of John Beckett, MP*, 1999

Beckman, Morris, *The Forty-Three Group*, 1993

Bellamy, Richard Reynell, 'We Marched With Mosley' (unpub. dated between 1958 and 1968)

Benewick, Robert, *The Fascist Movement in Britain*, 1972

Bergmeier, Horst J. P. and Lotz, Rainer E., *Hitler's Airwaves: The Inside Story of Nazi Radio Broadcasting and Propaganda Swing*, 1997

Bernays, Robert, *Robert Bernays 1932–1939: An Insider's Account of the House of Commons*, Lewiston, 1996

Berry, Paul and Bostridge, Mark, *Vera Brittain: A Life*, 1995

Bianchi, Gianfranco (ed.), *Dino Grandi racconta L'Evitabile 'Asse'*, Milan, 1984

Boca, Angelo del and Giovana, Mario, *Fascism Today: A World Survey*, 1969

Bondy, Louis, *Racketeers of Hatred: Julius Streicher and the Jew-Baiters' International*, Newman Wolsey, 1973

Boothby, Robert, *I Fight to Live*, 1947

Bourne, Richard, *Lords of Fleet Street: The Harmsworth Dynasty*, 1990

Bowra, C. M., *Memories 1898–1939*, 1966
Boyce, D. G., *Englishmen and Irish Troubles: British Public Opinion and the Making of Irish Policy 1918–1922*, 1972
Bradford, Sarah, *Sacheverell Sitwell: Splendours and Miseries*, 1993
Brandon, Piers, *The Dark Valley: A Panorama of the 1930s*, 2001
Brewer, John, *Mosley's Men: The British Union of Fascists in the West Midlands*, 1984
Brittain, Vera, Bishop, Alan (ed.), *Diary of the Thirties 1932–1939: Chronicle of Friendship*, 1986
Brockway, Fenner, *Inside Left*, 1942
—— *Towards Tomorrow*, 1977
Brown, W. J., *So Far*, 1943
Bryan, J. and Murphy, Charles J. V., *The Windsor Story*, 1981
Bullock, Alan, *The Life and Times of Ernest Bevin*, Vol. I: *Trade Union Leader 1881–1940*, 1960
Cain, Peter, *Political Economy in Edwardian England: The Tariff-Reform Controversy*, 1978
Campbell, John, *F. E. Smith, First Earl of Birkenhead*, 1983
—— *Nye Bevan and the Mirage of British Socialism*, 1987
Cannadine, David, *Aspects of Aristocracy: Grandeur and Decline in Modern Britain*, Yale University Press, 1994
Cartland, Barbara, *We Danced All Night*, 1994
Catlin, Sir George, *For God's Sake, Go!*, 1972
Charney, John, *Blackshirts and Roses*, 1990
Chesterton, A. K., *Oswald Mosley: Portrait of a Leader*, 1937
Cheyette, Bryan, *Construction of 'The Jew' in English Literature and Society: Racial Representations, 1875–1945*, Cambridge, 1994
Chisholm, Anne and Davie, Michael, *Beaverbrook: A Life*, 1992
Chodorow, Nancy, *The Reproduction of Mothering: Psychoanalysis and Sociology of Gender*, Berkeley, California, 1977
Clark, Alan, *The Tories, Conservatives and the Nation State 1922–1997*, 1998
Clarke, Peter, *The Keynesian Revolution in the Making 1924–1936*, Oxford, 1970
Cline, Catherine Ann, *Recruits to Labour: The British Labour Party 1914–1931*, Syracuse, 1963
Cole, J. A., *Lord Haw-Haw: The Full Story of William Joyce*, 1964
Coogan, Kevin, *Dreamer of the Day: Francis Parker Yockey and the Postwar Fascist International*, New York, 1999
Cross, Colin, *The Fascists in Britain*, 1961
Crowson, N. J., *Facing Fascism: The Conservative Party and the European Dictators, 1935–1940*, 1997
—— (ed.), *Fleet Street, Press Barons and Politics: The Journals of Collin Brooks, 1932–1940*, 1998
Cudlipp, Hugh, *The Prerogative of the Harlot: Press Barons and Power*, 1980
Curry, Jack, *The Security Service 1908–1945: The Official History*, 1999
Dalley, Jan, *Diana Mosley: A Life*, 1999

Dalton, Hugh, *The Fateful Years: Memoirs 1939–45*, 1953
Davenport-Hines, Richard, *The Macmillans*, 1993
De Courcy, Anne, *The Viceroy's Daughters*, 2000
—— *Diana Mosley*, 2003
Donoughe, Bernard and Jones, G. W., *Herbert Morrison: Portrait of a Politician*, 1986
Douglas, M., *Feminist Freikorps: The British Voluntary Women Police, 1914–1940*, USA, 1999
Dowse, Robert E., *Left in the Centre: The Independent Labour Party 1893–1940*, 1966
Drennan, James (Allen, W. E. D.), *Oswald Mosley and British Fascism*, 1934
Durham, Martin, *Women and Fascism*, 1998
Eckersley, Myles, *Prospero's Wireless: A Biography of Peter Pendleton Eckersley*, Romsey, 1998
Edwards, H. W. J., *Young England*, 1938
Edwards, Ruth Dudley, *Newspapermen: Hugh Cudlipp, Cecil Harmsworth King and the Glory Days of Fleet Street*, 2003
Eisenberg, Dennis, *The Re-Emergence of Fascism*, 1967
Farago, Ladislas, *The Game of Foxes*, 1971
Farr, Barbara Storm, *The Development and Impact of Right-Wing Politics in Britain, 1903–1932*, Illinois, USA, 1987
Feldman, David, *English and Jews: Social Relations and Political Culture 1840–1914*, 1994
Finlay, John L., *Social Credit: The English Origins*, Montreal, Canada, 1972
Floud, Roderick and McCloskey, Donald (eds), *The Economic History of Britain since 1700*, vol. II: *1860–1939*, Cambridge, 1994
Foot, Michael, *Aneurin Bevan: A Biography*, vol. 1: *1897–1945*, 1962
Frohlich, Elke (ed.), *The Diaries of Joseph Goebbels: Collected Fragments*, Part 1, *Notes 1924–1941*, vol. III: *1/1/1937–31/12/1939*, Berlin, 1987
Gannon, Dr Franklin Reid, *The British Press and Germany, 1936–1939*, Oxford, 1971
Gilbert, Martin, *Winston S. Churchill: Finest Hour*, 1986
—— *Winston S. Churchill: Road to Victory*, 1986
—— *The Churchill War Papers*, vol. II: *Never Surrender, May 1940–December 1940*, 1994
Glass, S. T., *The Responsible Society: The Ideas of the English Guild Socialist*, 1966
Gordon, Anne Wolrige, *Peter Howard: Life and Letters*, 1969
Gottlieb, Julie V., *Feminine Fascism: Women in Britain's Fascist Movement 1923–1945*, 2000
Green, E. H. H., *Ideologies of Conservatism: Conservative Political Ideas in the Twentieth Century*, Oxford, 2002
Green, Martin, *Children of the Sun: A Narrative of Decadence in England after 1918*, 1977
Griffiths, Richard, *Fellow Travellers of the Right*, 1983

—— *Patriotism Perverted: Captain Ramsay, The Right Club and British Anti-Semitism 1939–40*, 1998
Grundy, Trevor, *Memoir of a Fascist Childhood*, 1998
Guinness, Jonathan with Guinness, Catherine, *The House of Mitford*, 1984
Hamm, Jeffrey, *Action Replay: An Autobiography*, 1983
Harris, Kenneth, *Attlee*, 1982
Hastings, Selina, *Nancy Mitford: A Biography*, 1985
Headlam, Sir Cuthbert, *Parliament and Politics in the Age of Baldwin and MacDonald: the Headlam Diaries 1923–1935*, 1992
Higginbottom, Melvyn David, *Intellectuals and British Fascism: A Study of Henry Williamson*, 1992
Higham, Charles, *Wallis: Secret Lives of the Duchess of Windsor*, 1988
Hill, Ray, *The Other Side of Terror: Inside Europe's Neo-Nazi Network*, 1988
Hodge, Herbert, *It's Draughty in Front: The Autobiography of a London Taxidriver*, 1938
Hollis, Patricia, *Jennie Lee: A Life*, Oxford, 1997
Holmes, Colin, *Anti-Semitism in British Society, 1876–1939*, 1979
Holroyd, Michael, *Bernard Shaw*, vol. III: *1918–1950: The Lure of Fantasy*, 1991
Holton, Bob, *British Syndicalism 1900–1914: Myths and Realities*, 1975
Horrie, Chris, *Tabloid Nation: The Birth of the* Daily Mirror *to the Death of the Tabloid*, 2003
Irving, David, *Goebbels: Mastermind of the Third Reich*, 1996
Jacobs, Joe, *Out of the Ghetto: My Youth in the East End, Communism and Fascism 1913–1939*, 1978
Jaeger, H., *The Reappearance of the Swastika, Neo-Nazism and Fascist International*, 1960
James, Robert Rhodes, *Bob Boothby: A Portrait*, 1992
—— (ed.), *The Diaries of Sir Henry Chips Channon*, 1993
Jameson, Frederic, *Fables of Aggression: Wyndham Lewis, the Modernist as Fascist*, Berkeley, California, 1979
Jeffrey, Andrew, *This Present Emergency: Edinburgh, the River Forth and South-East Scotland and the Second World War*, Edinburgh, 1992
Jones, Jack, *Unfinished Journey*, Oxford, 1937
Jones, Thomas, *Whitehall Diary*, vol. II: *1926–1930*, Oxford, 1969
—— *A Diary with Letters, 1931–1950*, Oxford, 1969
Jowitt, The Earl, *Some Were Spies*, 1947
Kahn, David, *The Codebreakers*, 1973
Kennedy, Paul and Nicholls, Anthony (eds), *Nationalist and Racialist Movements in Britain and Germany before 1914*, 1981
Kenny, Mary, *Germany Calling: A Personal Biography of William Joyce, 'Lord Haw-Haw'*, 2003
King, Cecil, *Diary 1965–1970*, 1972
Koss, Stephen, *The Rise and Fall of the Politicial Press in Britain*, 1984
Kramnick, Isaac and Sheerman, Barry, *Harold Laski: A Life on the Left*, 1993

Kushner, Tony, *The Persistence of Prejudice: Antisemitism in British Society During the Second World War*, Manchester, 1989
—— with Lunn, Kenneth (eds), *Traditions of Intolerance: Historical Perspectives on Fascism and Race Discourse in Britain*, Manchester, 1989
—— *The Politics of Marginality: Race, the Radical Right and Minorities in Twentieth-Century Britain*, 1990
—— with Valman, Nadia (eds), *Remembering Cable Street: Fascism and Anti-Fascism in British Society*, 2000
Lasch, Christopher, *The Culture of Narcissism: American Life in an Age of Diminishing Expectations*, New York, 1979
—— *The Minimal Self: Psychic Survival in Troubled Times*, 1984
Laybourn, Keith, *Philip Snowden: A Biography 1864–1937*, 1988
—— and Murphy, Dylan, *Under the Red Flag: A History of Communism in Britain, c. 1849–1991*, 1999
Lee, Jennie, *My Life with Nye*, 1980
Lee, Martin A., *The Beast Reawakens*, 1997
Leeden, Michael Arthur, *Universal Fascism: The Theory and Practice of the Fascist International 1928–36*, New York, 1972
Lees-Milne, James, *Ancient as the Hills, Diaries 1973–1974*, 1974
—— *Harold Nicolson: A Biography 1930–1968*, 1981
—— *Another Self*, 1984
—— *A Mingled Measure, Diaries 1953–1972*, 1994
—— *Through Wood and Dale, Diaries 1975–1978*, 1998
—— *Deep Romantic Chasm, Diaries 1979–1981*, 2000
Lewis, D. S., *Illusions of Grandeur: Mosley, Fascism and British Society, 1931–81*, Manchester, 1987
Linehan, Thomas, *British Fascism 1918–39: Parties, Ideology and Culture*, Manchester, 2000
Lovell, Mary S., *The Mitford Girls: The Biography of an Extraordinary Family*, 2001
Lunn, Kenneth and Thurlow, Richard, *British Fascism: Essays on the Radical Right in Inter-War Britain*, 1980
McCleod, I. and Kelly, D. (eds), *The Ironside Diaries 1937–40*, 1962
MacKenzie, Norman and Jeanne (eds), *The Letters of Sidney and Beatrice Webb*, vol. III, Cambridge, 1978
—— *The Diary of Beatrice Webb*, vol. II: *1905–1924, The Power to Alter Things*, 1984
—— *The Diary of Beatrice Webb*, vol. III: *1924–1943, The Wheel of Life*, 1985
McKibbin, Ross, *Classes and Culture: England 1918–1951*, Oxford, 1998
Marquand, David, *Ramsay MacDonald*, 1998
Martel, Gordon (ed.), *'The Times' and Appeasement: The Journals of A. L. Kennedy, 1932–1939*, Cambridge, 2000
Marwick, Arthur, *The Deluge: British Society and the First World War*, 1965
Masters, Anthony, *The Man Who Was M: The Life of Maxwell Knight*, Oxford, 1984

Meyers, Jeremy, *The Enemy: A Biography of Wyndham Lewis*, 1980
Michaelis, Meir, *Mussolini and the Jews: German–Italian Relations and the Jewish Question in Italy 1922–1945*, Oxford, 1978
Miller, Joan, *One Girl's War: Personal Exploits in MI5's Most Secret Station*, Dublin, 1986
Morgan, Kenneth O., *Consensus and Disunity: The Lloyd George Coalition Government 1918–1922*, 1979
Morrison, Paul, *The Poetics of Fascism: Ezra Pound, T. S. Eliot, Paul de Man*, Oxford, 1996
Mosley, Charlotte (ed.), *The Letters of Nancy Mitford: Love from Nancy*, 1993
Mosley, Diana, *A Life of Contrasts*, 1977
—— *Loved Ones: Pen Portraits*, 1985
Mosley, Nicholas, *Rules of the Game/Beyond the Pale*, 1993
—— *Efforts at Truth*, 1994
Mosley, Sir Oswald, *My Answer*, Ramsbury, 1946
—— *The Alternative*, 1948
—— *My Life*, 1968
Newman, Michael, *John Strachey*, Manchester, 1989
Newton, Scott and Porter, Dilwyn, *Modernization Frustrated: The Politics of Industrial Decline in Britain since 1900*, 1988
Nicolson, Harold, *Diaries and Letters 1930–1964* (condensed version with previously unpublished additions by Stanley Olson), 1990
Nicolson, Nigel (ed.), *Harold Nicolson: Diaries and Letters 1930–1939*, 1966
—— *Mary Curzon*, 1977
—— *Long Life*, 1997
Normand, Tom, *Wyndham Lewis the Artist: Holding the Mirror up to Politics*, Cambridge, 1992
Nugent, Neill (ed.), *The British Right: Conservative and Right-Wing Politics in Britain*, Farnborough, 1977
O'Keefe, Paul, *Some Kind of Genius: A Life of Wyndham Lewis*, 2000
Overy, R. J., *William Morris: Viscount Nuffield*, 1976
Paton, Jon, *Left Turn!*, 1936
Peele, Gillian and Cook, Chris (eds), *The Politics of Reappraisal*, 1975
Phillips, Mike and Windrush, Trevor, *The Irresistible Rise of Multi-Racial Britain*, 1998
Pimlott, Ben, *Labour and the Left in the 1930s*, Cambridge, 1977
—— *Hugh Dalton*, 1985
—— (ed.), *The Political Diary of Hugh Dalton: 1918–60*, 1986
Postgate, Raymond, *The Life of George Lansbury*, 1951
Pryce-Jones, David, *Unity Mitford: A Quest*, 1996
Pugh, Martin, *Women and the Women's Movement in Britain 1914–1955*, 1992
—— *'Hurrah for the Blackshirts!': Fascists and Fascism in Britain Between the Wars*, 2005
Ramsden, John, *The Age of Balfour and Baldwin, 1902–1940*, 1998
Ravensdale, Baroness, *In Many Rhythms: An Autobiography*, 1953

Redman, Tim, *Ezra Pound and Italian Fascism*, Cambridge, 1991
Renton, David, *Fascism, Anti-Fascism and Britain in the 1940s*, Macmillan, 2000
Reid, Brian Holden, *J. F. C. Fuller: Military Thinker*, 1987
—— *Studies in British Military Thought: Debates with Fuller and Liddell Hart*, Lincoln, Nebraska, 1998
Ridley, Jasper, *Mussolini*, 1997
Ritschell, Daniel, *The Politics of Planning: The Debate on Economic Planning in Britain in the 1930s*, Oxford, 1997
Roberts, Andrew, *The Holy Fox: The Life of Lord Halifax*, 1997
Roberts, Michael, *T. E. Hulme*, Manchester, 1982
Scaffardi, Sylvia, *Fire Under the Carpet: Working for Civil Liberties in the Thirties*, 1986
Scanlon, John, *Decline and Fall of the Labour Party*, 1966
Schellenberg, Walter, *Invasion 1940: The Nazi Invasion Plan for Britain*, 2000
Seaman, L. C. B., *Post-Victorian Britain 1902–1951*, 1966
Selwyn, Francis, *Hitler's Englishman: The Crime of 'Lord Haw-Haw'*, 1987
Semmel, Bernard, *Impression and Social Reform: English Social-Imperial Thought 1895–1914*, 1960
Shepherd, John, *George Lansbury: At the Heart of Old Labour*, Oxford, 2002
Skidelsky, Robert, *Politicians and the Slump: The Labour Government of 1929–31*, 1967
—— *Mosley*, 1981
—— *John Maynard Keynes: The Economist as Saviour, 1920–1937*, 1992
—— *Interests and Obsessions: Historical Essays*, 1996
Smart, Nick (ed.), *The Diaries and Letters of Robert Bernays, 1932–1939: An Insider's Account of the House of Commons*, Lewiston, 1996
—— *The National Government, 1931–40*, 2000
Smith, Denis Mack, *Mussolini's Roman Empire*, 1976
Snowden, Philip, *An Autobiography*, Vol. II, 1934
Speer, Albert, *Inside the Third Reich*, 1970
Srebrnik, Henry Felix, *London Jews and British Communism, 1935–1945*, 1995
Steele, Tom, *Alfred Orage and the Leeds Arts Club, 1893–1923*, Aldershot, 1990
Sternhell, Zeev with Sznajder, Mario and Asheri, Maia, *The Birth of Fascist Ideology: From Cultural Rebellion to Political Revolution*, Princeton, USA, 1994
Stevenson, John and Cook, Chris, *The Slump, Society and Politics during the Depression*, 1977
Stewart, Graham, *Burying Caesar: Churchill, Chamberlain and the Battle for the Tory Party*, 1999
Strachey, John, *The Menace of Fascism*, 1933
Tauber, Kurt P., *Beyond Eagle and Swastika: German Nationalism Since 1945*, vols I and II, New Haven, Connecticut, 1967
Taylor, A. J. P., *English History, 1914–1945*, Oxford, 1965
—— *Beaverbrook*, 1972
Taylor, Gary, *Orage and the New Age*, Sheffield, 2000
—— *G. D. H. Cole and the National Guilds League*, Sheffield, 2002

Taylor, Philip M., *British Propaganda in the 20th Century: Selling Democracy*, Edinburgh, 1999
Taylor, S. J., *The Great Outsiders: Northcliffe, Rothermere and the* Daily Mail, Phoenix, 1999
Thayer, George, *The British Political Fringe: A Profile*, 1965
Thomas, Hugh, *John Strachey*, 1973
Thompson, Doug, *State Control in Fascist Italy: Culture and Conformity, 1925–43*, Manchester, 1991
Thompson, Noel, *John Strachey: An Intellectual Biography*, 1993
Thurlow, Richard, *Fascism in Britain: A History, 1918–85*, 1987
—— *The Secret State: British Internal Security in the Twentieth Century*, 1994
—— *Fascism in Modern Britain*, 2000
Townshend, Jules, *Lives of the Left: J. A. Hobson*, Manchester, 1990
Trythall, Anthony John, *'Boney' Fuller: The Intellectual General 1878–1966*, 1977
Trzebinski, Errol with Perry, Emma, *The Life of Lord Erroll: The Truth Behind the Happy Valley Murder*, 2000
Tyndall, John, *The Eleventh Hour: A Call for British Rebirth*, Welling, 1998
Vaill, Amanda, *Everybody Was So Young: Gerald and Sara Murphy, A Lost Generation Love Story*, 1998
Walker, Martin, *The National Front*, 1977
Webb, James, *The Occult Establishment*, vol. II: *The Age of the Irrational*, Edinburgh, 1981
Weber, G. C., *The Ideology of the British Right 1918–1939*, 1986
Weir, L. MacNeill, *The Tragedy of Ramsay MacDonald*, 1938
Wertheimer, Egon, *Portrait of the Labour Party*, 1930
West, W. J., *Truth Betrayed*, 1984
White, Dan S., *Lost Comrades: Socialists of the Front Generation 1918–1945*, 1992
Wilkinson, Ellen, *Peeps at Politicians*, 1930
Williams-Ellis, Amabel, *All Stracheys Are Cousins*, 1983
Williamson, Anne, *Henry Williamson: Tarka and the Last Romantic*, 1995
Witherell, Larry L., *Rebel on the Right: Henry Page Croft and the Crisis of British Conservatism, 1903–1914*, 1997
Wohl, Robert, *The Generation of 1914*, 1980
—— *A Passion for Wings: Aviation and the Western Imagination*, 1994
Wood, Ian S., *Lives of the Left: John Wheatley*, Manchester, 1990
Wrench, John Evelyn, *Francis Yeats-Brown 1886–1944*, 1948
Wright, A. M., *G. D. H. Cole*, Oxford, 1979
Wright, Patrick, *Tank: The Progress of a Monstrous War Machine*, 2000
Young, Kenneth (ed.), *The Diaries of Sir Robert Bruce Lockhart*, vol. I: *1915–1938*, 1973
Ziegler, Philip, *King Edward VIII: The Official Biography*, 1990

Index

OM indicates Sir Oswald Mosley

ABC (Spanish paper) 379
Abd-el-Krim 339, 379
Abeilli, Tuli 582
Abend Post 584
Action (BUF) 371, 404, 414, 432, 441, 444, 447, 452–4, 456, 465, 468, 471–2, 478, 482, 484, 492, 494, 500–1, 515
Action (NP) 174, 179, 185, 188, 191, 277, 345, 441
Action (UM) 616, 618, 622–3, 629–31
Action Française 74, 208, 317
Action Press 338
Acton, Harold 201
Acworth, Bernard 529
Adam, Sergeant Major 12
Adams, Eddie 617
Adams, Len 589
Addison, Colin 46
Adenauer, Chancellor Konrad 588, 602, 638
Adler 534
Advisory Committee (Birkett Committee) 382, 386, 472, 476–7, 481, 507–8, 510, 514–5, 517–8, 520
Aerial Navigation Bill (1918) 41
Aeroplane, The 22, 41, 262, 328, 421, 452, 473
Aeschylus 534
Age of Plenty 196, 251
Agenda 601
Agnew, Peter 230
Aigner, Dietrich 306, 397
Aiken-Sneath, Francis 236, 484, 518
Air Board 31
Air League 267, 325
Air Time 416, 435, 460
Aird, John 294
Airlie, Earl of 51
Airmen 17–8, 41, 267, 328–9, 356, 369, 403
Airwork Services 379
Aitken, Janet 609
Aitken, Max 174, 206
Alba, Duke of 69, 379, 478
Albertini, Georges 586, 596
Aldington, Richard 178
Alexander, A. V. 121
Alexander, Derek 616
Algerian National Liberation Front 603
Allen, Lord 388
Allen, Mrs 437
Allen, Barbara 486
Allen, Cissy 153
Allen, Clifford 78, 82, 98
Allen, Drennan 153
Allen, Geoffrey 415
Allen, Lydia 50
Allen, Commandant Mary 189, 258, 267, 282, 316. 335, 389, 400, 424, 451–2, 454, 459, 473, 480, 487, 492–3, 549
Allen, Natasha 606
Allen, Sam 486
Allen, W. E. D. 'Bill' 145, 152–5, 165, 169, 172, 174, 177, 191, 206, 214, 234, 245, 247, 267, 278–9, 290, 311, 314, 337, 370–2, 386–8, 393, 415–6, 420, 427, 437, 440, 497, 570–1, 606, 638
Allens, David and Sons 387–8, 430, 435, 437, 440–1
Allom, Charles 427
All Quiet on the Western Front (1929) 178
Almirante, Giorgio 582, 586
Alpenruf 585
Alternative, The 534, 553, 564, 566, 575, 584, 587
Amateur Fencing Association 209
Amaudruz, Guy 586, 596, 632–3
American Club 486

Amery, John 530–2, 551
Amery, Leo 38, 40, 182, 183, 256, 326, 530
Amherst, Lord Jeffrey 379, 410
Amor, Majorie (Mrs Majorie Mackie) 473–4, 479, 482, 486, 490, 495
Anderson, Sir John 481, 485, 495, 498–9, 500, 502, 505–6
Anfuso, Filipo 582
Anglo-French Supreme War Council 469
Anglo-German Agency for Domestic Servants 230, 251
Anglo-German Association 424
Anglo-German Club 168
Anglo-German Fellowship 362–3, 372, 387, 415, 424, 438–9, 450, 453, 460, 468, 470, 532
Anglo-German Information Service 424
Anglo-German Naval Treaty (1935) 341
Anglo-German Review 424
Animal Defence Society 586
Anslow, Lord 4, 239
Antieuropa 212
Anti-Fascist League 577
Anti-German Union (AGU) 195
Anti-Sanctionist League 374
Anti-Socialist Union 196
Anti-Suffrage League 44
Anti-Waste League 47, 50
Arab Commercial Bank 603
Archbishop of Canterbury 238
Argyll, Duke of 609
Aristotle 534
Arlosoroff, Victor 382
Arnaud, Madame 268
Arnold, Lord 453, 479, 489
Arriba 577
Ashley, Lady Sylvia 320
Asquith, Herbert (PM) 16, 23, 30–1, 36, 63, 70
Asquith, Margaret 41, 58, 168
Associated Press 405
Association Argentina-Europa 595
Association of Jewish Ex-Servicemen (AJEX) 558, 578, 584
Astor, Lady 28, 41, 52, 105, 110, 127, 239, 440, 494
Atkinson, Justice 521
Atlantic Charter 561
Attlee, Clement 140, 143, 154, 375, 494, 498, 500, 548
Auden, W. H. 185
Auslands Organization 284–5, 362, 472
Avanti 74

'B, Mrs' 263
Baarova, Lida 382
Bacmeister, Walter 288, 290, 294, 301–2
Badiglio, General Peitro 359
Bailey, Sir Abe 144, 426
Bailey, 'Bill' 370, 630
Bailey, Edward (Fred) 229–30, 349–50
Bailey, L. W. 295
Baille, Sir Adrian 237
Bakers Records 444
Baldwin, Oliver 151, 164–5, 167, 179
Baldwin, Stanley 49, 68, 70, 102, 118–9, 128, 155, 164, 165, 180, 224, 256, 271, 292, 364, 367, 370, 388, 403, 422, 458
Bale, Jeffrey 595
Balfour Declaration 65
Ball, Sir Joseph 312–3, 439–40, 504, 506, 518
Bank of International Settlement 372
Banker's Record 444
Bankhead, Talluah 69
Banks, J. C. 569
Bardeche, Maurice 561, 565, 571, 586, 588, 590–1, 594, 632
Barker, Dudley 583
Barnes, James Strachey 199, 234
Baron, Bernard 169
Baron, Edward 310
Barr, Hazel 197, 200, 411
Barry, Andy 301
Barry, Gerald 152, 297, 298
Barrymore, Blanche 108
Bartlett, E. J. 168
BAT 379
Bath Club 519
Battle of Loos 23, 379
Battle of the Somme 24
Battle of Ypres 20–1, 372, 464
Bauer, Christian 410, 439, 459, 464
Bayer 462
Bayreuth (Wagner Festival) 382–3, 640
Beamish, Henry Hamilton 77, 196, 203, 236, 426
Bean, John 569, 584, 590, 597, 604, 622, 625, 636
Beaton, Cecil 111, 179, 180
Beaumont, Colin 415–6, 419, 430
Beaumont, J. M. 416

Beaumont, Michael 267, 299, 327
Beavan, Arthur 229, 529
Beaverbrook, Lord 31, 44, 103–4, 114–5, 125, 128–9, 132, 142, 148, 150, 153–5, 158, 165, 167, 169, 174, 181, 192, 205, 212, 228, 269, 292, 376, 403–4, 483, 489, 537, 549, 605, 609
Bebb, Captain Cecil 379–80
Beck-Broichsitter, Major Helmut 562, 582, 587, 595
Beckett, Francis 189
Beckett, John 122, 134, 143, 146, 150, 189, 251, 277, 292–3, 322, 326, 330, 350, 358–60, 366, 371, 389, 394, 404, 407, 409, 412–3, 445, 452, 459, 471, 474, 476, 479, 484, 490, 501, 506, 509, 511, 547
Beckman, Maurice 569, 593
Bedaux, Charles 483
Bedford, Duke of (Tavistock) 501, 515, 524, 529, 547
Bedford, Richard 614
Behn, Dr Richard 345, 427–8, 430, 446
Belgian Workers Party 205
Belgium, King and Queen of 51
Bell, Quentin 75, 275
Bellairs, Carlyon 37, 128, 215, 293
Bellamy, Richard R. 34, 65, 247, 249, 293, 312, 476, 547
Bellew, Kyrle 251
Belloc, Hilaire 57, 74, 205, 208, 251, 447
Belsen 548, 567
Bene, Otto 236, 253, 262, 302, 318
Benewick, Robert 414
Benn, Ernest 456
Benn, Tony 141
Benn, Wedgwood (Lord Stansgate) 141
Bennett, Charles 349–50
Bennett, Wilfred 111
Benton, Kenneth 523–4
Berger, Gottlob 532
Bergery, Gaston 582, 589
Bergon, Henri 75
Berlin-Grunewald 441
Berlin Lokal-Anzeiger 377, 393, 421
Berlin Philarmonic Orchestra 571
Bernays, Robert 207, 278, 286, 325
Berners, Lord Gerald 202, 249, 295, 373, 377, 541, 543, 549
Bernhardt, Dr Johannes 441, 586
Besant, Mrs Annie 27, 89–90
Betjeman, John 201, 541, 549
Bevan, Aneurin 126, 150–1, 154–5, 159, 160, 163–4, 175, 275, 548, 551
Bevin, Ernest 130, 142, 151, 452, 536, 639, 554, 565, 570
'Bianchi, Mr' (Italian agent) 377
Bibiesco, Priscilia 605
'biff boys' 172, 175, 182
Bingham, John (Lord Clanmorris) 197, 296, 488
Bingham, Ralph 184, 189
Binot, Rene 591, 596
Birch, Nigel 224, 248
Birkett, Lord (Sir Norman) 304, 439, 476, 481, 510, 514–5, 517–8, 520–1, 555
Bismarck, Prince Otto von 241, 287, 293, 300–1, 309, 319–20
'Black, Miss' (BU) 409
Black and Tans 26, 56, 58, 61, 197, 247
'Black Book' (MI5) 520
'Black Book' (Nazi) 516
Black Gang, The (1922) 195
'Black House' (BUF) 246, 260–1, 285, 293–4, 311, 336, 356, 366, 530
Blackshirt, The 200, 224, 231–2, 237, 254–5, 267–8, 277, 285, 306–7, 309, 314, 325, 335–6, 344, 355, 358, 360, 369, 371, 374, 383, 390, 394, 417
'Black Thursday' 126
'Black Tuesday' 126
Blackeney, Brig. Gen. R. B. D. 196, 425
Blackett, Sir Basil 211
Blair, Sir Reginald 370
Blair, Tony 647
Blake, (Lord) Robert 638
'Blanchet' (agent) 528
Blavatsky, Madame Helena 27
Bledisloe, Lord 292
Blinkhorn, Martin 313, 646
Blockey, Robert 414
Blonstein, Dr J. 310
Bluebird 356
Blueshirts (Ireland) 316
Blumenfeld, Ralph 38, 124, 132, 196, 258, 292

Blunt, Anthony 522–3
Board of Deputies of British Jews 380, 396, 450–1, 454, 545, 547, 401, 414, 436, 554, 567
Boer War 38
Bohle, Dr Ernst-Wilhelm 302, 362, 454
Bolin, Luis 379
Bolingbrooke, Lord 217
Bonfield, Margaret 57
Bonham Carter, Lady Violet 57, 499, 539
Book, The 488
'Book Clubs' 554
Books and Bookmen 643
Bookseller and Stationer 444
Boothby, Robert 45, 51–2, 85, 128, 130, 132, 135, 137, 142, 152–3, 155, 158–60, 182, 193–4, 213, 215, 228, 271, 298, 387, 430, 435–6, 440, 522, 605, 641, 644
Borghese, Prince Valerio 586
Bormann, Martin 334, 461, 526, 603
Borremann, F. K. 602
Borth, Fred 630
Bosworth, R. J. B. 192
Bothamley, Margaret 451, 454, 459, 474
Bouverd, Jean-Marie 601
Bow Group 634
Bowden, Sir Robert 115
Bowles, Commander (MP) 426
Bowra, C. M. 96
Box, F. M. 171, 186, 188, 311, 320, 322, 330–2, 365–6
Bracken, Brendan 45, 153, 155, 176, 186, 228, 233, 298, 524, 536
Bradford, Charles 227, 322
Brailsford, H. N. 78, 79, 85, 101
Braithwaite, Rudy 618
Brand, Phyllis 43
Brand, Robert 91
Braun, Eva 455
Brenan, Gerald 501
Brewer, John 326, 632
Briscoe, Norah 506
Bristol, Arnold 200
Britain First (aircraft) 340
British Array 439, 445
British Brothers' League 350
British Council 620
British Council Against European Commitments 439, 452, 460
British Council for a Christian Settlement in Europe (BCCSE) 471, 473–4, 486, 489–90
British Democratic Party 545
British Empire Union 195, 197, 454
British Fascist 204
British Fascisti/s (BF) 109, 128, 194, 196, 198, 199, 203, 204, 244, 245, 254, 268, 293
British Free Coprs (BFC) 532, 552, 561
British Glycerine Co. 427
British-Italian Bulletin 361
British League of Ex-Servicemen and Women 542, 547, 549, 553, 557–8, 566–7, 569
British League Review 566
British Legion (SS) 405
British Movietone News 356
British National Party 622, 636
British People's Party (BPP) 452–3, 458, 471, 473, 484, 501, 525, 547
British Resistance Organization 508–9
British Shorthorn Society 427
British Traders Bureau (BU) 349, 444
British Union for the Abolition of Vivisection 373
British Union of Fascists (BUF) and British Union of Fascists and National Socialists (BU) 76, 128, 217, 371, 373–4:
anti-semitism 224, 237, 259, 263, 302, 304–5, 318, 334, 348, 360, 370, 383, 395–6, 414–5, 420, 423; FUBW 226–7; Women's Section 227, 258, 282, 332, 492; 'Fascist feminism' 281–2; Funds/ Mussolini 236, 255, 269–70, 277–8, 306, 330, 337, 345, 355, 365, 369–71, 378, 409, 517, 546; membership 247, 288–9, 368, 449, 489; Olympia 295–300, 304, 310; Nazis links 254, 302, 308, 317, 363, 419, 515, 517; Nazi funds 377, 403, 414, 448, 517, 520; Cotton campaigns 314, 326, 329, 367; organization 321, 330, 331–2, 365;

court marshall 322; East End 350–1, 375–6, 380–1, 383, 396, 410, 447–8; 'Mind Britain's Business' 354–5, 360–1, 368, 374; decline 310, 312, 329, 336, 346, 366–7, 376, 443, 449; elections 376, 380, 395, 410–1, 487; organization 401, 412, 414, 428, 444; anti-fascism/Cable Street 389–95; Abdication Crisis 403; approach of war 440, 449, 467–8; internment 502, 505–6, 524–5, 544; 'roll of honour' 552
British Union of Freemen 525
British Union Quaterly 399–400
British United Press 356
Britons Society 77, 426, 551
Britons Vigilantes Action League 549
Brittain (*Mail* executive) 329
Brittain, Vera 388
Brocket, Lord 373, 426, 453
Brock-Griggs, Anne 374, 455, 487, 492
Brocking, George 467
Brocklehurst, Philip 487
Brockway, Fenner 85, 86, 103, 122, 129, 143, 151, 158, 165
Brooke, General Sir 483, 512, 517, 525
Brooks, Collin 269, 296, 308, 329, 334, 340, 353–4, 375, 397, 401–5, 414, 430, 433–4, 445, 447, 456, 460, 470, 489, 547
Brooks, Jack 373
Brousse, Jacques 601
Brown, John 531
Brown, Noel 610
Brown, W. J. 138, 143, 150, 153, 155, 156, 159, 160, 162, 165
Bruce Lockhart, Robert 14, 124, 134, 148, 162, 169, 182, 190–1, 367, 429, 495
Bruderschaft (Brotherhood) 559, 561, 574, 583, 602
Brunning, Clement 497
Brunswick, Duchess of 342
Brust, Det. Insp. Harold 184
Bryan, Dan 599
Bryant, Arthur 408, 445, 474
Bryce, Lord 60
Bucard, Marcel 317, 327, 33
Buccleuch, Duke of 258. 328, 453, 470, 486, 495, 523
Buchanan, George 447, 479
Buchanan, Jack 387
Buchanan, Tom 399
Buchenwald 567
Bugle and Tiger 14
'Bulldog Drummond' 195, 421
Bullitt, William C. 496, 507
Bureau Concordia 526
Burgess, Guy 440, 488, 522, 606
Burgess, Victor 542, 556, 566, 576, 580, 597
Burke, Edmund 554
Burke, Owen 350, 410
Burns, Michael 357
Burt, Deputy Commander Len 573
Burwitz, Gudman (nee Himmler) 608–9
Buswell, Detective Sergeant 541
Butler, H. B. 127, 129–30
Butler, Rab 615
Butterwick, Mr 502
Byron, Robert 201

Cadogan, Sir Alexander 483, 501, 516
Cairns, Professor (Unity's doctor) 481
Callan, Paul 642
Cambridge University Fascist Association 416
Cameron, Helen 13
Camogna, Carlo 361
Campbell, Eric 225
Campbell, Jeannie 609
Campbell, Sir Malcolm 356
Campbell, Roy 399–400, 601
Camrose, Lord 371
Canaris, Admiral 356, 517
Cannadine, David 46, 70
Canning, George 338
Canning, Supt. (SB) 266
Canock, Lord 426
Capel, H. J. (Air Vice Marshal) 19
Car and General Insurance 421
Carlberg, Carl 586, 591
'Carlos Network' 603
Carlton Club 63
Carlyle, Thomas 26, 73, 116, 217, 291, 310, 492, 543
Carlyon, A. K. 63
Carroll, C. E. 424, 462
Carson, Sir Edward 16, 56, 256
Carter, Lt. Col. John 195

Cartland, Barbara 53, 69, 112
Casa Maury, Marquis 112, 124
Casa Maury, Paula (Gellibrand) 112, 124, 145, 153
Castlerosse, Doris 180
Catholic Herald 379, 410, 456
Catholic Times 456
Catlin, George 137, 141, 142, 146, 150, 165, 166, 168, 272, 296, 300
Cavendish-Bentinck, Henry 32, 55–7
Cazalet, Victor 155
Cecil, Algernon 364
Cecil, David 56
Cecil, Lord Hugh 20, 55, 206
Cecil, Lord Robert 32, 47, 49–50, 55, 58, 64, 68, 70
Celli, John 233
Centre International d'Estudes sur le Fascisme (CINEF) 199
Cerrecoundo, Mademoiselle 605
Cesarani, David 383
Chadwick, (British diplomat) 600
Chalet, Emil 291, 301
Challen, Charles 549
Chamberlain, Austen 50, 206, 207, 312
Chamberlain, Houston Stewart 383
Chamberlain, Joseph 37–40, 46, 154
Chamberlain, Neville 84, 104, 122, 171, 184, 417, 438–440, 467, 469, 474, 482, 494–5, 499, 501, 509
Chandos Group 205
Channon, Chips 260, 403, 538
Chaplin, Lord 456
Charles, Hilary 53
Charnley, John 323, 370, 457, 585, 599–600, 616
Chastelain, Major de 526
Chatham, Earl of (Pitt the Elder) 25, 39, 41
Chaumier, Air Commodore J. A. 258, 267, 278
Cheke, Marcus 510
Chesham, Guy 575–6
Chesterton, A. K. 251–2, 304–5, 309, 320, 324, 366, 417, 420, 429, 433, 445, 454, 452, 563, 605, 636
Chesterton, Cecil 251
Chesterton, G. K. 61, 74, 208, 251, 350, 365
Cheyette, Bryan 207
Cheyney, Peter 184, 189
Chicago Tribune 570
Children of the Sun 45
Chivalry 184
Christian Defence Movement 473
Christiansen, Arthur 537
Churchill, Clementine 63, 513, 524, 535
Churchill, Diana 320
Churchill, Lord Ivor 377
Churchill, Lord Randolph 25, 41, 135, 214, 334–5, 457, 609
Churchill, Randolph 179, 181, 182, 202, 205, 282
Churchill, Sarah 377
Churchill, Winston 29, 68, 116, 150, 153, 154, 176, 181, 188, 205, 228, 239, 314, 367, 397, 415, 470, 478, 484, 486, 489–90, 524, 598, 641, 646: Romanes lecture 141; 'Suicide club' 159; fencing 13; on Lloyd George 23; Minister of Air 47; on OM 44; on Snowden 122; Young Tories 128; India 257, 326, 334; Hitler 377–8, 432; Abdication 403–10; on Rothermere 340; 'Fifth Column' 464; attacks Fascism 432; PM 495, 497, 504, 508, 510–1, 522, 523, 538; internment 497–8, 506, 513, 524
Ciano, Count Galeazzo 234, 245, 333, 365, 395
Cimmie Mosley Day Nursery (Kensington) 498
Citrine, Walter 253
Clark, Dorothy 169
Clark, James 387, 448
Clarke, Edward 'Mick' 348, 350, 370, 395, 410, 432, 501, 546, 600
Clarke, Kenneth 623
Clausen, Dr 327, 333
Cline, J. R. 137
Clive, Lord 460
'Cliveden Set' 532
Clynes, J. R. 56, 131, 245
Coates, Capt. R. 284
Cochrane, Kelso 616
Cockburn, Claud 249
Cohen, (Lord Justice) Sir Lionel 310
Cohen, Richard 174
Cohn, Norman 646
Cole, Commander E. H. 425–6, 452
Cole, G. D. H. 73–5, 116, 117, 123, 125, 126, 129, 133, 141, 143, 157, 182, 226
Cole, Margaret 134

Colefax, Lady (Sibyl) 27–8, 53, 175, 372
Collier, Vincent (Captain 'X') 203, 381, 413, 454,
Collins, Michael 58, 60
Colman, Ronald 344
Cologne Chamber of Commerce 441
Colville, John 513, 522
Comintern (Communist International) 231, 351
Comitati d'azione per l'Univeralita di Roma (CAUR) 235, 270, 283, 327, 333
Committee on Fascism 553
Committee of Imperial Defence 354
Communist Party of Great Britain 77, 102, 189–90, 195, 197, 198, 204, 222, 231, 263, 295, 301, 305, 318–9, 351, 362, 375, 390, 396, 423, 487, 537
Common Sense 58
Commonwealth Party 569–70
Congress of Nazi Groups Abroad 356
Conner, 545
Connolly, Cyril 203
Connor, J. D. 56
Conservative Research Department 313
Constitutional Research Association 525
Coogan, Kevin 562, 575
Conway, Martin 316
Cook, Arthur 102, 110, 150, 156
Cook, Colin 41
Cooper, Lady Diana 69, 238, 465
Cooper, Duff 69, 167, 405, 465, 482
Cooper, Thomas 531, 552
Co-ordinating Committee for Anti-Fascist Activities 318
Co-ordinating Committee of Patriotic Societies 454
Coote, Colin 45–6, 202, 214, 215, 638
Cornwallis-Evans, T. P. 327
Corporate Book Club 554
Corporate Club 577
Corporatism 39, 141, 157, 185, 188, 190
Coselochi (Italian fascist) 327
Costa, General 582
Costigan, D. 592
Coston, 632
Cottenham, Lord (Mark) 484, 487
Cottentin, Maurice 583
Cotter, James 558
Cotton Factory Times 314
Coty, Francois 317
Counter-Intelligence Corps (US) 345, 356, 559, 563, 585–6, 596
Courlander, Roy 531
Courtauld, Sir Samuel 128, 313
Cowdray, Lord 31, 55, 60, 64
Cowling, Maurice 509
Cox, Anthony 405
Cox, Hubert 284
Craigavon, Lord 284
Craik, Lady 116
Craven, William F. 472
Creasey, Ronald 250
Cripps, Sir Stafford 146, 222, 256, 257, 266, 271, 274, 314, 526
Crisis (BU paper) 404
Crisis (NP film) 186
Croft, Sir Henry Page 35, 128, 183, 469, 502
Croker, William 505, 518
Crome, Werner 421
Cromwell, Oliver 143, 310, 343, 445, 526, 647
Cross, Colin 32, 366, 411, 544, 627
Cross, John Carlton 454
Crossman, Richard 13
Crowle, William 484–5
Crowley, Aleister 26, 90, 311
Croyden Airport 373
Crowood 543, 548
Crozier, W. P. 225. 535
Crux Easton 541, 543
Cudlipp, Hugh 309, 637, 641
Cullen, Stephen 228
Cumings, Leslie 165, 173, 176, 205, 210, 314
Cunard 197
Cunard, Lady (Maud) 28, 53, 201, 328
Cunliffe-Owen, Sir Hugh 128, 132, 134, 159, 169, 379
Curragh, The (County Kildare) 16, 23
Currey, Muriel 234, 256, 258, 359, 361
Curry, Jack 285
Curzon, Lord 31, 43–4, 48–9, 62, 66, 168, 344
Curzon, Alexandra (Baba Metcalfe), 112, 124, 221, 240, 319–20, 385, 402–3, 409, 457, 477, 607, 642:
childhood 43; Cimmie marriage 51; personality 62; attracted to OM 144, 223, 248, 260, 352, 445, 535–6; joins BUF 282; on Diana 333, 513; Grandi 337; Halifax 477

Curzon, Lady Cynthia (Cimmie Mosley), 103, 112, 116, 124, 156, 161, 168, 340, 344, 382, 642: childhood/teenager 43–4; end of WWI 33; Paris 48–9; OM 51–2, 119; personality 52; politics 119–20, 127, 145, 150; OM women 108, 112, 145–6, 213, 232; In Turkey/ Russia 144–5; NP 163, 176–7, 191, 207; children 180, 193, 204; BUF 226; ill 209, 213, 238; death 239; will 301
Curzon, Irene (Lady Ravensdale), 112, 124, 211, 233, 260, 320, 420, 439, 457: childhood/personality 43, 61; Cimmie marriage/problems 51, 110, 119–20, 232; on OM 221, 469, 495, 506, 551; Cimmie's illness/death 238; on Diana 333, 445, 469, 481; guardian to OM children 240, 340, 409, 465, 511
Curzon, Mary (Leiter) 43–4, 98

Dachau 548
Dairyman, The 444
Dallas, George 150
Dalton, Lady 225
Dalton, Hugh 85, 109, 114, 116, 146, 150, 152, 154, 157, 167, 501, 539
Dansey, Claude 528
Darnley, Lord 483, 489
Darrell, Margaret 372
Davidson, Colin 242, 406
Davidson, J. C. C. 41, 155, 406
Davies, Dan 168, 169, 170
Davies, Sellick 166, 187, 188
'Dawes Plan' 372
Dawn Patrol (1930) 178
Dawnay, Alan 358
Dawson, Lord 535–6
Dawson (BU member) 421
Day, James Wentworth 460
Day, Kenneth 467
'Deacon, Richard' (aka Patrick McCormick) 523
Dearborn Independent 100
Deardon, Dr Harold 505, 518
Deat, Marcel 206, 530, 560, 586
Death of a Hero (1928) 178
Dehler, Dr 603
Der Deutsche Block (DDB) 583, 596
D'Erlanger, Catherine 28
de Beaumont, Charles 174, 184, 209, 320
de Brogueville, Graf 345
de Courcy, Anne 352, 526, 548, 606
de Courcy, Kenneth 406
Deedes, W. F. 220, 391, 396, 541
de Gaulle, General 630
Degrelle, Leon 316, 427, 561, 591, 602
de Havilland, Sir Geoffrey 19, 328, 451
de Havilland, Lt Hereward 19
de la Cierva, Juan 379
de Lassoe, Major 526, 581
de Laubespin, Comte Antoine 474
de Leon, Ponce 623
del Boca, Angelo 628
Delmer, Sefton 393, 607–8
del Monte, Count Antonio 500
del Vayo, Julio Alvarez 400
de Maeztu, Ramiro 75–6
de Man, Henrik 206, 560
de Marsanich, Augusto 595
de Munck, Helene 486, 492, 494–5
'Department Z' (BUF) 265, 274
de Rivera, Jose Antonio Primo 316, 510, 582
De Ropp, Baron 476
Der Sturmer 283, 325, 346, 420, 423, 425, 475
Desert Island Discs 645
Deterding, Sir Henry 278, 306, 337
Deutsche-Englische Gesellschaft 362
Deutsche Partei (DP) 596
Deutsche Reichspartei (DRP) 602, 607, 623–4, 631
Deutsche Soziale Bewegung 591
Deutsches Flugblatt 577
De Valera, Eamon 61, 553
de Walzin, Baron Brugmann 427
Dewette, Elsa 575
De Wolfe, Elsie 53
Dickens, Rear Admiral Gerald 225
Dickoff, (German Foreign Minister) 300, 301
Dickson, Lovat 399
Dienststelle Ribbentrop (Buro) 330, 362, 383, 392, 420
Dietrich, Otto 333, 377, 458

Dietze, Dr Roderich 526
Dinamico Social 601
Direction de la Surveillance du territoire (DST) 581, 589
Di San Faustino, Princess Jane 53, 192
Disraeli, Benjamin 25
Diston, Marshall 205
Distributist League 251, 350, 644
Dixon, Piers 554
Dohring, Herbert 341
Dolan, Charles 263–5, 311–2
Dollan, Patrick 84
Dollfus, Chancellor (Austria) 317
Dollmore, Eugen 591
Domvile, Admiral Sir Barry 424, 450–1, 456, 458, 460, 462, 471, 473–4, 476–7, 482, 486–7, 505, 509, 515, 519
Domvile, Lady 460, 487, 524
Domvile, Compton 519
Don, Sir William Bt 447
Donner, Sir Patrick 207, 299, 364
Donovan, Capt. Brian 246, 366, 401, 455, 468, 474, 484–5, 501, 644
Doran, Edward 230
Dorchester Agricultural Society 586
Doriot, Jacques 530
Dorman, Geoffrey 21, 267, 329, 340
Dorman, Pamela 267
Douglas, Major Clifford 76–7
Douglas-Hamilton, Lord 426
Douglas-Hamilton, Lady Nina 450
Downe, Lady 189, 254, 278, 367, 430, 455, 463, 487, 501
'Drew, Colonel' 524
Driberg, Tom 430
Drieu la Rochelle, Pierre 29
'Driver, Dick' 69
Driver, Nellie 376
Druids 459
Drummond, Edwina 373
Drummond, Eric 317
Drummond, George 372–3, 425, 456, 457
Drummond's Bank 373, 456
Drummond Wolff, Henry 278, 289, 299, 364, 470
Duckworth-King, Sir George 258
Dufferin, Lord 225
Dugdale, Thomas 406
Duggan, Grace 44
Dunbar, Mr 256
Dundas, Admiral Sir Charles 233, 234
Dundas, Ian Hope 233, 234, 245, 255, 267, 274, 307, 318, 330, 340, 361, 365, 369, 403, 412, 419
Dundas, Lynette (daughter) 233, 365
Dunlop, George 529, 541–2, 545–6
Dunn, Lady 260, 415, 426, 452, 473, 502
Dunn, Sir James 132, 502
Du Pont (family) 372
Dupow, Otto Karl 591
Duprat (post-WWII neo-Nazi) 632
Durrell, Lawrence 400
Dutt, Rajani Palme 205, 318
Duvivier, Claude 451, 484–5, 515
Dyer, Lady (Schroeder) 436
Earls Court Exhibition Hall 457
East African Standard 327
Eatwell, Roger 560
Eccles, Lt-Col. (WWI) 23
Eccles, David 512
Eckersley, Frances 451, 454
Eckersley, Peter 168–9, 387–8, 415–7, 419 430, 437, 448, 451, 454, 460, 463
Economic Freedom League 205
Economic Policy Association (Berlin) 268
Economist, The 228
Ede, Chuter 236, 551, 553, 570
Eden, Anthony 358, 360, 373, 423, 469
Edmonds, Major Harry 525
Edward I, King 425
Edward VII, King 103, 353
Edward VIII, King 369, 373, 393, 403–4, 406–7, 422
Edwards, H. W. J. 74
'Egalite, Philippe' 116
Eggenfelden Printing Co. 596
Ehrhardt, Arthur 586, 591
18B Detainees Aid Fund 529–30, 541–2, 545
18B Publicity Council 529, 541–2
Einsatzgruppen Kommando 516, 571
Eisentraeger, Lothar 356
Elam, E. Dudley 468, 484, 487, 528
Elam, Norah 282, 468, 480, 484, 487, 501, 528
Eliot, Maxine 29, 32

Eliot, T. S. 26, 74
Elizabeth I, Queen 3, 416
Elliott, Walter 45–6, 103, 128, 132, 135, 142, 153, 155, 250, 255, 292
Elton, Lord 458
Elton, Geoffrey 102
Elwyn Jones, (Lord) Frederich 405
Emmanuel, King Victor 373
Empire Crusade 129, 132, 152, 164, 167, 202
Empire Day 12
Empire Economic Union 256
Empire Free Trade 115, 124, 260
Empire Industries Association 128
'Enderle, Dottore' 245
Engdahl, Per 563, 586, 590–1, 594
Engel, Major Gerd 398, 461, 508, 517
England Komitee 516, 530–1
English Mystery 250, 296, 327
English National Association 529
English Review 256, 258, 379
English Speaking Union 226
Errol, Earl of (Josslyn Hay) 69, 311, 327, 364
Erskine, Lord 258
Euphorian Books 610
Euripides 534
Europafront 630
Europa Unita 562, 582
Europe-Africa Association 616
European, The 616
European Court of Human Rights 634
European Economic Community (EEC) 610
European Liaison office 596, 600
European National Movement 616
European New Order 607
European People's Movement 600
European Press Agency 427, 430
Europan Situation, The (1948) 565, 574
European Study centre (MSI) 562
Evans, Captain Dudley M. 415, 434
Evans, Dr Geoffrey 535–6
Evening Dispatch 172
Evening Standard 81, 124, 139, 151, 154, 194, 215, 248, 457, 460, 540, 558, 609
Everyman 256
Evola, Professor J. 591
Express, Daily 105, 124, 141, 159, 172, 196, 303, 320, 345, 365, 393–4, 428, 430, 444, 458, 537
Eyre and Spottiswoode 311

'F, Michael' 403
Fabre-Luce, Alfred 180, 589
Fabre-Luce, Lottsie 180, 589
Fairbanks, Douglas 51, 82, 112, 122
Fairfax-Lucy, Sir Henry 256, 258, 339, 364
Falange Espanola 316, 363, 400, 586, 596
Farinacci, Roberto 326
Farman, Maurice 22
Farrer, Philip 425, 456, 460
Farson, Dan 628
Fascist, The 203
Fascist Quarterly 383, 413
Fascist Union of British Workers (FUBW) 226–7, 247, 301, 322–3
Fascist Week 249, 277
Fawcett, Arthur 229
Fawcett, E. 472
Featherstone-Hammond, Charles 473
Federal Reserve Board 101
Federation of British Industry (FBI) 98, 100, 133
Federation of Progressive Societies and Individuals 251
FBI 570, 577, 622, 628
Feisal, King 65
Fellowes, Daisy 541, 549
Fenton, Dr (Brixton prison) 536
Ferdinand, Prince Louis 244
Feversham, Lord 277
'Fifth Column' 473, 475, 488–91, 495–6, 498, 504, 506, 512, 516, 518, 521
Figaro, Le 601
Fighting Fund for Freedom 549
Findlay, Archibald 322, 338, 412, 419, 448
Findlay, Richard 334–5, 425, 452, 454, 473, 475, 515
Fine Gael 316
Fishman, William J. 350
Fitzgerald, Scott 69
Fitzgibbon, Constantine 634
FitzRandolph, Sigismund 308, 357
Fleming, Ian 523

Fleming, Peter 477
Flockhart, Alfred 545–6, 558, 566–7, 583, 590, 608
Focus 505
Foliogno, Cesare 361
Follett, Mary 99
Fontuyn, Pim 647
Foot, Isaac 298
Foot, Michael 107, 166, 641
Foot, Paul 622
Ford (BU member) 421
Ford, Henry 99–100
Fordham, Montague 586
Ford Motor Company 99
Foreign Policy Institute (Nazi) 561
Forgan, Dr Robert 150–1, 156, 163, 177, 179, 186, 188, 194, 204, 213, 220, 251, 257–8, 268, 274, 277, 301, 309–10, 312, 321
Forster, Frau 113, 117, 132
Forster, E. M. 447
Fortnightly Review 171, 219
43 Group 558–9, 568, 569–70, 577, 583
Forward 68, 80, 456
Forwood, Sir Dudley 9
Fountain, Andrew 622
Fourcade, Marie-Madeleine 528
Fox, James 570
Fox, Quentin 647
Foyle, Christine 408
Francis Hawkins, Neil 197, 200, 204, 210, 245, 246, 270, 306, 332, 330, 337, 366, 401, 407, 412, 414, 429, 446, 452, 468, 471, 473, 501, 567
Franciste 317
Franciste, Le 317
Franco, Generalissimo Francisco 379, 390, 399–400, 581–2
Frank, General Hans 459
Franke-Gricksch, Dr Alfred 559, 561–2, 564, 574, 578, 583, 587, 595, 597
Frankel, Dan 375
Frankel, William 634–5
Frankfurter, Felix 397
Frankfurter Zeitung 392
Frankische Tageszeitung 346–7, 356
Franklin (BU) 546
Franzero, Signor C. M. 378
Fredericks, Kay 262, 266, 289, 297–8, 321
Freeman, Benson 552
French, Sir (Field Marshal Lord) John 21, 23, 111
Frenz, Wolfgang 631
Freud 534
Friedlander, max 382
'Friend X' (radio project) 438
Friends of Italy 258
Friends of Mosley 645
Fromm, Bela 422
'Front Generation' 29, 34, 67, 75, 99, 101, 105, 205, 530, 560
Fronte Universaitario di Azione Nazionale 590
Frost Programme (BBC) 637
Fuller, Maj.Gen. J. F. C. 103, 251, 275, 310, 321, 324, 329–30, 337, 352, 354, 359–400, 414, 418, 424–5, 430, 450, 452–3, 457, 460, 473, 478, 487, 494, 501, 509, 511–2, 517, 547, 571, 591, 604
'Funny Money' 76
Fyfe, H. Hamilton 9, 295

Gable, Gerry 631
Gainer, St Clair 394
Galinsky, Dr Karl-Hans 358
Gallacher, Willie 95, 550
Game, Sir Philip 381, 390–1, 395–6, 411, 423, 496
Gannon, Anthony 563, 566, 576
Gardiner, Rolf 10, 92, 445
Gargoyle Club 111, 320
Gartner, Dr Margarete 265, 362
Garvin, J. L. 38, 155–6, 176, 351
Gazetta de Popolo 517
Gellibrand, Paula (*see* Casa Maury)
Gemona AG 419, 435, 440, 463
General Motors 372
General Strike (1926) 102
Genoud, Francois 603–4
George V, King 51, 233, 360, 369
George VI, King 373, 453, 469, 489–9, 507, 516
George, Prince (Duke of Kent) 62
Georgia Committee 279
Gerarchia 225
Gerault, C. S. 312
Gessner, Rudolph 300
Gilbert, Henri 601
Gilbert, John 124
Gilbert, Oliver C, 425, 465, 471–2
Gillies, Miss (Diana's maid) 513
Gilmour, Sir John 276, 285
Giornale d'Italia 360
Giovane Europe 629
Giovane Nazione 629
'Gladio' 624, 629–30

Glasgow, Earl of 278
Glass, James 107, 647
Glenconner, Lord 301
Gloucester, Duke of 495
Glyn, Elinor 48, 52
Goacher, Denis 601
Goad, Capt. Harold 199, 233, 256–7, 361
Godfrey, Edward 529
Godman, Commander Thomas 267, 356
Goebbels, Dr Josef 231, 244, 282, 327, 330, 342, 349, 354, 362, 368, 372, 376–7, 381–2, 389, 393–4, 398, 402, 409–10, 412, 415, 417, 419, 423, 427–8, 434, 444, 448–50, 456, 485, 488–9, 494, 501, 512, 575, 603, 645
Goering, Hermann 232, 342, 356, 388, 418, 424, 432, 441
Goethe 533, 617, 644
Goldberg, Alf 373
Goldsmith, Sir James 641
Gollancz, Victor 408
Gordon-Canning, Louise 339
Gordon-Canning, Robert 338–9, , 35, 353, 357, 378–9, 386, 393, 419, 425, 444–5, 452, 471–2, 482, 490, 551
Gordon Walker, Patrick 375
Gottlieb, Julie 227, 242
Gough, Gen. Sir Hubert 258, 275
Gowing, Horace 566
Graf Reischach Agency 421
Graham, Marquess of 327
Graham, Col. Henry 23
Graham, Miles 238
Graham, Sir (Lord) Ronald 192, 364, 451, 454, 487, 491, 494
Gran, Maurice 645
Grand, Major Lawrence 440
Grandi, Dino 199, 210, 211, 234, 236, 245, 255, 263, 269, 273–4, 285, 291, 320, 337, 355, 359, 361, 364, 373
Grant, Nellie 327
Gravelli, Asvero 235
Graves, Robert 178
Gray, John 15
Graziani, General Rudolfo 359
Greater Britain Movement 636
Green, Martin 178
Green, Richard 45
Green Badge 444
Green Shirt Movement for Social Credit 251
Greene, Ben 445, 452–3, 454, 471, 474, 484, 487, 506, 516, 547
Greene, Sir Hugh 628, 634
Greenwood, Arthur 129, 133, 135, 494, 498, 500
Gregoire, Armand 317, 428
Gregor, A. James 601
Greville, Mrs Ronnie 27, 53
Grey, C. G. 41, 329, 452, 473
Grey, Lord 58, 60, 258
Griffiths, James 61
Grigg, Sir Edward 259, 326
Grimm, Frederick 560
Grimm, Hans 591
Grosvenor Kin 296
Group 'Collaboration' 560
Grumfeld, Walter 569
Grundy, Edna 608
Grundy, Sidney 608
Grundy, Trevor 608
Guderion, General Heinz 504
Guest, Freddie 32, 46, 329
Guild Socialism 73–4, 77, 99
Guinness, Beatrice 180, 242
Guinness, Bryan 378
Guinness, Desmond 201, 501, 573
Guinness, Jonathan 201–2, 377, 455, 502, 513, 573
Guinness, Mrs Richard 241
Gummer, John 623

Hacking, Alfred 128
Haider, Jorg 646
Haigh-Wood, Vivienne 287
Hailsham, Viscount 206
Hale, Jim 513
Halifax, Lord 54, 373, 470, 477, 482–3, 492, 500
Hall, Howard 502
Hall, J. H. 375
Hamilton, Duke of 523, 532
Hamilton, Cecily 267
Hamilton, Gerald 488, 511, 519, 570
Hamilton, Sir Ian 206, 405, 453
Hamilton, Mary 239
Hamlyn (*Action* editor) 179
Hamlyn, Michael 627
Hamm, Jeffrey 395, 542, 547, 549, 553–8, 566–7, 575–6, 579, 587, 599, 609, 611, 613, 616, 630

Hammersley, Violet 621
Hammond, Charles 468
Hammond, J. L. 60
Hanfstaengl, Dr Ernst 'Putzi' 193, 241, 248, 326, 357, 410, 472
Handley Page 258
Hankey, Lord 470
Hankey, Maurice 133
'Hannay, Richard' 450
Hannon, Sir Patrick 128, 183, 299
Hanseatic League 73
Harding, Lawrence 468
Hardinge, Lady Alexander 426, 459
Hargreave, John 92, 251
Harker, Alan 506
Harker, Brig. Jaspar 197, 265, 447
Harmsdon, Danny 627, 630, 639
Harmsworth, Lord Cecil 456, 470
Harmsworth, Esmond 45, 154, 176, 191, 200, 205, 271, 309, 405
Harmsworth, Harold 50
Harpers 313
Harrod, Roy 249, 377, 529
Harrow Gazette 55, 61
Harrow Observer 32, 37, 61
Hart, E. D. 505
Hart, Jenifer (Williams) 480, 518–9
Hartshorn, Vernon 138
Harvey, Oliver 523
Hastings, Patrick 68
Haushofer, Albrecht 330, 383–4, 523, 532
Haushofer, Karl 330, 383, 385
Hawker, Capt. 'Johnny' 17–9, 22
Hawks, Olive 280, 349, 455, 487
Hay, Norman 452
Hayter, Sir William 623
Hayter, U. C. S. 364
Headlam, Sir Cuthbert 148, 276, 300
Hearst, Randolph 174
Heathcote, Sir Justin 4, 372
Heathcotes 4
Heidegger, Martin 564
Helbert, Lionel 10
Held, James 416, 442, 460, 463
Held, Stephen 488
Henderson, Arthur 60, 82, 121, 124, 129, 137, 151, 159, 167, 180
Henderson, Nevile 449
Henlein, Konrad 459
Hepburn, Audrey 242
Hepburn-Ruston, Joseph 242, 343, 427, 430, 446, 544
Herald, The 105, 137, 142, 159, 169, 173, 210, 272, 345–6, 518
Herbert, Aubrey 32, 55–6, 64
Herbert, David 548
Hesketh, Walter 623–4
Hess, Rudolf 248, 253, 330, 362, 422, 448, 459, 523–4, 555–6, 640
Hesse, Dr Fritz 345, 370, 383, 428, 526, 528, 530
Hesse, Prince Philip of 192
Hesse, Silke 227
Hetzler, Dr Erich 424
Hewel, Walter 362
Hewins, W. A. S. 37–8
Hewitt, Gerald 552
Heywood, Sir John 185, 357
Hickson, Oswald 529, 535
'Hickey, William' 430
Higgs, Nanny 540
Higham, Charles 372
Hildebrand, Herr 358
Hilliard, A. R. 553
Himmler, Henrich 344, 347, 354, 389, 425, 428, 449, 455, 459, 479, 512, 520, 526, 448, 561, 591
Hinchingbrooke, Lord (Victor Montague) 248, 388, 457
Hindenburg, Chancellor 202
Hirota (Japanese Foreign Minister) 329
Hiscox, 'Mollie' 506
Hitler, Adolf, 114, 181, 193–4, 202, 209, 232, 237, 241, 248, 255, 283, 287, 301, 317, 330, 335, 339, 353–4, 360, 362, 365, 370, 373, 379, 398, 410–1, 419–20, 423, 430, 435, 439, 448, 459, 469, 490, 502, 512–3, 526, 530, 545, 564, 598, 600, 603, 626, 628, 645:
  WWI 20, 464; end of war 35; *Hitler* (Lewis, 1930) 167; 'Chauffeureska' 241, 333, 472; Chancellor 224, 228–9; Night of the Long Knives 303; forbids spying 330; OM wedding 393; Chamberlain/ Redesdales 383; radio 427, 430; Table Talk 461–2; Mussolini 369, 423; OM 341–2, 343, 458, 476–7, 507, 509, 517, 526; supports BU 376–7, 403; invasion of GB 516–7; 'Secret Book' 525, 560

Hoare, Oliver 388, 427, 430, 435, 466
Hoare, Sir Samuel, 56, 228, 364, 388, 405, 451, 462, 464, 507, 526, 540
Hoare-Lavel Pact 364
Hobbes 217
Hobshouse, Christopher 172
Hobson, J. A. 78–9, 85, 103, 208
Hobson, S. G. 73–4, 76
Hodge, Herbert 169–70, 173, 177, 184, 186, 189, 194
Hoffman, H. R. 425
Hoffman, Heinrich 333, 357, 393
Hoffman, Henriette 593
Hogg, Quintin 206
Holderness, Sir Ernest 497
Hollis, Christopher 251
Hollis, Roger 540
Holmes, Colin 350
Holocaust 548, 563, 567, 571, 645
Holtby, Winifred 280
Holt-Wilson, Sir 520
Holz, Karl 283
Holzer, Lady 206
Hone, J. H. 468
Hoop, Dr (Liechtenstein minister) 430
Hoover, J. Edgar 570, 577, 622, 628
Horabin, Frank 84
Horchem, Dr Hans 608
Hore-Belisha, Leslie 45, 107, 142, 176, 282, 438, 469, 475, 482
Horner, Arthur 102
Horrie, Chris 637
Houston, Lady 175, 249, 256–7, 334–5, 340, 351, 370
Houston, Richard 'Jock' 348
Howard, Brian 201, 488
Howard, Michael 623
Howard, Peter 171, 179, 184, 186, 188, 202
Howard, T. F. 299
Howe, Lord 198
Hoy, James 602
Hudson, C. E. 468
Hughes, Arthur 197
Hughes, James McGuirk (*see* P. J. Taylor) 197, 262, 454, 478, 491, 515, 551
Hulme, T. E. 74–5
Hulton, Sir Edward 128
Humanist Society (Oxford) 635
Hunt, Antonia 531
Hunter, Dr 159
Huth Jackson, Mrs Annabel 480, 485, 487
Huxley, Aldous 112, 647
Huxley, Elspeth 327
Huxley, Julian 329
Huxley-Blythe, Peter 576, 580
Hyde, Douglas 542, 545, 552, 558
Hydleman, Louis 567
Hyslop, 'Nanny' 66

ICI 313
Il Giornale d'Italia 307
Illuminated politics 26–7
Illustrated London News 367
Imperial Defence League 563, 566
Imperial Fascist League 194, 203–4, 207, 236, 262, 276, 425–6, 465, 472, 547, 559
Imperial Fascists 200
Imperial Policy Group 405, 456
Imperial Zollverin 38–9
Imperium (1948) 571, 575
Inchape, Lord 169, 278
Independent Labour Party (ILP) 73, 77–80, 85, 101, 116, 231, 522
Independent Nationalists 545–6
India Defence League 207, 257
India Empire Society 364
Industrial Intelligence Board 195–6
Information and Policy 474
Ingham, Geoffrey 639
Ingram, Marie 507
Inskip, Sir Thomas 384, 435
Institute for the Rights of Nations 472
Intelligence Persons' Club 198
'intelligentzia' 150
International Broadcasting Co. 387, 440
International Broadcasting Union 419
International Fascist Exhibition (Rome) 232
International Publishing Corporation 637
International Union of Nationalists 283
Investigator 472
Iregun Zvai Leumi 557
Ireland 55–9
Ironside, Lord (son) 483
Ironside, Field Marshal Edmund (Lord) 36, 310, 449–50, 469, 474–5, 478, 482–3, 494, 504, 506, 517
Isherwood, Christopher 185
Ishiguro, Kazu 373
Isis 622
Ismay, Sir Hastings 389
Ismay, General 'Pug' 512
Italia Nostra 234

Jackson, Derek 320–1, 537–8, 540, 590–1
Jackson, Pamela 642
Jackson, Vivian 320
Jacobs, Joe 186, 318, 350–1, 375
James, Edward 202
James, Zita 144, 204, 242
Jameson, Dr 535
'Janitor' 116
January Club 237, 258, 260, 271, 275, 278, 272, 293, 309, 311–2, 324, 339, 357–8, 408
Jebb, Cynthia 551
Jebb, Sir Gladwyn 512, 600
Jebb, Ralph Gladwyn 468, 553
Jenks, Jorian 278, 417, 445, 468, 585–6
Jerrod, Douglas 251, 256–7, 311, 339, 364, 379, 400, 408
Jeune Europe (JE) 624, 630
Jeune Europe International 620
Jeunesse de l'Europe Nouvelle 560
Jewish Agency 382
Jewish Chronicle 210, 224, 230, 244, 259, 273, 277, 454, 487, 537, 625, 634–5, 638
Jewish People's Council against Fascism and Anti-Semitism 390
Joad, Cyril 142, 172, 173, 177, 179
Johannesburg Sunday Times 616
'John Bull' 8, 617
Johnson, Herschel V. 497, 499
Johnson, J. 84, 119, 168
Johnston, Tom 80, 121, 123, 130, 137, 183
Johnstone, Lt. Col. H. W. 205
Joint Broadcasting Committee (BBC) 440, 460
Jones, Inspector 501
Jones, Inigo 3
Jones, Jack 169, 170–1, 173, 187
Jones, John 545
Jones, Mervyn 583
Jones, Thomas 299, 389
Jordan, Colin 622, 625
Jordan, Michael 213, 229, 264
Josephs, Noel 179
Journey's End 178
Jowitt, (Lord) William 125, 152, 551
Joyce, Joan 464
Joyce, Margaret 411, 464
Joyce, Quentin 200, 439, 459, 472
Joyce, William 237–8, 248, 260, 273, 278, 318, 366, 399–400, 404, 464, 486, 497, 515, 523, 550, 552, 575:
biography 197–8; Carlyle influence 26; Knight/MI5 200, 238, 265, 330; anti-semitism 304–5, 351, 360, 394, 409; rival to OM 312, 318, 385, 401; India 348; marriage 411; leaves BU/NSL 412–3, 433, 439; Germany/'Lord Haw Haw' 459, 481, 491, 526–7, 530, 551
Joynson-Hicks 198
Jung 534
Junger, Ernst 586
Jungman, Nico 108
Jungman, Zita 108, 111, 180
Junior Imperial League 200

Kahn, David 446
Kameradenwerk 595
Karlowa, Karl 385
Karlowa, Otto 330
Kauffer, Ted McKnight 217
Kaye, Doris 558
Kaye, Solly 637
Kebble, Inspector 464
Keenes, Capt. 229
Kell, Sir Vernon 195, 198, 285, 290, 312, 425, 455, 464, 489, 504
Keller, Hans 283, 327, 472
Kelsey, Andrea 621
Kemsley, Lord 549
Kendrick, C. F. 187
'Kenmare' 419, 455
Kennedy, Aubrey Leo 20, 58
Kennedy, John F. 461
Kennedy, Joseph 492
Kensington Fascists 200
Kent, Tyler 486–7, 490, 495, 498–90, 500, 506, 521–2, 551
Kenworthy, J. M. 203
Keppel, Alice 353
Keppel, Celia 210, 223
Kerr, Admiral Mark 329
Keynes 69, 79–80, 83, 103–4, 108–9, 115–6, 120, 122, 124, 128, 130–1, 133, 141, 149, 157, 160, 171, 179, 185, 190, 242–3
Kibbo Kraft 92
Kieztoushi (radio project) 415
King, Cecil 516, 637, 640
King, Lady Phyllis 153
King David Hotel 557
Kirkpatrick, Sir Ivone 602
Kirkwood, Dr 238
Kitson, Arthur 76, 93, 147

Kleinwort Benson 379
Klemmer, Harvey 496, 520
Klindworths (German family) 382
Knickerbocker, H. P. 284, 289–90
Knight, Maxwell 296, 318, 346, 430, 473, 481, 490, 516, 606: BF 197, 198, 200; MI5 200, 265, 285; M Section 285, 446–8; agents 354, 473, 477, 482, 488, 494; Joyce 312, 330, 401, 409, 439, 464; Right Club 474, 497–8, 500
Knoechlein, Lt.Co. Fritz 572
Knowles, Frederick 438
Knox, James 201
Kogel, Arthur 591
Kordt, Theodor 426
Kredit Anstalt 171, 176
Krieger, Heinz 438
Kristallnacht 441
Kruger, Dr 484
Kruger, Peter and Lisa 478
Krupps 268
K Society 198
Ku Klux Klan 425
Kurtz, Harald (Cort, 'X') 447, 470, 482, 506, 515, 551
Kushner, Tony 498

Labour League of Youth 350
Lacarriere, Maurice 582
Ladies Carlton Club 480
Lamb, Lady Pansy 213
Lambrianou, Tony and Jimmy 627
Lammers, Dr (Nazi official) 261–2, 290
Lammont, Thomas 372
Landini, Amadeo 245
Lanfree, Giovanni 623–4, 631
Lansbury, George 121, 123, 130, 133, 135, 137, 150
Lansdowne Club 476
Larouche, Baroness 291
Laski, Harold 68, 71, 118, 121, 143, 146, 304, 310, 378, 380, 396–7, 451, 467
Lassalle (German Socialist leader) 286
Latchmere House 478, 518–9
Laurie, Professor A. P. 424, 452, 460, 462, 472
Laval, Pierre 365
Lavoro Fascista 258
Law, Bonar 48, 181
Lawrence, D. H. 178
Lawrence, Jon 299
Lawrence, T. E. (Lawrence of Arabia) 246, 357
Lawther, William 156
Lawton, Frederick 416, 421, 427, 434, 436, 441–2
Lawton, Launcelot 452
Lazarus, Jack 198
League of Empire Loyalists 605, 636
League of Ex-Servicemen 529
League of Industry 313
League of Nations 55, 60, 66, 169, 219, 352, 355, 360–1, 364, 383, 388, 482
League of Nations Union 55, 359
League of St George 642
League of Youth and Social Progress 48
Leaper, William 'Bill' 213, 314, 358
Lee, General (US attache) 494
Lee, Jennie 126, 138, 151, 153, 162, 275
Leeper, Rex 358
Lees, Aubrey 451–3, 454, 472, 477, 482, 487, 489, 493, 547
Lees-Milne, James 172, 187, 201–2, 310, 342, 406, 541, 605, 641, 643–4
Leese, Arnold 203, 204, 236, 262, 426, 551, 559, 622
Legion of Loyalists 200, 439
Legion of St George (SS) 530–1
Legion Wallonie (SS) 591
Lehane, Jerry 606
Lehmann, Rosamond 213
Leighton, Margaret 346
Leiter, Levi 43
Leiter Trust 113, 191, 239
Leitner, Elizabeth 530
Lemonnier, Guy 586, 596
Leopold, Josef 431
Le Pen, Jean-Marie 625, 646
Le Quesne, C. T. KC 416
Lesley-Jones, Peter 557
Levin, Bernard 625
Lewis, Capt. Charles 231, 233, 253
Lewis, Edward 'Kid' (Solomon Mendeloff) 182, 186, 187, 188, 194
Lewis, Morten (son) 194
Lewis, Oswald 402
Lewis, Wyndham 74, 77, 112, 144, 168–9, 185, 314, 399, 447
L'Humantie 462
Liberty Restoration League 426, 451, 454
Liddel, Capt. John 19
Liddell, Cecil 495
Liddell, Guy 306, 365, 448, 455, 481, 496–7
Liddell Hart, Basil 103, 258, 311, 418, 572, 591

Liddle, Peter 19, 280
Lindemann, Professor 320
L'Independence Belge 428
Lindsay, Sir Ronald 428
Link, The 424–5, 439, 444, 451–2, 459, 462, 470–1, 489, 506, 515, 523, 530, 532, 550
Linton-Orman, Rotha 196, 198, 204
'Living Wage, The' 79
Lloyd, Lord 154, 183, 207, 256–7, 278, 292, 326, 334–5
Lloyd, E. M. H. 30, 78, 79
Lloyd, Geoffrey 298
Lloyd George, David 19, 23–4, 29–31, 36, 40, 46, 55–9, 63–4, 70, 115–7, 130, 148, 153–4, 157–8, 176, 181, 193, 201, 224–5, 228, 292, 389, 397, 393, 470, 476, 489, 494–5, 507–9, 517, 523–4, 554, 598, 641, 647
Lloyd George, Megan 226
Locker-Lampson, Commander Godfrey 36, 540
Lockhart, J. G. 116
'Loch Lommond Wireless' 480
Lonciari, Fabio 582, 590–1
London Assurance 258
London Films 224
London General Press 454
London Mercury 185, 256, 314
London and Provincial Anti-Vivisection Society 468, 470, 480, 485
London Society of Compositors 405
London Tidings 563
Londonderry, Lady 53
Londonderry, Lord 328, 641
Longate, Norman 508
Lopokova, Lydia 108
'Lord Haw Haw' 365, 464, 478, 481, 490, 551
Loredan, Count Alvise 586, 621, 624
Losch, Tilly 202
Lothian, Lord 103, 155, 313, 508
Lovat-Frazer, J. 164
Lovelace, Earl of 153
Lovely, Percy Thomas 493
Lowther (Speaker of the House) 54
Lucas, Major 322
Lucas, Sir Jocelyn 460
Ludlam, H. F. 92, 251
Ludovici, Anthony 445
Luke, Rita 607
Lunn, Arnold 256
Luttman-Johnson, Capt. H. W. 257–8, 339, 364, 425, 471, 473, 515
Lutyens, Sir Edward 239
Lutyens, Robert (son) 239
Luxemburg 387, 439, 449
Lymington, Lord 250, 256, 327, 364, 439, 445, 452, 472, 474, 477, 479, 489
Lynn, Robert 174
Lyons 309

'Macaroni, Mr' 495, 500
MacCarthy, Desmond 89
McCormich, Colonel Robert 570
MacDonald, Ramsay 57, 71, 79, 104, 110, 112, 116, 121, 123, 127, 129, 132–3, 135, 143, 151, 165, 180, 187, 193, 205, 224, 239, 262
MacEntee 603
McGovern, John 156, 165, 479, 490, 522
McGowan, Sir Harry 147
McGuirk, Katherine 197
Macindoe, Rosemary 325
McKenna, Reginald 109, 122, 128
McKechnie, Hector G. 468, 501, 567, 623
Mackenzie, Sir Compton 288
MacKenzie-King (Canadian PM) 504
McKibben, Ross 222, 226, 639–40
Mackinder, H. J. 38
Macksey, Kenneth 509
McLean, Michael 577
Macmillan, Dorothy 142
Macmillan, Harold 120, 128, 142, 143, 153, 158, 163, 168, 214, 215
Macmillan, Norman 329
McNab, John 413, 439, 464
McNeil, Hector 570
McNeil Weir, L 159–60, 286, 323
Macquisten, F. A. 299
McWhirter (*Mail* executive) 329
Maddocks, J. 210
'Madison, Philip' (OM) 464–5
Maglinise, General Henri 427
Magnus-Allcroft, Sir Philip 258, 310
Maguire, Francis 552
Mail, Daily 9, 16, 19, 104, 146, 154, 191, 198, 224, 244, 271, 277, 288, 30–3, 309, 322, 330, 340, 352, 354, 359, 375, 420, 445, 456, 474, 537
Mairer, Charles 99

Mairet, Philip 205
Majoribanks, Edward 155
Makgill, Sir Donald 195, 258
Makgill, Lady Esther 258, 269, 280
Makgill, Sir George 195, 196, 258
Malan Afrikaner Party 572
Mallet, Sir Louis 270
Mallet, Robert 402
Malmo International 594–5, 600
Manchester Cotton Exchange 3
Manchester Guardian 132, 133, 138, 167, 187, 319, 345, 376, 536, 566
Manderville-Roe, E. G. 204, 205, 255, 279, 425, 451, 454–5
Mandle, W. F. 7, 143, 157
Mann (BU member) 421
Mar, Earl of 258, 452–3, 475, 479, 489
Marchbanks, John 311–2
Marconi, Guglielmo 233, 388
Marendez, Captain D. M. K. 356
Margesson, David 203, 405, 524
Marina, Princess 328
Markham, Frank 165
Marks and Spencer 211
Marley, Lord 275, 276
'Marovna, Baroness' (*see* Mary Tavener) 260
Marquand, David 131, 149
Marsden, K. E. 468
Martin, Kingsley 221, 372, 408
Mary, Queen 463, 502
MASK (codename) 362
Massi, Ernesto 582
Massingham, H. W. 64, 142
Masterman, J. C. 446
Matheson, Hilda 127, 440
Matteotti (murder of) 193
Maudling, Reginald 602
Maughan, Somerset 112
Maurras, Charles 39, 75, 208
Maxton, James 83, 110, 122, 124, 127, 134, 156, 157, 225
Maxwell, Sir Alexander 480–1, 521
Mayhew, Christopher 375
Mayne, Ferdy 447
Medical Society for the Study of Venereal Diseases 151
Meijer, Gerhard 559
Mein Kampf 167, 244, 336, 382, 408, 445, 537, 575
Meinertzhagen, Richard 362
Meissner, Karl 583, 586, 607
Melchett, Lord 127, 147
Melville, Cecil 130, 135, 136, 171, 175, 182, 208, 209, 225
Mendl, Sir Charles 53, 69, 112, 144
Mensdorff, Count Albert 263
Menzies, Stewart 523, 544
'Merrie England' socialists 39
Mesopotamia (Iraq) 65
Messel, Oliver 111, 179
Metcalfe, Capt. Dudley 'Fruity' 62, 144, 224, 294, 428, 477
Metexa, Doe 179
Methuen, Mr (medical commissioner) 536
Michaelis, Meir 360
Michelini, Arturo 594
Mignard, Gerard 533
Mikardo, Iain 165, 185
Miles, Alexander 197, 222, 227, 234, 242, 274, 293, 295, 301, 312, 323
Militant Christian Patriots 426, 450, 454
Miller, Joan 492
Millington, Commander (MP) 570
Mills, H. T. V. 'Bertie' 445, 451–2, 472, 547
Mills and Allen 387
Milner, Lord 30, 37–8, 40, 128
Minchin, Alfred 532
Miner, The 102
Miners' Federation 102, 165, 334
Ministry of Munitions (MoM) 23, 30–1, 128
Mirror, Daily 272, 547, 637
Mission 101 480
Mitchison, Naomi 251
Mitford, Lady Clementine 206
Mitford, Deborah (Duchess of Devonshire) 481, 591, 642
Mitford, Decca 346, 436, 638, 642
Mitford, Diana Freeman- (Guinness, Lady Mosley) 205, 223–4, 232, 246–7, 260–1, 263, 282, 296, 298, 303, 346, 354, 383, 440, 455–6, 475, 505, 511–2, 522, 553:
meets OM 201; politics 201, 377, 617, 639; car crash 252; social 210, 377; OM/ womanising 220, 336, 353, 366, 642; on

Cimmie 233, 238, 240; meets Putzi 241; Germany 247, 319, 325, 335, 356–7, 371–2, 385, 398, 402, 415, 418; Hitler 248, 335–6, 343, 345, 354, 363, 370, 389, 405, 410, 421, 448, 453, 462; Goebbels 362, 405; Olympic Games/ Bayreuth 381–2, 461; wedding 393–4, 445; Wotton 378, 406; radio project 416–7, 419–20, 434–5; anti-semitism 376, 520, 607; arrest/internment 501–2, 513–4, 520, 525–6, 532–4, 537; war 465–7; brother 541; post-WWII 555–6, 573, 575–9, 583, 617, 635, 589, 597, 605, 621, 632, 645; *A Life of Contrasts* (1977) 643; OM death 644–5; death 646
Mitford, Nancy 112, 223, 260, 280, 296, 314–5, 347–8, 503, 512, 553, 583, 598, 606–7, 623, 638, 642
Mitford, Pamela (nee Jackson) 320, 328
Mitford, Tom 194, 202, 206, 247, 319, 346, 357, 381, 394, 416, 457, 541, 543
Mitford, Unity 210, 243, 282, 298, 346–7, 363, 389, 433, 450, 461, 484, 540:
meets OM 223, 238, 300; meets Putzi 241; biography 241; Germany 247, 291, 303, 319, 335, 356–7, 415; Hitler, 333, 342–3, 345, 370, 398, 400, 421–2, 432, 435, 455; OM wedding 393–4; Olympic Games 381–2; Nazi informant 461–2; suicide 462, 467, 481, 576
Mitrinovi, Dimitri 205
'Modern Thought' Groups 554
Moir, Patrick 204, 208, 210
Moloney (UM official) 630
Monckton, Walter 429, 483, 490, 535
Mond, Henry 176
Monday Club 632, 636
Monk, Miss E. R. 501
Mont, Michael 601
Montague, C. E. M. 34
Montague, Margaret 27
Montrose, Duke of 451
Moore, Andrew 381
Moore, Sir Thomas 289, 299
Moore-Brabazon, Lt J. T. C. 'Ivan' 14, 41, 81, 164, 173, 282, 289, 299
Moral Rearmament 202
Moran, Lord (Dr) 539
Moran, 'Tommy' 326, 380, 391, 487, 505, 566, 580
Moreau, General 592
Morgan, J. P. (US bank) 372
Morgan, Kenneth 61
Morgan Grenfell 258
Morning Post 68, 105, 152, 299, 319, 399
Morpicati, Arturo 232
Morrell, Dr Theodor 333
Morris Cars 100
Morris, (Sir) William (Lord Nuffield) 73, 100, 125, 128, 147, 148, 157, 160, 165, 169, 179 195, 277, 313
Morrison, Harry 353
Morrison, Herbert 81, 104–5, 125, 129, 131, 150, 157, 167, 276, 290, 396–7, 408, 420, 472, 505,-6, 521, 524, 529, 535–7
Morrison, W. S. 405
Mortimer, John 408
Mortimer, Raymond 185
Morton, Desmond 505
Mosley, Alexander 445, 525, 540–1, 581, 592, 608, 619–20, 635, 643
Mosley, Lady Cynthia (*see* Cimmie Curzon)
Mosley, Lady Diana (*see* Diana Mitford)
Mosley, Edward (brother) 10–1, 14, 112, 239, 577, 644
Mosley, Ivor 641
Mosley, John (brother) 1,14, 577
Mosley, Lady (Katherine Heathcote) 'Maud' (mother) 1, 3–4, 6–8, 14, 71, 140, 227, 277, 311, 332, 340, 410, 457, 460, 480, 511, 577
Mosley, Max 492, 502, 513, 525, 540–1, 581, 592, 598, 613, 619, 622–3, 635, 643
Mosley, Michael (son) 204, 240, 340, 465, 621
Mosley, Nicholas (1527–1612) 3–4

Mosley, Nicholas (son), 240, 419, 437, 511, 642:
diary 1; on father 8, 50, 108, 233, 378, 392, 612, 615; on mother 233; OM circle 110–1; OM arrest 501; WWII 533, 536, 544; post-war 548–9, 556, 564, 587, 608, 618–9, 621, 644–5
Mosley, Sir Oswald (1729) 3
Mosley, Sir Oswald (great-grandfather) 4
Mosley, Sir Oswald (grandfather) 8, 20, 309
Mosley, Sir Oswald:
birth/diary 1–3; childhood 4–8; school 10–13; personality traits 7–8, 146; affairs with women 27–8, 65, 69, 108, 126, 145–6, 223; social life 29, 52–3; finances 112, 239; army/ Sandhurst, RFC 16–19, 20–2, 28; WWI 20–2; Politics/ reading 25–6, 48; social imperialism 115, 125, 142, 150; MoM/FO/War Office 30–3; 1918 General Election/MP 36–40; Cimmie 44, 49; Ireland 56–8; ILP/ Labour Party 81–xx; Revolution by Reason 101; Parliament/ minister 107, 118–9, 121, 136; McDonald's affair 113–6, 132–3, 143; economic rebel 131, 136–9, 141; defeat in Party 125, 148, 150; Mosley manifesto 155–7; Young Tories 128, 153, 155, 159; funds from Morris 161, 169, 179; New Party 162–4, , 168, 181, 185–6; fencing 174, 184, 209, 220, 320, 33, 381; Mussolini/Rome 193–3, 232, 269–70, 285; anti-semitism 194, 207–8, 212; end of NP 202–3; Diana 201; *The Greater Britain* 207, 211, 217, 219, 271, 288; BUF 217–9, 226, 279–80; Rothermere 269–72, 284, 309; BUF finances 235, 266, 269–70, 277, 285, 330, 337, 351, 361, 366, 371, 409, 412, 421, 428, 437; anti-semitism 224, 231, 244, 254, 259, 264, 273, 287, 288, 291, 303–6, 309, 318, 320, 324, 339, 348, 354, 360, 365, 397, 402, 410, 438, 447; Universal Fascism 283–4, 327; anti-communism 221–3, 275; violence/Fascist Defence Force 220, 225, 228–30, 246, 264, 293, 295, 297–8, 321; Abyssinia campaign 354–5, 358, 374; Nazi links/funds 290–1, 301, 317, 338, 377, 381, 406, 409, 414, 422, 430, 458; Hitler 341–3, 354; East End 380, 396; commercial activities/radio project 372, 386, 388, 416–7, 419–20, 435–6, 460, 463; Cable Street 390–4; wedding 392; Abdication Crisis 403–7; Peace campaign 432, 436, 456, 469, 475, 485, 493–4; co-operation with Right 451–2, 460; WWII/secret meetings 470–8, 482, 493; coup d'etat/ quisling 490, 496, 500, 503–4, 507–10, 532, 527–8; internment 514–5, 525, 535; release/ end of war 537–8; Crux Easton/Crowood 541–4, 591; Nazi atrocities 548, 563–4, 567; Fascist revival 545–5, 552–6; post-war neo-Nazi links 559–61, 602–3; Union Movement 566; Europe a Nation/ Euro-Africa 565–6, 572–4, 584, 588; Ireland/France 592, 598; Fascist International 577–8, 586, 588, 594, 596, 607, 623–5, 629–30; South Africa/Rhodesia 612, 632, 635; Notting Hill/ immigration 614–7; USA 628; end of UM 630–3; Venice 628–31; rehabilitation/King 637–8, 640; autobiography 638–9;

assessment 640–7; death 644–5
Mosley, Simon (son of John) 14, 239–40
Mosley, Vivien (daughter) 58, 240, 340, 352, 445, 511
Mosley, 'Waldie' (father) 3, 5–7, 9, 81, 102, 113
Mossman, James 638
Mottistone, Lord (J. E. Seeley) 148, 355, 470
Mountbatten, Lord Louis 637
Mount Temple, Lord 362
Mouvement Social European/ Europaische Soziale Bewegung 595–6, 624
Mouvement d'Action Civique (MAC) 620–1, 624–5, 630
Mouvement Jeune Nation 625
Moviemento Social Italiano (MSI) 562, 582, 586, 590, 594, 596, 607, 623, 636
Moyne, Lord 201, 223, 513
Muggeridge, Malcolm 486, 494, 517, 521, 628
Mullally, Frederick 645
Munro, E. 454
Munster, Count Paul 428
Murphy, Esther 114, 118
Murphy, Gerald 69
Murphy, Patrick 114
Murray, Basil 325
Murray, Gladstone 352
Museum Trust 460
Mussolini, Anna Maria (daughter) 586
Mussolini, Benito 138, 174, 191–2, 194, 198, 209, 210, 228, 244, 250–1, 256, 257, 263, 285, 373, 422, 496, 527, 586, 595, 600, 645: WWI 22; League of Nations 68; OM 192–3, 220, 386; anti-semitism 233, 283, 291, 438; Hitler/ Axis 317, 353, 402, 423, 427, 496; Abyssinia 351–2, 358–9, 361, 365, 369; Universal Fascism 199, 234, 327, 353; funds BUF 236, 255, 266, 269, 337, 261, 378, 412, 428, 484; turns against BU 340, 412, 448; Salo/Verona 560–1
Mussolini, Edda (daughter) 233
My Life (1968– OM) 637–8

Naldera (Broadstairs) 43, 344
Nathan, H. L. 310
Nation, The 255, 285
Nation Europa 581, 591, 595–6, 601, 604
National Book Association 408
National Citizens Union 200, 424, 454, 473, 549
National Council for Civil Liberties 552, 580
National Council of Industry and Commerce (NCIC) 147, 148, 154, 157, 160
National Credit Association 205
National Democratic Party (NPD) 631
National Executive Committee (NEC – Labour Party) 104, 109, 116, 120, 129, 149
National Farmers Union 250, 586, 629
National Fascisti (NF) 184, 199, 203
National Front 578, 636, 642
National Front After Victory 542, 547, 549
National Government 187, 188, 271, 313, 318, 351, 364, 375
National Industrial Council 40
National Labour Party 622
National League of Airmen 329, 334, 340
National Minority Movement 197, 198
National Newsagent 444
National Party 195–6
National Party (SA) 627, 629
National Party of Europe (NPE) 624, 631
National Publicity Bureau 313
National Renaissance Party 596
National Socialist League 413, 433, 460, 525
National Socialist Movement 622, 626
National Unemployed Workers Movement (NUWM) 222, 226, 323
National Union (Norway) 316
National Union of Ex-Servicemen 123
National Union of Railwaymen 121, 311
National Zeitung 424
Naumann, Klaus 608

Naumann, Dr Walter 588, 595–6, 602
Nazi-Soviet Pact 467
Neame, Alan, 601
Nelson (OM publisher) 637
New Age, The 69, 73–6, 217
New British Broadcasting Station 525
New English Weekly 205
New Epoch Products 307
New Era Securities 416
New Fabian Group 157
New Guard 225, 381
'New Labour' 150
New Leader, The 79, 114, 124, 130
New Look 634
New Museum Investment Trust 416, 419
Newnham, Henry 434, 465, 473, 549
New Order (SA) 572
New Party, 387:
origins 162–3; National policy 164–5; funds 169, 191; 'A National Plan for a National Crisis' 185; general election (1931) 187; Hitlerism 188, 209; eugenics 190; Rome delegation 191; New Movement 189–200; Kings Road, Chelsea 189; NUPA 189, 192, 205, 207, 208; Jews 194; dissolved 202; assessment 214
New Pioneer 445, 452, 476
New Political Economics 196
New Republic 569
New Statesman 226, 230, 242
New Swedish Movement 591
New Times, The 208, 212, 595
New York Times 521
News Chronicle 274, 297
News Letter 556, 564
New Society 636
News of the World 591
Newsam, Frank 498
Newton, Sir Issac 534
Nicholas II, Tsar 328
Nichols, Beverly 234
Nicholson, Mrs Christabel 454, 479, 496
Nicolson, Harold 27, 121, 130, 132, 143, 154–5, 157, 160–1, 180, 199, 202, 249, 255, 298, 353, 440, 483, 508, 539, 647:
on OM 26; literary works 26; FO 32; OM circle 45; biography 113; Young Tories 132; NP 163, 165, 169, 173–4, 181, 183, 188, 205; *Action* 185–6; Fascism 189, 193; Rome 192–4; anti-semitism 194; leaves NP 202; Cimmie's death 239; visits OM in prison 522
Nicolson, Max 152, 211
Nietzsche, Frederich 73–4, 217, 533
Niermans, Guy 474
Nieuwenhus, Jean 474
'Night of the Long Knives' (1934) 303, 311
Noel-Buxton, Lord 447, 470
No More War Movement 122
Non-Sectarian Anti-Nazi Council 363
Nordic League 425–6, 450–1, 454, 459, 465, 471–2, 478, 482, 493
Nordische gessellschaft 425
Norman, Montague 83, 183, 242, 309
Northcliffe, Lord 9, 30
Northern Council against Fascism 626
Northumberland, Duke of 68
Norwich, John Julius 606
Nouvel Ordre Europeen (NOE) 596, 623
Nuffield, Lord (*see* William Morris) 547
No. 1 Wing (RFC) 17
No. 6 Wing (RFC) 17, 20
Nunan, Sean 553, 592, 599
Nuova Antologia 374, 402
NUPA 189–92, 194, 202–4, 205, 208, 210:
anti-semitism 208, 210, 212
Nuremburg War trials 555, 563
Nusvenska Rorelsen 586

Observer, The 152, 154, 156, 239, 272, 351, 634
O'Connor, T. P. 61, 153, 299
ODESSA 562, 603, 610
O'Duffy, General Eoin 316, 327
O'Dwyer, Sir Michael 426
Officer Training Corps (OTC) 12, 198
Ogilive-Grant, Mark 503
O'Hagen, Robert 204
Ohlendorf, Lt.Col. Otto 571
Ohnesorge, Dr Wilhelm 434
Olley Air Services 379
'Omega' (OM) 32

On Guard 558, 568
Operation Barbarossa 524
Operation Lion 516
Operation Sealion 517
Operation Yellow 495
Orage, A. R. 69, 73, 77, 205
Organization for the Maintenance of Supply (OMS) 184, 198, 200
'Orange Book' 117
Ormsby-Gore, Mary 422
Ormsby-Gore, William 153
Orwell, George, 8, 227, 246, 366–7, 371, 401, 444, 517, 525
Other Club 153, 378
Otter, Laurens 570
Ottobre 217, 235
Oulthwaite, Alison 444
Owen, Arthur (SNOW-JOHNNY) 446
Owen, Frank 154
Owen, Robert 77, 206

Pakenham, Frank (Lord Longford) 140, 375, 641
Paleswski, Colonel Gaston 583
Pall Mall Club 358
Panorama (BBC) 638
Papineau, Mr 174
Paramour, Lord 266
Parisy, George 630
Parker, Lord Chief Justice 634
Parker, John 642
Parris, Matthew 647
Paternosters Club 430
Paton. J. 226
Paton, Jon 86, 103
Patriot, The 147, 196, 529, 547
Pavey, Inspector (agent) 451, 545, 554
Peace Aims Group 475, 489
Peace and Progressive Information Service 474
'Peace Party' 470, 474, 476, 483–4, 507
Peace Pledge Union (PPU) 453, 456, 471, 490
Peace with Ireland Council 56
Pearson, Lady 242, 249, 278, 451–2, 487, 502
Pelizzi, Camillo 259, 361
Pelling, H. 367
Pemberton, Sir Max 308
Penty, A. J. 73, 76, 205, 250, 251
Penty, Michael (son) 251
People's Campaign Against War and Usury 452
People's Common Law Parliament 525
People's League for Economy 48
Pepler (*Weekly Review*) 547
Pepys, Sir Mark 405
Peron, President (Argentine) 610, 631
Perth, Lord 318, 435, 460
Petain, Marshal 507, 509, 517, 523
Peterloo Massacre (1918) 4
Petrie, Sir Charles 233, 256–7, 278, 327, 408
Petter, Sir Ernest 147, 164
Pfister, Dr Georg 284, 287–8, 290, 294, 301–3, 307, 317–8, 338
Philby, Harry St John 458
Philby, Kim 438, 570, 606
Philips, Wogan 165, 213
Philips Price 156
Philips, Trevor and Mike 613
Phillimore, Lord 364, 456
Phillpott, R. H. S. 231, 235
Phillpotts, Christopher 606
Phipps, Sir Eric 398
Phipps, Lady 345
Phoenix Book Club 554
Piercy, Eric Hamilton 229–30, 322, 323, 411, 515
Pile, Duke 559
Pineton, Charles 365
Pini, Giorgio 636
Pinter, Harold 580
Pioneer, The 410
Pioneer Clubs 184
Piratin, Phil 351, 375, 570
Pirow, Oswald 572, 577, 587, 591
Pitt, the Elder (Earl of Chatham) 25, 107, 545
Pitt, the Younger 25, 545
Pitt-Rivers, George Lane-Fox 327–8, 452, 473, 487, 513
Plathen, Dick 250
Plato 534
Platt-Mills, John 570
Plugge, Captain Leonard 387, 415, 440
Plumb, Sir Henry 586, 629
Pocock, Tom 559
Point Counter Point (1928) 12
Pole, Sir Felix 128, 147, 158
Political Economic Planning (PEP) 211
Political Quarterly 202
Pollard, Major Hugh 379
Pollitt, Harry 198, 222, 288, 318, 358, 396–7, 487, 537
Ponsonby, (Lord) Arthur 85, 355

Ponsonby, Elizabeth 85
Pope, Ernest 422
Pope-Hennessy, James 589
Por, Odon 74, 205
Portal, Charles (Air Marshal) 173
Portal, Peter (Viscount) 13
Portal, (Viscount) Wyndham 147, 158, 160, 169, 175, 278
Portals (paper manufacturer) 147
Porter, Cole 69
Portland, Duke of 32
Portsmouth, Lord 547
Potato Marketing Board 450
Potter, Sydney 86
Pound, Ezra 26, 74, 77, 205, 251, 287, 361, 399, 561, 601
Preen, J. C. 421
Preston, Anne 280
Priester, Karl-Heinz 590–2, 594, 596
Prince of Wales ('Bertie', Edward VII) 9
Prince of Wales (Edward VIII) 62, 69, 174, 179, 244, 258, 263, 278, 294, 328, 333, 356, 367, 369, 373
Protocols of the Elders of Zion 77, 204, 425, 501
Proud, Cynthia 608
Proud, Sid 608, 620
Proust, Marcel 605
Pryce-Jones, Alan 185
Pryce-Jones, David 346
Public Order Act (POA) 276, 392, 402, 407–8, 411, 415–7, 423
Public Trustees Department 543
Pugh, Michael 355
Puller, H. P. 515
Purdy, Ken 552
Purcell, Hugh 639, 646

'Q' (*see* Mayne) 446
Quaderni Neri 629
Queen's Quarterly 160
Queen's Westminster Territorials 457
Queensbury, Lord 460
Quennell, Peter 185
Query 438
Quill, Michael 557, 578–80, 630
Quisling, Vidkun 316, 327, 490, 495, 510, 512

Racial Preservation Society 636
Radical Party (France) 72
Radio Athlone 415
Radio Bari 419
Radio Leesen 419
Radio Luxemburg 416, 495, 510, 512
Radio Normandy 387
Radio Toulouse 388, 415, 437
Railton, Ruth 641
Ramcke, General Barnhard 604
Ramsay, Captain Archibald Maule 425, 450–2, 454, 456, 460, 470, 473, 477–8, 482, 489, 498, 501, 506, 509–10, 515, 520–1, 550
Ramsay, Mrs 473, 479
Randall, E. D. 212, 280, 323, 358
Rand Daily Mail 616
Rathenau, Walter 99
Rawnsley, Stuart 289, 444
Read, Herbert 444
Reavely, Captain 322
Redesdale, Bertie 382
Redesdale, Lady (Sydney) 201, 372, 440, 457, 479, 535, 539, 577
Redesdale, Lord (David Mitford) 201, 372, 386, 439–40, 543, 555
Rees, Philip 205
Reichspartei Day (Nuremburg) 309, 320, 325, 356, 389, 436, 463–4
Reith, Sir John (Lord) 168, 184, 186, 314, 358, 405
Remains of the Day, The (1989) 373
Remer, Major-General Otto 602–3
Rendell, Dr 12
Renton, David 579
Rentoul, John 647
Resio, Arturo 245, 255
Reuter 359
Review of Reviews 399
Rexists (Belgium) 316, 427, 561, 563
Reynolds News 239, 580
Rhodes, Sir John 295
Rhondda, Lady 167
Ribbentrop, Adolf von 608
Ribbentrop, Joachim von 237, 293, 330, 349, 362, 372, 393, 398, 402, 406, 422–5, 428, 430, 444, 453, 463, 517, 528
Richardson, George 274, 275
Richardson, Mary 280
Richter, Dr Franz (aka Fritz Roessler) 594
Rickett, Maurice 205
Ridell, Lord 320
Riddell, Enid 495
Riefenstahl, Leni 356–7
Rifle Brigade (WWII) 536

Right Book Club 408
Right Club, The 230, 440, 454, 459, 470, 473–4, 479, 482, 486, 489–90, 497, 498, 500, 505–6, 515, 520, 532, 550
Risden, Wilfred ('Bill') 84–5, 165, 169, 205, 212, 286, 311, 326, 367
Ritschell, Daniel 94, 139, 157
Ritter, Nikolaus 445
Robb, J. H. 599
'Roberts' (MI5 agent) 488
Roberts, Andrew 646
Robertson, T. A. R. 523
Rodd, Francis 372
Rodd, Peter 179, 194, 260, 280, 348, 372
Rodd, (Lord) Sir Rennell 249, 260, 296
Roditi International 419, 455
Roe, Sir Alliot Verdon 251, 278
Roesel, Dr Gottfried 424, 450, 526
Rogers, Alan 627
Rogers, George 614
Rogers, William 334
Rohm, Ernst 303, 422
Rolleston Hall (Derbyshire) 5, 12, 49
Romilly, Esmond 175
Roosevelt, President (FDR) 100, 275, 372, 439, 486, 489, 496–7, 504, 508
Rose, Lionel 558–9, 573
Rosenberg, Alfred 181, 190, 236, 325, 341, 345, 374, 383, 410, 476
Rosenberg, Charlie 569
Ross, Colin 383, 560
Rosslyn, Earl of 260
Rothermere, Lord 31, 104, 146, 153, 158, 168, 191, 193, 205, 228, 258, 266, 275, 276, 291, 307, 317, 324, 335, 340, 356, 418, 455, 516, 637: Anti-Waste League 47, 50; Empire Free Trade 128, 129, 132; United Empire Party 132, 200; supports OM 194, 217, 269, 272, 284, 300; on Hitler 244, 303; pro-fascist 245; India 257; Jewish boycott 303, 308–9; drops OM 307, 309–10; Abyssinia 352, 369; abdication 403–4
Rothschild, Lord 83, 254
Rothschild, Baron Louis 432, 455
Rothschild, (Lord) Victor 201, 488, 506, 522
Round Table 313
Row, Robert 567, 587, 600–1, 604
Rowe, T. Victor 425, 454, 471
Rowse, A. L. 126
Royal Army Service Corps 377
Royal Bank of Scotland 373
Royal Flying Corps (RFC) 16–8, 31
Royal Institute of International Affairs (RUSI) 194, 233
Royal Society of St George 460
RSPCA 586
Rudel, Colonel Hans-Ulrich 562, 586, 588, 591, 595, 621, 624
Rueff, Bill 435
Rumbold, Anthony 242
Rural Reconstruction Association 250, 417, 586
Rushcliffe, Lord 470
Russell, A. E. 56
Russell, Lord 258
Russian Tea Rooms (Kensington) 328, 426, 492, 496
Ryan, Sergeant 12
Ryan, Michael 566, 569, 576

Sackville-West, Vita 113, 183, 185, 194, 353, 440
St Barbe, T. 474
St Barbe Baker, Richard 453
St Clair Erskine, Hamish 179, 260
St Clair Erskine, Mary (*see* Lady Dunn) 320
Salazar, President 572
Salisbury, Lord 47–8, 364, 460
Salmon, Judge 615
Salo Republic 560, 562
Samuel, Mrs Osborne 452
Sandhurst 14–16, 110, 379, 450
Sanden, Henrich 601
Sanducetti, Jullio 258
Sandys, Duncan 335
Santa, General villa 359
'Sapper' 195
Sark, Dame of (Sibyl) 415
Sasson, Sir Philip, 254
Saturday Review 152, 191, 249, 335, 351, 460
Saunders, Robert 552, 567, 585–6, 619, 629
Saxe-Coburg-Gotha, Duke of 369
Sayer, Dick 545
Scanlon, John 81–2, 151, 453–4, 479
Scarsdale, Lord 43
Schacht, Hjalmar 337–8, 356, 588, 603

Schaub, Julius 333
Scheel, Dr Gustav 595
Schilling, Dr Walter 572
Schmidt, Albert 610
Schmidt, Ernst 596
Schmidt, Paul 341, 526–7
Schmidt-Lorenzen, Gunther 254–5, 261
Schopenhauer 382
Schroeder, Lucy (*see* Dyer) 436
Schurch, Theodore 377, 532, 552
Schuster, Sir Claude 354, 426
Schutz, Waldemar 595
Scrimgeour, Alex 278, 414
Scrimgeour, J. and A. 128
Scobie, Edward 613
Scott, Sir Harold 554, 573
Scott, Sir Russell 285, 329, 409
Scott, Lord William 258
Sebastian, Mr (British consul) 509
Secret Army Organization (OAS) 620, 625, 629, 632
'Section D' (*see* IIB) 197
Section D (MI6) 440, 448, 488
Seeley, Sir John 38
Semphill, Master of 20, 415, 453
Senhouse, Roger 379
Sermoneta, Duchess of 373
Seton Hutchinson, Lt. Col. 426
17th Lancers 16
Sewell, Father Brocard 644
Shackleton, Ernest 267
Shape of Things to Come, The (1933) 267
Shaw, Captain (BBC) 350
Shaw, George Bernard 38, 73, 107, 112, 118, 162, 168, 180, 221, 508, 537, 548
Sherriff, R. C. 178
Sherwood, Hugh 581
Shinwell, Manny 171, 551
Siemens 258
Sieff, Israel 211, 212, 220, 221
Sieff, Marcus (son) 212
Silent Help 608
Silverman, Sydney 540
Silver Shirts 563
Simmons, Jim 148, 156
Simon, Sir John 57, 276, 380, 391, 402, 408
Simpson, Professor Brian 472, 524
Simpson, Celia (aka Strachey) 141
Simpson, Wallis (Duchess of Windsor) 328, 393, 403–4, 406, 428, 598, 644
Sinclair, Sir Archibald 66, 146, 176, 298
Sinclair, Sir John (MI6) 10
Sitwell, George (17th century) 178
Sitwell, Georgia 111, 112, 113, 132, 144, 174, 202, 203, 209, 239, 297
Sitwell, Osbert, 111, 133, 177–8, 361, 529, 541, 543
Sitwell, Sachverell (Sachie) 111, 178, 182, 209, 258
Six, Franz, 526, 532, 561
16th Lancers 16
62 Group 626, 628
Skeels, 'Professor' Serrocald 426
Skidelsky, Robert 141, 157, 228, 237, 295, 306, 346, 416, 456, 463, 557, 560, 568, 611, 623, 635–6, 639–40, 642–3
Skorzeny, Colonel Otto 318, 562, 586, 588, 591, 594, 608, 610, 621
Skorzeny, Waltraut (daughter) 608
Smart, Mariette 532
Smart, Nick 300
Smiley, David 480
Smirnoff, Eugene 492
Smith, Albie 186, 189
Smith, F. E. (Lord Birkenhead) 29, 44–6, 66, 115, 153–4
Smith, Gerald K. 578
Smith, Ian 632
Smith, Simon Harcourt 388
Smithers, Sir Waldron 549
SNOW (*see* A. Owens) 446
Snowden, Philip 79, 82–3, 104–5, 109, 115, 129, 133, 136, 141, 151, 176, 180, 182, 640
Social Imperialism 30, 36–8, 194, 215, 349
Socialist League 271, 275, 368, 421
Socialist Reich Party 588, 594
Society of Motor Manufacturers 128
Soil Association 586
Soloman, Dorothy 251
Sonnenkinder 45, 178–9
Sonnemann, Emmy 342
Sons of St George 566
Sophocles 534
Soref, Harold 632
Sorel, George 75, 217, 219
Spanish Travel Agency 608
Spears, Brig. Gen. E. L. 275
Special Operations Executive 480, 528
Spectator, The 157, 164, 477

Speer, Albert 333, 343, 398
Spengler, Oswald 205, 230, 253, 279–80, 311, 572, 575
Spengler Book Club 554
Sphere, The 11
Spicer (BU) 546
Spitzy, Richard 398, 531
Spot, Jack 392
Spranklin, Philip 357–8, 422, 434–5, 444, 497
Spurling, Skinner and Tudor 239
'Squadramania' 47
Squire, Sir J. C. 178, 256, 257–8
Stalin, Josef 574
Stammer (Nazi official) 386
Stanford, Molly 474, 479
Stanley, Oliver 121, 132, 142, 152–3, 163
Stanley, Sidney 579
Starace, Achille 192, 229
Starmer, Major Sir Lovelace 16
Steel, Johannes 235, 285
Steel-Maitland, Sir Arthur 147, 326
Stephens, Peter 637
Stephens, Colonel 'Tin-Eye' 518–9
Sternhell, Zeev 34, 75
Stevas, Norman St John 638
Stevenson, John 366
Stevenson, W. H. 256
Stewart, Desmond 577, 601
Stewart, Graham 135, 141
Stock, Noel 601
Stokes, Richard 475, 489, 499, 501, 517, 522
Stourton, J. J. 230
Strachey, James 85
Strachey, John (Evelyn) 72, 85, 101, 108–9, 111, 114, 118, 125, 129, 138, 141, 150, 153–4, 164–5, 169, 172, 175–6, 206, 215, 234, 251, 277, 321
Strachey, Lytton 85
Strachey, Mrs Ray 64
Strachey, St Leo 85
Strange, Capt. Louis 18, 20
Strasser, Dr Otto 562, 565, 601
Strauss, George 137–8, 165
Strauss, Richard 381
Streatfield, A. C. 457
Streicher, Elmar 319, 415
Streicher, Julius 283, 293, 302, 317, 345, 356, 370, 420, 448–9, 479, 637
Streicher, Lothar 317
Stuart, Sir Louis 426
Sueter, Admiral Sir Murray 329
Sunday Dispatch 296, 300, 308, 330, 334, 474
Sunday People 539
Sunday Pictorial 519, 550, 558
Sunday Telegraph 626
Sunday Times 627
Sundermann, Helmut 458
Suner, Serrano 581–2
Suner, Zita 581
'Suspect List' (MI5) 415, 425, 471, 488, 506, 515, 525
Susser, Leslie 400
Sutherland, J. F. 'Duke' 348
Sutherst, G. P. 278
Sutton, George 247, 501, 556
Sutton, Sir George 329
Swaffer, Hannen 214
Swann, Robert 541
Swift, William 507
Swinburne, Algernon 26
Swinton, Lord 504–5, 513, 515, 518–9
Swiss Nazi Party 603
Swope, Herbert 114
Sydenham, Lady 199
Sydenham, Lord 220
Sykes, Mark 32, 55
Sykes, Lady (Mark) 57
Sylvester, David 194 (son)
Sylvester, Philip 194
Syndicalists 39

Tablet, The 379
Tabor, Major G. J. H. 236, 278
Ta Fari, Emperor Ras 351
Tahan, Valerie Taylor 198
Tambroni (Italian PM) 623
Tariff Reform League 38, 40, 124
Tatler, The 54, 69, 258, 294, 422
Taubet, Dr Eberhard 595
Tavener, Mary 260–1
Tavistock, Lord (Duke of Bedford) 205, 424, 452–3, 471, 473, 479, 482, 484, 486, 488, 515
Taylor, Vice-Admiral A. E. 299
Taylor, A. J. P. 141, 214, 220, 226
Taylor, Frederick 'Speedy' 99
'Taylor, P. G.' (aka James McGuirk Hughes) 197–8, 262–5, 274, 276, 294–5, 301, 322, 323, 414, 421, 454, 494, 507
Taylor, Sterling 279
Taylour, Miss Fay 479
Tchelichew, Pavel 606
Tea with Mussolini (film) 353

Technique of Planning (TEC) 211
Teichmann, Paul 620
Telegraph, The 131, 156, 166, 298, 319, 371, 427, 445, 489, 501, 609, 621, 643, 647
Telesio, Giovanni 258
Temple-Cotton, Rafe 465, 567–8
Templeton, Viscount 293
Tennant, David 111, 320–1
Tennant, Diana 335
Tennant, Eleonora 549
Tennant, Stephen 111
Tenniel, Sir John 8
Terje Ballsrud 316
Tester, Dr Arthur Albert 344–5, 377, 427, 430, 446, 448, 485
Thayer, George 630
Theosophical Society 27
Theosophists 77
Thierack (Saxony's Minister of Justice) 261
3rd Cavalry Brigade 16
Thiriart, Jean 620, 623–4, 629
Thomas, Eric 472, 476
Thomas, J. H. 104, 121, 123, 124, 127, 129, 131, 133, 135, 140, 144, 193, 203
Thomas, Linda (nee Porter) 69
Thomas, P. 577
Thompson, Major 173
Thomsen, Hans 255, 290
Thomson, Lord 124, 148
Thomson, Alexander Raven 205, 230, 251–3, 258, 260, 262, 279, 317, 383, 410, 445–7, 493, 497, 501, 550, 553–4, 559, 563, 574–5, 581, 583, 585–7, 591, 596–7, 600, 604, 609
Thomson, Hanning 482
Thornton, A. P. 40
Thorpe, Jeremy 622
Thost, Dr Hans-Wilhelm 168, 203, 244, 294, 425, 460
Thurlow, Richard 27, 40, 205, 581, 605
Thwaites, Norman 256–7, 267
Tiechen, Hendrik 559
Time and Tide 167
Times, The 33, 105, 112, 137, 141, 147, 156, 158, 166, 177, 186, 189, 191, 224, 260, 293, 297, 364, 506, 613, 625, 638, 644–5
Tindell, Kenneth 10
'Tithe Wars' 250–2
Todd, Colonel Alfred 364
Tomorrow We Live (1937 – OM) 430, 553
Town Crier 86, 102, 105, 148
Transport and General Workers' Union 91, 566
Travel Association 440
Trefusis, Violet 249, 353
Trenchard, Hugh (Lord) 17, 266, 276, 293, 295, 307, 504
Trevelyan, Charles 83, 116, 125, 152, 165
Trevor-Roper, Hugh 555
Tribune 613
Troost, Frau 357
Trotsky, Leon 144
Troughton, Rupert 179
Truman's Brewery 531
Truth 313, 434, 440, 447, 465, 470, 486, 504, 529, 542, 547
Tryon, Major G. C. 435
TUC 133, 142, 149, 253, 263, 540, 614
Tucker, Justice 552
Turner, Wendy 558
TW3 (BBC) 625
Tyndall, John 578, 622, 626, 636

Uckert, Arthur 344
UFA Films (Germany) 357
Ulster Fascists 284
Ulster Volunteer Association 16
Union 572, 579, 591, 599, 604, 613
Union of British Freedom 556, 566
Union Movement: origin 566; funds 570, 627; European Contacts Section 571, 574; membership 573, 576, 583–6, 590, 615, 627; anti-immigration 579, 599, 612–6; anti-semitism 579–80, 599; elections 580, 597, 622; Special Propaganda Section 597; violence 626–7; NOE 624
United Christian Front 450
United Empire Party 132, 141
United Europe Movement 583
United Ratepayers Association 454
Unity Band 200
Unwin, Captain VC 378
Upton, H. M. 293
Ustinov, 'Klop' 426

Vaegen Framat 583
Valeriani, Mr 542
Van Heemstra, Baroness Ella 262, 343, 427

Vansittart, (Lord) Sir Robert 253, 358, 364, 409, 428, 499, 517, 547
Varsity 623
Vaughen-Henry, Dr Leigh 473, 494
Vernon, Major Wilfred 421–2
Verona Programme 561, 565
Versailles Peace Treaty 46
Vickers 258, 405, 540
Vickers, Vincent 278
Victoria, Queen 342
Vignon (architect) 592
Viking Brigade (SS) 561
Villari, Luigi 258–9, 361, 374
Villiers-Stuart, James and Emily 606
Vitkowitz (steel works) 432, 455
Vivian, Dr Margaret 552, 559
Voight, Frederick 167
Volkischer Beobachter 168, 181, 203, 300, 374, 537
Volksbund fur Frieden und Frieheit (VFF) 595
von Bulow, Nicholas 422
von Dirksen, Herbert 447, 458
von Dornberg, Alexander 610
von Hoesch, Karl 526
von Hoesch, Leopold 258, 334, 370
von Kanstein, Baron Fritz 644
von Kaufmann 422, 460, 463
von Killinger (Nazi official) 527
von Lagen, Herr 421
von Leers, Colonel Johann 591
von Mackensen, Hans Georg 487
von Oven, Wilfred 362, 427, 595
von Pflugl, Baroness Alice 574–6
von Rohrsschiedt (Nazi official) 527
von Scheppenburg (Nazi official) 450
von Schroeder, Baron Bruno 372
von Schroeder, Helmut 372
von Schroeder, Kurt 373, 441
von Schuschnigg, Kurt 431
von Thadden, Adolf 591, 602, 607, 623–4, 631
von Trott, Adam 508
von Zech-Burkersroda 483
Vorwaites 82

Wagner, Adolf 333
Wagner, Richard 342, 382–3, 462
Wagner, Siegfried 382–3
Wagner, Winnifred 342, 382–3, 461, 608
Waley, Daniel 355
Walker, Danton 556
Walker, Martin 636
Wall, Alfred 505
Wallace, Doreen 250
'Wall Street Crash' 126–7
Walsh, Gladys 391
Walter, Bruno 275
Walters, Detective Sergeant 615
Walton, William 111
Warburton, Edmond 488, 630
Warburton, John 265, 349, 363, 396, 466, 502, 548, 550, 557, 566, 578–9, 587, 609, 630, 636
Ward, M. Dudley 586
Ward Price, George 147, 244, 269, 271, 286, 300, 307, 389, 408, 420, 460, 474
Wardell, Mike 15, 62
Wardrop, Oliver 278
Warwick, Lady 103
Waterman, L. G. 208
Waters, Frank 458
Watson-Cheyne, Sir William 24
Watts, Charlie 524–5, 529, 542, 550, 574, 585, 589
Waugh, Evelyn 179, 201, 357, 359, 582–3
Webb, Beatrice 37, 67, 71, 82–5, 102, 104, 115, 124, 127, 136, 140, 143, 163, 168, 187
Webb, Sidney 37, 62, 71, 85, 266
Webster, Martin 622, 636
Webster, Nestor 196
Webster, William 627
Weedon Cavalry School 14
Week-End Review 152, 157, 160, 175, 177, 211
Weekly Review 547
Wegg-Prosser, Charles 414
Welles, Sumner 489
Wellesley, Dorothy 440
Wellesley, Lord George (Duke of Wellington) 20, 426, 440
Wellesley, Gerald (7th Duke of Wellington) 249, 440, 549
Wells, H. G. 103, 162, 168, 180, 181, 193, 211, 221, 251, 267–8, 287
Wells, Inspector 237
Werlin (Mercedes director) 342
Wertheimer, Egon 81–2, 109, 114, 119

Wessex Agricultural Defence Association 327
West, Rebecca 553, 558, 576
West Downs School 10
Westfront (1918) 178
Westminster, Duke of 38, 132, 329, 334, 424, 465, 470, 495
Westminster Gazette 65
Westropa Press 576
Weymouth, Lord 24
Wheatley, Denis 430
Wheatley, John 79, 84, 93, 105, 110, 122, 134
Whinfield, Lt.Col. H. C. and Muriel 478
Whinfield, Peter 478, 480, 484
Whistler, James 202
White, John Baker 196–8
White, Margaret 411
White Knights 425
'White List' 509, 516, 526
White Rose 588
White's Club 81, 112, 379
Whitfield, Edward 487
Wiedemann (Hitler's adjutant) 422, 427, 430, 441
Wigham, Peter 601
Wilhelm II, Kaiser 192
Wilhelmina, Queen (Holland) 344
Wilkinson, Ellen 107, 108, 143, 539
Willart, Paul 345
Willey, Vernon 98, 100
Williams, Glyn 182
Williams, Dr Sir John 3
Williams-Ellis, Amabel 72, 85, 96, 103, 107, 163
Williams-Ellis, Clough 96, 103, 125
Williamson, Henry 24, 33, 178, 357, 417, 456, 464–5. 487, 506, 529, 547, 566, 601
Williamson, Hugh Ross 453, 490, 494, 529
Wilson, A. N. 646
Wilson, Sir Arnold 256, 364, 408
Wilson, Colin 619
Wilson, Harold 637, 639
Wilson, Sir Henry 28, 55, 60
Wilson, Horace 124, 429
Winchester School 11–12
Windsor, Duke of 422, 428–9, 469–70, 474, 483, 494, 507, 510, 512, 516, 531–2
Windsor Club 339, 361, 364, 408, 425, 428, 471
Winkworth, Peter 173, 175
Winterton, Earl of 299
Wire Broadcasting 442
Wired Wireless System 388
Wireless Publicity 440
Wise, E. Frank 30, 77–9, 85–6, 126
Wise, Leonard 437, 502
Wistrich, Robert 349
Wodehouse, Lady 21
Wodehouse, P. G. 249, 443
Wolkoff, Admiral 328
Wolkoff, Anna 328, 426, 454, 459, 474, 486–7, 490, 492, 494–5, 498, 500, 506, 521, 551
Wolkoff, Gabriel 328
Wollheim, Eric 291
Wollner, Senator 435
Women's League of Health and Beauty 240
Women's Reserve 267, 389
Wood, Edward (Lord Halifax) 52, 56
Woods, George 540
Woolf, Leonard 168
Woolf, Virginia 168, 275
Worker, The Daily 84, 167, 331, 295, 391, 459, 540, 545, 550–1, 577
World Alternative, The (1936) 560
World Review 444
World's Press News 309
Worral, Albert 540
Wrede, Franz 377, 381, 406, 409, 420
Wrench, John 297
Wright, Elwin 362
Wyatt, Woodrow 579
Wybot, Roger 581, 589
Wyndham, Patrick 111
Wyndham, Richard 'Dick' 111–2, 124, 144, 145

'X' (*see* Kurtz) 446

Yeats-Brown, Colonel Francis 52, 256–7, 297, 311, 325, 342, 361, 408, 437, 452, 458, 473, 529
'Yellow Book' 115
Yellow Star Movement 626
Yockey, Francis Parker 563–4, 571–2, 574–5
York, Edward 284
Yorkshire Post 298
Young, Allan 84, 85, 103, 124, 129, 149, 163–4, 168, 170, 172, 173, 175–6
Young Communist League 319
'Young England' 25, 38, 47
'Young Plan' 372
Younger, Sir George 32
'Young Tories' 155, 157, 159, 160, 182

Zeffirelli, Franco 353
Zepplin company 525
Zetland, Lord 403
Ziegveld (Nazi official) 530
Zietschrift fur Geopolitik 383
Zimmermann, General Paul 602
Zinoviev Letter 313
zu Christian, Major Walter 516
zu Putlitz, Wolfgang 426

UNIVERSITY OF WOLVERHAMPTON
LEARNING & INFORMATION SERVICES

He just wanted a decent book to read …

Not too much to ask, is it? It was in 1935 when Allen Lane, Managing Director of Bodley Head Publishers, stood on a platform at Exeter railway station looking for something good to read on his journey back to London. His choice was limited to popular magazines and poor-quality paperbacks – the same choice faced every day by the vast majority of readers, few of whom could afford hardbacks. Lane's disappointment and subsequent anger at the range of books generally available led him to found a company – and change the world.

'We believed in the existence in this country of a vast reading public for intelligent books at a low price, and staked everything on it'
Sir Allen Lane, 1902–1970, founder of Penguin Books

The quality paperback had arrived – and not just in bookshops. Lane was adamant that his Penguins should appear in chain stores and tobacconists, and should cost no more than a packet of cigarettes.

Reading habits (and cigarette prices) have changed since 1935, but Penguin still believes in publishing the best books for everybody to enjoy. We still believe that good design costs no more than bad design, and we still believe that quality books published passionately and responsibly make the world a better place.

So wherever you see the little bird – whether it's on a piece of prize-winning literary fiction or a celebrity autobiography, political tour de force or historical masterpiece, a serial-killer thriller, reference book, world classic or a piece of pure escapism – you can bet that it represents the very best that the genre has to offer.

Whatever you like to read – trust Penguin.

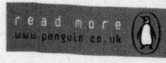

read more
www.penguin.co.uk

for the pukin'. Sovereign for what ails ye, the maker says, and I'm sure that includes gunshot wounds and cold." He handed the bottle to Grey. The smell was mildly alarming, but Grey hesitated no more than an instant before taking a modest gulp.

He coughed. He coughed until his eyes streamed and his chest heaved, but there was an undeniable sense of warmth stealing through his center.

Quinn, meanwhile, had got down onto the boards in order to rewrap Tom's arm and was now holding the bottle for the young man to drink. Tom swallowed twice, stopped to cough explosively, and, wordless, gestured for Grey to take another turn.

Out of concern for Tom, Grey drank abstemiously, taking only a few more sips, but it was enough to make his head swim pleasantly. He'd stopped shivering, and a feeling of drowsy peace laid its hand upon him. By Grey's feet, Quinn put the final touches on a fresh bandage torn from his shirttail and, patting Grey on the shoulder, clambered back behind him.

In front, Jamie Fraser still bent to his oars but, hearing Quinn's movement, called back, "How are ye, wee Byrd?"

Tom's only answer was a gentle snore; he had fallen asleep in the midst of the bandaging. Quinn leaned forward to answer.

"Well enough for the moment. The ball's still in him, though. He'll need to be brought to a doctor, I'm thinking."

"Ye know one?" Fraser sounded skeptical.

"Aye, and so do you. We'll take him to the monks at Inchcleraun."

Fraser stiffened. He stopped rowing, turned, and gave Quinn a hard look, visible even by starlight.

"It's ten miles at least to Inchcleraun. I canna row that far!"

"Ye'll not need to, you ignorant jackeen. What d'ye think the sail's for?"

Grey tilted back his head. Sure enough, he thought, with a

sort of muzzy interest, there was a sail. It was a small sail, but still.

"I was under the impression that the use of a sail required wind," Fraser said, elaborately courteous. "There is none, if ye hadna noticed."

"And wind we shall have, my rosy-bearded friend." Quinn was beginning to sound like his old expansive self. "Come sunrise, the wind comes up off Lough Derg, and 'twill bear us on the very breath of dawn, as the Good Book says."

"How long is it 'til dawn?" Fraser sounded suspicious. Quinn sighed and clicked his tongue reprovingly.

"About four hours, O ye o' little faith. Row just that wee bit longer, will ye, and we'll be into the waters of Lough Ree. We can turn aside out o' the current and find a resting place until daylight."

Fraser made a low Scottish sound in his throat but turned back to his oars, and the slow heave against the Shannon's current resumed. Left to silence and the softly rhythmic slosh of the oars, Grey's head dropped and he gave himself over to dreams.

These were bizarre, as opium dreams so often were, and he half-woke from a vision of himself erotically enmeshed with a naked Quinn, this sufficiently vivid that he scrubbed at his mouth and spat to rid himself of the taste. The taste proved to be not of the Irishman but of the tonic he had drunk; a ginger-tasting belch rose up the back of Grey's nose and he subsided against the side of the boat, feeling unequal to the occasion.

He was enmeshed with Tom, he found. Byrd was lying close against him, breathing stertorously; his face was pressed against Grey's chest, his flushed cheek hot even through Grey's half-dry shirt. All motion had stopped, and they were alone in the boat.

It was still dark, but the cloud cover had thinned, and the

faded look of the few visible stars told him that it was no more than an hour 'til dawn. He lay flat on the wet boards, fighting to keep his eyes open—and fighting not to recall any of the details of the recent dream.

So groggy was he that it hadn't occurred to him even to wonder where Fraser and Quinn had gone, until he heard their voices. They were near the boat, on land—*well, of course they're on land,* he thought vaguely, but his drugged mind furnished him with a surreptitious vision of the two of them sitting on clouds, arguing with each other as they drifted through a midnight sky spangled with the most beautiful stars.

"I said I wouldna do it, and that's flat!" Fraser's voice was low, intense.

"Ye'll turn your back on the men ye fought with, all the blood spilt for the Cause?"

"Aye, I will. And so would you, if ye'd half the sense of a day-old chick."

The words faded, and Grey's vision of Quinn melted into one of a red-eyed banty rooster, crowing in Irish and flapping its wings, darting pecks at Fraser's feet. Fraser seemed to be naked but was somewhat disguised by drifts of vapor from the cloud he was sitting on.

The vision melted slowly into a vaguely erotic twinning of Stephan von Namtzen with Percy Wainwright, which he watched in a pleasant state of ennui, until von Namtzen evolved into Gerald Siverly, the ghastly wound in his head not seeming to hamper his movements.

Loud moaning from Tom woke him, sweating and queasy, to find the little boat gliding under sail along the shore of a flat green island—Inchcleraun.

Feeling mildly disembodied, and with only the crudest notion how to walk, he staggered up the path behind Fraser and Quinn, who were hauling Tom Byrd along as gently as they could, making encouraging noises. The remnants of his dreams mingled with the mist through which they walked, and he remembered the words he had overheard. He wished very much that he knew how that particular conversation had ended.

27

Loyalty and Duty

JAMIE WAS GREETED WITH CONCERNED WELCOME BY THE monks, who took Tom Byrd away at once to Brother Infirmarian. He left Quinn and Grey to be given food and went in to see Father Michael, disturbed in mind.

The abbot looked him over with fascination and offered him a seat and a glass of whiskey, both of which he accepted with deep gratitude.

"You do lead the most interesting life, Jamie dear," he said, having been given a brief explanation of recent events. "So you've come to seek sanctuary, is it? And your friends—these would be the two gentlemen you told me of before, I make no doubt?"

"They would, Father. As for sanctuary . . ." He tried for a smile, though weariness weighed down even the muscles of his face. "If ye might see to the poor lad's arm, we'll be off as soon as he's fettled. I wouldna put ye in danger. And I think perhaps the deputy justiciar of Athlone might not respect your sanctuary, should he come to hear about Colonel Grey's presence."

"Do you think the colonel did in fact murder Major Siverly?" the abbot asked with interest.

"I'm sure he did not. I think the miscreant is a man called Edward Twelvetrees, who has—had, I mean—some associations with Siverly."

"What sort of associations?"

Jamie lifted his hand in a vague gesture. His bruised right shoulder burned like fire when he moved it and ached down to the bone when he didn't. His arse wasn't in much better case after hours of rowing on a hard slat.

"I dinna ken exactly. Money, certainly—and maybe politics." He saw the abbot's white brows rise, green eyes grow more intent. Jamie smiled wearily.

"The man I brought with me—Tobias Quinn. It's him I told ye of, when I made my confession before."

"I remember," murmured the abbot. "But I could not, of course, make use of that information, given as it was under the seal."

Jamie's smile grew a little more genuine.

"Aye, Father. I ken that. So now I tell ye outside that seal that Toby Quinn has it in his heart to take up the destiny I laid aside. Will ye maybe speak to him about it? Pray with him?"

"I will indeed, *mo mhic,*" Father Michael said, his face alight with wary interest. "And you say he knows about the *Cupán*?"

An unexpected shudder ran over Jamie from his crown to the base of his spine.

"He does," he said, a little tersely. "I leave that between you and him, Father. I should be pleased never to see or hear of it again."

The abbot considered him for a moment, then raised a hand.

"Go in peace, then, *mo mhic,*" he said quietly. "And may God and Mary and Padraic go with you."

JAMIE WAS SITTING on a stone bench by the monastery's graveyard when Grey came to find him. Grey looked exhausted, white-faced and disheveled, with an unfocused look in his eyes that Jamie recognized as the aftereffects of Quinn's tonic.

"Give ye dreams, did it?" he asked, not without sympathy.

Grey nodded and sat down beside him.

"I don't want to tell you about them, and you don't want to know," he said. "Believe me."

Jamie thought both statements were likely true, and asked instead, "How's our wee Byrd, then?"

Grey looked a little better at this and went so far as to smile wanly.

"Brother Infirmarian's got the ball out. He says the wound is in the muscle, the bone's not broken, the boy has a little small fever but, with the blessing, all will be well in a day or two. When last seen, Tom was sitting up in bed eating porridge with milk and honey."

Jamie's wame gurgled loudly at thought of food. There were things to be discussed first, though.

"D'ye think it was worth it?" he asked, one brow raised.

"What?" Grey slumped a little, rubbing the itching bristle on his chin with the palm of his hand.

"Tom Byrd. He'll likely do fine, but ye ken well enough he might have been killed—and yourself, too. Or taken."

"And you and Quinn. Yes. We all might." He sat for a moment, watching a fuzzy green worm of some kind inching along the edge of the bench. "You mean you think I was a fool to ask you to get me out of Athlone."

"If I thought that, I wouldna have done it," Jamie said bluntly. "But I like to know why I'm riskin' my life when I do it."

"Fair enough." Grey put down a finger, trying to entice the worm to climb on it, but the creature, having prodded blindly at his fingertip, decided that it offered no edible prospects and, with a sudden jerk, dropped from the bench, dangling briefly from a silken tether before swinging out on the wind and dropping away altogether into the grass.

"Edward Twelvetrees," he said. "I'm morally sure he killed Siverly."

"Why?"

"Why might he have done it, or why do I think he did?" Without waiting for Jamie's reply, Grey proceeded to answer both questions.

"*Cui bono,* to begin with," he said. "I think that there is or was some financial arrangement between the two men. I told you about the papers they were looking at when I went there the first time? I am no bookkeeper, but even I recognize pounds, shillings, and pence written down on a piece of paper. They were looking over accounts of some sort. And that very interesting chest was probably not filled with gooseberries.

"Now, Siverly had money—we know that—and was obviously involved in what looks very like a Jacobite conspiracy of some kind. It's possible that Twelvetrees was not involved in that—I can't say." He rubbed his face again, beginning to look more lively. "I have difficulty believing that he is, really; his family is . . . well, they're hard-faced buggers to a man, but loyal to the bone, been soldiers for generations. I can't see him committing treason."

"So ye think that he might have discovered what Siverly was into—perhaps as a result of your visit—and killed him to prevent his carrying out the scheme? Whatever scheme it was?"

"Yes. That's the honorable theory. The dishonorable one is that, discovering that Siverly held all this money—presumably on behalf of the conspiracy—he might simply have decided to do away with Siverly and pocket the lot. But the point is . . ." He spoke more slowly, choosing his words. "Whichever it was, if it had to do with money, then there may be proof of it in the papers that Siverly had."

Grey's hand had curled into a fist as he spoke, and he struck it lightly on his knee, unconscious of the movement.

"I need to get into the house and get those papers. If there's any proof of Siverly's involvement in a political conspiracy, or Twelvetrees's relations with him, it must lie there."

Jamie had been wondering, during these last conjectures, whether to mention the Duchess of Pardloe's information regarding Twelvetrees and money. Apparently, she hadn't chosen to share it with her husband or her brother-in-law, and he wondered why not.

The answer to that presented itself almost immediately: her wicked old father. Andrew Rennie was undoubtedly the source of her information, and she likely didn't want Pardloe finding out that she still dabbled in intelligence work for the old man. He didn't blame her. At the same time, the situation now seemed more serious than whatever marital strife the revelation might cause, if it got back to the duke.

"*The entire Twelvetrees family harbors feelings of the deepest hatred for my husband.*" The duchess's words came back to him. Ah, he'd forgotten that. It wasn't only her father she was concerned with; it was what might happen if Pardloe crossed swords—either figuratively or literally—with Edward Twelvetrees.

Aye, well—he might be able to save her confidence, even while sharing the information.

"There's a thing ye ought to know," Jamie said abruptly. "For some time, Twelvetrees has been moving large quantities of money to Ireland. *To* Ireland," he emphasized. "I didna ken where it was going—nor did the person who told me—but what d'ye think the odds are that it was going to Siverly?"

Grey's face went almost comically blank. Then he pursed his lips and breathed in slowly, thinking.

"Well," he said at last. "That does alter the probabilities. If that's true, and if it means that Twelvetrees was involved in the conspiracy, then it may be a case of plotters falling out—or . . ." A second thought brightened his face; clearly he didn't like the notion of Twelvetrees being a traitor, which Jamie thought very interesting. "Or he was misled in what the money was to be used for and, discovering the truth, decided to put Siverly out of commission before he could put anything into action. I suppose your source didn't tell you exactly what this particular conspiracy had in mind to accomplish?" He shot Jamie a sharp look.

"No," Jamie said, with absolute truth. "But I suppose ye're right about the need to see the papers, if ye can. What makes ye think Twelvetrees hasn't already got them?"

Grey took a deep breath and blew it out, shaking his head.

"He might. But it was only yesterday—God, was it only yesterday?—that Siverly was killed. Twelvetrees wasn't staying in the house; the butler told me. The servants will be in a great taking, and Siverly does—did—have a wife, who presumably inherits the place. The constable said he was sealing the house until the coroner could come; I can't see the butler just letting Twelvetrees march in, open the chest, and make off with everything in it.

"Besides," he glanced toward the stone cottage where Tom Byrd lay, "I'd thought that once you got me out, we'd go straight back to Glastuig, and I'd almost certainly be there before Twelvetrees could worm his way in. But things happen, don't they?"

"They do," Jamie agreed, with a certain grimness.

They sat for a moment in silence, each alone with his thoughts. At last Grey stretched and sat up straight.

"The other thing about Siverly's papers," he said, looking

Jamie in the eye, "and why I must have them, is that whatever they do or don't say about Twelvetrees, they're very likely to reveal the names of other men involved in the conspiracy. The members of the Wild Hunt, if you will."

This aspect of the matter had not escaped Jamie, but he could hardly contradict Grey's conclusion, no matter how much he hated it. He nodded, wordless. Grey sat for a minute longer, then stood up with an air of decision.

"I'll go and speak to the abbot, thank him, and make provision for Tom to stay until we come back for him. Do you think Mr. Quinn will see us ashore?"

"I expect he will."

"Good." Grey started toward the main building, but then stopped and turned round. "You asked me if I thought it was worth it. I don't know. But it is my duty, regardless."

Jamie sat watching as Grey walked away, and an instant before he reached the door of the building, the Englishman stopped dead, hand already stretched out for the latch.

"He's just thought that he didna ask me whether I'd go with him," Jamie murmured. For with Siverly's death, Jamie's word to Pardloe was kept and his own obligation in the matter technically ended. Any further assistance Grey might need would be asked—or offered—as one man to another.

Grey stood fixed for a long moment, then shook his head as though annoyed by a fly and went inside. Jamie didn't think the gesture meant that Grey had dismissed the issue; only that he had decided to do his business with Father Michael before mentioning it to Jamie.

And what will I tell him?

The questions of Siverly's death or Twelvetrees's possible guilt mattered not a whit to him. The possibility of exposure of the Jacobite conspirators, though . . .

"Ye've thought it all out once already," he muttered to himself, impatient. "Why can ye not leave it alone?"

I, James Alexander Malcolm MacKenzie Fraser, do swear, and as I shall answer to God at the great day of judgment, I have not, nor shall have, in my possession any gun, sword, pistol, or arm whatsoever, and never use tartan, plaid, or any part of the Highland garb; and if I do so, may I be cursed in my undertakings, family, and property. May I never see my wife and children, father, mother, or relations. May I be killed in battle as a coward and lie without Christian burial in a strange land, far from the graves of my forefathers and kindred; may all this come across me if I break my oath.

The words of the oath they'd made him speak when they spared his life had burned his lips when he spoke them; they burned his heart now. He likely knew none of the Wild Hunt personally—but that didn't make betrayal of those men any the lighter a burden.

But. The memory of a tiny skull with long brown hair lying under a gorse bush came to his mind as vividly as the memory of that foul oath—and weighed heavier. To leave these Irish lunatics to their business—or to keep Grey from stopping them, which amounted to the same thing—was to betray wee Mairi, or Beathag, or Cairistiona, and all those like them.

Well, then, he thought calmly. *That is* my *duty. And I think the price is not too high.*

He should eat, but he lacked the will to get up and go inside. He took the rosary from his pocket instead, but didn't begin any of the mysteries, merely held it in his hand for comfort. He twisted round on the bench, turning his back on the silent dead, letting the tiredness flow out of him as the living peace of the place settled on him.

The small bell rang from the church, marking the hour of Nones; he saw the lay brothers in the garden lay down their hoes and shake the dirt from their sandals, ready to go in.

And he saw a boy of fourteen or so, his head neatly tonsured, fresh and white as a mushroom, come round the shattered wall, looking from side to side. The boy saw Jamie and his face lighted with satisfaction.

"Mr. Fraser you'll be," he said, and held out a piece of paper. "Mr. Quinn asked me would I be handing this to you." He thrust it into Jamie's hand and was hurrying back toward the chapel before Jamie could thank him.

He knew what it was: Quinn's farewell. So he'd gone, then—to use the cup. John Grey would have to find another ferryman. Ironic, considering where he'd just decided his duty lay—but he had promised Quinn to speak to the abbot and would just have to leave the matter now to God and hope the Almighty shared his view of the situation.

He nearly threw the note away, but some obscure impulse of civility made him open it. He glanced cursorily at it, then stiffened.

It was neither addressed nor signed.

You've a great loyalty to your friends, and God himself will surely bless you for it on the last day. But I should be less than a friend myself, did I not tell you the truth.

It was the Englishman who did for Major Siverly. I saw him with my own eyes, as I was watching from the wood behind the summerhouse.

Captain Twelvetrees is a great friend to our cause, and with

Major Siverly dead, the means lie now in his hand. I urge you to protect him and give him what help you can when you return to London.

God willing, we will meet there and, with our other friends, see the green branch burst into flower.

By reflex, he crumpled the note in his hand. John Grey had come out of the abbot's office, pausing there to turn and say something to Brother Ambrose.

"Friends!" he said aloud. "God help me." He grimaced and, putting the rosary back in his pocket, tore the note to tiny pieces, which he scattered to the wind.

28

Amplexus

JAMIE REFUSED TO ALLOW GREY TO TRY TO HIRE HORSES, ON grounds that the Irish liked gossip as much as did Highlanders, and were Grey to be seen in his uniform, the castle would know it by noon of the following day.

So they walked through the night from Lough Ree, keeping to the fields in the crepuscule, resting in the woods during light of day—when Jamie went into Ballybonaggin for food—then coming out onto the roads again at dark, where they kept up a fine pace, lighted by a sympathetic moon that rose above them huge, pale, and mottled as a ball of gleaming alabaster.

The countryside was empty of people—and anything else.

They had passed from open meadows into a wooded area, and the trees clustered thick and dark, roots intruding into the road, branches overhanging, so that they walked through pools of darkness, the road invisible beneath their feet, emerging suddenly into clearer spots where the trees drew back a little, and the moon caught the sudden white flash of face or shirtfront, the glint of a sword hilt.

Even the shuffle of their feet was lost in the murmur of the woods, a fresh wind rising, rattling the new leaves. John felt the night as something wild creeping upon him, the force of spring itself rising from the ground into his feet, his legs, bursting through his body 'til the blood throbbed in his fingers, pulsed in his chest.

Perhaps it was freedom, the exhilaration of their escape. Perhaps the excitement of a hunt by night, adventure and danger before them. Or the knowledge that he was an outlaw—with pursuit and danger certainly behind him.

The road was narrow, and they jostled against each other now and then, blinded between the dark wood and the brilliance of the rising moon. He could hear Jamie's breath, or thought he could—it seemed part of the soft wind that touched his face. He could smell Jamie, smell the musk of his body, the dried sweat and dust in his clothes, and felt suddenly wolflike and feral, longing changed to outright hunger.

He wanted.

Master me, he thought, breathing deep, *or shall I your master be?*

There were frogs in the ditches, in the bogs that lay beyond the scrim of trees. They called, high and low, shrill and bass, cascading over one another in a vast, pulsating chorus. At a distance, sitting on a lawn with that chorus as background, watching the stars come out, the sound might be no more than a pastoral, the song of spring.

This close, it was still the song of spring, but that song was revealed to be what the pagans had always known it to be—the blind urge to seize, to mate, to spill blood and seed heedlessly into the earth, wallow in crushed flowers, writhe in the juices of grass and mud.

Those bloody frogs were *shrieking* their passion, raw-throated and triumphant. Hundreds of them. The racket was deafening.

Distracted by the vision of amphibians in their thousands

locked in slime-wrapped sexual congress amid the dark waters, he caught his foot in a root and fell heavily.

Fraser, close beside, felt him go and grabbed him, catching him round the middle and jerking him upright again.

"Are ye all right?" he asked, low-voiced, his breath warm on Grey's cheek.

"Croakle dum-ho," he said, breathless and dazed. Fraser's hands were still tight on his arms, steadying him.

"What?"

"Great Lord Frog to Lady Mouse. It's a song. I'll sing it to you later."

Fraser made a sound in his throat that might have been either derision or amusement—maybe both—and let go Grey's arms. He swayed, almost staggering, and put out a hand to steady himself. He touched Fraser's chest, warm and solid through his clothes, swallowed hard, and took his hand away.

"This seems the sort of night on which one might meet the Wild Hunt itself," Grey said, starting to walk again. His skin prickled and jumped, and he would not in fact have been surprised in the slightest to see the Queen of Faerie come riding out of the wood, fair and spectral as the sailing moon, terrible in her hunting, her pack of attendants all young men, lithe and sharp-toothed, hungry as wolves. "What are they hunting, do you suppose?"

"Men," Fraser said without hesitation. "Souls. I was thinking the same myself. Though ye see them more on a storm-tossed night."

"Have you actually seen them?" He believed for an instant that it was quite possible, and put the question in all seriousness. Rather to Grey's surprise, Fraser took it the same way.

"No," he said, but in a tone verging on doubt. "At least—that is—"

"Tell me."

They walked in silence for a few moments, but he could feel Fraser gathering his thoughts and kept silent himself, waiting, feeling the shifting rhythms of the bigger man's body as he moved, soft-footed, on the uneven ground.

"Years back," Fraser said at last. "It was after Culloden. I lived on my own land then, but hidden. In a wee cavern in the rocks. I'd come out at night, though, to hunt. And sometimes I'd have need to go far afield, if the hunting was poor, and often it was."

They had emerged momentarily into a spot where the trees fell away, and the light of the moon shone bright enough for Grey to see Fraser tilt his head back, as though considering the orb.

"It wasna a night like this, really," he said. "Nay moon at all, and the wind going through your bones and moaning like a thousand lost souls in your ears. But it—it was wild, ye might say. Wild in the way this is," he added, dropping his voice a little and gesturing briefly at the dark countryside surrounding them. "A night when ye might expect to meet wi' things, should ye venture out."

He spoke quite matter-of-factly, as though it were entirely commonplace to meet with "things." On a night like this, Grey could believe that completely and wondered suddenly how many nights the other had spent roaming alone beneath blazing stars or a clouded vault, with no touch on his skin save the wind's rough caress.

"I'd run down a deer and killed it," Fraser said, also as though this was commonplace. "And I'd sat down by the carcass to catch my breath before the gralloching—that's the cutting out o' the bowels, ken. I'd slit the throat, of course, to bleed the meat, but I hadna yet said the prayer for it—I wondered later if it was maybe that that called them."

Grey wondered whether "that" referred to the hot scent of the pumping blood or the lack of a sanctifying word, but didn't want to risk stopping the story by asking.

"Them?" he said after a moment, encouraging.

Fraser's shoulders moved in a shrug. "Perhaps," he said. "Only all of a sudden, I felt afraid. Nay—worse than afraid. A terrible fear came upon me, and then I heard it. *Then* I heard it," he repeated, for emphasis. "I was afraid before I heard it—them."

What he had heard was the sound of hooves and voices, half-swallowed by the moaning wind.

"Was it some years before, I should ha' thought it was the Watch," he said. "But there wasna any such thing after Culloden. My next thought was that it was English soldiers—but I couldna hear any words in English, and usually I'd hear them easily at a distance. English sounds different, ken, than the *Gàidhlig,* even when ye dinna make out the words."

"I would suppose it does," Grey murmured.

"The other thing," Fraser went on, as though Grey hadn't spoken, "was that I couldna tell which direction the sound came from. And I should have. The wind was strong but steady, from the northwest. And yet the sounds came sometimes out o' the wind but just as often from the south or the east. And then they would disappear, and then come back."

By this time he had been standing, hovering near the body of the slain deer, wondering whether to run and, if so, which way?

"And then I heard a woman scream. She . . . ah." Fraser's voice sounded a little odd, suddenly careful. Why? Grey wondered. "It . . . wasna a scream of fear, or even anger. It . . . ehm . . . well, it was the way a woman will scream, sometimes, if she's . . . pleased."

"In bed, you mean." It wasn't a question. "So do men. Sometimes."

You idiot! Of all the things you might have said . . .

He would have berated himself further for having brought back the echo of his unfortunate remark in the stable at Helwater, that injudicious—that criminally stupid remark—

But Fraser merely made a deep "mmphm" sound in his throat, seeming to acknowledge Grey's present remark at face value.

"I thought for an instant, perhaps, rape . . . but there were nay English soldiers in the district—"

"Scots do not commit rapine?" Annoyance with himself sharpened Grey's tone.

"Not often," Fraser said briefly. "Not Highlanders. But as I say, it didna sound like that. And then I heard other noises—screeching and skellochs, and the screaming of horses, aye, but not the noise of battle. More like folk who are roaring drunk—and the horses, too. And it was coming closer to me."

It was the notion of drunken horses that at this point had put the vision of the Wild Hunt into Jamie's mind. It was not a common tale of the Highlands, but he had heard such stories. And heard more, from other mercenaries, when he'd fought in France as a young man.

"The queen, they said, rides a great white horse, white as moonlight," he said quietly. "Shining in the dark."

Jamie had spent enough time on the moors and in the high crags to know how much lay hidden in the land, how many ghosts and spirits lingered there, how much unknown to man—and the thought of supernatural creatures was not foreign to him at all. Once the thought of the Wild Hunt had come to him, he spared not a moment in leaving the deer's carcass, as fast as he could go.

"I thought they smelled the blood, ken," he explained. "I'd not said the rightful prayer to bless it. They'd think it was their lawful prey."

The matter-of-fact tone of this statement made the small hairs prickle on John's nape.

"I see," he said, rather faintly. He saw all too well, in his mind's eye: a helter-skelter rush of the unearthly, horses' coats and faerie faces glowing with a spectral light, spilling down out of the dark, screaming like the wind, howling for blood. The shrieking of the lust-crazed frogs now struck him differently; he heard the blind hunger in it.

"Sidhe," Fraser said softly. *Sheee,* the word sounded like, to Grey; much like the sigh of the wind.

"It's the same word, in the *Gàidhlig* and the *Gaeilge.* It means the creatures of the other world. But sometimes when they come forth out o' the stony duns where they live—they dinna go back alone."

He had run for a nearby burn, out of some half-heard, half-recollected notion that the *sidhe* could not cross running water, thrown himself over a high bank, and crouched among the boulders at its foot, staggering against the force of water that surged to mid-thigh, half-drowned in the spray, blind in the dark but keeping his eyes tight shut nonetheless.

"Ye dinna want to look upon them," he said. "If ye do, they can call ye to them. Cast their glamour upon you. And then ye're lost."

"Do they kill people?"

Fraser shook his head.

"They take people," he corrected. "Lure them. Take them back into the rocks, down to their ain world. Sometimes"—he cleared his throat—"sometimes, the stolen ones come back. But they come back two hundred years later. And all—all they knew and loved—are dead."

"How terrible," John said quietly. He could hear Fraser's breathing, heavy, like a man struggling against tears, and wondered why this aspect of the tale should move him so.

Fraser cleared his throat again, explosively.

"Aye, well," he said, voice steady once more. "So I spent the rest o' the night in the burn and nearly froze to death. If it hadna been near dawn when I went in, I shouldna have come out again. I could barely move when I did, and had to wait for the sun to rise high enough to warm me, before I could make my way back to where I'd left my deer."

"Was it still there?" Grey asked with interest. "As you'd left it?"

"Most of it was. Something—someone," he corrected himself, "had gralloched it neat as a tailor's seam and taken away the head and the entrails and one of the haunches."

"The huntsman's share," Grey murmured under his breath, but Fraser heard him.

"Aye."

"And were there tracks around it? Other than your own, I mean."

"There were not," Fraser said, the words clipped and precise. And he would know, Grey thought. Anyone who could hunt a deer like that could certainly discern the traces. Despite Grey's attempt at logic, a brief shiver went over him, visualizing the headless carcass, clean and butchered, the blood-soaked ground left trackless in the mist of dawn, save for the deep-gouged prints of the fleeing deer and the man who had felled it.

"Did you—take the rest?"

Fraser raised one shoulder and let it fall.

"I couldna leave it," he said simply. "I had a family to feed."

They walked on then in silence, each alone with his thoughts.

THE MOON HAD BEGUN to sink before they reached Glastuig, and exertion had calmed Grey's rush of spirits somewhat. These revived abruptly, though, when they found the gate shut but not locked and, passing through, saw a glimmer of light on the distant lawn. It was coming from one of the windows on the right.

"Do you know which room that is?" he murmured to Jamie, nodding toward the lighted window.

"Aye, it's the library," Fraser replied, equally low-voiced. "What do ye want to do?"

Grey took a deep breath, considering. Then touched Jamie's elbow, inclining his head toward the house.

"We'll go in. Come with me."

They approached the house cautiously, skirting the lawn and keeping to the shrubberies, but there was no sign of any servants or watchmen being on the premises. At one point, Fraser lifted his head and sniffed the air, taking two or three deep breaths before gesturing toward an outbuilding and whispering, "The stable is that way. The horses are gone."

Jamie's cautious researches had indicated as much; word in the village was that all the servants had left, unwilling to remain in a house where murder had been done. The livestock would have been taken away to the village, too, Grey supposed.

Could this nocturnal visitor be the executor? Grey could think of no reason why a legitimate executor of the estate would need to make a surreptitious visit—but then, perhaps the man had come in daylight, as was proper, but then lingered at his work? He glanced up at the moon; it was past midnight. Surely that argued more dedication to duty than he was accustomed to find among lawyers. Perhaps the man was just staying in the house and, finding himself wakeful, had come down in search of a book, Grey thought with a mental shrug. Occam's razor worked more often than not.

They were within pistol shot of the house now. Grey glanced to and fro, and then, feeling self-consciously dramatic, stepped out onto the lawn. It was lit like a stage, and his shadow puddled dark at his feet, the bright moon almost overhead. No dog barked, no voice called out demanding to know his purpose, but still he walked gingerly, footfalls soundless on the untidy lawn.

The casements were well above eye level. Well above his eye level, at least. With some irritation, he saw that Fraser, who had come silently out behind him, was able by standing on his toes to see into the house. The big Scot shifted to and fro, craning to see—and then froze. He said something out loud, in bloody Gaelic. Grey thought from the tone and the clearly visible expression on his face that it must be a curse.

"What do you see?" he hissed, plucking impatiently at Fraser's sleeve. The Scot thumped down on his heels and stared down at him.

"It's that wee arse-wipe, Twelvetrees," he said. "He's going through Siverly's papers."

Grey barely heard the second part of this; he was already headed for the front door and quite ready to break it down, should it offer him the least resistance.

It didn't. It was unlocked, and he heaved it open with such force that it crashed into the wall of the foyer. The sound coincided with a startled yelp from the library, and Grey charged toward the open door through which light was streaming, barely aware of Fraser, at his heels, saying urgently, "I'm no going to break ye out of that bloody castle again, just you remember that!"

There was a louder yelp as he burst into the library to find Edward Twelvetrees crouched beside the mantelpiece, the poker clutched in both hands and poised like a cricket bat.

"Put that down, you bloody nit," Grey said, halting just short of striking range. "What the devil are you doing here?"

Twelvetrees straightened up, his expression going from alarm to outrage.

"What the devil are *you* doing here, you infamous fiend?"

Fraser laughed, and both Grey and Twelvetrees glared at him.

"I beg your pardon, gentlemen," he said mildly, though his broad face still bore a look of amusement. He waved his fingers, in the manner of one urging a small child to go and say hello to an aged relative. "Be going on wi' your business. Dinna mind me."

Jamie looked around, picked up a small wing chair that Grey had knocked over in his precipitous entry, and sat in it, leaning back with an air of pleased expectation.

Twelvetrees glared back and forth between Grey and Fraser, but an air of uncertainty had entered his expression. He looked like a rat baffled of its cheese rind, and Grey suppressed an urge to laugh, too, despite his anger.

"I repeat," he said more mildly, "what are you doing here?"

Twelvetrees laid down his weapon but didn't alter his attitude of hostility.

"And I repeat—what are *you* doing here? How dare you enter the house of the man you have so foully murdered!?"

Grey blinked. For the last little while, taken up by the magic of the moonlit night, he had quite forgotten that he was an outlaw.

"I didn't murder Major Siverly," he said. "I should very much like to know who did, though. Was it you?"

Twelvetrees's mouth dropped open. "You . . . cur!" he said, and, seizing the poker up, made to brain Grey with it.

Grey caught his wrist with both hands and managed to pull him off balance as he lunged, so that Twelvetrees lurched and staggered, but he kept his feet sufficiently as to elbow Grey in the face with his free arm.

Eyes watering, Grey dodged a reckless swipe with the poker, leapt backward, and caught his bootheel in the edge of a rug. He staggered in his turn, and Twelvetrees, with a triumphant grunt, swung the poker at his midsection.

It was a glancing blow but knocked the wind out of him briefly, and he doubled over and sat down hard on the floor. Unable to breathe, he rolled to the side, avoiding another blow that clanged off the slates of the hearth, and, seizing Twelvetrees by the ankle, jerked as hard as he could. The other man went over backward with a whoop and the poker flew through the air, crashing into one of the casement windows.

Twelvetrees appeared to have stunned himself momentarily, having knocked his head against the battered mantelpiece. He lay sprawled on the hearth, his outflung hand dangerously close to the unshielded fire. With a relieving gasp, Grey rediscovered how to breathe, and lay still, doing it. He felt the vibration of a large body through the floorboards and, wiping a sleeve across his streaming face—God damn it, the bastard had bloodied his nose; he hoped it wasn't broken—saw Fraser reach down delicately and haul Twelvetrees clear of the fire. Then, frowning, Fraser rose swiftly and, grabbing the ash shovel, scraped a smoking mass of papers out of the hearth, scattering them hastily over the floor, seizing chunks that had not yet quite caught fire, and separating them from the baulk of burning pages. He ripped off his coat and flung it over the half-charred papers to smother the sparks.

Twelvetrees uttered a strangled protest, reaching for the papers, but Fraser hauled him to his feet and deposited him with some force on a settee upholstered in blue- and white-striped silk. He glanced back at Grey, as though inquiring whether he required some similar service.

Grey shook his head and, wheezing gently, one hand to his

bruised ribs, got awkwardly to his feet and hobbled to the wing chair.

"You could . . . have helped," he said to Fraser.

"Ye managed brawly on your own," Fraser assured him gravely, and to his mortification, Grey found that this word of praise gratified him exceedingly. He coughed and wiped his nose gingerly on his sleeve, leaving a long streak of blood.

Twelvetrees groaned and raised his head, looking dazed.

"I'll . . . take that . . . as a no, . . . shall I?" Grey managed. "You say you did *not* kill Major Siverly?"

"No," Twelvetrees answered, looking rather blank. Then his wits returned and his eyes focused on Grey with a profound expression of dislike.

"No," he repeated, more sharply. "Of course I did not kill Gerald Siverly. What kind of flapdoodle is that?"

Grey thought briefly of inquiring whether there was more than one sort of flapdoodle and, if so, what the categories might be, but thought better of it and ignored the question as rhetorical. Before he could formulate another question, he noticed that Fraser was calmly engaged in going through the piles of paper on the desk.

"Put those down!" Twelvetrees barked, staggering to his feet. "Stop that at once!"

Fraser glanced up at him and raised one thick red brow.

"How d'ye mean to stop me?"

Twelvetrees slapped at his waist, as do men who are accustomed to wearing a sword.Then sat down, very slowly, reason returning.

"You have no right to examine these papers," he said to Grey, calmly by comparison with his earlier outbursts. "You are a murderer and evidently an escaped outlaw—for I misdoubt that you have been released officially?"

Grey understood this was intended as sarcasm and didn't bother replying. "By what right were you examining them, may I ask?"

"By right of law," Twelvetrees replied promptly. "I am the executor of Gerald Siverly's will, charged with the discharge of his debts and the disposition of his property."

So put that in your pipe and smoke it, his expression added. Grey was in fact taken aback at this revelation.

"Gerald Siverly was my friend," Twelvetrees added, and his lips compressed briefly. "A particular friend."

Grey had known that much, from Harry Quarry, but it hadn't occurred to him that Twelvetrees would be so intimate with Siverly as to have been appointed executor of his estate. Had Siverly no family, bar his wife?

And if Twelvetrees was so intimate—what did he know concerning Siverly's actions?

Whatever it was, he obviously wasn't about to confide his knowledge to Grey. John got to his feet and, manfully trying not to wheeze in the smoke-filled air, went to the bay window and threw back the lid of the blanket chest. The ironbound box was gone.

"What have you done with the money?" he demanded, swinging back to Twelvetrees. The man glared at him with profound dislike.

"So sorry," he sneered. "It's where you'll never get your thieving hands on it."

Jamie was collecting the half-charred bits of paper he had saved from the fire, handling each with ginger care, but looked up at this, glancing from Twelvetrees to Grey.

"D'ye want me to search the house?"

Grey's eyes were on Twelvetrees, and he saw the man's nostrils flare, his lips compress in disgust—but there was no hint of agitation or fear in his red-rimmed eyes.

"No," Jamie said, echoing Grey's thoughts. "He's right; he's carried it away already."

"You're quite good at this business of outlawry," Grey said dryly.

"Aye, well. I've had practice." The Scot had a small collection of singed papers in his hand. He carefully pulled one free and handed it to Grey.

"I think this is the only one that might be of interest, my lord."

It was written in a different hand, but Grey recognized the sheet at once. It was the Wild Hunt poem—and he did wonder where the devil the rest of it was; why only this one page?—much singed and smeared with ash.

"Why—" he began, but then, seeing Fraser jerk his chin upward, turned the paper over. He heard Twelvetrees's breath hiss in, but paid no attention.

The Wild Hunt

Capt. Ronald Dougan
Wm. Scarry Spender
Robert Wilson Bishop
Fordham O'Toole
Èamonn Ó Chriadha
Patrick Bannion Laverty

Grey whistled softly through his teeth. He knew none of the names on the list but had a good idea what it was—an idea reinforced by the look of fury on Twelvetrees's face. He wouldn't go back to Hal *quite* empty-handed.

If he wasn't mistaken, what he held in his hand was a list of conspirators, almost certainly Irish Jacobites. Someone—had it been Fraser or himself?—had suggested that the Wild Hunt poem was a recognition signal, and he had wondered at the time, a signal for whom? Here was the answer—or part of one. Men who did not know one another personally would recognize others in their group by the showing of the poem—on its face a bit of half-finished, innocuous verse, but in reality a code, readable by those who held the key.

Fraser nodded casually toward Twelvetrees. "Is there anything ye want me to beat out of him?"

Twelvetrees's eyes sprang wide. Grey wanted to laugh, in spite of everything, but didn't.

"The temptation is considerable," he said. "But I doubt the experiment would prove productive. Just keep him there, if you would, while I have a quick look round."

He could tell from Twelvetrees's dour expression that there was nothing further to be found in the house, but, for form's sake, he went through the desk and the bookshelves and made a brief foray upstairs with a candlestick, in case Siverly should have kept anything secret in his bedchamber.

He felt a strong sense of oppression, walking through the empty darkness of the house, and something akin to sadness, standing in the dead man's chamber. The servants had stripped the bed, rolled up the mattress, and tidily covered the furniture in dust sheets. Only the moving gleam of candlelight from the damask wallpaper gave a hint of life.

He felt curiously empty, as though he himself might be a ghost, viewing the remnants of his own life without emotion. The heat and excitement of his confrontation with Twelvetrees had quite drained away, leaving a sense of flatness in its wake. There was nothing further he could do here; he could not arrest Twelvetrees or compel answers from him. Whatever might yet be discovered, the end of the matter was that Siverly was dead, and his crimes with him.

"And his place shall know him no more," he said softly, and the words fell and vanished among the silent shapes of the sleeping furniture. He turned and left, leaving the door open on darkness.

SECTION IV

A Tithe to Hell

29

The Wild Hunt

THEY STRAGGLED INTO LONDON ON THE LATE MAIL COACH, unwashed, unshaven, and smelling strongly of vomit. The channel crossing had again been rough, and even Grey had been sick.

"If you can hold on to your stomach when all about you are losing theirs . . ." he muttered, thinking that this would be a good line for a poem. He must remember to tell Harry; perhaps he could think of a decent rhyme. "Boozing lairs" was the only thing that came to his own mind, and the thought of boozing kens, dark cellars full of drunken, sweating, cohabiting humanity, combined with the reek of his companions and the coach's jolting, made him queasy again.

The thought of explaining things to Hal made him queasier still, but there was no help for it.

They reached Argus House near sunset, and Minnie, hearing the noise of their arrival, came hurrying down the stairs to greet them. A quick, appalled glance at them having told her all she wanted to know, she forbade them to speak, rang for footmen and chambermaids, and ordered brandy and baths all round.

"Hal . . . ?" Grey asked, glancing warily toward the library.

"He's in the House, making a speech about tin mining. I'll

send a note to bring him back." She took a step away, holding her nose with one hand and gesturing him toward the stairs with the other. "Shoo, John."

CLEAN AND STILL relatively sober, despite a lavish application of brandy, Grey made his way down to the larger drawing room, where his nose told him tea was being served. He heard the soft rumble of Jamie Fraser's voice, talking to Minnie, and found them cozily ensconced on the blue settee; they looked up at his entrance with the slightly startled air of conspirators.

He had no time to wonder about this before Hal arrived, dressed for the House of Lords and flushed from the heat of the day. The duke collapsed into a chair with a groan and pried his red-heeled shoes off, dropping them into Nasonby's hands with a sigh of relief. The butler bore them off as though they were made of fine china, leaving Hal to examine a hole in his stocking.

"The press of carriages and wagons was so great, I got out and walked," he said, as though he'd last seen his brother at breakfast, rather than weeks before. He glanced up at Grey. "I've got a blister on my heel the size of a pigeon's egg, and it looks better than you do. What the devil's happened?"

With this introduction, it proved easier than Grey had thought to lay things out. This he did as succinctly as possible, referring to Fraser now and then to provide details.

Hal's lips twitched a bit at the part about Siverly's attack upon Jamie Fraser, but he sobered immediately upon hearing of Grey's two visits to Siverly's estate.

"Good God, John." Tea had now appeared, and he absently took a slice of fruitcake, which he held uneaten in one hand while stirring sugar into his tea. "So you escaped from Athlone

Castle and fled Ireland, suspected of murder. You do realize that the justiciar will recognize you from your description?"

"I hadn't time to worry about it," Grey retorted, "and I don't plan to start now. We have more important things to think of."

Hal leaned forward and set down the fruitcake, very carefully. "Tell me," he said.

Grey obliged, bringing out the half-charred pages they had retrieved from Twelvetrees's bonfire. Finally, he deposited the smudged and crumpled sheet of poetry, with the list of names on the back, and explained what he thought these signified.

Hal picked it up, whistled between his teeth, and said something scabrous in German.

"Nicely put," said Grey. His throat was raw from seasickness and talking. He took up his cup of tea and inhaled it thankfully. "I see one man on that list who holds a commission; if any of the others are in the army, it should be possible to locate them fairly easily."

Hal put the singed pages carefully on the table.

"Well. I think it behooves us to proceed carefully, but quickly. I'll put Harry on to these names; he knows everyone and can find out who they are, if they're in the army, and what their history may be. Plainly most *are* Irish; I think we ought to have a very cautious look at the Irish Brigades—don't want to offend them unduly. As for Twelvetrees . . ." He noticed the fruitcake, picked it up, and took a bite, chewing absently as he thought.

"He already knows he's under suspicion of something," Grey pointed out, "whether he knows what or not. Do we approach him directly or just follow him about London to see who he talks to?"

Hal's face lighted in a smile, as he looked his younger brother up and down.

"You going to black your face and follow him yourself? Or did you have in mind setting Mr. Fraser on him? Neither of you is what I'd call inconspicuous."

"No, I thought I'd let you do it," Grey said. He reached for the brandy decanter and poured some into his teacup. He was so tired that his hand shook, splashing a little into the saucer.

"I'll talk to Mr. Beasley," Hal said thoughtfully. "I believe he knows where those O'Higgins rascals are; they might be of use."

"They *are* Irish," Grey pointed out. The O'Higgins brothers, Rafe and Mick, were soldiers—when it suited them. When it didn't, they disappeared like will-o'-the-wisps. They did, however, know everyone in the Rookery, that raucous, uncivilized bit of London where the Irish émigrés congregated. And if there was a job to be done involving things that weren't strictly legal, the O'Higginses were your men.

"Being Irish doesn't necessarily imply treasonous proclivities," Hal said reprovingly. "They were certainly helpful with regard to Bernard Adams."

"All right." Grey leaned back in his chair and closed his eyes, feeling fatigue flow through his body like sand through an hourglass. "On your head be it."

Minnie cleared her throat. She'd been sitting quietly, stitching something, while the men conversed.

"What about Major Siverly?" she asked.

Grey opened his eyes, regarding her blearily.

"He's dead," he said. "Were you not listening, Minerva?"

She gave him a cold look. "And doubtless he deserved it. But did you not begin this hegira with the intent of bringing him to justice and making him account publicly for his crimes?"

"Can you court-martial a dead man?"

She cleared her throat again and looked pleased.

"Actually," she said, "I rather think you can."

Hal stopped chewing fruitcake.

"I collected any number of records of general courts-martial, you know," she said, with a quick glance at Grey. "When . . . when poor Percy . . ." She coughed, and looked away. "But the point is, you can have a posthumous court-martial. *A man's deeds live after him* and all that, apparently—though I think it's mostly intended to provide a record of truly stunning peccability, for the edification of the troops and to enable the wicked officer's superiors to indicate that they weren't actually asleep or conniving while all the dirty dealings were going on."

"I've never heard of such a thing," Grey said. From the corner of his eye, he could see Jamie Fraser examining a crumpet as though he'd never seen one before, lips tight. Jamie Fraser was the only person in the world—besides Percy—who knew the truth of Grey's relationship with his stepbrother.

"How often has it been done?" Hal asked, fascinated.

"Well, once that I know about," Minnie admitted. "But once is enough, isn't it?"

Hal pursed his lips and nodded, eyes narrowed as he envisioned the possibilities. It would have to be a general court-martial, rather than a regimental one; they'd known that to begin with. Siverly's regiment might wish to prefer charges against him, given the scale of his crimes, but the records of a regimental court-martial were not public, whereas those of a general court-martial necessarily were, involving the judge advocate's office and its tediously detailed records.

"And it does give you a public arena, should you want one," Minnie added delicately, "in which to explore Major Siverly's relations with Edward Twelvetrees. Or anyone else you like." She nodded at the singed paper lying next to the teapot.

Hal began to laugh. It was a low, joyous sound, and one Grey hadn't heard in some time.

"Minnie, my dear," he said affectionately. "You are a pearl of great price."

"Well, yes," she said modestly. "I am. Captain Fraser, would you care for more tea?"

THOMAS, COMTE DE LALLY, Baron de Tollendal, was lodged in a small private house near Spitalfields. So much Jamie had discovered from the duchess, who didn't ask him why he required the information; nor did he ask her why she wanted to know whether he had spoken with Edward Twelvetrees and, if so, whether Twelvetrees had mentioned the name Raphael Wattiswade.

He wondered briefly who Wattiswade was but made no inquiries of Grey or Pardloe; if the duchess respected his confidence, he would respect hers. He had asked her whether she had heard of Tobias Quinn; she had not.

He wasn't surprised at that; if Quinn was in London—and knowing what he knew about Quinn's plans, he was almost sure of it—he would be keeping himself quiet. Still, he might be using the Druid cup as inspiration to those followers whose dedication was not quite sure—and if he had the cup and had been showing the dreadful thing about, there might well be rumors of it.

He walked through the narrow streets, feeling the alien strangeness of the city. Once, he had had men he knew—both those he commanded and those who sought him out—and networks of information. Once, he could have put out word and found a man like Quinn within hours.

Once.

He put the thought firmly away from him; that part of his life was over. He had made up his mind to it and did not mean to turn back; why did such thoughts still come to him?

"Because ye've still to finish it, clot-heid," he muttered to himself. He had to find Quinn. Whether it was to put a stop to the Irish Brigades' plot before it became action, dooming those involved in it, or for the sake of Quinn himself, he wasn't sure—but he must find the man. And Thomas Lally was still a man such as he had been himself. Lally was also a prisoner, true, but one still with followers, informants, one who listened and planned. A man who would leave the stage of war only when carried off it feetfirst. *A man who hasn't given up,* he thought, with a tinge of bitterness.

He'd come unannounced. It wasn't courteous, but he wasn't interested in courtesy. He needed information and had a better chance of getting it if Lally hadn't time to decide whether it was wise to give it to him.

The sun was high by the time he arrived; Pardloe had invited him to make use of the Greys' coach, but he didn't want anyone knowing his destination and so had walked halfway across London. They weren't bothering to follow him anymore; they were much too busy looking for the members of the Wild Hunt. How long might he have before one of those names led them to someone who would talk? He knocked at the door.

"Captain Fraser." It was Lally himself who answered the door, to Jamie's surprise. Lally was surprised, too, but cordial—he stepped back, gesturing Jamie inside.

"I am alone," Jamie said, seeing Lally peer down the street before closing the door.

"So am I," said Lally, casting a bleak look round the tiny front room. It was disordered, with smeared crockery and crumbs on the table, a cold, unswept hearth, and a general feel of neglect.

"My servant has left, I'm afraid. Can I offer you . . ." He swung round, eyeing a shelf that held two or three bottles, picked one up and shook it, looking relieved when it sloshed. "A glass of ale?"

"Aye, thank ye." He knew better than to refuse hospitality, particularly under such circumstances, and they sat down at the table—there was no place else to sit—pushing aside the dirty dishes, green cheese rinds, and a dead cockroach. Jamie wondered if the thing had died of starvation or poisoning.

"So," said Lally, after a minimal exchange of commonplaces, "did you find your Wild Hunt?"

"The English think they have," Jamie said. "Though it may be naught but a mare's nest."

Lally's eyes widened in interest, but he was still reserved.

"I heard that you went to Ireland with Lord John Grey," he remarked, and sighed a little. "I haven't seen it in many years. Is it still green, then, and beautiful?"

"Wet as a bath sponge and mud to the knees, but, aye, it was green enough."

That made Lally laugh; Jamie thought he didn't laugh often. It didn't come easily to him.

"It's true that I was obliged to go wi' his lordship," Jamie said, "but I had another companion, as well—one less official. D'ye recall Tobias Quinn, by chance?"

Indeed he did; Jamie saw the knowledge flicker deep in Lally's eyes, though his face stayed calm, slightly quizzical.

"From the Rising. One of the Irish who came with O'Sullivan, was he not?"

"Aye, that'll be the man. He met us in Ireland and traveled with us, in the guise of a traveler met by accident."

"Indeed." Lally sipped ale—it was flat and stale, and he made a face and threw it out the open window. "What was his purpose?"

"He told me he sought a thing—the *Cupán Druid riogh,* he called it. Ye've heard of it?"

Lally was not a good natural liar.

"No," he said, but his hands curled on the tabletop and he stiffened a little. "A Druid king's cup? What on earth is that?"

"Ye've seen it, then," Jamie said, friendly but firm. Lally stiffened further, torn between denial and answer. So he had seen it. Which in turn meant that he'd seen Quinn, for surely Quinn would surrender it to no man save Charles Stuart.

"I need to speak with him," Jamie said, leaning forward to indicate sincerity and urgency—neither one feigned. "It is a matter of his own safety, as well as that of the men with whom he's involved. Can ye get word to him? I shall meet him anywhere he likes."

Lally sat back a bit, suspicion darkening his eyes.

"Meet him and betray him to the English?" he said.

"Ye believe that of me?" Oddly, the idea that Lally might believe it hurt him.

Lally grimaced and looked down.

"I don't know," he said, low-voiced, and Jamie saw how drawn he was, the muscles of his face hard under the skin. "So many men I thought I knew . . ." He gave a small, despairing shake of the head. "I don't know whom to trust—or whether there is anyone who can be trusted, anymore."

That, at least, held the ring of truth.

"Aye," said Jamie quietly. "I, too." He spread his hands out, flat on the table. "And yet I have come to you."

And yet . . . He could almost hear Lally thinking. Furious things were going on behind that pale, twitching face.

Ye're in it up to your eyebrows, poor wee fool, he thought, not unkindly. Add one more to the tally, then; one more man who might go to his doom if this harebrained scheme came to the point of action. One more who might be saved, if . . .

He pushed his chair back from the table and stood up.

"Hear me, *a Tomás MacGerealt,*" he said formally. "Quinn will maybe have told ye what he said to me, and I to him. If not, ask him. I said it not from cowardice, not from treachery, nor unwillingness to stand wi' friends and comrades. I said it from sure knowledge. Ye kent my wife?"

"The Sassenach woman?" The ghost of a smile touched Lally's mouth, sardonic.

"La Dame Blanche, they called her in Paris, and for good reason. She saw the end of the Cause—and its death. Believe me, Thomas. This venture, too, is doomed, and I ken that fine. I wouldna have it take ye down wi' it. For the sake of our shared past, I beg ye—stand clear."

He hesitated, waiting for an answer, but Lally kept his eyes on the table, one finger circling in a puddle of spilled ale. At last, he spoke.

"If the English do not send me back to France to clear my name, what is there for me here?"

There was no answer to that. Lally lived at the sufferance of his captors, as Jamie did. How would a true man not be tempted by the possibility of regaining his life? Jamie sighed, helpless, and Lally glanced up, his gaze sharpening as he perceived pity on Jamie's face.

"Ah, don't worry about me, old comrade," he said, and there was as much affection as irony in his voice. "The Marquise of Pelham comes back from her country house next week. She has a *tendresse* for me, La Marquise—she will not let me starve."

30

Particular Friends

HAROLD, DUKE OF PARDLOE, COLONEL OF THE 46TH FOOT, visited the Judge Advocate's office, attended by both his regimental colonels and by his brother, Lieutenant Colonel Lord John Grey, to file the necessary documents to call a posthumous general court-martial of one Major Gerald Siverly, on a variety of charges ranging from theft and corruption, to failure to suppress mutiny, to willful murder—and treason.

After hours of discussion, they had decided to proceed with the court-martial at once and to add the charge of treason. It would cause talk—an immense amount of talk—and perhaps bring more of Siverly's connections to the surface. Meanwhile, those men they had managed to identify from Siverly's list of the Wild Hunt—a half dozen or so—would be carefully watched, to see whether news of the court-martial might cause them to run, to act, or to seek out others in the plot.

Even with the documents filed, it would be nearly a month before the court-martial was convened. Unable to bear the inactivity of waiting, Grey invited Jamie Fraser to go with him to a race meeting at Newmarket. Returning two days later, they stopped at the Beefsteak, where they took rooms, intending to dine and change before going on to a play in the evening.

By unspoken mutual consent, they had avoided any reference to Ireland, Siverly, Twelvetrees, court-martials, or poetry. Fraser was quiet, occasionally withdrawn—but he relaxed in the presence of horses, and Grey felt a small relaxation of his own tension in seeing it. He had arranged for Jamie's parole at Helwater because of the horses and the relative degree of freedom, and while he could not deceive himself that Jamie was content as a prisoner, at least he had some hope that he was not completely unhappy.

Am I right to treat him thus? he wondered, watching Fraser's broad back as the Scot preceded him from the dining room. *Will it give him something to remember, to recollect with pleasure when he goes back—or only increase the bitterness of his position? God, I wish I knew.*

But then . . . there was the possibility of freedom. He felt his stomach knot at the thought but wasn't sure whether it was from fear that Fraser would gain his freedom—or that he wouldn't. Hal had certainly mentioned it as a possibility, but if there proved to be a fresh Jacobite plot, the country would be swept up once more in fear and hysteria; it would be nearly impossible to have Fraser pardoned in such circumstances.

He was so caught up in these reflections that it was some moments before he realized that he knew the voice coming from the billiards room to his right.

Edward Twelvetrees was at the green-baize table. He looked up from a successful shot, his face alight with pleasure, then caught a glimpse of Grey in the hallway, and his face went stiff, the smile freezing into a tooth-baring rictus. The friend with whom he'd been playing stared at him in astonishment, then turned a bewildered face toward Grey.

"Colonel Grey?" he said, tentative. It was Major Berkeley Tarleton, the father of Richard Tarleton, who had been Grey's ensign at Crefeld. He knew Grey, of course, but plainly could not understand the sudden hostility that had sprung up like a wall of thorns between the two men.

"Major Tarleton," Grey said, with a nod that did not take his eyes away from Twelvetrees. The tip of Twelvetrees's nose had gone white. He'd received his summons to the court-martial, then.

"You unspeakable whelp." Twelvetrees's voice was almost conversational.

Grey bowed.

"Your servant, sir," he said. He felt Jamie come up behind him and saw Twelvetrees's eyes narrow at sight of the Scot.

"And you." Twelvetrees shook his head, as though so appalled that he could find no speech to address the situation. He turned his gaze upon Grey again. "I wonder at it, sir. Indeed, I wonder at it. Who would bring such as this fellow, this depraved Scotch creature, a convicted traitor"—his voice rose a little on the word—"into the sacred precincts of this club?" He was still holding his cue, clutching it like a quarterstaff.

"Captain Fraser is my particular friend, sir," Grey said coldly.

Twelvetrees uttered a most unpleasant laugh.

"I daresay he is. A very *close* friend, I have heard." The edge of his lip lifted in a sneer.

"What do you imply, sir?" Fraser's voice came from behind him, calm, and so formal as almost to lack his usual accent. Twelvetrees's hot eyes left Grey, rising to Fraser's face.

"Why, sir, since you are so civil as to inquire, I *imply* that this arse-wipe is your"—he hesitated for an instant, and then said, elaborately sardonic—"not merely your most particular friend. For surely only the loyalty of a bedfellow can have led him to do your bidding."

Grey felt a ringing in his ears, like the aftereffects of cannon fire. He was dimly conscious of thoughts pinging off the inside of his skull like the shards of an exploding grenade, even as he shifted his weight: *He's trying to goad you, does he want to provoke a fight—he'll bloody get one!—or does he want a challenge, if so, why not give one? Because he wants to look the aggrieved party? He's just called me a sodomite in public, he means to discredit me, I'll have to kill him.* This last thought arrived simultaneously with the flexing of his knees—and the grasp of Tarleton's fingers on his arm.

"Gentlemen!" Tarleton was shocked but firm. "Surely you cannot mean such things as your conversation might suggest. I say you should command your passions for the moment, go and have a cooling drink, take sober thought, perhaps sleep on the matter. I am sure that in the morning—"

Grey wrenched his arm free.

"You bloody murderer!" he said. "I'll—"

"You'll what? Fucking sodomite!" Twelvetrees's hands were clenched on the cue stick, his knuckles white.

A much bigger hand came down on Grey's shoulder and dragged him out of the way. Fraser stepped in front of him, reached across the corner of the table, and plucked the cue out of Twelvetrees's hands as though it were a broomstraw. He took it in his hands and, with a visible effort, broke it neatly in two and laid the pieces on the table.

"Do you call me traitor, sir?" he said politely to Twelvetrees. "I take no offense at this, for I stand convicted of that crime. But I say to you that you are a greater traitor still."

"You—what?" Twelvetrees looked mildly stunned.

"You speak of particular friends, sir. Your own most particular friend, Major Siverly, faces a posthumous court-martial for corruption and treason of a most heinous kind. And I say that you should be tried along with him, for you have been partner to his crimes—and if justice is served, doubtless you will be. And if the justice of the Almighty be served, you will then join him in hell. I pray it may be swift."

Tarleton made a small gobbling noise that Grey would have found funny in other circumstances.

Twelvetrees stood stock-still, beady eyes a-bulge, and then his face convulsed and he leapt upon the table, launching himself from it at Jamie Fraser. Fraser dodged aside, and Twelvetrees struck him no more than a glancing blow, falling to the floor at Grey's feet.

He remained in a crumpled heap for a moment, panting heavily, then rose slowly to his feet. No one tried to assist him.

He stood up, slowly straightened his clothing, and then walked toward Fraser, who had withdrawn into the hall. He reached the Scotsman, looked up as though gauging the distance, then, drawing back his arm, slapped Fraser bare-handed across the face with a sound like a pistol shot.

"Let your seconds call upon me, sir," he said, in a voice little more than a whisper.

The hall was full of men, emerged from smoking room, library, and dining room at the sound of raised voices. They parted like the waves of the Red Sea for Twelvetrees, who walked deliberately away, back ramrod-straight and eyes fixed straight ahead.

Major Tarleton, with some presence of mind, had fished a handkerchief out of his sleeve and handed it to Fraser, who was wiping his face with it, Twelvetrees's blow having been hard enough to make his eyes water and slightly bloody his nose.

"Sorry about that," Grey said to Tarleton. He could breathe again, though his muscles were jumping with the need to move. He put a hand on the edge of the billiards table, not to steady himself but merely to keep himself from flying out in some unsuitable way. He saw that Twelvetrees's bootheel had made a small tear in the baize of the table.

"I cannot imagine what—" Tarleton swallowed, looking deeply unhappy. "I cannot imagine what should have led the captain to speak in such a—to say such—" He flung out his hands in total helplessness.

Fraser had regained his self-possession—well, in justice, Grey thought, he'd never lost it—and now handed Tarleton back his handkerchief, neatly folded.

"He spoke so in an effort to discredit Colonel Grey's testimony," he said quietly—but audibly enough to be heard by everyone in the hallway. "For what I said to him is the truth. He is a Jacobite traitor and deeply involved, both in Siverly's treason—and in his death."

"Oh," said Tarleton. He coughed and turned a helpless face on Grey, who shrugged apologetically. The witnesses out in the hallway—for he realized that this was what they were, what Fraser had intended them to be—had begun to whisper and buzz among themselves.

"Your servant, sir," Fraser said to Tarleton, and bowing politely he turned and went out. He didn't go toward the front door, as Twelvetrees had, but rather toward the stairway, which he ascended in apparent unawareness of the many eyes fixed on his broad back.

Tarleton coughed again. "I say, Colonel. Will you take a glass of brandy with me in the library?"

Grey closed his eyes for an instant, flooded with gratitude for Tarleton's support. "Thank you, Major," he said. "I could do with a drink. Possibly two."

IN THE END, they shared the bottle, Grey taking the lion's share. Various friends of Grey's joined them, tentatively at first, but then with more confidence, until there were more than a dozen men clustered round three tiny tables shoved together, the tables crowded with glasses, coffee dishes, bottles, decanters, plates of cake and sandwich crumbs, and crumpled napkins. The talk, at first carefully casual, swung round quickly to loudly expressed shock at Twelvetrees's effrontery, with a general consensus that the man must be mad. No word was said regarding Fraser's remarks.

Grey knew they did not think Twelvetrees mad, but as he was in no way prepared to discuss the matter himself, he merely shook his head and murmured a general bewildered agreement with this assessment.

Twelvetrees had his supporters, too, of course, but there were fewer of them, and they had retreated to a stronghold in the smoking room, from which a stream of uneasy but decidedly hostile murmuring flowed like the tobacco smoke that shielded them. Mr. Bodley's face was pinched as the steward set down a fresh tray of savories in the library. The Beefsteak was no stranger to controversy—no London club was—but the staff disliked the sort of argument that led to broken furniture.

What the devil made him do it? was the refrain that pulsed in Grey's temples, along with the brandy. He didn't mean Twelvetrees, though he wondered that, as well; he meant James Fraser. He wanted urgently to go find out but made himself sit until the bottle was empty and the conversation had turned to other things.

Only until they get outside, he thought. The news would spread like ink on white linen—and be just as impossible to eradicate. He stood up, wondering vaguely what he'd tell Hal, took his leave of Tarleton and the remaining company, and walked—very steadily, concentrating—up the stairs to the bedrooms.

The door to Fraser's room stood open, and a male servant—the Beefsteak employed no chambermaids—knelt on the hearth, sweeping out the ashes. The room was otherwise empty.

"Where is Mr. Fraser?" he asked, putting a hand on the door-jamb and looking carefully from corner to corner of the room, lest he might have overlooked a large Scotsman somewhere among the furnishings.

" 'E's gone out, sir," said the servant, scrambling to his feet and bowing respectfully. " 'E didn't say where."

"Thank you," Grey said after a pause, and walked—a little less steadily—to his own room, where he carefully shut the door, lay on his bed, and fell asleep.

I CALLED HIM a murderer.

That was the thought in his mind when he woke an hour later. *I called him a murderer, he called me a sodomite . . . and yet it's Fraser he called out. Why?*

Because Fraser accused him, point-blank and publicly, of treason. He had to challenge that; he couldn't let the statement stand. An accusation of murder might be mere insult, but not an accusation of treason. And particularly not if there was any truth in it.

Of course. He'd known that, really. What he didn't know was what had possessed Fraser to make the accusation now, and in such a public manner.

He got up, used the pot, then splashed water from the ewer over his face and, tilting the pitcher, drank most of the rest. It was nearly evening; his room was growing dark, and he could smell the luscious scents of tea preparing downstairs: fried sardines, fresh buttered crumpets, lemon sponge, cucumber sandwiches, sliced ham. He swallowed, suddenly ravenous.

He was strongly tempted to go down and have his tea instantly, but there were things he wanted more than food. Clarity, for one.

He can't have done it for me. The thought carried some regret; he wished it were true. But he was realist enough to know that Fraser wouldn't have gone to such lengths merely to distract attention from Twelvetrees's accusation of sodomy, no matter what he personally thought of Grey at the moment—and Grey didn't even know that.

He realized that he was unlikely to divine Fraser's motives without asking the man. And he was reasonably sure where Fraser had gone; there weren't many places he could go, in all justice.

Justice. There were a good many different ways to achieve that enigmatic state of affairs, in descending levels of social acceptability. Statute. Court-martial. Duello. Murder.

He sat down on the bed and thought for a few moments. Then he rang for paper and ink, wrote a brief note, folded it, and, without sealing it, gave it to the servant with instructions for its delivery.

He at once felt better, having taken action, and, smoothing his crumpled neckcloth, went in search of fried sardines.

31

Betrayal

FRASER HAD, AS GREY THOUGHT, GONE BACK TO ARGUS
House. When he arrived himself, Grey had barely ascertained as
much from Nasonby when Hal came storming up the steps be
hind him, his tempestuous entrance nearly jerking the door from
the butler's grasp.

"Where is that bloody Scotchman?" he demanded, dividing a
glare between Grey and Nasonby.

That was fast, Grey thought. News of what had happened a
the Beefsteak had clearly spread through the coffeehouses and
clubs of London within hours.

"Here, Your Grace," said a deep, cold voice, and Jamie Frase
emerged from the library, Edmund Burke's *A Philosophical En
quiry into the Origin of Our Ideas of the Sublime and Beautiful* in hi
hand. "Did you wish to speak with me?"

Grey had a moment's relief that Fraser had finished the col
lected disputations of Marcus Tullius Cicero; Burke would make
much less of a dent in Hal's skull if it came to blows—which
looked likely at the moment.

"Yes, I bloody wish to speak with you! Come in here! You

too!" He turned to glower at Grey, including him in this command, then swept past Fraser into the library.

Jamie walked across the room and sat down deliberately, looking coolly at Hal. The door had barely closed behind them when Hal swung round to face Fraser, face livid with shock and fury.

"What have you done?" Hal was making an effort to control himself, but his right hand was flexing, closing and unclosing, as though he were keeping himself with an effort from hitting something. "You knew what I—what we"—he corrected himself, with a brief nod at Grey—"intended. We have done you the honor of including you in all our counsels, and this is how you repay—"

He stopped abruptly, because Fraser had risen to his feet. Fast. He took a quick step toward Hal, and Hal, by pure reflex, took a step back. His face was flushed now, but his color was nothing to Fraser's.

"Honor," Fraser said, and his voice shook with fury. "You dare speak to me of honor?"

"I—"

A large fist crashed down on the table, and all the ornaments rattled. The bud vase fell over.

"Be still! Ye seize a man who is your captive—and your captive by honor alone, sir, for believe me, if I had none, I should have been in France these four years past! Seize and compel him by threat to do your bidding, and by that bidding to betray ancient comrades, to forswear vows, betray friendship and loyalty, to become your very creature . . . and ye think ye do me *honor* to count me an Englishman!?"

The air seemed to shiver with the force of his words. No one spoke for a long moment, and there was no sound save the drip of water from the fallen vase, dropping from the edge of the table.

"Why, then?" Grey said quietly, at last.

Fraser rounded on him, dangerous—and beautiful—as a red stag at bay, and Grey felt his heart seize in his chest.

Fraser's own chest heaved visibly, as he sought to control his emotions.

"Why," he repeated, and it was not a question, but the preface to a statement. He closed his eyes for an instant, then opened them, fixing them on Grey with great intensity.

"Because what I said of Twelvetrees is true. With Siverly dead, he holds the finances of the rising in his hands. He must not be allowed to act. *Must* not."

"The rising?" Hal had subsided into his chair as Fraser spoke but now sprang to his feet. "There is a rising, then? You know this for a fact?"

Fraser spared him a single glance of contempt.

"I know it." And in a few words, he laid the plan before them: Quinn's acquisition of the Druid king's cup, the involvement of the Irish regiments, and the Wild Hunt's plan. His voice shook with some strong emotion at moments in the telling; Grey could not tell whether it was rage at them or fear at the enormity of what he said. Perhaps it was sorrow.

He seemed to have stopped speaking, letting his head fall forward. But then he drew a deep, trembling breath and looked up again.

"If I thought that there was the slightest chance of success," he said, "I should ha' kept my own counsel. But there is not, and I know it. I canna let it happen again."

Grey heard the desolation in his voice and glanced briefly at Hal. Did his brother know the enormity of what Fraser had just done? He doubted it, though Hal's face was intent, his eyes live as coals.

"A minute," Hal said abruptly, and left the room. Grey heard him in the hall, urgently summoning the footmen, sending them at once for Harry Quarry and the other senior officers of the regiment. Calling for his secretary.

"A note to the prime minister, Andrews," Hal's voice floated back from the hallway, tense. "Ask if I may wait upon him this evening. A matter of the greatest importance."

A murmur from Andrews, a great rush of exodus, then a silence, and Hal's footsteps on the stairs.

"He's gone to tell Minnie," Grey said aloud, listening.

Fraser sat by the hearth, elbow on his knee and his head sunk upon one hand. He didn't answer or move.

After a few moments, Grey cleared his throat.

"Dinna speak to me," Fraser said softly. "Not now."

THEY SAT IN SILENCE for half an hour by the carriage clock on the mantelpiece, which chimed the quarter in a small silver voice. The only interruption was the entrance of the butler, coming in first to light the candles, and then again, bringing a note for Grey. He opened this, read it briefly, and thrust it into his waistcoat pocket, hearing Hal's footsteps on the stair, coming down.

His brother was pale when he came in and clearly excited, though plainly in command of himself.

"Claret and biscuits, please, Nasonby," he said to the butler, and waited 'til the man had left before speaking further. Fraser had risen to his feet when Hal came in—not out of respect, Grey thought, but only to be ready for whatever bloody thing was coming next.

Hal folded his hands behind him and essayed a small smile, meant to be cordial.

"As you point out, Mr. Fraser, you are not an Englishman," Hal said. Fraser gave him a blank stare, and the smile died a-borning. Hal pressed his lips together, breathed in through his nose, and went on.

"You are, however, a paroled prisoner of war, and my responsibility. I must reluctantly forbid you to fight Twelvetrees. Much as I agree that the man needs killing," he added.

"Forbid me," Fraser said, in a neutral tone. He stood looking at Hal as he might have examined something found on the bottom of his shoe, with a mix of curiosity and disgust.

"You cause me to betray my friends," Jamie said, as reasonably as one might lay out a geometric proof, "to betray my nation, my king, and myself—and now you suppose that you will deprive me of my honor as a man? I think not, sir."

And, without another word, he strode out of the library, brushing past a surprised Nasonby, coming in with the refreshments. The butler, nobly concealing any response to current goings-on—he had worked for the family for some time, after all—set down his tray and retired.

"That went well," said Grey. "Minnie's advice?" His brother gave him a look of measured dislike.

"I didn't need Minnie to tell me the sort of trouble that will happen if this duel takes place."

"You could stop him," Grey observed, and poured claret into one of the crystal cups, the wine dark red and fragrant.

Hal snorted.

"Could I? Yes, possibly—if I wanted to lock him up. Nothing else would work." He noticed the fallen bud vase and absently righted it, picking up the small daisy it had held. "He has the choice of weapon." Hal frowned. "Sword, do you think? It's surer than a pistol if you truly mean to kill someone."

Grey made no reply to this; Hal had killed Nathaniel Twelvetrees with a pistol; he himself had killed Edwin Nicholls with a pistol much more recently—though, granted, it had been sheer accident. Nonetheless, Hal was technically right. Pistols were prone to misfire, and very few were accurate at distances beyond a few feet.

"I don't know how he is with a sword," Hal went on, frowning, "but I've seen the way he moves, and he's got a six-inch reach on Twelvetrees, at least."

"To the best of my knowledge—which is reasonably good—he hasn't had any sort of weapon in his hands for the last seven or eight years. I don't doubt his reflexes"—a fleeting memory of Fraser's catching him as he fell on a dark Irish road, the scream of frogs and toads in his ears—"but it's you who is constantly prating on at me about the necessity of practice, is it not?"

"I never prate," Hal said, offended. He twiddled the daisy's stem between his fingers, shedding white petals on the rug. "If I let him fight Twelvetrees and Twelvetrees kills him . . . that would cause trouble for you, he being nominally under your protection as the officer in charge of his parole."

Grey felt a sudden clench in the belly. "I should not consider damage to my reputation the worst result arising from that situation," he said, imagining—all too well—Jamie Fraser dying in some bleak dawn, his pumping blood hot on Grey's guilty hands. He took a gulp of wine, not tasting it.

"Well, neither would I," Hal admitted, putting down the tattered stem. "I'd rather he wasn't killed. I like the man, stubborn and contentious as he is."

"To say nothing of the fact that he has rendered us a signal service," Grey said, with a noticeable edge to his voice. "Have you any notion what it cost him to tell us?"

Hal gave him a quick, hard look, but then glanced away and nodded.

"Yes, I have," he said quietly. "You know the oath of loyalty that they made the Jacobite prisoners swear—those who were allowed to live?"

"Of course I do," Grey muttered, rolling the cup restlessly between his palms. It had been his duty to administer that oath to incoming prisoners at Ardsmuir.

May I never see my wife and children, father, mother, or relations. May I be killed in battle as a coward and lie without Christian burial in a strange land, far from the graves of my forefathers and kindred . . .

He could only thank God that Fraser had been in the prison already for some time when Grey was appointed governor. He hadn't had to hear Jamie speak that oath or see the look on his face when he did so.

"You're right," Hal said, sighing deeply and reaching for a biscuit. "We owe him. But if he should kill Twelvetrees—there's no chance of it stopping with a mere drawing of blood, I don't suppose? No, of course not." He began to pace to and fro slowly, nibbling the biscuit.

"If he kills Twelvetrees, there'll be the devil to pay and no pitch hot, as the sailors say. Reginald Twelvetrees won't rest until he's got Fraser imprisoned for life, if not hanged for murder. And we won't fare much better." He grimaced and brushed biscuit crumbs from his fingers, plainly reliving the scandal that had followed his duel with Nathaniel Twelvetrees, twenty years before. This one would be worse, much worse, with the Greys accused of failing to stop a prisoner under their control—and if they were not openly accused of using Fraser as a pawn to accomplish a private vengeance, certainly that would be said privately.

"We have used him. Badly," Grey said, answering the thought, and his brother grimaced again.

"Depends on how you look at the results," Hal said, but his voice lacked conviction.

Grey rose, stretching his back.

"No," he said, and was surprised to find that he felt very calm. "No, the results may justify it—but the means . . . I think we must admit the means."

Hal swung round to look at him, one brow raised. "And if we do?"

"Then you can't stop him, if he's decided to fight. Or not 'can't,'" Grey corrected himself. "But you won't. It's his choice to make."

Hal snorted a little, but didn't disagree. "Do you think he does want it?" he asked after a moment. "He intimates that he threw Twelvetrees's treason in his face publicly to stop his machinations before they could go too far—and he certainly accomplished that much. But do you think he foresaw that Twelvetrees would call him out? Well, yes, I suppose he did," Hal answered himself. "Twelvetrees couldn't do otherwise. But does Fraser want this duel?"

Grey saw what his brother was getting at and shook his head. "You mean that we might be doing him a favor by preventing his fighting. No." He smiled affectionately at his brother and put down his cup. "It's simple, Hal. Put yourself in his place, and think what you'd do. He may not be an Englishman, but his honor is equal to yours, and so is his determination. I could not pay him a greater compliment."

"Hmmph," said Hal, and flushed a little. "Well. Had you better take him to the *salle des armes* tomorrow, then? Give him a bit of practice before he meets Twelvetrees? Supposing he does choose swords."

"I don't think there will be time." The feeling of calm was spreading; he felt almost as though he floated in the warm light of fire and candles, as though it bore him up.

Hal was staring at him suspiciously.

"What do you mean by that?"

"I thought it out this afternoon, and reached the same conclusions that we have just come to. Then I sent a note to Edward Twelvetrees, demanding satisfaction for his insult to me at the club."

Hal's jaw dropped.

"You . . . what?"

Grey reached into the pocket of his waistcoat and pulled out the crumpled note.

"And he's replied. Six o'clock tomorrow morning, in the gardens behind Lambeth Palace. Sabers. Odd, that. I should have thought he'd be a rapier man."

32

Duello

MUCH TO HIS SURPRISE, HE SLEPT THAT NIGHT. A DEEP, dreamless sleep from which he woke quite suddenly in the dark, aware that the day was coming.

An instant later, the door opened, and Tom Byrd came in with a candle and his tea tray, a can of hot shaving water balanced in the crook of his arm.

"Will you have some breakfast, me lord?" he asked. "I brought rolls with butter and jam, but Cook thinks you should have a proper cooked breakfast. To keep up your strength, like."

"Thank Cook for me, Tom," Grey said, smiling. He sat up on the side of the bed and scratched himself. He felt surprisingly well.

"No," he said, taking the roll to which Tom had just applied a lavish knifeful of apricot preserve, "this will do." If he were facing a daylong battle, he'd tuck solidly into the ham and eggs, black pudding, and anything else on offer—but whatever happened today wouldn't last more than a few minutes, and he wanted to feel light on his feet.

Tom laid out his clothes and stirred up the shaving soap while Grey ate, then the valet turned round, razor in hand and a determined look on his face.

"I'm a-going with you, me lord. This morning."

"You are?"

Tom nodded, jaw set.

"Yes, I am. I heard the duke and you talk about it last night, saying he oughtn't to be there, and that's all well and good; I see that him being there would just make more trouble. I can't second you, of course. But somebody ought to—to be there, at least. So I'm going."

Grey looked down into his tea, quite moved.

"Thank you, Tom," he said, when he could trust his voice. "I shall be very happy to have you with me."

IN FACT, he was glad of Tom's company. The young man didn't speak, seeing that Grey was in no mood for conversation, but sat opposite him in the carriage, Grey's best cavalry saber balanced carefully on his knees.

He would have a second, though. Hal had asked Harry Quarry to meet Grey at the ground.

"Not only for moral support," Hal had said. "I want there to be a witness." His mouth thinned. "Just in case."

Grey had wondered, in case of what? Some chicanery on the part of Twelvetrees? The sudden appearance of the Archbishop of Canterbury, roused by the noise? He didn't ask, though, fearing that the "just in case" Hal had in mind involved having someone present to memorize Grey's dying words—unless you took the blade through the eye or the roof of the mouth, you usually did have a few moments while bleeding to death in which to compose your epitaph or send an elegantly phrased farewell to your beloved.

He thought of that now and wondered briefly just what Jamie Fraser would do, if made the recipient of some particularly florid sentiment of a personal nature, with Grey safely out of neck-breaking range. The thought made him grin. He caught sight of Tom's shocked expression and hastily erased the grin, replacing it with a grave look more suitable to the occasion.

Maybe Harry would write his epitaph. In verse.

Master me . . . Damn, he never had found the other line to his couplet. Or did he need two lines? Me/be—that rhymed. Maybe it was two lines, not one. If it was really two lines he had, then he clearly needed two more to make a quatrain . . .

The carriage pulled to a halt.

He emerged into a fresh, cool dawn and stood still, breathing, while Tom made his way out, handling the sword gingerly in its scabbard. There were two other carriages pulled up, waiting under the dripping trees; it had rained in the night, though the sky had cleared.

The grass will be wet. Bad footing.

Little jolts of electricity were running through him, tightening his muscles. The feeling reminded him—vividly—of his experience of being shocked by an electric eel the year before, and he paused to stretch, easing the tightness in chest and arm. It was the bloody eel that had led to his last duel, the one in which Nicholls was killed. At least if he killed Twelvetrees this morning, it would be on purpose . . .

Not if.

"Come on," he said to Tom, and they walked past the other carriages, nodding to the coachmen, who returned their salutes, sober-faced. The horses' breath rose steaming.

The last time he had been here, it was for a garden party to which his mother had required him to escort her.

Mother . . . Well, Hal would tell her if . . . He put the thought aside. It didn't do to think too much.

The big wrought-iron gates were closed and padlocked, but

the small man-gate beside them was open. He passed through and walked toward the open ground on the far side of the garden, his heels ringing on the wet flagstones.

Best fight in stocking feet, he thought—*no, barefoot,* and then came out from under an archway covered with climbing roses into the open ground. Twelvetrees stood at the far side, under some kind of tree flocked with white blossoms. Grey was interested—and relieved—to see that Reginald Twelvetrees was not with his brother. He recognized Joseph Honey, a captain of the Lancers, who was evidently Twelvetrees's second, and a man with his back turned, who from his dress—and the box by his feet—appeared to be a surgeon. Apparently, Twelvetrees planned to survive, if wounded.

Well, he would, wouldn't he? he thought, almost absently. He was already beginning the withdrawal from conscious thought, his body relaxing, easing, rising into eagerness for the fight. He felt well, very well. The western sky had changed to a luminous violet, the final stars almost gone. Behind him, the eastern sky had gone to pink and gold; he felt the breath of dawn on the back of his neck.

He heard footsteps on the path behind him. Harry, no doubt. But it wasn't Harry who ducked his way under the rose-covered arch and came toward him. His heart jumped; he felt it distinctly.

"What the devil are you doing here?" he blurted.

"I am your second." Fraser spoke matter-of-factly, as though Grey ought to have expected this. He was dressed soberly, in the borrowed blue livery he had worn on his first night at Argus House, and wore a sword. Where had he got that?

"You are? But how did you find out—"

"The duchess told me."

"Oh. Well, she would, wouldn't she?" He didn't bother being annoyed with Minnie for minding his business. "But Harry Quarry—"

"I spoke with Colonel Quarry. We agreed that I should have the honor of seconding you." Grey wondered for an instant whether "agreed" was a euphemism for "knocked on the head," as he couldn't see Quarry yielding his office with any grace. Still and all, he couldn't help smiling at Fraser, who gave him a small, formal inclination of the head.

He then reached into his pocket and withdrew a slip of paper, folded once. "Your brother bade me give ye this."

"Thank you." He took the paper and put it into his bosom. There was no need to open it; he knew what it said. *Luck.—H.*

Jamie Fraser looked across the field to where Twelvetrees stood with his two companions, then looked soberly down at Grey. "He must not live. Ye may trust me to see to that."

"If he kills me, you mean," Grey said. The electricity that ran in little jolts through his veins had settled now to a fine constant hum. He could hear his heartbeat, thumping in his ears, fast and strong. "I'm much obliged to you, Mr. Fraser."

To his astonishment, Fraser smiled at him.

"It will be my pleasure to avenge ye, my lord. If necessary."

"Call me John," he blurted. "Please."

The Scot's face went blank with his own astonishment. He cast down his eyes for a moment, thinking. Then he put a hand solidly on Grey's shoulder and said something softly in the Gaelic, but in the midst of the odd, sibilant words, Grey thought he heard his father's name. *Iain mac Gerard . . .* was that him?

The hand lifted, leaving the feel of its weight behind.

"What—" he said, but Fraser interrupted him.

"It is the blessing for a warrior going out. The blessing of Michael of the Red Domain." His eyes met Grey's squarely, a darker blue than the dawning sky. "May the grace of Michael Archangel strengthen your arm . . . John."

GREY SAID SOMETHING very obscene under his breath, and Jamie looked sharply in the direction of his gaze, though he saw nothing more than Edward Twelvetrees, already stripped to shirt and breeks, looking like a chilled ferret without his wig, talking to an officer in uniform—presumably his second—and a man whom Jamie supposed to be a surgeon.

"It's Dr. John Hunter," Grey said, nodding at the surgeon, whom he was regarding narrowly. "The Body-Snatcher himself." He caught his lower lip in his teeth for a moment, then turned to Jamie.

"If I'm killed, you take my body from the field. Take me home. Under no circumstances let Dr. Hunter anywhere near me."

"Surely he—"

"Yes, he bloody would. Without an instant's hesitation. Swear you will not let him touch me."

Jamie gave Dr. Hunter a closer look, but the man didn't look overtly like a ghoul. He was short—a good four inches shorter than John Grey—but very broad in the shoulder and plainly a vigorous man. He glanced back at Grey, mentally envisioning Hunter tossing Grey's limp body over his shoulder and loping off with it. Grey caught and interpreted this glance.

"Swear," he said fiercely.

"I swear upon my hope of heaven."

Grey drew breath and relaxed a little.

"Good." He was pale, but his eyes were blazing and his face alert, excited but not afraid. "You go and talk to Honey, then. That's Twelvetrees's second, Captain Joseph Honey."

Jamie nodded and strode toward the little group under the trees. He'd fought two duels himself, but neither had been with seconds; he'd never undertaken this office before, but Harry Quarry had given him a brief instruction on his role:

"The seconds are meant to discuss the situation and see whether it can be resolved without an actual fight—if the party of the first part will withdraw or rephrase the insult, say, or the insulted party will agree to some other form of redress. In this instance, I'd say the odds of it being resolved without a fight are approximately three million to one, so don't strain yourself in the cause of diplomacy. If he happens to kill Grey quickly, though, you'll take care of him, won't you?"

Captain Honey saw him coming and met him halfway. Honey was young, perhaps in his early twenties, and much paler than either of the combatants.

"Joseph Honey, your servant, sir," he said, offering his hand. "I—I am not sure what to say, really."

"That makes the two of us," Jamie assured him. "I take it Captain Twelvetrees doesna intend to withdraw his assertion that Lord John is a sodomite?"

The word made Captain Honey blush, and he looked down.

"Er . . . no. And I quite understand that your principal will not brook the insult?"

"Certainly not," Jamie said. "Ye wouldna expect it, would ye?"

"Oh, no!" Honey looked aghast at the suggestion. "But I did have to ask." He swallowed. "Well. Um . . . terms. Sabers—I see your principal is suitably equipped; I'd brought an extra, just in case. At ten—oh, no, you don't do paces when it's swords, naturally not . . . er . . . Will your principal agree to first blood?"

Jamie smiled, but not in a friendly fashion.

"Would yours?"

"Worth a try, isn't it?" Honey rallied bravely, looking up at Jamie. "If Lord John would be willing—"

"He is not."

Honey nodded, looking unhappy.

"Right. Well, then . . . there's not much more to say, is there?" He bowed to Jamie and turned away, but then turned back. "Oh—we have brought a surgeon. He is of course at Lord John's service, should that be necessary."

Jamie saw Honey's eyes travel past him, and he glanced over his shoulder to see Lord John, stripped to shirt and breeches, barefoot on the wet grass, warming his muscles with a series of slashes and lunges that, while not showy, clearly indicated that he knew how to use a saber. Honey exhaled audibly.

"I dinna think ye'll have to fight him," Jamie said gently. He looked toward the trees and saw Twelvetrees openly gauging him. Eyes meeting the other man's, Jamie very slowly stretched himself, displaying both reach and confidence. Twelvetrees's mouth quirked up at one corner, acknowledging the information—but in no way disturbed at the possibilities. Either he thought there was no chance of his having to fight Jamie—or he thought he could win if he did. Jamie inclined his head in a slight bow.

Grey had turned his back on Twelvetrees and was tossing the sword lightly from hand to hand.

The weight of the saber felt good in his hand, solid, heavy. The freshly sharpened edge glittered in the light; he could still smell the oil of the sharpening stone; it made the hairs prickle agreeably down his arms.

Jamie walked back, to find that Harry Quarry had joined Lord John and Tom Byrd. The colonel nodded at him.

"Couldn't stay away," he said, half-apologetically.

"Ye mean His Grace doesna quite trust me to give him a complete report of the outcome—should that be necessary?"

"Partly that. Mostly—dammit, he's my friend."

Grey had barely registered Harry's arrival, absorbed as he was in his own preparations, but he heard that and smiled.

"Thank you, Harry." He walked to his supporters, suffused with a sudden overwhelming affection for the three of them. The lines of the old folk song drifted through his mind: *God send each noble man at his end / Such hawks, such hounds, and such a friend.* He wondered briefly which was which and decided that Tom must be his faithful hound, Harry of course the friend, and Jamie Fraser his hawk, untamed and ferocious but there with him at the last—if that's what it was, though in all honesty he thought not.

I can feel my heart beating. Feel my breath. How can it stop?

Harry reached out and clasped his hand quickly. He smiled reassuringly at Tom, who was standing there clutching his coat, waistcoat, and stockings, looking as though he might faint. Some unspoken signal ran among the men, and the opponents walked out to face each other.

Wet grass feels wonderful, cold, fresh. Bastard's been up all night, his eyes are red. He does look like a ferret—or a badger—without his wig. Should have polled my hair, but what the hell, too late now . . .

His saber touched Twelvetrees's sword with a tiny chime of metal, and electricity ran smoothly up his back and over him, out to the tips of his fingers. He took a harder grip.

"Go," said Captain Honey, and sprang back out of the way.

Jamie could see at a glance that both men were excellent swordsmen. Neither one was concerned with showing away, though; this was deadly business, and they set about each other with a concentrated ferocity, seeking advantage. A flock of doves erupted out of the trees in an uproar of wings, frightened by the noise.

It couldn't last long. Jamie knew that. Most sword fights were decided in a matter of minutes, and no one could keep up such effort with a heavy saber for much more than a quarter hour. Yet he felt as though it had already lasted much longer. Sweat crawled down his back, in spite of the cool morning.

He was so attuned to the fight that he felt his own muscles twitch, echoing the surge, the lunge, the gasp and grunt of effort, and his hands were clenched at his sides, clenched so hard that the knuckles and joints of his bad hand popped and grated.

Grey knew what he was about; he'd got a knee between Twelvetrees's thighs and a hand behind the other man's neck, his sword hand held out of the way as he grappled to bring Twelvetrees's head down. Twelvetrees was no novice, either, though, and pushed forward into Grey's hold rather than pulling back. Grey staggered, off balance for an instant, and Twelvetrees broke loose and leapt back with a loud cry, swiping at Grey.

Grey dodged back, too, but not quickly enough, and Jamie heard a strangled cry of protest from his own throat as a line of red opened as if by magic across the top of Grey's leg, followed by a rapid curtain of blood crawling down the cloth of his breeches.

Shit.

Grey lunged, disregarding—or not noticing—the injury, and though his hurt leg gave way and he fell to one knee, he caught Twelvetrees a ringing blow with the flat of his saber, over the left ear. Twelvetrees staggered, shaking his head, and Grey got laboriously to his feet and lunged, missing his aim and slicing through the meat of Twelvetrees's arm.

Got you. Bastard. Got you!

"Pity it's not his sword arm," muttered Quarry. "That would end it."

"Nothing will end this but death," said Captain Honey. The young man was white to the lips, and Jamie wondered briefly if he'd ever seen a man killed before.

Twelvetrees fell back, opening himself, and Grey rushed him, realizing too late that it was a trap; Twelvetrees brought the pommel of his sword down in a vicious thunk on Grey's head, half-stunning him. Grey dropped his sword and lurched forward into Twelvetrees, though, flung his arms about the other man's body, and fell back onto his good leg, lifting Twelvetrees over his hip and slamming him to the ground.

Take that, *arse-wipe! Christ, my ears are ringing, damn you . . . damn . . .*

"Oh, very pretty, sir, very pretty!" cried Dr. Hunter, beating his hands enthusiastically. "Did you ever see a more beautiful cross-buttock throw?"

"Well, not in a duel, no," Quarry said, blinking.

Grey stood, mouth open and chest heaving. He picked up his saber, half-leaning on it as he fought for breath. Wisps of hair clung wetly to his face, and rivulets of blood coursed slowly down his cheek and his bare calf.

"Do you . . . yield, sir?" he said.

Come on, come on! Get up, let's finish it! Hurry!

Twelvetrees, winded from the fall, did not reply but, after a moment, succeeded in rolling over, slowly managing to get to his knees. He crawled to his fallen sword, picked it up, and got slowly to his feet, but in such a manner of deliberate menace as made his answer clear.

Grey got his own sword up in time, and the sabers met with a sliding clash that locked their hilts. Without hesitation, Grey punched Twelvetrees in the face with his free hand. Twelvetrees grabbed at Grey's head, caught his clubbed hair, and yanked hard, pulling Grey off balance. His arm was weakened by the cut, though, spattering blood, and he could not keep his grip—Grey got his saber loose and hacked viciously at the other's body with a loud grunt.

Jamie winced, hearing Twelvetrees's hoarse cry and feeling that blow go home. He had a curving scar across his own ribs, inflicted by an English saber at Prestonpans.

Grey pressed his advantage as Twelvetrees staggered back, but the ferret was wily and ducked under Grey's lunge, collapsing onto one hand and thrusting upward, straight into Grey's unprotected chest.

Fuck!

There was a gasp from all the watchers. Grey pulled loose, reeled backward, coughing, his shirt reddening. Twelvetrees got his legs under him, but it took him two tries to stand, his legs shaking visibly.

Grey collapsed slowly to his knees, swaying to and fro, the saber hanging from his hand.

Fuck . . .

"Get up, me lord. Get up, please get up," Tom was whispering in anguish, his hand clutching Quarry's coat sleeve. Quarry was breathing like a boiling kettle.

"He's got to ask him to yield," Quarry was muttering. "Got to. Infamous not to—oh, God."

Twelvetrees took a step toward Grey, unsteady, face set in a rictus that showed his sharp teeth. His mouth moved, but no words came out. He drew one step closer, drawing back his bloodied sword. One more step.

One . . . more . . .

And Grey's saber rose fast and smooth, Grey rising after it, driving it home, hard into the ferret's belly. There was an inhuman noise, but Jamie couldn't tell which of them had made it. Grey let go of his sword and sat down suddenly on the grass, looking surprised. He looked up and smiled vaguely at Tom, then his eyes rolled up into his head and he fell backward, sprawled on the wet grass, welling blood.

Oh . . . Jesus . . .

Twelvetrees was still standing, hands closed around the blade in his belly, looking bemused. Dr. Hunter and Captain Honey were running across the grass and reached him just as he fell, catching him between them.

Jamie wondered briefly whether Twelvetrees had given Captain Honey instructions regarding his body, but dismissed the thought as he ran across the grass to his friend.

Take me . . . ho

33

Billets-Doux

"IF THE BLOW HAD GONE BETWEEN YOUR RIBS, YOU'D BE dead, you know."

It wasn't the first time Grey had heard this—it wasn't even the first time he'd heard it from Hal—but it was the first time he'd had the strength to reply to it.

"I know." The thrust had in fact—he'd been told, first by Dr. Hunter, and then by Dr. Maguire, the Greys' family physician, and finally by Dr. Latham, the regimental surgeon—struck him in the third rib, then sliced sideways for two or three inches before the tip of the saber had stuck in the bone of his sternum. It hadn't hurt at the time; he'd just been conscious of the jolting force of the blow.

"Hurt much?" Hal sat on his bed, peering closely at him.

"Yes. Get off."

Hal didn't move.

"In your right mind, are you?"

"Certainly. Are you?" Grey felt extremely cross. It did hurt, his bum had lost all feeling from sitting in bed, and now that the fever had passed, he was very hungry.

"Twelvetrees died this morning."

"Oh." He closed his eyes for a moment, then opened them again, feeling an apologetic gratitude for hunger and pain. "God rest his soul."

He'd known Twelvetrees was almost certain to die; it was rare to recover from a serious wound to the abdomen, and he'd felt his sword strike bone somewhere deep inside Twelvetrees; he'd gone through the man's guts, entire. If blood loss and shock didn't do for a man, infection would. Still, there was a somber finality to the news that jarred him.

"Well," he said, clearing his throat. "Has Reginald Twelvetrees sent round an official demand for my head yet? Or at least my arrest?"

Hal shook his head, unamused.

"He can't say a word, not with everyone thinking—and saying—that Edward was a traitor. You're more or less being hailed as a public hero."

Grey was staggered. "What? What for?"

Hal gave him a raised eyebrow. "After you exposed Bernard Adams as a Jacobite plotter two years ago? And then what Fraser said to Twelvetrees at the Beefsteak? Everyone thinks you challenged him because of his treasonous behavior—not that they know what that was, thank God."

"But that—I didn't—"

"Well, I know you didn't, ass," his brother said. "But as you didn't take out a notice in the newpapers saying he'd called you a pederast and you took exception to it—and he didn't take out a notice saying he thought you were a menace to society and proposed to support his opinion by force of arms—the public has as usual made up its own mind."

Grey's left arm was in a sling, but he rubbed his right hand hard over his stubbled face. He was disturbed by the news but not sure what to do about it, if anything could be done, once—

"Oh, bloody hell," he said. "The newspapers have got hold of it."

"Oh, yes." A muscle twitched at the corner of Hal's mouth. "Minnie's saved a few of the better ones for you. When you're feeling up to it."

Grey gave Hal a look. "When I feel up to it," he said, "I have a thing or two to say to your wife."

Hal smiled broadly at that. "Be my guest," he said. "And I hope you've a fine day for it." He got up, jostling Grey's bad leg. "Are you hungry? Cook has some revolting gruel for you. Also burnt toast with calf's-foot jelly."

"For God's sake, Hal!" The mingled outrage and pleading in his voice appeared to move his brother.

"I'll see what I can do." Hal leaned over and patted him quite gently on his good shoulder.

"I'm glad you're not dead. Wasn't sure for a bit."

Hal went out before he could reply. Tears welled in John's eyes, and he dashed at them with the sleeve of his nightshirt, muttering irritably in a vain attempt to convince himself that he wasn't moved.

Before he got very far with this, his attention was distracted by noise in the hallway: the sort of disturbance caused by small boys attempting to be quiet, with loud whisperings and shushings, punctuated by shoving and bumping into walls.

"Come in," he called, and the door opened. A small head poked cautiously round the corner.

"Hallo, Ben. What's a-do?"

Benjamin's face, apprehensive, relaxed at once in delight.

"You all right, Uncle? Mama said if the sword—"

"I know, I'd be dead. But I'm not, now, am I?"

Ben squinted carefully at him, dubious, but decided to take this statement at face value and, turning round, rushed to the door, hissing something into the passage. He came dashing back, now followed by his younger brothers, Adam and Henry. All of them leapt on the bed, though Benjamin and Adam prevented Henry—who was only five and didn't know better—from trying to sit in Grey's lap.

"Can we see where the sword went in, Uncle?" Adam asked.

"I suppose so." The wound had a dressing, but the doctor was coming later to change it, so no harm in pulling it off, he supposed. He unbuttoned his nightshirt one-handed and rather gingerly detached the bandage. His nephews' awed admiration was more than adequate recompense for the discomfort involved.

After the initial chorus of "Ooh!" Ben leaned forward to look more closely. It was a fairly impressive wound, Grey admitted, glancing down; whichever surgeon had seen to him—he hadn't been in any condition to notice—had lengthened the original slash so as to be able to pick out the fragments of his sternum that Twelvetrees's saber had dislodged and the bits of his shirt that had been driven into the wound. The result was a six-inch gash across the already scarred left side of his upper chest, a nasty dark red crisscrossed with coarse black stitches.

"Does it hurt?" Ben asked seriously.

"Not so bad," Grey said. "The itching on my leg's worse."

"Lemme see!" Henry began to scrabble at the bedclothes. The resultant squabble among the three brothers nearly pitched Grey onto the floor, but he managed to raise his voice enough to restore order, whereupon he pulled back the blanket and lifted his nightshirt to display the slash across the top of his thigh.

It was a shallow wound, though impressively long, and while it did still hurt a bit, he'd been honest in saying the itching was worse. Doctor Maguire had recommended a poultice of magnesium sulfate, soap, and sugar, to draw the poisons from the wounds. Doctor Latham, arriving an hour later, had removed the poultice, saying this was all great nonsense, and air would help to dry the stitches.

Grey had lain inert through both processes, having only enough strength to feel gratitude that Doctor Hunter had not come to give his opinion—he would probably have whipped out his saw and made off with the leg, thus settling the argument. Having renewed his acquaintance with the good doctor, he had somewhat more sympathy with Tobias Quinn and his horror of being anatomized after death.

"You've got a big willy, Uncle John," Adam observed.

"About the usual for a grown man, I think. Though I believe it's given fairly general satisfaction."

The boys all sniggered, though Grey thought that only Benjamin had any idea why, and wondered with interest where Ben's tutor had been taking him. Adam and Henry were too young yet to go anywhere, being still in the nursery with Nanny, but Ben had a young man named Whibley who was meant to be teaching him the rudiments of Latin. Minnie said Mr. Whibley spent much more time making sheep's eyes at the assistant cook than he did in dividing Gaul into three parts, but he did take Ben to the theater now and then, in the name of culture.

"Mama says you killed the other man," Adam remarked. "Where did you stick him?"

"In the belly."

"Colonel Quarry said the other man was an uncon-she-ubble tick," Benjamin said, working out the syllables carefully.

"Unconscionable. Yes, I suppose so. I hope so."

"For why?" asked Adam.

"If you have to kill someone, it's best to have a reason."

All three boys nodded solemnly, like a nestful of owls, but then demanded more details of the duel, eager to hear how much blood there had been, how many times Uncle John had stuck the bad fellow, and what they had said to each other.

"Did he call you vile names and utter foul oaths?" asked Benjamin.

"Foul oafs," Henry murmured happily to himself. "Foul oafs, foul oafs."

"I don't think we said anything, really. That's what your second does—he goes and talks to the other fellow's second, and they try to see if things can be arranged so that you don't need to fight."

This seemed a most peculiar notion to his audience, and the struggle to explain just why one wouldn't always want to fight someone exhausted him, so that he greeted with relief the arrival of a footman bearing a tray—even though the tray bore nothing more than a bowl of gray slop that he assumed was gruel and another of bread and milk.

The boys ate the bread and milk, passing the bowl round the bed in a companionable way, dribbling on the covers and vying with one another to tell him the news of the household: Nasonby had fallen down the front stair and had to have his ankle strapped up; Cook had had a disagreement with the fishmonger, who sent plaice instead of salmon, and so the fishmonger wouldn't bring any more fish, and so supper last night was pancakes and they all pretended it was Shrove Tuesday; Lucy the spaniel had had her pups in the bottom of the upstairs linen closet, and Mrs. Weston the housekeeper had had a fit—

"Did she fall down and foam at the mouth?" Grey asked, interested.

"Probably," Benjamin said cheerfully. "We didn't get to look. Cook gave her sherry, though."

Henry and Adam were by now cuddling against his sides,

their wriggly warmth and the sweet smell of their heads a comfort that, in his weakness, threatened to make him tearful again. To avoid this, Grey cleared his throat and asked Ben to recite something for him.

Ben frowned thoughtfully, looking so much like Hal considering a hand of cards that Grey's emotion changed abruptly to amusement. He managed not to laugh—it hurt his chest very much to laugh—and relaxed, listening to an execrably performed rendition of "The Twelve Days of Christmas," this interrupted by the entrance of Minnie, followed by Pilcock with a second tray from which appetizing smells wafted.

"Whatever are you doing to your poor uncle John?" she demanded. "Look what you've done to his bed! Off with the lot of you!"

The bedroom purged, she looked down her nose at John and shook her head. She had on a tiny lace cap, with her ripe-wheat hair put up, and looked charmingly domestic.

"Hal says the doctor be damned and Cook, too: you are to have steak and eggs, with a mixed grill. So steak you shall have, and if you die or burst or rot as a result, it will be your own fault."

Grey had already plunged a fork into a succulent grilled tomato and was chewing blissfully.

"Oh, God," he said. "Thank you. Thank Hal. Thank Cook. Thank everybody." He swallowed and speared a mushroom.

Despite her earlier disavowal, Minnie looked pleased. She loved feeding people. She motioned the footman off and sat down on the edge of the bed to enjoy the spectacle.

"Hal said you wanted to scold me about something." She didn't look at all apprehensive at the prospect.

"I didn't say that," Grey protested, pausing with a chunk of bloody steak held in transit. "I just said I could do with a word."

She folded her hands and looked at him, not quite batting her eyelashes.

"Well, actually, I meant to reproach you with sharing your insights regarding my motives with Mr. Fraser, but as it is . . ."

"As it is, I was right about them?"

He shrugged, mouth too full of steak to answer.

"Of course I was," she answered for him. "And as Mr. Fraser is no fool, I doubt he needed telling. He did, however, ask me why I thought you'd challenged Edward Twelvetrees. So I told him."

"Where . . . um . . . where is Mr. Fraser at the moment?" he asked, swallowing and reaching at once for a forkful of egg.

"I suppose he's where he has been for the last three days, reading his way through Hal's library. And speaking of reading . . ." She lifted a small stack of letters—which he hadn't noticed, his whole attention being focused on food—off the tray and deposited them on his stomach.

They were tinted pink or blue and smelled of perfume. He looked at her, brows raised in inquiry.

"Billets-doux," she said sweetly. "From your admirers."

"What admirers?" he demanded, setting down his fork in order to remove the letters. "And how do you know what's in them?"

"I read them," she said without the faintest blush. "As for whom, I doubt you know many of the ladies, though you've likely danced with some of them. There are a great many women, though—particularly young and giddy ones—who positively swoon over men who fight duels. The ones who survive, that is," she added pragmatically.

He opened a letter with his thumb and held it in one hand, going on eating with the other as he read it. His brows went up.

"I've never met this woman. Yet she professes herself besotted with me—well, she's certainly besotted, I'll say that much—

consumed with admiration for my valor, my excessive courage, my . . . Oh, dear." He felt a slow blush rising in his own cheeks and put the letter down. "Are they all like that?"

"Some much worse," Minnie assured him, laughing. "Do you never think of marriage, John? It is the only way to preserve yourself from this sort of attention, you know."

"No," he said absently, scanning another of the missives as he wiped sauce from his plate with a chunk of bread. "I should be a most unsatisfactory husband. Holy Lord! *I am enraptured by the vision of your valiance, the power of your puissant sword*— Stop laughing, Minerva, you'll rupture something. This didn't happen when I fought Edwin Nicholls."

"Actually, it did," she said, picking up the discarded letters, some of which had fallen to the floor. "You weren't here, having absconded to Canada in the most craven fashion, and all just to avoid marrying Caroline Woodford. Putting aside the question of a wife, do you not long for children, John? Do you not want a son?"

"Having just spent half an hour with yours, no," he said, though in fact this was not true, and Minerva knew it; she merely laughed again and handed him the tidy pile of letters.

"Well, in fact, the public response to your duel with Nicholls was quite subdued compared with this. For one thing, it was hushed up as much as possible, and for another, it was only fought over the honor of a lady rather than the honor of the kingdom. Hal said I needn't forward the letters to you in Canada, so I didn't."

"Thank you." He made to hand the letters back to her. "Here, burn them."

"If you insist." She dimpled at him, but took the pile and stood up. "Oh, wait—you haven't opened this one."

"I thought you'd read them all."

"Only the female ones. This looked more like business." She picked a plain cover from the stack of hued and scented ones and handed it over. There was no return direction upon the cover, but there was a name, written in a neat, small hand. *H. Bowles.*

A most extraordinary feeling of revulsion came over him at sight of it, and he suddenly lost his appetite.

"No," he said, and gave it back. "Burn that one, too."

34

All Heads Turn as the Hunt Goes By

HUBERT BOWLES WAS A SPYMASTER. GREY HAD MET HIM some years previously, in connection with a private matter, and had hoped never to meet him again. He couldn't imagine what the little beast wanted with him now and didn't propose to find out.

Still, the boys' visit and the meal had restored him to such an extent that when Tom appeared—as he did with the regularity of a cuckoo clock—to ensure that Grey had not managed to die since last inspected, he let Tom shave him and brush out and plait his hair. Then, greatly daring, he stood up, clinging to Tom's arm.

"Easy, me lord, easy does it now . . ." The room wavered slightly, but he steadied himself and, after a moment, the dizziness passed. He limped slowly about, hanging on to Tom, until he was reasonably sure that he would neither fall down nor rip the stitching out of his leg—it pulled a bit, but so long as he was careful, it would likely do.

"All right. I'm going downstairs."

"No, you're no—er . . . yes, me lord," Tom replied meekly, his initial response quelled by a glare from Grey. "I'll just, ah, go down in front of you, shall I?"

"So that I can fall on you, if necessary? That's truly noble, Tom, but I think not. You can follow me and pick up the pieces, if you like."

He made his way slowly down the main stair, Tom behind him muttering something about all the king's horses and all the king's men, and then along the main hallway to the library, nodding cordially to Nasonby and inquiring after his bad ankle.

Fraser was indeed sitting in a wing chair near the window, a plate of biscuits and a decanter of sherry at his side, reading *Robinson Crusoe.* He glanced up at the sound of Grey's footsteps, and his eyebrows went up—perhaps in surprise at seeing him up and about, or perhaps only in astonishment at his banyan, which was silk, with green and purple stripes.

"Are you not going to tell me that had the sword gone between my ribs, I'd be dead? Everyone else does," Grey remarked, lowering himself gingerly into the matching wing chair.

Fraser looked faintly puzzled.

"I kent it hadna done that. Ye weren't dead when I picked ye up."

"You picked me up?"

"You asked me to, did ye not?" Fraser gave him a look of mild exasperation. "Ye were bleeding like a stuck hog, but it wasna spurting out, and I could feel ye breathing and your heart beating all right while I carried ye back to the coach."

"Oh. Thank you." Dammit, couldn't he have waited a few moments longer to pass out?

To distract himself from pointless regret, he took a biscuit and asked, "Have you spoken with my brother lately?"

"I have. Nay more than an hour ago." He hesitated, a thumb stuck inside the book to keep his place. "He offered me a sum of money. In reward of my assistance, as he was pleased to put it."

"Well deserved," Grey said heartily, hoping that Hal hadn't been an ass about it.

"I told him it had the stink of blood money and I wouldna touch it . . . but he pointed out that I hadna done what I'd done for money—and that's true enough. In fact, he said, he'd forced me to do it—which is not entirely true, but I wasna disposed to argue the fine points—and that he wished to recompense me for the inconvenience to which he had put me." He gave Grey a wry look. "I said I thought this a jesuitical piece o' reasoning, but he replied that as I'm a Papist, he supposed I could have no reasonable objection on those grounds.

"He also pointed out," Fraser went on, "that I was under no obligation to keep the money myself; he would be pleased to pay it out to anyone I specified. And, after all, there were still folk who were under my protection, were there not?"

Grey sent up a silent prayer of thanksgiving. Hal hadn't been an ass.

"Indeed there are," Grey said. "Who do you propose to help?"

Fraser narrowed his eyes a bit but had plainly been thinking about it.

"Well, there's my sister and her husband. They've the six bairns—and there are my tenants—" He caught himself, lips compressed for a moment "Families who *were* my tenants," he corrected.

"How many?" Grey asked, curious.

"Maybe forty families—maybe not so many now. But still . . ."

Hal must have come well up to scratch on the reward, Grey thought.

Grey didn't wish to dwell on the matter. He coughed and rang the bell for a footman to bring him a drink. His chances of getting anything stronger than barley water in his bedroom were slim, and he wasn't fond of sherry.

"Returning to my brother," he said, having given his order for brandy, "I wondered whether he has said anything to you regarding the court-martial or the progress of . . . er . . . the, um, military operation." The arrest of the incriminated officers of the Irish Brigades, he meant.

The frown returned, this time troubled and somewhat fierce.

"He has," Fraser replied shortly. "The court-martial is set for Friday. He wished me to remain, in case my testimony is required."

Grey was shaken; he hadn't thought Hal would have Fraser testify. If Jamie did, he would be a marked man. The testimony of a general court-martial became by law part of the public record of the Judge Advocate's court; it would be impossible to hide Fraser's part in the investigation of Siverly's affairs or the revelation of Twelvetrees's treachery. Even if there were no direct linkage made to the quashing of the Irish Brigades' plot, Jacobite sympathizers—and there were still many, even in London—would draw conclusions. The Irish as a race were known to be vengeful.

A lesser emotion was one of dismay at the thought that Hal might send Fraser back to Helwater so quickly—though in justice there was no reason to keep him in London. He'd done what Hal required of him, however unwillingly.

Was that what Hal was thinking? That if Fraser testified, he could then be quickly sent back to the remote countryside to resume a hidden life as Alexander MacKenzie, safe from retribution?

"As to the . . . military operation . . ." The broad mouth compressed in a brief grimace. "I believe it is satisfactory. I am naturally not in His Grace's entire confidence, but I heard Colonel Quarry telling him that there had been several significant arrests made yesterday."

"Ah," Grey said, trying to sound neutral. The arrests couldn't help but cause Fraser pain, even though he had agreed with the necessity. "Was . . . er . . . was Mr. Quinn's name among them?"

"No." Fraser looked disturbed at this. "Are they hunting Quinn?"

Grey shrugged a little and took a sip of his brandy. It burned agreeably going down.

"They know his name, his involvement," he said, a little hoarsely, and cleared his throat. "And he is a loose cannon. He quite possibly knows who some members of the Wild Hunt are. Do you not think he would make an effort to warn them, if he knows they are exposed?"

"He would, aye." Fraser rose suddenly and went to look out the window, leaning on the frame, his face turned away.

"Do you know where he is?" Grey asked quietly, and Fraser shook his head.

"I wouldna tell ye if I did," he said, just as quietly. "But I don't."

"Would you warn him—if you could?" Grey asked. He oughtn't, but was possessed by curiosity.

"I would," Fraser replied without hesitation. He turned round now and looked down at Grey, expressionless. "He was once my friend."

So was I, Grey thought, and took more brandy. *Am I now again?* But not even the most exigent curiosity would make him ask.

35

Justice

THE COURT-MARTIAL OF MAJOR GERALD SIVERLY (DECEASED) was well attended. Everyone from the Duke of Cumberland (who had tried to appoint himself to the board of judges, but been prevented by Hal) to the lowest Fleet Street hack crowded into the Guildhall, this being the largest venue available.

Lord John Grey, pale and limping but steady of eye and voice, testified before the board, this consisting of five officers drawn from various regiments—none of them Siverly's—and the Judge Advocate, that he had received the papers now presented to the board from Captain Charles Carruthers in Canada, where Carruthers had served under Major Siverly and been witness to the actions described herein, and that he, Grey, had heard such further testimony from Carruthers in person as inclined him to believe the documentary evidence as it stood.

Courts-martial had no set procedure, no dock, no Bible, no barristers, no rules of evidence. Anyone who wished to do so might testify or ask questions, and a number of people did so—including the Duke of Cumberland, who thrust his bulk forward before Grey could sit down and came straight up to him, glowering directly into his face from a distance of six inches.

"Is it not true, my lord," Cumberland asked, with heavy sarcasm, "that Major Siverly saved your life at the siege of Quebec?"

"It is, Your Grace."

"And have you no shame at thus betraying your debt to a brother-in-arms?"

"No, I haven't," Grey replied calmly, though his heart was thumping erratically. "Major Siverly's behavior on the field of battle was honorable and valorous—but he would have done the same for any soldier, as would I. For me to withhold evidence of his corruption and his peculations off that field would be a betrayal of the entire army in which I have the honor to serve and a betrayal of all those comrades with whom I have fought through the years."

"Hear him! Hear him!" shouted a voice from the back of the hall, which he rather thought was Harry Quarry's. A general rumbling of approval filled the hall, and Cumberland receded, still glaring.

The testimony went on all day, with various officers of Siverly's regiment coming to offer their own witness, some speaking well of the dead man's character, but others—many others—recounting incidents that supported Carruthers's account. Regimental loyalty counted for a great deal, Grey thought—but regimental honor counted for more, and the thought pleased him.

For Grey, the day gradually blurred into a confusion of faces, voices, uniforms, hard chairs, shouts echoing from the huge beams of the ceiling, the occasional shoving match broken up by the sergeant-at-arms . . . and, at the end of it, he found himself in the street outside, momentarily apart from the tumultuous crowd that had spilled out of the Guildhall.

Hal, who had been the most senior officer on the court, was

across the street, talking intently to the Judge Advocate, who was nodding. It was late afternoon, and the chimneys of London were all belching forth as the fires were built up for evening. Grey took a grateful lungful of the smoky air, fresh by comparison with the close atmosphere inside the Guildhall, which was composed in equal parts of sweat, trampled food, tobacco, and the smell of rage—and fear. He'd been aware of that, the tiny thrilling of the nerves among the crowd, the faces that quietly vanished as the testimony mounted.

Hal had been careful to avoid any mention of the Irish Brigades, the Wild Hunt, or the plan to seize the king; there were too many plotters as yet unaccounted for, and no need to alarm the public *a priori.* He had brought up Edward Twelvetrees, though, and his role as Siverly's confidant and co-conspirator—and Grey shivered suddenly, recalling the look on Reginald Twelvetrees's face, the old colonel sitting like a stone near the front of the room, burning eyes fixed on Hal without blinking as the damning words came out, one after another in an overwhelming flood.

Reginald Twelvetrees hadn't said a word, though. What, after all, could he say? He'd left just before the final verdict—guilty, of course, on all charges.

Grey supposed he should feel victorious, or at least vindicated. He'd kept his promise to Charlie, found the truth—a good deal more of it than he'd expected or wanted—and, he supposed, achieved justice.

If you could call it that, he thought dimly, seeing three or four Fleet Street scribblers elbowing one another in an effort to talk to young Eldon Garlock, the ensign who had been the youngest member of the court and thus first to give his verdict.

God knew what they'd write. He only hoped none of it would be about him; he'd experienced the attentions of the press before, though in an entirely favorable way. Having seen the favors of the printers at close range, he could only hope that God would have mercy on those they didn't like.

He had walked away from the crowd, but with no real direction in mind, only wanting to put distance between himself and this day. Absorbed in his thoughts—at least Jamie Fraser had not been required to testify; that was something—he failed for some time to realize that he was accompanied. Some faint sense of arrhythmia disturbed him, though, an echo of his own footsteps, and at last he glanced aside to see what might be causing it.

He stopped dead, and Hubert Bowles, who had been walking a half step behind him, came up even and stopped, bowing.

"My lord," he said politely. "How do you do?"

"Not that well," he said. "I must ask you to excuse me, Mr. Bowles." He turned to go on, but Bowles stopped him with a hand on his arm. Affronted by the familiarity, Grey jerked back.

"I must ask your forbearance, my lord," Bowles said, with a faint lisp that made it almost "forbearanth." He spoke mildly but with an authority that stopped Grey's making any protest. "I have something to say that you must hear."

Hubert Bowles was small and shapeless, with a round head and rounded back, and with his shabby wig and worn coat, no one would have looked at him twice. Even his face was bland as a boiled pudding, with deceptively vague blue eyes put in. Nonetheless, Grey slowly inclined his head in unwilling acknowledgment.

"Shall we take coffee?" he said, nodding toward a nearby coffeehouse. He wasn't about to invite something like Bowles into any of the clubs where he had membership. He had no notion of the man's antecedents, but his presence made Grey want to wash.

Bowles shook his head. "I think it better if we merely walk," he said, suiting his actions to his words and compelling Grey by a touch on the elbow.

"I am most annoyed with you, my lord," he said in a conversational tone, as they made their way slowly into Gresham Street.

"Are you," Grey said shortly. "I am concerned to hear it."

"You should be. You have killed one of my most valued agents."

"One of—what?"

He stopped, staring down at Bowles, but was urged on by the other's gesture.

"Edward Twelvetrees hath been for some years involved in the suppression of Jacobite plots." A shadow of annoyance crossed Bowles's face at his lisp's struggle with the word "suppression," but Grey was too disturbed at Bowles's statement to take much pleasure in it.

"What, you mean that he has been working for *you*?" He didn't even try to stop it sounding rude, but Bowles didn't react to his tone.

"I mean precisely that, my lord. He had spent a great deal of time and effort in insinuating himself with Major Siverly, once we had determined that Siverly was a person of interest in that regard. His father had been one of the Wild Geese who flew from Limerick, did you know?"

"Yes," Grey said. His lips felt stiff. "I did."

"It is a great inconvenience," Bowles said reprovingly, "when gentlemen will be conducting their own investigations, rather than leaving such things to those whose profession it is."

"So sorry to inconvenience you," Grey said, beginning to grow angry. "Do you mean to tell me that Edward Twelvetrees was *not* a traitor?"

"Quite the reverse, my lord. He served his country in the noblest fashion, working in secrecy and in danger to defeat her enemies." For once, there was a note of warmth in that colorless voice, and, glancing down at his unwelcome companion, Grey realized that Bowles was himself angry—very angry.

"Why the devil did he not say something to me privately?"

"Why should he have trusted you, my lord?" Bowles riposted smartly. "You come from a family whose own background bears the shadow of treason—"

"It does not!"

"Perhaps not in fact but in perception," Bowles agreed with a nod. "You did well in rooting out Bernard Adams and his fellow plotters, but even the clearing of your father's name will not erase the stain—only time will do that. Time, and the actions of yourself and your brother."

"What do you bloody mean by that, damn you?"

Bowles lifted one sloping shoulder but forbore to reply directly.

"And to speak of his activities to anyone—anyone at all, my lord—was for Edward Twelvetrees to risk the destruction of all his—all our—work. True, Major Siverly was dead, but—"

"Wait. If what you tell me is true, why did Edward Twelvetrees kill Siverly?"

"Oh, he didn't," Bowles said, as though this was a matter of no importance.

"What? Who did, then? I assure you, it wasn't me!"

Bowles actually laughed at that, a small creaking noise that made his hunched back hunch further.

"Of course not, my lord. Edward told me that it was an Irishman—a thin man with curly hair—who struck down Gerald Siverly. He heard raised voices and, upon coming to see the cause, overheard an Irish voice in a passion, denouncing Major Siverly, saying that he knew Siverly had stolen the money.

"In any case, there was an argument, then the sounds of a scuffle. Twelvetrees did not wish to reveal himself but advanced cautiously toward the folly, whereupon he saw a man leap over the railing, spattered with blood, and rush into the wood. He pursued the man but failed to stop him. He saw you run past shortly thereafter and thus hid in the wood until you had passed, then left quietly in the other direction.

"He hadn't seen the Irish gentleman before, though, and was unable to find anyone in the area who knew him. Under the circumstances, he was reluctant to make too many inquiries." He looked up at Grey, mildly inquiring. "I do not suppose you know who he was?"

"His name is Tobias Quinn," Grey said shortly. "And if I were forced to ascribe a motive to him, I imagine it would be that he was a fervid Jacobite himself, and he thought that Siverly proposed to abscond with the money he had collected on behalf of the Stuarts."

"Ah," said Bowles, pleased. "Just so. You see, my lord, that is what I meant about you and your brother. You are in a position to acquire many useful bits of information.

"Captain Twelvetrees had in fact informed me that he thought Siverly was about to abscond with the funds to Sweden; we intended to allow this, as it would have crippled the Irish plan beyond repair. I cannot say how the Irish Jacobites learned of it, but plainly they did."

There was a brief pause, during which Bowles withdrew a clean handkerchief from his pocket—a silk one with lace edging, Grey saw—and blew his nose daintily.

"Do you know Mr. Quinn's present whereabouts, my lord? Or if not, might you make discreet inquiries amongst your Irish acquaintances?"

Grey rounded on him, furious.

"You are inviting me to spy for you, sir?"

"Certainly." Bowles didn't seem discomposed by Grey's clenched fists. "But returning to the subject of Edward Twelvetrees—you must forgive me for seeming to harp upon it, but he really was a most valuable man—he could not say anything regarding his activities, even in private, for fear of those activities being revealed before our plans were complete."

Realization was beginning to push its way through the veil of shock and anger, and Grey felt ill, an unhealthy sweat breaking out on his face.

"What . . . plans?"

"Why, the arrest of the Irish Brigade officers involved in the conspiracy. You know about that, I believe?"

"Yes, I do. How do you know about it?"

"Edward Twelvetrees. He brought me the outline of the plan but hadn't yet collected a full list of those involved. 'The Wild Hunt,' they called themselves—most poetic, but what can you expect from the Irish? Edward's untimely death"—a small note of irony was detectable in Mr. Bowles's voice—"kept us from knowing the names of all the men involved. And while your brother's worthy attempt to arrest the conspirators succeeded in bagging some of the prey, it alarmed others, who have either fled the country to cause trouble elsewhere or who have merely sunk into hiding."

Grey opened his mouth, but could find nothing to say. The wound in his chest throbbed hotly with his heartbeat, but what was worse, what burned across his mind, was his memory of Reginald Twelvetrees's face, set like granite, witnessing the destruction of his brother's name.

"I thought you ought to know," Bowles said, almost kindly. "Good day, my lord."

❦

HE'D ONCE SEEN Minnie's cook take a sharpened spoon and cut the flesh of a melon out in little balls. He felt as though each of Bowles's words had been a jab of that spoon, slicing out neat chunks of his heart and bowels, one at a time, scraping him to the rind.

He didn't remember coming back to Argus House. Just suddenly found himself at the door, Nasonby blinking at him in consternation. The man said something; he waved a hand in vague dismissal and walked into the library—*thank God Hal's not here; I have to tell him, but, God, not now!*—and out through the French doors, across the garden. His only thought was to find refuge, though he knew there could be none.

Behind the shed, he sat down carefully on the upturned bucket, put his elbows on his knees, and sank his head in his hands.

He could hear the watch ticking in his pocket, each tiny sound seeming to last forever, the stream of them endless. How impossibly long it would be before he died, for only that could put an end to the echo of Bowles's words in the hollow of his mind.

He had no idea how long he sat there, eyes closed, listening to the reproach of his own heartbeat. He didn't bother opening his eyes when footsteps came to a stop before him and the coolness of someone's shadow fell on his hot face.

There was a brief sigh, then big hands took him by the arms and lifted him bodily to his feet.

"Come wi' me," Fraser said quietly. "Walk. It will be easier to say what's happened, walking."

He opened his mouth to protest but hadn't the strength to resist. Fraser took his arm and propelled him firmly through the back gate. There was a narrow lane there, wide enough for barrows and tradesmen's wagons, but at this hour of the day—it was late, he thought dimly, the whole of the lane was in shadow—there were only a few female servants loitering near the gates of the big houses, gossiping or waiting to walk out with a young man. These glanced at the two men sidelong but turned their heads away, lowering their voices as they continued their conversations. He wished passionately that he was one of those women, had a right still to engage in the ordinariness of life.

There was a lump in his throat, hard and round as a walnut. He didn't see how words would ever find their way past it. But Fraser kept hold of his arm, guiding him out into the street, into Hyde Park.

It was nearly dark, save for the pinprick campfires of the tramps and gypsies who came into the park by night, and there were few of these. At the corner where pamphleteers, electioneers, and those possessed of strong opinions stood to speak, a larger fire was burning, dying down unattended, with a smell of charred paper. A figure hung from the branch of a nearby tree, an effigy that someone had tried to set on fire, but the fire had gone out, leaving the figure blackened and stinking, the pale square of paper pinned to its chest unreadable in the dark.

They'd made nearly half a circuit of the park before he found the first words, Fraser walking patiently beside him, no longer holding his arm, and he missed the touch . . . but the words came at last, at first disjointed, reluctant, and then in a burst like a musket volley. He was surprised that it could be said so briefly.

Fraser made a small sound, a sort of soft grunt, as though he'd been punched in the belly, but then listened in silence. They walked for some time after Grey had finished speaking.

"Kyrie, eleison," Fraser said at last, very quietly. Lord, have mercy.

"Well enough for you," Grey said without rancor. "It must help, to think there is some ultimate sense to things."

Fraser turned his head to look at him curiously.

"Do ye not think so? Whether ye call the ultimate cause—or the ultimate effect, I suppose—God or merely Reason? I have heard ye speak with admiration of logic and reason."

"Where is the logic in this?" Grey burst out, flinging out his hands.

"Ye ken that as well as I do," Fraser said rather sharply. "The logic of duty, and what each man of us—you, me, and Edward Twelvetrees—conceived that to be."

"I—" Grey stopped, unable to formulate his thoughts coherently; there were too many of them.

"Aye, we're guilty of that man's death—the two of us, and dinna think I say so out of kindness. I ken well what ye mean—and what ye feel." Fraser stopped for a moment, turning to face Grey, his eyes intent. They stood outside the house of the Earl of Prestwick; the lanterns had been lit and the light fell through the wrought-iron bars of the fence, striping them both.

"I accused him of treason in public, to stop him executing actions that would have injured folk who are mine. He challenged me, to prevent any suspicion attaching to him, so that he could carry out his schemes, though they were not the schemes I—we—assumed him to have. You then challenged him, to—" He halted suddenly and stared hard at Grey. "Ostensibly," he said, more slowly, "ye challenged him to preserve your honor, to refute the slur of sodomy." His lips compressed into a tight line.

"Ostensibly," Grey echoed. "Why the bloody hell else would I have done it?"

Fraser's eyes searched his face. Grey felt the touch of the other man's gaze, an odd sensation, but kept his own face composed. Or hoped he did.

"Her Grace says that ye did it for the sake of your friendship with me," Fraser said at last, quietly. "And I am inclined to think her right."

"Her Grace should mind her own bloody business." Grey turned away abruptly and began walking. Fraser caught him up within a pace or two, bootheels muffled on the sandy path. Small forms darted in and out of the scattered light from the lanterns of the big houses: children, mostly, scavenging the piles of horse droppings left on the riding path.

Grey had noticed the nice distinction: *"for the sake of your friendship with me,"* as opposed to the simpler—but far more threatening—*"for me."* He didn't know if the distinction was Minnie's or Fraser's, but supposed it didn't matter. Both statements were true, and if Fraser preferred the greater distance of the former, he was welcome to it.

"We are both guilty in his death," Fraser repeated doggedly. "But so is he."

"How? He couldn't have suffered your accusation without response. And he couldn't have told you, even privately, what the truth of his position was."

"He could," Fraser corrected, "save that he saw it as his duty not to."

Grey looked at him blankly. "Of course."

Fraser turned his head away, but Grey thought he detected the glimmer of a smile among the shadows. "You *are* an Englishman," Fraser said dryly. "So was he. And had he not tried to kill ye at the last—"

"He had to," Grey interrupted. "His only other choice would have been to ask me to yield—and he knew bloody well wouldn't."

Fraser gave a cursory nod of acknowledgment. "Did I not say it was logical?"

"You did. But . . ." He let his voice trail away. In the enormity of his own regret, he hadn't paused to think that what Fraser said was true: he also had a share in Twelvetrees's death—and therefore in the regret.

"Aye, but," Fraser said with a sigh, "I would have done the same. But ye've killed men before, and likely better men than Twelvetrees."

"Quite possibly. But I killed them as—as enemies. From duty." Would it have come to this pass if not for Esmé and Nathaniel? Yes, likely it would.

"Ye killed him as an enemy, did ye not? The fact that he wasna one in fact is not your fault."

"That is a very specious argument."

"Doesna mean it's not true."

"Do you think you can argue me out of guilt? Out of horror and melancholy?" Grey demanded, annoyed.

"I do, aye. It isna possible to feel urgent emotion and engage in rational discourse at the same time."

"Oh, yes, it is," Grey began, with some warmth, but as it was that unfortunate conversation in the stable at Helwater that would have formed his prime example, he abandoned this tack. "Do you truly consider all impassioned speech to be illogical? What about the bloody Declaration of Arbroath?"

"A speech may be conceived in passion," Fraser conceded, "but it's executed in cold blood, for the most part. The declaration was written—or at least subscribed—by a number of men. They canna all have been in the grip of passion when they did it."

Grey actually laughed, though shortly, then shook his head.

"You are trying to distract me from the point at issue."

"No," said Fraser thoughtfully. "I think I am trying to lead ye to the point at issue—which is that no matter how much a man may try to do what is right, the outcome may not be one that he either foresees or desires. And that's grounds for regret—sometimes verra great regret," he added more softly, "but not for everlasting guilt. For it is there we must throw ourselves on God's mercy and hope to receive it."

"And you speak from experience." Grey had not meant this statement to sound challenging, but it did, and Fraser exhaled strongly through his long Scottish nose.

"I do," he said, after a moment's silence. He sighed. "When I was laird of Lallybroch, one of my tenants came to ask my help. She was an auld woman, concerned for one of her grandsons. His father beat him, she said, and she was feart that he would kill the lad. Would I not take him to be a stable-lad at my house?

"I said that I would. But when I spoke to the father, he'd have none of it and reproached me for tryin' to take his son away from him." He sighed again.

"I was young, and a fool. I struck him. In fact . . . I beat him, and he yielded to me. I took the lad. Rabbie, his name was; Rabbie MacNab."

Grey gave a small start, but said nothing.

"Well. Ronnie—that was the father's name; he was Ronald MacNab—betrayed me to the Watch, out of his fury and bereavement, and I was arrested and taken to an English prison. I . . . escaped . . ." He hesitated, as though wondering whether to say more, but decided against it and went on. "But later, when I came back to Lallybroch in the early days of the Rising, I found MacNab's croft burnt out, and him gone up in smoke and ashes on his own hearthstone."

"I take it this was no accident?"

Fraser shook his head, the movement barely perceptible, as they were passing under the great row of elms along the east side of the park.

"No," he said softly. "My other tenants did it, for they ken vell who had betrayed me. They did what seemed right—their luty to me—as I had done what seemed right and my duty as aird. And yet the end of it was death, and nothing I intended."

Their steps were soft, nearly shuffling as they walked more lowly.

"I take your point," Grey said at last, quietly. "What became of the boy? Rabbie?"

One large shoulder moved slightly.

"He lived in my house—he and his mother—during the Ris-ng. Afterward . . . my sister said he had made up his mind to go outh, to see if he might find work, for there was nothing left in he Highlands for a young man, save the army, and that he vouldna do."

Greatly daring, Grey touched Jamie's arm, very gently.

"You said that a man cannot foresee the outcome of his ac-ions, and that's true. But in this case, I can tell you one of yours."

"What?" Fraser spoke sharply, whether from the touch or rom Grey's words, but did not jerk away.

"Rabbie MacNab. I know what became of him. He is—or was, vhen last I saw him—a London chairman and contemplating narriage." He forbore to tell Fraser that Rab's intended was his cquaintance, Nessie, not knowing whether a Scotch Catholic's iew of prostitution might be similar to that of a Scotch Presby-erian, who tended in Grey's experience to be rather rigid and ensorious about the pleasures of the flesh.

Fraser's hand closed on his forearm, startling Grey consider-bly.

"Ye ken where he is?" Fraser's voice showed his excitement. Can ye tell me where I might find him?"

Grey rummaged hastily through his scattered thoughts, trying o recall where Agnes had said: *My new house . . . The end o' Brydges treet. . . . Mrs. Donoghue . . .*

"Yes," he said, feeling his spirit rise a little. "I can find him fo
you, I'm sure."

"I—thank ye, my lord," Jamie said abruptly.

"Don't call me that." John felt a little better but suddenl
unutterably tired. "If we share blood guilt and remorse for wha
we did to that bastard Twelvetrees, you can for God's sake ca
me by my Christian name, can you not?"

Fraser paced in silence for a bit, thinking.

"I could," he said slowly. "For now. But I shall go back to—t
my place, and it willna do then. I . . . should find it disagreeabl
to become accustomed to such a degree of familiarity an
then . . ." He made a small, dismissive gesture.

"You needn't go back," Grey said, reckless. He had no powe
to commute Fraser's sentence nor pardon him and no busines
to suggest such a thing—not without Hal's assent. But h
thought it could be done.

He'd shocked the Scot, he saw; Fraser drew a little away, eve
as they walked together.

"I . . . am much obliged to your lordship for the thought," h
said at last. His voice sounded queer, Grey thought, and won
dered why. "I . . . even if it should be possible . . . I—I do not wis
to leave Helwater."

Grey misunderstood for a moment and sought to reassur
him. "I do not mean you should be committed to prison agair
nor even released to a new parole in London. I mean, in light c
your great service to—to the government . . . it might be possib
to arrange a pardon. You could be . . . free."

The word hung in the air between them, small and solid. Fra
ser drew a long, tremulous breath, but when he spoke, his word
were firm.

"I take your meaning, my lord. And I am truly very muc
obliged for the kindness ye intend. But there is—I have . .

omeone . . . at Helwater. Someone for whose sake I must re-
urn."

"Who?" Grey asked, very startled by this.

"Her name is Betty Mitchell. One of the lady's maids."

"Really," Grey said blankly, then, coming to the realization
hat this sounded very discourteous, hastened to make amends.
I—I congratulate you."

"Aye, well, ye needna do that just yet," Fraser said. "I havena
poken to her—formally, I mean. But there is . . . what ye might
all an understanding."

Grey felt rather as though he'd stepped on a garden rake
which had leapt up and banged him on the nose. It was the last
hing he would have expected—not only in light of the social
lifferences that must exist between a lady's maid and a laird
though a brief thought of Hal and Minnie drifted through the
back of his mind, together with a vision of the scorched hearth
ug), no matter how far the laird's fortunes had fallen, but in
ight of what Grey had always assumed to be Fraser's very exigent feelings toward his dead wife.

He knew the lady's maid slightly, from his visits to Helwater,
nd while she was a fine-looking young woman, she was dis-
inctly . . . well, common. Fraser's first wife had been distinctly
ıncommon.

"Christ, Sassenach. I need ye."

He felt shocked—and rather disapproving. He was more
hocked still to realize this and did his best to dismiss the feel-
ng; it wasn't his business to be shocked, and even if it were . . .
vell, it had been a very long time since Fraser's wife had died,
nd he was a man. And an honorable one. *Better to marry than
urn, they say,* he thought cynically. *I wouldn't know.*

"I wish you every happiness," he said, very formal. They had
come to a stop near the Alexandra Gate. The night air was soft,

full of the scent of tree sap and chimney smoke and the distant reeks of the city. He realized with a lesser shock that he felt very hungry—and, with a mingled sense of shame and resignation that he was pleased to be alive.

They were more than late for supper.

"You'd best send for a tray," Grey said, as they climbed the marble steps. "I'll have to tell Hal what Bowles said, but there's no need for you to be involved any further. In any of this."

"Is there not?" Fraser looked at him, serious in the light of the lantern that hung by the door. "Ye'll be going to speak wi' Reginald Twelvetrees, will ye not?"

"Oh, yes." The thought of that necessity had been pushed to the back of his mind during the recent conversation but had not left him; it hung like a weight suspended by a spider's thread Damocles' sword. "Tomorrow."

"I'll go with ye." The Scotsman's voice was quiet but firm.

Grey heaved a deep sigh and shook his head.

"No. I thank you . . . Mr. Fraser," he said, and tried to smile at the formality. "My brother will second me."

36

Teind

THE GREY BROTHERS WENT THE NEXT MORNING TO PAY their call on Reginald Twelvetrees. They left, grim and silent, and came back the same way, Grey going out to the conservatory, Hal to his den of papers, speaking to no one.

Jamie had some sympathy for the Greys—and for the Twelvetrees brothers, come to that—and, finding his favorite chair in the library, took out his rosary and said a few decades for the eventual peace of all souls concerned. There were, after all, many situations that simply had to be handed over to God, as no human agency was capable of dealing with them.

He found himself losing his place, though, distracted by his memory of the Greys going off together, shoulder-to-shoulder, to face what must be faced. And the thought of Reginald Twelvetrees, privately mourning two lost brothers.

He had lost his own brother very young; Willie had been eleven when he died of the smallpox—Jamie, six. He didn't think of Willie much, but the ache of his absence was always there, along with the other scars on his heart left when someone was torn away. He envied the Greys their possession of each other.

Thought of Willie, though, reminded him of another William, and his heart lifted a little with the thought. If life stole dear ones from you, sometimes it gave you others. Ian Murray had become his blood brother after Willie died; sometime he would see Ian again, and meanwhile the knowledge of his presence in the world—looking after things at Lallybroch—was a true comfort. And his son . . .

When this was over—and pray God it would be soon—he would see William again. Be with him. He might—

"Sir."

At first, he didn't realize that it was himself the butler meant. But Nasonby repeated, "Sir," more insistently, and when he looked up, the butler presented his silver tray, upon which reposed a sheet of rough paper sealed with a daub of candle wax and marked with the print of a broad thumb.

He took it with a nod of thanks and, putting his rosary away, brought the letter upstairs to his room. By the rainy light from the window, he opened it and found a note penned with a careful elegance, much at odds with its crude materials.

Shéamais Mac Bhrian, the salutation read. The rest was in the Irish, too, but was simple enough for him to understand:

For the love of God and Mary and Patrick, come to me now.

Tobias Mac Gréagair,
of the Quinns of Portkerry

At the bottom of the page was drawn a neat line with several boxes perched atop it, and below it written "Civet Cat Alley." One of the boxes had an "X" marked through it.

An extraordinary feeling ran through him, a cold grue that fell over him like an icy blanket. This wasn't merely Quinn's usual drama—still less the intended mischief of his note denouncing Grey as a murderer. The simplicity of it, plus the fact that Quinn had signed it with his formal name, carried an undeniable urgency.

He was halfway down the stairs when he met Lord John, coming up.

"Where is Civet Cat Alley?" he asked abruptly. Grey blinked, glanced at the paper in Jamie's hand for an instant, then said, "In the Rookery—the Irish quarter. I've been there. Shall I take you?"

"I—" He started to say that he would go alone, but he knew nothing of London. If he went on foot, asking his way, it would take a great while. And he had a deep certainty that there was not a great while to spare.

He was prey to the most profound anxiety. Was Quinn threatened with imminent arrest? If so, he should certainly not take Grey to him, but . . . Or it might be that the Jacobite plotters, learning that they were betrayed, had decided that it was Quinn who had betrayed them. Oh, Jesus. If that were the case—

Yet something in the dark cavern of his heart gave off a metallic echo, a note of doom, small and inexorable as the chime of Grey's pocket watch. Ticking off the moments of Quinn's life.

"Yes," he said abruptly. "Now."

OF COURSE he had known, from the moment the note was put into his hand. But still, he urged the carriage on by force of will and, in Civet Cat Alley, went in to the house with heart hammering and scarcely able to breathe. He seized a young slattern with a baby in her arms in the first room he came to and demanded the whereabouts of Tobias Quinn.

"Upstairs," she said, affronted but frightened of his size and his ferocity. "The fourth floor back. What are ye wantin' wit' him?" she added in a bawl after him, but he was pounding up the stairs to what he knew was there, leaving Grey to deal with the gathering crowd of curious, half-hostile Irish who had followed the carriage through the streets.

The door was unlocked and the room orderly and peaceful, save for the blood.

Quinn had lain down on his bed, fully clothed save for his coat, which was neatly folded at the foot of the bed, the checkered silk outermost. He had not cut his throat but had turned back his cuff with great care and cut his wrist, which dangled over the *Cupán,* set on the floor beneath. The blood had overflowed and run red across the sloping floor almost to the door, like an unfurled carpet laid for royalty. And neatly, as neatly as a man could print with a finger dipped in his own blood, he had written the word "TEIND" on the wall above his shabby cot. A tithe to hell.

Jamie stood, trying not to breathe, though his chest heaved with the need for air.

"May God rest his soul," said Grey's voice, quiet behind him. "Is that it? The cup?"

Jamie nodded, unable to speak for the glut of grief and guilt that filled him. Grey had come beside him, to look. He shook his head, gave a little sigh, and, saying, "I'll get Tom Byrd," left Jamie alone.

37

Sole Witness

Inchcleraun

QUINN COULD NOT BE LAID TO REST IN CONSECRATED ground, of course. Still, Abbot Michael had offered the aid of some of the brothers for the burial. Jamie declined this offer—though with gratitude—and with the wooden coffin perched on the sledge that the monks used to fetch home peats from the moss-hag, he set off across the bog, a rope round his shoulder and his burden bumping and floating by turns behind him.

When they had reached the rocky small hill in the middle of the bog, he took up the wooden spade Brother Ambrose had given him and began to dig.

Sole witness, sole mourner. He had told the Grey brothers that he would come alone to Ireland to bury Quinn. They had looked at each other, their faces reflecting the same thought, and had made neither objection nor condition. They knew he would come back.

Others had seen the body, but he knew he was the sole true witness to Quinn's death. God knew he understood this death as few others could. Knew what it was to have lost the meaning of your life. Had God not bound him to the earth with the ties of flesh and blood, he might well have come to such an end himself. Might come to it now, were it not for those same ties.

The soil was rocky and hard-packed, but only for the first few inches. Below that was a rich, soft earth of lake silt and decayed peat moss, and the grave opened easily, deepening with the rhythm of his shoveling.

Teind. Which of them was it who was meant to be the tithe to hell? Quinn, or him? He supposed Quinn had meant himself, for surely he expected to go to hell, as a suicide. But the nagging thought recurred: Why leave the word written there in his blood? Was it confession . . . or accusation? Surely if Quinn had known what Jamie had done, he would have written *"fealltóir"*. Traitor. And yet the man was an Irishman, and therefore poetical by nature. *"Teind"* carried a good bit more weight, as a word, than did *"fealltóir."*

The day was warm, and after a bit he took off his breeches and a little later his shirt, working naked to the air, wearing nothing but sandals and a handkerchief bound round his brow to keep the sweat from running into his eyes. There was no one to see his scars, no one but Quinn, and he was welcome.

It was late when at last he'd made the grave square and seemly. Deep enough that the water began to seep into the hole at the bottom, deep enough that no digging fox would scrabble at the coffin lid. Would the coffin and the body rot at once? he wondered. Or would the dark-brown water of the bog preserve Quinn as it had once preserved the thrice-killed man with the gold ring on his finger?

He glanced up the slope at that other unmarked grave. At least Quinn would not lie alone.

He'd brought the cup, the *Cupán Druid riogh*. It lay wrapped in his cloak, awaiting restoration. To whom? Beyond asking whether the cup was the *Cupán Druid riogh,* Grey had never mentioned it again. Neither had the abbot asked after it. Jamie realized that the thing was given into his hands, to do with as he wished. The only thing he wished was to get rid of it.

"Lord, let this cup pass away," he muttered, dragging the coffin to the lip of the grave. He gave it a tremendous shove and it shot forward, falling with a loud *crunk!* into the earth. The effort left him trembling, and he stood for a moment gasping, wiping his face with the back of his hand. He checked to see that the lid had not come off and that the coffin had not burst or turned sideways in its fall, and then once more took up the spade.

The sun was dropping toward the horizon, and he worked fast, not wanting to risk being stranded on the islet for the night. The air cooled, and the midges came out, and he paused to put his shirt on. The light came in low and flat now, gilding the drifting clouds, and the dark surface of the bog glimmered below like gold and jet. He took up the spade again, but before he could resume his shoveling, he heard a sound that made him turn round.

Not a bird, he thought, nor yet the abbey's bell. It was a sound he'd never heard before and yet somehow familiar. The bog had fallen silent; even the hum of the midges had ceased. He listened, but the sound did not repeat itself, and slowly he began to shovel again, pausing now and then, listening—for what, he did not know.

It came again as he had nearly finished. The grave lay neatly mounded, though with an opening at the head. He had it in mind to lay the cup there, let Quinn take the bloody thing to hell with him, if he liked. But as he lifted his cloak to unwrap the cup, twilight began to rise from the earth, and the sound came clear to him through the still air. A horn.

Horns. Like the blowing of trumpets, but trumpets such as he had never heard, and the hairs rippled on his body.

They're coming. He didn't pause to ask himself who it was that was coming but hastily put on his breeks and coat. It didn't occur to him to flee, and for an instant he wondered why not, for the very air around him quivered with strangeness.

Because they're not coming for you, the calm voice within his mind replied. *Stand still.*

They were in sight now, figures coming slowly out of the distance, taking shape as they came, as though they materialized from thin air. Which, he thought, was precisely what they'd just done.

There was no mist, no fog over the water. But the party coming toward him—men and women both, he thought—had come from nowhere, for there was nowhere from which to come; nothing lay behind them save a stretch of bog that reached clear to the shore of the lake beyond.

Again the horns sounded, a flat, discordant sound—would he know if they were tuneful? he wondered—and now he saw the horns themselves, curving tubes that caught the rays of the sinking sun and shone like gold. And it came to him what they sounded like: it was the honking of wild geese.

They were closer now, close enough to make out faces and the details of their clothing. They were dressed plain, for the most part, dressed in drab and homespun, save for one woman dressed in white—*why is her skirt no spattered wi' the mud?* And he saw with a little thrill of horror that her feet did not touch the ground; none of them did—who carried in one hand a knife with a long, curved blade and a glinting hilt. *I must remember to tell Father Michael that it wasna a sword.*

Now he saw another exception to the plain appearance of the crowd—for it was a crowd, thirty people at least. Following the woman came a tall man, dressed in simple knee-length breeks and bare-chested but with a cloak made in a checkered weave. The tall man wore a rope around his neck, and Jamie gulped air as though he felt the noose tighten around his own throat.

What were the names Father Michael had told him?

"Esus," he said, not aware that he spoke aloud. "Taranis. Teutates." And, like clockwork, one man's head turned toward him, then another—and finally the woman looked at him.

He crossed himself, invoking the Trinity loudly, and the older gods turned their gaze away. One, he saw now, carried a maul.

He'd always wondered about Lot's wife and how it was that she turned to a pillar of salt, but now he saw how that could be. He watched, frozen, as the horns blew a third time and the crowd came to a stop, hovering a few inches above the glimmering surface of the bog, and formed a circle around the tall man—he stood a head taller than anyone else, and now the sun lit his hair with a gleam of fire. The woman in white came near, lifting her blade, the man with the maul moved ceremoniously behind the tall man, and a third reached for the end of the rope round his neck.

"No!" Jamie shouted, suddenly released from his captive spectatorship. He drew back his arm and hurled the *Cupán* as hard as he could, into the midst of the eerie crowd. It hit the bog with a splash, and the people vanished.

He blinked, then squinted against the glare of the setting sun. Nothing moved on the surface of the silent bog, and no bird sang. With the sudden energy of a madman, he seized his spade and shoveled dirt furiously, tamped it down, and then, catching up his cloak under his arm, ran, water splashing from his sandals as he found the wooden causeway, half-submerged.

Behind him, he thought he heard the echo of wild geese calling and, despite himself, looked back.

There they were, now walking away, backs turned to him, into the face of the setting sun, and no glinting sight of the curving horns. But he thought he saw the flash of checkered cloth in the crowd. It might have been the tall man's cloak. It must only be a trick of the fading light that made the checkered cloth glow pink.

SECTION V

Succession

38

Redux

THEY DIDN'T TALK MUCH ON THE WAY TO HELWATER. TOM was with them, of course—but beyond that, there wasn't much that could be said.

It was early autumn, but the weather had been foul. Pouring rain turned the roads to mud, and wind lashed the leaves from the trees, so they were either damp or soaked to the skin, plastered with mud, but absurdly spangled with gaudy blots of red and gold. They came to each inn at night shaken with cold, blue-lipped, and wanting nothing save warmth and food.

They shared a room, never a bed. If there were not beds enough, Jamie slept on the floor with Tom, wrapped in his cloak. John would have liked to lie in the darkness, listening to them breathe, but fatigue usually overwhelmed him the moment he lay down.

He felt almost as though he were escorting Jamie to his execution. While Fraser would of course continue to live—in contentment, he hoped—their arrival at Helwater would be the death of the relationship that had grown up between them. They could no longer behave as equals.

They would speak now and then, he supposed; they had, before. But it would be the stiff, formal conversation of gaoler and prisoner. And infrequent.

I'll miss you, John thought, watching the back of Jamie's head as the Scot negotiated a plunging slope ahead of him, leaning far back in the saddle, red plait swinging as the horse picked its way, slewing and skittering through the mud. He wondered, a little wistfully, whether Jamie would likewise miss their conversations—but knew better than to dwell on the thought.

He clicked his tongue, and his horse began the last descent to Helwater.

The drive was long and winding, but as they came into the last turn, he saw several well-bundled figures taking the air on the lawn, all women: Lady Dunsany and Isobel, and with them a couple of maid-servants. Peggy the nurse-maid, with William in her arms . . . and Betty Mitchell.

Beside him, he felt Fraser stiffen, rising slightly in his saddle at the sight. Grey's heart contracted suddenly, feeling the Scot's sudden surge of eagerness.

His choice, he reminded himself silently, and followed his prisoner back into captivity.

HANKS WAS DEAD.

"Quicker than he deserved, the sod," Crusoe observed dispassionately. "Slipped going down the ladder one morning and broke his neck. We picked him up dead." Crusoe gave Jamie a sidelong glance; it was plain that he wasn't sure how he felt about Jamie's reappearance. On the one hand, Crusoe couldn't handle all the work himself, or even half of it, and Jamie needed no training. On the other . . . with Hanks dead, Jamie might take over as head groom, and Crusoe might well fear the consequences of that.

"God rest his soul," Jamie said, and crossed himself. He'd let the question of who was to be head groom bide for now. If Crusoe could handle the responsibilities, he was welcome to them. If not . . . time enough to deal with that later.

"I'll take Eugenie's string out, then, aye?" he said, casual. Crusoe nodded, a little unsure, and Jamie went up the ladder to the loft, to leave his sack of belongings.

He'd come back better clothed than he left; his shirt and breeks were still rough, but new, and he had three pair of woolen stockings in his sack, a good leather belt, and a slouch hat of black felt—the latter, a gift from Tom Byrd. He disposed these items in the box that stood beside his pallet, checking as he did so to see that the things he had left in it were still there.

They were. The little statue of the Virgin that his sister had sent him, a dried mole's foot, to be carried against the rheumatism—he took that out and put it in the small goatskin pouch at his waist; his right knee had begun to ache on wet mornings, since Ireland—the stub of a pencil, a tinderbox, and a chipped pottery candlestick, an inch of melted wax still in it. A scatter of stones, picked up because of their feel in the hand or a pretty color. He counted them; there were eleven: one each for his sister, for Ian, for Young Jamie, Maggie, Kitty, Janet, Michael, and Young Ian; one for his daughter, Faith, who had died at birth; another for the child Claire had carried when she went; the last—a piece of rough amethyst—for Claire herself. He must look out for another now: the right stone for William. He wondered briefly why he had not done that before. Because he hadn't felt the right to claim William even in the privacy of his own heart, he supposed.

He was pleased, if surprised, to find his things intact. It might be only that there was nothing there worth the taking, of course. Or it might be that they expected him to come back and were afraid to tamper with his box. Someone *had* taken his blanket, he saw.

His most intimate keepsake was one that could not be lost or stolen, though. He flexed his left hand, where the thin white line of the letter "C"—carved a little crookedly, but still perfectly legible—showed on the mound at the base of his thumb. The "J" he had left on her would be likewise still visible, he supposed. He hoped.

One more thing to be put away. He took the heavy little purse from the bottom of the bag and tucked it under the balled-up stockings, then closed the box and went down the ladder, sure-footed as a goat.

For now Jamie was surprised at the sense of peace he felt in the stable. It wasn't homecoming, precisely—this place would never be home to him—but it was a place he knew, familiar in its daily rhythms, and with open air and the calm sweet presence of the horses always there at the bottom of it, no matter what the people were like.

He took his string of horses out along the road past the mere, then up a little way—not onto the fells but beyond the outer paddocks, where a grassy track led the way up and over a series of small hills. He paused at the summit of the highest, to breathe the horses and to look down over Helwater. It was a view he liked, when the weather was clear enough to see it: the big old house couched comfortably in its grove of copper beeches, the silver of the water beyond, rippling in the wind, its lacy edging of cattails spattered with blackbirds in spring and summer, their clear high song reaching him if the breeze lay right.

Just now there were no birds visible save a small hawk circling below the crest of the hill, alert for mice in the dead grass. There were tiny figures coming out along the drive, though; two men, mounted—Lord Dunsany and Lord John. He recognized the first by his stooped shoulders and the way his head jutted forward, the second by his square, solid seat and his easy, one-handed way with the reins.

"God be with ye, Englishman," he said. Whatever John Grey had thought of Jamie's announcement that he meant to court Betty Mitchell—Jamie grinned to himself at memory of Lord John's face, comically trying to suppress his astonishment in the name of courtesy—he'd brought Jamie back to Helwater.

Grey would leave in a few days, he supposed. He wondered if they would speak again before that happened, and, if so, how. The odd half-friendship they had forged from necessity could not in justice be forgotten—but neither could the resumption of their present positions as, essentially, master and slave. Was there any ground that would let them meet again as equals?

"A posse ad esse," he muttered to himself. From possibility to actuality. And, gathering up his leading rein, shouted, "Hup!" to the horses, and they thundered happily down the hill toward home.

THE DAY WAS COLD and windy but bright, and leaves from the copper beeches flew past in wild flurries, as though pursued. Grey had worried momentarily when Dunsany suggested a ride, for the old man was very frail, noticeably more so than on Grey's last visit. The giddy flights of sun, wind, and leaves lent the day a sense of mild excitement, though, which seemed to communicate itself to Dunsany, for his face took on a faint glow and his hands seemed strong enough on the reins. Nonetheless, Grey took care to keep their pace moderate and one eye on his ancient friend.

Once out of the drive, they took the lake road. It was muddy—Grey had never known it not—and the churned earth showed numerous hoof hollows slowly filling with water; a number of horses had passed this way not long before. Grey felt the small spurt of excitement that he had been experiencing whenever horses or stables were mentioned at Helwater—a more or less hourly occurrence—though he knew that encountering Jamie Fraser out with a horse was a long shot, there being other grooms on the estate. Still, he couldn't help a quick glance ahead.

The road lay empty before them, though, and he bent his attention to Lord Dunsany, who had slowed his horse to a walk.

"Has he picked up a stone?" he asked, reining in and preparing to dismount and attend to it.

"No, no." Dunsany waved him back into his saddle. "I wished to talk with you, Lord John. Privately, you know."

"Oh. Yes, of course," he said, cautiously. "Er . . . about Fraser?"

Dunsany looked surprised, but then considered.

"Well, no. But since you mention him, do you wish to . . . make other arrangements for him?"

Grey bit the inside of his cheek. "No," he said carefully. "Not for the present."

Dunsany nodded, not seeming bothered at the prospect. "He's a very good groom," he said. "The other servants don't make things easy for him—well, they wouldn't, would they?—but he keeps much to himself."

"He keeps much to himself." Those casual words gave Grey a sudden insight into Fraser's life at Helwater—and a slight pang. Had he not kept Fraser from transportation, he would have remained in the company of the other Scots, would have had companionship.

If he hadn't died of seasickness, he thought, and the pang faded, to be replaced by another moment of insight. Was this the explanation for Fraser's decision to marry Betty Mitchell?

Grey knew Betty fairly well; she'd been Geneva Dunsany's

lady's maid since Geneva's childhood and, with Geneva's death, had become Isobel's maid. She was quick-witted, good-looking in a common way, and seemed to be popular with the other servants. With her as wife, Jamie would be much less strange to the Helwater servants, much more a part of their community.

Little as Grey liked that idea, he had to admit that it was a sensible way of dealing with isolation and loneliness. But—

His thoughts were abruptly jerked back to Dunsany.

"You—I beg your pardon, sir. I didn't quite hear . . . ?" He'd heard, all right; he just didn't believe it.

"I said," Dunsany repeated patiently, leaning closer and raising his voice, "that I propose to amend my will and wish to ask your permission to add a provision appointing you as guardian to my grandson, William."

"I—well . . . yes. Yes, of course, if you wish it." Grey felt as though he'd been struck behind the ear with a stocking full of sand. "But surely there are other men much better qualified for the office. A male relative—someone on William's father's side of the family?"

"There really is no one," Dunsany said, with a helpless, one-shouldered shrug. "There are no male relations at all; only a couple of distant female cousins, neither of them married. And there is no one in my own family who is near enough, either in terms of geography or degree of relation, to make a competent guardian. I would not have the boy shipped off to Halifax or Virginia."

"No, of course not," Grey murmured, wondering how to get out of this. He could see why Dunsany wanted to amend his will; the old man was feeling his years, and with good reason. He was ill and frail and might easily be carried off by the winter's chills. It would be irresponsible to die without providing for William's guardianship. But the possible imminence of Dunsany's demise also meant that Grey's putative guardianship had an uncomfortable immediacy, as well.

"Besides not wanting to uproot the child so drastically—and my wife and Isobel would be quite desolate without him—he is the heir to Ellesmere. He has considerable property here; he should be raised with a knowledge of it."

"Yes, I see that." Grey pulled his horse's head away from the clump of grass it was nosing after.

"I know this is gross presumption on my part," Dunsany said, perceiving his hesitation. "And doubtless you were not expecting such a request. Should you like time to consider it?"

"I—no." Grey made up his mind on the moment. He hadn't seen that much of William but did like the little boy. While he was small, he wouldn't need that much in the way of help; Lady Dunsany and Isobel could care for him very well, and Grey could stay longer on his visits to Helwater. As William grew older . . . he'd need to go to school, of course. He could divide his holidays, perhaps, coming with John to London sometimes, the two of them coming to Helwater.

Just as he had once come with his friend Gordon Dunsany. When Gordon had been killed at Culloden, Grey had come then alone, to grieve and to comfort. Over time, he had become not Gordon's replacement, of course, but almost an adopted son of the house. It was that intimacy that had allowed him to make his arrangements with Dunsany for Fraser's parole. And if a son had privileges within his family, he had also responsibilities.

"I'm most honored by your request, sir. I promise you, I will execute the office to the very best of my ability."

Dunsany's withered face lighted with relief.

"Oh, you relieve my mind exceedingly, Lord John! I confess, the matter has been pressing upon me to a terrible degree." He smiled, looking much healthier. "Let us finish our ride and then go back for our tea; I believe I shall have an appetite for the first time in months!"

Grey smiled back and accepted the old baronet's hand on the bargain, then followed him as they sped up to a canter past the ruffled waves of the mere. Movement in the distance caught his eye, and he saw a string of horses running down the slope of a distant hill, graceful and wild as a flurry of leaves, led by a horseman.

It was too far to be sure, but he was sure, nonetheless. He couldn't take his eyes off the distant horses until they had rounded the bottom of the slope and disappeared.

Only then did his interrupted chain of thought restring itself. Yes, marrying Betty would make Jamie Fraser more comfortable at Helwater—but he need not stay at Helwater; it had been his choice to return. So it must in fact be Betty that drew him back.

"Well, bloody hell," Grey muttered. "It's his life." He spurred up, passing Dunsany on the road.

JAMIE WAS SURPRISED at how quickly Helwater reabsorbed him, though he supposed he shouldn't have been. A farm—and Helwater was a working farm, for all its grand manor house—has a life of its own, with a great, slow-beating heart, and everything on a farm listens to that beat and lives to its rhythm.

He knew that, for the rhythm of Lallybroch was deep in his bones, always would be. That knowledge was both sorrow and comfort, but more of the latter, for he knew that should he ever go back, that familiar heartbeat would still be there.

. . . *and his place shall know him no more,* the Bible said. He didn't think that was exactly what was meant; his place would always know him, should he come again.

But he would not come to Lallybroch again for a long time. *If ever,* he thought, but quickly put that thought out of his head. He turned his ear to the ground and felt the beating of Helwater, a quicker sound, one that would support him in his weakness, comfort him in loneliness. He could hear the speaking of its waters and the growing of the grass, the movement of horses and the silence of its rocks. The people were part of it—a more transient part, but not an unimportant part. And one of those was Betty Mitchell.

It couldn't be put off. And one benefit of the inexorable daily rhythm of a farm was that the people were part of it. He lingered for a moment after breakfast, to speak to Keren-happuch, the middle-aged Welsh kitchen maid, who liked him in a reserved, thin-lipped, dour sort of way. She was deeply religious, Keren—as evidenced by her name—thought him a Roman heretic, and wouldn't stand for carryings-on in any case, but when he told her that he had come back with news for Betty of a kinsman, she was willing to take his message. Everyone would know, of course, but under the circumstances, that wouldn't matter. At least he hoped not.

And so in the quiet part of the afternoon, an hour before tea, he came to the kitchen garden and found Betty waiting.

She turned at his step, and he saw that she'd put on a clean fichu and a little silver brooch. She lifted her chin and looked at him under her straight dark brows, a woman not quite sure of her power but clearly thinking she had some. He must be careful.

"Mrs. Betty," he said, bowing his head to her, formal. She had stretched out her hand, and he was obliged to take it but was careful not to squeeze or breathe on it.

"I came to tell ye about Toby," he said at once, before she could say anything. She blinked and her gaze sharpened, but she left her hand in his.

"Toby Quinn? What's happened to him, then?"

"He's died, lass. I'm sorry for it."

Her fingers curled over his and she gripped his hand.

"Died! How?"

"In the service of his king," he said. "He's buried safe in Ireland."

She was plainly shocked but gave him a sharp look.

"I said how. Who killed him?"

I did, he thought, but said, "He died by his own hand, lass," and said again, "I'm sorry for it."

She let go his hand and, turning, walked blindly for a few steps, put out her hand, and held tight to one of the espaliered pear trees that stood against the garden wall, spindly and vulnerable without its leaves.

She stood for some minutes, holding on to the branch, head bowed, breathing with a thickness in the sound. He'd thought she was fond of the man.

"Were you with him?" she said at last, not looking at him.

"If I had been, I should have stopped him."

She turned round then, lips pressed tight.

"Not then. Were you with him when you . . . went away?" Her fingers fluttered briefly.

"Yes. Some of the time."

"The soldiers who took you—did they catch *him*?"

"No." He understood what she was asking: whether it was the prospect of captivity, transportation, or hanging that had made Toby do it.

"Then why?" she cried, fists curling. "Why would he do it?"

He swallowed, seeing again the tiny dark room and smelling blood and excrement. Seeing *"Teind"* on the wall.

"Despair," he said quietly.

She made a small huffing sound, shaking her head doggedly to and fro.

"He was a Papist. Despair's a sin to a Papist, isn't it?"

"Folk do a great many things they think are sins."

She made a little noise through her nose.

"Yes, they do." She stood for a moment staring at the stones in the walk, then looked up suddenly at him, fierce. "I don't understand at all how he could have—what made him despair?"

Oh, God. Guide my tongue.

"Ye ken he was a Jacobite, aye? Well, there was a plot he was involved in—a great matter, with great consequences, did it either fail or succeed. It failed, and the heart went out o' the man."

She let out her breath in a sigh that sank her shoulders, seeming to deflate before his eyes. She shook her head.

"Men," she said flatly. "Men are fools."

"Aye, well . . . ye're no wrong there," he said ruefully, hoping that she would not ask whether he had been involved in the great matter—or why the soldiers had taken him to start with.

He needed to go before the conversation became personal. She took his hand again, though, holding it between both of hers, and he could see that she was about to say something he didn't want her to say. He'd shifted his weight, about to pull loose, when he heard footsteps on the walk behind him, heavy and quick.

"What's going on here?" Sure enough, it was Roberts, face flushed and lowering. Jamie could have kissed the man.

"I brought sad news to Mistress Betty," he said quickly, taking back his hand. "The death of a kinsman."

Roberts looked back and forth between them, clearly suspicious, but Betty's air of shock and desolation was unfeigned and obvious. Roberts, who was not, after all, a stupid man, went rapidly to her, taking her by the arm and bending solicitously down to her.

"Are you all right, my dear?"

"I—yes. It's only . . . oh, poor Toby!"

Betty was not stupid, either, and burst into tears, burying her face in Roberts's shoulder.

Jamie, being the third wise party present, silently praised God and backed hastily away, murmuring inconsequent regrets.

The wind was cold outside the shelter of the kitchen garden, but he was sweating. He made his way back toward the stables, nodding to Keren-happuch, who was standing outside the kitchen garden, holding a vegetable basin and waiting patiently for the godless behavior inside the walls to cease.

"A death, was it?" she said, having obviously come along to ensure that his aim had not been wicked canoodling, after all.

"A sad death. Would ye say a prayer, maybe, for the soul of Tobias Quinn?"

A look of surprised distaste crossed her face.

"For a Papist?" she said.

"For a poor sinner."

She pushed out her thin lips, considering, but reluctantly nodded. "I suppose so."

He nodded, touched her shoulder in thanks, and went on his way.

The Church did call despair a sin, and suicide an unforgivable sin, as the sinner could not repent. A suicide was therefore condemned to hell, and prayers thus useless. But neither Keren nor Betty was a Papist, and perhaps their Protestant prayers might be heard.

For himself, he prayed each night for Quinn. After all, he reasoned, it couldn't hurt.

39

The Fog Comes Down

BOWNESS-ON-WINDERMERE WAS A SMALL, PROSPEROUS town, with a maze of narrow stone-paved streets clustered cozily in the town center, these spreading out into a gentle slope of scattered houses and cottages that ran down to the lake's edge, where a fleet of little fishing boats swayed at anchor. It was a considerable coach ride from Helwater, and Lord Dunsany apologized for the effort required, explaining that his solicitor chose to live here, having left the London stews for what he assumed to be the bucolic pleasures of the country.

"Little did he know what sorts of things go on in the country," Dunsany said darkly.

"What sorts of things?" Grey asked, fascinated.

"Oh." Dunsany seemed mildly taken aback at being thus challenged, but furrowed his brow in thought, his cane tapping gently on the stones as he limped slowly toward the street where the solicitor's office lay.

"Well, there was Morris Huckabee and his wife—only it seemed she was, in fact, his daughter. And *her* daughter was in fact not Morris's at all but born to the ostler at the Grapes, as the mother admitted in court. Now, ordinarily, the wife would inherit—old Morris had died, you see, thus precipitating the trouble—but the question arose: was a common-law marriage (for of course the old creature had never gone through with a proper marriage, just told everyone she was his wife, and no one thought to ask for details) based on an incestuous relationship valid? Because if it wasn't, you see, then the daughter—the wife daughter, I mean, not the daughter of the wife—couldn't inherit his estate.

"Now, under those circumstances, the money would then normally pass to the child or children of the marriage, save that in this case, the child—the younger daughter—wasn't really Morris's, and while in law, any child born in wedlock is considered to be the child of that marriage, regardless of whether he or she was really fathered by the butcher or the baker or the candlestick maker, in *this* case . . ."

"Yes, I see," Grey said hastily. "Dear me."

"Yes, it was quite a revelation to Mr. Trowbridge," Dunsany said, with a grin that showed he still had the majority of his teeth, if somewhat worn and yellowed with age. "I think he considered selling up and going straight back to London, but he stuck it out."

"Trowbridge? I thought your solicitor was a Mr. Wilberforce."

"Oh," Dunsany said again, but less happily. "He was, indeed. Still is, for matters of conveyancing. But I did not quite like to employ him for this particular matter, you know."

Grey did not know, but nodded understandingly.

Dunsany sighed and shook his head.

"I do worry about poor Isobel," he said.

"You do?" Grey thought he must have missed some remark that established a relationship in the conversation between Mr. Wilberforce and Isobel, but—

"Oh!" Grey exclaimed himself. He'd forgotten that Lady Dunsany had said that Mr. Wilberforce was paying considerable *attention* to Isobel—this remark being made in a significant tone that made it clear that Lady Dunsany had her doubts about Wilberforce.

"Yes, I see." And he did. They were visiting the solicitor for the purpose of adding the new provision to Dunsany's will, establishing Lord John's guardianship of William. If Mr. Wilberforce had aspirations to Isobel's hand in marriage, the last thing Lord Dunsany would want was for the lawyer to be familiar with the provisions of his will.

"Her sister's marriage was so—" Dunsany's lips disappeared into the wrinkles of his face, so hard pressed were they. "Well. I have concerns, as I say. Still, that is neither here nor there. Come, Lord John, we must not be late."

IT WAS A RARE and beautiful day, one last warm breath of what the local people called "St. Martin's summer," before the chill rains and fogs of autumn fell like a curtain over the fells. Even so, Crusoe looked sourly up toward the distant rocks and rolled an eye at the sky.

"Something's coming," he said. "Feel it in me bones." He straightened his back with an alarming crack, as though to make the point, and groaned.

Jamie surreptitiously flexed his right hand. He also frequently felt weather coming; the badly mended bones seemed to have odd spaces that cold crept into. He felt nothing now, but he wasn't going to call Crusoe a liar.

"Aye, it might be," he said equably. "But Miss Isobel and Lady Dunsany are wanting to take Master Willie up to the old shepherd's hut for a wee wander." Having heard the screams and roarings from the nursery as he passed under its windows after breakfast, he had the impression that the proposed outing was the outcome of a domestic counsel of desperation.

According to kitchen gossip, Master William had a new tooth coming, a back tooth, and it was coming hard—particularly for those who had to deal with him. Opinion was divided as to the best treatment for this ailment, some advising a leech upon the gums, some bleeding, others a poultice of hot mustard at the back of the neck. Jamie supposed that all these things would at least distract the child from his suffering by giving him something else to roar about but would himself have rubbed the lad's gums with whisky.

"Use enough of it," his sister had told him, a practiced finger in his new niece's squalling mouth, *"and they'll go quiet. It helps to take a wee dram for yourself, too, in case they don't."* He smiled briefly at the memory.

Isobel, though, had evidently decided that an outing would take Willie's mind off his tooth and had sent word for horses and a groom. Lady Dunsany, Lady Isobel, Betty—old Nanny Elspeth had flatly refused to countenance getting on a horse, and Peggy had a bad leg, so Betty had been dragooned to mind the child, and Jamie wished her well of that job—Mr. Wilberforce, and Jamie himself would complete the party.

Jamie wondered what Lady Isobel would say when she found that he was to escort the party, but he was too pleased with the prospect of seeing Willie—roaring or not—for a few hours to worry about it.

In the event, Lady Isobel seemed barely to notice his presence. She was flushed and cheerful, doubtless because of lawyer Wilberforce's presence, though her gaiety had a strange edge to it. Even Lady Dunsany, most of her attention fixed on Willie, noticed Isobel's mood and smiled a little.

"You're in good spirits, daughter," she said.

"Who could not be?" Isobel said, throwing back her head dramatically and raising her face to the sun. "So intoxicating a day!"

It was a fine day. A sky you could fall into, and never mind how far. The copper beeches near the house had gone to gold and rust, and a sweet, nippy little breeze whirled the fallen leaves round in skittish circles. Jamie remembered another day with air like blue wine, and Claire in it.

Lord, that she may be safe. She and the child. For an odd moment, he felt as though he stood outside himself, outside time, sensing Claire's hand warm on his arm, her smile as she looked at Willie—red-faced, tearstained, and obviously miserable, but still his bonnie wee lad.

Then the world snapped into place, and he picked up the boy to set him on Betty's saddle. William kicked him in the stomach, scrunched his face, and howled.

"NOOoooooo! Don't want her, don't want HER, wanna ride with YOUuuuu, Mac!"

Jamie tucked Willie under one arm, so that his sturdy legs churned harmlessly in the air, and looked to the ladies for advice, one eyebrow raised.

Betty looked as though she would prefer to share her horse with a wildcat but didn't say anything. Lady Dunsany glanced dubiously from the maidservant to Jamie, but Lady Isobel—her conversation with Mr. Wilberforce interrupted—drew up her reins and said impatiently, "Oh, let him."

And so they rode up toward the fells, skirting the moss, though at this time of year it was dry and mostly safe. Willie was breathing thickly through his mouth, his nose being blocked from crying, and was drooling now and then, but Jamie found his small, solid presence a pleasure, though he was disturbed to find that the boy was wearing a corset under his shirt.

As soon as the party reached a place where the horses were

not compelled to follow one another, he maneuvered his own mount so as to drop back and ride beside Betty, who affected not to notice him.

"Is the wean not ower-young to be trussed up like a Christmas goose?" he asked bluntly.

Betty blinked at him, taken by surprise.

"Like . . . Oh, you mean the corset? It's only a light thing, barely any boning. He won't have a real one 'til he's five, but his grandmother and his aunt thought he might as well grow used to it now. While they can still overpower him," she added in an undertone, with an unwilling twitch of amusement. "The little bugger kicked a hole in the wall of the nursery yesterday and broke six of the best teacups the day before. Stole them off the table and flung them against the wall to hear them smash, laughing all the time. He'll be a right devil when he's grown, you mark my words," she said, nodding at William, who had a thumb in his mouth and was dreamily lost in the horse's motion and the soothing proximity of Jamie's body.

Jamie contented himself with a neutral sound in his throat, though he felt his ears grow hot. They would not discipline the boy, and yet they meant to case his sweet small body in linen and whalebone, to narrow his shoulders and sway his back to meet the demands of what they thought fashionable?

He knew that the custom of corseting children was common among the wealthy English—to form their bodies into the slope-shouldered, high-chested figure thought most fashionable—but such things were not done in the Highlands, save perhaps among the nobles. The odious garment—he could feel the hard edge of it pressing into Willie's soft flesh, just below his oxter—made Jamie want to spur up and ride hell-bent for the Border, pausing only to strip the thing off and throw it into the mere as they passed.

But he couldn't do that and so rode on, one arm tight around William, seething.

"He's selling," Betty murmured, distracting him from his dark thoughts, "but Lady D's not buying. Poor Isobel!"

"Eh?"

She nodded and he looked ahead, seeing Mr. Wilberforce riding between the two ladies, now and then casting a quick, possessive glance at Isobel but turning the most of his winsome charm on Lady Dunsany. Who, as Betty said, seemed less than overwhelmed.

"Why poor Isobel?" Jamie asked, watching this byplay with interest.

"Why, she's sweet on him, you great nit. Surely even you can see that?"

"Aye, so?"

Betty sighed and rolled her eyes dramatically but was sufficiently bored as to put aside her pose of disinterest.

"So," she said, "Lady Isobel wants to marry him. Well," she added fairly, "she wants to be married, and he's the only one in the county that's halfway presentable. But only halfway, and I don't think that'll be enough," she said, squinting judiciously at Wilberforce, who was nearly falling out of his saddle in the effort to pay a compliment to Lady Dunsany, who was pretending to be hard of hearing.

On Wilberforce's other side, Isobel was glaring at her mother, with a look of mingled frustration and apprehension on her face. Lady Dunsany rode tranquilly, rocking a little on her sidesaddle, glancing vaguely at Wilberforce's importunate face from time to time, with an expression that said plainly, *"Oh, are you still here?"*

"Why do they not like him for their daughter, then?" Jamie asked, interested despite himself. "Do they not wish her to be married?"

Betty snorted. "After what happened to Geneva?" she asked, and looked pointedly at William, then raised her face to Jamie, with a tiny smirk. He kept his own face carefully blank, despite a lurch of the innards, and did not reply.

They rode in silence for a bit, but Betty's innate restlessness would not tolerate silence for long.

"They'd let her marry *well,* I s'pose," she said, grudging. "But they don't mean to let her throw herself away on a lawyer. And one that's talked about, too."

"Aye? What's said about him?" Jamie didn't give a fig for Wilberforce—and not much more for Lady Isobel—but the conversation took his mind off Willie's corset.

Betty pursed her lips, with a knowing, sly sort of look.

"They say he spends a good bit of time with his clients what are ladies with no husbands—more than he needs to. And he lives beyond his means," she added primly. "Well beyond."

That was likely the more serious charge, Jamie reflected. He supposed that Isobel had a decent portion. She was the Dunsanys' only remaining child, though of course William would inherit the estate.

As they climbed the path to the old shepherd's hut, he felt a tightening of the belly, but there was no sign of anyone, and he gave a small sigh of relief and said a quick prayer for the repose of Quinn's soul. A basket had been brought, with a roast chicken, a loaf, some good cheese and a bottle of wine. Willie, emerging from his daze, was irascible and whiny, rejecting all offers of food. Mr. Wilberforce, in an attempt at ingratiation, ruffled the boy's hair and tried to jolly him out of his sulks, being severely bitten in the hand for his pains.

"Why, you little—" The lawyer's face went red, but he wisely coughed and said, "You poor little child. How sorry I am that you should be so miserable!"

Jamie, his face kept carefully straight, happened to catch Lady Dunsany's eye at this point, and they exchanged a glance of perfect understanding. Had it lasted more than an instant, one or both of them would have burst into laughter, but Lady Dunsany looked away, coughed, and reached for a napkin, which she offered to the lawyer.

"Are you bleeding, Mr. Wilberforce?" she inquired sympathetically.

"William!" said Isobel. "That is very wicked! You must apologize to Mr. Wilberforce this minute."

"No," said William briefly, and, plumping down on his backside, turned his attention to a passing beetle.

Isobel hovered in indecision, plainly not wanting to appear before the lawyer as anything other than the personification of womanly gentleness and not sure how to reconcile this desire with the equally plain urge to clout Willie over the ear. Mr. Wilberforce begged her to sit down and have a glass of wine, though and Betty—with a deep sigh of resignation—went to crouch beside William and distract him with plucked blades of grass showing him how to chivvy the hapless beetle to and fro.

Jamie had the horses hobbled, grazing on the short turf beyond the ruined hut. They needed no attention, but he took the bread and cheese Cook had given him for the journey and went to look at them, enjoying a moment's solitude.

He must be careful not to spend too much time in watching William, lest his fascination show, and he sat down on the ruined wall, back turned to the party—though he was unable to avoid hearing the stramash that broke out when William put the doomed beetle up his nose and then shrieked at the result.

The unfortunate Betty came in for a dreadful scolding, all three of the others reproaching her at once. The clishmaclaver was made worse by William, who started roaring again, apparently wanting the beetle put back.

"Go away!" Isobel shouted at Betty. "Go right away to the house; you're no use at all!"

Jamie's mouth was full of bread and cheese, and he nearly choked when Betty broke away from the group and ran toward him, sobbing.

"Horse," she said, her bosom heaving. "Get my horse!"

He rose at once and fetched her animal, swallowing the last of his meal.

"Did they—" he began, but she didn't stay for question or comfort but put her foot in his offered hand and swung into the saddle in a furious flurry of petticoats. She lashed the startled horse across the neck with the end of the rein, and the poor beast shot down the trail as though its tail was on fire.

The others were fussing over William, who seemed to have lost his mind and had no idea what he wanted, only that he didn't want whatever he was offered. Jamie turned round and walked up the fell, out of earshot. The wean would wear himself out soon enough—and sooner if they'd leave him be.

Up higher, there was no shelter from the wind, and its soft, high whistle drowned the noise from below. Looking down, he could see William curled up in a ball beside his auntie, with his jacket over his head, his breeches filthy, and the damned corset almost round his neck. He looked deliberately away and saw Betty, halfway across the moss. His mouth tightened. He hoped the horse wouldn't step into one of the boggy spots and break a leg.

"Wee gomerel," he muttered, shaking his head. Despite their history, he felt a bit sorry for Betty. He was also curious about her.

She hadn't been friendly to him today, not quite that. Bu
she'd spoken to him with more intimacy than she'd ever show
before. He would have expected her to ignore him, or be shor
with him, after what had passed between them. But no. Wh
was that?

"She wants to be married," the lass had said of Isobel. Perhap
Mrs. Betty did, as well. She was the age for it, or a wee bit be
yond. He'd thought—and blushed at his presumption—that sh
only wanted to bed him, whether out of lewdness or curiosity, h
couldn't tell. He was nearly sure that she knew about Genev
and him. But what if she'd fixed on him as a husband, in prefer
ence to George Roberts? God, had Grey said anything to her
The thought disturbed him very much.

On the face of it, he thought no woman in her right min
would consider him in that light. He'd neither money, propert
nor freedom, doubted he even *could* wed, without the permissio
of Lord John Grey. Betty could be in no ignorance of his circum
stances; the entire estate knew exactly what—if not exactl
who—he was.

Who. Aye, who. Examining his feelings—a mixture of sur
prise, alarm, and a mild revulsion—he was a bit bothered to fin
that part of it was pride, and pride of a particularly sinful kind
Betty was a common girl, the daughter of a poor tenant o
Dunsany's—and he was both startled and discomfited to fin
that, in spite of present circumstance, he still thought of himsel
as the laird of Lallybroch.

"Well, that's foolish," he muttered, batting away a cloud o
whining small flies that clustered round his head. He'd marrie
Claire without a single thought of his place or hers. For all he'
known then, she was a—well, no. He smiled a little, involun
tarily. He'd been an exile and an outlaw, with a price on his head
And he'd never have taken her for a slattern or peasant.

"I would have taken ye even if that was so, lass," he said softly. "I'd have had ye, no matter if I'd known the truth from the start."

He felt a little better, about himself, at least. That was the main root of his feeling regarding Betty, after all. Only that he could not countenance the thought of marrying again. That—

He stopped dead, catching sight of the corner of the wall where Quinn had sat, the Irishman's strange light eyes glowing with fervor. Betty was Quinn's sister-in-law; of course she knew who Jamie was. Had been.

The wind touched his neck with a sudden, different chill, and he turned at once, to see the fog coming down. He stood up in haste. Fogs on the fells were swift, sudden, and dangerous. He could see this one moving, a dirty great swell like a wild beast poking its head above the rocks, tendrils of mist creeping over the ground like the tentacles of an octopus.

He was running down the slope and looking to the horses, who had all stopped feeding and were standing with their heads up, looking toward the fog and switching their tails uneasily. He'd have the hobbles off in seconds—best run to the Dunsanys and make them pack up at once; he'd get the horses while they were about their business.

Thinking this, he looked for the party and found them. Counted them automatically. Three heads and a—Three. Only three. He flung himself down the hill, leaping rocks and stumbling over tussocks.

"Where's William?" he gasped, as the three adults turned shocked faces on him. "The boy? Where is he?"

THE BOY WAS NOT quite three; he could not have gone far. He *ouldn't.* So Jamie told himself, trying to control the panic that was creeping into his mind as fast as the fog was covering the ground.

"Stay here, and stay together!" he said to Isobel and Lady Dunsany, both of whom blinked at him in surprise. "Call out for the lad, keep calling out—but dinna move a step. Here, hold the horses." He thrust the bundled reins into Wilberforce's hand, and the lawyer opened his mouth as though to protest, but Jamie didn't stay to hear it.

"William!" he bellowed, plunging into the fog.

"Willie! Willie!" The women's higher voices obligingly took up the call, regular as a bell on a ship's buoy, and serving the same purpose. "Willie! Where are youuuu?"

The air had changed quite suddenly, no longer clear but soft and echoing; sound seemed to come from everywhere and nowhere.

"William!" The sound bounced off the stones and the short, leathery turf. "William!"

He was moving up the slope, Jamie could tell that much. Perhaps William had gone to explore the shepherd's hut. Wilberforce had joined the women now in calling out but was doing it in counterpoint, rather than in unison with them.

Jamie had the feeling that he could not breathe, that the fog was choking him—but this was nonsense. Pure illusion.

"William!"

His shins thumped into the fallen wall of the shepherd's hut. He could not see more than the faintest outline of the stones but felt his way inside and crawled quickly along the walls, calling out for the boy. Nothing.

Fogs might last an hour, or a day.

"Willie-iam-Wil-Willy-iam-WILLIE!"

Jamie gritted his teeth. If they didn't keep quiet now and then, he couldn't hear Willie shouting back. If the boy was capable of shouting. The footing was treacherous, the grass slippery, the ground rocky. And if he went all the way to the bottom of the slope, the moss . . .

He went higher, among the tumbled stones. Staggered from one to another, feeling round their bases, stubbing his toes. The fog was cold in his chest, aching. His foot came down on something soft—Willie's jacket—and his heart leapt.

"WILLIAM!"

Was that a sound, a whimper? He stopped dead, trying to listen, trying to hear through the whisper of the moving fog and the distant voices, cacophonous as a ring of church bells.

And then, quite suddenly, he saw the boy curled up in a rocky hollow, the yellow of his shirt showing briefly through an eddy in the fog. He lunged and seized William before he could disappear, clutched him to his bosom, saying, "It's all right, *a chuisle,* it's all right now, dinna be troubled, we'll go and see your grannie, aye?"

"Mac! Mac, Mac! Oh, *Mac*!"

Willie clung to him like a leech, trying to burrow into his chest, and he wrapped his arms tight around the boy, too overcome to speak.

To this point, he could not really have said that he loved William. Feel the terror of responsibility for him, yes. Carry thought of him like a gem in his pocket, certainly, reaching now and then to touch it, marveling. But now he felt the perfection of the tiny bones of William's spine through his clothes, smooth as marbles under his fingers, smelled the scent of him, rich with the incense of innocence and the faint tang of shit and clean linen. And hought his heart would break with love.

40

Gambit

GREY SAW JAMIE NOW AND THEN, MOSTLY IN THE DISTANC as he went about his work. They had had no opportunity t speak, though—and he could not seem to invent a pretext, le alone think what he might say if he found one. He felt amazingl self-conscious, like a boy unable to say anything to an attractiv girl. He'd be blushing, next thing, he thought, disgusted wit himself.

Still, the fact remained that he really had nothing to say t Jamie anymore—or Jamie to him. *Well, not nothing,* he correcte himself. They'd always had a great deal to say to each other. Bu there was no excuse for conversation now.

Three days before his scheduled departure, he rose in th morning with the conviction that he must speak with Frase somehow. Not in the stiff manner of an interview between pa roled prisoner and officer of the Crown—simply a few words, a man to man. If he could have that, he could go back to Londo with an easy heart, knowing that sometime, somewhere, ther was the possibility that they might be friends again, even if tha time and place could not be here and now.

It was no good anticipating an unknown battle. He ate hi

breakfast and told Tom to dress him for riding. Then he put on his hat and, heart beating a little faster than usual, went down oward the stables.

He saw Jamie from a long way off; he couldn't be mistaken for any other man, even without the signal fire of his dark-red hair. He had it tailed today, not plaited, and the ends fluttered against he white of his shirt like tiny flames.

William was with him, trotting at his heels, chattering like a magpie. Grey smiled to see him; the little boy was in his tiny breeches and a loose shirt and looked a proper little horseman.

He hesitated for a moment, waiting to see what Fraser was about; better if he did not interrupt the day's work. But they were headed for the paddock, and he followed them at a distance.

A young man he didn't know was waiting there; he bobbed his head at Fraser, who offered a hand and said something to him. Perhaps this was the new groom; Dunsany had said something about needing a new man to replace Hanks, over tea last night.

The men spoke for a few minutes, Fraser gesturing toward the group of horses in the paddock. There were three horses there, frisky two-year-old stallions, who nipped and shoved one another, galloping up and down in play. Fraser took a coiled halter rope from the fence post, and a bag of oats, and handed these to he young man.

The new groom took them gingerly, then opened the gate and went into the paddock. Grey saw that his nervousness vanished as soon as he was in with the horses; that was a good sign. Fraser seemed to think so, too—he gave a small nod to himself and crossed his forearms on the top rail, settling himself to watch.

Willie yanked at the side of Fraser's breeches, obviously wanting to get up and see. Rather than pick the boy up, though,

Fraser nodded, bent, and showed Willie how to put a foot up on the rail and then pull himself up. With a large hand cupped under his bottom to supply a boost, William made it to the upper rail and clung there, crowing with pleasure. Fraser smiled at him and said something, then turned back to watch how the groom was getting on.

Perfect. Grey could go and watch, too: nothing more natural.

He came up beside Fraser, nodded briefly to him, and leaned in his turn on the fence. They watched in silence for a few moments; the new man had successfully whistled the stallions in shaking his bagful of oats, and had slipped the halter rope around the neck of one of the young horses. The others, finding the oats gone, shook their manes and frisked away; the roped one tried to go with them and, displeased to find himself tied, jerked back.

Grey watched with interest to see what the groom would do; he didn't pull on the rope but rather swarmed inward along it and, with a hand on the stallion's mane, was on his back in an instant. He turned his face toward Fraser, flashing a grin, and Fraser laughed, turning up his thumb in approval.

"Well done!" he called. "Take him round a few times, aye?"

"Well done!" Willie piped, and hopped up and down on the fence rail like a sparrow.

Fraser put out a hand to touch the boy's shoulder, and he quieted at once. All three of them watched the groom take the horse barebacked round the paddock, sticking in spite of all attempts to shake or rear, until the stallion gave up and trotted peacefully along.

The sense of excitement ebbed to one of pleasant half attention. And, quite suddenly, Grey knew what to say.

"Queen's knight," he said quietly. "To queen three." It was, he knew, a dangerous opening.

Fraser didn't move, but Grey felt his sideways glance. After an instant's hesitation, he replied, "King's pawn to king four," and Grey felt his heart lighten. It was the answer to the Torremolinos Gambit, the one he had used on that far-off, disastrous evening at Ardsmuir, when he had first laid his hand on Jamie Fraser's.

"Well done, well done, well done," Willie was chanting softly to himself. "Well done, well done, well done!"

41

A Moonlicht Flicht

IT WAS NOT YET TEATIME, BUT THE SUN HOVERED JUST above the leafless copper beeches; the dark came earlier every day. Jamie was walking up to the distant barn where the farm horses were kept. Three young men from the village tended these, feeding, brushing, and mucking out; Jamie came daily when the horses were brought in, to check for injury, lameness, cough, and general ill health, for the farm horses were, in their own way, nearly as valuable as the stud.

Joe Gore, one of the farmhands, was outside the barn, looking out for him, and looking anxious. The instant he saw Jamie, he broke into a clumsy run, waving his arms.

"Fanny's gone missing!" he blurted.

"How?" Jamie asked, startled. Fanny was a big Belgian draft horse, fawn in color, who stood seventeen hands at the shoulder. Not easily mislaid, even in the fading light.

"Well, I dunno, do I?" Joe was scared, and defensive with it. "Ike hit a stone and bent t' wheel rim, so'm he unhitched wagon and left her while he brung wheel to smithy. I go up to get her and she's nay bloody there, is she?"

"Ye checked the walls and hedges, aye?" Jamie was already moving, heading for the distant cornfield, Joe at his heels. That field was not fenced but was bordered by drystone dikes on three sides, a windbreak hedgerow to the north. The notion of Fanny jumping the walls was just this side of absurd, but she might conceivably have broken through the hedge; she was a powerful horse.

"Think I'm green? 'Course I did!"

"We'll go round by the road." Jamie jerked his chin toward the road that edged the property to the east; it was the border of Helwater's land and made along the high ground, offering a view of the whole of the back fields.

They had barely reached the road, though, when Joe gave a shout of relief, pointing. "There she is! Who the devil's that atop her?"

Jamie squinted for a moment into the glare of the fading sun and felt a lurch of alarm—for the small figure perched on Fanny's back, kicking its heels in frustration against the draft horse's great placid sides, was Betty Mitchell.

Fanny had been plodding stolidly along when first sighted, but now the big head reared up, nostrils flaring, and she broke into a thumping gallop. Betty screamed and fell off.

Jamie left Fanny to Joe, who seized the horse by the mane and was half-dragged toward the barn as Fanny made single-mindedly for her manger. Jamie squatted by Betty but was relieved to see her already struggling to rise, using the most unladylike language he'd heard since Claire had left him.

"What—" he began, seizing her under the arms, but she didn't wait for him to finish.

"Isobel!" she gasped. "That frigging lawyer's got her! You've got to go!"

"Go where?" He set her firmly on her feet, but she swayed alarmingly, and he gripped her arms to steady her. "Mr. Wilberforce, ye mean?"

"Who bloody else?" she snapped. "He came to take her driving, in a gig. She was already out in the yard with her bonnet on, getting in, when I saw her from the window. I ran down and said, whatever was she thinking? She wasn't going off with him by herself—Lady D would have my head!"

She paused to breathe heavily, gathering herself.

"She tried to make me stay, but he laughed and said I was quite right; 'twasn't proper for an unmarried young woman to be out with a man unchaperoned. She made a face, but she giggled at him and said, oh, all right, then, she supposed I could come."

Betty's hair was coming down in thick hanks round her face; she brushed one back with a "Tcha!" of irritation, then turned round and pointed up the road.

"We got up to the edge of Helwater, and he stops to look at the view. We all got out, and I'm standing there thinking it's perishing cold and me come out with no more than my shawl and cross with Isobel for being a thoughtless ninny, and all of a sudden Mr. Wilberforce grabs me by the shoulders and pushes me off the road and into a ditch, the fucking bastard! Look at that, just look!" She seized a handful of her muddied skirt and shook it under Jamie's nose, showing him a great rent in the fabric.

"Where's he gone, do ye know?"

"I can bloody guess! Gretna fucking Green, that's where!"

"Jesus Christ!" He took a deep breath, trying to think. "He'll never get there tonight—not in a gig."

She shrugged, exasperated. "Why are you standing here? You've got to go after them!"

"Me? Why, for God's sake?"

"Because you can ride fast! And because you're big enough to make her bloody come back with you! And you can keep it quiet!"

When he did not move at once, she stamped her foot. "Are you deaf? You have to go now! If he takes her maidenhead, she's stuffed more ways than one. The bugger's got a wife already."

"What? A wife?"

"Will you stop saying 'What' like a bloody parrot?" she snapped. "Yes! He married a girl in Perthshire, five or six years back. She left him and went back to her parents, and he came to Derwentwater. I heard it from—well, never bloody mind! Just—just—go!"

"But you—"

"I'll manage! GO!" she bellowed, her face scarlet in the glare of the sinking sun.

He went.

HIS FIRST IMPULSE was to go back to the house, to the main stable. But that would take too long—and embroil him in awkward explanations that would not only delay his leaving but rouse the whole household.

"And you can keep it quiet," Betty had said.

"Aye, fat chance," he muttered, half-running for the barn. But if there was any chance of keeping this from becoming an open scandal, he had to admit that it probably lay with him, little as he liked it.

There was no possibility of pursuing Wilberforce on one of the farm horses, even were they not knackered from the day's work. But there were two fine mules, Whitey and Mike, who were kept to draw the hay wagon. They were broken to the saddle, at least, and had spent the day in pasture. He might just . . .

By the time he'd reached this point in his thoughts, he was already rifling through the tack in search of a snaffle and, ten minutes later, was mounted on a surprised and affronted Whitey, trotting toward the road, the three stable-hands staring after them with their mouths hanging open. He saw Betty in the distance, limping toward the house, her entire figure emanating indignation.

He felt no small amount of this emotion himself. His impulse was to think that Isobel had made her bed and could lie in it—but, after all, she was very young and knew nothing of men, let alone a scoundrel like Wilberforce.

And she would indeed be stuffed, as Betty inelegantly put it, once Wilberforce had taken her maidenhead. Quite simply, her life would be ruined. And her family would be badly damaged—more damaged. They'd lost two of their three children already.

He pressed his lips tight. He supposed he owed it to Geneva Dunsany and her parents to save her little sister.

He wished he had thought to tell Betty to seek out Lord John and let him know what was to do—but it was too late for that, and he couldn't have waited for Grey to come, in any case. The sun had sunk below the trees now, though the sky remained light; he'd have an hour, maybe, before full dark. He might reach the coaching road in that time.

If Wilberforce meant to reach Gretna Green, just over the Scottish border, where he could marry Isobel without the consent of her parents—and without anything in the way of questions asked—he must be taking the coaching road that led from London to Edinburgh. This passed within a few miles of Helwater. And it had inns along the way.

Not even an eloping scoundrel would try to drive a gig all the way to Gretna at night. They'd have to stop overnight and go on in the morning.

He might catch them in time.

IT WAS A GOOD deal safer to ride a mule in the dark than to drive a gig, but still nothing a sane man would want to do. He was shivering—and not entirely from the cold, though he was wearing only a leather jerkin over his shirt—and cursing in a manner that would have outdone Betty, by the time he saw the lights of the first posthouse.

He gave the mule to an ostler to water, asking as he did whether a gig had stopped, with a well-dressed man and a young woman in it?

It had not, though the ostler had seen such a conveyance go by, just before dark, and thought the driver an idiot.

"Aye," Jamie said briefly. "How far's the next inn?"

"Two miles," the man replied, peering at him curiously. "You're after him, are you? What's he done?"

"Nothing," Jamie assured him. "He's a solicitor, hurryin' to a dying client who needs a will changed. He's left behind some papers he needs, so they sent me on to bring them."

"Oh." The ostler—like everyone else in the world—had no interest in legal matters.

Jamie had no money, so shared the mule's water, scooping it up with his hand. The ostler took his lack of money personally, but Jamie loomed menacingly at him, and the ostler took his disgruntlement off to a safe distance, muttering insults.

Back to the road, after a brief contest of wills between Jamie and the mule, and on into the night. There was a half-moon, barely up, and as it rose, he was at least able to see the edge of the road and thus not fear going badly astray in the dark.

Biddle was not a posthouse but rather a small hamlet boasting one tavern—outside which stood the Helwater gig, its traces unhitched. Jamie said a quick Hail Mary in thanks, added an Our Father for strength, and swung grimly off the mule.

He tied Whitey to the rail and stood for a moment, rubbing his stubbled chin and thinking how to proceed. One way if they were in separate rooms—but another if they were together. And if solicitor Wilberforce was the man that Betty thought him, Jamie would put money on together. The man wouldn't want to risk being caught before he'd put the matter beyond question; he wouldn't wait for marriage before deflowering the girl, for once he'd taken her virginity, there was no going back.

The simplest thing would be to walk in and demand to know the whereabouts of Wilberforce and Isobel—but if the aim was as much to prevent scandal as it was to rescue the fat-heided wee lassie from her peril, he'd best not do that. Instead, he walked quietly round behind the tavern, looking at the windows.

It was a small place: only two rooms upstairs, and only one of those windows was lit. The shutters were drawn, but he saw a shadow pass by the crack, and as he stood there in the sharp-smelling dark, he heard Isobel's giggle, high and nervous, and then the rumble of Wilberforce's voice.

Not too late, then. He drew a deep breath and flexed his hands, stiff with cold and long riding.

The words of an old Highland song echoed in his mind as he rummaged about the ramshackle shed behind the tavern. He had no notion of the music, but it was a ballad, and he recalled the story, which had to do with an abducted bride.

. . . in one bed they were laid, were laid, in one bed they were laid.

In the song, the young woman hadn't wanted to be abducted, though, and fiercely resisted the attempts of her would-be bridegroom to consummate the marriage.

"Before I lose my maidenheid, I'll fight wi' you 'til dawn, 'til dawn, I'll fight wi' you 'til dawn," he murmured absently, feeling round the walls. A good-size beer barrel would be enough; tall as he was, he could reach the sill, he thought.

The valiant maid succeeded—owing as much, Jamie thought, to the unmanly feebleness of her would-be husband as to her own efforts—and, come dawn, emerged triumphant from the boudoir, insisting that her abductors restore her to her home, . . . *virgin as I came, I came—virgin as I came!*

Well, he hadn't heard any screeching yet, so there was a chance Isobel would come home in the same condition. He didn't find a suitable barrel but did come across something better—a thatcher's ladder, laid on its side. He carried this out, walking as softly as he could, and laid it carefully against the wall.

There were noises from inside the tavern—the usual clatter and voices, and a smell of roasted meat that made his mouth water, despite his preoccupation. He swallowed saliva and set foot on the ladder.

Isobel screamed.

The sound was cut off abruptly, as by a hand placed over her mouth, and three seconds later Jamie smashed in the shutter with a ferocious kick and dived headfirst into the room.

Lawyer Wilberforce yelped in shock. So did Isobel. The man had her pressed to the bed, and was on top of her in only his shirt, his hairy arse protruding obscenely between her white round thighs, glimmering in the candlelight.

Jamie reached the bed in two steps, grabbed Wilberforce by the shoulders, pulled him off Isobel, punched him in the face, and sent him staggering into the wall. He picked up the candlestick and bent to take one hasty glance between Isobel's legs, but saw neither blood nor any other sign of recent intrusion, so put down the candlestick, yanked her night rail down over her legs, lifted her off the bed, and headed for the window, then on second thought went back for a blanket.

Someone was calling up the stairs, wanting to know was anything wrong?

Jamie bared his teeth at Wilberforce and ripped the side of his hand across his own throat, ordering silence. The lawyer was on the floor, back pressed against the door, but at this made an earnest attempt to scrabble backward through it.

"I can't, I can't," Isobel was saying, breathless. He didn't know if she meant she couldn't climb down the ladder in the dark or was only hysterical, but he hadn't time to ask her. He hoisted her over his shoulder, threw the blanket on top of her, stood on the sill, and stepped backward out into the night.

The ladder, while stout enough for its purpose, hadn't been intended for elopements. The rung snapped under his foot and he slid most of the way to the ground, clinging to the rails in terror as the ladder slewed sideways. He hit the ground—still standing—and lost both his grip and Isobel. The ladder fell sideways with a clattering thud, Isobel with a thump and a stifled shriek.

He picked up the lass and ran for the mule, Isobel whimpering and digging her fingernails into his neck. He slapped her briefly on the bum to make her stop, put her up on the mule, untied it, and made for the road as the door of the inn opened and a truculent male voice said—from the safety of the lighted interior—"I see you, you bugger! I see you!"

Isobel said not a word on the way back to Helwater.

JOHN GREY WAS LYING in his bed, contentedly reading Mrs. Haywood's *Love in Excess; or, The Fatal Enquiry,* when he heard a great rustling and bumping in the corridor outside. Tom had gone to bed long since in the servants' attic, so Grey flung back the covers, reaching for his banyan. He had barely got this on when there was a brief, imperative thump at his door that shivered its boards, as though someone had kicked it.

Someone had.

He wrenched the door open and Jamie Fraser walked in, dripping wet, carrying someone wrapped in a blanket. Breathing heavily, he crossed the room and deposited his burden on Grey's rumpled bed with a grunt. The burden let out a small squeak and clutched the blanket round itself.

"Isobel?" Grey glanced wildly at Fraser. "What's happened? Is she hurt?"

"You need to soothe her and put her back where she belongs," Fraser said, in very decent German. This startled Grey nearly as much as the intrusion, though an instant's thought supplied the explanation—Isobel spoke French but not German.

"Jawohl," he replied, giving Fraser a sideways look. He hadn't known Fraser spoke German, and a brief thought of Stephan von Namtzen flashed through his mind. Christ, what might they have said to each other in Fraser's hearing? That didn't matter now, though.

"What's happened, my dear?"

Isobel was hunched on the edge of the bed, snuffling and hiccuping. Her face was bloated and red, her blond hair loose, damp and tangled about her shoulders. Grey sat down gingerly beside her and rubbed her back gently.

"I'b ad idiot," Isobel said thickly, and buried her face in her hands.

"She tried to elope with the lawyer—Wilberforce," Jamie said in English. "Her maid came and got me and I went after them." Jamie returned to German and acquainted Grey with the situation in a few blunt sentences, including his intelligence regarding Wilberforce's wife and the precise situation in which he had found the lawyer and Isobel.

"The *schwanzlutscher* hadn't penetrated her, but it was close enough to give her a shock," he said, looking down dispassionately on Isobel, who was slumping with exhaustion, her head leaning on Grey's shoulder as he put his arm about her.

"Bastard," Grey said. It was the same word in English and German, and Isobel shuddered convulsively. "You're safe, sweetheart," he murmured to her. "Don't worry. Everything will be all right." The wet blanket had slipped off her shoulders and puddled round her, and he saw with a pang that she was wearing a nightdress of sheer lawn, with *broderie Anglaise* inserts and pale pink ribbon at the neck. She'd gone prepared for her wedding night—only she hadn't been prepared at all, poor little creature.

"What did you do to the lawyer?" he asked Jamie in German. "You didn't kill him, did you?" It was pouring outside; he hoped he wouldn't have to go and hide Wilberforce's body.

"Nein." Fraser didn't elaborate, but squatted in front of Isobel.

"No one knows," he said to her softly, eyes intent on her face. "No one needs to know. Ever."

She didn't want to look at him; Grey could feel her resistance. But after a moment she lifted her head and nodded, her mouth compressed to stop it trembling.

"I—thank you," she blurted. Tears ran down her cheeks, but she wasn't sobbing or shivering anymore, and her body had begun to relax.

"It's all right, lass," Fraser said to her, still softly. He rose then and went to the door, hesitating there. Grey patted Isobel's hand and, leaving her, came across to see Fraser out.

"If you can get her back to her room without being seen, Betty will take care of her," Jamie said to Grey in a low voice. And then in German, "When she's calm, tell her to forget it. She won't, but I don't want her to feel that she is in my debt. It would be awkward for us both."

"She is, nonetheless. And she is an honorable woman. She'll want to repay you in some way. Let me think how best to handle it."

"I am obliged." Fraser spoke abstractedly, though, and his eyes were still on Isobel. "There is . . . if she . . ." His gaze switched suddenly to Grey's face.

Jamie's own face was rough with red stubble and lined with tiredness, his eyes dark and bloodshot. Grey could see that the knuckles of his left hand were swollen and the skin was broken; he'd likely punched Wilberforce in the mouth.

"There is a thing I want," Fraser said, very low-voiced, still in German. "But it cannot be blackmail or look like it in any way. If there were some means to suggest it very tactfully . . ."

"I see your opinion of my diplomacy has improved. What is it that you want?"

A brief smile touched Fraser's face, though it vanished almost at once.

"The wee lad," he said. "They make him wear a corset. I would like to see him free of it."

Grey was extremely surprised, but merely nodded.

"All right. I'll see about it."

"Not tonight," Fraser said hastily. Isobel had collapsed with a little sigh, her head on Grey's pillow, feet trailing on the floor.

"No," he agreed. "Not tonight."

He closed the door quietly behind Fraser and went to deal with the girl in his bed.

42

Point of Departure

TOM HAD THE LUGGAGE LOADED ONTO THE MULE, AND THE horses were waiting. Lord John embraced Lady Dunsany and—very gently—Isobel and shook hands with Lord Dunsany in farewell. The old man's hands were cold, and the bones as fragile in his grasp as dried twigs. He felt a pang, wondering if he would see Dunsany alive the next time he came—and a deeper pang of concern, realizing what the old man's death might mean to him, beyond the loss of a dear old friend.

Well . . . he'd cross that bridge when he came to it, and God send he wasn't coming to it just yet.

Outside, the weather was lowering, the first drops of rain already making wet spots on the flags. The horses' ears twitched and turned to and fro; they didn't mind rain and were fresh and eager to be off.

Jamie was holding Grey's gelding. He inclined his head respectfully and stood back to allow Grey to mount by himself. As Grey put his hand on the pommel, he heard a low Scots voice murmur in his ear:

"Queen's rook to king eight. Check."

Grey laughed out loud, a burst of exhilaration pushing aside his disquiet.

"Ha," he said, though without raising his voice. "Queen's bishop to knight four. Check. *And* mate, Mr . . . MacKenzie."

JAMIE COULDN'T ENLIST Keren's help this time. Instead, when Peggy the nursemaid came to fetch Willie back to the nursery for his tea, he asked her to take a note from him to Betty. Peggy couldn't read, and while she might tell someone he was meeting Betty, she couldn't know where. He particularly didn't wish to be overheard.

Betty was waiting for him behind the hay shed, fastidiously eyeing the immense manure pile with a curled lip. She switched the expression to him, raising one brow in inquiry.

"I've a wee thing for ye, Mrs. Betty," he said without preliminary.

"About time," she said, the curl melting into a coquettish smile. "Though not so wee as all *that,* I hope. And I also hope you have a better place than this for it, too," she added, with a glance at the manure. It was too late in the season for flies, and Jamie personally found the smell rather pleasant, but he could see she didn't share this opinion.

"The place will do well enough," he said. "Give me your hand, lass."

She did, looking expectant. The look changed to one of astonishment when he put the little purse into her palm.

"What's this?" she asked, but the chink of coins as she weighed the purse was answer enough.

"That's your dowry, lass," he said, smiling.

She looked at him suspiciously, plainly not knowing whether this was a joke or something else.

"A lass like you should be marrit," he said. "But it's not me ye should be marrying."

"Who says so?" she asked, fixing him with a fishy eye.

"I do," he replied equably. "Like the wicked Mr. Wilberforce, lass—I've got a wife."

She blinked.

"You do? Where?"

Ah, where indeed?

"She couldna come with me, when I was captured after Culloden. But she's alive still."

Lord, that she may be safe . . .

"But there's a man that wants ye bad, lass, and well ye know it. George Roberts is a fine man, and with that wee bawbee"—he nodded at the purse in her hand—"the two of ye could set up in a bit wee cottage, maybe."

She didn't say anything but pursed her lips, and he could see her envisioning the prospect.

"Ye should have your own hearth, lass—and a cradle by it, wi' your own bairn in it."

She swallowed and, for the first time since he'd known her, looked tremulous and uncertain.

"I—but—why?" She made a tentative gesture toward him with the purse, not quite offering it back to him. "Surely you need this?"

He shook his head and took a definite step back, waving her off.

"Believe me, lass. There's nothing I'd rather do with it. Take it wi' my blessing—and if ye like, ye can call your firstborn Jamie." He smiled at her, feeling the warmth in his chest rise into the back of his eyes.

She made an incoherent sound and took a pace toward him, rose onto her toes, and kissed him on the mouth.

A strangled gasp broke them apart, and Jamie turned to see Crusoe goggling at them from the corner of the shed.

"What the devil are *you* looking at?" Betty snapped at him.

"Not a thing, miss," Crusoe assured her, and put one large palm over his mouth.

43

Succession

October 26, 1760

GREY ARRIVED IN LONDON TO THE TOLLING OF PASSING BELLS.

"The king is dead!" cried the ballad sellers, the news chanters, the scribblers, the street urchins, their voices echoing through the city. "Long live the king!"

In the furious preparations and public preoccupations that attend a state funeral, the final arrests of the Irish Jacobite plotters who had called themselves the Wild Hunt took place without notice. Harold, Duke of Pardloe, neither ate nor slept for several days during this effort, nor did his brother, and it was in a state of mind somewhere between sleep and death that they came to Westminster Abbey on the night of the king's obsequies.

The Duke of Cumberland did not look well either. Grey saw Hal's eyes rest on Cumberland with an odd expression, somewhere between grim satisfaction and grudging sympathy. Cumberland had suffered a stroke not long before, and one side of his face still sagged, the eye on that side almost closed. The other was still pugnacious, though, and looked daggers at

Hal from the other side of Henry VII's chapel. Then the duke's attention was distracted by his own uncle, the Duke of Newcastle, who was crying, alternately mopping his eyes and using his glass to spy out the crowd and see who was there. A look of disgust crossed Cumberland's face, and he looked back down into the vault, where the huge purple-draped coffin sat somber and majestic in the light of six enormous silver candelabra, all ablaze.

"Cumberland's thinking he will descend there himself in no short time, I fear." Horace Walpole's soft whisper came from behind Grey, but he couldn't tell whether it was directed to him or merely Walpole making observations to himself. Horry talked all the time, and it seemed to make little difference whether anyone was listening.

Whatever you wanted to say about the royal family—and there was quite a lot you could say—they mostly displayed a becoming fortitude in their time of sorrow. The funeral of George II had been going on for more than two hours now, and Grey's own feet were mere blocks of ice from standing on the cold marble of the abbey floor, though Tom had made him put on two pair of stockings and his woolen drawers. His shins ached.

Newcastle had surreptitiously stepped onto the five-foot train of Cumberland's black cloak in order to avoid the mortal chill of the marble floor; Grey hoped he would neglect to get off before his brother started walking again. But Cumberland stood like a rock, despite a bad leg. He'd chosen—God knew why—to wear a dark-brown wig in the style called "Adonis," which went oddly with his distorted, bloated face. Maybe Horry was right.

The view down into the vault was impressive; he'd admit that much. George II was now once and forever safe from the Wild Hunt—and every other earthly threat. Three officers of the Irish

Brigades—so far—had been court-martialed quietly and condemned to hang for treason. The executions would be private, too. The monarchy was safe; the public would never know.

You did it, Charlie, Grey thought. *Goodbye.* And sudden tears made the candle flames blur bright and huge. No one noticed; there were a number of people moved to tears by the emotion of the occasion. Charles Carruthers had died alone in an attic in Canada and had no resting place. Grey had had Charlie's body burned, his ashes scattered, that carefully assembled packet of papers his only memorial.

"Such a relief, my dear," Walpole—who was exceedingly slight—was saying to Grenville. "I was positive they would pair me with a ten-year-old boy, and the young have so little conversation."

The huge fretted vault of the abbey rustled and chirped as though it were full of roosting bats, the noise a counterpoint to the constant tolling of bells overhead and the firing of minute guns outside. One went off, quite close, and Grey saw Hal close his eyes in sudden pain; his brother had one of his sick headaches and was having trouble staying on his feet. If there had been incense, it would likely have finished him off; he'd thought Hal was about to vomit when Newcastle scampered past him earlier, reeking loudly of bergamot and vetiver.

For all the lack of frankincense and priests saying Masses for the late king's soul, the ceremony was lavish enough to have pleased a cardinal. The bishop had blundered badly through the prayers, but no one noticed. Now the interminable anthem droned on and on, unmeasurably tedious. Grey found himself wondering whether it sounded any better to him than it would have to Jamie Fraser, with his inability to hear music. Mere rhythmic noise, in either case. It wasn't doing Hal any good; he gave a stifled moan.

He pulled his thoughts hurriedly away from Fraser, moving a little closer to Hal in case he fell over. His undisciplined thoughts promptly veered to Percy Wainwright. He'd stood thus in church with Percy—his new stepbrother—at the marriage of Grey's mother to Percy's stepfather. Close enough that their hands had found each other, hidden in the full skirts of their coats.

He didn't want to think about Percy. Obligingly, his thoughts veered straight back in the direction of Jamie Fraser.

Will you bloody go away? he thought irritably, and jerked his attention firmly to the sight before him: people were crammed into every crevice of the chapel, sitting on anything they could find. The white breath of the crowd mingled with the smell of smoke from the torches in the nave. If Hal did pass out, Grey thought, he wouldn't fall down; there wasn't room. Nonetheless, he moved closer, his elbow brushing Hal's.

"At least now we'll have a ruler who speaks English. More or less." Walpole's cynical remark drew Grey's wandering eye to the heir—the king, he should say. The new George looked just like all the Hanovers, he thought, the beaky nose and heavy-lidded, gelid eyes undiluted by any softer maternal influence; doubtless they'd all looked that way for a thousand years and would do so for another thousand. George III was only twenty-two, though, and Grey wondered how well he might withstand the influence of his uncle Cumberland, should the latter decide to shift his concerns from horse racing to politics.

Though perhaps his health would not recover enough to allow any meddling. He looked almost as ill as Hal did. Grey didn't suppose that the outcome of Siverly's court-martial had actually caused Cumberland to have a paralytic stroke, but the timing was coincidental.

The anthem plodded toward a conclusion, and people began to draw breath in relief—but it was a false amnesty; the ponderous refrain started up again, this time sung by a bevy of angel-faced little boys, and the audience relapsed into glazed endurance. Perhaps the point of funerals was to exhaust the mourners, thus numbing the more exigent emotions.

In spite of the tedium, Grey found something reassuring about the service, with its sheer solidity, its insistence upon permanence in the face of transience, the reliability of succession. Life was fragile, but life went on. King to king, father to son . . .

Father to son. And with that thought, all the disconnected, fragmentary, scattered fancies in his brain dropped suddenly into a single, vivid image: Jamie Fraser, seen from the back, looking over the horses in the paddock at Helwater. And beside him, standing on a rail and clinging to a higher one, William, Earl of Ellesmere. The alert cock of their heads, the set of their shoulders, the wide stance—just the same. If one had eyes to see, it was plain as the nose on the new king's face.

And now a great sense of peace filled his soul, as the anthem at last came to an end and a huge sigh filled the abbey. He remembered Jamie's face as they rode in to Helwater, alight as they saw the women on the lawn—with William.

He'd suspected it when he'd found Fraser in the chapel with Geneva Dunsany's coffin, just before her funeral. But now he knew, beyond doubt. Knew, too, why Fraser did not desire his freedom.

A sudden poke in the back jerked him from his revelation.

"I do believe Pardloe's going to die," Walpole said. A small, neat hand came through the narrow gap between the Grey brothers, holding a corked glass vial. "Would you care to use my salts?"

Startled, Grey looked at his brother. Hal's face was white as a sheet and running with sweat, his eyes huge and dilated, absolutely black with pain. He was swaying. Grey grabbed the salts with one hand, Hal's arm with the other.

By the combined effect of smelling salts and force of will, Hal remained on his feet, and the service came mercifully to an end ten minutes later.

George Grenville had come in a sedan chair, and his bearers were waiting on the embankment. Grenville generously put these at Hal's service, and he was taken off at the trot for Argus House, nearly insensible. Grey took leave of his friends as soon as he decently could and made his own way home on foot.

The dark streets near the abbey were thronged with the people of London, come out to pay their respects; they would file through all night, and much of the next day, before the vault was sealed again. Within a few minutes, though, Grey had made his way through the press and found himself more or less alone under the night sky, cloudy and cold with autumn's chill, nearly the same purple as the velvet shroud on the old king's coffin.

He felt both elated and peaceful, almost valedictory: a strange state of mind to experience in the wake of a funeral.

Part of it was Charlie, of course, and the knowledge that he had not failed his dead friend. Beyond that, though, was the knowledge that it lay within his power to do something equally important for the living one. He could keep James Fraser prisoner.

Rain began to fall, but it was a light drizzle, no more, and he did not hurry his step on that account. When he reached Argus House, he was fresh and damp, the smoke and stink of the crowd blown away, and in possession of a fine appetite. When he came in, though, his thoughts of supper were delayed by discovery of an equerry, waiting patiently in the foyer.

Stephan, he thought, seeing the distinctive mauve and green of the outlandish livery of the house of von Erdberg, and his heart jumped. Had something happened to the graf?

"My lord," said the servant, bowing. He bent and picked up a large, round, lidded basket that had been sitting on the floor and presented it as though it contained something of immense value, though the basket itself was rough and common. "His excellency the graf hopes you will accept this token of his friendship."

Deeply puzzled, Grey lifted the lid of the basket and, in the light of the candles, found a pair of bright dark eyes staring up at him from the face of a tiny, long-nosed black puppy, curled up on a white linen towel. The little hound had floppy ears and absurdly stumpy, powerful legs, with huge paws and a long, graceful tail whose tip beat in tentative greeting.

Grey laughed, utterly charmed, and gently picked the puppy up. It was a badger hound, specially bred by Stephan; he called them *Dackels,* an affectionate diminutive for *dachs-hund*—"badger hound." It put out a tiny pink tongue and very delicately licked his knuckles.

"Hallo, there," he said to the puppy. "Hungry? I am. Let's go and find some milk for you, shall we?" He dug in his pocket and offered a coin to the servant but found the man now holding a sealed note, which he put into Grey's hand with another obsequious bow.

Not wanting to set down the dog, he managed to break the seal with his thumb and open the note. In the light of the nearest sconce, he read Stephan's words, set down in German in a firm black hand.

Bring him when you come to visit me. We will perhaps hunt together again.

—S.

Helwater
December 21

It was cold in the loft, and his sleep-mazed mind groped among the icy drafts after the words still ringing in his mind.

Bonnie lad.

Wind struck the barn and went booming round the roof. A strong chilly draft with a scent of snow stirred the somnolence, and two or three of the horses shifted below, grunting and whickering. *Helwater.* The knowledge of the place settled on him, and the fragments of Scotland and Lallybroch cracked and flaked away, fragile as a skin of dried mud.

Helwater. Straw rustling under him, the ends poking through the rough ticking, prickling through his shirt. Dark air, alive around him.

Bonnie lad . . .

They'd brought down the Yule log to the house that afternoon, all the household taking part, the women bundled to the eyebrows, the men ruddy, flushed with the labor, staggering, singing, dragging the monstrous log with ropes, its rough skin packed with snow, a great furrow left where it passed, the snow plowed high on either side.

Willie rode atop the log, screeching with excitement, clinging to the rope. Once back at the house, Isobel had tried to teach him to sing "Good King Wenceslas," but it was beyond him, and he dashed to and fro, into everything, until his grandmother declared that he would drive her to distraction and told Peggy to take him to the stable to help Jamie and Crusoe bring in the fresh-cut branches of pine and fir.

Thrilled, Willie rode on Jamie's saddlebow to the grove and stood obediently on a stump where Jamie had put him, safe out of the way of the axes while the boughs were cut down. Then he helped to load the greenery, clutching two or three fragrant, mangled twigs to his chest, dutifully chucking these in the general direction of the huge basket, then running back again for more, heedless of where his burden actually landed.

Jamie turned over, wriggling deeper into the nest of blankets, drowsy, remembering. He'd kept it up, the wean had, back and forth, back and forth, though red in the face and panting, until he dropped the very last branch on the pile. Jamie had looked down to find Willie beaming up at him with pride, laughed, and said on impulse, "Aye, that's a bonnie lad. Come on. Let's go home."

William had fallen asleep on the ride home, his head heavy as a cannonball in its woolen cap against Jamie's chest. Jamie had dismounted carefully, holding the child in one arm, but Willie had wakened, blinked groggily at Jamie, and said, "WEN-sess-loss," clear as a bell, then fallen promptly back asleep. He'd waked properly by the time he was handed over to Nanny Elspeth, though, and as Jamie walked away, he had heard Willie, as he walked away, telling Nanny, "I a bonnie lad!"

But those words came out of his dreams from somewhere else, and long ago. Had his own father said that to him once?

He thought so, and for an instant—just an instant—was with his father and his brother, Willie, excited beyond bearing, holding the first fish he'd ever caught by himself, slimy and flapping, both of them laughing at him, with him in joy. *"Bonnie lad!"*

Willie. God, Willie. I'm so glad they gave him your name. He seldom thought of his brother, but every now and then, he could feel Willie with him; sometimes his mother or his father. More often, Claire.

I wish ye could see him, Sassenach, he thought. *He's a bonnie lad. Loud and obnoxious,* he added with honesty, *but bonnie.*

What would his own parents think of William? They had neither of them lived to see any of their children's children.

He lay for some time, his throat aching, listening to the dark, hearing the voices of his dead pass by in the wind. His thoughts grew vague and his grief eased, comforted by the knowledge of love, still alive in the world. Sleep came near again.

He touched the rough crucifix that lay against his chest and whispered to the moving air, "Lord, that she might be safe, she and my children."

Then turned his cheek to her reaching hand and touched her through the veils of time.

Author's Notes

The Wild Hunt

The concept of the Wild Hunt—a spectral horde seen rushing through the night skies or above the ground, hunting for things unknown—doesn't come from Celtic mythology but from that of Central/Northern/Western Europe. Celtic mythology being the very plastic and inclusive thing that it is (*vide* the way it historically entwined itself easily with Catholic theology in Scotland and Ireland, where people might say a prayer to St. Bride in one breath, and a charm against piskies in the next)—and the inability of any Celt to pass up a good story—and it's no wonder that you find variations on the Wild Hunt in the Celtic lands as well.

In some forms of these stories, the horde consists of faeries, in others, the "hunt" consists of the souls of the dead. Either way, it isn't something you want to meet on a dark night—or a moonlit one, either. In the British forms, the best-known "wild hunt" tales are "Tam Lin" and "Thomas the Rhymer" (there are dozens of variations), in which a young man meets the Queen of Faerie and is more or less abducted by her.

The notion of abduction of humans by the hunt is common to almost all hunt tales, though—and it may be this aspect that caused our Irish Jacobite plotters to adopt this *nom de guerre*, as they planned to abduct George II. Then again, it might have been a reference to and natural extension from the older name, "Wild Geese," as the Irish Jacobites of the late seventeenth century called themselves. The idea of the *teind*—the tithe to hell—is from "Tam Lin," and likely a word that would have resonance to people who lived by a code of honor, to whom betrayal and treason would carry a heavy price.

The host is riding from Knocknarea
And over the grave of Clooth-na-Bare;
Caoilte tossing his burning hair,
And Niamh calling Away, come away:
Empty your heart of its mortal dream.
The winds awaken, the leaves whirl round,
Our cheeks are pale, our hair is unbound,
Our breasts are heaving our eyes are agleam,
Our arms are waving our lips are apart;
And if any gaze on our rushing band,
We come between him and the deed of his hand,
We come between him and the hope of his heart.
The host is rushing 'twixt night and day,
And where is there hope or deed as fair?
Caoilte tossing his burning hair,
And Niamh calling Away, come away.
—William Butler Yeats, "The Hosting of the Sidhe"

[Footnote: An interesting modern variation on the Wild Hunt is the BBC television series *Quatermass and the Pit,* by Nigel Kneale, broadcast in December/January of 1958/59. In this science fiction serial, the concept of the Wild Hunt is used as a very literal metaphor for the murderous and bestial impulses of humanity (truly creepy in spots, hilarious in others; great acting!).]

Thomas Lally

Thomas Arthur, Comte de Lally, Baron Tollendal, is one of the real historical figures who appear in this book, along with George II, George III, and Horace Walpole. Born of an Irish father and a French mother (from whom he inherited his titles), he served with the famous Irish Brigade at Fontenoy and was a French general during the Seven Years War. He did in fact serve as Charles Edward Stuart's aide de camp during the battle of Falkirk, in the '45, and was mixed up in various Jacobite plots, including one hatched in Ireland in the 1760's.

I *have* taken one small liberty with Thomas Lally, though. He was captured by the British following the Siege of Pondicherry, in India, and taken to England in 1761, not 1760. Given his real involvement with the Irish Jacobites—and his obvious spiritual kinship with Jamie Fraser as a prisoner of the English—I thought the minor temporal dislocation was worth it.

An interesting—if grim—footnote to Lally's life is that he was indeed Just Furious about slurs cast on his reputation in France, following the French defeat at Pondicherry, and agitated to be sent back to France to defend himself at a court-martial. After five years of steady badgering, the British *did* send him back to France—where, in 1766, he was promptly convicted of treason and beheaded.

Twenty years later, a French court reviewed the evidence and reversed his conviction, which I trust he found satisfying.

Bog Bodies

I've always found bog bodies—the corpses of people found preserved in peat bogs—fascinating. The garb and accoutrements of the body found on Inchcleraun (which is a real place, and has a real monastery) are a composite of such items found on or with bog bodies from Europe. My thanks to the Los Angeles Museum of Natural History for hosting a special exhibition on bog bodies that provided me with a great deal of useful information, and to the British Museum, whose Lindow Man has always spoken powerfully to me.

George II, George III, and Horace Walpole

I love Horace Walpole, as does anyone with an interest in eighteenth-century English society. The fourth son of Robert Walpole, who was

England's first prime minister (though he himself never used the title), Horace was not politically active, nor was he socially important, physically attractive, or otherwise very noticeable. He was, however, intelligent, observant, witty, sarcastic, and apparently never suffered from writer's cramp. His letters provide one of the most detailed and intimate views of English society during the mid-eighteenth century, and I'm indebted to one of these missives for Lord John's experience of King George II's state funeral.

Below is the text of Walpole's account of the funeral; you may find it interesting to compare this with the fictionalized view in Chapter 43. The temptation, when presented with such eloquent historical largesse, is to use it all, but that's a temptation that should, by and large, be resisted. The point of fiction is to tell a particular story, and too much embroidery can't but detract, no matter how fascinating.

In this instance, the point of showing you the king's funeral was primarily that it provided Lord John with his moment of enlightenment regarding Jamie's motive for remaining at Helwater. Secondarily, it shows a historical turning point that a) anchors the reader in time, b) metaphorically underlines the conclusion of the Grey brothers' quest, c) marks a turning point in Lord John's relationship with Jamie Fraser, and d) opens the door to a new phase of both personal and public history—for George III (who was the grandson, not the son, of George II) is, of course, the king from whom the American colonies revolted, and we see in the later books of the Outlander series just how *that* affects the lives of Lord John, Jamie Fraser, and William.

To George Montagu, Esq.
Arlington-street, November 13, 1760.

. . . Do you know, I had the curiosity to go to the burying t'other night; I had never seen a royal funeral; nay, I walked as a rag of quality, which I found would be, and so it was, the easiest way of seeing it. It is absolutely a noble sight. The prince's chamber, hung

with purple, and a quantity of silver lamps, the coffin under a canopy of purple velvet, and six vast chandeliers of silver on high stands, had a very good effect. The ambassador from Tripoli and his son were carried to see that chamber. The procession, through a line of foot-guards, every seventh man bearing a torch, the horse-guards lining the outside, their officers with drawn sabres and crape sashes on horseback, the drums muffled, the fifes, bells tolling, and minute guns,—all this was very solemn. But the charm was the entrance of the abbey, where we were received by the dean and chapter in rich robes, the choir and almsmen bearing torches; the whole abbey so illuminated, that one saw it to greater advantage than by day; the tombs, long aisles, and fretted roof, all appearing distinctly, and with the happiest chiara scuro. There wanted nothing but incense, and little chapels here and there, with priests saying mass for the repose of the defunct; yet one could not complain of its not being catholic enough. I had been in dread of being coupled with some boy of ten years old; but the heralds were not very accurate, and I walked with George Grenville, taller and older, to keep me in countenance. When we came to the chapel of Henry the seventh, all solemnity and decorum ceased; no order was observed, people sat or stood where they could or would; the yeomen of the guard were crying out for help, oppressed by the immense weight of the coffin; the bishop read sadly, and blundered in the prayers; the fine chapter, Man that is born of a woman, was chaunted, not read; and the anthem, besides being immeasurably tedious, would have served as well for a nuptial. The real serious part was the figure of the duke of Cumberland, heightened by a thousand melancholy circumstances. He had a dark brown adonis, and a cloak of black cloth, with a train of five yards. Attending the funeral of a father could not be pleasant: his leg extremely bad, yet forced to stand upon it near two hours; his face bloated and distorted with his late paralytic stroke, which has affected too one of his eyes, and placed over the mouth of the vault, into which, in all probability, he must himself so soon descend; think how unpleasant a situation! He bore it all with a firm and unaffected countenance. This grave scene was fully contrasted by the burlesque duke of Newcastle. He fell into a fit of crying the moment he came into the chapel, and flung himself back in a stall, the archbishop hovering over him with a smelling-bottle; but in two minutes his curiosity got the better of his hypocrisy, and he ran about the chapel with his glass to spy who was or was not there, spying with one hand, and mopping his eyes with the other. Then returned the fear of catching cold; and the duke of Cumberland, who was sinking with heat, felt himself weighed down, and turning round, found it was the duke of Newcastle standing upon his train, to avoid the chill of the marble. It was very theatric to look down into the vault, where the coffin lay, attended by mourners with lights. Clavering, the groom of the bed-chamber, refused to sit up with the body, and was dismissed by the king's order.

I have nothing more to tell you, but a trifle, a very trifle. The king of Prussia has totally defeated marshal Daun. This, which would have been prodigious news a month ago, is nothing today; it only takes its turn among the questions, "Who is to be groom of the bed-chamber? what is sir T. Robinson to have?" I have been to Leicester-fields today; the crowd was immoderate; I don't believe it will continue so. Good night.

Yours ever.

Remarks on Some Eighteenth-Century Words and Foreign Phrases

"making love"—This term, like some other period phrases, exists in modern speech, but has changed its meaning. It was not a synonym for "engaging in sexual relations," but was strictly a male activity and meant any sort of amorous wooing behavior, including the writing or reading of romantic poetry to a young woman, giving her flowers, whispering sweet nothings in her ear, or going so far as kissing, cupping (breasts, we assume), toying (pretty open-ended), etc.—but certainly not including sexual intercourse.

"gagging" (e.g., "What had the gagging wee bitch been saying?")—This is a Scots word (not Gaelic), meaning "hoaxing," from which we might deduce an etymology that led to the present-day "gag," meaning a joke of some sort.

"imbranglement"—period colloquialism; an onomatopoetic word that means just what it sounds like: complicated and involuntary entanglement, whether physical, legal, or emotional.

whisky vs. whiskey—Scotch whisky is spelled without an "e" and Irish whiskey is spelled with an "e." Consequently, I've observed this geographical peculiarity, depending on the location where the substance is produced and/or being ingested.

pixilated—nowadays, you occasionally see this term (spelled as "pixelated") used to mean "rendered digitally, in pixels," or "of unusably low-resolution," in reference to a photographic image. It was used as a reference to stop-frame photographic technique even before the development of digital photography, and spelled as "pixilated" it was used as a synonym for drunkenness from the mid-nineteenth century. The original meaning, though, was very probably a literal reference to being "away with the pixies (fairies)"—i.e., delusional, and Jamie uses the word in this fashion.

Humpty-Dumpty—The first known *published* version of this nursery rhyme is from 1803, but there's considerable evidence for the name and general concept—as well as, perhaps, earlier versions of the rhyme—existing prior to this. "Humpty dumpty" is a documented slang term from the eighteenth century, used to refer to a short, clumsy person, and while Tom Byrd doesn't use the name, he's obviously familiar with the concept.

Plan B—I had some concern from one editor and one beta-reader as to whether "Plan B" sounded anachronistic. I didn't think so, and explained my reasoning thus:

Dear Bill—

Well, I thought about that. On the one hand, there is "Plan 9 from Outer Space" and the like, which would certainly lead one to suppose "Plan B" is modern. And it certainly is common (modern) short-hand for any backup contingency.

On the other hand . . . they certainly had plans (as used in Lord John's sense) in the 18th century—and presumably, a man with an orderly mind would have listed his plans either as 1, 2, 3, or A, B, C (if not I, II, III). WhatImeantersay is, it could reasonably be regarded as simple common-sense usage, rather than as a figure of speech—and IF so, it isn't anachronistic.

If you think it might trouble folk unduly, though, I can certainly reorder his lordship's language, if not his plans.

To which the editor luckily replied:

Dear Diana

That all makes perfect sense. In fact, the more I think about it, the more it sounds like the natural expression of an orderly 18th-century mind. So let's keep it.

Scots/Scottish/Scotch—As I've observed in the notes to other books, the word "Scotch," as used to refer to natives of Scotland, dropped out of favor in the mid-twentieth century, when the SNP started gaining power. Prior to that point in history, though, it was commonly used by both Scots and non-Scots—certainly by English people. I don't hold with foisting anachronistic attitudes of political correctness onto historical persons, so have retained the common period usage.

"**Yellow-johns**" and "**swarthy-johns**" were both common Irish insults of the period used in reference to the English, God knows why (cf. *Ireland and the Jacobite Cause, 1685–1766: A Fatal Attachment,* by Éamonn Ó Ciardha).

Gàidhlig/Gaeilge

The Celtic tongue spoken in Ireland and Scotland was essentially the same language—called "Erse"—until about 1600, at which point local variations became more pronounced, followed by a big spelling shift that made the Gaelic of the Highlands (*Gàidhlig*) distinct from the Irish Gaelic (*Gaeilge*). The two languages still have much in common (rather like the relation between Spanish and Italian), but would have been recognizably different even in 1760.

Now, with reference to my own novels, I did know that Gaelic was the native tongue of the Scottish Highlands, when I began writing *Outlander.* Finding someone in Phoenix, Arizona (in 1988), who *spoke* Gaelic was something else. I finally found a bookseller (Steinhof's Foreign Books, in Boston) who could provide me with an English/Gaelic dictionary, and that's what I used as a source when writing *Outlander.*

When the book was sold and the publisher gave me a three-book contract, I said to my husband, "I think I really must *see* the place," and we went to Scotland. Here I found a much bigger and more sophisticated Gaelic/English dictionary, and that's what I used while writing *Dragonfly in Amber.*

And then I met Iain. I got a wonderful letter from Iain MacKinnon Taylor, who said all kinds of delightful things regarding my books, and then said, "There is just this one small thing, which I hesitate to mention. I was born on the Isle of Harris and am a native Gaelic-speaker—and I think you must be getting your Gaelic from a dictionary." He then generously volunteered his time and talent to provide translations for the Gaelic in subsequent books, and the Gaelic in *Voyager, Drums of Autumn, The Fiery Cross, The Outlandish Companion,* and *A Breath of Snow and Ashes* is due to Iain's efforts, and those of his twin brother Hamish and other members of his family still residing on Harris.

At this point, Iain was no longer able to continue doing the translations, but I was extremely fortunate in that a friend, Catherine MacGregor, was not only a student of Gaelic herself but was also a friend of Catherine-Ann MacPhee, world-famous Gaelic singer, and a native speaker from Barra. The two Cathys very generously did the Gaelic for *The Exile* and *An Echo in the Bone.*

And then I rashly wrote a book that not only involved Scottish Gaelic *and* Irish, but actually employed the language as a plot element. Fortunately, Cathy and Cathy-Ann were more than equal to the challenge and dragooned their friend Kevin Dooley, musician, author, and fluent Irish speaker, to provide those bits as well.

One thing about Gaelic is that it doesn't look *anything* like it sounds—and so my ever-helpful Gaelic translators kindly offered to make a recording of themselves reading the bits of Gaelic dialogue in the book aloud, for those curious as to what it really sounds like. You can find this recording (and a phonetic pronunciation guide) on my website at www.DianaGabaldon.com, or on my Facebook page at www.facebook.com/AuthorDianaGabaldon.

Gaelic and Other Non-English Terms

Here, I've just listed brief common expressions that aren't explicitly translated in context.

Moran taing—thank you

Oidhche mhath—good night

Mo mhic—my son

Scheisse!—Shit! (German)

Carte blanche—literally "white card," used as an expression in picquet to note that one holds a hand with no points. In more general parlance, it means one has the freedom to do anything in a given situation, as no rules apply.

Sixième—Sixth

Septième—Seventh

Turn the page for a
special early preview of

Written in My Own
Heart's Blood,

the next Outlander novel after
An Echo in the Bone.

laire, having just discovered that Jamie is alive, meets Jamie's ister, the recently widowed Jenny Murray, in Philadelphia, n the wake of other traumatic discoveries . . .

IRS. FIGG WAS SMOOTHLY SPHERICAL, GLEAMINGLY BLACK, nd inclined to glide silently up behind one like a menacing ball-earing.

"What's *this?*" she barked, manifesting herself suddenly be-ind Jenny.

"Holy Mother of God!" Jenny whirled, eyes round and hand ressed to her chest. "Who in God's name are you?"

"This is Mrs. Figg," I said, feeling a surreal urge to laugh, lespite—or maybe because of—recent events. "Lord John Grey's cook. And Mrs. Figg, this is Mrs. Murray. My, um . . . ny . . ."

"Your good-sister," Jenny said firmly. She raised one black yebrow. "If ye'll have me, still?" Her look was straight and open, nd the urge to laugh changed abruptly into an equally strong rge to burst into tears. Of all the unlikely sources of succor I ould have imagined. . . . I took a deep breath and put out my and.

"I'll have you."

Her small firm fingers wove through mine, and as simply as

that, it was done. No need for apologies or spoken forgiveness. She'd never had to wear the mask that Jamie did. What she thought and felt was there in her eyes, those slanted blue cat-eyes she shared with her brother. She knew me, now, for what I was—and knew I loved—had always loved—her brother with all my heart and soul—despite the minor complications of being presently married to someone else. And that knowledge obliterated years of mistrust, suspicion, and injury.

She heaved a sigh, eyes closing for an instant, then opened them and smiled at me, mouth trembling only a little.

"Well, fine and dandy," said Mrs. Figg, shortly. She narrowed her eyes and rotated smoothly on her axis, taking in the panorama of destruction. The railing at the top of the stair had been ripped off, and cracked banisters, dented walls, and bloody smudges marked the path of William's descent. Shattered crystals from the chandelier littered the floor, glinting festively in the light that poured through the open front door, the door itsel hanging drunkenly from one hinge.

"*Merde* on toast," Mrs. Figg murmured. She turned abruptly to me, her small black-currant eyes still narrowed. "Where's hi lordship?"

"Ah," I said. This was going to be rather sticky, I saw. Whil deeply disapproving of most people, Mrs. Figg was devoted t John. She wasn't going to be at all pleased to hear that he'd bee abducted by—

"For that matter, where's my brother?" Jenny inquired, glanc ing round as though expecting Jamie to appear suddenly ou from under the settee.

"Oh," I said. "Hm. Well . . ." Possibly worse than sticky. Be cause . . .

"And where's my Sweet William?" Mrs. Figg demanded, snif ing the air. "He's been here; I smell that stinky cologne he put on his linen." She nudged a dislodged chunk of plaster disapprovingly with the toe of her shoe.

I took another long, deep breath, and a tight grip on what remained of my sanity.

"Mrs. Figg," I said, "perhaps you would be so kind as to make us all a cup of tea?"

Having just discovered Jamie Fraser is his true father, William leaves Lord John's house in a whirlwind of shock and rage . . .

WILLIAM RANSOM, NINTH EARL OF ELLESMERE, VISCOUNT Ashness, shoved his way through the crowds on Broad Street, oblivious to the complaints of those rebounding from his impact.

He didn't know where he was going, or what he might do when he got there. All he knew was that he'd burst if he stood still.

His head throbbed like an inflamed boil. Everything throbbed. His hand—he'd probably broken something, but he didn't care. His heart, pounding and sore inside his chest. His foot, for God's sake, what, had he kicked something? He lashed out viciously at a loose cobblestone and sent it rocketing through a crowd of geese, who set up a huge cackle and lunged at him, hissing and beating at his shins with their wings.

Feathers and goose shit flew wide, and the crowd scattered in all directions.

"Bastard!" shrieked the goose-girl, and struck at him with her crook, catching him a shrewd thump on the ear. "Devil take you, *Schmutziger Bastard*!"

This sentiment was echoed by a number of other angry voices, and he veered into an alley, pursued by shouts and honks of agitation.

He rubbed his throbbing ear, lurching into buildings as he passed, oblivious to everything but the one word throbbing ever louder in his head. *Bastard*.

"Bastard!" he said out loud, and shouted, "Bastard, bastard, *bastard*!!" at the top of his lungs, hammering at the brick wall next to him with a clenched fist.

"Who's a bastard?" said a curious voice behind him. He swung round to see a young woman looking at him with some interest. Her eyes moved slowly down his frame, taking note of the heaving chest, the bloodstains on the facings of his uniform coat and green smears of goose shit on his breeches, reached his silver buckled shoes, and returned to his face with more interest.

"I am," he said, hoarse and bitter.

"Oh, really?" She left the shelter of the doorway in which she'd been standing, and came across the alley to stand right in front of him. She was tall and slim, and had a very fine pair of high young breasts—which were clearly visible under the thin muslin of her shift, because while she had a silk petticoat, she wore neither stays nor bodice. No cap, either—her hair fell loose over her shoulders. A whore.

"I'm partial to bastards, myself," she said, and touched him lightly on the arm. "What kind of bastard are you? A wicked one? An evil one?"

"A sorry one," he said, and scowled when she laughed. She saw the scowl, but didn't pull back.

"Come in," she said, and took his hand. "You look as though you could do with a drink." He saw her glance at his knuckles, burst and bleeding, and she caught her lower lip behind small white teeth. She didn't seem afraid, though, and he found himself drawn unprotesting into the shadowed doorway after her.

What did it matter? he thought, with a sudden savage weariness. *What did anything matter?*

IT WASN'T YET MIDDAY, and the only voices in the house were the distant chitter of women. No one was visible in the parlor as they passed, and no one appeared as she led him up a foot-marked staircase to her room. It gave him an odd feeling, as though he might be invisible. He found the notion a comfort; he couldn't bear himself.

She went in before him and threw open the shutters. He wanted to tell her to close them; he felt wretchedly exposed in the flood of sunlight. But it was summer; the room was hot and airless, and he was already sweating heavily. Air swirled in, heavy with the odor of tree sap, and the sun glowed briefly on the smooth top of her head, like the gloss on a fresh conker. She turned and smiled at him.

"First things first," she announced briskly. "Throw off your coat and waistcoat before you suffocate." Not waiting to see whether he would take this suggestion, she turned to reach for the basin and ewer. She filled the basin and stepped back, motioning him toward the wash-stand, where a towel and a much-used sliver of soap stood on worn wood.

"I'll fetch us a drink, shall I?" And with that, she was gone, bare feet pattering busily down the stairs.

Mechanically, he began to undress. He blinked stupidly at the basin, but then recalled that in the better sort of house, sometimes a man was required to wash his parts first. He'd encountered the custom once before, but on that occasion, the whore had performed the ablution for him—plying the soap to such effect that the first encounter had ended right there in the washbasin.

The memory made the blood flame up in his face again, and he ripped at his flies, popping off a button. He was still throbbing all over, but the sensation was becoming more centralized.

His hands were unsteady, and he cursed under his breath, reminded by the broken skin on his knuckles of his unceremonious exit from his father's—no, *not* his bloody father's house. Lord John's.

"You bloody *bastard*!" he said under his breath. "You knew, you knew all along!" That infuriated him almost more than the horrifying revelation of his own paternity—that his stepfather, whom he'd loved, whom he'd trusted more than anyone on earth—that Lord John bloody Grey had lied to him his whole life!

Everyone had lied to him.

Everyone.

He felt suddenly as though he'd broken through a crust of frozen snow and plunged straight down into an unsuspected river beneath. Swept away into black breathlessness beneath the ice, helpless, voiceless, a feral chill clawing at his heart.

There was a small sound behind him and he whirled by instinct, aware only when he saw the young whore's appalled face that he was weeping savagely, tears running down his own face, and his wet, half-hard cock flopping out of his breeches.

"Go away," he croaked, making a frantic effort to tuck himself away.

She didn't go away, but came toward him, decanter in one hand and a pair of pewter cups in the other.

"Are you all right?" she asked, eyeing him sideways. "Here, let me pour you a drink. You can tell me all about it."

"No!"

She came on toward him, but more slowly. Through his swimming eyes he saw the twitch of her mouth as she saw his cock.

"I meant the water for your poor hands," she said, clearly trying not to laugh. "I will say as you're a real gentleman, though."

"I'm not!"

She blinked.

"Is it an insult to call you a gentleman?"

Overcome with fury at the word, he lashed out blindly, knock-ng the decanter from her hand. It burst in a spray of glass and heap wine, and she cried out as the red soaked through her pet-icoat.

"You *bastard*!" she shrieked, and drawing back her arm, threw he cups at his head. She didn't hit him, and they clanged and olled away across the floor. She was turning toward the door, rying out, "Ned! Ned!" when he lunged and caught her.

He only wanted to stop her shrieking, stop her bringing up vhatever male enforcement the house employed. He got a hand n her mouth, yanking her back from the door, grappling one-anded to try to control her flailing arms.

"I'm sorry, I'm sorry!" he kept saying. "I didn't mean—I don't nean—oh, bloody *hell*!" She caught him abruptly in the nose vith her elbow and he dropped her, backing away with a hand to is face, blood dripping through his fingers.

Her face was marked with red where he'd held her, and her yes were wild. She backed away, scrubbing at her mouth with he back of her hand.

"Get . . . *out*!" she gasped.

He didn't need telling twice. He rushed past her, shouldered is way past a burly man charging up the stairs, and ran down he alley, realizing only when he reached the street that he was in is shirtsleeves, having left coat and waistcoat behind, and his reeches were undone.

"Ellesmere!" said an appalled voice nearby. He looked up in orror, to find himself the cynosure of several English officers, ncluding Alexander Lindsay, Earl Balcarres.

"Good Christ, Ellesmere, what happened?" Sandy was by way

of being a friend, and was already pulling a voluminous, snow handkerchief from his sleeve. He clapped this to William's nose pinching his nostrils and insisting that he put his head back.

"Have you been set upon and robbed?" one of the others de manded. "God! This filthy place!"

He felt at once comforted by their company—and hideousl embarrassed by it. He was not one of them; not any longer.

"Was it? Was it robbery?" another said, glaring round eagerl "We'll find the bastards who did it, 'pon my honor we will! We' get your property back and teach whoever did it a lesson!"

Blood was running down the back of his throat, harsh an iron-tasting, and he coughed, but did his best to nod and shru simultaneously. He *had* been robbed. But no one was ever goin to give him back what he'd lost today.

Meanwhile, outside Philadelphia, Lord John and Jamie con tinue an Interesting Conversation . . .

HE'D BEEN QUITE RESIGNED TO DYING; HAD EXPECTED I from the moment that he'd blurted out, "I have had carn knowledge of your wife." The only question in his mind ha been whether Fraser would shoot him, stab him, or eviscerat him with his bare hands.

To have the injured husband regard him calmly and sa merely, "Oh? Why?" was not merely unexpected, but . . . inf mous. Absolutely infamous.

"Why?" John Grey repeated, incredulous. "Did you say '*why*'?

"I did. And I should appreciate an answer."

Now that Grey had both eyes open, he could see that Fraser outward calm was not quite so impervious as he'd first suppose There was a pulse beating in Fraser's temple, and he'd shifted hi veight a little, like a man might do in the vicinity of a tavern rawl, not quite ready to commit violence, but readying himself o meet it. Perversely, Grey found this sight steadying.

"What do you bloody *mean,* 'why'?" he said, suddenly irriated. "And why aren't you fucking dead?"

"I often wonder that myself," Fraser replied politely. "I take it e thought I was?"

"Yes, and so did your wife! Do you have the faintest idea what he knowledge of your death *did* to her?"

The dark blue eyes narrowed just a trifle.

"Are ye implying that the news of my death deranged her to uch an extent that she lost her reason and took ye to her bed by orce? Because," he went on, neatly cutting off Grey's heated eply, "unless I've been seriously misled regarding your own naure, it would take substantial force to compel ye to any such ction. Or am I wrong?"

The eyes stayed narrow. Grey stared back at them. Then he losed his own eyes briefly and rubbed both hands hard over his ace, like a man waking from a nightmare. He dropped his hands nd opened his eyes again.

"You are not misled," he said through clenched teeth. "And ou *are* wrong."

Fraser's ruddy eyebrows shot up—in genuine astonishment, e thought.

"Ye went to her because—from *desire*?" His voice rose, too. And she let ye? I dinna believe it."

The color was creeping up Fraser's tanned neck, vivid as a limbing rose. Grey had seen that happen before, and decided ecklessly that the best—the only—defense was to lose his own emper first. It was a relief.

"We thought you were *dead,* you bloody arsehole!" he said, urious. "Both of us! Dead! And we—we—took too much to drink one night—very much too much . . . we spoke of you . . . and . . . Damn you, neither one of us was making love to the other—we were fucking *you!*"

Fraser's face went abruptly blank and his jaw dropped. Grey enjoyed one split-second of satisfaction at the sight, before a massive fist came up hard beneath his ribs and he hurtled backward, staggered a few steps further, and fell. He lay in the leaves, completely winded, mouth opening and closing like an automaton's.

All right, then, he thought dimly. *Bare hands it is.*

The hands wrapped themselves in his shirt and jerked him to his feet. He managed to stand, and a wisp of air seeped into his lungs. Fraser's face was an inch from his. Fraser was in fact so close that he couldn't see the man's expression—only a close-up view of two bloodshot blue eyes, both of them berserk. That was enough. He felt quite calm now. It wouldn't take long.

"You tell me exactly what happened, ye filthy wee pervert," Fraser whispered, his breath hot on Grey's face and smelling of ale. He shook Grey slightly. "Every word. Every motion. *Everything.*"

Grey got just enough breath to answer.

"No," he said definitely. "Go ahead and kill me."

Kidnapped and imprisoned in a hydroelectric maintenance tunnel under a dam, Jem rides the workers' train toward whatever awaits him in the dark . . .

HE MUST BE GETTING NEAR THE END OF THE TUNNEL. JEM could tell by the way the air pushed back against his face. All he could see was the little red light on the train's dashboard—di

ou call it a dashboard on a train? he wondered. He didn't want
) stop, because that meant he'd have to get out of the train,
ıto the dark. But the train was running out of track, so there
'asn't much else he could do.

He pulled back a little bit on the lever that made the train go,
nd it slowed down. More. Just a little more, and the lever clicked
ıto a kind of slot and the train stopped with a little jerk that
ıade him stumble and grab the edge of the cab.

An electric train didn't make any engine noise, but the wheels
ıttled on the track and the train made squeaks and clunks as it
ıoved. When it stopped, the noise stopped too. It was really
uiet.

"Hey!" he said out loud, because he didn't want to listen to
is heart beating. The sound echoed, and he looked up, startled.
1um had said the tunnel was really high, more than thirty feet,
ut he'd forgot that. The idea that there was a lot of empty space
anging over him that he couldn't see bothered him a lot. He
wallowed, and stepped out of the tiny engine, holding on to the
ame with one hand.

"Hey!" he shouted at the invisible ceiling. "Are there any bats
p there?"

Silence. He'd kind of been hoping there *were* bats. He wasn't
fraid of them—there were bats in the old broch, and he liked to
t and watch them come out to hunt in the summer evenings.
ut he was alone. Except for the dark.

His hands were sweating. He let go of the metal cab and
rubbed both hands on his jeans. Now he could hear himself
reathing, too.

"Crap," he whispered under his breath. That made him feel
etter, so he said it again. Maybe he ought to be praying instead,
ut he didn't feel like that, not yet.

There was a door, Mum said. At the end of the tunnel. It led into the service chamber, where the big turbines could be lifte up from the dam if they needed fixing. Would the door b locked?

Suddenly he realized that he'd stepped away from the trai and he didn't know whether he was facing the end of the tunn or back the way he'd come. In a panic, he blundered to and fr hands out, looking for the train. He tripped over part of th track and fell sprawling. He lay there for a second saying, "Cra crap-crap-crap-*crap*!" because he'd skinned both knees and th palm of his hand, but he was OK, really, and now he knew whe the track was, so he could follow it and not get lost.

He got up, wiped his nose, and shuffled slowly along, kickin the track every few steps to be sure he stayed with it. He though he was in front of where the train had stopped, so it didn't reall matter which way he was going—either he'd find the train c he'd find the end of the tunnel. And then the door. If it *w* locked, maybe—

Something like an electric shock ran right through him. H gasped and fell over backward. The only thing in his mind wa the idea that somebody had hit him with a light saber like Luk Skywalker's, and for a minute, he thought maybe whoever it wa had cut off his head.

He couldn't feel his body, and could see in his mind his bod lying bleeding in the dark and his head sitting right there on th train tracks in the dark, not being able to see his body and n even knowing it wasn't attached anymore. He made a breathle kind of a noise that was trying to be a scream, but it made h stomach move and he felt that, he *felt* it, and suddenly he felt lot more like praying.

"Gratia . . . Deo!" he managed to gasp. It was what Grandd said when he talked about a fight or killing something and th

wasn't quite that sort of thing, but it seemed like a good thing to say anyway.

Now he could feel all of himself again, but he sat up and grabbed his neck, just to be sure his head was still on. His skin was jumping in the weirdest way. Like a horse's does when a horse-fly bites it, but all over. He swallowed and tasted sugared silver and he gasped again, because now he knew what had hit him. Sort of.

This wasn't quite like it had been, when they'd all walked into the rocks on Ocracoke. One minute, he'd been in his father's arms and the next minute it was like he was scattered everywhere in little wiggly pieces like the spilled quicksilver in Grannie's surgery. Then he was back together again and Da was still holding him tight enough to squeeze his breath out, and he could hear Da sobbing and that scared him and he had a funny taste in his mouth and little pieces of him were still wiggling around trying to get away but they were trapped inside his skin. . . .

Yeah. That was what was making his skin jump now, and he breathed easier, knowing what it was. That was OK, then, he was OK, it would stop.

It was stopping already, the twitchy feeling going away. He still felt a little shaky, but he stood up. Careful, because he didn't know where it was.

Wait . . . he *did* know. He knew exactly.

"That's weird," he said out loud without really noticing, because he wasn't scared by the dark anymore, it wasn't important.

He couldn't really *see* it, not with his eyes, not exactly. He squinted, trying to think how he *was* seeing it, but there wasn't a word for what he was doing. Kind of like hearing or smelling or touching, but not really any of those.

But he knew where it was. It was right *there*, a kind of . . .

shiver . . . in the air, and when he stared at it, he had a feeling i
the back of his mind like really pretty sparkly things, like sun o
the sea and the way a candle flame looked when it shone throug
a ruby, but he knew he wasn't really *seeing* anything like that.

It went all the way across the tunnel, and up to the high roo
too, he could tell. But it wasn't thick at all, it was thin as air.

He guessed that was why it hadn't swallowed him like th
thing in the rocks on Ocracoke had. At least . . . he thought i
hadn't, and for an instant, worried that maybe he'd gone some
time else. But he didn't think so. The tunnel felt just the same
and so did he, now his skin had stopped jumping. When they'
done it, on Ocracoke, he'd known right away it was different.

He stood there for a minute, just looking and thinking, an
then shook his head and turned around, feeling with his foo
for the track. He wasn't going back through *that*, no matter wha
He'd just have to hope the door wasn't locked.

Chronology of the Outlander series

The Outlander series includes three kinds of stories:

- The Big, Enormous Books that have no discernible genre (or all of them).
- The Shorter, Less Indescribable Novels that are more or less historical mysteries (though dealing also with battles, eels, and mildly deviant sexual practices).

And,

- The Bulges—These being short(er) pieces that fit somewhere inside the storylines of the novels, much in the nature of squirming prey swallowed by a large snake. These deal frequently—but not exclusively—with secondary characters, are prequels or sequels, and/or fill some lacuna left in the original storylines.

Now. Most of the shorter novels (so far) fit within a large lacuna left in the middle of *Voyager*, in the years between 1757 and 1761. Some of the Bulges also fall in this period; others don't.

So, for the reader's convenience, here is a detailed chronology, showing the sequence of the various elements in terms of the storyline. However, it should be noted that the shorter novels and novellas are all designed suchly that they may be read alone, without reference either to each other or to the Big, Enormous Books—should you be in the mood for a light literary snack instead of the nine-course meal with wine pairings and dessert trolley.

CROSS STITCH (novel)—If you've never read any of the series, I'd suggest starting here. If you're unsure about it, open the book anywhere and read three pages; if you can put it down again, I'll give you a dollar. (1946/1743). [Published in the US as Outlander.]

DRAGONFLY IN AMBER (novel)—It doesn't start where you think it's going to. And it doesn't end how you think it's going to, either. Just keep reading; it'll be fine. (1968/1744–46)

VOYAGER (novel)—This won an award from *EW* magazine for "Best Opening Line." (To save you having to find a copy just to read the opening, it was: "He was dead. However, his nose throbbed painfully, which he thought odd, in the circumstances.") If you're reading the series in order, rather than piecemeal, you do want to read this book before tackling the shorter novels or novellas. (1968/1766–67)

LORD JOHN AND THE HAND OF DEVILS/ "Lord John and the Hellfire Club" (novella)—Just to add an extra layer of confusion, *The Hand of Devils* is a collection that includes three novellas. The first one, "Lord John and the Hellfire Club," is set in London in 1757, and deals with a red-haired man who approaches Lord John Grey with an urgent plea for help, just before dying in front of him. [Originally published in the anthology *Past Poisons*, ed. Maxim Jakubowski, 1998.]

LORD JOHN AND THE PRIVATE MATTER (novel)—Set in London, in 1758, this is a historical mystery steeped in blood and even less savory substances, in which Lord John meets (in short order) a valet, a traitor, an apothecary with a sure cure for syphilis, a bumptious German, and an unscrupulous merchant prince.

LORD JOHN AND THE HAND OF DEVILS/"Lord John and the Succubus" (novella)—The second novella in *The Hand of Devils* collection finds Lord John in Germany in 1758, having unsettling dreams about Jamie Fraser, unnerving encounters with Saxon princesses, night hags, and a really disturbing encounter with a big, blond Hanoverian graf. [Originally published in the anthology *Legends II*, ed. Robert Silverberg, 2004.]

LORD JOHN AND THE BROTHERHOOD OF THE BLADE (novel)—The second full-length novel focused on Lord John (but it does include Jamie Fraser) is set in 1759, deals with a twenty-year-old family scandal, and sees Lord John engaged at close range with exploding cannons and even more dangerously explosive emotions.

LORD JOHN AND THE HAND OF DEVILS/"Lord John and the Haunted Soldier" (novella)—The third novella in this collection is set in 1759, in London and the Woolwich Arsenal. In which Lord John faces a court of inquiry into the explosion of a cannon, and learns that there are more dangerous things in the world than gunpowder.

"The Custom of the Army" (novella)—Set in 1759. In which his lordship attends an electric-eel party in London and ends up at the Battle of Quebec. He's just the sort of person things like that happen to. [Originally published in *Warriors*, eds. George R. R. Martin and Gardner Dozois, 2010.]

THE SCOTTISH PRISONER (novel)—This one's set in 1760, in the Lake District, London, and Ireland. A sort of hybrid novel, it's divided evenly between Jamie Fraser and Lord John Grey, who are recounting their different perspectives in a tale of politics, corruption, murder, opium dreams, horses, and illegitimate sons.

"Plague of Zombies" (novella)—Set in 1761, in Jamaica, when Lord John is sent in command of a battalion to put down a slave rebellion and discovers a hitherto unsuspected affinity for snakes, cockroaches, and zombies. [Originally published in *Down These Strange Streets*, eds. George R. R. Martin and Gardner Dozois, 2011.]

DRUMS OF AUTUMN (novel)—This one begins in 1766, in the New World, where Jamie and Claire find a foothold in the mountains of North Carolina, and their daughter, Brianna, finds a whole lot of things she didn't expect when a sinister newspaper clipping sends her in search of her parents. (1968-1969/1766–67)

THE FIERY CROSS (novel)—The historical background to this one is the War of the Regulation in North Carolina (1767–1768), which was more or less a dress rehearsal for the oncoming Revolution. In which Jamie Fraser becomes a reluctant Rebel, his wife, Claire, becomes a conjure woman, and their grandson Jeremiah gets drunk on cherry bounce. Something Much Worse happens to Brianna's husband, Roger, but I'm not telling you what. This won several awards for "Best Last Line," but I'm not telling you that, either. (Mid-1760s)

A BREATH OF SNOW AND ASHES (novel)—Winner of the 2006 Corine International Prize for Fiction, and a Quill Award (this book beat novels by both George R. R. Martin *and* Stephen King, which I thought Very Entertaining Indeed). All the books have an internal "shape" that I see while I'm writing hem. This one looks like the Hokusai print titled "The Great Vave Off Kanagawa." Think tsunami—two of them. (Early to nid-1770s/1970–71)

N ECHO IN THE BONE (novel)—Set in America, Lonon, Canada, and Scotland. The book's US cover image reflects he internal shape of the novel: a caltrop. That's an ancient miliary weapon that looks like a child's jack with sharp points; the Romans used them to deter elephants, and the Highway Patrol till use them to stop fleeing perps in cars. This book has four najor storylines: Jamie and Claire; Roger and Brianna (and famly); Lord John and William; and Young Ian, all intersecting in he nexus of the American Revolution—and all of them with harp points. (1777–1778/1972)

VRITTEN IN MY OWN HEART'S BLOOD (novel)—The eighth of the Big Enormous Books, this will probably be ublished in 2013. It begins where *An Echo in the Bone* leaves off, n the summer of 1778 (and the autumn of 1973—or possibly 974, I forget exactly).

"A Leaf on the Wind of All Hallows" (short story (no, really, it is))— Set (mostly) in 1941–43, this is the story of What Really Happened to Roger MacKenzie's parents. [Originally published in the anthology *Songs of Love and Death*, eds. George R. R. Martin and Gardner Dozois, 2010.]

"The Space Between" (novella)—Set in 1778, mostly in Paris, this novella deals with Michael Murray (Young Ian's elder brother), Joan MacKimmie (Marsali's younger sister), the Comte St. Germain (who is Not Dead After All), Mother Hildegarde, and a few other persons of interest. The space between *what?* It depends who you're talking to.

[To be published in early 2013 in the anthology *The Ma*
Scientist's Guide to World Domination, ed. John Josep
Adams.]

"Virgins" (novella)—Set in 1740, in France. In which Jami
Fraser (aged nineteen) and his friend Ian Murray (aged twenty) become young mercenaries. [To be published in late 2012
in the anthology *Dangerous Women*, eds. George R. R. Marti
and Gardner Dozois.]

NOW REMEMBER . . .

You can read the short novels and novellas by themselves, or i
any order you like. I would recommend reading the Big, Enormous Books in order, though.